February 1885

Amy sat at John's side as the buggy rattled its way homewards. It was as though nothing had changed during their few minutes in the courthouse. The only thing that felt different was the ring on her finger. She twisted the thin band absently and from time to time glanced at her new husband. Charlie rode beside the buggy, close to Amy's seat. Jack attempted to converse with him, but got only an occasional monosyllable in reply.

Thomas soon began to irritate Susannah by demanding to sit with Amy. 'He'll crease your dress, dear,' Susannah protested.

'It doesn't matter. Come on, Tommy.' Thomas clambered over the seat and onto Amy's lap. She held him close, welcoming the distraction of his prattle.

It was almost milking time, and Charlie left them at his gate. 'When do I come over to fetch her?' he asked.

'Come at dinner time, Mr Stewart,' Susannah said. 'We'll have a nice little family meal together.'

Harry was nowhere to be seen when the Leiths pulled up to the house, but John assured his father that Harry would meet them at the cow shed. Amy replaced her silk dress with a pink gingham frock, and helped Susannah with dinner preparations until her stepmother glanced at the clock and shooed Amy off to her room.

'You'd better get your things packed—not your pretty dress, though, you can put that on again for dinner. You'll want to wear it when you go to your new home.'

Amy took a large drawstring bag she sometimes kept mending in and loaded her clothes into it, wrapping her shoes in paper so as not to soil anything else. It did not take long to pack her few dresses and all her underwear. She left the two maternity dresses lying on the bed and looked around the room at her other possessions.

There was her work box; it had been her mother's, and Amy knew Susannah would not want it. And of course her precious photograph. Amy wrapped it carefully in a chemise and put it into the centre of the bundle. Her eyes went to her neglected books. They only took up one small shelf, but they would be heavy to carry. But the books had been friends to her, before her reality had become too harsh to escape from. It didn't seem right to abandon them. *I can carry them. I'm strong again now. I wonder if he'll let me put them up somewhere.*

She slipped her brush and hand mirror into the growing bundle, along with the little box that held her grandmother's tortoise-shell comb and cameo brooch. Amy hesitated for a moment over the crocheted mats on her dressing table, then packed them away with her clothes. She had made them herself, under her grandmother's instruction, so surely they belonged to her.

The same reasoning applied to her bedspread, though it seemed a large thing to take without permission. But she did not want to leave the beautiful thing behind when she left her home to go to this man who was still a stranger.

She was still fretting over the bedspread when Susannah came in.

'I've fed the children and put them to bed early, so they won't get in the way while we're trying to eat. Have you nearly finished packing?'

'Almost. Susannah, do you mind if I take my bedspread? Granny and I made it together, and I'd like to have it with me. Is that all right?'

'I'll have to get your father to buy another one for this room if you do… oh, I suppose it doesn't matter. That one's not very practical, anyway, being white. Yes, go on, take it.'

Susannah sat down on a chair and watched as Amy folded the bedspread. 'You know, if you were as you should be, I'd have to give you a little talk now. Your father even suggested it this morning. That's just like him, of course. He's never been very good at facing facts when it doesn't suit him to.'

'A talk? What about?'

'About what to expect, of course. Your duties as a wife. Just like my mother had a little talk with me. She could have told me rather more, too,' Susannah said with a trace of bitterness. 'Ah well, you've saved me that job, anyway. I doubt if there's much I could tell you.' She glanced at the maternity dresses, which Amy had put on the dressing table before folding her bedspread. 'Why haven't you packed those?'

'They're yours, not mine. I thought you'd want them back.'

'Of course I don't. Why would I want those horrible things? I'm not going to have any more children.'

'I don't want any more babies, either,' Amy said quietly, fingering the soft cotton of her bedspread.

'Don't say that,' Susannah said sharply. She studied Amy's downcast face. 'Amy, I will give you some advice after all. Don't say anything like that to your husband. He's likely to have quite different ideas.'

'You told Pa you didn't want any more babies.'

'That's completely different. I'd done my duty, giving him two sons. Even if I hadn't, he already had grown children, he didn't really care whether he had more or not. Anyway,' Susannah seemed to be choosing her words with care, 'your father's different. Here's a little bit more advice, Amy. Men expect to get their own way. Your father's become quite bossy the last few months, but he could be worse—I can still manage him. But I think your husband's going to be... well, a little more difficult. You must do your very best to please him.'

'How can I do that?' Amy asked.

'Do whatever he wants, and do it well. At least you won't have stepchildren to put up with. Now, pack those dresses away and make yourself pretty again for dinner. I'm going to put my good dress on now.' Susannah went out, closing the door behind her.

Amy changed back into her blue dress, and joined Susannah in the kitchen. It was not long before Jack and John came in from milking. 'Where's Harry?' Susannah asked.

'Sloped off,' said Jack. 'He's got himself invited to the Forsters' place for dinner.'

'I do think he might have let me know before I started cooking,' Susannah complained. 'Though he'd probably sit there looking grumpy all through the meal, anyway. You two had better hurry up and get changed before Charlie arrives.'

'I'm going over to Uncle Arthur's for dinner,' John said. 'You don't mind, do you Amy?'

'No, John. You do whatever you want.' She managed a smile for him as he went out.

'Well, really,' Susannah said. 'Those two haven't a good manner between them.' She was still grumbling when Charlie arrived, putting a stop to her flow.

Susannah was attempting to treat the occasion as a genuine celebration, using her best cloth and china and even decorating the table with flowers. It appeared to be wasted on Charlie, who sat grim-faced throughout the meal. Amy was glad she had baked the bread herself that morning; she thought Charlie would look even grimmer if he had to contend with one of Susannah's leathery loaves.

'And what do you think of your beautiful bride, Charlie?' Jack said. 'Quite a picture, isn't she?'

'She looks well enough,' Charlie said, looking up for a moment from his plate, then returning his attention to the roast chicken set before him.

The worst moment came after dessert, when Jack decided toasts were in order.

'First a salute to our gracious sovereign lady, Victoria,' he announced. He and Susannah got to their feet. Amy had just begun to rise in her turn, when Charlie caught hold of her wrist and pulled her forcibly back down into her chair.

'I don't drink the health of that German woman who calls herself Queen of Great Britain,' he told the room at large. 'And neither does my wife.'

There was a shocked silence. Everyone in the valley knew that Charlie had some strange ideas about the royal family, but none of them had ever realised it went as far as outright disloyalty to the Queen.

Jack cleared his throat. 'Yes, well, let's not talk politics in front of the ladies.' He drank a sip of his wine, and Susannah followed suit.

Having shown their loyalty, Jack tried again. 'A toast to the happy couple.' This time he took a hearty swig from his glass. Susannah took a dainty sip from hers, and the awkward moment passed.

Amy tried to react as she knew her father wanted her to, but it was not easy to conjure a smile when she looked at the stern man opposite her. A life sentence, Mr Leveston had said. It sounded a very long time.

As dusk set in Charlie had a last piece of cake, then pushed back his chair and got to his feet. 'We'll be off now,' he announced.

'Don't worry about your milking tomorrow morning—I'll send the boys over,' Jack said. 'You have a lie-in.'

'There'll be no need for that,' said Charlie. 'I don't care to have other people messing about with my stock. Thank you,' he added as an afterthought. 'Come, Amy.' It was the first time she had ever heard him use her name.

Amy hurried off to her bedroom, which was no longer her bedroom, and gathered up the bundle she had made of her possessions. She put her beautiful hat on and gave the room one last glance. It looked bare and impersonal now. Amy closed the door on the sight.

At the farmhouse gate Amy got a bear hug from Jack and a peck on the cheek from Susannah. She set off beside Charlie down the track in the deepening dusk.

Jack watched his daughter struggling to match her husband's long stride. 'He could offer to carry that bundle for her.'

'Charlie's not used to polite manners. Don't worry, he'll improve now he's got a wife,' said Susannah.

Amy looked a small child beside Charlie. 'She's too young,' Jack murmured.

'That's why it's good she's married a man old enough to be her father. He'll look after her. You wouldn't want to see her going off with a boy of eighteen, would you?'

'I suppose not.' Jack refrained from saying he would rather see Amy with the fellow of twenty who had caused all this. Best to forget all that now. Amy had found a husband, and she'd make the best of it. It was easy to believe that Charlie would be charmed by her.

He watched till Amy was almost out of sight, then Susannah surprised him by taking his arm. 'Come inside now, and stop worrying,' she said. 'You'll catch a chill if you stand out here much longer.'

Amy walked beside Charlie in silence. Watching her footing in the gloom took all her concentration. And she had no idea what she should say to him.

She looked up at her old home, and immediately regretted having done so. She saw a dim, yellow light in the parlour window; it looked homely and familiar, and she could picture her father sitting in his comfortable armchair, smiling at her. She had never yet seen a smile on the face of this stranger who walked beside her with such an awkwardly long stride. Even Susannah seemed familiar and safe. Amy suddenly realised that she had not kissed the little boys good night. She wondered if Thomas would ask for her when he woke up in the morning. *I won't be there if he looks in my room. I'll be in Charlie's room.*

They turned off the valley road and onto a track leading up to the house. Charlie barely slowed his pace as they climbed the hill. Amy's bundle was uncomfortably heavy by the time they reached the cottage.

She could just make out the shape of the building, a shadow against the dim sky. Charlie went up to the small porch. Amy heard the rattling of a handle, followed by a creak as he pushed open the door. She stood at the foot of the steps and waited to be asked into his house.

Our house. My house—a house of my own. This is what I'm supposed to want.

'Come on,' Charlie said from the doorway, turning away as he spoke.

Amy climbed the steps and entered the house. It seemed pitch dark after the lingering dusk outside, but she guessed she was passing through the kitchen. She followed Charlie through a door on the opposite wall, a few steps across another room, and through an open doorway. Charlie lit a candle. By its flickering light Amy saw she was in a bedroom. His bedroom.

The room was tiny, dominated by the bed. There was a wardrobe; a chest with five drawers, a cut-down kerosene tin on it serving instead of ewer and basin; and a chair beside the bed. Amy stood just inside the doorway, clutching her bundle and waiting to be told what to do next.

Charlie placed the candle on the chest of drawers, its light casting a looming shadow behind him. He turned to face Amy.

'I want you to understand a few things from the start,' he said. 'Then there won't be trouble later. I expect to be obeyed in my own house. I won't have arguments or talking back. Your shame will never be mentioned—I've given you an honourable name, and I'll not bring up your past against you if you behave like a decent woman. You are never to speak of your bastard. Understand?'

Amy felt her face burning. She could only manage a nod.

'I'll have your word on that. Swear to me you'll never raise the subject.'

'I... I promise I won't.' *Ann. I'm not allowed to talk about you. He can't stop me thinking about you, though.*

'See that you remember. I don't want to have to speak of this again. You'll be wanting to get ready for bed now.'

Oh, God, he's going to stand there and watch me get undressed. I can't do it. Not with him staring at me. But Charlie took something from a drawer and went back out to the other room, closing the door behind him.

Amy took off her precious hat and placed it on the chest, well away from the candle, then slipped the pins from her hair to let it tumble down over her shoulders. She undressed as quickly as possible, tugging at the laces of her stays with clumsy fingers, and pulled on her nightdress. What to do with her clothes? Leave them draped over the back of the chair? That seemed slovenly. She shoved them into her bundle and placed it on the chair; tonight was not the time to explore the drawers and wardrobe.

She heard the door open, and scrambled into bed. It smelt musty, as though the bedding had not been aired in a long time. Charlie came through the doorway wearing a long nightshirt and thick woollen socks. He bent over the candle to blow it out, and Amy heard the blood pounding in her ears. She lay very still, listening to his heavy tread on the bare wooden floor, then felt the bed sink as he climbed in. What would he expect of her? Jimmy's soft words and careful urging seemed a long time ago.

Charlie took hold of her shoulder with one hand, while the other pulled up her nightdress. The fabric twisted awkwardly as he tugged at it, and Amy felt it cutting into her thigh. She gasped at the shock of his weight as he heaved himself onto her and forced her legs apart.

Pain stabbed through Amy, burning and rasping with every thrust. She might have cried out from it if she had not been struggling for breath under the crushing load of the body bearing down on hers. The bed swayed and creaked, and Amy held herself rigid, clutching at the sheet beneath her fingers.

It didn't last long. Charlie heaved himself off her and rolled away. When his snoring told Amy he was asleep, she slid closer to the edge of the bed and curled herself into a ball. Her shoulders hurt from the grip of Charlie's hands. One thigh was stinging where her nightdress had dug into it. And up through her centre a line of pain throbbed.

The room seemed full of the smell of unwashed sheets and of the man beside her. The house creaked from time to time, as it gave up the last of the day's heat. Amy lay trembling, and trying to make no noise as she wept.

This was more horrible than she could have imagined; worse than anything in her life except losing her baby. It was worse than losing Jimmy, worse than hurting her father. She had tied herself to this man. There was no escape.

In the early hours, Charlie roused and came at her again, hauling her onto her back as she scrabbled to lift her nightdress out of his way. It lasted much longer this time. Amy lay awake through what was left of the night, too terrified to move.

Charlie stirred as dawn broke. For a moment Amy thought he was going to take her again, with the added ordeal of having it happen in daylight, but he pushed back the covers and sat up. He stared down at Amy with something like astonishment. She knew her face must betray the hours of weeping, and she tried to turn away. But he grasped her chin in his hand and forced her to look at him.

'What the hell's wrong with you? Trying to play the bashful virgin? It can't have come as much of a surprise.' Through the fear raking her, Amy was dimly aware that his promise not to mention her 'past' had not survived the night.

He got out of bed, turned his back on her and got dressed. This morning he would make no attempt to spare any modesty she might have. 'Straighten yourself up and get out to the kitchen,' he growled. 'I expect my breakfast on the table when I come in from milking.' He stomped out of the room. A moment later she heard the back door slam.

That bed held no temptation for her to linger. Amy eased herself out from under the covers and stood up carefully, her legs trembling as she put weight on them. A smoky old mirror hung on the wall above the chest of drawers. She peered into it and grimaced at the face that stared back at her: red-blotched, swollen, and surrounded by a tangle of hair.

'There's no sense in grizzling over what you can't change,' her grandmother had always said. Granny had had a saying for every occasion. Charlie might have defeated even her determined optimism, but she was right about things that couldn't be changed. 'Things always look brighter in the morning' had been another of her sayings; Amy looked at her own puffy, tear-streaked face in the mirror and found herself unable to agree.

She splashed her face with the small amount of water that was all the kerosene tin contained, drying herself on her nightdress as there was no towel. She untied her bundle and retrieved her hairbrush, along with some underwear and a badly creased work gown and apron. Her hair took much painful tugging to get into a semblance of order, but Amy felt stronger when she was dressed and tidy. She gave her face one last inspection in the mirror, checking for any traces of tears. Weeping annoyed Charlie, so there had best be no more of it.

Laundering the linen and giving the blankets a much-needed airing would have to wait till washing day, but at least the bed looked tidy when Amy had made it. That done, she made herself look in the chest, and was relieved to find the lowest three drawers were empty. No need to disturb Charlie's things. Her clothes only took up two of the drawers, and she jammed her books and bedspread into the third one. There was enough space in the wardrobe next to Charlie's clothes for her dresses, and the shelf above was just high enough for her hat.

Exploring the cottage took only moments. The bedroom door led into a tiny parlour, sparsely furnished with a sofa and a pair of old armchairs. The kitchen opened off the parlour, and another door led from it into the cottage's other bedroom. Those four rooms made up the house.

The kitchen faced west, and was cool and dim in the early morning light. It had a big, black range, which struck Amy as rather new-looking, set into one wall, with a small stack of wood beside it and an iron kettle on the hob; two or three saucepans and a frying pan hung on hooks above the range. A heavy wooden table and four chairs stood against the opposite wall. There was a small dresser with a few plates on it in front of the third wall, and against the last one stood a rough wooden bench with another cut-down kerosene tin and a chipped enamel bowl on it. Beside this bench were some food bins and a few shelves. The room was tidy enough (it was too bare to be otherwise), but the floor showed half-swept traces of dirty boots, the range had obviously not been cleaned at all during its short life, and the pans had had only cursory attention from the scrubbing brush.

'That's what a man calls clean!' She could hear Granny saying it now with a disgusted sniff. In Granny's opinion men were incapable of performing any household task satisfactorily. Charlie obviously fitted the mould; though Amy thought back to the state Frank's house had been in when she and Lizzie had visited, and she wondered if Charlie had, in fact, made an effort to tidy up.

Well, she was used to cooking and cleaning. And it would be nice to have her own kitchen again, even though she was going to have to spend days getting everything cleaned up. But the first task was to prepare Charlie's breakfast. Amy did not know how many cows he had, so had no idea how long he was likely to take over milking.

A side of bacon hung from a hook in the ceiling, there was a plate of dripping on one of the shelves, and Amy found knives in a drawer of the sideboard. The eggs would still be under the hens, so she would have to go searching for them.

She found a large, wooden barrel at one corner of the house, and was pleased to think she had found the water supply. But when she looked inside she saw that its base was rotten, so any water that fell into it from the guttering simply trickled away. There would be no water from that source.

Amy disturbed a sitting hen under a tree close to the porch and retrieved two warm, brown eggs, but she had to search under hedges all around the house before she had gathered six, which she carried carefully back to the house in her apron.

Finding the eggs had taken longer than she had expected, and Amy began to get flustered. She had to have everything ready before Charlie came back, and he surely couldn't be much longer. She ran through the tasks in her head: put the kettle on to boil, fry the bacon, then keep it warm on the side of the range while she fried the eggs. Water! There was none in the kitchen, she had used the last few drops from the tin in the bedroom, and the rain barrel was useless. Did she have time to go searching for the well? Did she dare not have a pot of tea ready for Charlie? She decided it was more important to get the food ready; she could fetch water while Charlie ate if necessary.

Amy knew she should sweep the previous day's ashes from the range's fire box before using it, but it seemed safer to leave that till after breakfast. The next blow came when she attempted to light the range and found there were no matches. She hurriedly searched the kitchen for them without success. Had she but known it, the matches were at that moment in Charlie's pocket as he sat in the cow shed. In desperation, she opened up the fire box and found that a few of the embers were still glowing; she spent a valuable few minutes coaxing these into flame using some newspaper and blowing at the cinders. Her face was hot and she was short of breath by the time she had a fire going.

There was no time to let the flames settle down to the steady heat she needed, so she just threw the bacon into a pan with some dripping and hoped for the best. The fat hissed and smoked, and the bacon became badly singed around the edges before she had time to pull it off the heat. She shoved the pan to one side, and broke the eggs into another pan with more dripping. Clumsy with nervousness, she managed to break the yolks of four of the eggs. She watched in dismay as the edges of the whites burned while the yolks of the unbroken eggs remained uncooked. Suddenly overcome with weariness, Amy felt tears starting from her eyes.

It was at this moment the back door opened and Charlie came in, carrying a billy of milk. He stared at the scene: a kitchen full of smoke, bacon half blackened and half raw, a pan containing something that might once have been eggs, and in the midst of it all Amy standing with tears streaming unchecked down her face.

'I'm sorry, I couldn't find—'Amy's words were cut off when Charlie lashed her face with the back of his hand. She fingered her tender cheek in shock while he stood over her, glowering.

'I thought you'd be competent in women's work, not a useless, whining child! Is it too much for a man to ask a bit of breakfast when he's been up labouring since dawn? Are you capable of boiling a kettle? Is there a pot of tea ready?'

Amy shook her head helplessly. 'I... I didn't know where to get the water from.'

'And it was too much trouble to look outside the door, was it? Did you think I'd fetch it for you?' He took her by the shoulders and shook her roughly. 'Stop that bawling, or I'll give you something to cry about. You've ruined my breakfast, let's see you be of some use.' He half-led, half-dragged her out to the back doorstep, where he picked up a large kerosene tin and thrust it into her hand. 'The well is over there,' he said, pointing out a direction and giving her a shove.

Nearly blinded by tears, her face burning from the slap, Amy stumbled down the slight slope to the well. She pumped water until her container was full, then struggled back up to the house with the heavy load, the tin bumping painfully against her leg as she went.

Charlie had gone inside again. When Amy entered the kitchen he was sitting at the table, a half-eaten slice of bread and jam in one hand. She managed to lift the tin onto the bench, then wiped the back of her hand across her tear-streaked face, belatedly realising she must have left a black smear on one cheek to go with the red mark on the other. Her hands shook as she filled the kettle and placed it on the hob, aware of Charlie's baleful glare.

12

The kettle seemed to take hours to boil, but at last she was able to fill the teapot. She carried it to the table and placed it in front of Charlie with a cup and saucer and a sugar bowl. She filled a cracked jug with milk and put some into the cup, poured the tea when she judged it had drawn, then stood waiting, hoping for some sign of approval, as Charlie stirred sugar into the tea and drank it. She did not dare sit down at the table and pour herself a cup.

Charlie drank his tea in silence, then pushed the cup away and stood up from the table.

'I'll be back at lunch-time. There'd best be something fit to eat.' He pulled a box of matches from his pocket and flung it down on the table, then left the room.

When she was alone Amy sank into a chair with her arms on the table, laid her head on them and for a few minutes gave way to weeping.

But tears were no use, and they brought no lasting relief. Amy roused herself and began putting the room in order, first opening the windows to let the smoke escape. She boiled water on the range and used it to wash all the dishes on the dresser as well as the cutlery from the drawer and the pots and pans, then scrubbed the bench and table. The floor could have done with being washed, but Amy instead decided to give herself plenty of time to prepare lunch.

After she had composed her face into decency with plenty of cold water, Amy went exploring once more. She found a sack of potatoes in a shed near the house, along with some turnips and onions in an untidy pile on the dirt floor of the same shed. There was a neglected vegetable patch with a few weed-choked carrots. Amy scrabbled around with her fingers and found enough to take back to the house. A few clumps of spinach had survived the weeds; that would do for greens with their meat. She set the bacon bone left over from breakfast to simmer in a pot of water while she chopped the vegetables; she wished she had some barley to make the soup more substantial, but Charlie's kitchen did not run to such delicacies. Amy added plenty of salt and hoped it would be flavoursome enough. She looked with distaste at the loaf of bread on one shelf; it was obviously shop-bought, and none too fresh at that, but it would have to do for today.

When the soup was bubbling, Amy went outside again, searching for meat. She found a meat safe hanging from a puriri tree on the shady side of the house, and retrieved six small chops from it. Back in the kitchen, she boiled up a large pot full of potatoes, ready to be mashed with a little milk and butter. It was difficult to think of a pudding to make when Charlie's kitchen was devoid of all fruits and spices, but she managed to concoct a jam sponge which, though unavoidably heavy given the lack of baking powder, would at least be filling.

Amy watched all the pots carefully, timing her preparations so the food would all be ready in the right order. When she heard a heavy tread on the doorstep, she filled a bowl with soup. Charlie stomped across the room, leaving a trail of dirt as he did so, sat down at the table and looked expectantly at her. Amy placed the bowl in front of him, then stood anxiously waiting for his approval. He took a cautious spoonful, and Amy could see from his expression that he liked what he tasted. He nodded towards another chair; she poured soup for herself and sat down opposite him. She had done something right at last!

Her work of the morning had given Amy a good appetite, and she tucked into her food as enthusiastically as Charlie did. She had held a tiny hope that he might praise the meal, but she had to be content with not being rebuked.

After a second helping of pudding and two cups of tea, Charlie pushed his chair back and lit his pipe, while Amy carried their empty plates to the bench. She was pouring hot water into the basin, trying to ignore the feeling that Charlie was watching her, when she heard him get up from the table.

'I like to have a cup of tea and a wee bite to eat about three o'clock,' he said, and with that he was gone.

It was easy for Amy to keep herself busy all afternoon. She scrubbed the floor and gave the range as thorough a cleaning as she could manage without letting it cool down, and made some plain biscuits for Charlie's 'wee bite'. She started to make a mental list of the things she would like to see added to her kitchen supplies so she could cook more appetising meals, but it quickly grew to an alarming length. Amy knew she would not have the courage to ask Charlie to buy so many things at once.

When she had scrubbed all the shelves it was time to start making dinner. Amy was a little less anxious about the meal after the successful lunch. She was sure that stew and dumplings, with plenty of boiled potatoes and some more spinach, would make a filling main course after soup left over from lunch, and her baked jam custard had set beautifully when she pulled it from the oven to cool on the bench.

Charlie's silence over dinner told Amy he was pleased with it, and she looked up from her own plate hoping to see approval in his face. Instead she saw hunger. That seemed natural enough when he was barely halfway through his soup, but his expression did not change as he ploughed through the rest of the meal; if anything it became more intense. He scarcely glanced at his food as he shovelled it from his plate;

all he seemed to want to do was stare at Amy with the same grim expression, making her more and more nervous.

Amy began to worry that she had not cooked enough, but Charlie's plate was piled so high she was sure he could not possibly want any more. She tried to avoid meeting his gaze.

She ran through the rest of the evening in her head. *We'll finish dinner, then I'll wash up, then I'll—oh, I can't make bread, I don't have any yeast. I'll have to do something about that tomorrow. I might do some sewing—Charlie's sure to have some things that need mending. I suppose he'll want to sit in the parlour, but if I'm busy sewing it won't matter that he doesn't seem to talk to me. Maybe he'll read the paper. Or maybe...*

Her eyes swung back to Charlie. That wasn't hunger for food she could see in his gaze. A hard knot formed in the pit of Amy's stomach as memories of the terrifying night flooded back. How long would he let her sit in the parlour before he ordered her into that bedroom?

2

February 1885

Frank rode down the road from Lizzie's house feeling warm and content. Another good meal, another pleasant few hours with the Leiths, and a rewarding little stroll with Lizzie along the banks of the creek to walk off some of the food. He felt part of the family already. Arthur had long ago got over his inexplicable grumpiness, and as far as Frank could tell his soon-to-be father-in-law treated him with the same rough affection as he did his own sons. Even when he had caught Frank and Lizzie having a farewell kiss in the porch he had laughed and given Frank a wink.

Yes, a very pleasant few hours. Lizzie certainly could cook. She had been particularly affectionate today, too; down at the creek she had definitely kissed back, and had pressed so hard against him while they were kissing that there had been no need for Frank to risk a scolding by reaching for those forbidden bumps of hers. He wondered if Lizzie had noticed the hard lump in his trousers while they embraced; he suspected it must have been difficult to miss.

Only two more months and Lizzie would be coming home with him. Frank was sure life would be very, very good when she did, and not just because of her skill in the kitchen. The thought of Lizzie in his bed made Frank's trousers feel tight all over again; that was going to be the best thing of all. As long as he could figure out what to do with her once he got her there. He brushed that thought aside for the moment; it was a problem that would have to be solved, but he would not let apprehension spoil his good mood. He wanted to keep hold of the courage his delightful afternoon had given him.

Today he felt strong and brave; brave enough to tackle a task he had put off for eight long months. Today he was going to tell Ben.

He knew he had been foolish to put it off so long. If Ben hadn't been such a hermit Frank would never have got away with keeping his engagement secret all this time; but if Ben wasn't so unfriendly to people it wouldn't be so hard to tell him he was going to have to get used to a woman in the house. What would Ben say about it? Frank knew his brother wouldn't be pleased, and he was grateful that Ben was not a great one for talking. Perhaps he wouldn't say much at all.

Frank glanced to the side of the road and noticed he was passing Charlie Stewart's farm. What a surprise that had been, hearing Amy had married Charlie. She was quite a pretty girl, really, and even younger than

Lizzie; it seemed strange that her father had given her to someone like Charlie. Lizzie didn't seem to want to talk about it; when Frank had asked her why she hadn't mentioned the wedding till it was over, she had said something about hoping Amy would back out of it. That seemed an odd way to talk about a wedding.

He dragged his thoughts back to the task at hand and started running through phrases in his mind. Should he butter Ben up first? Should he be matter-of-fact or solemn? Maybe try to make a joke about it? Ben probably wouldn't find it very funny, though.

'By the way, Ben, did I tell you I'm getting married in April?' No, that was too casual. Perhaps he should work up to it gradually, try to get Ben to see how nice it would be to have a woman's touch around the place. Frank grinned as he remembered trying to work Arthur around to the subject of letting him have Lizzie. Arthur had certainly made him suffer before he had relented.

By the time he reached home Frank had decided a straightforward approach would be best. After all, Ben was his brother, not the wary father of a young girl. Ben would be all right. He'd tell Ben while they were milking.

But during milking Ben's attention was so taken up with the cows that Frank was reluctant to distract him, and perhaps annoy him. Over dinner might be a better time.

Then again, perhaps after dinner. Ben would be in a good mood when he had a full stomach, Frank thought as he gnawed at a chop. It seemed a particularly tough chop, and Frank remembered the tasty stew he had had for lunch. The chops didn't seem the kind of food to put anyone into a good mood. When should he bring up the subject? After Ben had had a cup of tea? When he started reading the paper? Why not right now?

Frank watched Ben hack another slice of bread from the loaf, then took a deep breath and spoke before he had time to change his mind.

'I've got a bit of news, Ben.'

'Uh?' Ben grunted, showing more interest in his piece of bread and butter.

'Yes. Good news.' Ben was looking expectantly at him now. 'It's about Lizzie.'

Ben's eyes narrowed. 'That girl? What about her?'

'Lizzie and me are going to get married.' There, it was said.

Ben's mouth dropped open, and he looked at Frank in stunned silence for several seconds. 'You bloody idiot!' he said, finding his voice at last. 'What the hell do you want to do a fool thing like that for?'

This was not going well. 'Calm down, Ben. There's no need to go crook about it.'

'You've asked her, have you? It's too late to get out of it?' Ben pressed.

'I don't want to get out of it! I want to get married. It'll be really good to have a woman around the place.'

'Why? What's so good about having a woman telling you what to do?'

'She'll make things nice. She'll clean the place up—we won't have to bother with washing and dishes and things any more. She's a really good cook, too. No more tough chops.'

'What's wrong with my chops?'

'Nothing's wrong with them, but Lizzie cooks roasts and things, and she makes beaut puddings.'

'Make things nice, will she?' Ben said in disgust. 'What, cloths on the table, I suppose? Leave your boots at the door and all that rubbish. Frilly things lying around. Ugh.'

This was an aspect that had not occurred to Frank. But he would gladly put up with cloths on the table if it meant not having to eat out of saucepans. And mention of frilly things made him imagine Lizzie's underwear. He wondered just what she kept hidden under those long skirts of hers. He would find out soon.

'What are you grinning about?' Ben asked. 'That girl's already got you dancing to her tune, eh?'

'No!' Frank protested. 'Lizzie's a really nice girl, Ben. You'll like her when you get to know her.'

'Not bloody likely,' Ben grumbled. 'Well, what's she like, then? Is she the sort of woman who keeps her mouth shut? I don't want some rowdy woman wagging her tongue all day long.'

'Oh, Lizzie's not a noisy person,' Frank assured him. That was true enough, he told himself. No one would call Lizzie quiet, but it wouldn't be fair to call her noisy. After all, she never seemed to shout. She just never stopped talking. Perhaps he could have a word with her, and tell her not to say too much around Ben.

'Will she do as she's told?'

'Ahh…' Frank hesitated, reluctant to tell an outright lie.

'You'd better keep her in line, Frank. No woman's going to rule this place while I'm here. You get her sorted out right from the start.'

'Lizzie'll be all right, don't you worry.' He really would have to have a word with Lizzie.

'She might be all right if you show her who's boss. I'm warning you, if she doesn't behave I'll sort her out myself.'

'What are you talking about, Ben?'

'If you're too stupid to keep the little bitch in line—'

'Don't call my wife a bitch!' Frank interrupted angrily. 'And you can keep your hands off her, too.'

'I don't want the little tart,' Ben snarled. 'You can tumble her all you want. Dunno why you can't go to the whorehouse if you're that desperate for a woman.'

'Shut up!' Frank shouted. 'I'm going to marry Lizzie, and you'll just have to put up with it. And if there's any sorting out to be done I'll do it myself. You can shut up about whorehouses, too.' As if he would go to a place like that and have his ignorance laughed at by bold-faced women. It was going to be hard enough with Lizzie, and he knew she wouldn't laugh at him.

'Shit,' Ben spat. 'You've been bloody well sucked in, haven't you?'

'It's my look out if I have.' Frank took a deep breath and unclenched his fingers from the edge of the table. 'Just calm down, Ben. You'll get used to it, and it's too late to row about it, anyway.'

'Huh!' Ben grunted. 'Too bloody late. A woman around the place!' He cut himself another slice of bread and stabbed at the slab of butter. 'She'd better not try telling me what to do.'

Charlie rose from the breakfast table and went out, leaving Amy with the sense of relief his absence already, after only two days of marriage, gave her. When she had washed the dishes she looked around her kitchen in frustration. There really was nothing in it to make anything very tasty with. Charlie had told her he would go into town for supplies the next day, but in the meantime she couldn't even make something as simple as scones without so much as a bit of baking powder. And she was tired of stale shop bread, but she couldn't make bread without yeast. There was only one thing for it: she would have to borrow a few things from Susannah. She loosened her hair on one side and pulled a lock forward to cover the bruise Charlie's back-hander had left, then set out.

As she clambered over the boundary fence Amy reflected that if corsets were uncomfortable simply to stand around in, they were doubly so when climbing fences.

It was a strange feeling to be back on her father's farm and not be allowed to think of it as home. Charlie's house wasn't home; it was merely where she had to live now.

Susannah was rolling out scone dough while the little boys scoffed handfuls of raisins. She looked up when the door opened, and when she saw it was Amy an uneasy expression flitted across her face.

Thomas and George rushed over and demanded cuddles. Amy knelt and gave them each a squeeze, then straightened up and turned to Susannah.

'I've only come to borrow a few things,' she said. 'Just until Charlie goes into town. I haven't got much in the kitchen yet.'

'Oh,' Susannah said, clearly relieved. 'That's all right then, help yourself.'

'I need some baking powder, and a few of those raisins if you can spare them?'

'If these monsters have left any—oh, you've been treading them into the floor, you horrible little creatures—don't pick them up and eat them, George, that's disgusting.' She slapped George's hand away.

Amy picked the guilty raisins off the floor and dropped them into the slops bucket. 'Could I take a bottle of yeast?'

'I'm not sure if I've got much left, and I hate making it.'

'You've got lots. I made a big batch the other day so you wouldn't have to bother for a while. See?' Amy opened a cupboard and pointed to the row of bottles.

'Did you? I hadn't noticed. Take one, then.'

Amy took a bottle of yeast, then found two empty jars and spooned a little baking powder into one and put a handful of raisins in the other.

'Do you want anything else?' Susannah asked.

'I don't think so—oh, I know! Can I take a few cloves?' An apple pie made spicy with cloves; Amy was sure Charlie would like that. Everyone seemed to like apple pies, and Amy knew she made good ones.

'Take as many as you like.' Susannah watched Amy stow her jars into the large front pocket of her apron.

'Amy, come and see,' Thomas said, taking hold of her hand.

'Come and see what, Tommy?'

'Come and see,' he insisted. Amy let herself be pulled through the door into the passage.

'See?' Thomas said proudly, leading Amy through the door of her old bedroom. 'I got my own room now!'

'So you have, Tommy,' Amy said, fighting back tears. A few toys were lying on the floor, and some of Thomas's clothes were on the bed.

Susannah followed them into the room. 'I thought Thomas was old enough to move out of our room. I'll put George in here with him in a few months.'

'You can sleep in my bed with me,' Thomas said, beaming up at Amy.

'No, I can't, Tommy.' This time Amy could not hide the catch in her voice. 'I've got another bedroom now.'

'Don't you want to sleep with me?' There was disappointment in the little boy's voice.

'Shh, that's enough of that,' Susannah cut in. 'Come out of here, Thomas, I don't want you making this room any more untidy than it is.' She took hold of Thomas's arm and led him back to the kitchen, with Amy following at their heels. 'Do you want to have a cup of tea before you go home, Amy?'

Amy pictured herself sitting at the familiar table in the comfortable kitchen. 'Thank you. But I'd better get back. Charlie'll want a cup of tea himself soon.'

'Where you going, Amy?' Thomas asked.

'She's going home. Don't you go making a fuss, Thomas,' Susannah said. 'Amy will come back and visit soon. Here, have some more raisins.'

With Thomas successfully distracted, Susannah walked Amy to the door. 'Your hair looks rather odd hanging down on one side like that, Amy—here, I'll tidy it for you.'

'Don't,' Amy said, but it was too late. Susannah lifted the stray lock, revealing Amy's bruised cheek.

'I see.' Susannah let the hair drop. 'That didn't take long, did it? What did you get that for?'

Amy looked down at the floor. 'Burning breakfast.'

'Is that all? I thought you might have done something silly, like tried to fight him off. He is difficult, isn't he? You'll have to be more careful.'

'I know,' Amy said through clenched teeth. 'Please don't tell Pa.'

'Of course I won't. He'd only go making a fool of himself. It's none of his business now, anyway.'

'It won't happen again, as long as I'm careful,' Amy said, trying to sound confident. *Charlie will like the apple pie. Maybe he'll even say something nice about it.*

She walked back across the paddocks, holding the bottle of yeast in one hand so it would not get too shaken about. When she saw the back door standing open she was grateful that she had refused Susannah's offer of a cup of tea; Charlie had come home a little early for his own.

Amy took her boots off in the porch and hurried into the kitchen, vaguely taking in the fact that every door in the house seemed to be open. 'You haven't been waiting long, have you, Charlie? I've just—'

Charlie rushed at her and took hold of her shoulders. 'Where the hell have you been?' he roared.

'I-I went next door,' Amy stammered. His face was wild with rage, but something else seemed mixed with his anger. If the idea had not been so ridiculous, Amy might have thought it was fear. 'I needed to borrow a few things from Susannah.'

'Don't you ever,' he punctuated each word with a shake that jerked Amy's head painfully back and forth, 'don't you ever set foot off my land without asking me. I'll not have you roaming around wild. You *ask* me. You understand?'

'I d-didn't know,' Amy gasped out between shakes. 'I didn't know I w-wasn't allowed. I'm s-sorry.'

'Your pa let you run around where you pleased, didn't he?'

'Y-yes. I w-was allowed out b-by myself.'

'And look what you did! You found a man to roll in the grass with. Didn't you! I'll not have you making a fool of me, you little bitch.' He gave her a hard shove, slamming her against the wall. Her head snapped back, hitting the wall with a thud, then her legs gave way under her and she slid to the floor, still cradling the bottle of yeast in her hands.

Amy looked at the angry face glaring down at her and watched it blur as tears of pain and bewilderment brimmed in her eyes. 'I'm sorry,' she whispered. 'I only wanted to make you something nice for your dinner.'

Charlie's enraged expression faltered. 'That's a poor excuse,' he said gruffly. 'Don't wander off like that again.'

'I won't.'

'And for God's sake stop bawling all the time! I hardly touched you.'

Amy dried her tears on her apron, then carefully picked herself up, wincing from the pain in her shoulder blades, and placed her borrowings on a shelf before putting the kettle on to boil. She didn't make herself a cup; instead she busied herself at the bench while Charlie drank his tea. That way he would not see the tears that kept welling up afresh.

When she heard the back door close behind him Amy poured herself some tea and sat down at the table. Her head was beginning to throb from being banged against the wall, and every movement made it hurt more. *I can't please him. Whatever I try just seems to annoy him. All these rules that I don't know about until I break them, then he hits me. What if it keeps getting worse? What if I can't bear it?* Her father's house, such a short run across the paddocks, made an enticing picture. What would happen if she just took to her heels and ran home? *Pa wouldn't make me come back here, not if I told him Charlie hit me. I'd still be married—I wonder if it would still count as making me respectable if I didn't live here.*

She took a gulp of the hot tea, hardly noticing as it scalded her mouth. *I can't do that. Charlie would want to divorce me or something, and it would be a terrible scandal. Anyway, I belong to Charlie now, and if he said he wanted me Pa would have to give me back to him. Pa would be really upset then.* She replaced the cup on its saucer, spilling a little as her hand shook. *All those people who wanted me to back out of it, and I was so sure I could bear it. Can I?*

Amy picked up the spoon Charlie had left beside his cup and stirred her tea, quite unnecessarily as there was no sugar in it. *I'll just have to bear it. There's no use being miserable. Things are awful, but they might get better when I get more used to them. It's always worst when it's the first time. Last night wasn't as bad as the first time—well, he only did it once instead of twice, so that was better, anyway. And I was so tired that I went to sleep as soon as he finished. He only hits me when I annoy him, so when I learn all the rules that won't happen any more. And he was right to be annoyed with me about going home. I used to be allowed to go wherever I wanted, and I did sneak off and do bad things with Jimmy. No wonder Charlie doesn't trust me. I don't deserve to be trusted.* New tears welled up. *I hope I can learn to be good. I hope he won't hit me too much.*

Charlie ate a generous share of the golden-crusted apple pie without comment, but Amy was sure he had enjoyed it. While he was still lingering over his second cup of tea, she took the largest basin the kitchen held and put it on the table. She measured flour into it along with a little sugar and salt before carefully pouring in yeast from her borrowed bottle. Charlie watched as Amy stirred in some lukewarm water and started working the mixture.

'Are you making bread?' he asked.

'Yes.' Amy shot a sideways look at him, and was gratified to see interest in his face. 'I'll bake it in the morning, then you can have some nice and fresh for breakfast.'

Amy got up next morning as soon as Charlie had dressed and left the room. Her dough had risen beautifully overnight. She gave it a good, long kneading and filled two loaf pans. The loaves had risen and were ready for baking by the time she had the range cleaned and heated and had gathered fresh eggs. By the time Charlie came in for his breakfast Amy had turned the golden brown loaves on to a rack.

The room smelt deliciously of fresh, warm bread. Amy cut the first few slices, and Charlie took one and buttered it. The butter melted into the bread as he lifted it to his mouth. Charlie chewed his slice slowly, and Amy watched, hardly daring to breathe. He reached for another slice, turned to her and said, 'That's not bad bread. Not bad at all.'

It felt the most lavish praise anyone had ever given her. 'I'm glad you like it,' Amy said. She smiled hesitantly at Charlie and watched him eat several more slices before he even started on his bacon and eggs. *I've done something he likes. I'm learning.*

After the success of her bread, Amy felt brave enough to rattle off a long list when Charlie asked what she needed from town later that morning. She stopped when she noticed he was looking incredulous.

'What do you want all that stuff for?' he asked. 'What do you need hops for? And caustic soda?'

'Hops are for making yeast, and soda—' she picked up a bar of soap that was lying on the bench. She had already noticed its suspiciously regular shape. 'Do you buy this?'

'I don't get it out of a cow's backside. Where do you think it comes from?'

'It's just that I always made it at home. I'm sure it's cheaper making it myself. That's what I need the soda for.'

Charlie grunted. 'Well, you can't have all that stuff, anyway. Tell me two things you really need.' That was discouraging, but Amy resigned herself to building up her kitchen stocks gradually over a few months.

When the evening meal was over, Charlie announced, 'We're going to church tomorrow. My mare's quiet enough, you can ride her.'

'I'm sorry, I can't ride a horse, Charlie.'

'What are you talking about? I used to see you riding to school, years ago.'

Fancy him remembering that. It was so long ago—I was only twelve when I finished school. 'I used to ride like a boy then—you know, just throw a blanket across the horse and ride astride. But I can't really do that now. And you haven't got a side-saddle.' She had already checked the shed that held Charlie's tack.

'Oh. Well, it's maybe for the best. It would only encourage you to wander if you could ride. I'll go over and see your pa first thing, see if he'll take you in his buggy. I can't put you behind me on Smokey, too hard on his back to have you bouncing around all the way into town.'

Pretty hard on my bottom, too. And I wish he didn't make me sound like a straying cow.

'I suppose you'll want a bath tonight,' Charlie said.

'Yes, please—if it's not too much trouble. I'd better start fetching some water.'

'I'll do it,' Charlie said in the tone of one making a great sacrifice. 'It'd take you half the night to fetch enough.'

Amy draped her nightdress and Charlie's nightshirt over two of the chairs. Charlie carried a tin bath into the kitchen from one of the sheds, then made several journeys to the well carrying a large bucket in each hand. He watched Amy heat up water on the stove and pour it into the bath. He seemed to be thinking through a problem, and at last he said, 'You can have the bath water first. Don't let it get cold.'

'Thank you. I'll try and be quick.'

When Charlie had left her alone, Amy undressed and climbed into the little bath. She had to suppress a foolish urge to giggle. *So there is something good about being married after all. No more having to use Susannah's bath water.* A small laugh escaped her; she stifled it before it turned into hysteria. She squirmed around to check her shoulders and found a livid bruise on each side. *That doesn't matter. No one will see those. And the bruise on my cheek's faded a lot now. As long as he doesn't hit me on the face before tomorrow no one will notice anything.*

Amy found small bruises at the tops of her thighs, and knew they must be from Charlie's rough thrusting. Like the bruises on her shoulders, they were tender to the touch, but she ignored the discomfort and scrubbed herself all over. After three nights of Charlie's demands it was blissful to feel clean again. Perhaps she would only stay clean for a few more hours, but in the meantime she was going to enjoy it.

Amy woke on Monday morning feeling weary and despondent. Sunday had got off to a good start, with Charlie leaving her alone on Saturday night. At first Amy had been afraid he was annoyed with her, but he had said nothing, just groped half-heartedly then rolled away and gone to sleep. After his importunity of the first three nights it had puzzled Amy, though she was grateful for it. She had no way of knowing it was one of the differences between a man of twenty and one well past forty.

The service had been something to endure, with Amy only too aware everyone was staring at her as she sat near the back of the church at Charlie's side. It had been even worse afterwards, with everyone rushing up to give meaningless good wishes and congratulations. Amy knew they were all speculating on why she had married Charlie. She had seen a gleam in Mrs Carr's eye, and was sure Mrs Carr had been eyeing her belly, expecting to see a guilty swelling there.

After the humiliation of being inspected by everyone, Amy had had to fight off feeling sorry for herself all the rest of that day. It hadn't helped that, being Sunday, she had not been able to weary herself by working as hard as usual. That meant she had been wide awake at bedtime, when Charlie had seemed to want to make up for his wasted time on Saturday night. He had taken a long time over it, too, leaving Amy feeling bruised and battered. The final stroke had come when Charlie at last rolled away from her, and Amy, lying awake with her mind racing, had remembered the date: it was once again the eighth of February. One year since Jimmy had proposed to her, and one year since they had lain together under the stars. *I used to like it with him, and I hate it now. I must be really bad to hate it with my husband. And we made Ann together, and I gave her away.* She had sobbed into her pillow for much of the night before drifting into an uneasy slumber.

And now she had washing day to cope with. At home Amy would have sorted the clothes into piles and put the dirtiest ones in soak on the Sunday, but there were no washtubs here, so she would just have to scrub them harder. She had found a filthy washboard on the earth floor of one shed, where it had obviously lain neglected for years, but there was no copper or any other sign of laundry facilities. Over breakfast she asked, 'Charlie, where do you do the washing?'

'That's your job!' he said indignantly. 'It's woman's work!'

'I know it is, I didn't mean it like that. It's just that I don't know where things are yet, and I wasn't sure where I'm meant to do it.'

'Oh. I used to give things a bit of a splash down at the creek. I expect you to do it properly, though. I want things nice around the place now there's a woman here.'

Doing it properly without anything to boil the clothes in was going to be difficult. Amy thought hard while she did the dishes, then went through to the bedroom, pulled the sheets off the bed and bundled the dirty clothes up in them. At least there was only two people's worth of washing to do.

She checked her wood heap, and was relieved to find it full. She dragged the tin bath out of its shed and piled the firewood into it along with a cake of soap, some newspaper and matches, with the clothes on top. There were several empty kerosene tins lying in the shed. Amy carried out two of them and managed to fit one into the bath with the wash board inside it. She looped the second tin over one arm and struggled down the hill to the creek, juggling her awkward load.

She lit a fire on a level spot close to the creek, filled both kerosene tins with water and set them on the fire. It took load after load to fill the bath with boiling water, and the sun had been up for hours before she had enough.

The washboard came clean when she dipped it in boiling water and rubbed it hard with soap, and after a rinse in the creek it was ready for use. Amy managed to get all the underwear, her work dress and aprons, and Charlie's shirts and socks washed before the bathful of water was soiled enough to need emptying. She tipped it over, narrowly avoiding a nasty scald, and looped the steaming clothes over a stick to carry them from the tub. The creek was the best place to do her rinsing, though it meant keeping a tight hold on each item as she swished it about in the water.

After stopping for an hour to make lunch and bolt down her share, it was time to carry on. Her fire needed stoking again and a fresh bathful of water had to be boiled before she could wash the sheets and the rest of the clothes. She left Charlie's work trousers soaking in the hot water while she finished rinsing the sheets, which were particularly awkward to hold on to in the creek. Although she added more boiling water, Amy could not keep the bath of water at a high enough temperature for the dirtiest clothes. Even after having been soaked, the trousers took a long session of hard rubbing against the washboard before they came clean, and Amy skinned her knuckles against the wooden board.

The edges of the tin bath had cut into her hands when she carried it down the hill, and wringing the steaming hot clothes by hand wore the skin raw. Her head ached from being out in the hot sun for so long, despite her straw bonnet, and her bruised shoulders protested painfully. Amy sat on the grass for a few minutes to rest her back, which was aching from hours of hunching over the washing. She tried not to think too longingly of her lovely big copper with the two tubs beside it where she had done the washing so many times over the years.

I shouldn't complain. Pa told me Mama had to do the washing down by the creek for years, before he got the proper house built. There were four of them to wash for, too. Pa used to carry the wet washing up to the clothesline for her afterwards, because it was so heavy. I won't even try asking Charlie—that's woman's work.

With that, the next problem struck her: there was no clothesline. *Why does everything have to be so hard?* But she had no time to waste on the luxury of feeling sorry for herself.

She sought out Charlie, and found him checking his potato paddock. 'Charlie, can I please have a bit of rope?' she asked.

'What for?'

'To hang the clothes on.'

He stared hard at her. 'Is that the truth?'

'Yes,' Amy assured him, wondering at his earnestness.

He studied her puzzled expression, and seemed satisfied. 'There's plenty in the cowshed. You can fetch it yourself.'

What did he think I wanted it for? Maybe he thought I might hang myself with it. Amy smiled at the foolishness of the idea, until it occurred to her to wonder if it really was such a ridiculous notion. No more struggling to please Charlie, never knowing whether he would approve or lash out at her. No more being mauled in bed, then lying awake wondering if he would do it again. *How would Charlie feel if he found me swinging from one of the trees?* She shuddered at the picture. *Maybe he'd feel guilty. I don't think so. He'd be angry, but it would be too late. That would get the tongues wagging—oh, it would be terrible,* Amy realised abruptly. *Everyone would say Pa forced me to marry Charlie, then I hung myself because I couldn't bear it. Pa would never get over that. It would be the worst thing I could ever do to him.*

Amy found a coil of rope, noting the grubby butter churn lying neglected in a corner of the same shed; she would have to clean that up and start making butter when she had a little time to spare. She looked for two trees a convenient distance apart, and saw a suitable pair some way further up the hill from the house, in a spot sufficiently exposed to catch the sun. Attaching the rope high enough so the clothes would not drag on the ground was going to be a problem. Amy studied the branches, and decided there was only one way to do it.

If there was one thing even more difficult than clambering over fences in a corset, Amy found, it was climbing trees. But it had to be done, and by taking off her shoes and stockings she had at least given herself a chance of getting a grip on the tree trunk. She knew she would make a strange sight, clinging to a tree branch with her skirt and petticoats tucked into her apron strings, but no one was likely to see her. One leg had a deep scratch by the time she had secured the rope.

The wet clothes *were* heavy, and it took Amy several trips to bring them up from the creek. She had to drape them over the makeshift clothesline and hope they would stay there, as there were no clothes pegs. That was another thing she would have to ask for one shopping day.

Amy stood back from her clothesline and studied the washing. It did not look as clean as she would have wished, certainly not as clean as she was used to, but it was a good deal better than it had been before. The sun was hot enough to dry everything in what was left of the afternoon. It was essential that they did dry quickly, as Charlie only seemed to possess one pair of sheets. *No wonder he never bothered washing them.*

By the time dinner was over and Amy had her bread dough warming in front of the range she was drooping with exhaustion, but she welcomed her weariness as a friend. *I'm so tired I'm sure to drop off as soon as he's finished. Maybe I'll even go to sleep during it.* That, she decided, was too much to hope for. But another first had been conquered: her first washing day. The sheets were back on the bed, smelling fresh and clean instead of musty, and the clothes were all dry and ready for ironing. It had been far more difficult than she could have imagined, but next time would be easier. She wondered fleetingly how she would manage during the scanty daylight hours of winter, especially when the creek began to run muddy, but she thrust that thought aside. *I'll just be miserable all the time if I think about things like that. One day at a time, that's the best way to be. And at least I've got a clothesline now. I won't have to do that again. I'm not much good at climbing trees.* She rubbed at her scratched leg through her dress.

Charlie put down his cup and rose to go through to the parlour. At the door he turned. 'You left my good bit of rope tied to those trees,' he said, frowning. 'I had to get it down and put it away. Now, don't go bawling whenever you're told off, you silly bitch.'

3

February – April 1885

One day at a time, Amy told herself whenever things threatened to weigh her down beyond bearing. She was used to working hard, and strong enough to cope with the drudgery of this house.

Charlie allowed her to bring out her bedspread, but he announced that her lacy doilies were too fussy for his room, so they lay neglected in a drawer. Amy did not risk asking permission to bring out her books, and she could not bear to think of her mother looking down at the bed and all its horrors with her loving smile. She left the photograph in a drawer with her books.

Her beautiful white bedspread looked out of place in the starkness of Charlie's room. Sometimes its familiarity gave Amy comfort; she liked to stroke it as she climbed into bed, remembering her grandmother's hugs. At other times she regretted having brought it from home to cover what took place in that bed.

Desperation taught her ways of coping with the ordeal of her nights. She learned to make her body relax when her instinct was to go rigid, and she slowly trained herself to let her mind wander as Charlie grunted and moaned above her. She would lie very still and plan what meals to cook the next day, what she might ask Charlie to buy at the general store that week, how she could make time to weed the neglected vegetable patch. As the days wore on into weeks Amy often found herself left to lie in peace for two or even three nights in a row, but she never knew just when a hand would reach out in the darkness and pull up her nightdress. She soon learned always to sleep on her back.

Loneliness made things even harder. Lizzie was too far away and too busy with wedding preparations to pop over, and there was no one else to visit her. It was a week before Amy managed to pluck up her courage and ask permission to visit her old home so she could return her borrowings, but she was not allowed to stay long enough to have a cup of tea with her father.

On Sundays she saw her family on the drive to and from church, and it gradually became less of a trial to be inspected by the other churchgoers as her hasty marriage became less of a novelty. But even after the service she had little opportunity to talk to Lizzie. There always seemed to be someone talking to Lizzie and Frank about their approaching wedding, and Amy was reluctant to butt in on such conversations. If she did, some well-meaning woman would make a remark about Amy's being a happy young bride, and Amy would feel like a liar. If her father was nearby she would have to make a special effort to smile.

On the third Sunday after her wedding, Amy stood outside the church waiting for her father to take her home. The previous week Jack had invited them for Sunday lunch that day, and after some thought Charlie had agreed. As she watched Charlie walking towards his horse, she heard a voice at her shoulder.

'Hello, Amy, you keeping well?'

Amy turned and saw Matt Aitken, with his two older children at his heels.

'I'm very well, thank you,' she replied automatically. 'Hello, Bessie.' She smiled at the little girl. 'You're getting so big! You must be eight now.'

'I'll be nine soon,' Bessie said proudly. 'I'm in the fourth row at school.'

'Are you? You must be working hard.' Her brief spell of teaching seemed so long ago that it was almost as if it had happened to someone else. Someone who still believed in dreams.

Amy turned back to Matt. 'How's Rachel?' She knew Rachel was only a month or two away from having her fifth child.

Matt grimaced. 'Fed up with being stuck at home, poor old girl, specially in this heat. She's well enough, though. You should come and see her some time, she'd like that.'

'Maybe I will, if I'm allow… I mean, if I have time. Tell her I was asking after her.'

'I hope you can come around, Amy. It'd cheer her up.'

Amy opened her mouth to say she would try, but instead she gave a startled cry as her arm was grasped. She turned and saw Charlie there.

'Charlie, I was just telling your wife she should—' Matt began, but Charlie ignored him. He tugged at Amy, giving her no choice but to walk with him away from the church and towards the horse paddock.

His fingers dug into the flesh of her arm. 'You're hurting me, Charlie.'

'I'll hurt you worse if you don't behave yourself,' he said, gripping her arm more tightly. Amy bit her lip to keep back a cry of pain. 'Don't you talk to that Matt Aitken,' Charlie growled.

'Why? Don't you like him?'

'I don't like seeing my wife talking to him. Understand?'

'We were talking about Rachel, that's all. He asked me—'

Charlie gave her arm a shake, and this time Amy could not hold back a yelp. 'Are you arguing with me, woman?'

'No! I'm sorry, I won't talk to him again. I didn't know—'

'You'll know another time.' He led Amy over to her father's buggy. 'You just wait there and stay out of trouble until your pa comes.' Charlie went over to Smokey, but made no move to leave. Instead he stood rubbing the horse's nose and fiddling with the bridle, occasionally casting a glance in Amy's direction. Only when Jack and Susannah arrived at the buggy with their children did he mount and ride off ahead of them.

When the buggy reached Charlie's gate he was standing there waiting. 'Hop in, we'll give you a lift,' Jack said, halting the horses.

'We're not coming,' Charlie said. 'We're stopping home.' He reached out a hand to guide Amy down from the buggy.

'But you're coming for lunch,' Jack protested.

'I've changed my mind. Hurry up, Amy.' Amy avoided her father's eyes as she got down.

'Now, Jack, it's only natural Charlie wants to have Sunday lunch at home,' Susannah came in smoothly, covering the awkward moment. 'They've only been married a few weeks, and Amy *is* a very good cook. Leave them in peace, they can come another day.'

Jack laughed. 'You're right. Come next week, then, Charlie—I miss my girl, you know. Bring her over to see me soon.'

'We'll see,' said Charlie.

Jack drove off, and Charlie took Amy's arm, digging his fingers into the tender spots he had made earlier. He marched her up the slope, making Amy half-trot to match his stride, and did not release his hold until they reached the house.

Amy rubbed at her sore arm. 'I haven't got anything ready for lunch, Charlie,' she said in a small voice, wondering just why she was in trouble.

'Get on with it, then.' Charlie glowered at her. 'If it wasn't the Sabbath I'd teach you not to make a spectacle of yourself with men.'

'I'm sorry. I didn't know I wasn't allowed to talk to him.'

'You keep away from men, you little bitch. I'll not be made a fool of. I'll not have people saying my wife's a whore. Whatever you were before I wed you, you'll do as I say and act like a decent woman now. Understand?' He shook her. 'Understand?'

'Y-yes,' Amy stammered. 'I'm sorry. I didn't mean to annoy you.' Charlie gave her a dark look and stalked inside, leaving Amy to follow in his wake.

As she lay in bed that night struggling for breath under Charlie's weight, Amy thought about his words. *He thinks I'd do this with another man if I got the chance. He thinks I'm a whore. That must be a woman who does this with lots of men. I wish he trusted me. I wish I hadn't been so bad.*

A more cheerful thought struck her, and Amy mentally counted days, trying to estimate when her bleeding might start. She dreaded the thought of having to explain to Charlie why he wouldn't be able to touch her for a few days, but the relief would be worth the fearful task.

She counted twice to be sure, then once more, but each time the sum came out the same way. Her bleeding was already a few days late.

I've only had one lot since Ann was born, maybe it's not regular yet. Or maybe I've remembered the dates wrong. Amy pushed back against the knowledge that was seeping into her awareness. She was with child again; Charlie's child. *I don't want it. I don't want it!*

In early April the days were still warm, and Amy had still not told Charlie about the child on its way. Telling would make it seem a certainty, and she clung desperately to the hope that she might be wrong. She did not want to go through the misery of pregnancy and then be ripped apart again to bear this child of her degradation; the child of a union not of love, but of fear and revulsion on her part and contempt coupled with lust on his. So she ignored it, and hoped it would go away.

April had seemed safely in the distance for so long that it came as a shock to Frank when he realised the month of his wedding had arrived. Only two more weeks and he would be bringing Lizzie home with him. The thought of sharing his life and his house with Lizzie made him feel warm and comfortable; when he thought about sharing his bed with her excitement fought a war with nervousness, and each day that the wedding drew closer the two emotions became stronger.

He knew that whatever went on in married couples' bedrooms couldn't be very difficult to learn; after all, people seemed to have babies all the time. But just how did they learn? He had got the impression from hay paddock jokes that most men seemed to know all about it, even the ones who weren't married. There were always plenty of remarks about lacy drawers, and about women letting down their rigging, which he suspected referred to corsets.

He supposed he would figure it out, given time, but what if he hurt Lizzie first, doing it the wrong way? He never, ever wanted to hurt Lizzie. And how would he know if he had done it wrong? Lizzie would have no more idea than he did; this was going to be one area where she would not try to tell him what to do. He was the man; it was up to him to know. And he had no real idea.

Frank was so preoccupied with his weighty problem that it was some time before he noticed how strangely Ben was acting. His stay-at-home brother had taken to making mysterious trips into town; trips which he refused to discuss when asked, beyond saying he was 'arranging a few things'. When Frank told Ben he wanted him to be his best man Ben scoffed at the idea; when Frank pressed him he swore and muttered, 'Please yourself. Shut up about it.' Frank didn't mention Ben's reluctance to Lizzie; he was sure she would say there was no point making Ben be best man if he didn't want to, but Ben was, after all, his brother, and the only family he had. Until he gained his new wife, of course. At least Ben had stopped his complaints and threats against Lizzie's arrival. Frank had enough to make him nervous without that.

A week before the wedding, Frank was still none the wiser about what would happen in seven nights. His mind was full of his problem as he loaded his empty milk cans onto the spring cart after dropping the milk off at the cheese factory, so it was some time before he became aware of the conversation going on around him.

'Reckon that Charlie Stewart's got a glint in his eye these days,' one of the men said. Frank looked up from the cart to see Charlie driving away.

'Yep. Tasty little wife in his bed, that's why,' another voice replied. Frank looked at the speakers and saw they were Mr Carr and old Mr Aitken.

'Bet he makes her squeal,' Mr Carr commented. Squeal? How would he make her squeal? Did they mean Charlie hurt Amy?

'First night, anyway. They let out a good yell then—even the ones who've got no need to.'

'Well, my old woman reckons Charlie had a bite at that cherry a while before the wedding—reckons that's why they got married in such a rush. So she did her screaming out in the paddock, I guess.'

'You reckon? Now, how did he talk a good looker like her into rolling in the grass with him?'

Mr Carr shrugged. 'Dunno. But I suppose he must have—don't see why else Jack would've given her to him.' He noticed Frank looking at him. 'Hey, Frank! Your big day's coming up soon, eh? And your big night!' He winked, and Frank felt himself redden.

'Bet he hopes it's *big* that night,' Mr Aitken said, and both men guffawed.

Frank smiled nervously. He climbed onto his cart and drove off as quickly as possible, hearing the laughter die away behind him. That did it. All that talk of making women scream. He was sorry for Amy if it was true, and it was easy to believe Charlie might hurt her, but Amy was not his responsibility. Lizzie was, and he had no intention of hurting Lizzie.

He was just going to have to find out how to do it properly.

When Frank went to Lizzie's house for lunch the next day he felt brave and determined, but his boldness soon evaporated. It was only seeing Lizzie smiling across the table at him that gave him the courage to do what he intended. Lizzie trusted him; he could see it in her face.

Lizzie suggested a walk after lunch, and she looked surprised when Frank refused.

'Maybe later,' he said, looking out the window to see which direction Arthur had taken. 'I want to have a bit of a talk with your pa first.'

'Why?' Lizzie asked.

'I just… I just want to ask him some things.'

'Oh, well, if you're that keen.' For a moment Frank thought Lizzie was going to be huffy, but she soon relented. 'All right, I'll do the dishes now instead of later, then we can go for a walk when you've finished with Pa.'

Frank gave her a grateful peck on the cheek when he thought Edie was not looking, then hurried out the door and after Arthur.

'Wait a minute, Mr Leith,' Frank called when he was close. 'Can I walk with you for a bit?'

'Frank! I'm flattered,' Arthur said, laughing. 'Now, why am I suddenly more interesting than my daughter?'

'I like talking with you.'

'You don't need to butter me up any more, Frank. I've said you can have her, and it's a bit late to change my mind now.'

'I'm not trying to butter you up—I really do like talking with you.'

'Just don't get me mixed up with Lizzie and try to kiss me.' Arthur gave Frank a friendly slap on the back. 'Now, what do you want to talk about?'

Don't muck about, Frank told himself. Come straight to the point. At least it wouldn't be as hard as asking for Lizzie's hand. Arthur wouldn't hit him for asking this. He might laugh, though.

'I… I'm really glad me and Lizzie are going to get married,' he began.

'I should hope so. Lizzie'll make you a fine wife.'

'Yes, she will. But… I'm glad I'll be part of your family as well. That means a lot to me.'

Arthur gave him an indulgent smile. 'It means a lot to me, too, Frank, even if you can be a bit stupid sometimes.'

'Thank you,' Frank said absently. 'I mean… well, I was pretty young when Pa died, so I haven't had a father for a long time. I'm really glad you're going to be my pa now. I sort of think maybe… can I call you Pa?'

'Well, you could wait till next week! Now, I'm only joking, don't look so crushed. Call me Pa. I'd like you to.'

'Thanks, Pa. You know, I've been thinking, maybe my pa would be telling me some things now. I sort of wondered if... if maybe you could tell me them instead?'

Arthur looked at him blankly. 'What are you talking about, Frank? What things?'

'Things about getting married.' There, it was out now.

'Ah. Right. You want some advice about marriage, do you?'

'Yes, please.' This was going well; Arthur had caught on beautifully.

'Hmm.' Arthur looked thoughtful. 'Let's sit down for a bit,' he said when they neared a fallen log. They sat beside each other, and Arthur was silent for a few moments.

'Now, Lizzie's my daughter, and she's a good girl really, but it has to be said—she's bossy. All women like their own way, but Lizzie's keener on it than most. I don't know where she gets that from, I've never had much trouble with Edie, but it's a fact. You're going to have a bit of bother with her.'

'I am?' Frank asked in confusion. He seemed to have lost track of the conversation rather suddenly.

'Unless you get things sorted out early on. That's the secret, Frank— never let a woman rule you, and let her know you're not going to allow it right from the start. If she thinks she can get away with her nonsense she'll get worse and worse. The first time she tries it, you'll have to come down hard on her.'

'Ah... how do I do that?' This wasn't really what he needed to hear, but maybe it would be useful. It might get wearing, being told what to do all the time.

'Now, mind, I'm not talking about being rough, Frank. I don't want to see my daughter covered in bruises. I'd have something to say about it if she was, husband or no husband.'

'Bruises?' Frank echoed in alarm.

Arthur patted him on the shoulder. 'I don't really need to tell you that, do I, Frank? You're not a violent man, any more than I am. No, there's no need to be cruel just to show a woman who's boss. One or two hidings, that's all it should take.' He stopped and thought for a while. 'Though being Lizzie, it might take three or four.'

'Are... are you saying I should hit Lizzie?' Frank asked hesitantly, hoping he had misunderstood.

'Not all the time, just until she gets the idea. She's not stupid—she's pretty smart, come to that. She'll catch on soon enough. After that you just need to give her a look or a sharp word if she plays up, just to remind her.'

'I don't think I could,' Frank admitted. 'I mean, I'm fond of Lizzie—I don't want to hurt her.' That reminded him of the real reason for this discussion, but Arthur was not to be diverted just now.

'Of course you're fond of her—that's why you want to do the right thing by her. It's not natural for a woman to rule a house, Frank. You'll only end up both being miserable if you let that happen, you mark my words.'

'Will we?'

Arthur nodded. 'Did you ever hear any good of a house where the woman wears the trousers? She'd make your life a misery, and you'd be a laughing-stock. It wouldn't make her happy, either, though she might think it would. Women need a man to tell them what to do, even the bossy ones.'

Frank chewed at his lip. 'How would I do it?' he asked. It was hard to imagine Lizzie meekly standing still to let herself be hit. And even harder to imagine himself doing the hitting.

'It's important to be fair, remember that. Give her a warning the first time she plays up, then the next time you let her have it. You can use your hand...' He stopped and studied Frank. 'Though you're not all that much bigger than Lizzie, are you? You might have trouble making a good job of it with just your hand. No, you'd be better to use a belt or a strap. I don't approve of using a stick on a woman, that's too harsh.'

Would this really be the best for Lizzie? Frank wondered. He wanted to make her happy, but... 'Where's the best place to do it?'

'Bedroom, of course. It's the only place private enough.'

'No, I meant sort of... where on her?'

Arthur laughed. 'On the part with the best padding, of course! Right on the backside. You're not aiming to damage her, remember, just make her take a bit of notice of you.'

'Hmm.' Try as he might, Frank could not picture himself taking a belt to Lizzie. She would just tell him not to be so stupid.

'You'll get on just fine, Frank, as long as you start as you mean to go on. All right? Has that been any help?' Frank could see that Arthur was ready to stand up and move away.

'Well...' Frank said, 'I think so—I mean, I'm sure it has, but...'

'Hmm? What else do you want me to tell you about?'

'I was sort of wondering... I don't really know...' Now the right words refused to come. Frank took a deep breath and tried again. 'Lizzie and me are getting married next week.'

'I know that, Frank. I should know, it's going to cost me enough money.'

'We'll get married, and then we'll go to my place.'

'That's the general idea, yes.'

'That's right. We'll go to my place, and we'll… well, I suppose we'll go inside, maybe make a cup of tea or something.'

'I don't think you'll bother with that,' Arthur said with a knowing smile.

'Maybe not. Maybe we'll just…' Frank trailed off and felt himself redden. 'Maybe we'll go straight to bed,' he said to the ground between his feet.

'I expect you will. Lord knows I've made you wait long enough, you're not going to want to waste any more time.'

Frank nudged at a clod of earth with one foot. 'So we'll go to bed, and then—'

'Yes, yes, we don't need all the details,' Arthur interrupted. 'I think I've got the general idea. You don't need to ask my permission, you know.' He peered at Frank's expression. 'Is something wrong, Frank? What's on your mind?'

'I don't…' Frank raised his eyes to meet Arthur's, and was reassured by the friendly concern he saw there. 'I don't know what to do,' he said in a rush, then looked down again.

There was a long silence. 'I see,' Arthur said at last. 'Well, I needn't have worried about you two getting up to mischief, eh? So you've never been around the back and upstairs at the Royal Hotel, then?'

'Where the whores are?' Frank asked, shocked. 'No, never!'

'And a good thing, too,' Arthur said quickly. 'That's not a fit place for married men to be going—I wouldn't like to think of you spending your evenings there. Still,' he looked thoughtful, 'it's not a bad place to find out—no, that's enough talk about whores.' He lapsed into silence once more, until Frank began to fear that the conversation might be over. Arthur cleared his throat and started speaking again.

'The most important thing to remember,' he said portentously, 'is to be very gentle with her.'

'Yes, right,' Frank said, storing Arthur's remark away. This was certainly more encouraging than talk of making women yell.

'Very gentle,' Arthur repeated. 'Start off nice and slow, then just sort of gentle her along a bit.'

He was becoming disconcertingly vague. 'Ah, what exactly should I do?' Frank asked, desperation overcoming reticence.

Arthur seemed reluctant to meet his eyes. 'Well, you've been around animals all your life, Frank. You must have the general idea.'

'I suppose so,' Frank said doubtfully.

'And of course you've heard the men's talk out in the paddocks? That'd tell you a bit, too.'

Maybe it would if he could understand any of it. 'Yes,' Frank said miserably.

'Right, then. So all you have to do is… well, you get her into bed with you, then you have a bit of a cuddle, then you… well, you just do what comes naturally.'

If only he could be sure it would come naturally.

'Remembering what I said about being gentle, of course,' Arthur added.

'Of course,' Frank echoed.

'So, you're all sorted out now. That's good.'

'Thank you,' Frank said, feeling that some sort of response was expected.

Amy saw Frank riding home while she was carrying a bucket of water up from the well. She waved, but Frank was obviously too absorbed in his thoughts to look away from the road in front of him.

He's thinking about Lizzie, Amy thought fondly. *He's going to make her a nice husband. She was right to pick him. And I thought I was so clever—I used to think Frank was boring. Serves me right.*

The bucket banged painfully against her leg, diverting her thoughts from their fruitless course. *Carrying this water's going to get hard soon, when I start getting big. If I am having a baby—maybe I'm just really, really late. I don't know how long it takes for the bleeding to get regular again.* She did her best to ignore the voice that told her she would have to face the truth soon.

A whinny from the horse paddock startled her as she passed it. 'Hello, Smokey,' she called to the grey gelding. 'Are you a bit lonely in there?'

Something about the way Smokey tossed his head did not seem quite right. Amy put down her bucket and walked over to the paddock. She looked down and saw that the horse had entangled his front fetlock in a coil of rusting wire lying near the fence. 'Oh, poor Smokey, no wonder you're frightened.' She reached through the lower two rails and tried to grasp the twisted wire, but it was just beyond her reach.

Smokey tossed his head and snorted nervously. He stamped his foot, rattling the wire. 'Stop that, Smokey—you'll make it worse. Oh, I'll have to climb over and untangle you.'

Amy started to clamber over the fence, holding on to a post and careful to avoid the section of the top rail where the wood had split into two jagged spikes. Just as she reached out towards Smokey's halter, a gust of wind caught her skirts and set them flapping. Smokey whinnied in alarm and tried to rear, then let out a horsey scream of pain as the end of the wire bit into his leg.

'What the hell are you doing?' came a shout behind Amy. 'Get away from my horse!'

Amy turned to see Charlie running towards her. 'He's caught in some wire—I was trying to get him out of it.'

'Trying to cripple him, more like. Get down off there.' He yanked at Amy, pulling her off the fence. She heard her skirt rip as the split in the wood caught it. Charlie pushed her away from him. She lost her balance and fell to the ground.

Charlie made soothing noises to the horse, caught him by the halter, and tethered it to the fence with some twine from his pocket. He soon had the wire safely away from Smokey's leg. He threw it over the fence, climbed back to Amy's side, and untied the halter. Smokey moved off with only a slight limp.

Amy picked herself up and raised her eyes to meet Charlie's. She winced at the anger she saw there. 'I'm sorry,' she said in a small voice. 'I was only trying to help Smokey.'

She cried out as Charlie smacked the back of his hand against her cheek. 'You had no business interfering with my horse! You keep away from my animals, you stupid bitch! The kitchen's your place. You could have lamed him!' He caught her another blow, this time across the side of her head, making Amy's ears ring, then took hold of her bodice and shook her. 'I'll teach you your place!' He slapped her hard on both cheeks, still gripping her bodice with one hand, while Amy sobbed with pain. When he let go she sank to her knees and cradled her face between her hands.

'I'm sorry,' her voice came out indistinctly. 'I'm sorry, Charlie.'

He snarled a curse at her and stalked away, bumping against Amy's bucket of water and knocking it flying as he went.

Amy crouched on the ground until the roaring in her ears stopped, then fumbled for her now-empty bucket. *I've done the wrong thing again. I'm going to have another bruise now. I hope it's gone before Lizzie's wedding.*

4

April 1885

On the day before his wedding Frank managed to persuade his brother to take the milk to the factory, giving Frank a valuable hour or two alone. It was best that Ben did not see what Frank was about to do.

When Ben returned he wandered into the kitchen, then stood and looked aghast at the scene. All the dishes had been washed and stacked, the table and bench wiped down, and Frank was attacking the stubborn dried mud on the floor with a stiff broom.

'I thought you said that woman of yours was going to do the work,' Ben said indignantly.

'She is—of course she is,' Frank assured him. 'She'll keep the place really nice. But it's not fair to expect her to clean up all this mess, is it?'

'Why not?'

'Well… it's just not. It's really old dirt, Ben. I can't remember the last time we cleaned this kitchen.'

'It was clean enough before.' Ben shook his head in disgust. 'You make me sick, you know that? Mooning around over the first lot of skirts you ever noticed.'

'All right, shut up about it. You'll like Lizzie once you get to know her.'

'I never thought you were that stupid. You're going to regret it one day, you know. You just remember, I warned you not to bring a woman into the house.'

'I won't need to remember. You'll keep telling me.'

'No I won't,' Ben said. 'You'll never hear anything about it from me after tomorrow.'

Frank found that hard to believe, but let it pass. 'Hey, Ben,' he said cautiously, 'I sort of wondered…' He stopped himself. Why on earth was he nervous about making a perfectly reasonable request of his own brother, when a few days before he had managed to ask his future father-in-law for the most intimate advice possible?

'I want me and Lizzie to have Ma and Pa's old room,' he began again boldly. 'I think Lizzie should have the best bedroom. Do you mind?'

'I don't care a damn,' Ben said. 'Just as long as you keep her out of my room—even that doesn't matter, come to think of it. Not after tomorrow.'

Ben was beginning to sound mysterious. Perhaps he was just trying to be annoying. 'Lizzie won't go in your room, Ben—not unless you want her to make your bed or something. But you're still the oldest. If you get married, you can have the good bedroom and Lizzie and me will move out of it.'

'Huh! I'll never be that bloody stupid—no woman's ever going to get her claws into me.'

'Please yourself, Ben.'

Frank suspected that the parlour would start being used a lot more once Lizzie arrived. He opened its windows and waved a cloth around the furniture, raising clouds of dust. That looked good enough, he decided, as he made his way out of the room in a fit of coughing. He couldn't possibly get all the dust off the mantelpiece and tables; much of it seemed to have set in place.

He opened the window in the front bedroom and gave its furniture the same cursory attention the parlour's had received, but when he shook the mattresses they made so much dust that his work was undone at once. He dragged the mattresses out to the verandah, where they could have a good airing. After all, the bed had not been slept in for years.

That afternoon Frank hunted out clean sheets and made up the bed. With its pretty blue coverlet, the brass bedstead looked inviting. Frank could picture his mother propped up against the pillows, smiling at him. She had often let him sneak in to have a cuddle in the morning, while Frank was still too young to go off with his father and Ben. In the last few years of her life she had had to spend more and more time in that bed, and in her final months she had been too weak to get out of it at all.

But after tomorrow it wouldn't be his mother smiling up at him from the pillows. It would be Lizzie. At least he hoped she would be smiling; that would depend on how good a job he made of things.

Frank sighed. He would do his best, and that was all he could do. He ran through his scraps of information and made his plans. Tomorrow morning he would leave a clean nightshirt under the pillow; no, he would leave it in his own bedroom. Lizzie might be shy the first night; Frank was quite sure he would be. He would let her get undressed in private.

He hoped Ben would stay out late the night of the wedding; either that or go to bed very early. Despite Arthur's comments about not wasting time, Frank had decided it would be a good idea for him and Lizzie to share a cup of tea before they went to bed, and he was sure Ben's presence at the table would do nothing to help them relax.

After a nice, quiet supper together, he would suggest that Lizzie get ready for bed while he got undressed in his old room. When she was ready, he would join her in the bedroom; in the bed, in fact. Then what? Put out the lamp, of course; neither of them was going to want to be seen. Cuddling in the dark would be fun, and he knew Lizzie would let him fondle anything he liked once they were safely married.

His step-by-step plan gave Frank a small amount of confidence. Now all he had to do was pray that by the time his knowledge ran out, at the cuddling stage, 'Doing what comes naturally' would have taken over. He smiled at the thought of Lizzie's body snuggling up against his. Even if he couldn't figure it all out at first, they were going to have some good cuddles.

The day of Lizzie and Frank's wedding dawned beautifully clear and sunny. After breakfast Amy timidly asked permission to go to her uncle's house in time to help Lizzie get ready. To her relief, Charlie gave his consent with nothing more than an admonition to 'Behave yourself'. She put the slight feeling of nausea with which she had woken down to fear that Charlie might have refused her request.

Amy walked up the road wearing a faded print frock and carrying her good dress and beautiful hat; she had decided the occasion was special enough to take the hat from its shelf. She felt like a child let out of school on the first day of the holidays as she revelled in the luxury of being alone. Apart from the ill-fated visit to Susannah just after her marriage, and a hurried second visit to return her borrowings, it was the first time she had left Charlie's farm by herself in the two months since her wedding.

Once she had rounded a bend in the road and Charlie's property was out of sight, Amy managed to shake off an uneasy sense of being watched. She looked around her at the beauty of the bush. It was as if she had not seen it for years, and she almost felt like giving a little skip as she went along. The long walk to Arthur's farm did not seem weary; it was like a pleasant Sunday stroll. Even the mild churning in her stomach failed to lower her spirits.

When she got to the farm, Bill and Alf were busy setting out all the chairs the Leiths owned or had been able to borrow on the lawn in front of the verandah. Amy waved to them as she went into the house and sought out Lizzie.

Lizzie and her mother had been up from first light, putting the finishing touches to the wedding breakfast then preparing Lizzie for display. Amy let out a gasp when she saw her. All the romantic notions she and Lizzie had talked about as children, of brides glowing with joy on their wedding days, were made real in Lizzie. The round, cheerful face had taken on a radiance that lifted it beyond ordinary prettiness and into something Amy supposed must be beauty. She had never seen anyone looking so happy.

Lizzie was standing in the parlour beside a table groaning under its load. The centrepiece was a three-tier wedding cake surrounded by vases of flowers, and Lizzie looked like the cake come to life. Her gown was of pale pink satin stitched into a mass of gathers and ruffles. The bodice had tiny pin-tucks either side of a row of ivory buttons, and was edged with cream lace. The same lace made a frill around the neck and cuffs, and the sleeves were smocked above the elbows. She had a puffed train over her bustle and spilling around her feet, on which she wore white satin shoes.

'Amy, you've got nimble fingers, help me with this blessed thing,' Edie asked, struggling with Lizzie's veil. Amy helped her secure it to Lizzie's hair with pins before they placed a wreath of orange blossom over the tulle.

'Doesn't she look fine?' Edie said, beaming all over her broad, good-natured face as she and Amy stood back to admire their handiwork.

'Lovely. Just lovely,' Amy agreed.

Edie clucked in alarm when the mantel clock struck nine. The two girls sent her off to finish her own toilette. Amy turned back to Lizzie, and stood drinking in the sight.

'You look beautiful.' She gave Lizzie a careful hug, anxious not to disturb any of her finery. 'Frank is a very lucky man.'

'I'll make sure he knows it, don't you worry.' Lizzie studied her, and Amy instinctively shied away from the inspection. 'I haven't seen you much lately. I've really missed you since you got married. But, you know, there's been all this stuff to do, getting ready for the wedding… are you well, Amy?'

Amy felt her face take on a closed expression, and she replied more sharply than she had intended.

'Quite well enough, thank you. There's no need to worry about me.'

'You look so tired—you've got shadows under your eyes, and I think you've lost a bit of weight. Your face looks sort of drawn. Haven't you been sleeping well?'

'A husband takes a bit of getting used to, you'll find.' Amy attempted a laugh, but failed. 'There's a lot to get used to with a new house, too.' *Washing clothes by the creek. Hauling wet washing up the hill. Dragging water all the way from the well.*

'Is he treating you all right?'

Amy gave a tired sigh. 'He's my husband. He can do whatever he likes. I try to please him, and sometimes I get it right. I'll get better at it.'

'How did you get this?' Lizzie asked, fingering the fading purple bruise on Amy's cheek.

'That's from not getting it right,' Amy snapped, pushing Lizzie's hand away. 'What do you want, Lizzie—do you want me to burst out crying and tell you that you were right, I shouldn't have done it? I've made my bed, and I'm the one who has to lie in it.' *I have to lie in that bed every night and wonder if he'll hurt me, or if he'll just start snoring.* 'You're the one who was always so keen on getting married, anyway. Don't you like what you see of the real thing? Should I tell *you* to back out of it while you still can?'

She regretted her last words at once, but Lizzie ignored them. She put an arm around Amy and held her close. Dry sobs racked Amy, but she would not allow herself the relief of tears. Not tears on a wedding morning; her grandmother had always said that was terribly bad luck.

'You're right,' Lizzie said. 'I'm being an interfering busybody and I should learn to keep my mouth shut. But I do love you, and I hate to see you unhappy. I *hate* to think of him hurting you. If I wasn't practising keeping my mouth shut...'

Amy recovered herself and gave Lizzie a quick kiss on the cheek. 'I wouldn't have you any other way,' she said, managing a smile. 'But you mustn't worry about me on your special day. I brought it all on myself, you know, it's no good complaining now. I'll be all right, really I will. I'm just a bit tired, and I'm still not very good at pleasing Charlie. Now, let's finish getting you ready! Where's your bouquet?'

'In my bedroom. You'd better get changed, too, come on.'

Amy put on her pretty dress and Lizzie helped pin on her hat. Amy had to clench her teeth to avoid crying out when Lizzie's hand knocked against the side of her head where Charlie had hit her, but Lizzie didn't seem to notice.

Amy carried Lizzie's huge bouquet out to the parlour for her. They fussed about with the flowers, Amy twitched at the veil and train, and by the time Lizzie's mother came bustling back out of her bedroom Lizzie was ready.

'Now what do I do, Ma?' Lizzie asked. 'I've got ready too early! I can't even sit down, can I?'

'No, you'll crease your dress,' Edie agreed. 'Oh, I don't know, walk around the room or something. Don't walk too much, though, you'll disturb your veil.'

'Ma!' Lizzie complained. She took small, mincing steps around the room while Amy helped her aunt carry even more food out from the kitchen.

Amy delighted in working with her aunt. It was easy to pretend she was a little girl again and staying with Lizzie; easy to smile back when Edie beamed at her. Even the uncomfortable feeling in her stomach was forgotten as she scurried about. When the tables in the parlour were hopelessly full, Amy and Edie left the remaining food in the kitchen and collapsed onto a couch. Lizzie stood in front of the mantelpiece and tried to glare balefully at them, but her glow of happiness defeated any attempt at looking resentful.

Amy heard her uncle come in. When he had changed into his best suit he joined them in the parlour.

'You look good, girl,' he said, gazing proudly at Lizzie. 'You look really good. So you should—that dress cost a fortune! That dressmaker saw you and your ma coming.'

He turned to Amy, and she felt shy. Her uncle had always been like a second father to her, but she knew he had disapproved of her ever since her disgrace. Today all that seemed to be forgotten, and he smiled affectionately at her. 'At least you didn't bankrupt your pa with your wedding, eh, Amy? I've just about had to mortgage the place to pay for all this.' He patted Amy on the shoulder. 'And you beat her to it! For all her chasing after Frank, you got a husband first.' Amy knew he meant it kindly. She managed to smile back at him.

Arthur sat on the couch beside Edie and gave his wife a squeeze. 'Brings back a few memories, eh, Edie?' Edie giggled like a girl. 'Now we've got to sit around and wait for everyone to arrive. Don't worry, Lizzie, if Frank doesn't turn up I'll go looking for him. I'd better make sure I get rid of you after spending all this money!'

'Frank'll turn up,' Lizzie said, smiling confidently.

'I don't know,' Arthur said with a wicked grin. 'He might take fright and make a bolt for it!'

'No, he won't,' Lizzie said in a voice full of certainty.

Frank got up at his usual early hour that morning. At the milking shed his mind was full of Lizzie, and Ben was as taciturn as usual, so they worked in silence. They had just turned the last cow out into the yard when Ben announced, 'I'm not coming to your wedding, boy.'

'Eh? But you're to be best man!' Frank said in dismay.

Ben gave a snort of derision. 'It's all a lot of rot. I don't want anything to do with it. You can put the ball and chain around your ankle without me helping. I'm going away for a bit—it'll give that girl a chance to settle in and start ordering you about.' And with that he walked back to the house.

Frank hurried after him and asked just where he was going, but Ben refused to answer. Frank persisted until it was time for him to start getting ready, then shook his head and went off to his bedroom where his suit was laid out on the bed.

By the time he had shaved, given himself a stand-up wash and put on clean underwear the shock of Ben's announcement had worn off, and Frank was quietly grateful for his brother's strange decision; bringing Lizzie home for the first time was going to be far easier without Ben scowling at her, or perhaps even giving her his opinions on how women should behave, as soon as she walked in the door.

He put on his suit and brushed it down. Without thinking, he reached for his battered old felt hat. He caught himself in time and left the hat on its shelf. Today of all days Frank wished he could hide under the broad, floppy brim, but he had to face the world looking his best, and that meant wearing a good hat.

Ben watched as Frank saddled up Belle and mounted. 'Good luck,' he said. 'You'll need it.'

'Thanks, Ben.' Frank turned in the saddle and called back over his shoulder as he rode away. 'Take care. I'll see you in a couple of days.' There was no reply from Ben.

Lizzie was chased from the parlour and told to stay out of sight when the first guests began to arrive. She and Amy took refuge in Lizzie's bedroom, from where they could peep through the curtains as buggies pulled up.

'Such a lot of people!' Amy exclaimed. 'Who's Uncle Arthur invited?'

'Everyone,' Lizzie said with deep satisfaction. 'Fifty or sixty at least, not counting children. I didn't tell Frank there'd be so many people, or he really might have been too frightened to turn up. There'll be lots of presents, eh?'

'Oh, I'm sorry Lizzie, I meant to say earlier—I haven't got you anything.'

'It doesn't matter, we'll get plenty.'

'But I wanted to give you a present. I don't get into town, you see, and I didn't like to ask Charlie. I would have made something, except... well, I would have had to ask Charlie to buy me some material or suchlike, and—'

'It doesn't matter, Amy,' Lizzie interrupted. 'Presents are for people who don't really care about me and Frank, just so's they can feel good. You don't need to go giving me things to show you want us to be happy.'

'I do want that. I want you to be happy with Frank—and you will be, I'm sure. You deserve to be.'

'So do you,' Lizzie said, a look of sadness passing over her face.

'I know what I deserve. Come on, Lizzie, smile again! Brides are meant to look happy.'

Edie bustled into the room, with Bill close at her heels. 'Frank's arrived,' she announced. 'He's sitting in the parlour with your pa, saying hello to everyone. But his brother hasn't come with him.'

'What? Why not?'

'Frank said he's gone away for a day or two.'

'But Ben's meant to be best man!' Lizzie said. 'I don't need a bridesmaid, I didn't want anyone but Amy, but Frank needs a best man. Who's going to do that?'

'Don't worry, Lizzie,' Bill said, smiling. 'I've told Frank I'll help him out. He might need someone to hold him up in case he feels faint.'

'What about the ring?' Lizzie demanded. 'Frank might have forgotten and left it with Ben.'

Bill patted his jacket pocket. 'Frank's not that silly. I've got it right here.'

'Bless me, I nearly forgot,' Edie said. 'Your husband's here, Amy. You'd better go and see him, he's asking for you. I expect he misses you when you go out.' She smiled, and Amy wondered if her aunt had managed to forget that there had been anything hasty or unsavoury about Amy's marriage. She kissed Lizzie and went outside to find Charlie.

Even with all their borrowed chairs the Leiths could not possibly provide seating for all the guests. Amy found Charlie standing behind the mass of chairs that had been appropriated by the oldest people present.

'You haven't been waiting long, have you, Charlie?' she asked. 'Aunt Edie forgot to tell me you were here.'

'Long enough,' Charlie grunted, but he did not look any grimmer than usual.

Amy smiled at her father when she caught his eye. She noticed that Susannah looked somewhat embarrassed at having been classified as needing a seat. But there were chairs left over when all the older folk had been seated, and Susannah recovered her composure when Marion Forster sat next to her. Jane Neill slipped away from her sister's side, and Amy was not surprised to see her standing beside Harry a small distance from the seated guests.

People chatted among themselves until there was a small stir and the minister came out of the house onto the verandah, followed by Frank and Bill. Amy was sure Frank's step faltered when he saw the sea of faces staring at him, but Bill gave him a nudge forward. Mothers gathered up their wandering offspring, and everyone waited expectantly for the bride to appear.

Lizzie took her time coming. Amy wished Charlie had found a spot in the shade as the sun mounted and the day grew warmer. The heat began to make her feel faint, and her earlier nausea returned. But at last she heard murmurs of appreciation, and Arthur emerged from the house with Lizzie on his arm. He led her over to Frank's side, and Amy was glad she could see a little of Frank's face when he turned and saw Lizzie in all her glory. He stared open-mouthed, and gave her a look so full of love that Amy felt tears pricking her eyes.

Reverend Hill waited for silence, then he began to speak.

'Dearly beloved, we are gathered together here in the sight of God...'

Amy listened to the words, distracted from her growing discomfort by their gravity.

'... Therefore is not by any to be enterprized, nor taken in hand, unadvisedly, lightly, or wantonly, to satisfy men's carnal lusts and appetites, like brute beasts that have no understanding...'

Carnal lusts and appetites. That's what Charlie wants me for.

'It was ordained for the procreation of children...'

But I had my baby without being married. I don't want any more babies now. I only want Ann.

'It was ordained as a remedy against sin, and to avoid fornication...'

That's what I did. I sinned and fornicated—I never knew what fornication meant. I was bad. That's why I wasn't allowed to keep Ann. That's why I had to make it right by marrying Charlie. Amy's upbringing had been too firmly Protestant for her to have even heard of penance, but she would have recognised the concept had it been explained to her.

'It was ordained for the mutual society, help, and comfort, that the one ought to have of the other...'

Lizzie and Frank will be like that. They'll be happy together. She cast a sidelong glance at Charlie's stern face. *I must try to make Charlie happy. It's my duty to.*

Arthur passed Lizzie's hand to Reverend Hill, and Amy watched Frank take the hand in his. He stared intently at Lizzie as he repeated his vows, so quietly that Amy could only just hear him.

'I Frank take thee Elizabeth to my wedded wife, to have and to hold from this day forward, for better for worse, for richer for poorer, in sickness and in health, to love and to cherish, till death us do part, according to God's holy ordinance; and thereto I plight thee my troth.'

Lizzie took Frank's hand in a firm grip and spoke in a ringing voice.

'I Elizabeth take thee Frank to my wedded husband, to have and to hold from this day forward, for better for worse, for richer for poorer, in sickness and in health, to love, cherish, and to obey, till death us do part, according to God's holy ordinance; and thereto I plight thee my troth.'

I'm glad I didn't have a church wedding. I couldn't promise to love Charlie. I have to obey him, of course, and show him proper respect, too. That's only right, he's my husband. But I can't love him. I can't.

'I pronounce that they be man and wife together, In the Name of the Father, and of the Son, and of the Holy Ghost. Amen.'

They're married. Amy saw a radiant smile of triumph spread across Lizzie's face. She slipped away to go inside and help her aunt.

After the service the guests invaded Arthur's house and filled it to overflowing; they spilled out to the broad verandah and even onto the lawn. The mountain of food slowly disappeared, and Edie looked anxious for a while; but it soon became clear that there was plenty for even the greediest of guests and the family would be eating leftovers for days afterwards.

Amy had snatched the chance of spending a few moments talking with her father and giving Thomas and George a cuddle, when Harry led Jane over to the family.

'Pa, this is Jane,' Harry said, shuffling his feet and looking awkward.

'Jane? You're young Bob Forster's sister-in-law, aren't you?' Jack smiled at Jane but looked puzzled.

'That's right, Mr Leith.' Jane flashed a smile. 'I've been staying with Marion all summer, but I have to go home soon.' She glanced at Harry then looked meaningfully at Susannah. When Harry failed to respond, Jane nudged him with her elbow. 'You haven't introduced me to Mrs Leith, Harry.'

'That's all right, dear,' Susannah said sweetly. 'Harry's just forgotten his manners.' She smiled at Harry; he scowled back. 'I'm so pleased to meet you.' She extended her hand, and Jane shook it.

'Well, anyway, Pa, I wondered if Jane could come around for lunch one day.'

'Lunch? I suppose so—Susannah, do you mind if the girl comes for lunch?'

'Not by herself, Jack.' Susannah looked a little shocked. 'You meant with Mr and Mrs Forster, didn't you, Harry? They'd be most welcome, of course. Perhaps next Sunday?'

Harry said nothing, but Jane came in quickly. 'That's very kind of you,

Mrs Leith. I'll tell my sister you invited us. I'm sure we'll be able to come.'

Jack watched as Harry and Jane walked away. 'Is something going on with those two? Do you know anything about it, Amy?'

'Well, I think they are a bit keen on each other, Pa.' Harry was obviously no longer trying to keep it a secret. 'They got to know each other last summer when Jane came to stay.' *When I was falling in love with Jimmy. When I was sinning.*

Jack glanced at John. 'What are you smirking about?'

'You've never noticed, Pa.' John grinned. 'All summer Harry's been taking the milk to the factory and taking half the morning to get home again, and you've never even noticed. He's been visiting Jane!'

'Has he?' Jack looked thunderstruck. 'Courting on the sly when he should have been working? The young rascal!' He laughed. 'Well, I suppose we'd better get to know the girl. Harry's too young to think about getting wed for a few years yet, of course, but there's no harm in him getting friendly.'

'He's not as young as all that, Jack,' said Susannah. 'And he is rather difficult, you know. He might be easier to get along with if he had a wife to calm him down, and I could certainly do with some help around the house.'

'He's only twenty, Susannah. Don't talk silly.' Susannah raised her eyebrows, but said nothing.

The day wore on, getting hotter as the sun passed the zenith. Lizzie and Frank, along with Lizzie's family, were photographed in the garden, the session taking hours as every conceivable combination was assembled for portraits. The guests stood around in small groups, the laughter getting more raucous as the men emptied the large barrel of beer Arthur had supplied; the women contented themselves with Edie's fresh lemonade and ginger beer. Amy was kept busy for much of the day helping her aunt, carrying food out from the kitchen and clearing away plates as they were emptied. The heat inside the house was almost unbearable, but she forced herself to keep going, despite a growing feeling of nausea. She caught a glimpse of Charlie from time to time, standing in a corner of the verandah by himself. In the middle of the afternoon Edie shooed her away.

'You'll want to go and talk to your husband,' she said cheerfully. 'I know what you young brides are like! Anyway, you look all in, dear,' she added, looking at Amy in some concern. 'You're white as a sheet. You go and sit on the verandah, out of this crush.' She took Amy by the hand and led her outside. 'Here you go, Charlie, you look after this girl. She wants to get the weight off her feet.'

Amy was aware that Charlie had been drinking all day in the heat, and that it had not improved his temper. She avoided his eyes and sat beside him in silence, watching Frank and Lizzie as they stood on the lawn under a large jacaranda tree. They made a handsome couple, even though Frank was squirming uncomfortably in his good suit by this time and looking as though he didn't know where to put his feet. Lizzie had slipped her arm through his and he was holding it in a proprietorial way. Amy smiled at the sight, distracted for the moment from the churning in her stomach.

Charlie followed her gaze. He bent down and said in a low growl, 'What are you staring at? Did you fancy young Kelly for yourself, then? Wouldn't he have you?' Amy looked at him in shocked disbelief.

'He didn't want a little slut like you, did he? He's got a decent woman now, it's no good you making cow's eyes at him,' he snarled; still too softly for the people around them to hear, Amy hoped.

'Please don't talk like that here, Charlie,' she said quietly. 'It's not fitting.'

'I'll talk to you however I want,' he said, raising his voice a little. The group nearest them stopped talking for a moment and stared, then quickly turned away. 'Don't you presume to tell me what's fitting, you little bitch.'

Amy rose from her seat and went down the verandah steps. Charlie got up and followed her. She slipped around the corner of the house and behind a large lemon tree, which she hoped would hide them from prying eyes. She did not want people gossiping about her any more than could be avoided. To her humiliation, she found the rapid movement had been too much for her nausea. When Charlie walked around the tree she was bent over the ground vomiting.

'What's wrong with you? Eaten too much rich food?'

Amy's body was racked with fierce retching. When the fit passed she got slowly to her feet and turned to face him, wiping a small trail of vomit from her mouth with the back of her hand. She felt weak but relieved. 'What's wrong with you?' Charlie asked again, taking her by the shoulders and shaking her, but not as roughly as she expected.

Amy looked away from him to the repulsive mess she had left on the ground. This was how low she had been brought: to be vomiting in her aunt's garden, where anyone might come around the corner and see her. But it was no use trying to cling to any shreds of pride, not when she knew what she had to go through before the year was out. She raised her eyes to his.

'I'm with child.'

Again, she added to herself.

The effect on Charlie was startling. His eyes opened wide, and his face took on a softer expression than Amy had ever seen on it.

'You're sure?' he demanded. She nodded. Yes, she was sure now. It was as though telling Charlie had made it true when before it had been only an imagined fear.

'Come on,' he said abruptly. 'We're going home.'

'What? But we can't go yet, not until Lizzie and Frank go. And I haven't said goodbye to Lizzie.'

'Don't worry about that, her mind's on other things. She'll not be missing you. You need to get your feet up and have a bit of peace and quiet.'

This was unlike anything Amy had ever seen from Charlie, but he was still to be obeyed without argument. He lifted her onto Smokey's back to perch sideways in the saddle. She held the mane while Charlie led the horse by the reins.

Charlie asked her several times if she felt quite well as they walked home. He insisted that she lie down when they got to the house, and even brought her a cup of tea. He sat on the chair beside the bed while she drank it.

'So, a child on the way. We'll have to get things ready for him. When do you judge your time will be?'

'November, I think. It's a long time yet, Charlie. There's no need to rush.'

'A cradle, he'll need a cradle. And clothes and suchlike, I suppose— you know all about that, anyway.'

Amy, whose real experience of what a baby needed came from her little brothers rather than her daughter, noticed it was the first time Charlie had ever managed to refer to her past without reviling her. She did not risk spoiling his new softness by pointing out that the child might be a girl. Muttering to himself, Charlie went outside to stamp about in his timber store looking for wood suitable for a cradle, leaving Amy to drift off into a light slumber. She did not expect Charlie's good temper to last, but she might as well enjoy it while it did.

Charlie was wrong. Lizzie did miss Amy when the time came to leave for her new home, and was concerned when she could not find her. But the flurry of gathering up her belongings, kisses and tears from her mother, and climbing into her father's buggy put Amy out of her head. Arthur had insisted they borrow his buggy; it was hardly fitting for his daughter to leave her wedding walking up the road in the dust or bouncing behind her husband's saddle.

'I'll send the boys over in the morning to do the milking,' he said to Frank while the two of them were waiting for Lizzie to reappear. 'They can bring the buggy back then. You have a lie-in.' He dug his new son-in-law in the ribs, and Frank felt his ears go red. 'You'll be all right,' Arthur added in a low voice, smiling encouragingly.

Arthur's confidence in him gave Frank a warm glow. 'Yes, I think I will.'

'Just you remember,' Arthur said, wagging his finger to emphasise his words, 'start as you mean to go on with Lizzie. Get things sorted out right from the start.'

'Right, yes, I'll do that, Pa,' Frank assured him.

Frank helped Lizzie into the buggy and climbed in beside her, while all the guests stood and waved, calling out their good wishes.

The harness was more complicated than the one Frank was used to on his spring cart. He fumbled with the reins, causing the horses to shy. Lizzie was jerked against the seat, and turned from waving to everyone. 'What are you doing?' she said under her breath. 'Don't you know how to do it?'

'Not really,' Frank admitted. 'I'll manage, though.' To his dismay, he saw that he was getting the reins into a knot.

'Not like that,' Lizzie hissed. 'You're making a mess of it. You need to… oh, just hold them steady for a bit, don't try steering or you'll get in a worse muddle.' She looked back over her shoulder again and smiled and waved until they rounded a bend in the road and were out of sight from the house. Then she leaned across to Frank and took the reins out of his hands.

Frank was about to protest, but he had to admit that Lizzie was right; he had been making a mess of driving. She knew what she was doing, so it seemed only sensible to let Lizzie take over.

5

April – August 1885

It seemed to Amy that Charlie was now obsessed with her health. Several times a day he asked her how she felt.

'You were sick this morning,' he said at breakfast time a few days after Lizzie's wedding.

'I'm sick every morning now. It won't last much longer, maybe a few more weeks.'

Charlie stared anxiously at her. 'You're sure that's normal?'

'I think so. It doesn't always happen, I remember Susannah was sick a lot when she was having Georgie, but she was fine with Tommy.' *I didn't get sick with Ann, either.* 'It's nothing to worry about, I'm sure it isn't.'

'Well… just be careful, then.'

What's that supposed to mean? 'I'll try.'

It was hard to get used to expressions of concern from Charlie. Amy had hardly had a sharp word from him over the previous few days, let alone a blow.

'You're not showing any sign yet,' Charlie said, looking at Amy's belly. 'You're sure about it?'

'Quite sure. I'll start showing soon enough.' *I'll soon be heaving myself around like a great bloated cow. Then I have to go through all that.* Amy hid a shudder, and busied herself with dishing up Charlie's breakfast.

'Where's yours?' he asked when she put his plate in front of him.

'I can't face bacon and eggs, I'll just have some dry bread and a cup of tea.'

'Bread? You can't live on bread and tea! You've got to eat, woman—good food, too.'

'I'll eat at lunch-time, when my stomach's settled. I really can't face anything heavy, Charlie.' Even the smell of Charlie's breakfast was making her queasy.

Charlie frowned at her. 'You've got to eat. Dish yourself up some breakfast.'

'I don't want—'

'Eat!' he shouted. Amy cringed and waited for a blow to go with the words, but it did not happen. Charlie's fist was clenched, but he pressed it against the table, clearly making an effort to restrain himself. 'Do as I say. That's not some man's bastard you're carrying this time—it's my son. I expect you to take proper care of him.'

And I thought it was me he was worrying about. That was stupid of me. Amy dished herself up a small plateful and forced down some bacon and eggs under Charlie's watchful gaze.

She fought back nausea with each unwanted mouthful, until it became too much of a struggle. She hurried outside and emptied her stomach onto the grass, then sat on the ground enjoying the sense of relief vomiting had brought. Charlie came out and glared at the sight, but said nothing. Amy suspected it would be the last time he forced her to eat in the morning.

Every day Amy saw Charlie studying her belly closely. It was as much to make him happy as for her own comfort that she started lacing less tightly, then in mid-May abandoned her corset altogether apart from on her Sunday outings to church.

'You're looking thicker around the middle,' Charlie said on the first morning he saw her fully dressed without it.

'Yes, I am.' Amy did not tell him that he was merely seeing her natural waist rather than the line of her corset.

But in another few weeks she had a definite bulge; so much so that when she put on her good dress one Sunday she shook her head at her reflection and replaced the close-fitting dress with a looser woollen frock.

'I won't be going to church today, Charlie,' she told him. 'I'm going to have to stay home from now on. I'm really showing now, see?' She pressed her dress flat over the bulge.

'Mmm, you are.' Charlie looked at her belly with a satisfied expression. 'I'll stop home too.'

'Oh. Just as you like, Charlie.' Amy had looked forward to a peaceful morning alone, but she kept her thoughts to herself.

'I suppose I could go without you,' Charlie said. 'People will ask where you are, though. No one knows about the bairn except your kin. What'll I say?'

'You just say I'm a bit poorly, and they won't see me around for a few months. People will know what you mean.'

'Will they?'

Amy nodded. 'That's what husbands say when their wives are with child.'

'Hmm. I might go, then.'

Charlie did go off to church alone, and he arrived home looking pleased with himself. 'People asked after you. I told them what you said—I think they knew.'

'I'm sure they did, Charlie.'

Her bulge was not yet an encumbrance, but Amy knew that in a few more weeks she would become awkward. Taking care of Charlie's baby meant taking care of herself. One evening as they sat in the parlour, Amy sewing a baby gown while Charlie read the *Weekly News*, she chose a moment when she saw him look up from his newspaper to glance at her thickening middle.

'Charlie, things are going to start getting a bit hard for me soon.'

'What are you talking about? What things?'

'When I get bigger I won't be able to do all the things I do now. Some of them I'll just have to leave, like scrubbing the floor—I'm afraid we'll have to put up with it for a few weeks.'

Charlie grunted. 'That doesn't matter. Floor's clean enough.'

'And butter, too—I don't think I'll be able to manage the churn. You don't mind buying it at the factory for a while, do you?' Charlie shook his head.

'That's good. But some things can't be left. I'm sure I'll be all right with the cooking, but doing the washing and fetching water for the kitchen's going to be hard.'

'I'm not doing it for you!' Charlie said indignantly. 'Don't go thinking you'll get out of all your work just because you're with child.'

'I'm not trying to get out of it. But women aren't meant to carry heavy things when they're with child—honestly they're not, Charlie. Aunt Edie told me that when Susannah was having her babies. I think it can make things go wrong.'

Charlie looked anxious. 'Can it? What do you do, then? What did your pa's wife do?'

'She had me, so she didn't need to do heavy work.' *And Pa made Susannah do the heavy work for me when I was carrying Ann.*

'It's the water, mainly,' she hurried on, not giving Charlie time to comment. 'Up and down to the well for all the cooking. Do you think you could get a new rain barrel? Then I wouldn't have to carry it so far. And as long as it rained enough to keep the barrel full, I could do the washing up here instead of taking the clothes down to the creek and back—that's very heavy, especially carrying the wet clothes up the hill.'

Charlie grunted and went back to reading his paper, and Amy said no more. But when he returned from his next weekly trip to the store he unloaded a large barrel from the cart and put it in the place of the rotten one.

It's something, Amy thought as she knelt over the tin bath scrubbing Charlie's trousers the following Monday. *It's not like a copper and tubs, but it's easier than washing by the creek.* She knew that later in her pregnancy she would be unable to crouch on the grass over her makeshift tubs, but she put that problem off for the moment. Even with the status pregnancy gave her in Charlie's eyes, it was not easy to ask him for favours.

Frank drifted through his first few days of marriage in a happy daze. He had guessed from men's talk and jokes over the years that it must be fun, but he had had no idea anything could be quite *that* good.

Their shyness evaporated after the first night, and their clumsiness lasted only a day or two longer. When Frank emerged from church with Lizzie on his arm the Sunday after their wedding, their first public appearance since the wedding itself, he was feeling thoroughly smug. He had even managed, albeit with difficulty, to stay awake during the long sermon, though he and Lizzie had both had to smother yawns all through the service.

They were soon surrounded by a crowd of well-wishers; the sea of smiling faces made Frank feel awkward. The thought that all those people knew just what he had been doing all week brought a blush to his face. He was amazed that Lizzie could talk to them all with no sign of embarrassment; but then, that was Lizzie. Nothing ever seemed to discomfort her.

Frank noticed Amy hovering on the edge of the crowd, patiently waiting for a chance to talk to Lizzie. He was about to point her out to Lizzie when Arthur put a hand on his arm and manœuvred him off to one side.

'Everything going all right, Frank?' Arthur asked quietly.

Frank gave him a smile that turned into a grin. 'Yes. It's going really well, Pa.' He stifled a yawn as he spoke.

'Good lad. I knew you wouldn't have any trouble,' Arthur said. Frank yawned again, belatedly covering his mouth with his hand. 'Well, Frank, I would tell you to start getting a bit more sleep,' Arthur said with mock sternness. 'Except I know that's one piece of advice you wouldn't take a bit of notice of!'

Yes, marriage was the best thing that had ever happened to him, Frank decided as the days wore on into weeks. Life had become so comfortable with Lizzie around. The house was spotless, and tasty meals appeared on the table without any effort on his part. His clothes were washed and ironed, and his own clumsy attempts at mending were replaced with neat stitches. And best of all, every night instead of a cold bed he had Lizzie's soft body snuggling up against him in the warm darkness.

Ben's 'few days' stretched on, and Frank was relieved when he could dry off his herd. Milking the cows, even once a day, was a long, wearying task when he had to do it with Lizzie's help instead of Ben's. Lizzie did her best, but she had not milked in years, and was much slower than Ben. Frank wondered occasionally where Ben had got to, but life with Lizzie was too full for him to think about his brother very often.

Lizzie seemed to feel the need to rearrange the house as soon as she was installed as its mistress. She announced it needed tidying up, and Frank left her to it. All the dishes were moved around on the dresser until Lizzie was satisfied, and the larder was completely reorganised. She shifted the parlour furniture into a new arrangement and moved rugs from room to room. It made her happy and it didn't do any harm, though Frank was taken aback when he opened a drawer in the bedroom one morning and found it full of Lizzie's underwear instead of his own.

'Where's my stuff, Lizzie?'

'Oh, I moved it. You had it all shoved in that drawer, and it looked really untidy, so I pulled it out and went through it. Some of your things needed chucking out, but they'll make good rags. The rest is all folded nicely in that drawer there.' She indicated a lower drawer. 'You need some new combinations, Frank.'

'Do I?'

'Yes. You've only got three pairs, and one of them can't be mended much more. You can buy some this week. I went through all your clothes yesterday and rearranged them, they were all in a muddle. It'll be much easier for you to find things now.'

Getting used to his clothes' being in different places didn't seem much to ask, especially when the bedroom was new to him anyway. There were other changes, but Lizzie had good reasons for them all. She liked to serve dinner half an hour earlier than Frank was used to, because it gave her more time to get the bread made afterwards. Fresh bread every morning was worth the small effort of adjusting to a different meal time. And Frank could understand why Lizzie didn't want him to wear his boots to the table, though it was difficult to remember to take them off in the porch.

'Frank, you've done it again,' Lizzie said one lunch-time, shaking her head at him.

'Sorry.' Frank pulled the boots off, dislodging a few clods in the process.

'Careful! And don't just drop them in the porch like that. Put them tidily against the wall.'

'Is that all right?'

'That's nice. Now, hurry up before your soup gets cold.' And very good soup it was, too, Frank thought as he spooned it up.

'I've got most of my work done this morning. Ben's room must need an airing by now, I might give it a tidy up this afternoon.'

Frank looked up from his soup in alarm. 'No, don't do that, Lizzie. Ben wouldn't want you to interfere with his things.'

'I'm sure he'd like to have his room tidied and nice, and men never do that sort of thing for themselves. Look what a muddle your drawers were in before I sorted them out.'

'I don't think you should, Lizzie. I'd rather you left Ben's room alone.' Frank realised that he never had got around to warning Lizzie how she should behave around Ben. 'Hey, I was going to talk to you about Ben, too. When he comes back I want—'

'Don't be silly, Ben'll be pleased. Eat up your soup, it's getting cold.'

It was hard to argue with Lizzie when she was so sure about everything. Frank wondered briefly what Arthur would have to say if he were there, but he brushed the uncomfortable thought aside.

Lizzie was a good wife, and she was making him very happy even if she was a bit bossy. Well, if he was honest, she was very bossy. Was she getting worse? Frank wondered. Arthur had warned him that she would. But what could he do about it? He couldn't hit her, he just couldn't. Surely they could talk about things.

'Lizzie, I wish you wouldn't tell me what to do all the time,' Frank said, trying to sound stern.

'I don't. Are you going to eat that soup or not? I've cooked some nice chops, they'll get all dry if we leave them too long.'

'You do a bit, Lizzie.'

'Don't you like the soup? I thought you liked vegetable soup. You told me you did.'

'I do, I just want—'

'I won't make it again if you don't like it. I wish you'd told me.'

'I *do* like it. But Lizzie—'

'Why don't you eat it, then? Oh, I'll tip it out for the pigs. I *think* my cooking's good enough for them.' She reached over for Frank's bowl, giving him a hurt look.

Frank knew when he was beaten. 'Don't do that, Lizzie, I'll eat it now.' Maybe he would try talking to Lizzie that evening when they sat in the parlour. Then again, maybe they would go to bed as soon as Lizzie had set her bread dough to rise; they often seemed to be in bed by half-past seven.

Frank smiled at the thought. He would certainly find it hard to scold Lizzie in bed, and he had no intention of wasting time trying to threaten her with the strap. As long as Lizzie wasn't bossy to him in front of other people she couldn't make him a laughing-stock. And it *was* very good soup.

When Frank realised he and Lizzie had been married two months, he felt a stab of guilt at not having even thought about Ben for weeks. Where could Ben possibly have gone for so long? When was he going to come home? And what would he say to Lizzie when he got there? Fighting with his brother to protect his wife did not appeal, but it might yet come to that.

'I've got to find out about Ben,' he announced one morning. 'It's stupid not knowing where he is. He can't be in Ruatane, not for two whole months without us seeing him.'

'I suppose he's gone away on holiday somewhere,' Lizzie said. 'It's funny he hasn't written, though.'

'He wouldn't write.'

'Why not? Just a few lines to let you know where he is, that's not much to ask.'

'He...' Frank struggled between loyalty to his brother and a reluctance to keep secrets from Lizzie. 'Ben's not much good at writing.'

'Lots of men aren't.'

'No. But Ben... he can't really write, Lizzie.'

Lizzie looked astonished. 'Can't he? Why not?'

'Well, Ben was fourteen when the school started. Pa said he could go for a few months if he wanted, and Ma tried to talk him into it, but Ben didn't want to sit with a lot of little kids. I was only ten, so it wasn't so bad for me—there were kids there older than me. Ma taught us our letters when we were little, and to read a bit, but that was all. Ben can sign his name, and he can read easy things if he takes his time, but nothing else.'

'Oh. That was silly of him not to go to school. He'll be all right, though, wherever he's got to.'

'He should be back by now. I'm going to find out.'

That morning Frank went into town and started asking questions. He spoke to Sam Craig at the general store, but Mr Craig had no particular memory of seeing Ben. Sergeant Riley, Ruatane's sole policeman, was no help, either, though he promised to keep an ear open for any news.

Then Frank remembered that Ben's horse had thrown a shoe a few days before Ben's sudden departure. He rode over to the blacksmith's shop, where he found the broad-shouldered Mr Winskill working at the forge.

'Shoe his horse?' Mr Winskill laughed. 'I *bought* his horse off him! Not a bad animal, either. He's in the paddock over the back.'

Frank checked the paddock behind the shop; sure enough, Ben's gelding was munching contentedly from a nosebag. Why on earth would Ben sell his horse? Especially since the horses belonged to the farm rather than to either brother.

'Did Ben say where he was going?'

'Said he was escaping from a woman! Was some female after him?'

'Not exactly. Didn't he say anything else?'

'No. Not a great one for talking, your brother.'

Frank thanked Mr Winskill and went on his way, thinking hard.

Ben had obviously wanted some money, and it was this thought that led Frank to the Bank of New Zealand.

The manager, Mr Callaghan, was behind the counter. 'Goodness me, Frank, I only usually see you when your milk cheque's in or you've sold your potato crop and you're settling up at the store. And now you turn up when your brother was here only a few weeks ago! What's got into you Kellys? Wanderlust?'

'Ben was here? What did he say? Do you know where he's gone?'

Mr Callaghan looked startled. 'You don't know? I assumed he'd discussed it with you. This is rather awkward, though your account was such that… come and sit down a minute, Frank.' He ushered Frank into his tiny office and closed the door.

'Your brother said you were dissolving your partnership. Well, he didn't say it quite like that, but that's what it amounted to. He said he was going to take his share and start out somewhere else. I got the impression he wasn't too happy about…' Mr Callaghan trailed off awkwardly.

'Wasn't too happy about me getting married,' Frank finished for him.

'Well, yes. Your farm's in both your names, so either of you has the right to borrow money on it. And to draw money out of your account, of course, though you don't usually have much money in it! Your brother borrowed two hundred pounds against the farm—'

'Two hundred pounds!' Frank echoed in astonishment.

'That's right. There's no hurry to pay it back, you can take a few years if you like.'

'I'll have to.' Two hundred pounds? How much did the farm make in a year? Not enough to spare two hundred pounds out of, Frank was quite sure of that.

'Ben left something for you,' Mr Callaghan said. He opened a drawer and pulled out an envelope. 'He asked me to give it to you the next time you came in—he said there was no particular hurry.'

Frank ripped open the envelope. Inside were two sheets of paper, both with the same neat handwriting. Frank took the top sheet and sounded the words under his breath as he read:

' "I have gone away to get away from women with wagging tongues. I won't be back. Don't worry about me. Good luck. Ben." '

Under the short message a note had been added in the same hand.

' "Written at the express"…'

Frank stumbled on the next word. 'What does this say?' he asked, passing the page to Mr Callaghan.

'Dictation. "Written at the express dictation of Mr Benjamin Kelly".' Mr Callaghan glanced at the rest of the page and a slight smile passed over his face. 'He's got the lawyer to write it for him, you see, and Mr Jamieson is making it clear that it's your brother's own words, not what Mr Jamieson wanted to write.'

'I see.' Frank studied the other sheet. This had obviously been composed by the lawyer, but he recognised Ben's spidery 'B. Kelly' at the foot of the page.

'I can't make out all these long words—what does it mean?'

Mr Callaghan obligingly took the piece of paper. 'It's lawyer's talk, full of "thereinafters" and "heretofores". But in plain English, it says your brother gives up his share in the farm to you in return for the two hundred pounds he's taken. That's quite a bargain—your farm's certainly worth more than four hundred pounds. The farm belongs to you now, Frank. Except for the bank's share, that is.' He smiled, but Frank did not feel able to return the smile.

Frank rode home unsure whether to feel angry, guilty or hurt. Ben had saddled him with a debt that Frank had no idea how long it would take to repay. But Ben must have been desperate to get away, and it was Frank's action that had driven his brother from his home. Why couldn't Ben have talked to him about it? Why hadn't Ben trusted him to keep Lizzie in line?

He gave a snort of disgust. Ben wasn't stupid. He didn't know Lizzie, but he knew Frank. Why should Ben trust him? It was true, after all: he couldn't tell Lizzie what to do. She didn't take the slightest bit of notice when he did.

Amy struggled against the sluggishness of pregnancy to get all her work done to Charlie's satisfaction. As she increased in bulk all her tasks took longer, but she did not want to have to excuse herself to him. She soon had to let some of her work slip. Charlie had never shown any sign of noticing if the floor had been scrubbed or not, so Amy made do with regular sweeping. And the rugs would have to manage without being beaten for a few months.

Washing was becoming more and more of a burden, especially when there was not enough water in the barrel and she had to fetch it from the well. Edie described the baby as 'A difficult little fellow' when she paid Amy a brief visit on her way home from town one day; according to her the child was lying awkwardly, which meant it pressed uncomfortably against Amy whenever she bent over or twisted around.

'You're a nuisance,' Amy murmured to the intruder in her womb one day in her sixth month as she struggled up from the well with a heavy kerosene tin of water for rinsing. 'You make everything so hard.' Bending over the washing was now so difficult that she had to stop every few minutes and walk around with her hands braced against her back. That meant the task took even longer than usual.

She did her best to get lunch ready on time, but she barely had the chops in the pan before Charlie came in. He had been ploughing all morning, and the moment she saw his face Amy knew he was tired and irritable.

'Where's my lunch?' he demanded.

'It'll be ready in a few minutes. I'm a bit slow today, I'm sorry.'

'You lazy bitch! I expect my meals ready on time, woman!'

His hand took Amy by surprise as it swung out and caught her a slap on the side of her head. She stumbled and made a grab for a chair, missed it and managed to catch the edge of the table. A violent burst of kicking from inside her womb took Amy's breath away. She stood gripping the table.

'What's wrong?' Charlie asked, seeing her panting for breath. 'Is it the child? Has he started coming?'

'Yes, it's the baby, but it's not coming yet,' Amy said when she got her voice back. 'It got a fright when you... when I tripped then, and it's complaining.'

She saw the wild-eyed look of fear on Charlie's face. On an impulse, she took hold of his hand and placed it on her belly. 'Here, you feel.'

The baby obliged with a powerful kick. 'I felt it!' Charlie said in wonder. 'I felt my son!'

He kept his hand pressed firmly against Amy until the baby quietened, then he helped her into a chair and sat opposite her. 'For God's sake don't keep aggravating me. I don't want to do you any harm, but if you push me...' He rubbed a hand across his forehead. 'I've waited a long time for this child. I don't want anything to go wrong now.'

Amy could not help but be moved by the intensity in his voice. 'I'm sorry, Charlie. I don't mean to annoy you, but I honestly can't help being slow. It's the baby—it makes me clumsy, so I can't move as fast. Aunt Edie says she thinks it's a big baby, too, so I'll get worse, I'm afraid. And it keeps me awake at night with all that kicking, so I'm tired, and that makes me even slower.'

'Kicks a lot, does he?' Charlie asked, looking absorbed.

'An awful lot. Really hard, too. Aunt Edie says that means it's a big, healthy baby.' Edie had also said, after studying Amy's abdomen, that judging by her shape she was probably carrying a boy, but Amy was anxious enough about Charlie's reaction if she were to have a girl without making things even worse by building up his hopes.

'More than the other fellow's?'

'What?' Amy asked blankly.

'Does he kick more than your bastard did?'

I thought I wasn't allowed to talk about her. But Charlie had raised the subject, and he obviously expected to be answered. 'Yes,' Amy said quietly. 'Much, much more.'

'Good.' Charlie looked smug. 'I suppose it's natural you're slow, then. Take your time over lunch.'

While they were eating, Amy studied Charlie's face. He looked tired, but she thought he had frightened himself over losing his temper. It seemed a sensible time to try for a favour. In any case, she was tired of struggling.

'Charlie, I can't really manage any more. The washing's just too hard for me like this, and it's going to get harder.'

'What do you expect me to do about it?' Charlie demanded indignantly. 'Get you a servant?'

Despite his tone, Amy could see he was anxious. 'I think—no, I'm sure I could do it if I only had a copper and tubs. Please could you get me one?'

'You cost a lot of money, you know that? I bought a proper range before we got wed so you'd be able to cook decent meals. Then you wanted a wire clothesline, not to mention a new rain barrel. Now you want a copper?'

'I'm sorry I'm such a nuisance, but… well, I'm scared something will go wrong if I have to keep bending all the time. Aunt Edie said I shouldn't, and she knows all about babies.'

'Did she? Hmm. It'd mean a bricklayer to make a proper chimney for it and set it in place—that wouldn't come cheap. I'll have to think about it.'

Charlie picked up his newspaper, signalling that the conversation was at an end, and Amy tackled her food with a sense of relief. He was going to buy her a copper; she was quite sure of it.

After her initial indignation at Ben's having left such a debt, Lizzie was quite unconcerned over his disappearance.

'One less for me to cook for, anyway,' she said. 'I did think his room looked a bit empty when I cleaned it up. I'll give it a real sort out now we know he's not coming back.'

'I hope he's all right. Ben's not much good at mixing with people.'

'Oh, for goodness sake! He's a grown man, not a child. Don't be so stupid, Frank.'

She *was* getting worse. 'Don't call me stupid, Lizzie. I don't like it when you do that.'

'Don't *be* stupid then. I don't know what you're so upset about. Ben didn't worry about you, did he? Just took off and left you to run the farm by yourself.'

'I wish he'd told me he was going,' Frank fretted. 'It's pretty bad when I've driven my own brother away.'

'Driven him away? What rubbish! You didn't make him go.'

'He wouldn't have gone if I hadn't got married. He'd still be here.'

'But I wouldn't be, Frank. Would you rather have that?'

'Of course I wouldn't. Ben's not much use as company, and you're… come here.' Frank reached out and pulled Lizzie onto his lap. She put her arms around his neck and nestled obligingly against him. 'You're neat. But Ben's the only family I've got. I can't just forget about him.'

'I'll be your family now. Me and the babies, when they finally start coming.'

'No sign of it yet?'

'No. I suppose two months isn't long, though. Ma just laughed and told me to be patient when I moaned about it.'

Frank kissed her hair. 'It's not for want of trying, anyway,' he murmured in Lizzie's ear.

When he thought back over the years, Frank recalled that often whole days had gone by without more than two words being spoken by Ben. His brother had never provided much in the way of conversation, while Lizzie did more than her share. He realised now that he had often been lonely with only Ben for company; no one could be lonely with Lizzie around.

If only she wasn't so bossy. She told him what clothes to wear, what time to go into town for supplies, even how to hold his knife and fork. If he tried remonstrating with her she either looked hurt and said she was only trying to help, or told him not to be so silly.

He began to worry that she would start bossing him in front of other people; most of all that she might do it in front of her father. She had come close to it a few times. Frank dreaded to think how Arthur would react to *that*. Once or twice when he was sharpening his razor he looked thoughtfully at the strap and tried to picture himself following Arthur's advice. He didn't think things were that desperate yet. Then again, by the time they were that desperate perhaps Lizzie would be beyond taking any notice of him at all. Or perhaps she was already beyond it. Frank was unwilling to make the trial.

One Tuesday in August Frank was lingering over his afternoon tea while Lizzie did the ironing. She gave a sudden yelp.

'I can hear a few drops of rain on the roof, and I've still got some things on the line from yesterday. Can you give me a hand getting them in?'

They raced out to the clothesline together and started grabbing at the clothes, but the stray cloud passed overhead and the sun returned.

'That's good,' said Lizzie. 'Now, I didn't leave an iron on the table, did I? Oh no, I think I might have! I'd better run back.'

'I'll get the rest in,' Frank said. 'It'll only take a minute.'

He was reaching for the last sheet when he glanced down the hill and saw that two riders had halted on the road to look up at the house. He recognised them as Arthur and Alf, and wondered if they were going to drop in for a visit on their way back up the valley, but they started their horses trotting and disappeared from sight.

Frank thought nothing of the incident until he and Lizzie visited her old home for dinner a few days later. It was Arthur's birthday, and he was more generous than usual about beer. He even broke open a bottle of whisky to share with Frank and Bill.

Despite his father-in-law's generosity, Frank began to sense disapproval in Arthur's manner. Arthur was certainly more reserved than usual with him, and several times Frank thought he saw Alf smirking. Frank drank rather more beer than he had intended, as well as several whiskies, in an attempt to bolster his courage.

'How many drinks have you had, Frank?' Lizzie asked, glancing over from the couch where she had been deep in conversation with her mother.

'Leave him alone, Lizzie,' Arthur said.

'I just—'

'Lizzie!' Arthur raised his voice slightly, and Lizzie subsided. How did he do it? Frank wondered. How did Arthur get Lizzie to be so respectful? She never told Arthur he was being stupid. He poured himself another whisky.

'I think it's time we went home,' Lizzie said a few minutes later. 'It's starting to get dark.'

'Have another beer first, Frank,' Bill suggested.

'No, he's had enough,' Lizzie said firmly. 'Hurry up and get your coat, Frank, I want to get going.' She left the room to fetch her cloak.

Frank stood up to obey, conscious of an unpleasant thickness in his head.

'Yes, hurry up, Frank,' Alf echoed, grinning. 'You might have some more washing to hang out.' He broke into a laugh.

'Shut up, Alf,' Arthur growled.

'But you said—' Alf began indignantly.

'I told you to shut up. If he wants to make a fool of himself it's his affair.' Arthur looked at Frank and shook his head. 'You've made a rod for your own back, Frank, but that's your look-out. You can't say I didn't warn you.'

Lizzie prattled away without seeming to notice Frank's silence as they rode down the valley together. He paid no attention to her words, but her voice was too insistent to be ignored. It was like a mosquito whining away in his ear, on and on without a rest, a background to his uncomfortable musings. Arthur thought he was a fool. The whole family did. Soon the whole town would. Everyone would be laughing at him, not just Alf. Maybe they already were.

Lizzie was still going strong when they went into the house after turning their horses into a paddock.

'Do you want a cup of tea before we go to bed? I think you should, a hot drink would be good for you after all that beer.'

'No.'

'I'll make one. You shouldn't have drunk so much, Frank, you'll have trouble waking up in the morning. Don't do it again.'

'I don't want a cup of tea.'

'Stop being so silly. I'm making a cup of tea and you're going to drink it.'

'I'm *not!*' Frank was dimly surprised by the unfamiliar sound of his own voice raised in a shout. He was even more surprised to find that he had taken hold of Lizzie's bodice with one hand and was shaking her by it. 'You're turning into a real bitch, you know that? I'm sick of you nagging at me, Lizzie. I'm sick of you telling me what to do—bossing me in front of everyone as if I was a little kid. It's to stop. Do you understand?' He glared at her. There was barely an inch in height between them; Frank was grateful that the slight difference was in his favour.

Lizzie's mouth hung open in amazement, then shut like a trap. Her eyes flicked to Frank's right; he stopped shaking her to follow their movement. He saw his own fist waving ineffectually at nothing in particular; he dropped it to his side, and let go of Lizzie's bodice. She stared back at him, white-lipped with what he at first thought was fear but soon realised was tightly controlled rage. It took all Frank's self-control not to quail before her look and apologise. Lizzie turned on her heel and left the room, slamming the passage door behind her.

Frank sat at the kitchen table until his head stopped spinning quite so alarmingly, then made his rather unsteady way after her. The bedroom was in darkness; Frank did not bother to light the lamp. He undressed, leaving his clothes on the floor, and climbed into bed, fully intending to take his pleasure with Lizzie. But once he was between the covers it seemed too much like hard work. He rolled onto his side and went to sleep.

He woke next morning with a throbbing head and a dry mouth. When he stood up he groaned at the stabbing pain behind his eyeballs. Lizzie was already up; Frank found her in the kitchen in front of the range, banging pots and dishes with a noise that seemed to echo in his skull. When he sat down at the table she put his plate in front of him and made to leave the room.

'Where's your breakfast?' he asked.

'I've already eaten.' Lizzie closed the door and left him alone.

It was the same at lunch-time: Frank came into the kitchen and found a single place set at the table, with Lizzie's empty plate on the bench. Again Lizzie served his meal and left the room. At dinner time she sat at the table and ate with him, but apart from an 'Amen' at the end of Frank's grace she did not say a word.

'Why aren't you talking, Lizzie?' he asked.

Lizzie tossed her head. 'It seems I only give offence when I *do* speak, so I'm better to keep silent.'

Frank tried to hide his amazement. Had he really subdued Lizzie? Now that his headache had gone he felt pleased with himself. There had been no need to put off disciplining her for so long. It hadn't been as hard as all that, and it had had such a dramatic result. There was no nagging this evening.

Tonight he was determined to celebrate his victory by taking Lizzie. He climbed into bed and reached out in the darkness to where she lay close to the opposite edge, lying on her back. Frank felt his way down her body and found that her nightdress had been firmly pulled down instead of conveniently riding up to her thighs as it usually seemed to. And her legs were closed.

Frank gave a grunt of irritation as he took hold of her nearer thigh, but when he gave it a tug it moved readily enough. He lifted her nightdress and clambered on top of her.

Why was it so difficult tonight? It wasn't even much fun. Lizzie lay inert with her arms at her sides, not showing any sign that she was even aware of his presence. It was like cuddling something dead. Frank took hold of one of her shoulders and gave it a small shake. 'Lizzie, behave yourself.'

'I'm not stopping you, am I?' came an aloof voice through the darkness.

'You're not exactly *helping.*'

'I'm sure I don't know what you're talking about.' Lizzie did not make another sound. Frank finished, but it was no use trying to pretend he had got any great pleasure from his efforts.

Well, at least it was peaceful now Lizzie had stopped nagging. He saw now that she was not in the least subdued; she was angry and had her own way of showing it. But the effect was much the same.

Frank tried to convince himself over the next few days that he was enjoying the peace and quiet. There was no more constant stream of chatter at the meal table, so he could eat his food in peace. In fact he generally had to eat it in solitude, as Lizzie contrived to have her own meals before he came in as often as not. It seemed strange to sit at the table all by himself. He missed sharing all the little incidents of the day with Lizzie. Their bedroom was even more silent than the kitchen, and the nights had become rather dull, though Lizzie made no attempt to prevent his doing whatever he wanted. Frank wondered fleetingly how long Lizzie could keep it up, but he soon brushed that thought aside. Lizzie was strong; she could keep it up as long as she wanted to.

But he had stopped her from telling him what to do. He had shown her he wouldn't put up with being made a fool of, and the lesson must have sunk in. She was a different woman, really. It wasn't like living with Lizzie at all. In fact it was like...

Oh, God, it was like living with Ben again. Whole days going by with hardly a word spoken. Feeling lonely while sharing a house; while sharing a bed, even. The picture of years dragging on like this was too stark to be borne. This wasn't what he had got married for. Surely it was better to put up with being laughed at than to lose his wife.

'Lizzie,' Frank called as she was about to leave the room, having placed his lunch in front of him.

She turned and looked at him. 'What?' she asked haughtily.

'Those things I said the other night... look, it was only the beer talking. Are you going to make my life a misery for ever over it?'

'I've only been trying not to annoy you. Can't I do anything right?' Lizzie gave him a hurt look, but somehow it did not take long to turn into a smile. She sat down at the table, and in a few minutes she was chattering away as if nothing had happened. That night when Frank put out the lamp and climbed between the sheets Lizzie snuggled up to him, and Frank found he had his warm, soft wife again.

It seemed like wishful thinking when he began to feel that Lizzie wasn't being quite so bossy. Maybe he was just getting used to it; and he would have to get used to it. He had tried to assert his authority and had been soundly defeated; not that Lizzie was trying to lord it over him. She was just being Lizzie.

Frank tried to ignore his discomfort when he had to face Lizzie's family after church the next Sunday, especially when he saw Alf's superior grin and Arthur's frown of disapproval. Even Bill's look of sympathy was hard to take.

'Do you want to come for lunch today?' Edie asked, blissfully unaware of any tension within her family. 'I made a big batch of marmalade on Friday, you can take a few jars home with you.'

'I'd like to come, Ma,' Lizzie said. 'But I'll have to ask Frank first. Frank, dear, is it all right with you if we go to Ma's today? Only if you want to, of course.' She slipped her hand through Frank's arm and smiled sweetly.

Frank stared at her in amazement, then recovered himself. 'I think that'd be all right, Lizzie,' he said after what he thought was due time for consideration.

'Thank you, Frank.' Lizzie gazed adoringly at him for a few moments, then moved off to talk to her mother, leaving Frank standing next to Arthur.

He allowed himself to catch Arthur's eye, and saw a look of astonishment slowly give way to a broad smile.

'That's the way, Frank,' Arthur said. 'You've sorted her out, haven't you? She's hanging on your every word now. You know, for a while there I thought you didn't have it in you. I certainly thought you'd left it too late with Lizzie. I'm glad to say I was wrong.'

'So am I,' Frank agreed.

6

Months before Jane Neill made her reluctant departure from Ruatane at the end of April, she and Harry had come to an understanding. Harry found his father harder to convince than Jane had been that he was old enough to get married, but he had an unexpected ally in Susannah.

'They're so fond of each other, Jack, why make them wait?' Susannah said. 'Jane seems a terribly suitable wife for Harry, too. She's a farm girl, she's used to the life, and she looks a strong sort of girl.'

'I don't know, I think Harry should be older. He's not old enough to know his own mind.'

'But you like Jane, don't you?'

'Yes, she's a nice girl,' Jack said. 'I've got quite fond of her, really.'

'Well, there you are, then. *You're* certainly old enough to judge, even if Harry isn't. Is he going to find a nicer girl than Jane? And she's twenty, you know. If you make them wait too long she might get sick of it and find someone else. Wouldn't that be rather hard on Harry?'

That hit home. Jack did not want to see another of his children forced to take second best. His initial flat 'No—not for years' was soon modified to 'Maybe next year, when you're a bit older', and by mid-May Harry's pleading and Susannah's soft words had done their work. Jack agreed that Harry could get married later in the year, when he had turned twenty-one.

Jack had hoped that would be the end of the issue for a few months, but he soon found Harry was not to be satisfied with merely sharing his bedroom with Jane. He wanted a house of his own.

'I don't want Jane to have to work for *her*,' Harry protested, softening his language from that used when talking privately to John. 'I'm not going to bring Jane here just to be ordered around all the time.'

'Don't bring her, then,' Jack responded irritably, wishing the whole business was over.

'You *said* we could get married! I'm not going to hang around here if I can't have Jane—I'll go and work for someone else. Bob Forster would have me.'

'You're not sloping off after I've fed you for years, you ungrateful young—'

'Jack,' Susannah interposed, coming to Harry's rescue once more. 'Just think it over before you fly off the handle. I'm hurt, of course, that Harry begrudges me the bit of help Jane might be, but he'd only poison her against me if she was living in the same house. I'd have two of them giving me dark looks all the time and making nasty remarks. And at least it'll be one less to cook for and clean up after if Harry has his own place.'

So once again Harry had his way. Jack agreed that Harry could use the quiet winter months to put up a new cottage on the farm with John's help whenever their labour could be spared. Harry went to Te Puke for a few days to meet Jane's parents and get their permission to marry their daughter, then spent the next few months frantically working on a tiny two-roomed cottage. It was barely fit for habitation when September came and it was time for Harry to pay another visit to Te Puke, this time to get married.

Amy had had to follow the progress of her brother's courtship third-hand, through Lizzie's reports, so she was delighted when Harry visited her the day before he was to leave. She was relieved Harry chose a time when Charlie was out on the farm; Amy did not quite trust her brother to be tactful when talking to Charlie.

'I'd have had the house properly finished if Pa had let me have more time off,' Harry grumbled. 'No chance of painting it or anything, I haven't even got the inside walls lined. I just hope the roof doesn't leak, some of the roofing iron's a bit dodgy.'

'She won't mind, Harry,' Amy said. 'As long as you're together, that's all Jane will be thinking about. You can finish the house later.'

'I suppose so. I wanted things nice for her, though. I want to make Jane happy.'

'Just be kind to her. That'll make her happy.'

'Mmm. That won't be hard.' Harry grinned. He glanced at Amy, studiously avoiding looking at her abdomen. 'You all right? Keeping well and everything?'

'Yes, I'm all right.' *Big and awkward and uncomfortable, but I'm not sick.*

'Is he treating you right?'

'I'm all right, Harry,' Amy repeated.

'Good. You tell me if he ever gives you any trouble.'

And what good would that do? But she smiled at Harry. He was only trying to be kind.

'Wish me luck, then,' Harry said. Amy put her arms around his neck and kissed him. They both pretended not to notice her great swollen belly squashed between them.

Amy was grateful when Lizzie devoted an afternoon one day in early October to filling Amy's biscuit tins in a shared session of baking. She tried to work fast enough to do her share, but Lizzie soon noticed how uncomfortable any sort of movement made Amy, and ordered her to sit at the table with a small box as a footstool.

'I'm not used to sitting around doing nothing,' Amy protested.

'Well, you should be. If you can't have a rest when you're in this state I'd like to know when you can. You're all puffy-looking, too.'

'That happens when I get tired. Especially when I stand up for too long.'

'I won't let you stand up, then. I can finish off by myself.'

'Don't burn anything, Lizzie.'

'Humph! I hardly ever burn things. I'm going to make you some fruit pies after I've done these biscuits, then you won't have to cook any puddings for a few days.'

'You're very kind to me, Lizzie.'

'You'd do the same for me. I don't suppose *he* helps you with anything.'

'Cooking's women's work,' Amy said, trying to make her voice light. 'I can manage, anyway.'

'There,' Lizzie said, shutting the oven door with a flourish. 'Now I can sit down for a few minutes while those are cooking. I'll put the kettle on and we can try some of these scones.'

'We should wait for Charlie.'

'We'll have another cup when he comes in.'

Lizzie buttered hot scones and poured the tea when it had drawn, then sat back in her chair with an exaggerated sigh. 'I'm ready for a rest.' She gave Amy a warm smile. 'Only about a month to go now, eh?'

'Don't talk about it, Lizzie. There's no sense worrying before I have to.'

'Worry? You're not worried about it, are you?'

'Having a baby's not very easy. Talk about something else.'

'But it's *natural.*'

'So is dying, and I don't suppose you're in any great hurry to see me do that?' Amy snapped. 'Oh, I'm sorry, Lizzie, I don't mean to be so sour. I'm just fed up with being in this state, and I'm...' *I'm scared.* 'I'm not looking forward to what comes at the end of it.'

'It doesn't last very long, though, does it? And then afterwards you've got a baby. Things'll be much better once you've got a baby.'

'Will they?' It was what all her family seemed to believe.

'Of course they will! I'm really looking forward to seeing your baby. I *wish* I had one.'

I don't want it. 'You will. Don't wish it on yourself too soon.'

'But I *do* wish it!' Lizzie's face creased in a frown. 'Amy, I'm worried.'

'You? What on earth have you got to be worried about?'

'I'm still not expecting. We've been married nearly six months now, and there's no sign of it. What do you think I should do?'

Amy twisted in her chair to get a better view of Lizzie's face, and at once regretted it as a shaft of pain went through her. 'Be thankful,' she said bitterly. 'It's not much fun being in this state. Especially with an awkward baby like this one.'

'Must take after its father. But why is it taking me so long? Amy, what if there's something wrong with me? What if I'm barren?'

'Don't talk rot, Lizzie. There's nothing wrong with you, anyone can see that.'

'Why aren't I having a baby, then? It didn't take you long, did it?'

'No. It seems a man only has to touch me and I'm with child. I don't know, Lizzie, I suppose some women are more fruitful than others.'

'You're fruitful, anyway. You're lucky.'

'Am I? Nobody seemed to think so last year.' *Ann. Everyone thinks you're something shameful, but they all make such a fuss about this one. It's not fair. It's not your fault I did wrong.* Lizzie studiously ignored her remark, and Amy dragged her concentration back to her cousin's worried face. 'Lizzie, I don't know what to tell you. Have you asked Aunt Edie about it?'

'Yes. Ma says six months isn't long. She said Bill was born on her and Pa's first wedding anniversary, so it took three months for them to start him, but she's heard of people taking a bit longer.'

'There you are, then. And you're so strong and healthy, I can't believe you're barren.'

'I don't *feel* barren,' Lizzie agreed. 'But… well, there could be another reason.'

'What are you talking about now? It's just taking a while, like Aunt Edie said.'

'Maybe. Or maybe…' Lizzie drifted into silence.

Amy was tempted to try and change the subject, but it was so unusual to see Lizzie feeling awkward that she felt obliged to try and draw her cousin out. 'Maybe what, Lizzie? What's worrying you?'

'Well, what if… what if we're doing it wrong?'

'What do you mean?'

'You know, what men and women do. What if me and Frank aren't doing it right? We'll never have a baby if we're not.'

'Lizzie! Don't talk like that.' Even talking about pregnancy was preferable to this most distasteful of subjects.

'But how would we know if we were doing it wrong?' Lizzie persisted.

'What nonsense! It's just... well, obvious, isn't it? Men all know how to do it.'

'Frank didn't,' Lizzie said with conviction.

'He must have.'

'No, I'm sure he didn't. He didn't have a clue, Amy.'

'Really?' Amy said dubiously.

'Mmm. Honestly, that first time... well, Frank's been around animals too much. We were cuddling for a bit, then he started sort of shoving at me. I'm sure he was trying to roll me over onto my front. You know, like cows and sheep do it. Ma didn't tell me much, but she said to lie on my back, so I knew that must be right. So when he shoved I just lay still, and after a bit he seemed to get the idea.'

'You shouldn't be telling me all this, Lizzie. Frank would be annoyed if he heard you, and anyway I don't like hearing it.'

'Frank doesn't know I'm telling you, and you wouldn't tell anyone else. I have to tell you, Amy. I need you to tell me if we're doing it right.'

'No!' Amy protested. 'It's bad enough having to do it without having to talk about it! That's one good thing about being in this state—at least this great big belly stops him.'

'Don't you like it?'

'I *hate* it,' Amy burst out. 'Every night before I got big I'd lie there and just shake, I was so scared he'd do it again. It hurts me, and it makes me feel all used and dirty. It's the worst thing of all. You know what, Lizzie? I hate it when he hits me, but sometimes when he does *that* to me I wish... I wish he'd hit me instead.' She put her hands to her face and sobbed.

Lizzie rose from her chair and slid her arms around Amy. When Amy quietened she heard Lizzie murmur, 'We must be doing it wrong.'

'Why? Because you don't hate it?' Amy's voice came muffled.

'Yes. I quite like it,' Lizzie admitted.

'I don't think that means you're doing it wrong, Lizzie. It probably just means you're a good wife.' Amy disentangled herself from Lizzie's embrace. 'You said Aunt Edie told you what to expect, so you must know.'

'She wasn't much use, really. I expect she thought Frank would know all about it, so she was just telling me enough so I wouldn't be scared.'

'What did she say?' Amy asked resignedly. Lizzie was not to be put off, so it was better to get the subject over with.

'Let's see... she said it would hurt a bit the first time, but just to lie on my back and let him get on with it. She reckoned it'd be all right after that—she got this silly sort of look on her face when she said that. She started going on about how happy it makes your husband, so that makes you happy too.' Lizzie's face took on a look that Amy was sure must be at least as 'silly' as Edie's had been. 'That's true, isn't it? It does make them very happy.'

'It must do,' Amy said tartly. 'They seem to want to do it often enough.'

'I know! For a while there I was so *tired!* Frank never seemed to want to sleep.' She gave a little laugh. 'He's a bit better now, but not much. He's terrible,' she said, a fond smile on her face.

'That was enough, wasn't it? You must know whether you're doing it right or not.'

'I *thought* we were. It did hurt the first time—it hurt a lot! I was ready for it, I was sure I could keep quiet when it happened, 'cause I knew Frank would get upset if I let on that it hurt me. Hurt a bit! It really hurt, Amy. And I let out a yell like a pig having its throat cut. I was so annoyed with myself. Oh, Frank was so upset. He sort of jumped away from me and started going on about how it was all his fault, he'd hurt me, he didn't want to hurt me, he should have gone somewhere and found out how—I don't know what he meant by that. It took me ages to shut him up and get it into his head that it was meant to hurt. Then he said that wasn't fair on me. So I told him that's how he could know it was the first time for me. I think he quite liked that.'

'He would,' Amy said quietly, but Lizzie was in full flow and carried on as if she had not heard.

'I finally convinced him it wouldn't hurt me again and he should have another go. It was all right after that. But then, wouldn't you know it? The next week what should come along but my bleeding. Just when we'd really got the hang of it. I asked Ma what I should tell Frank. "Just say it's not convenient," she said. "He'll know what you mean." How on earth was Frank supposed to know that? I said it anyway, and Frank looked all sort of hurt. "I wish you'd just tell me if you don't like it, Lizzie," he said. So then I had to tell him I was bleeding down there. What a fuss *that* caused! Frank started going on again about how he'd done it wrong and damaged me. I had to put my hand on my heart and swear it was normal for women before he'd believe me.' Lizzie gave a sigh. 'And the bleeding's been coming back every month ever since!'

Amy looked at her in amazement. 'Frank's awfully sweet to you, Lizzie. You're a very lucky woman.' *I mustn't feel sorry for myself. I've no right to.* 'It sounds to me like you two are doing it right. Just be patient.'

'Couldn't you just tell me how it's done?' Lizzie wheedled. 'Just so's I could be sure? Please?'

'No. That's enough about it, Lizzie.' Amy tried to sound firm.

Lizzie looked crestfallen. 'Well, if you won't tell me I suppose I'll have to ask Ma. I'll have to tell her we might be doing it wrong. I don't want to do that, Amy. She's sure to tell Pa, then he'll take Frank aside and have a talk to him. Frank would be *so* embarrassed if Pa did that— imagine having his father-in-law find out he's been married six months and still doesn't know what he's doing. Frank hates people laughing at him. I sort of forgot that for a bit, but Frank reminded me.' Lizzie sighed heavily. 'I'll have to ask her, though, if you won't tell me.'

'Oh, for goodness sake! All right, I'll tell you if you'll just shut up about it afterwards. You lie on your back and the man gets on top of you, then he sticks that thing up between your legs and moves about.' Amy gave a shudder at the memory. 'And the next thing you know you're the size of a house. Are you satisfied?'

'Yes!' Lizzie looked delighted. 'That's just what we do! And that's really all there is to it?' Amy nodded. 'So do you think I'll have a baby soon?'

'I expect you will, Lizzie. You're pretty good at getting what you want.'

Amy had not thought it possible for her to become any more uncomfortable, but she continued to grow bigger and more awkward. With the end of October the memory of Ann's birth, never far from her mind, became stronger, and with it the pain of loss. She spent the second of November weeping for her little girl, now one year old, whenever she was alone. Charlie frowned at the sight of her red-rimmed eyes, but said nothing.

'Don't you dare come today,' Amy murmured over and over to the creature causing her such discomfort. 'Don't you dare take Ann's birthday.'

But the day passed with no sign of labour. Another week went by before Amy felt a sharp twinge one morning while she was cooking breakfast. She brushed it off as the baby moving, though she had not felt it move for the previous day or two. But the spasm was followed by another, half an hour later, then another while Charlie was loading milk cans onto his cart.

It's started. Amy was sure it would be many hours before the baby arrived, and Charlie had to get his milk to the factory or it would spoil, so she sat quietly until she heard the cart rattle away down the road. Then she hastily assembled the clothes she thought she would need and wrapped them in a large shawl, placing the whole in her drawstring bag.

She put her cloak beside the bundle; the sky looked grey and threatening, and she might need the cloak's shelter while Charlie took her into town.

Charlie had refused to accept the idea of a strange woman's staying in his house and running the household, even to deliver his precious child, so Edie had helpfully arranged for Amy to stay with Mrs Coulson, a maternity nurse who occasionally took women from particularly isolated farms into her house for their confinements. Amy barely knew Mrs Coulson by sight. As she carried her bundle out to the kitchen she wondered what the nurse would be like. *She'll probably be horrible*, she thought with a shudder, remembering Sister Prescott's rough handling. A wave of pain gripped her, and she forgot about everything else.

When Amy heard Charlie return from the factory, she walked awkwardly to the door and called to him. Charlie took one look at her face and ran over.

'It's started?'

'Yes. I think you'd better take me into town now.'

Amy put on her cloak, then stood and watched as Charlie unharnessed the horse from the spring cart and let it out into the horse paddock. He did not bother to take the empty milk cans off the cart; they tipped over noisily as it tilted. He caught a fresh horse and harnessed it to his new gig, then hoisted Amy's bundle onto the seat and helped her climb in.

It was the first time Amy had ridden in the gig. Charlie had proudly brought it home a few weeks before, announcing that Mr Winskill had said it was just the thing now Charlie was a family man.

'I'll maybe need a bigger carriage as more bairns come along,' Charlie had said, 'but this one'll do for now. It'll carry you and me with a couple of little ones.'

The gig was solid enough, but Amy soon found that its builder had not been generous with springs. It was far bumpier than her father's buggy. As they jolted their way along the beach Amy's contractions merged into the bone-shaking bumps until the whole ride seemed one continuous labour pain. The only respite came when the heavens opened, drenching them within moments, and Charlie stopped to remove his own coat and place it over Amy's head and shoulders.

'You'll get cold, Charlie,' Amy protested feebly, but he ignored her.

The rain had turned into drizzle by the time they pulled up in front of a neat little house with a tiny flower garden, close to the centre of Ruatane. Amy clambered out of the gig with Charlie's help, and waited while he lifted her bundle off the seat. She walked beside him up to the gate, but when Charlie pushed it open Amy froze in fear. Suddenly she could not bear the thought of walking up that path and into a stranger's house to be pushed and bullied and abused; to lie screaming on a hard bed with no sympathy, only contempt; to abandon herself to the pain that was surely worse than dying could ever be.

The door of the house opened, and a wiry-looking grey-haired woman of about fifty came out onto the verandah. 'Mrs Stewart?' she called. 'Hurry up, dear, come inside out of this wet.' She smiled encouragingly at Amy, but Amy remembered the smile Sister Prescott had given her under Jack's watchful gaze. She was sure this woman's apparent kindness was for Charlie's benefit.

'Hurry up,' Charlie said irritably. 'What are you doing, standing there like an idiot?'

'I'm scared,' Amy whispered. She reached a hand towards Charlie's sleeve. At least he was familiar.

But Charlie was not someone to cling to. Amy let her hand drop, and did not resist when Charlie took her by the elbow and propelled her up the path.

Mrs Coulson held the door open until they were in a small passage. She tut-tutted over Amy's sodden state.

'Never mind, dear, I'll soon have you warm and dry. Now, Mr Stewart, off you go home. I don't want you under my feet.'

Amy waited for Charlie to erupt in fury, but Mrs Coulson's matter-of fact orders left him dumbfounded. He retrieved his coat from Amy's shoulders, walked to the door, then turned and asked, 'When do I come back?'

'Tomorrow morning's soon enough. I expect we'll have a little someone for you to meet by then. Goodbye, Mr Stewart.' She gave Charlie a small shove out towards the rain and closed the door firmly behind him, then turned to Amy.

'Let's get these wet things off you, my dear,' she said brightly. 'Oh, what a frightened little face! Don't worry, we'll soon have you comfortable.' Mrs Coulson slipped an arm around Amy's shoulders, and Amy gave a shudder. She backed away from Mrs Coulson, whimpering in fear.

'Goodness me, you *are* frightened, aren't you, dear? Has some old woman been telling you terrible stories? Don't you take any notice— some women enjoy frightening young girls like you. It won't be as bad as all that. Come on, sweetheart.'

Amy tried to take another step backwards, but a powerful contraction gripped her. She clutched her belly and moaned, then leaned against Mrs Coulson and let the woman lead her a short way down the passage and into a bedroom.

Mrs Coulson sat her on the edge of the bed and deftly removed Amy's shoes and stockings. Amy let her do as she wished. If she closed her eyes she could imagine it was her grandmother undressing her for bed, until another shaft of pain brought her back to the present.

'Why are you being so nice to me?' she asked when the pain subsided enough to let her speak.

'Now, why shouldn't I be?' Mrs Coulson said with a laugh. 'Aren't people usually nice to you? Put your arms up, darling.'

Mrs Coulson undressed her, then got the nightdress out of Amy's bundle and helped her into it.

'There we are, now we can get on with things. Lie back, sweetheart.' Amy lay on the bed and lifted her knees, then let them drop outwards. 'That's a good girl,' Mrs Coulson said. 'I'm going to have a little look to see how you're going, you tell me if I hurt you.' But she didn't hurt. Her touch was firm but gentle, and Amy found it almost comforting.

Mrs Coulson stood back from Amy and raised her eyebrows. 'My goodness, dear, it's a good thing you didn't leave it much longer getting here. You're well on the way. Why did you wait so long?'

'I-I didn't want to be any trouble. My husband was busy with the milk, and I thought nothing would happen for hours and hours.'

'You were wrong there! Another hour or two, three at the most, that's all. And you would have troubled your husband a lot more if he'd had to deliver your child out on the road.'

'I'm sorry,' Amy began, then she cried out as pain gripped her.

'Never mind, dear, you're here now. Lie still for a bit, I'll be back in a jiffy.'

She disappeared from the room and came back holding a thick pad of cloth over a dark brown bottle, just as Amy let out a shriek of pain. 'Yes, poor little thing, it hurts, doesn't it?' Mrs Coulson crooned. 'Don't be frightened, this'll make the pain go away. Take a deep breath.' She tilted the bottle for a moment, turned it upright and replaced its cork, then held the pad close to Amy's face.

'What's that? Is that chloroform?'

'That's right, darling. Come on, don't twist your face away.'

The pain was making it hard to think. Amy struggled to concentrate on Mrs Coulson's kind face, but it kept fading into Sister Prescott's grim scowl of disapproval. 'I thought I couldn't have that. I thought it had to hurt.'

Mrs Coulson suddenly looked fierce, and Amy cringed, but her anger was directed elsewhere. 'Is that what the old women have been saying to you?' she demanded. 'Just because they suffered in childbirth they want every woman to, and they tell girls like you that the good Lord meant women to suffer. They're wrong, child. I had my first three with nothing to take the pain away, and I've blessed the Lord for this wonderful thing every day since I bore my fourth with hardly more pain than cutting my finger. This is God's gift to women.'

'I'm not allowed,' Amy said, desperately longing to take hold of that cloth and the relief it promised.

'Who said you're not allowed? Did your husband tell you that? You can be sure he'd be yelling for the chloroform if he had a broken leg that needed setting. I'll tell you what, my dear—the day a man bears a child is the day I'll take notice of any man's opinion on the subject. Anyway, I won't tell him and you won't either. Come on now, be a good girl.' She held the pad over Amy's face just as a sharp pain made Amy cry out louder than ever.

Amy gasped for air and felt a delicious numbness creep over her body. She breathed deeply again and again until the pad was taken away. 'It doesn't hurt now,' she said in wonder. She closed her eyes and savoured the strange, floating feeling that had taken hold of her in place of the pain.

She was still unconscious two hours later when a lusty cry broke the silence of the room. 'A fine big boy,' Mrs Coulson murmured to herself. 'That should cheer the poor, frightened little thing.'

7

This was the strangest dream Amy had ever had. She struggled to wake from it, but hands seemed to be pulling her down into the thick darkness. There were muffled noises around her; they slowly resolved into voices, and even more slowly into audible speech.

'Come on, darling,' a voice said. 'Time to wake up now.'

Granny? Is that Granny calling me? Have I slept in? I'll be late for school. I mustn't be late, Miss Evans said I could start on the new reading book today.

She felt a hand patting her cheek. 'Wake up, dear.'

It's not Granny. Granny's dead. I don't want to wake up.

'Open your eyes, darling. You want to see your baby, don't you?'

My baby? Ann's here? Amy forced her eyes to open, but everything around her seemed dim and unfocussed. 'My baby,' she slurred. 'Where's my baby? I want her.'

'*Him*, you mean. Here's your fine big son.'

Amy began to see a little more clearly. An ugly, wrinkled face topped with a fuzz of red hair was thrust near her own.

'Look at your baby, dear.'

'That's not my baby. What have you done with my baby? I *want* her.' Amy tried to push herself upright in the bed, but her body refused to obey.

'Why does she say it's not her baby, Mrs Coulson?' Amy heard the voice of a young girl. 'It is, isn't it?'

'Hush, girl, of course it is. She's muddled in her mind, she's still stupid from the chloroform. Don't take any notice of what she says, she'll be right as rain when she's woken up properly.'

'I want my baby,' Amy whimpered. She felt tears running down her face, but it seemed too much effort to wipe them away.

'I'll put him to her breast for a bit. That should steady her, and I want him to suck—it encourages the milk to come in. Undo her buttons for me, Nellie.'

Amy felt hands fumbling at the yoke of her nightdress. She blinked away the tears and tried to focus on the red-headed creature. Its face was twisted in what looked like anger, and a thin wail came from its mouth. For a moment the small face blurred into Charlie's large one, contorted with rage as he swung his hand at her. Amy closed her eyes against the sight. 'Please don't hurt me.'

'No one's going to hurt you, darling. The little fellow wants a drink, that's all. My Lord, Nellie, I've never seen a girl as frightened as this one. Have you got her bodice undone yet? That's the way, pull it right open.'

A hand was reaching for her breasts. Amy opened her eyes, and now the face that she saw, half Charlie's face and half a strange creature's, was full of hunger. 'Don't,' she begged. 'I don't want to. Please don't make me. I don't want to!' She waved her hands feebly, trying to ward off the assault on her body.

'Now you're being silly,' a voice said sternly. 'Hold her arms down for me, Nellie. She nearly caught the little fellow a clout then.'

Strong hands gripped Amy's own and forced them down to her sides. *I mustn't struggle. Charlie will be angry with me now. He'll hit me.* 'I'm sorry I was bad. I'll be good now. I'm sorry, Charlie.' She closed her eyes and waited for a blow; instead she felt her breasts being fumbled with and tugged at. Amy lay limp and unresisting. *I belong to him. It's his right to do whatever he likes.*

'Who's she talking to, Mrs Coulson? Who's Charlie?'

'That's her husband. Stop prattling, girl, you pop out to the kitchen and put the kettle on for me. She'll want a nice, hot cup of tea when she comes around properly.'

The mild discomfort of having her nipples sucked at cleared the last of the clouds from Amy's head. When the sucking stopped she opened her eyes and recognised Mrs Coulson, holding a blanket-wrapped bundle.

'Are you all right, dear?' Mrs Coulson asked. 'Do you know where you are now?'

'Yes, thank you. Wasn't someone else here a minute ago?'

'That's Nellie, Mrs Finch's girl from next door. She helps me around the house when I've got mothers staying here—she loves babies, that one. Of course I keep her well out of the way while the real business is going on, but she's a good, useful sort of girl.'

'Oh. Did I… did I say silly things before?'

'No sillier than hundreds of women. Don't worry, dear, I didn't take any notice. Now, have a proper look at your baby.'

Amy tried to drag herself up into a sitting position, but as soon as she moved pain stabbed through her, making her cry out.

'You're a bit tender, aren't you? Take it slowly. You just lie still and I'll move the pillows.' Mrs Coulson held the baby in one arm while she adjusted the pillows behind Amy's back till she was half-upright. 'I'm afraid you'll be sore for a while. This great big boy of yours was in a hurry to get into the world, and he didn't mind tearing you in the process. But I've stitched you up nice and neat, and you'll heal up given time. There you are,' she said, patting the pillows. 'You want to have a little cuddle with your baby now, don't you?'

Amy looked at the creature in Mrs Coulson's arms. It had come from her body, and yet it seemed to have nothing to do with her. 'No, thank you.'

'Don't be frightened, you won't hurt him. Babies aren't as delicate as they look. Come on,' she encouraged. She laid the baby on Amy's chest and curled Amy's left arm behind his head. 'That's the way. Isn't that nice?'

Amy said nothing. She lay quietly and looked at the baby, wondering how long Mrs Coulson would expect her to hold him. *I don't want you.* She felt nothing but weariness and resignation.

After a minute or two Mrs Coulson lifted the baby and placed him in a cradle close to the bed. 'He'll go off to sleep in a minute. He's a fine boy all right.'

'Why is he so ugly?'

'Well, most newborns aren't very pretty, darling, except to their mothers. But it's worse with such a big baby. His head's been all pushed out of shape on his way out. Don't worry, he'll look nice soon.'

'A boy. My husband will be pleased. He wanted a son.'

'Most men do, especially the first time.' Mrs Coulson sat on the bed and slipped an arm around Amy's shoulders. 'You wanted a girl, didn't you, dear?'

'No. I was scared I might have a girl—he would've been angry with me if I had.'

'Of course he wouldn't have been! Disappointed, maybe, but it's nothing to be annoyed over.'

'Yes, he would. He would've been really angry.'

'Does he often get angry with you? Got a bit of a temper, has he?' Mrs Coulson probed.

'Only when I annoy him.' Amy tried to smile. 'The trouble is, I seem to do it such a lot.' She wondered for a moment why she was talking so freely to a stranger; but Mrs Coulson did not seem like a stranger now, and she was so easy to talk to.

'Well, I find *that* hard to believe—a sweet little thing like you. Goodness me, some men don't know how fortunate they are.'

'It doesn't matter. It's a boy, and Charlie'll be pleased with me. That's all that matters.'

'You and the little fellow are both safe and well, and *that's* all that matters,' Mrs Coulson retorted. She gave Amy a gentle squeeze. 'You know what, dear? With all those stitches—and you lost a fair amount of blood when the little fellow was coming, too—I think I should keep you here with me for three weeks instead of two. It'll give you a bit more time to heal up and get stronger before you have to go home and manage by yourself. Would you like that?'

'I'd like to stay—if I won't be a nuisance?'

'Of course you won't! You'll be good company for me. And I've got Nellie to help with the work—now, why's that girl taking so long with the tea?' She bustled off to hurry along the tardy Nellie.

Amy slept late the next morning. It was after nine o'clock before Mrs Coulson brought in her breakfast on a tray. When Amy had had a leisurely meal and dozed a little more, Mrs Coulson sat her up against the pillows and fussed over her. Amy closed her eyes and savoured the pleasure of being treated like a much-loved child as the nurse washed her face and hands.

'I'll give your hair a good brush, you'll want to look nice when your husband comes. Such pretty hair,' Mrs Coulson exclaimed. 'So thick and wavy. I'm afraid your son won't take after you in that.'

Amy looked down at the cradle, where the baby lay sleeping. 'He looks much better today, like a real person. Do you think he looks like Charlie?'

'Mmm? Yes, I suppose he does. Yes, he'll look just like his Papa.'

'I hope so. Charlie would like that.'

Charlie arrived earlier than Amy would have thought possible; she knew he must have rushed through his milking and factory visit. Mrs Coulson had barely finished putting her own pretty mauve bed jacket around Amy's shoulders when there was a loud knocking at the front door and she hurried off to answer it.

'Come in, Mr Stewart,' Amy heard her say.

'What's happened? Is it all over? Is everything all right?' That was Charlie's voice.

'They're both doing very well. Come along, see for yourself.'

Charlie all but pushed his way past Mrs Coulson when they reached the bedroom door. Amy could see from his face that he must have hardly slept all night. He looked drawn and anxious, and she could not help but feel sorry for him.

'Come and see, Charlie.' She indicated the cradle, invisible from where Charlie stood just inside the doorway. 'Come and see your son.'

Charlie strode past the bed and dropped to one knee beside the cradle. He stared intently at the sleeping child, reaching out a hand towards the baby's cheek then letting it hover a few inches from the soft skin.

'My son,' he murmured wonderingly. 'My son.'

Amy and Mrs Coulson watched in silence, unwilling to intrude. When Charlie once again became aware that there were others in the room, he stood up and cleared his throat noisily.

'He's healthy?' he demanded.

'Yes, a fine, strong boy,' Mrs Coulson assured him.

Charlie glanced uncertainly down at the cradle. 'He's not very big.'

'Not very big!' Mrs Coulson exclaimed. 'Don't you go saying that in front of your wife too often or you'll hear all about it! Goodness me, if he'd been much bigger I think you'd still be waiting for him to arrive. I'll have you know that's one of the biggest babies I've ever brought into the world.'

'Is he?' Charlie stared avidly at Mrs Coulson. 'So he's bigger than most bairns?'

'I should say so. Well over nine pounds, he is, and out of a little scrap of a girl like your wife. You did very well, didn't you, dear?' She smiled at Amy.

'Nine pounds.' Charlie gazed at his son, glowing with pride.

'Closer to nine and a half, I'd say.'

'Nine and a half,' Charlie repeated, as if memorising. 'People will ask,' he said with a touch of defensiveness.

'Of course they will,' Mrs Coulson agreed. 'Everyone likes to hear about a new baby. Now I'll leave you alone for a bit and get the kettle on.'

Charlie sat on a chair close to the bed, from where he could see his son clearly. He dragged his eyes away to take notice of Amy for the first time. 'You're all right?'

'Yes, thank you. I'm tired, and it still...' Amy shied away from telling him where it still hurt. 'I'm tired,' she repeated awkwardly. 'But it wasn't too bad. Not as bad as...' *last time*. 'Not as bad as I expected.'

'That woman's looking after you and the boy properly?'

'Oh, yes, she's being lovely.'

'Good.' He turned his attention back to his son, and no more was said between them until it was time for Charlie to make his reluctant departure.

Charlie was only the first of several visitors Amy had over the next few days. Lizzie arrived the following afternoon, bursting into the room clutching a bunch of roses from her mother's garden. She flung her arms around Amy's neck and kissed her, then inspected the baby.

'He's big, isn't he? He's not very pretty, though.'

'No, not really. But he's healthy, and he's a boy. That's the main thing.'

'Humph! I suppose *he*,' a vague hand gesture indicated the absent Charlie, 'wanted a boy.' Without giving Amy time to comment, Lizzie plumped herself down on the bed and leaned close to her. 'Guess what?' she said, her eyes dancing with happiness. 'I'm going to have a baby!'

To Amy it seemed the last thing in the world anyone should be delighted over. 'That's good, Lizzie. I'm pleased for you.'

'I think I already was when I came to see you, you know, when I asked you about all that sort of thing. But I'm sure I am now. The end of June, Ma says it'll be. I hope I have a girl—but I won't really mind if it's a boy.'

'Frank must be pleased.'

'Oh, he is! He's really excited about it.'

'Where is he, anyway?'

'I left him outside. I thought you mightn't want to see men while you're in bed.'

'I'd love to see Frank, Lizzie. I haven't seen him for months and months—I've hardly seen anyone, really. And I'm decent enough like this.'

'All right. What's that girl called who opened the door for me?'

'Nellie.'

Lizzie summoned Nellie, a bright-eyed girl of about twelve, and sent her outside to fetch Frank. He came in looking shy at entering a woman's bedroom, but he smiled at Amy, asked after her health and dutifully admired her son. He and Lizzie exchanged what Amy could see were meant to be secret smiles, reminding one another of their own good news.

'That's enough visiting, Frank, you go and wait outside again,' Lizzie said after a few minutes. 'Amy's looking tired.' Frank gave her a startled look, and Lizzie's demeanour changed at once. 'You don't want to be stuck in a room with two women chattering, do you, dear? Can I stay and talk to Amy for a bit longer? Just for a minute or two? Do you mind?'

'No, that'll be all right, Lizzie,' Frank said, his composure regained. He left them alone again.

'Frank doesn't like me telling him what to do in front of other people,' Lizzie explained in a low voice. 'He's never said—well, only the once— but I can tell. Of course I don't really tell him what to do, just sort of encourage him, but he gets a bit funny about it. I'm careful now, especially in front of Pa, but I never thought about it with only you here—I didn't think he'd worry about you. Never mind, I made it up all right.'

'He looks really good, Lizzie. You must be looking after him well. Frank never used to look like that. He looks… well, *sleek*.'

'Doesn't he just?' Lizzie agreed. 'Well-fed, well-looked after and well pleased with himself.'

Jack and Susannah came next day with the two little boys. Jack looked proudly at the baby and squeezed Amy's hand.

'That's a fine grandson you've given me, girl. It's a great thing for a man to become a grandfather.'

You've been a grandfather for a year now, Pa. Amy managed an answering smile with difficulty.

'The boys'll be in to see you some time,' said Jack.

'I hope so,' Amy said. 'I'd like to see them.'

'Harry and Jane were meant to come in with us, but they never turned up. There was a bit of a row coming from their place this morning. I think they… ahh… fell out.'

'Poor Jane,' Susannah said with a sigh. 'She has a terrible time with him. Harry's so bad-tempered, I've always said so, though no one ever takes any notice of me.'

'Jane gives as good as she gets,' said Jack. 'Let them work it out for themselves.'

'Of course,' Susannah said. 'I wouldn't dream of interfering.'

Their visit was cut short when Thomas and George climbed on the bed and tried to clamber onto Amy's lap, wrestling each other out of the way. Amy cried out in pain when Thomas's foot slipped between her thighs. Mrs Coulson rushed into the room and swept both boys off the bed.

'Keep those children away from her,' she scolded Susannah. 'You should know better, Mrs Leith, letting them climb all over the poor girl like that.'

'They're fond of Amy,' Susannah said, gripping each of her sons firmly by one wrist.

Mrs Coulson stood close to her and hissed in a voice that Amy barely caught. 'The poor little thing's as full of stitches as a flour sack. She can do without great lumps of children tumbling about on her.'

'Well, I'm sure it's not *my* fault if she's delicate,' Susannah said haughtily. 'We'd better go, Jack. I know when I'm not wanted.' She swept out of the room. Amy knew it would be the last time Susannah came to see her.

Charlie came to visit every day, generally staying for an hour or two. He would sit beside Amy's bed and stare at his son, asking Amy questions about the boy's progress and health then lapsing into silence for minutes at a time. Sometimes he arrived while Amy had the baby at her breast, and watched fascinated as the child suckled. Amy knew it was foolish to feel shy at exposing her breasts to her husband, but she was always relieved when she could button up her nightdress again.

It was a new experience for them to be thrust into one another's company with neither work, newspapers nor food to cover their lack of affinity. When the long silences became too awkward Amy filled them with comments about the child, which always aroused Charlie's interest, even if she had made the same remarks the previous day.

Charlie arrived one day and informed Amy that he had registered their son's birth at the courthouse, and had named him Malcolm Charles. The first two minutes of conversation thus taken care of, Amy asked him questions about the farm, and was told the cows were producing well, there were plenty of eggs, and the grass was growing. Silence reigned until Malcolm woke and demanded to be fed, and when Charlie had watched the process he asked Amy yet again if the baby was growing, and was assured that he was.

But if the daily hour or two with Charlie was awkward, that did not seem much to complain about. Charlie's visits and feeding Malcolm were the parts of Amy's day that she thought of as her duty; the rest was gentle pleasure. Mrs Coulson sat with her each afternoon after she had done her morning's work, and Amy enjoyed talking with the older woman or sharing a companionable silence. Amy was not used to idleness, and begged Mrs Coulson to let her help with things, so the nurse gave her small tasks such as mending that she could do sitting down. Often one or both of them would doze for a time, making up for the broken nights Malcolm was giving them. Mrs Coulson told Amy of how she had come to the Bay of Plenty as a soldier's wife during the wars of the 1860s, and had been left a widow with young children to support.

'There was only one thing I knew how to do that could make me a bit of money, and that was birthing babies. So I started doing that when my youngest was seven years old. Many's the time I'd have a frantic husband knocking on my door in the middle of the night, and I'd have to saddle up and ride out to some farm in the back of beyond, with my oldest girl looking after the other four, and her only fourteen. Well, my little ones are all grown and settled now, none of them in Ruatane, I'm sorry to say. But they visit me when they can, and I see plenty of little ones still.'

In return, Amy told her of her own childhood, the little she remembered of her mother, what her grandmother had been like, and how Amy had run the household after her grandmother died. She even mentioned her dream of being a teacher, though briefly and in an offhand way. After a small hesitation, she confessed that she had never got on very well with Susannah, and she could see from Mrs Coulson's set expression that the nurse did not approve of her stepmother.

Safe though she felt with Mrs Coulson, Amy's confidences did not extend past the birth of her little brothers. She did not trust herself to speak of Jimmy's arrival with anything like nonchalance, and she would not risk being drawn on the reasons for her strange marriage. Not that Mrs Coulson showed any disposition to pry.

'You remind me of my granny,' Amy told Mrs Coulson one day, as the two of them basked in the afternoon sunshine.

'Goodness me, I know I'm ancient but I'm not old enough to be your grandmother, girl!' Mrs Coulson said, with a mock-fierce expression that took Amy in for a moment.

'I'm sorry, I didn't mean to be rude.'

'Now don't look so crushed, darling! I was only having a little joke. Where's your sense of humour?'

'I don't know,' Amy said thoughtfully. 'I used to have one. I think I lost it.'

'Not much to laugh about these days?' Mrs Coulson asked gently, with a kind smile that made Amy want to cry. 'Never mind, dear, make the best of it. You've got your little boy to cheer you up now.'

Mention of Malcolm made Amy feel guilty again. *I don't love him. There must be something wrong with me when I don't love my baby.* She fed Malcolm when Mrs Coulson placed him in her arms, held him when the nurse told her to give him a cuddle, and handed him back as soon as she could. When the baby's face was contorted with angry crying, making him look like his father in a rage, Amy sometimes had a twinge of fear she knew was foolish, but other than that she felt nothing for him at all. 'Yes, I've got Malcolm.'

Her three weeks with Mrs Coulson drew to an end all too quickly. On the appointed day, Charlie pulled up in the gig to collect his wife and son.

Amy walked down the path with Malcolm in her arms, Mrs Coulson beside her carrying Amy's bundle. At the gate, Amy impulsively flung one arm around the nurse's neck and kissed her, careful not to crush the baby as she did so. She turned and saw Charlie standing by the gig watching.

'She's been very kind to me,' Amy said, abashed at being caught in such an outburst of emotion.

Mrs Coulson smiled at her. 'Now, who could help being kind to you?' She turned to Charlie and fixed him with a serious look. 'You've a sweet little wife, Mr Stewart. I hope you look after her properly.'

Charlie frowned, but made no reply. He took Amy's bundle and loaded it into the gig, then helped her up to the seat. When Amy looked back at Mrs Coulson the nurse was dabbing at her eyes with a handkerchief, but she put it away quickly and waved them off.

Amy had worried that Malcolm might wake and want to be fed during the drive home, but the gig's motion seemed to soothe him. He was still sleeping in her arms when they went into the house. She put him in the cradle Charlie had made, and went out to start cooking dinner. She knew it would take her what was left of the afternoon; she still tired easily, and her body ached if she stood for long without a rest. Amy ignored the pile of dirty dishes for the moment; cleaning the house would have to be done a little at a time.

That evening Amy once again had her sewing and Charlie his newspaper to hide behind, so that their silence did not appear awkward. At nine o'clock Charlie stood up and said 'bed'. He put out the lamp, walked out of the parlour and into the bedroom. Amy sat on in her chair for a few moments, gathering strength for what was to come. She had never before denied Charlie anything he demanded.

When she had put on her nightdress, she made sure Malcolm was tucked snugly into his cradle by her side of the bed. He was sleeping soundly for the moment. The baby looked less disconcertingly like his father when he was asleep. *But I've never seen Charlie asleep*, Amy realised. She wondered if his face softened from its habitual scowl when he slept.

Charlie stood by the lamp waiting for her to get into bed. As soon as she rose from the cradle and climbed between the sheets, he put out the light. Amy was quite sure Charlie had not washed or aired the bedding during her absence. The stale smell of the room brought that horror-filled first night in this bed alive in her memory. *I thought I couldn't bear it. But I'm learning—things'll get better.*

She was so certain he would try to take her that she was ready to speak the moment she felt his hand on her shoulder: 'No, Charlie.' She was surprised at how calm her voice sounded; it gave no suggestion of the fear churning inside her.

There was the briefest of silences; then, as though he could not believe he had heard her properly, Charlie said, 'What?'

'There's bleeding... from having the child.' Amy spoke quickly, while

93

her courage held.

'Is something not right with him?'

'No, it's quite normal.' Amy could feel her face burning, and was glad the darkness hid it. 'Women always have this after a baby's born.'

She sensed he was debating whether to believe her or to test the truth of her words. When he finally spoke again she let out her breath with relief, and only then realised she had been holding it.

'How long?' he asked.

'Another three weeks,' Amy answered in a small voice. Charlie made a noise in his throat and rolled away from her.

Malcolm woke an hour later. His mewling cries seemed much louder in the darkened bedroom than they had at Mrs Coulson's, and Amy was awake at once. She took him up from his cradle, thankful that the moon gave just enough light for her to see by, and sat on the chair beside the bed while the baby nursed. Charlie stirred a little. She saw the dark outline he made against the window heave as he rolled over, but he did not wake.

When the baby woke next at one o'clock Amy tried to reach him again without Charlie's being woken, but Charlie gave a snort and sat up against the pillows.

'What's happening?' he said sleepily. 'What's wrong with him?'

'Nothing,' Amy said, putting the baby to her breast. 'I'm just feeding Malcolm.'

'Why are you sitting in the dark?'

'I didn't want to wake you up. I can see well enough.'

'Well, you *did* wake me up,' Charlie grumbled. But he rolled over, and she could soon hear from his breathing that he had gone back to sleep.

The sky was lightening when Malcolm woke once more, this time crying from wet napkins as well as hunger, as Amy realised when she picked him up. She glanced in Charlie's direction and saw him looking at her resentfully.

'He cries a lot,' he said.

As if I'm doing it on purpose. 'Babies do.' She turned away from Charlie to attend to Malcolm's napkin. The baby howled, waving his tiny fists in impotent protest against discomfort and hunger.

'Humph!' Charlie said, sitting up in bed. 'I might as well get up now, I won't get back to sleep with *that* going on.' Amy said nothing. There was nothing useful to say.

Malcolm *did* cry a lot, Amy had to admit. She looked at his angry little face, red and screwed up, as she walked around the kitchen floor with him later that morning, trying vainly to soothe him.

'What's wrong, baby?' she asked helplessly. 'You're not hungry, I've just fed you. You're not wet. Do you have a pain? I wish you could tell me.' But Malcolm just screamed. Amy didn't recall Thomas and George waking so much when they were tiny. *Maybe I've just forgotten—I didn't have to get up to them, only look after them in the daytime. Did Ann cry all the time like this? I don't think so—but I lost Ann when she was younger than Malcolm is now.*

After half an hour of Amy's pacing back and forth, Malcolm finally tired himself out with crying and closed his eyes. Amy put him back in his cradle with relief.

Amy found it difficult to get her work done during the short periods when Malcolm fell asleep, but she knew she had to keep the house running smoothly. Charlie was going to be difficult enough with his sleep being disturbed and her body being unavailable to him; if he didn't have his meals on time he would be unbearable.

Charlie came in at lunch-time, but instead of sitting down at the table he walked straight through the kitchen and into the parlour. Puzzled, Amy followed him, and found him in the bedroom standing over the cradle staring down at Malcolm. He looked so proud and self-satisfied that for a moment Amy forgot to be frightened of him. *Perhaps we really can be like an ordinary family.*

He turned and saw her looking at him. 'He's asleep,' he said.

'Yes, at last,' said Amy. 'Your lunch is ready.'

Charlie had something close to a smile on his face as he ate his lunch. 'He's a fine boy, isn't he?'

'Oh, yes, very healthy Mrs Coulson said. And big for his age, too. He'll be strong.' Charlie looked more smug than ever. 'He looks just like you,' Amy said, studying Charlie's reaction carefully.

'Don't talk rot—saying a little mite like that looks like a grown man.' But Amy could see he was pleased at the idea.

Charlie was less good-natured when Malcolm woke them an hour after they had gone to bed that night. 'How long is this going to keep up?' he grumbled as Amy sat in the chair nursing the baby.

'Quite a while, yet, I'm afraid,' Amy said into the darkness. 'He'll sleep a bit longer between feeds as he gets older, but he's going to wake in the night for months yet.'

'Months!' Charlie repeated, thunderstruck.

'Yes.' Charlie said nothing out loud, but she could hear him cursing under his breath. 'Would you like me to take him into the other bedroom and sleep there for a while—just until he starts sleeping a little bit longer?'

'No—you stay where you are,' Charlie said, surprising her with his vehemence. 'I suppose I can manage without sleep for a while,' he said in a martyred tone.

I suppose I can, too.

But it was hard to manage, Amy found. Malcolm wouldn't let her sleep for more than three hours at a time, sometimes much less. He often cried during the day, and took a good deal of soothing. He fed well and was thriving, but Amy felt herself becoming more and more worn out over the next few weeks.

It made things even harder that she had to be as careful as ever not to annoy Charlie. She had to speak softly when he grumbled, appear calm and collected when Malcolm's constant crying made him irritable, and do all her work properly, despite weariness from lack of sleep and lingering pain from the difficult birth.

'He's growing well, isn't he?' Lizzie said when she called in one afternoon on her way to visit her mother. 'How old is he now?'

'Six weeks.' Amy felt a sudden stab of fear. 'I've been home three weeks today,' she said, more to herself than to Lizzie.

'Is everything all right, Amy?'

'What? Oh, yes, everything's all right—I'm just tired, that's all, and I wish this one would start sleeping a bit more. He keeps us awake a lot.'

Afterwards Amy wondered if Charlie had been checking the calendar every evening to keep track of the time since that first night she had come home. He gave her a meaningful look as he bent over the lamp. 'You've been home three weeks now, haven't you?'

'Yes,' Amy said very quietly. She lay still, trying to will her muscles not to tense up.

The moment he started Amy knew it was too soon for her; the places where she had been torn during Malcolm's birth had not yet healed properly. But it would be worse than useless to ask Charlie to stop.

I can bear it. It won't last long.

Amy kept her teeth tightly clenched to stop herself from screaming with the pain. She felt herself going rigid, a reaction so strong that she knew Charlie must be aware of it. She tried to remember how she had learned to cope with it before: *Relax... go limp... think about something else.* But she hadn't been in agony then. Her pain took on the rhythm of his thrusting. When he had finished it took her a few moments to realise it was over. Her body was still throbbing.

Charlie gave her an angry shove as he pushed himself away. 'You're worse than ever.' Amy opened her mouth to say she was sorry, but the moment she did so she could tell that if she let her jaw relax she would cry out.

When Malcolm woke two hours later Charlie was snoring, while Amy was awake trying to muffle her sobs. She picked up the baby, still wrapped in his blankets, and slipped quietly out to the parlour, finding her way to the door by feel in the darkness. She sat down in one of the armchairs and unbuttoned her nightdress, then slipped a nipple into Malcolm's questing mouth and suckled him till he was satisfied. She buttoned up her bodice, lay back in the chair and closed her eyes.

I'd forgotten. I'd forgotten how awful it is. It's even worse now I'm all torn up. I wonder how long before I'll heal. Maybe I won't ever heal if he keeps doing that. A warm tear trickled down her face; she caught it with her tongue before it had the chance to drop onto the snugly wrapped baby.

Amy woke to find her shoulder being shaken, and saw that daylight had crept into the room.

'What are you doing out here?' Charlie asked grumpily.

Amy shook her head to try and clear it. 'I... I wanted...' *I wanted to get away from you.* 'I didn't want to wake you again. Malcolm slept right through,' she said in surprise. 'He must like being cuddled at night.'

'You're not taking him into bed with you,' Charlie said quickly. 'I'll not have my son being made soft. And I'll not have *you* sneaking out of my bedroom.'

'I'm sorry. Do... do you want me to come back to bed now?' The thought made Amy's stomach turn over. Tears brimmed in her eyes.

'Humph! It's time to get up, near enough.' He looked at her fear-filled face in disgust. 'What the hell's wrong with you, woman? Eh?'

'It... it hurts me.'

'Hurts you!' Charlie echoed scornfully. 'Are you made differently from other women, then?'

'I don't know. It just hurts me, that's all.' Amy cringed, waiting to be slapped, but Charlie was too conscious of the child in her arms to lash out at her.

'I suppose you think I don't know what I'm doing?'

'No, I don't think that. I'm sorry I annoyed you. I didn't mean to.' Amy closed her eyes and willed him to leave her alone. Charlie made an angry noise in his throat, then stalked off to the bedroom to get dressed.

Malcolm cried off and on all morning, as if reflecting Amy's own emotions. His noise hid his parents' silence over breakfast. Amy tried to avoid Charlie's eyes; when her own did meet them she saw resentment there.

After he returned from the factory Charlie had his morning tea, still staring balefully at Amy, then rose from the table.

'I'm going into town,' he announced.

Amy stopped pacing the floor with the baby for a moment.

'Can I come too? It would settle Malcolm down, he loves riding in the gig. And I need a couple of things in town.'

'No, you can't,' Charlie said gruffly. 'You can stop home and do your work.'

Amy was so startled by his refusal that she nearly asked why he would not take her, but stopped herself in time. That would sound too much like arguing with him. She followed him out the back door with the still wailing Malcolm in her arms and watched him saddle up Smokey.

'Will you be gone long?' she asked.

'If it suits me,' Charlie answered shortly.

'Can you get me some—'

'No, I can't. You can wait until Saturday. Useless bitch,' he flung at her as he swung his leg across the saddle and set Smokey moving with a hard kick. Amy saw the horse's ears flick in surprise.

'Your Papa's annoyed with us,' she told Malcolm. 'He's annoyed with you for crying all the time, and with me for not doing what he wants. No, that's not right—I do whatever he wants. I think it's because I don't *feel* what he wants. That's hard, isn't it? I can't help what I feel.' She sighed. 'I suppose if I was a good wife I'd feel the right things. Lizzie does.'

Amy sat down wearily on the grass and watched Malcolm waving his tiny fists in frustration. She felt a rush of sympathy for him. 'You're not really bad-tempered, are you, baby? You're just miserable, same as me. Poor little mite. Papa's angry all the time, and Mama didn't even want you. I do want you now, Mal. Well, even if I don't it doesn't really matter, does it? We're all stuck with each other and we've got to make the best of it. I'll be a good mother to you, Malcolm. I'll try and make you happy, you and your Papa both. I just wish I was better at it.'

She dragged herself to her feet. 'Come on, Malcolm, let's walk you around out here and see if all this fresh air and sunshine can wear you out. Maybe if I get you tired enough you'll sleep all through the night. I wish your Papa would.'

Amy looked down the road and watched Charlie disappearing. 'I wonder why he wouldn't take us today,' she said thoughtfully. 'He's usually so keen to show you off, Malcolm. It's strange he's gone off by himself, and it's not even a shopping day. I wonder where he's gone.' She shrugged and began pacing the grassy area, murmuring soothing noises to the baby in her arms.

8

June 1886

Frank lay in bed wondering what had woken him so abruptly out of a sound sleep. His head had somehow slipped off the pillow, and he slid slowly into a more comfortable position, careful not to disturb Lizzie. She was not sleeping well now that she was so big, and she needed her rest.

He had barely got his head back on the pillow before a sharp jolt shook the bed and set the windows rattling. Frank felt Lizzie awake with a start.

'What is it? What's happening?' she cried out in alarm.

Frank slipped his arms around her. 'Shh, Lizzie, it's all right. It's just an earthquake.' He held her close while the bed slowly stopped shaking.

'It gave me a fright. I was having such a good sleep, too.'

'Mmm, it was quite a strong one. Never mind, try and go back to sleep.'

'It took me ages to drop off,' Lizzie grumbled. Frank felt her wriggling around, trying to find a comfortable way to lie. She stopped moving, and Frank listened to the sound of her breathing, wondering if she had fallen asleep again.

He had almost nodded off himself when another tremor rolled them both into the centre of the bed. The windows rattled loudly and the bedstead creaked and groaned under them until the shaking stopped.

'That was even worse,' said Lizzie. 'I thought the bed was going to fall apart.'

'Nah, this bed's pretty strong—look what it put up with for a year.' Frank grinned into the darkness. The bed had had a quiet time for the previous few months since Lizzie's bulk had become too daunting, but the memories of pleasure were still vivid. He reached an arm across Lizzie and gave her a careful squeeze. 'Don't worry, it won't fall apart.'

Lizzie wriggled again. 'I won't get back to sleep now. Oh, I'm so uncomfortable tonight—even worse than usual.'

'What's wrong?'

'It's my back. It's really aching.'

'Roll over.' Frank helped Lizzie heave herself onto her side, then slid his hand slowly down her back. 'Here?'

'No, lower—oh, that's the spot.' He rubbed Lizzie's back through her nightdress, and she made little noises of pleasure. 'Mmm, that feels good.'

'This fellow playing up tonight, eh?' Frank slid his hand over Lizzie's belly and patted it, enjoying the feel of the firm, warm flesh through the fabric.

'Who says it's a fellow? Rub my back some more.'

'Bossy,' Frank teased. He nuzzled his way through Lizzie's hair and planted a soft kiss on her neck as he began to rub her back once again.

'You're good at that. I suppose husbands are some use.'

'Useful for making babies, anyway.' A soft pattering stole Frank's attention. 'Hey, it's raining.'

'So it is. That's good, isn't it?'

'Mmm. The ground's been getting really dry lately.'

The noise on the iron roof grew louder. When Frank had soothed the ache out of Lizzie's back, he put his arms around her and pressed his own body against hers. 'It's cold tonight. It's a good night for cuddles.'

'It's always a good night for cuddles,' Lizzie said drowsily. The next earthquake was so slight it almost seemed to be rocking them to sleep.

'Frank?' Lizzie's voice had an oddly strained note in it that penetrated Frank's slumber abruptly. The night seemed deeper than before. As he dragged himself back into wakefulness Frank realised he had been asleep for some time.

'What's wrong? Was it another quake?'

'No.' Lizzie's hand reached out in the darkness and clutched at the sleeve of Frank's nightshirt. 'It's the baby. I think it's started coming.'

'What? But—but it can't be. It's not time yet. You said not for another couple of weeks.'

'I know, but I think it is. You'll have to go and get the nurse.'

'Now? It's the middle of the night, Lizzie.'

'I can't help that!' Lizzie spoke sharply, but Frank could hear the nervousness in her voice. 'Hurry up!' She rolled over and pushed at him.

'Hey, hey, calm down, Lizzie—don't shove me out of bed,' Frank said, wishing he felt calmer himself. He slipped an arm behind Lizzie's shoulders and held it firmly in place when she tried to push it away. 'Are you sure it's the baby?'

'Yes! Well, not *sure*. What else could it be, though? I felt a pain right around my back—oh, there's another one! Ow!' Lizzie gave a yell, followed by a long, low moan. 'That was worse. It's working its way around to the front now.'

'Well… how long will it take?'

'How should I know? I've never had a baby before.'

'You must have some idea. Hasn't your ma told you anything about it?'

'Not that sort of thing. She just told me a bit about how it would feel, not all the ins and outs. I don't know—wait a minute, I'm sure Amy said it took hours.'

'Hours? How many? Two? Three?'

'I don't know! Stop asking stupid questions, just go and get the nurse.'

'Lizzie, it's going to take me well over an hour to get a nurse here. Maybe two hours—it's dark out there, I won't be able to go fast, you know. I can't leave you alone all that time. I think I'd better go and get your ma first, then I'll try and get into town.'

'Yes! Go and get Ma—please go and get her, Frank.'

'Do you think you can hang on that long?'

'I… I think so. You won't take long, will you? Please don't take long.'

'I'll be as quick as I can.' Frank rolled back the covers, shivering when he felt the chilly night air. He fumbled for the matches lying on the dressing table and lit the lamp. The clock beside the lamp showed three o'clock. Lizzie's face in the lamplight was white and full of fear. Frank crossed to the bed and put his arm around her. 'Will you be all right on your own, Lizzie?'

'If it's not for long. *Please* hurry, Frank.' Lizzie bit her lip, and Frank could see the beginnings of tears in her eyes. He forced himself to turn away from the sight; he knew he would not be able to leave her if he saw her get any more upset.

Frank dressed quickly, stopping for a few seconds when a small earthquake made the room tremble. He lit a candle from the lamp and carried it out to the kitchen. Catching sight of his face in the hall mirror, he saw that it was almost as white as Lizzie's. He went out the back door to the porch, where his hat and coat were hanging above his boots. The noise of the rain on the roof was louder out here, and Frank gave a groan. 'Hasn't rained for weeks—now it's got to start again the night Lizzie's having the baby,' he muttered under his breath as he shrugged on his coat.

There was a kerosene lantern hanging in the porch. Frank lit it and placed it on the porch floor while he pulled on his boots and reached for his hat. The night was black; there must be a heavy bank of cloud feeding the rain. Just catching a horse was going to be hard, let alone making his way up the road in the pitch darkness. The horses would be in a state with all those earthquakes, too; he could hear them snorting and whinnying nervously. He wouldn't be able to go faster than a walk; even fetching Edie was going to take close to an hour at that pace.

Frank stood at the top of the porch steps and peered uneasily into the gloom. There was something strange about that rain. The air seemed to have a close, stuffy feel about it instead of the freshness rain usually brought; there was even a hint of sulphur. He stretched his hand out into the night air, expecting to feel cool wetness.

How could water feel rough against his skin? His fingers felt gritty when he rubbed them together. Frank drew back his hand and saw it was covered with a coarse dust. A sick realisation came to him: it wasn't rain at all. It was ash.

Fear so intense that it left a bitter, metallic taste on his tongue sent a shudder through Frank, so strong that for a moment he thought it was another quake. What was going on out there? Why was the earth being convulsed while ash fell from the sky?

'And, lo, there was a great earthquake; and the sun became black as sackcloth of hair.... And the stars of heaven fell unto the earth.' Words half-remembered from a lesson in church crept unbidden into Frank's mind. Was this the end of the world?

'Frank?' Lizzie's voice came in a wail down the passage. 'Where are you? It hurts, Frank.'

The sound brought Frank back from the edge of panic to a sense of his responsibilities. He had to look after Lizzie. He couldn't go out into whatever was happening in the world; if ash was falling, maybe fire would soon shower from the sky. If that happened he had no way of being sure the house would protect them, but he knew it would mean certain death to anyone caught outside. That included his stock, but he could not risk himself to try and get the animals into shelter, even if he had had the barns to hold them. If he was injured there would be no one to look after Lizzie.

He pulled his boots off and left them lying in the porch with his hat and coat dropped heedlessly on top of them, stopping only to put out the lantern. Another quake struck when he was barely inside the kitchen door, and he stumbled against one wall as he hurried up the passage to the bedroom.

Frank rushed into the room and crouched beside the bed. He reached out and stroked Lizzie's face, not speaking until he was sure he could make his voice sound calm. She must not know how frightened he was. 'I can't get out, Lizzie. Not till daylight, anyway.'

'Why not? You've got to go out—you've got to get the nurse for me.'

'I can't. There's something really funny going on. That's not rain you can hear on the roof—it's ash.'

'Ash? How can it be ash?'

'I don't know. It's like all the hills are on fire, except it's pitch black out there. Don't worry, Lizzie,' he said quickly, seeing a new fear grow in her face. 'It won't hurt us here. We'll be safe inside the house.' He silently prayed he was telling the truth. 'But I can't go out in that—I'd never get the horse to move, it'd just go mad and throw me. And if that ash turns hot… well, it'd burn me up where I stood.'

'I want Ma. I want Ma!' Tears spilled out of Lizzie's eyes. Frank sat on the bed and held her close until her sobs quietened. 'You mustn't go out. I can see that. But I'm scared, Frank.'

Frank had never seen Lizzie frightened of anything. Now she needed him to be strong, and the knowledge made him brave. 'Don't be scared. I'll look after you.'

'What about the baby?'

'Maybe nothing'll happen for hours and hours. The minute it's light I'll go out—the horses won't be so frightened in daylight, and I'll be able to see if it's safe or not.' He did not voice his fear that there might not be any daylight under that thick pall of ash, or any morning at all if it really was the end of the world. Or perhaps they would both be dead, burned alive by whatever unnatural flame was producing that ash. But there was no sense letting himself think like that. Whatever was going on outside was beyond his control; within this room he could still do some good.

'What say it does? What if the baby comes before you can get out?'

'Then we'll just have to manage by ourselves.'

'How can we? We don't know anything about it. Frank, I don't really know what happens. Ma just said the nurse would tell me what to do, and it was nothing to be frightened of. She said the nurse would give me something to stop it hurting before it got too bad. I don't know how they get babies out.'

Unlike Lizzie, Frank had often had occasion to put his hand up the back end of a cow, helping reluctant calves into the world. 'I think I do. I can figure it out if I have to.'

'How do you know? You're not even a woman.'

'It can't be that different from cows—'

'I'm not a cow!' Lizzie flung at him.

'Of course you're not. You're my wife. You're the most important thing in the world to me, and I'm not going to let anything happen to you.'

'Am I really the most important thing in the world to you?' Lizzie had forgotten her fear for the moment. She rested her head on Frank's shoulder.

'Yes, you are.' He held her close in silence, his mind racing. He had seen cows die in calving. And from time to time he had heard of women dying, sometimes leaving tiny babies behind. He had a vague idea from something his mother had once said that Amy's mother had died that way. If anything happened to Lizzie… he could not bear to think of it. Losing Lizzie seemed a far worse disaster than anything else the world could do to him. 'We can manage if we have to, Lizzie, but it'll be better if we can wait for the nurse.' He disentangled himself and tucked the covers in on her side of the bed. 'I think you should lie still and try to stay calm—that might slow things down.'

'All right,' Lizzie said meekly. That small, frightened voice did not sound like his wife.

'Are you warm enough?'

'No. I want a cuddle.'

Frank unbuttoned his trousers and stepped out of them before climbing into bed beside Lizzie; keeping the rest of his clothes on would save a valuable minute or two when daylight finally came. If it came. He put an arm under Lizzie's shoulders and guided her head on to his chest, then stroked her hair with his other hand. 'Is that better?'

'Much better. Keep holding me like this.'

'I'll hold you all night if you want me to.'

Lizzie's body jerked. By the lamplight Frank saw her face twisted with the strain of holding back a cry. He kissed away a tear that had escaped from under her tightly closed eyelids, and waited until he felt the tension slip away from her. Lizzie had not made a sound.

'Are the pains really bad, Lizzie?'

'Not *really* bad—I'm just being a big baby. It's because I'm scared of what's going to happen later when it starts hurting a lot.'

'You're not a baby. You're brave. You didn't even yell out with that last one.'

Lizzie took hold of his hand and raised it to her mouth to kiss. 'I feel a lot braver with you cuddling me.'

As the long night dragged on Frank held Lizzie close, murmuring comforting noises and kissing her softly when she tensed in pain. Sometimes Lizzie dozed off for a few minutes between contractions, but Frank remained wakeful, trying to decide just what he would do if he had to deliver the baby himself. He wondered if he should look to see if there was any sign of it trying to make its way out, but he suspected that would distress Lizzie, and perhaps even hurt her. Although he knew his way well enough by feel he had never seen what Lizzie looked like down there, and this was probably not the right time to force that on her. No, it was safer to make do with trying to give her comfort by holding her, and hope desperately that he would be able to get help for her in the morning.

The lonely hours of silence gave him time to think about what might be going on outside. As he thought it over he was able to view things more calmly, especially when the earthquakes became less frequent and then stopped altogether. Ash in the sky: what could that mean? In his mind Frank pictured the view from the front verandah, down the valley and out to sea. White Island on the horizon, with its permanent cloud hovering above, sometimes bigger, sometimes smaller, but always there, even when the island itself was invisible. White Island was a volcano, he knew that, and he remembered that Miss Evans had said the cloud above it was ash, because the island was always on fire. *Erupting*, they called it in the newspapers.

That must be it, he decided. White Island was having a huge eruption, far bigger than any within living memory. The island was thirty miles off the coast; it couldn't possibly burn them up from there. The worst it could do was make a terrible mess, and perhaps keep the sky dark when the sun rose. Frank let out a deep sigh of relief. Now all he had to worry about was whether he would have to deliver the baby or could leave it to someone who knew what they were doing.

At first Frank thought it was wishful thinking when the darkness of the room seemed to lessen, but when the outline of the window took shape he knew morning had come at last, and had brought daylight with it. He disentangled himself from the sleeping Lizzie, trying not to disturb her, but she woke as soon as he moved and grasped his sleeve, trying to keep hold of him.

'Let go, Lizzie,' he said softly. 'It's light outside. I'm going out to get your ma now. I won't be long.'

Lizzie rubbed her eyes and sat up to watch Frank pulling on his trousers. He gently pushed her down against the pillows. 'Lie still till I get back.' He tucked her in and planted a kiss on her forehead before he left the room.

His coat and hat were still lying in an untidy heap in the porch on top of his boots. Frank reached for the coat, then stopped to stare in amazement at the scene below the steps. Everything around him was the same dull grey colour, as if an artist with only one hue in his palette had slashed it carelessly over the landscape. Trees, hedges, grass, all had the same soft-edged hazy appearance, and although there was no longer any ash falling a lowering sky closed the world in with a darker grey pall. Frank put on his coat and hat then pulled his boots on before stepping down into the greyness. An inch of his boots disappeared into the ash as he walked, and small clouds of dust rose around him.

The sombre colour invited silence, but instead Frank heard the mournful lowing of cows as they searched fruitlessly for grass. The doleful sound coupled with the eeriness of the grey-covered landscape seemed like a portent of death, and it made Frank shudder. Then he remembered Lizzie pressing close to him; trusting him. He walked faster, then broke into a run towards the horse paddock. No sense thinking about death when he was responsible for seeing that a birth went smoothly.

Belle let herself be caught without trying to run away; she almost seemed to want Frank's company. But she shied and rolled her eyes when he put on her saddle, and she performed an awkward sidestepping dance when Frank mounted her. Her ears went flat against her skull and she tried to rear, but Frank held the reins firmly and dug his heels in mercilessly, forcing her into a fast trot and then a canter. The horse's hooves threw up clouds of ash, coating both horse and rider in grey dust, but Frank ignored it as best he could. The picture of Lizzie lying alone and frightened in the big bed was far stronger than any discomfort from the rising ash. Belle's hooves thudding in the canter's triple time made a background to his thoughts. Lizzie waiting for him. Lizzie relying on him. Lizzie bearing his child.

The horse hung her head miserably when Frank at last took off her tack and let her out into the paddock. As soon as he had gasped out his news to Edie, and had seen her tell Alf to catch and saddle a horse for her, he had wasted no time in setting off for town to fetch Mrs Parsons. By the time he had led the way back home, with the nurse following on her own horse, Belle had been stumbling with weariness, and Frank had had to let her finish the ride at a walk.

Mrs Parsons had thrust her horse's reins into Frank's hand and made her own way to the house without waiting to be shown in. Frank found Edie's horse tied hastily to a fence by its bridle, and he saw to all three horses before following the nurse. The bedroom door was closed, but Frank opened it and went in without hesitation, only to be greeted by an indignant shout from Mrs Parsons.

'Mr Kelly, what do you think you're doing? Get out of here at once.'

Frank only had time for a brief glimpse of Lizzie lying on the bed with the covers pulled back and her nightdress up around her waist before Mrs Parsons came up to him and pushed him towards the door.

'But I want to see Lizzie,' Frank protested, at the same time giving way before Mrs Parsons' onslaught.

'Can't Frank stay?' Lizzie called plaintively from the bed.

'Certainly not! What a ridiculous idea.' The nurse glared at Frank as she gave him a final shove through the doorway. 'Keep out of the way, please. Surely you have some work you should be doing?' She shut the door firmly on him.

Frank sat miserably in the kitchen, wondering what to do next and listening to the faint cries he could hear from the bedroom, but it was not long before Edie came out to join him.

'How is she? Is she all right?' Frank asked, half rising from his chair.

'She's just fine,' Edie said. 'She was a bit frightened when I got here, but we've been having a nice little talk and she's quite happy now.'

'I've been that worried about her. I thought I mightn't be able to get you in time, and—'

'I know, Frank. Lizzie told me what you thought.' Edie gave him an affectionate pat on the shoulder before sitting down at the table. Her serene smile contrasted with her slightly bedraggled appearance. Frank had fetched her before she had had time to pin her hair up properly, and wisps of fair hair had escaped to twine around her face. As well, she seemed to have mismatched the buttons and buttonholes of her bodice in her hurry to put on a warm dress for riding.

'Frank,' she said gently, 'it's natural you were worried about Lizzie, what with it being your first, and coming a bit before its time, too, and you did the right thing to rush and get me. But nothing's going to happen before this afternoon, dear—maybe not till tonight if the little one decides to take its time.'

'Tonight?' Frank repeated. 'You mean it's going to be hours and hours yet?'

Edie nodded, a soft smile playing around her lips. 'They don't come all in a rush as a rule. Especially not first babies.'

'I've been pretty stupid, haven't I?'

'Of course you haven't, dear. You didn't know any better. The two of you are as innocent as a couple of babies yourselves.' Edie leaned across the corner of the table and gave Frank a conspiratorial grin. 'Anyway, if you hadn't rushed up to our place in such a panic, yelling your head off that I'd better come right away, Arthur might have thought to tell me I had to get home in time to make his lunch.'

'Perhaps you should go home,' Frank said, trying not to look disappointed. He knew Lizzie wanted her mother with her, and Edie's placid presence was a comfort to him.

'Stuff and nonsense! It won't hurt them to get their own lunch for once, and I want to be here to see my grandchild into the world.'

'But I don't want to get you in trouble.' Edie's rear was well padded, but Frank did not want to be responsible for getting it strapped.

'I won't get in trouble. Arthur's bark's worse than his bite. Of course if he'd told me I had to be home by such and such a time I'd have to do as he said, and quite right, too.' Edie stated this as an unarguable fact, one she accepted without question, and Frank wondered briefly how she could have had so little influence on her daughter's nature. 'You don't live with a man for twenty-two years without finding out how to keep him happy.'

She rose from her chair. 'Lizzie's quite comfortable now, and Mrs Parsons is seeing to her. Would you like me to make you a cup of tea? You must be ready for a drink.'

'I didn't have any breakfast,' Frank said, noticing his grinding hunger for the first time.

'Didn't you? Of course you didn't, poor boy, you've been rushing about since daybreak. You sit right there and I'll make you something.'

After he had eaten the huge plateful of bacon and eggs that Edie produced, Frank wandered about the farm doing his work, all the time listening anxiously for a cry from the house. He gave Belle a nosebag of oats to salve his conscience for his rough treatment earlier. He fed out hay to the unhappy cows stamping their feet in the ash-covered paddocks, and milked the two who were still in milk. Then he walked around the paddocks looking for any damage, but the wild, earthquake-filled night had left no sign except the ash. Being smothered by ash was not going to do the grass any good, Frank knew, and he was vaguely aware that he might have a problem finding enough grazing for the animals later in the year, but his mind was too full of Lizzie for any other worries to take root.

When he heard Edie's voice he ran to the house, but he arrived panting to find that she had only called him for lunch. Edie ate her own lunch hurriedly, then went off to sit with Lizzie, giving Mrs Parsons the chance to eat. The nurse looked so stern that Frank was reluctant to question her, but he plucked up his courage to ask how Lizzie was.

'There's nothing to worry about, Mr Kelly. I know my work,' Mrs Parsons said briskly, in a tone that did not encourage further questioning. She looked at Frank's downcast face and seemed to take pity on him. 'Your wife's asleep. I put her under the chloroform a few minutes ago. I don't think it'll be much more than two hours or so now.'

It seemed a very long two hours. Frank hovered about in the passage for some time. Then he stacked the dishes on the bench and began to wash them, but he dropped a plate when he thought he heard a noise from the bedroom. After he had picked up the broken pieces of china he sat at the table, idly fingering a corner of the tablecloth. He dropped the cloth guiltily when he saw the deep creases his twisting fingers had left in it.

He had just decided to go outside for a while and try to find something, anything, to do when the bedroom door opened and he heard Edie softly calling him. He started up the passage at a run, but Edie put her finger to her lips and Frank went the rest of the way on tiptoe.

'What's happened? Is she all right?' Frank asked, but one look at Edie's face told him that all was well.

'You've got a daughter, Frank,' Edie said, beaming with happiness. 'You can come in and see them, just for a minute.' She opened the door wide for him. He walked over to the bed, holding his breath in anticipation.

Lizzie lay back against the pillows. Her hair hung lank, much of it plastered to her scalp with perspiration. Her face was shiny and flushed with exertion, and her mouth could manage only a crooked smile. 'You look beautiful,' Frank told her. And he meant it.

Tucked into the curve of Lizzie's arm was a tiny, blanket-wrapped bundle. Lizzie could hardly keep her eyes open, but they were shining with delight. 'Look, Frank,' she said, slurring her words as if her mouth would not quite obey her. 'Isn't she lovely?'

Frank carefully turned down the top of the blanket and looked at his daughter. The baby's unfocussed gaze wandered about the room; then, as if she suddenly became aware of her father's presence, Frank found those blue eyes trained on him with what seemed a rather disapproving expression.

'She looks as though she's going to tell me off,' he said, a bubble of relieved laughter welling up inside him. 'She's going to take after you, Lizzie.' He carefully put his arms around both wife and daughter.

'Careful, Frank, don't squash her,' Lizzie warned.

'I won't squash her.' Indifferent to his audience, Frank lowered his face to Lizzie's and planted a soft kiss on her waiting mouth.

9

June – December 1886

Malcolm's eyelids were drooping, and Amy laid him gently in his cradle. It was a relief to straighten up without his weight dragging at her; at seven months he was a sturdy-limbed child and big for his age. But it seemed to make Malcolm more contented if she carried him around as often as she could whenever he was awake. She was determined to be a good mother to him, and if that meant balancing him on one hip while she stirred a pot of soup, collected eggs, pulled carrots out of the garden, or performed any other tasks that could be done, albeit awkwardly, one-handed, she would manage somehow. Amy almost welcomed the difficulty. It was all part of trying to make up for the guilt of not having wanted Malcolm.

She went outside to find Charlie for his afternoon tea. It was tempting to leave him to his own company, but he might be angry with her if she 'forgot' to call him. He had been in a foul temper for most of the day; the earthquakes had kept both of them awake during the early hours, and had disturbed Malcolm with their rough rocking of his cradle. Amy had had to sit shivering on the chair beside the bed holding Malcolm in her arms and soothing him back into drowsiness. It would have been much easier to take him into bed with her; but that was against the rules. That might make the boy soft.

And what a sight had greeted them when daylight came. 'That muck will kill every blade of grass!' Charlie had said, aghast. He had proceeded to track large quantities of 'that muck' over the floor as he went in and out of the house, swearing all the time. By lunch-time he had calmed down somewhat, but was still muttering under his breath about grazing. Amy had considered putting Malcolm on his father's lap; that usually softened Charlie's manner. But today Charlie seemed too sour for even Malcolm's influence to do any good, and there was always the risk that Malcolm might bring up some milk or soil his napkin. Charlie was in no mood to take that indignity calmly.

A faint, high-pitched sound caught her attention; Amy stopped and listened for a moment. Yes, it was Jane's voice. She and Harry were having one of their rows. They were already becoming proverbial in the valley for their fiery, though short-lived, altercations, and such small details as a night of earthquakes followed by an ash-covered morning would not distract them. Lizzie claimed that when the wind was right she could hear them from her home at the mouth of the valley, but Amy was sure that must be an exaggeration.

Amy shook her head over her brother and sister-in-law's mystifying relationship. When they were not hurling abuse they seemed so fond of each other; embarrassingly so at times. It was almost as though they enjoyed fighting. Perhaps they did; though Amy was sure it must be costing Harry a fortune to keep replacing all the china Jane delighted in throwing at him.

Charlie was in a paddock not far from the house, where some cows were nosing disconsolately at wisps of dried grass half-buried in the ash. 'Look at this hay,' he said, pointing to the ground at his feet. 'Half of it trodden into this muck—the cows'll never eat it now.'

'No,' Amy agreed. 'But they must have had a fair bit before they started treading it in.'

'They still look half-starved.'

'Couldn't you give them some more?' She had not thought her remark would annoy him, but Charlie turned on her and slapped her across the side of the head; a casual blow using his palm rather than the back of his hand, more to express his irritation than to punish her for speaking out of turn.

'Silly bitch,' he grumbled. 'Are you saying I should give them a week's worth of hay?'

It didn't hurt much. Certainly not enough for her to risk annoying Charlie more by letting herself cry. 'No. I'm sorry I said the wrong thing. I didn't think. Would you like some afternoon tea now?'

'What am I going to do when the hay runs out? Well?'

'I don't know. I've made scones.'

'There won't be any new grass coming on. What am I going to feed my cows on?'

I expect you'll have to buy some feed. But Charlie did not like her to talk about money. 'They're date scones.'

'I'll have to sell some of the calves as soon as they're born. I wanted to build up my herd this year, now I've got the boy to think about. I've got to keep you fed and clothed too, you know.'

Why don't you wait and see if the grass does start growing? You could always send some of the cows away for grazing, just till the ground comes right. That ash can't be everywhere. But you don't really want to hear what I think. 'I've put jam and cream on them.'

'Stop going on about your bloody scones.' He looked as though he was considering giving her another slap, but Amy had carefully stepped a little out of his range. 'What sort of jam?'

'Strawberry.' His favourite. Food was something she could usually rely on to soften Charlie's harsher moods. After sixteen months of marriage she knew all his likes and dislikes; and Charlie was, after so many years of living alone, a fussy eater and reluctant to try new things. But cooking was not something Amy found difficult, and after preparing meals for three men and a far fussier Susannah it was no hardship to cater to Charlie's finicky appetite. That particular hunger was readily satisfied; she only wished the other one could be so easily sated.

'All right, I'll come and have some. Can't do much good out here.' He kicked idly at a fallen branch and started back to the house, with Amy keeping up as best she could.

They had almost reached the back door when the noise of hooves on the road, muffled slightly by the ash, caught their attention. Amy recognised Frank approaching at a gentle trot.

'What's that idiot coming up here for?' Charlie grumbled. Amy wondered if he was worried he might have to share his scones. 'He should be sorting out his farm, same as me.'

'Perhaps it's about Lizzie. I hope everything's all right.'

As soon as Frank was close enough for her to see his expression, Amy knew that all was very well indeed. He jumped off his horse before it had quite stopped moving, and knotted the reins hurriedly around the top rail of a fence before running over to where Amy and Charlie stood watching him. His face was glowing as the words tumbled out.

'I've just been up to Arthur's to tell him the news—I saw you in the paddock just before, so I came up for a minute—I knew Lizzie would want me to tell you, Amy.' Frank stopped and caught his breath. 'I'm a father,' he said, his wonder at the fact making his voice shake. 'We've got a little girl.'

'Oh, Frank, that's lovely news,' Amy said. 'And they're all right? Lizzie and the baby?'

'They're… they're wonderful. It's a bit before the proper time, but Edie says the little one's perfect. Only six pounds, but healthy and strong. A daughter.' Frank's eyes were bright.

Charlie cleared his throat. 'Well, you'll maybe have a son next time,' he said magnanimously.

'Eh?' Frank looked at him blankly. 'Next time? I haven't got over the shock of *this* time yet!' He grinned, then let out a laugh. 'I just feel so… so *happy!*' Before she realised what he was doing, Frank took hold of Amy's shoulders and kissed her on the mouth.

The kiss was over before Amy had the chance to pull her face away. She took a step back when Frank released her, not daring to look at Charlie.

'I've got to get home, they might wake up soon, then I'll be able to see them again.' Frank was already striding back to his horse. When Amy risked a glance, she could see that Charlie was too stunned by Frank's audacity to protest. For the moment, anyway.

'What? Oh, yes… give my love to Lizzie, Frank. Tell her I'll come and see her as soon as I can.' Amy's voice shook a little, but she knew Frank would not notice.

Amy closed her eyes for a moment, wondering what her punishment might be, then opened them to see Charlie looming over her. He looked as angry as she had feared he would. She waited for him to start shouting at her, but for a long moment he was silent. That was even more frightening than shouting.

His voice when it came at last was a low growl. 'Is that the way of it? Did Frank Kelly practice on you before he started courting? Eh? Tried it out on a whore before he went looking for a decent woman to wed?'

'N-no,' Amy stammered.

'Am I the laughing-stock of this town? Did every boy between here and Ruatane get between your legs?'

'Please don't, Charlie, please. I don't know what to say when you talk like that.'

'Bitch!' he shouted. His fist caught her a blow on the side of her head that sent Amy sprawling. She raised herself onto her hands and knees, her ears ringing from the knock, and looked up to see Charlie standing over her, red-faced with rage. He reached down and took hold of her bodice front to haul her to her feet. He yanked at the fabric, forcing Amy to stand on tiptoe, and lowered his own face till it was close to hers. 'Tell me the truth. Has Frank Kelly been in you? Don't lie to me, woman.'

'Frank's never touched me before. I swear it, Charlie, I swear it's true.' She hurried on, trying desperately to convince him. 'Frank never seemed very interested in girls. He didn't even court Lizzie—she courted him.' She knew that was not very loyal to Lizzie and Frank, but her own need was more urgent.

Charlie's hold on her bodice relaxed, and Amy staggered backwards, barely regaining her balance in time to stop herself from falling. 'That sounds true enough. He doesn't look as if he ever had the gumption to get a woman for himself.'

His face took on a disdainful expression. 'All that fuss about a girl child! He maybe can't father boys, a runt like him. It's taken him long enough to get a bairn on her at all—they were wed only a couple of months after us, and the boy's six months old already.'

'Seven,' Amy put in. 'Malcolm's seven months old now.' She studied Charlie's face carefully. Pride at his own prowess seemed to have overshadowed his anger; she had got off lightly, she decided. Her head was beginning to pound from his blow, but the spot was mostly covered by her hair. Except where his knuckles had ground against her cheekbone it would not leave a visible bruise; she would only have to hide her face from other people for a few days. 'I think I was with child the first week we were married.'

'No sense wasting time,' Charlie said loftily. But he had not forgotten that kiss; Amy saw the resentment in his face as his eyes narrowed. 'Did you enjoy that? Did you like him kissing you?'

'No, I didn't,' Amy assured him.

'Why not? He wears trousers, that's all you're interested in, isn't it? Why didn't you like it?'

'I don't want other men kissing me.'

'Don't you?' Amy shook her head vehemently. He brought his face close to hers again. 'Do you want *me* to kiss you?' he asked in a low voice.

What do I say? 'If… if you want to.'

'What do *you* want?' he pressed.

Amy struggled for words that would not make him angry but would still be the truth. 'I want to please you. That's all.' She waited for Charlie's reply; when none came she dared to speak again. 'Can I go inside now, please?' She took his continued silence as permission.

Charlie followed her into the kitchen. Amy filled the teapot and carried it to the table, aware of his eyes on her. Perhaps she had not got off so lightly after all. She felt his heavy tread on the floor behind her. He placed a hand on her shoulder and turned her round to face him, then took hold of one of her heavy, milk-filled breasts through the thick fabric that covered them and squeezed it hard, at the same time pressing his mouth against hers. His beard rasped against her face. He smelt of tobacco and sweat. *Not now,* Amy begged silently. *Don't make me go to bed now. Not in the daytime. Not so I'll have to look at you.*

He let go of her and stood upright, towering over her. 'Did you like that?'

I hated it. But it was his right to do as he wished, and her duty to try and please him. 'I'm your wife. I want whatever you want.'

Charlie made a growling noise in his throat and sat down heavily at the table. Amy knew her response had not satisfied him, but affection was not like obedience. Fear and duty were not enough to make her feel whatever it was he wanted from her.

She poured the tea and put a cup in front of Charlie, along with the promised scones. At least he was not going to force her into bed then and there. That part of the punishment would not come till evening.

He had seemed so troubled earlier about the effects of the ash on his pasture that Amy was startled when Charlie announced after he had finished his snack that he was going into town.

'What for?' she asked.

'None of your business.'

'But… it's nearly four o'clock. I thought you wanted to check all the fences and see if they're all right after the earthquakes. You won't have time if you go out.'

'Don't tell me what to do, you meddling little bitch.' He gave her a slap across the cheek. Amy was grateful it wasn't her sore one.

'I'm sorry. I didn't mean to be rude. When do you think you'll be home?'

'Don't know,' he said shortly.

'It's just that…' Amy knew she was risking another slap, but Charlie hated to be kept waiting for his meals. Having his dinner ready late was a worse risk. 'I wondered when I should have dinner ready.'

'I mightn't be home for dinner.'

'What?' That startled her even more. Charlie had never been out at dinner time before.

'Are you deaf as well as stupid? I might be home for dinner, I might not.'

Charlie was not home for dinner. Amy kept the food warm until seven o'clock before eating her own, and it was almost eight before he returned. He smelt of beer and of something else Amy could not quite identify, though it seemed familiar, and she guessed that he had eaten at one of the hotels. But she asked no questions, knowing how prying would be rewarded, even though the looks Charlie cast at her as he ate half a plateful of the food she warmed for him almost seemed to be daring her to say something. He looked as though he could not make up his mind whether to be angry or to lord over her whatever secret he was holding.

That night she was almost as astonished as she had been by Charlie's strange outing when, instead of groping for her in the darkness, Charlie rolled over and went straight to sleep, his loud snores soon punctuating the silence of the bedroom. *It must be the beer*, she decided. Not that beer usually had that effect on him.

A few days after the wild night of the earthquakes and the birth of

Lizzie's baby, the *Bay of Plenty Times* arrived in Ruatane on the steamer and told the town of the real events of that night.

Frank sat on the chair beside Lizzie as she lay in bed feeding the baby, and he read out snippets of news to her. 'So it was Tarawera, eh, not White Island at all.'

'Mmm,' Lizzie agreed absently, watching the baby pulling at her breast.

'Mind you, White Island's been puffing out smoke like mad since Tarawera blew up. I wonder if they're sort of joined up somehow.'

'Eh? How can they be? Tarawera's miles away. Where is it, Frank?'

'Over by Rotorua. You know, you must have heard of the Pink and White Terraces.'

'Oh, *that* Tarawera. I know where you mean now. I read in the *Weekly News* one time about people going there on their honeymoon.'

'They won't be going there now. The whole mountain cracked open, and they think the terraces have broken up. It says in the paper that a whole village got buried in the ash. They don't know how many people were killed.'

'How terrible. Look at her, Frank.' Lizzie had put her finger on the baby's palm when the little girl stopped sucking, and the tiny fingers were closing around it.

Frank put the newspaper on the floor and devoted his attention to his family. 'Do you think Mrs Parsons will leave us alone for a bit?' he asked, glancing apprehensively at the bedroom door.

'Probably. She's making bread, so she'll be up to her elbows in dough.'

'Good.' He lay down on the bed close to Lizzie, with the baby between them. He coaxed the baby's hand to clutch one of his own fingers, smiling at the touch. 'Her fingers are so little—look at those tiny nails. But everything's perfect. Hello, Edith Maud,' he said, touching the baby's nose gently with one finger. 'I registered you today at the courthouse. You're all legal now. Edith Maud Kelly.'

'Look at Papa, Maudie,' Lizzie cajoled.

'Do you think we'll call her Maud?'

'Mmm. Two Edies at once would be too confusing.'

'Ma would have liked that. A little granddaughter with her name. Gee, I felt proud registering her, Lizzie. It feels good to be a father.' He stroked Maudie's downy cheek.

A noise from the direction of the kitchen made them both jump. Frank sat up guiltily and resumed his seat on the chair. 'Mrs Parsons would probably go crook if she saw me lying on the bed in my clothes. "You seem to have a good deal of spare time, Mr Kelly," ' he said in an attempt to imitate Mrs Parsons' disapproving tone.

'She'd say Maudie should be back in her cradle, too. She's very bossy. What are you grinning at, Frank?'

'You calling someone else bossy.'

'She is! You should have heard her when Maudie was coming. "Push harder." "Sit up." "Lie down." Ordering me around all the time!'

'Better than trying to manage by ourselves, though.'

'That's true. She wasn't horrible or anything, just bossy. I didn't really mind it then, 'cause I was a bit scared and it was good to have someone who knew all about it. I'm a bit sick of her now, though. She keeps telling you what to do, too—I don't like that. Don't you worry, I'll get her sorted out once I stop feeling so feeble.'

'Yes, I bet you will.' Frank was quite sure Mrs Parsons had more than met her match in Lizzie.

Amy had to wait a day longer than Frank to read about the eruption. When she was picking up Charlie's discarded newspaper in the parlour next morning, she took a few minutes to look at it. The paper had mournful reports of people buried alive, huddled together for comfort while they waited to die. She gave a shudder. *Buried alive. I should count my blessings like Granny used to say.*

She folded the newspaper and put it by the hearth, unwilling to read any further. Being buried alive, trapped and unable to escape, was uncomfortably easy to imagine.

The remaining months of winter were a pinched, anxious time, as the farmers watched their pasture to see if it would recover from the burden of ash. Amy read in another discarded newspaper that farmers in Tauranga had sent their cattle away towards Thames, where the ash had not fallen as thickly, to graze, but Ruatane had not been affected quite so badly. Charlie's haystacks were gone before July was over, fed out to hungry cows, and Amy knew it troubled him when he had to buy feed for them. She wondered if he had had to borrow money to do so.

But spring brought new growth, though less than usual, and Charlie began to look less grey and care-worn. Malcolm now regularly slept through the night, to the relief of his parents. He learned to crawl, and got his little gowns filthy in the process. Crawling was such an easy way of getting about that Malcolm seemed reluctant to abandon it for the more precarious two-legged method. Amy tried to encourage him to walk, but it was difficult to find the time, and it did not seem to matter. He would walk when he was ready; she knew that big children like him were often slower about walking.

She devoted more time to teaching Malcolm to talk. During the daytime, when the two of them were alone in the house, she would hold him on her lap and repeat over and over, 'Papa. Papa. Come on, Mal, you say it. Papa.' But Malcolm squirmed to get down, cried if she held him too long against his will, or jabbered away with his own meaningless sounds.

This year Ann's birthday brought a dull ache instead of the sharp pain of a year before. *My little girl. You're two now. I expect you're talking lots. I wonder what you're like. I bet you're pretty. Oh, Ann, I hope they love you.*

On Malcolm's first birthday Amy baked a cake, though she gave only a tiny portion to Malcolm himself. He made quite enough mess with his little chunk; Amy was careful to sweep up the crumbs before Charlie came in for lunch.

'I just want to mash some gravy in with the vegetables for Malcolm. Could you please hold him for me for a minute?' she asked.

'All right,' Charlie said in the tone of one bestowing a great favour, but Amy knew he enjoyed holding his son when she gave him an excuse to do so without appearing sentimental. He sat the boy on his lap, jiggling him on one knee when he thought Amy was not watching.

Malcolm chortled away at his father. *He never laughs for me like that. It's almost as if he knows I didn't want him.*

The little fist reached out to take hold of Charlie's beard. He gave it a tug, but before Charlie had a chance to prise his fingers away Malcolm gave a little giggle and said quite clearly, 'Papa.'

Charlie stared at him open-mouthed, then turned to Amy. 'Did you hear that?'

'Yes. That's the first word he's ever said.'

'Is it? He hasn't even called you Mama yet?'

'No, never.' It would be surprising if he had, after all her coaxing. But the look on Charlie's face was worth the effort.

'You know your Papa, eh?' He jiggled Malcolm, not caring now that Amy was watching the two of them.

'Papa. Papa,' Malcolm crowed.

Amy sat and watched them for some time, but she was aware of two plates of food, along with Malcolm's bowlful, getting cold on the table. 'I'd better take him now, I can give him his lunch while you're eating yours.' For a moment she thought Charlie was going to offer to feed Malcolm, but he appeared to think better of it and handed the baby over.

Malcolm grizzled briefly at being taken off his father's lap, but the food soon distracted him. When he had ploughed his way through a bowl of mashed vegetables, Amy turned sideways on her chair to give herself a little more privacy, unbuttoned her bodice and offered a nipple to Malcolm. He sucked greedily, though she knew he was no longer taking much nourishment from her now that he was eating so many solids.

'Don't bite, Mal,' she admonished, tapping the little boy's mouth gently. 'You've got too many teeth.'

'Does he still need that?' Charlie asked, startling her.

'I think so, Charlie. It's good for babies to feed off their mothers. Mal's certainly thriving.'

'He's hardly a baby any more. Look at him—he's nearly walking, and he's talking now. You look ridiculous suckling him—like a cow with last year's calf.'

Perhaps she did, now that Malcolm was so big. But Amy did not suckle him to look elegant. She did it for Malcolm's good… and for her own. She knew she would soon be with child again once she stopped. 'I suppose I could start weaning him in a little while,' she said reluctantly.

'You can start now,' Charlie declared. 'A year's long enough for that business. The boy's growing up, and I'll not have him turning into a Mama's boy.'

'I don't think he will—'

'I don't want to hear what you think, you silly bitch.' He used the term casually, not with any particular animosity. It was just how he thought of her, Amy knew. 'I want the boy weaned.'

And of course she did as he wished. By Christmas, with Malcolm thirteen months old, Amy was sure that she was, once again, with child.

10

December 1886 – January 1887

Just as she had with Malcolm, Amy put off telling Charlie about the coming child. But this time it was not because of any reluctance on her part to face the fact of her pregnancy; childbearing was something to be accepted as part of the duties of being a wife, just like cooking, cleaning and sharing Charlie's bed.

This time she held the news in reserve as a kind of insurance. The next time Charlie became violently angry, she would announce that she was with child, and thus avert his wrath.

But Amy was so anxious to please, so careful of Charlie's comfort, that there were no outbursts frightening enough for her to squander her news on. So she kept silent and let the days take their course.

On Christmas Day Amy and Charlie took Malcolm and went next door to Jack's house for lunch. They walked around the long way, using the road; climbing the fences, as Amy did when she visited without Charlie, offended his sense of the correct. Malcolm perched on his father's shoulders in what looked to Amy a precarious position for a one-year-old, but they were both happy that way, so she contented herself with keeping a wary eye on the baby.

She saw Thomas and George playing by the creek, and the little boys ran to join them. They both looked as though they had fallen over once or twice; their knees were filthy, and their faces liberally smudged with mud. Thomas slipped a grubby little hand into Amy's as they walked up the hill to the house, and Amy ruffled his hair affectionately.

As soon as they walked into the kitchen, Amy was aware of tenseness in the air. Her father had a weary expression, and Susannah was tight-lipped. John sat at the table looking as though he wished he were elsewhere.

Jack gave Amy a kiss and chucked Malcolm under the chin. 'Good to see you!' he said heartily. Amy guessed that he was glad of the interruption. 'How's my grandson?' he said as Charlie lowered Malcolm into Amy's waiting arms.

'Bigger and stronger than ever, Pa,' Amy told him with a smile.

'Excuse me if I don't rush over, Amy,' Susannah said, noisily jostling dishes on the bench. 'I've rather a lot to do, and I've had to get everything ready by myself.' She glared around the room, but Amy was the only one who met her eyes.

'Do you want me to help, Susannah?'

'I've all but finished, actually. Of course I've been on the go all morning. There's a lot of work in getting a meal ready for seven adults and three children, you know. Especially with no one to help.'

'You want a beer, Charlie?' Jack offered, ignoring his wife's complaints. Charlie did not need to be asked twice. He joined the other two men at the far end of the table where Jack had a jug and glasses ready.

Amy put Malcolm down to crawl, and he made his way across the room to where Thomas and George stood beside their father. She took an apron from the familiar hook behind the door. 'What can I do?'

'I hardly know whether I'm coming or going. I don't think I've sat down since breakfast,' Susannah said, moving pots about ineffectually.

'I'll make the gravy, shall I? Then I'll set the table. Everything else looks ready.' Amy set to work without waiting for instructions. 'Where's Jane?' she asked.

'*That* is a good question,' Susannah said grimly. 'I did think she might have given me a bit of help. She said she would, but there's been no sign of her this morning. Everyone just seems to take it for granted that I should do all the work by myself.'

'Had a bit of rain last night,' Amy heard her father explain as he filled the glasses. 'I think that roof of Harry's leaks a bit—there's always a row from his place when it rains. He looked as though he'd been sent out with a flea in his ear when he came down to the cow shed this morning. They must have started scrapping again when Harry went back home.' Charlie grunted an acknowledgement and reached for his glass.

'I would have come over and helped you if I'd known,' Amy told Susannah.

'Oh, you're busy, I know. After all, you've got a baby to look after as well as a husband. Not like some girls I could mention.'

'Don't start again, Susannah,' Jack put in from across the room.

'All I said was that I understand why *Amy* couldn't be expected to come and help me. What's wrong with that?'

'Nothing,' Jack said. He took a large gulp from his glass.

The final meal preparations were soon complete. Amy and Susannah left the food to keep warm on the range and joined the men at the table. Amy picked Malcolm up and sat him on her lap, but he whined at being held.

'He's rather a grizzly baby, isn't he?' Susannah remarked. 'He's always cried a lot.'

'He doesn't cry much now,' Amy said defensively. She gripped Malcolm more tightly as he struggled to get free.

'Give him here,' Charlie said, and Amy passed the little boy over to him. 'Stop that noise,' he told Malcolm. The grizzles stopped abruptly, and Malcolm gave his father a dubious look. His face broke into a smile as he tugged at Charlie's beard.

Amy studied the two of them. 'He likes his Papa best,' she said. *Much better than he likes me. But that's only fair—I didn't even want him before he was born. Charlie's wanted a son half his life, I think.*

'He's talking a bit now,' Charlie said. 'Walking, too.' He stood Malcolm on the floor between his knees. The little boy took a few steps on tiptoe while Charlie held his hands.

'They grow up fast, eh?' Jack said. 'It only seems the other day you were starting to walk, girl,' he said, smiling at Amy. 'Now you've got one of your own.'

Two. An image of her tiny, dark-haired daughter rose sharply in Amy's mind. To hide the sudden stab of memory she took hold of Malcolm's hand as Charlie lifted him back onto his lap. 'Show Grandpa what you can say, Mal,' she coaxed. 'Come on. Who's got you? Papa's got you.'

'Papa,' Malcolm repeated. 'Papa. Papa.' Charlie looked smug.

'There's nothing of you in that child, Amy,' Susannah said. 'He's just the image of his father.' Amy knew she did not say it to be kind, but Charlie looked more pleased with himself than ever.

'It's about time he started walking,' Susannah added. 'He's a little bit slow to be just starting now.'

Charlie looked affronted at the slight to his son. He turned to Amy for reassurance. 'No, he's not!' Amy said. 'He's just average. He's so big, too, it's harder work for him to walk.'

Susannah looked doubtful. 'I suppose that might be right. Oh, I expect he just seems slow to me because my children were so forward.'

'They were not,' Amy said. 'They were about the same as Malcolm.'

'Oh, I don't think so, Amy,' Susannah said. 'I'm quite sure Thomas walked before he was this age.'

'He didn't,' Amy insisted. Susannah was going to upset Charlie, going on like this, and she was talking a load of rubbish anyway. 'Tommy was thirteen months when he walked, exactly the same as Malcolm is now.'

'Well, I do think I'm more likely to remember when my own child started walking than you are,' Susannah said haughtily. 'What makes you so sure you're right and I'm wrong?'

'Because I taught Tommy to walk,' Amy shot back.

Susannah's composure was shaken for a moment. She looked away. 'Oh. Perhaps you did, I don't remember. Of course I would have been busy with George—I was probably rather ill, anyway. Perhaps it was

George who was early walking. Anyway,' she said, continuing the attack with renewed vigour, 'they both started talking early. They were certainly saying quite a few words by that age.'

'Leave the girl alone, Susannah,' Jack put in, forestalling Amy's retort. 'There's nothing wrong with this boy of hers.'

'I didn't say there was anything wrong with him,' Susannah said. 'I was just saying he was slower than my children.'

'Well, you've said it. Keep quiet about it now. When's lunch going to be ready?'

'It's ready now. As soon as Harry and Jane decide to turn up we can all eat. *If* they turn up.'

'They'll be here,' Jack said.

'Humph. I *thought* Jane was going to come this morning and she didn't.'

'Harry's stomach will tell him lunch is on. We'll wait a couple more minutes.'

'Well, all I can say is don't blame me if lunch is ruined, standing on the range for so long. Is it too much to expect people to turn up on time to eat it? The meat will dry out, and—'

'Shut up, Susannah.'

'I don't know what I've done to deserve being spoken to like that. After slaving all morning in this hot kitchen. Just because I said—'

'Oh, for God's sake, Susannah,' Jack interrupted. 'Give us a rest from it.' Susannah glared at him, but said nothing.

The ensuing few minutes' awkward silence was broken by an oblivious Thomas. 'I'm hungry, Mama. I want lunch.'

'Me too,' George chimed in.

'Your father says you have to wait for your big brother, darlings,' Susannah told them, casting a meaningful look at Jack. 'We're not allowed to talk about it, or Papa will growl.'

Jack barely suppressed a curse, then sighed. 'I'm fed up with waiting for those two myself. Amy, how about you hop down and give them a hurry up?'

Amy looked at him in alarm. If Harry and Jane really were having an argument, she had no desire to become part of it. As if that weren't enough, she caught Charlie's eye and realised she would have to ask his permission in front of everyone to 'wander' off by herself. But there seemed no way of avoiding it.

'Is it... is it all right if I go down to Harry's?' She spoke as quietly as she could, but she felt Jack's and Susannah's eyes on her, then saw them exchange a surprised glance. She cringed with embarrassment.

John spoke up, startling her. 'I'll come down with you, shall I, Amy? It won't take long.'

Amy looked a question at Charlie, and he gave a nod of approval. She smiled at John, grateful that he had broken the unpleasant moment.

'I'll go too,' Thomas announced.

'No, you won't,' Susannah said, noticing the grubby state of her sons for the first time. 'Look at the two of you! You look like nasty, rough children. I told you not to get dirty.'

'I want to go with Amy!' Thomas protested.

'Well, you can't. Come along, I'll have to wash your faces again.'

'Let me go with Amy, Mama,' Thomas pleaded.

'Don't want my face washed,' George said, looking rebellious.

'Do as you're told!' Susannah gave each of them a sharp slap on the bottom to reinforce her words, then dragged the yelling children out of the room.

'Have another beer, Charlie,' Amy heard her father say wearily as she and John closed the back door on the uproar.

'Thanks for saying you'd come with me, John,' Amy said as soon as they were clear of the house.

'That's all right. I wanted to get out of there, anyway.'

Neither of them referred to Amy's need to ask permission merely to leave the house by herself, but she knew that John had noticed. 'I think maybe you're the only one in the family with any sense,' Amy said, trying to make her voice light. 'At least you haven't rushed and got married.'

'Well, maybe it's not something to rush into.'

'Have the rest of us put you off, then?'

John looked thoughtful. 'Not exactly,' he said after a time. 'I guess it's made me... careful. I sure wouldn't want to end up with a... with someone like Susannah.' He gave a laugh. 'There must be something good about it, eh? Otherwise people wouldn't keep doing it. That Harry looks pretty smug half the time, when Jane's in a good mood with him.'

'Yes, he does. They're not really like Pa and Susannah.'

'What about you?' John asked, with a casualness Amy suspected was feigned. 'Are things all right with you and him?'

'Yes, they're fine,' Amy said, wishing she could raise a more enthusiastic tone. 'He loves Mal, he really does. We get on all right, as long as I'm not stupid about things. I haven't got anything to complain about.'

'You're easy enough to get on with. Charlie must think he's pretty lucky.' If he did, Amy reflected, he hid it well.

They reached the last small stand of bush before Harry and Jane's two-roomed cottage and came to a halt. Only a low murmur came through the open window that faced them. 'What do we do?' Amy asked. 'Knock on the door?'

'I suppose so,' John said uncertainly.

As he spoke, they heard two voices suddenly raised in altercation. They were close enough to distinguish Jane's soprano shrilling over Harry's deeper tones.

'I'd just as soon not go and knock,' John said. 'Maybe we could start talking loud so they'll hear us from here.'

'We'd have to make a lot of noise.'

'Mmm. Let's just wait a minute, they might stop.'

They stood and listened to the commotion Harry and Jane were making. It was difficult to think of it as eavesdropping when the contenders seemed to have no concern over whether or not they were overheard. The noise soon resolved into intelligible words.

'How do you expect me to keep this place clean when there's great huge puddles all over the floor every time it rains?' they heard Jane yell.

'A bit of water, that's all. You're making all this fuss over a few drops of water. Why didn't you put something down to catch it, anyway?'

'You've got a cheek saying that. How could I know the roof would leak again? It's *your* fault.' There was a sharp crash.

'Aw, Jane, that was the last cup. Why have you got to throw things all the time? You nearly got me with that one.'

'You'd drive a saint to it! You *said* you'd fixed it last week. You stamped about on the roof for long enough.'

'I thought I had.' Harry sounded defensive, but his volume did not drop. 'That was a real storm last night, it must have lifted the iron.'

'Storm!' Jane said derisively. 'It was a shower, that's all. If you'd built this house properly in the first place you wouldn't have to fix it now.'

'There's nothing wrong with this house! It's a bloody good house.'

'Don't you use that language to me, Harry Leith. And if it's such a wonderful house, why does the roof leak? Why does the door stick in the wet weather?'

'Why do you moan all the time?'

'I don't moan! Anyway, you'd moan if you had to clean up all this water whenever it's wet. *And* I'm sick of you stamping around in the house with your dirty boots all the time.'

'I do not! Not for ages and ages, anyway.'

'You did it yesterday! I'd just scrubbed the floor and you tramped right over it.'

'It's my floor. I'll walk on it when I want.'

'Your floor? I have to scrub it, don't I? And I have to mop up the water when *your* roof leaks. Just look at these puddles. Look at them!'

'Water, eh? You're sick of water. You're moaning about a couple of little puddles. I'll give you something to moan about. I'll show you water.'

'You keep away from me. What are you doing? Don't you dare!' Jane gave a shrill scream. They heard the sound of furniture scraping against the floor, as if Harry was chasing Jane around the room.

Amy turned to John in alarm. 'Maybe you should stop him.'

'Me?' John looked at her in amusement. 'No thanks. It's none of my business, anyway. They can sort it out for themselves.'

'But...' *he's going to hit her.* But John was right: it was no one else's business what Harry chose to do with Jane. Amy wondered why on earth Jane would want to bait her husband so; surely she knew he would hit her. Amy did not want to hear Jane's screams when he did. 'I want to go back now, John.'

'Why? The fun's just starting.'

'Fun? But he's going to hit her.'

'Course he isn't! Harry's all talk, he always has been. You should know that.'

Amy shook her head. What John said of Harry was true enough, but it did not fit her own experience of marriage.

Jane screamed again and the cottage door opened noisily. That door *did* stick, Amy noticed with a corner of her mind. Harry burst through the door with a loudly yelling Jane slung over one shoulder.

'You put me down!' Jane demanded. 'You put me down this minute.' She pummelled at Harry's back with her fists, but he took no notice. 'What are you doing? Stop it!'

'I told you. I'm going to show you some real water. That'll stop your moaning.'

Harry strode down the hill in front of the cottage, walking a little unsteadily under his struggling load. Amy and John saw where he was headed much earlier than Jane, whose head was upside down against Harry's back. It was only when Harry reached the bank of the creek that Jane realised what he intended.

'Don't you dare! You put me down!'

'All right,' Harry said agreeably. He grasped Jane around the waist and slid her forward over his shoulder until her feet were almost on the ground, then he thrust her out over the creek and let go.

Jane's yell of protest was cut off abruptly as water entered her mouth. She went right under for a few seconds, then sat up coughing and spluttering, water streaming down her face and hair on to her soaking bodice. Harry doubled over with laughter as he watched.

'You beast!' Jane flung at him as soon as she had her voice back. 'Look at me—I'm wet through!'

Harry was too convulsed with mirth to speak for some time. At last he gasped out, 'Are you wet enough now? Has that cooled you down, you little hothead?'

'You're horrible! Look at the state I'm in.'

'That'll teach you not to moan all the time. You just remember—aw, Janey, don't do that,' Harry said as Jane's face crumpled. 'Don't start crying.'

'I c-can't help it,' Jane choked out through a sob. 'You're annoyed with me. I hate it when you're annoyed with me. I shouldn't have gone on about the house, I know. I didn't mean to. Ohh, this water's cold,' she said, hugging herself.

'Get out of it, then. Hurry up, Jane, I don't want you to get cold.'

Jane struggled to lift herself upright, then sank down heavily. 'I c-can't.' Now her teeth were chattering. 'My skirts are full of water, they're too heavy for me to stand up. I'm so c-cold.'

Harry's look of glee had changed to concern. He scrambled down the bank into the shallows of the creek. 'Here, take my hand, I'll pull you out.'

Jane stretched out her arm towards him. 'I can't reach. Come a bit closer.'

Harry took a few tentative steps until the water was lapping over the tops of his feet. 'Can you reach now?'

'Not quite.'

He took another step and perched one foot awkwardly on a rock that jutted out of the creek bed. Jane reached up and took hold of his proffered hand. As he tried to get a firmer foothold Jane suddenly yanked at his hand, pulling him off balance. Harry fell into the water beside her with a loud splash.

Now it was Harry's turn to splutter. Jane shrieked with laughter as he sat up with his hair plastered to his head.

'That's fixed you! Hothead yourself. Serves you right.'

Harry glared as though he was mustering his strength to fling abuse at her, then he let out a guffaw. 'Jane Leith, you are a hell-cat. You're enough to drive a man to drink.' He held out his arms and Jane pressed herself against him. They carefully stood up, supporting one another as they did. 'Let's get back to the house. Must be nearly time for lunch now.'

'Oh! Oh, Harry, we're meant to go up to your pa's for lunch. I think we're a bit late.'

'Heck, I suppose we are. The bitch'll make a fuss about that. Too bad about her. We'd better hurry up and get changed, though—don't want you getting a chill. Come on.' They climbed up the bank and made their way back to the cottage, streaming water as they went.

John took his hand from his mouth, where he had clamped it firmly to stop his laughter escaping. 'Those two are mad. They were made for each other.'

'They'd drive anyone else mad, I suppose,' Amy said. She was unsure whether to laugh or cry at the sight of Harry and Jane with their wet arms around each other. 'I'm glad he didn't hit her.'

'I told you he wouldn't.' John looked as if he were debating whether or not to ask her a question, then seemed to decide against it. 'Let's get back and tell Pa they're on their way.'

Harry and Jane arrived arm in arm ten minutes after Amy and John got back to the house; Amy noticed that Jane's hair was still damp. Jane rushed to hug Amy with the warm affection she always showed her little sister-in-law. Jane was quick to love, or, in Susannah's case, to dislike. Amy suspected that Harry had told his wife about Amy's dark secret and Susannah's role in it.

Susannah was tight-lipped all through lunch, from time to time casting wounded glances at Jane, which were steadfastly ignored. Although they were both barely polite to Charlie, Harry and Jane made much of Malcolm.

'He's such a big, healthy baby,' Jane said. 'You must get a lot of pleasure from him.'

'Jane likes babies,' Harry said, gazing fondly at his wife.

'You two could get on and have one of your own if you didn't waste all your energy fighting,' Jack said. Jane blushed and looked to Harry for help.

'Jack! Don't be so coarse,' Susannah reproved.

'We will,' Harry said. 'There's no rush. I'll have to build an extension in a year or two, I suppose. That shouldn't be too much trouble—I know all about building houses now. I made a really good job of my house,' he said, warming to his subject. 'I reckon it must be the best house around here.'

'It's all right when it doesn't rain, dear,' Jane said with deceptive sweetness. 'When the roof doesn't leak, and the door doesn't stick.'

'Don't you start on that,' Harry said. 'There's nothing wrong—'

'Now, you two,' Jack broke in. 'There'll be no fighting in this house.'

Harry and Jane subsided, and Jane lowered her eyes with a suitably meek expression, but not before Amy had seen her poke her tongue at Harry for the briefest of moments.

Amy carried a sleepy Malcolm in her arms for the first part of their walk home later that afternoon, but Charlie took the load from her when they were out of sight of the house.

'What did she mean, saying the boy's slow?' he demanded. 'There's nothing wrong with him, is there?'

'Nothing at all,' Amy said. 'Anyone can see he's healthy and normal—he's much bigger than most children his age. Susannah likes to make trouble, that's all. She's always been like that, you just have to ignore her. Pa tries to.'

Charlie looked relieved at her words. 'They're mad in that house. They let the women carry on with a lot of nonsense—especially your pa's wife. All that back talk, and he let her go on and on and never even corrected her.' He did not seem to want a reply, so Amy said nothing.

'You behaved all right,' he added.

'Thank you,' Amy said, grateful for the small sign of approval.

'They've no idea how to handle women. No idea at all. No wonder he let you run wild. Look what that led to.'

The New Year came in warm and dry, and all the haystacks were safely finished before January was half over. One evening a few days after haymaking was finished Charlie announced, 'I'll be away over the back of the farm tomorrow.'

Amy looked up from the shirt she was sewing for him. 'What are you going to do over there?' Charlie did not usually spend much time in the wild area of the farm that nudged up against the bush.

'There's a couple of paddocks that are full of scrub. They were cleared once, a long while before I bought this place, but they were half-wild again by the time I got here. I'm going to break them in properly.' He glanced towards the bedroom, where Malcolm was asleep in his cradle. 'I'll be needing the extra grazing when I build the herd up—can't have wasted land. I've the boy to think about, you know.'

Amy thought it would be more sensible for Charlie to leave the heavy work of clearing scrub till the cooler weather of autumn, but she did not offer unwanted advice. 'I'll bring your lunch down if you like, that'd save you coming home for it.'

Charlie grunted an acknowledgement and turned his attention back to his newspaper.

Next day while Malcolm had his morning sleep Amy used the peaceful time to prepare lunch. She had just lifted a large, golden-crusted meat pie out of the oven when she heard Malcolm crying a complaint.

'I'm coming, Mal,' she called. She slid a tray of jam tarts into the range and closed the door on them before hurrying into the bedroom.

Malcolm was struggling to get out of his cradle, but as soon as he leaned against one side the cradle would tilt on its rockers, making him fall flat on his bottom again. The indignant look on his face made Amy smile. She knelt and lifted him out before his cries could turn into roars.

'You mustn't try and climb out by yourself, Mal. You have to wait for Mama, or you'll hurt yourself. You're getting too big for a cradle, aren't you? We'll have to ask Papa to make you a little bed.' And anyway, there would be another baby in the cradle by the end of the year.

She carried Malcolm out to the kitchen, sat him at the table and gave him a mug of milk, holding it to his lips as he sipped. The smell of cooked pastry caught her attention. She took the empty mug away before lifting the tray of jam tarts out of the oven.

Malcolm looked wide-eyed at the tarts. 'Me!' he said.

'Not yet, Mal. Wait till they're cold, then you can have one.'

'Me!' Malcolm demanded.

'No, you'd burn your mouth.' She winced when she saw Malcolm's face start to turn red as he opened his mouth to roar his disapproval. She reached up to a cake tin and pulled out a biscuit. 'Do you want a bikkie? Have this one. Go on, Mal.'

Malcolm took the biscuit in his hand and flung it onto the floor. 'No!' he yelled. 'Cake!'

'Malcolm! That's naughty.' She gave Malcolm's hand a small slap, which he did not seem to notice. 'I should give you a real smack for being so naughty. Papa wouldn't like it if he saw you doing that.' But she knew she would not hit him, and she suspected Malcolm knew it too.

Amy picked up the rejected biscuit and threw it into the slops bucket, then fetched a small plate and gingerly lifted two tarts on to it. 'Look, here's tarts for you and me. We just have to wait for them to cool down.' She put the plate on the windowsill, where the breeze from the open window would blow over them.

She turned around just in time to see Malcolm clamber down off the chair and make his unsteady way towards the range. 'Mal! Don't you touch that,' she called, but it was too late. Malcolm let out a shrill scream as his little hand touched the hot iron tray that held the remaining tarts.

Amy crossed the kitchen in a few steps and caught Malcolm up in her arms. He screamed and screamed, but she could see that it was mostly in anger at not having been able to snatch a tart. She sat with him on her lap and took the two reddened fingers into her mouth for a moment to cool them. 'Poor Mal,' she crooned. 'Poor little Mal.'

The jam jar was still on the table. Amy picked the spoon out of it and looked around guiltily, half expecting to see a disapproving Charlie in the doorway, then slipped a spoonful of jam into Malcolm's mouth. His cries stopped abruptly as he tasted the sweetness. Amy gave him another spoonful, then held him close as he slowly quietened, his sobs subsiding into whimpers.

'Oh, Mal, you do get in a state, don't you? You want your own way all the time, and you make such a fuss when you don't get it. What am I going to do with you?' *Give him what he wants*, part of her said. *Give him a smack for being so silly*, came a more pragmatic thought.

But she could not see Malcolm's tears without remembering that she had not wanted him; that she had felt nothing when he was first placed in her arms. She had to be as good a mother as she was capable of. She did not want to see Malcolm crying; far less did she want to make him cry by hitting him.

Amy brushed down a tuft of hair standing awry on his head. No one would call Malcolm a pretty baby; the kindest remark Edie could make was that he was 'a sturdy little fellow'. His hair, still sparse on the big, square head, was an orange flame. Malcolm's skin was very fair, and sure to freckle when he grew a little older. His eyes were small and the palest of blues, and just now they were wet with tears.

Malcolm nestled against her, seeking comfort, as he had not done since he was a small baby. Amy placed a light kiss on his head. 'You do like Mama a little bit, don't you, Mal? I think I love you like a mother's meant to. I love you as much as I can, anyway.' *Would I have loved Ann properly?* she wondered. *Yes*, the answer came clear and strong as she remembered the feeling of her little girl warm in her arms, pulling at her breasts; long black eyelashes framing those deep blue eyes that had stared so wisely at her.

Amy roused herself from her reverie when she saw that a large tear had dropped from her cheek on to Malcolm's head. She kissed it away. 'Ann's got a new mother now, you've only got me. It's not your fault you look like your Papa. It's not your fault Papa gets angry with me, either. It's my fault.'

Malcolm began to nuzzle against the cloth of her bodice, and Amy realised what he was trying to do. 'No, Mal, you mustn't do that.' She gently pushed his head away from her breasts. 'That's not allowed any more. There's no milk left, anyway. There'll be milk again in a few months. Milk for the new baby. A little brother for you—I hope it's another boy, anyway. Will you like that? You won't be jealous, will you?' Malcolm looked dubiously at her, and Amy laughed. 'It's a good thing you can't talk much yet, or you'd tell Papa about the new baby, and it's still my secret.'

She stood up and balanced Malcolm on one hip as she walked over to the window. 'Let's have our tarts now, Mal, they'll have cooled down. Then we'll take lunch down to Papa. We'll have a picnic, the three of us. Do you want to go and see Papa?'

'Papa, Papa,' Malcolm echoed as he reached for the tart Amy held out to him.

Charlie had cleared a wide swathe of manuka scrub, Amy saw when she rounded a corner and he came into view. She let Malcolm slither down from her hip as she lowered the basket of lunch to the ground.

'Papa,' Malcolm called in his shrill voice.

Charlie turned abruptly. 'You're a wee bit too early, I want to clear down to yon fence before I stop for my lunch,' he called back. 'Keep the boy away. I don't want him falling on this stuff.'

Amy could see what he meant. Every felled manuka bush left a lethal-looking spear of stem sticking out of the ground. A small child falling over in that deadly forest would be badly hurt, if not killed. 'Papa will be finished soon, Mal, let's just watch him for a bit,' she said, keeping a tight hold of Malcolm's hand.

'No!' Malcolm protested. 'Papa.' He struggled to pull away, and Amy saw the dangerous red tinge mounting in his face. Malcolm was going to yell soon if she did not distract him. He flailed his free hand, knocking his floppy-brimmed white bonnet askew, and when Amy tried to straighten the bonnet he pushed her hand away. 'No.'

'You've certainly learned that word, haven't you, Mal?' Amy said, grateful that Charlie was not close enough to see his son misbehaving. How was she going to keep this boy out of mischief until Charlie was ready to stop? 'I know! I'll show you how to climb a tree. Come on, Mal.'

She coaxed Malcolm into a patch of tall bush safely to the side of the scrub area and lifted him onto a broad tawa branch at her chest height. 'That's how your Uncle John and Uncle Harry taught me to climb trees, Mal,' she told him. 'Put me on a high branch and said I had to get down by myself, then they pretended they were going away.' She smiled at the memory. 'The bullies! I didn't know how to climb, so I just jumped. I got a big bruise on my arm—I ripped my dress, too. Granny gave me a hiding for ripping it, but only a little one. John and Harry got a real hiding from Pa, though. They taught me how to climb properly after that. You're a bit small for that yet. Now, come on, jump to Mama,' she coaxed, holding out her arms.

Malcolm flung himself off the branch, chortling with delight at the new game. 'Oof!' Amy exclaimed as she caught him. 'You *are* heavy, aren't you? Shall we do it again?'

'Yes!' Malcolm said.

They played the game for several minutes. Amy was so busy catching Malcolm that she did not notice Charlie come up to stand beside her.

'What are you doing?' he asked.

Amy turned with Malcolm in her arms. 'Oh! You gave me a start. I've just been playing with Mal. I'll set lunch out now.'

'Mama!' Malcolm complained, stretching out his arms towards the tree.

'No, it's time for lunch, Mal.' *Don't start grizzling, please*, she begged silently. 'One more time, just to show Papa.' Malcolm leaped once more into her arms, giggling happily, then Amy grasped him firmly and walked beside Charlie to where she had left the basket of food.

'He wasn't frightened to jump out of that tree,' Charlie said.

'Oh, no, Mal isn't frightened of anything.' Amy did not point out that Malcolm was too young to have the sense to be frightened.

'Good.' Charlie sat down heavily against the base of a tree and watched Amy spread a cloth and set out the food.

'You've done a lot,' Amy said, handing him a large slice of pie on a plate.

'Hell of a lot to go,' Charlie said through a mouthful of pie. His hand shook a little as he held the plate; Amy realised he was almost too weary to keep a grip on it. His forearms were criss-crossed with scratches, some of them oozing blood, from the tough, scrubby plants.

'It's hard work, isn't it?' she asked.

'Bloody hard,' he answered shortly.

Amy held Malcolm on her lap and fed him, then ate her own lunch. When Charlie had finished he pushed his plate away and made to rise. 'I'd better get back to it,' he said, then slumped against the tree trunk with his eyes half-closed. 'In a minute.'

Amy thought of the dusting, Malcolm's napkins to be washed, and the tins that needed to be filled with baking. 'We'll stay here a while, then,' she said. 'Mal and I will keep you company for a bit.'

Charlie said nothing. Amy tidied the remains of lunch away into the basket and settled herself on the grass.

They were half shaded by the tall tawa Charlie was leaning against, and the dappled sunlight warmed her without being uncomfortably hot.

Malcolm soon became drowsy from his games of the morning followed by a good lunch. He snuggled into the crook of Amy's arm for a few minutes, then crawled over to his father. Charlie roused himself to put his arm around him. Malcolm laid his head on Charlie's chest and went to sleep.

'Mal's always happy when he's with you,' Amy told Charlie. 'That's what he likes best.'

Charlie gave a grunt that she thought contained a note of happiness. He patted his son on the arm and closed his own eyes.

'There'll be another baby in the spring.' Until the words were out Amy had not known she was about to say them. And there it was, her secret told, just like that. But it seemed so natural to tell him, just now when the three of them were at peace together.

A look of calm satisfaction spread across Charlie's face, though he did not open his eyes. 'Good,' he murmured, drawing Malcolm a little closer.

Amy watched them, taking pleasure from the sight. *Charlie loves Mal so much. He's a good father, he really is.* She studied Charlie, noting the lines of weariness etched on his face. *He's been overdoing it a bit this morning. I wish I could tell him to take it easier, but he'd only growl at me—maybe hit me. No, I don't think he'd hit me today. He's not in a bad mood.*

His hair's got greyer since we got married. It's nearly all grey now. I wonder how old he is. She knew Charlie's age must be on their marriage certificate, but that was shut away in one of his drawers, and she would never dare go poking among his private things. *Not as old as Pa, I don't think. He's quite old, though. He must be well over forty. It must be hard for him to do all the farm work by himself.* She looked at Malcolm, sound asleep pressed close to his father's side. *I'm glad Mal's going to be big and strong. He'll be able to help Charlie. I hope the new baby's another boy.*

She slid her hands down until they rested on her belly, where the new life was taking shape inside her. *Charlie's pleased about the new baby—not excited like he was with Mal, but he's happy about it. I'm glad I've told him.*

Amy rolled onto her side to get a closer view of Charlie's face. *He does look tired. He works so hard, no wonder he gets grumpy. He's hard-working and he's a good father. That's quite a lot, really. He's not such a bad husband. I think maybe he trusts me a little bit more now, too. I just wish he'd like me. If only I could please him properly—if only I could really be a good wife, he'd like me then. I wish I knew how.*

For a moment she was tempted to reach out and smooth the lines of weariness from Charlie's forehead, but she let her half-raised hand drop back into her lap, fearful of annoying him. *I wonder what it would be like to snuggle up to him like Mal is. Maybe it'd be like when I used to have cuddles with*

Pa, before Susannah came. She smiled wistfully at the memory of sitting on her father's lap with his strong arms around her. *His beard's like Pa's, I bet he could do nice tickly kisses. I miss those. If he'd just give me a nice, soft kiss I wouldn't be frightened, I'm sure I wouldn't.*

She edged a little closer to Charlie, hardly aware of what she was doing. *A nice kiss, and then he might put his arms around me and squeeze—not too hard, just so's it was a real cuddle. He might even say he liked me. I wonder... I wonder if he'd like it if I kissed him?* She pondered the idea. *Maybe it's not right for women to do that. Jimmy used to say he liked me being like that—he said I wasn't to be aloof just because that's how ladies should behave. But Charlie calls me a whore because of what I did with Jimmy.* Taking the initiative seemed too risky.

She leaned even closer. *He's in quite a good mood, really, especially now I've told him about the baby. Maybe he really will give me a nice kiss. I think I'd like that—I'm sure I would. A nice, tickly kiss and a big cuddle.*

Amy's lips were parted slightly, ready for the kiss she had almost convinced herself she was going to receive. She breathed a little faster at the thought of being held in strong arms, pressing her face against a broad chest. When Charlie suddenly opened his eyes she smiled dreamily at him and tilted her face up a little.

'What have you got that dopey look on you for?'

It was like having a dash of cold water flung in her face. Amy turned away and looked at the ground in front of her feet. 'Have I? I'm sorry, I didn't know.'

'Well, I can't sit around here all day, I've work to do.' He disentangled his arm from the sleeping Malcolm. 'Bloody arm's gone to sleep,' he muttered, shaking it. 'Haven't you got any work to do, woman?'

'Yes, I have. Lots and lots.'

'Get on with it, then. I know what your trouble is,' he said, sounding self-satisfied. 'It's because you're broody. Makes you stupider than usual.'

Amy gathered up her basket and her sleeping child without a word, not trusting her voice to be steady.

'And see you go straight back to the house,' Charlie called after her. 'Don't go wandering about the place.'

It's hard to wander with a great lump of a child on one hip. 'I'll go straight home,' she called back, not turning her head.

He doesn't even trust me to walk up to the house without getting in trouble. I'm not stupid, I'm not! She kicked at a small piece of wood in her path.

Amy looked up the hill before her, with the tiny cottage on its far side. She glanced over one shoulder to see Charlie watching. The hills on either side marked the boundaries of her small prison. Malcolm dragged at her like a dead weight, then stirred and began to grizzle at having been disturbed.

My life. This is what I've made of it. People used to say I was clever. Charlie's right about me—I must be the stupidest woman that ever lived.

11

Frank gave the fence post a nudge with his foot, and at once regretted it when a large chunk of wood flaked off one side. Arthur was right: this section of fence was half-rotten and needed replacing.

He felt a mild irritation at Arthur; why did his father-in-law have to go poking around the farm finding work for him to do? He had plenty to keep him busy; too much, he sometimes thought. During the first months of their marriage Lizzie had helped him with the morning milking, but she had stopped that as soon as they had realised she was pregnant; the baby was far too precious to risk losing. Frank had not suggested that she start helping again; Lizzie had enough to do with Maudie to look after as well as all her cooking and cleaning. She always seemed to be working; even in the evenings when he could relax with a newspaper Lizzie would be sewing and mending. Frank grinned to himself as he reflected that however busy she was Lizzie could usually be persuaded into an early night.

He wiggled the fence post warily. No, it would hold for a bit longer, he decided. It would probably be all right until winter, when he'd have more time to do maintenance. Arthur had said he'd better get on and fix it or the cows would get through, but Arthur was inclined to be a worrier. If he did start mending the fence that afternoon, by the time he got back from milking Maudie would already be asleep, and he would not have the chance to play with her.

Frank turned his back on the sagging fence and went off to round up the cows. He did his best to ignore the weed-choked drain he was walking alongside. Arthur had said he'd better clear out that drain before winter, too. Arthur was fond of giving advice, and Frank was happy enough to listen to it. That didn't mean he had to do everything Arthur said straight away. He had better ways of spending his time now.

He rushed through milking, knowing that Arthur would disapprove of that, too. But it wasn't going to kill the cows if he didn't get every drop of milk out of them. Carefully stripping each cow for the last few drops took too long. It was all very well for Arthur, with two sons big enough to help him. Frank had already half-decided to sell all the calves born that year; he had too many cows to milk as it was. He had a feeling the last milk cheque had been a bit lower than usual, but that was nothing to worry about. They had the farm and they had plenty to eat; what more did they want?

The delicious smell of his dinner wafted through the open kitchen door to meet him as he walked up to the house.

'Boots!' Lizzie called when he stepped onto the porch.

'You always say that,' Frank said with a grin, placing his boots neatly outside the door.

'You always forget if I don't.' Lizzie offered her cheek for a kiss without leaving off stirring a pan of gravy. She held Maudie in her free arm. 'You're a bit early.'

'I got through milking pretty fast. I wanted to come and see my girls.'

'Make yourself useful, then—you can take this girl and keep her entertained.'

There was nothing Frank wanted more. He took Maudie from Lizzie and sat at the table with his little daughter on his lap. Maudie giggled and waved her arms about as he bounced her gently on one knee.

'Have you been a good girl, Maudie? Did you miss Papa today? You were asleep when I came in for lunch.'

'She slept till two o'clock, then she woke up a bit grumpy. I had her out here for a while but she started playing up. I put her back to bed and shut the door on her till she stopped bawling.'

'Playing up for Mama, eh?' Frank tried to look stern at Maudie, but it was difficult to frown when she was giving him a wide smile, showing her two teeth. 'It's no good trying that on, Maudie. Mama's pretty good at getting her own way.' He hoisted Maudie high in the air, making her squeal with delight.

Lizzie stood watching the two of them. 'She's going to be pretty good at getting her own way, too. Especially with you.'

'Yes,' Frank agreed. 'She's neat.' He lowered Maudie to his lap and planted a soft kiss on her forehead.

Lizzie chattered away about the details of her afternoon as she finished getting dinner ready, then she took the chair next to Frank. 'It'll be ready in ten minutes or so, when those peas are cooked. Give her here, I'll see if she wants a feed before I put her down.' She unbuttoned her bodice and held out her arms for Maudie. 'Look at you with all that around your face.' She wiped the dribble from Maudie's chin with a corner of her apron before putting the baby to her breast. 'I think you've got another tooth coming through.'

The baby sucked for a minute or two, then lost interest and gazed around the kitchen, waving her arms aimlessly. 'No, she's not very hungry,' Lizzie said. She closed her bodice and stood up with Maudie against one shoulder. The little girl looked over Lizzie's shoulder at Frank and stretched out her hands towards her father. She gave a small cry of frustration at being tightly held.

'Does she have to go yet, Lizzie?' Frank asked. 'Couldn't she stay out here with us a bit longer?'

'I'm going to dish up in a minute.'

'I'll hold her. I can eat my dinner with Maudie on my lap.'

'All right, as long as you don't drop any food on her.' Lizzie put Maudie back on Frank's lap, where the little girl laughed delightedly.

'Of course I won't drop anything.'

'Just be careful, she's inclined to wriggle.' Lizzie brought their plates to the table, then took her own seat and watched the two of them. 'You're going to spoil that girl, aren't you?' she said, smiling at the sight.

'No more than I do you.' Frank grinned at her.

'Humph! Eat your dinner before it gets cold. There's strawberries and cream for pudding.'

Frank ploughed his way through roast lamb followed by a huge pile of strawberries from Lizzie's garden, then leaned back in his chair to drink his tea, sipping it carefully to avoid spilling a single drop on Maudie. The little girl's eyelids were drooping as she snuggled into the crook of his free arm. Frank put both arms around her and squeezed. He looked across the table to see Lizzie beaming back at him, and he thought he must be the happiest man alive.

'I'd better get a bit of material when we go into town this week,' Lizzie remarked idly. 'I need a new dress.'

'Oh. How much will that cost?'

'I'm not sure—I need about seven yards, I suppose it'll be a shilling a yard. I'll just buy some cheap cotton, it's only a work dress.' Frank felt his brow crease in thought, and saw Lizzie frown at his expression. 'Is that all right, Frank?'

'Hmm? Yes, yes, that's fine. I was just thinking about something.' He tried to add up in his head just how much of a bill he had run up in town since he had last settled his accounts. He soon gave up; it was too hard to remember.

'I could make this one do until next summer, I suppose. It's got a bit of a rip in the back, but I could put a little patch on it—'

'No! I don't want you wearing patched clothes, Lizzie. You can buy all the material you want.'

'You're sure? That's all right, then. I can probably get some for ninepence a yard if I rat around in the shop. You could do with a new warm nightshirt before winter, too, I might see if Mrs Nichol's got any decent flannel.'

'What about Maudie?' Frank asked with a laugh. 'If we're both getting new things you'd better make her something, too.'

'Oh, Maudie's the best dressed of the lot of us—all those fancy things Aunt Susannah's mother sent from Auckland. They've done Tom and George and Mal, they're still not worn out. I'll have to give the littlest sizes back to Amy soon, now she's having another one.'

'That Charlie doesn't muck around, eh? They only got married a couple of months before us, and they're on their second one already.'

'Jealous?' Lizzie asked with a wry smile.

Frank gave a snort at the notion. How could he be jealous of anyone when he had a wife and daughter like Lizzie and Maudie? 'Of course not. I just thought he'd be too old for all that, that's all.'

'I think Amy wishes he was,' Lizzie said, more to herself than to Frank. For a moment she looked sad, then her face set in determined lines. 'But I can't do anything for Amy except be her friend. She's been much happier since she had Mal, too—much calmer, anyway.'

She leaned across and put her hand over Frank's where it rested on the table. 'We'll have more babies. Lots and lots of them.'

'You're not worried about it, like you were before we started Maudie?'

Lizzie shook her head. 'No, not now I'm sure we know what... I mean, I'm sure we can have babies. I'd rather have a couple of years between them.'

'Mmm.' Frank gripped her hand more tightly. 'Tired?'

'A bit. It's been really hot today.'

'How about an early night, then?'

Lizzie gave his hand a playful slap. 'Don't you ever think about anything else?' she scolded, though the twinkle in her eyes gave her away. 'We'll see. I've got a pile of mending to do after I've done these dishes—'

'I'll help you with the dishes,' Frank offered. After all, if he was honest with himself he had not done a lot of work that day.

'Promise?' She grinned at him. 'I'll still have to do all that mending... well, some of it, anyway. And now I really am going to put that child to bed.' She walked around the table and took the sleeping Maudie from Frank's lap. He gave Lizzie's bottom a light pat as she turned away; she looked back over her shoulder with an expression that made Frank quite sure most of Lizzie's mending would be left for another day.

Yes, Arthur took life too seriously, Frank thought as he carried the dirty dishes to the bench. Why should he waste his time worrying about a bit of fence or about the milk cheque being a few shillings down when he had Lizzie and Maudie to think about?

This time Amy was not going to risk giving birth on the beach. As soon as she felt the first pangs of labour she moved a large pot of soup off the heat of the range, thrust her nightdress and some extra pairs of drawers into the bundle she had had ready for several weeks, and made up a small parcel of clothes for Malcolm, then took him by the hand and went in search of Charlie.

'It's time,' she told Charlie when she found him checking the in-calf cows. 'Can you take Mal to Pa's?' She passed Malcolm's clothes to Charlie, and knelt awkwardly to lower herself to the little boy's level.

'Listen, Mal, you're going to stay with Grandpa and Aunt Susannah for a while.' She saw his mouth move to shape a determined 'No', and spoke hastily to prevent him. 'You'll be able to play with Tommy and Georgie—you'll like that, won't you?'

The idea of playing with the big boys brought a smile to Malcolm's face. 'Yes!' he said.

'That's the boy. Now, you be a good boy for Aunt Susannah.' *She won't put up with any nonsense*, Amy added silently. 'Papa will bring you to see me soon. Give Mama a kiss.'

'Uck,' Malcolm said, twisting away from her embrace. He went off with his father, and Amy made her slow way back to the house to wait for Charlie to collect her.

I'm not frightened about it this time, Amy thought as Charlie drove her into town. In fact she was looking forward to staying with Mrs Coulson.

When the nurse closed the door on Charlie and turned to face her young patient, Amy found it easy to return her smile.

'Here we go again,' Mrs Coulson said cheerfully. 'Now, let's take a look at the business end of you, then we'll see how long we've got.' She bustled Amy into the familiar bedroom and soon had her in her nightdress and lying in bed for the nurse to examine her.

'When did the pains start, dear?'

'Just this afternoon, about two hours ago, that's all. I haven't felt any for a while though.'

'I didn't think so.' Mrs Coulson lowered Amy's nightdress and sat on the bed beside her. 'Well, my dear,' she said, leaning close and giving Amy a conspiratorial smile, 'you and I are going to have a nice, quiet evening together. You've had a bit of a false alarm.'

'Oh, no!' Amy said in dismay. 'What am I going to tell Charlie when he comes tomorrow?'

'Don't you worry about that,' Mrs Coulson said, patting her on the arm. 'By the time he arrives I expect you'll be well away again, and I'll just tell him to come back the next day.' She looked away from Amy and spoke in an apparently offhand way. 'Even if you haven't started again, I probably won't let him see you tomorrow—unless you specially want him to, anyway. See how you feel then.'

'Thank you,' Amy said, glad to have the responsibility of dealing with Charlie's possible disapproval taken from her.

'Now, you just lie there and enjoy taking the weight off your feet, and I'll make us a nice cup of tea, then we'll have a chat until it's time for me to get dinner on. You can tell me how that great big boy of yours is doing.'

'I'll help you with dinner if you like, now the baby's settled down.'

'You certainly will not,' Mrs Coulson said. 'You look worn out, girl. You've been running around too much, haven't you?'

'Well, more waddling than running,' Amy admitted. 'Malcolm's at a difficult sort of age, he takes a lot of looking after.' She did not add that it took all her imagination to hide Malcolm's naughtiness from Charlie.

'I thought as much. You're going to stay in that bed and gather your strength for tomorrow. You can have a doze before dinner, after we've had a chat.'

'Oh, I don't think I can sleep in the daytime, I'm not used to—'

'Now, my girl,' Mrs Coulson interrupted, wagging her finger in a mock scolding, 'in my house you'll do as I say. And I say you're to take things easy. Understand?'

'Yes,' Amy agreed meekly. She leaned her head against Mrs Coulson's shoulder and smiled up at her. 'Thank you.'

The nurse hugged at her. 'You've a lovely smile, my dear. A pity you don't show it very often.'

Amy's pains had not started again by the following morning. Mrs Coulson let her get out of bed and sit in the parlour, wearing her nightdress and with a knitted blanket over her knees. When Charlie arrived Amy sat very quietly in the parlour and listened to Mrs Coulson sending him away.

'No, she's not finished yet, I'm afraid, Mr Stewart,' the nurse said airily. 'Everything's going well, there's no need for you to worry, we'll just let nature take its course. Sometimes these things take a while. You don't really want to see her just now, do you?' This last question was said in such a dubious tone that Amy was not at all surprised when Charlie went away without entering the house.

Amy got up from her armchair and peeked through the lace curtains to watch Charlie ride away. 'Maybe I should have seen him,' she said guiltily.

'Nonsense,' Mrs Coulson said. 'You'll see him soon enough. Stop worrying about him and put your feet back on that footstool. I want you properly rested up before we have to get down to business.'

In the early evening the contractions returned, this time so strong that there was no doubting they were the real thing. Around midnight Mrs Coulson announced that things were far enough advanced for Amy to have some chloroform. Amy breathed gratefully at the chloroform-soaked cloth, welcoming the numbness.

Sometime in the small hours of the next morning, Amy struggled through the muffling darkness of the anaesthetic and became aware of a warm bundle in her arms. She half-opened her heavy eyes and saw a small creature with a mop of dark hair.

'Ann,' she murmured in wonder. 'My little one.'

She held the baby close until she felt it being lifted away from her. She tried to hold on, but her arms would not obey her. 'Don't take her away,' she begged. 'Let me hold her a bit longer. Please don't take my baby away.'

'Baby needs a sleep now,' a soft voice said. Amy knew she should recognise it, but her mind refused to supply a name. 'You should go to sleep, too. You've been working hard.'

'Please,' Amy whispered.

A hand brushed tears from Amy's cheek. 'All right, darling, you can have a bit more of a cuddle. Just for a minute, though.' Amy lay back against the pillows with the baby on her chest and drifted off into an exhausted sleep.

When she opened her eyes again she saw cracks of light through the drapes. This time she knew where she was and who she was with. Mrs Coulson was sitting in a chair beside the bed; she stood up and leaned over Amy as soon as she saw her eyes open.

'Is the baby all right?' Amy asked.

'As pretty a baby as a mother could wish,' Mrs Coulson told her. 'But I'm afraid he won't be called Ann.'

Ann. A pang of loss went through Amy. 'I got a bit muddled. I thought it was a girl.'

Mrs Coulson bent over the cradle and lifted the baby boy from it. 'Have another cuddle, now you're properly awake.'

Amy opened her arms to hold the baby. 'He is pretty, isn't he? He looks just like... just like a little girl.'

'So he does, my dear,' Mrs Coulson agreed. 'It doesn't really make any difference till they're old enough to wear trousers.'

'I wanted another boy, really I did. A boy to help Charlie.'

'You're a good girl. Don't worry, you'll have a little girl to name after your mother one day.'

Amy shook her head. 'No, I couldn't do that. I… never mind. I only want boys.'

'Just as you say, dear,' Mrs Coulson said. Amy knew that the nurse was humouring her.

The chloroform had left Amy with a feeling of nausea, and whenever she moved even slightly her body sent a painful complaint. She was still weak and drowsy when Charlie arrived later that morning.

'You can come in for a minute, Mr Stewart, but only if you're very quiet,' she heard Mrs Coulson saying from the passage. 'She's very tired, and the little fellow's asleep.' The nurse led Charlie into the room and over to the cradle. Amy tried to manage a smile for him, but for the moment Charlie had eyes only for the baby. 'There he is,' Mrs Coulson said in a loud whisper. 'Your new son. A fine little fellow, isn't he? Not so little, either—nine pounds if he's an ounce.'

Charlie stood over the cradle and looked down at the sleeping baby. 'He's got black hair,' he said in surprise.

'Yes, Mr Stewart. So has your wife, you may have noticed.'

'I thought he'd look like the boy,' Charlie said.

'He'll look like your wife, which means he'll be a lovely child. He'll have your height, though—he's quite a lanky chap. I'd show you those long legs of his, except I don't want to disturb him.'

The nurse sat on the bed beside Amy and stroked her hair. 'Are you all right, dear? Having trouble keeping your eyes open, aren't you, darling?'

'A bit,' Amy admitted. 'It's another boy, Charlie,' she said, hoping for some sign of approval.

'Aye,' Charlie said, as if the thought that the baby might not be a boy had never entered his head. He took a proper look at Amy for the first time 'What's wrong with her?' he asked the nurse.

'She's just had a baby, Mr Stewart,' Mrs Coulson said sharply. 'That takes a bit more energy than making your breakfast. The poor girl's worn out.'

'Oh.' Charlie looked surprised at this idea. 'She'll get over it, won't she?'

'Yes, she will,' the nurse said. 'Women have to get over it. And she's young and strong. You can go now, I want her to get some rest.'

She came back muttering to herself when she had closed her front door on Charlie. 'Men have no idea,' Amy heard her say. 'No idea at all.' She popped her head round the bedroom door. 'Go to sleep, sweetheart. I'll come back and give you a bit more of a tidy-up later.'

Amy spent the next few hours in a half-doze, but was glad of the company when Mrs Coulson came back to her around midday. 'Don't sit up,' the nurse told her. 'I can do what's needed with you flat on your back. I just need to clean up the fresh lot of blood that's come since this morning.'

Amy felt the nurse sponging her loins. She winced at the touch, gentle though it was. 'Everything hurts so much,' she said. 'Oh, and I feel so awful. Why do I feel so sick? I'm worse than last time.'

'You lost more blood this time, dear—and last time was bad enough for that. Nothing dangerous, but it'll leave you feeling rather feeble for a while. It's these big babies of yours, darling.'

'I'm too small, aren't I?'

'Your husband's too big, that's another way of looking at it.' The nurse pulled Amy's nightdress back down over her thighs and sat on the chair by the bed. 'Don't worry, dear, you'll feel stronger soon. I'll look after you until you do.'

'Thank you.' Amy studied Mrs Coulson's tender expression. The kindness, coupled with her weakness, made her feel safe. 'Charlie's pleased about the baby, don't you think? He didn't say much, but he looked a bit pleased.'

Mrs Coulson pursed her lips. 'If that man doesn't wake up every day thinking he's the luckiest man in the world to have a wife like you and these two fine sons you've given him—now, don't shake your head at me like that.'

'No,' Amy said tiredly. There seemed no need to pretend with Mrs Coulson. 'He loves Mal, and he'll like the new baby too. But he doesn't like me.'

'Don't be silly, dear—who could help liking you?'

'Charlie doesn't. He's sort of got used to me, but he doesn't like me. I don't think he ever will.' Amy was too weary to feel more than a resigned sadness.

'Now, dear, you're just thinking like that because you're worn out. Of course he likes you—I doubt if anyone exactly twisted *his* arm to make him marry you.'

'I think…' Amy stopped to put her thoughts in order. 'I don't really understand it properly, but I think Charlie expected I'd be different from how I am. I'm not exactly sure what he wanted, but I know I'm not it. I've tried and tried, but I just can't seem to please him. I can't seem to make him happy.'

Amy had not even known she was weeping until she felt Mrs Coulson wiping her face with a handkerchief. 'If you can't make him happy, darling, then I don't think any woman on earth could.'

'But if I was a good wife he'd like me, wouldn't he?'

'If he wasn't a bigger fool than most men he'd worship the ground you walk on. Shh now, dear, or you'll have me saying something I shouldn't.'

Amy looked down at the cradle. 'Charlie's not going to love this baby as much as he does Mal. I think he'll like him, and he'll be a good father to him, but it won't be really special for him this time. Maybe it's because Mal was his first child—Mrs Coulson, do you think there's something special about a person's first baby? Something that makes them love it more than the other ones?' *Is that why I loved Ann so much? Or just because she was my baby, and these ones belong to Charlie?*

'There's something in that,' Mrs Coulson said thoughtfully. 'I don't know about loving the first one more—my oldest was certainly more of a trial to me than the others, till she grew up a bit, anyway. But the one that makes you a mother… well, that's the most special thing that can happen to a woman, isn't it?' She smiled at Amy. 'I'm sure you'll love this little fellow just as much as you do your Malcolm. Don't twist like that, darling,' she warned when Amy tried to roll onto her side to look at the baby more closely, but it was too late. Amy let out a gasp of pain.

'Oh, it hurts!'

Mrs Coulson nodded sympathetically. 'It's the stitches. Another big baby, another big tear in you. You'll have to lie as still as you can for a while.'

'Stitches. I'd forgotten about those.' Amy closed her eyes, trying to hide from the memory of those agonised nights after Malcolm's birth, when Charlie had decided she was ready to meet his demands.

'I'm afraid you'll have to have them every time now, dear. Once one baby's ripped you it makes your flesh a bit weak, so all the others tear you in the same places.'

'I see. I didn't know that.' She did not trust herself to speak further without breaking down. Mrs Coulson soon left her alone, with an injunction to try and sleep again.

Late that night Amy was woken by the feeble sound of the baby's crying. Mrs Coulson was beside the cradle in a flash, lifting the baby ready to hold him to Amy's breasts.

'Don't move, darling,' the nurse whispered to her. 'You don't even have to wake up properly. You just leave it all up to me.' She let the baby

146

suckle for a short time, then settled him back in the cradle and returned to the sofa she slept on while Amy used the big bed.

But Amy was wide awake now. The baby's cries had brought back other memories of Malcolm's babyhood: memories of broken nights, with Charlie complaining about his disturbed sleep when he wasn't inflicting agony on her, or shaking her angrily for not being able to hide how much she hated what he was doing to her.

The room was silent except for the tiny noises of the baby's snuffly breathing. When she could no longer weep silently, Amy muffled her small sobs in the pillow. She thought she was succeeding in keeping her misery secret until she felt a hand on her heaving shoulder, and turned her face to see Mrs Coulson kneeling beside the bed.

'What's wrong, darling?' the nurse asked quietly. 'What's upsetting you so much?'

'I'm sorry,' Amy choked out between sobs. 'I didn't mean to wake you up.'

'Never mind about me, I don't need much sleep anyway. Tell me what's wrong.'

'It's…' Amy took a gulp of air and tried to speak more calmly. 'The baby wakes up and cries. He'll wake up in the night for ages.'

'Well, yes, dear, babies do wake in the night. You knew that, why's it worrying you so much now?'

'I'd forgotten. It made Charlie so bad-tempered when Mal was doing it. Now it's all going to start again.'

'I'll give you some laudanum to take home, that'll make the little fellow sleep if the nights get too much for you. You've got to be careful using it on little ones, but sometimes there's nothing else to be done. But darling…'

Mrs Coulson was silent for a moment. She went on in a measured tone, as if trying hard to be fair. 'You have to remember, your husband's a bit old to be going through all this with small babies. Most men would be nigh on twenty years younger than him when their first child's born. People get less patient as they get older.'

'I know. I try and keep him happy, so the baby won't annoy him too much. But it's hard to be careful all the time, especially when there's a little baby to look after.'

'Don't try too hard, sweetheart. You mustn't run yourself ragged. The worst time passes soon enough with little ones.'

'But I have to try hard. I have to. I've got to do my best to make Charlie happy—that's my duty. That's how I have try and make up for all the wrong things I've done.'

'You?' Amy could hear the smile in Mrs Coulson's voice. 'I doubt if you've done anything in your life worse than sneaking extra biscuits from the tin.'

'I have. I've done terrible, terrible things.' *I was wicked with Jimmy. I made Pa so unhappy. I gave away my baby.* A sob racked her. She pressed her face into the pillow once again.

'Shh, shh,' Mrs Coulson soothed, rubbing her hand softly across Amy's shoulders. 'Everything seems worse in the middle of the night. You just forget about all the terrible things you imagine you've done—and I don't believe a word of it, by the way—and think about this lovely little baby you've got.'

'And I've got stitches,' Amy said into the pillow.

'What was that, dear?'

Amy rolled onto her back, the movement sending knife-thrusts of pain through her. 'Stitches. I didn't know I'd have to have them again.' The last word was almost a wail. She put her hand over her mouth to smother the sob.

'Are they really hurting you, darling?' There was concern in Mrs Coulson's voice. 'I'll have a good look at them in the morning to see if something's not right, but perhaps I'd better give you a bit of laudanum now to help you sleep.'

'It's the stitches. All those places where I got torn. It makes me so sore, and Ch-Charlie gets so angry with me, and...' Amy gave up trying to talk and abandoned herself to the tears.

'Ah, I see,' Mrs Coulson said. 'It takes you a long time to get back to normal down below because you're torn up so badly. So that's the trouble with him, is it? Gets grumpy because he has to do without for a while?'

Amy looked at the paler patch of shadow that was Mrs Coulson in her nightdress. It was easy to whisper into the darkness things she could never have said in the light. 'Do without?' she echoed in bewilderment. 'It's because I cry, and he can tell it's hurting me, and that makes him angry... I don't cry usually, really I don't. Only the first few weeks, when I was so frightened all the time. Then when Mal was born it all started again. I tried not to show it, but I couldn't help it. It hurt so much. And now it's g-going to happen again.'

There was silence in the room for a long moment. 'Are you telling me,' Mrs Coulson said slowly, 'he forced himself on you while you were in that state? All ripped up from bearing his great big son? My dear, you must have been nearly mad with the pain!'

'Forced?' Amy shook her head in confusion. 'But he's my husband.

148

It's his right. I just wish he wouldn't get so angry with me.'

'I think, dear,' Mrs Coulson said, her voice shaking slightly, 'you'd better not tell me anything else.'

'I'm sorry. I shouldn't be telling anyone things like that. Charlie wouldn't like it if he heard me.'

Mrs Coulson gripped Amy's arm. 'That's not what I meant. If I heard any more, I don't think I'd be able to send you home. I think I'd want to keep you here with me.' She slipped her arms around Amy and kissed her on the forehead. 'Poor child. What on earth were they thinking of, making you marry him?'

I wish I didn't have to go back. But Amy would not say the words aloud. She had to return to Charlie's house. She had to do her duty. 'Nobody made me marry him,' she said, trying to sound calm. 'It was my own decision. Nobody forced me.'

'There's more ways of forcing than holding a gun to your head,' Mrs Coulson said grimly, but Amy did not reply and the nurse did not press her further.

Mrs Coulson did not mention their midnight conversation again, although Amy saw the nurse looking at her with her brow furrowed many times over the next few days. Her strength seemed slower in returning this time; it was several days before she could sit up in bed for more than a few minutes at a stretch. But as soon as she felt able to spend half an hour or so propped up against the pillows, Mrs Coulson gave in and let her have the needle and thread she begged for. Lizzie brought in a length of flannelette, and Amy was soon busily hemming squares into napkins for the new baby.

'They go through so many, don't they?' Amy remarked as she finished yet another one. 'Especially while they're little. At least Mal doesn't dirty as many now—I don't think Susannah's too pleased at having all that extra washing while she's looking after him, though.'

'Mmm. She looks even more of an acid drop than usual lately,' Mrs Coulson agreed. 'You know, I often think men are the biggest babies of all, but at least you don't have to keep them in nappies.'

Amy laughed aloud at the idea of a grown man in napkins, and Mrs Coulson smiled back at her. 'It's good to see you laugh, dear.'

'I've been a real misery lately, haven't I?' Amy said. 'I'm sorry I've been so silly—'

'Stop that at once,' Mrs Coulson interrupted. 'I don't want to hear another "I'm sorry" from you. You spend far too much time apologising to the world.'

'I'm sor—' Amy began. She looked at Mrs Coulson and laughed again. 'All right, I'll try not to say it all day. Will that do?'

'It's a start,' Mrs Coulson conceded. 'Oh, I think the little fellow's stirring. Put that needle well out of the way and I'll fetch him up to you.'

Once the baby was suckling, Mrs Coulson took up her own needle and continued stitching away at a chemise she was mending. 'I'd better go and see what sort of a job young Nellie's making of getting those vegetables ready when this fellow's had his feed. What do you think you might like for pudding? I went over to the store this morning, so my larder's full.'

'Just anything,' Amy said in surprise. 'Whatever you want to have.'

'I want to make something *you* like. Now you've got your appetite back properly you can appreciate a decent feed. What's your favourite pudding?'

'I make a steamed pudding with jam quite a lot, that's one of Charlie's favourites.'

'Sweetheart, I'm not making your husband a pudding, I'm making *you* one. There must be something you specially like.'

'Um…' Amy tried to think back to life in her father's house before her marriage. 'I used to like that chocolate sort of pudding—you know, the one that makes its own sauce when you cook it. Charlie doesn't like chocolate, so I never make it now. But don't go to any trouble.'

'Chocolate pudding it is,' Mrs Coulson said triumphantly. 'That's one of my favourites, too. Goodness me, I've never heard of anyone not liking chocolate. What a fuss-pot your husband is.'

Amy felt she should defend Charlie against this slight. 'He's not really fussy, it's just that he only likes certain things and he doesn't like trying new things much.'

'Just as I said. Fussy.' Mrs Coulson sat and watched the baby suckling. 'He's feeding well. He's going to be another big fellow, all right, same as your Malcolm. What are you going to call him?'

'I don't know. Charlie hasn't said yet what his name's to be.'

'You do get some say in it, don't you?' Mrs Coulson said in surprise.

'I shouldn't think so. Why?'

'Well, because he's your son too. Did he name the first one?'

'Yes. Maybe he'll let me this time, I hadn't thought of it.' Amy looked down at the baby pulling at her breast. 'This one feels more like my baby than Mal did. I know that's silly, but he does. I'd like to name him after Pa, but we've already got a Jack and a John just next door. Maybe he could have John as a second name.'

But when Charlie arrived for his daily visit the next morning, he

150

announced to Amy that he had just registered the baby at the courthouse.

'Oh,' Amy said, trying not to show her disappointment. 'What have you called him?'

'Good, solid Scottish names. None of your English rubbish. James David Stewart.'

Amy's eyes opened wide in shock. 'No,' she said in a voice little more than a whisper. 'You can't call him that—you can't!'

'What are you talking about, woman?' Charlie said indignantly. 'I can call my son whatever I want. I suppose you wanted to name him after bloody Prince Albert or something?'

'Please, Charlie, no,' Amy begged. 'Please don't call him that. Not that name. Not… James,' she got the name out with difficulty.

'What's wrong with it? What's wrong with James for a name? He'll be Jamie, or maybe Jimmy…' His voice trailed away. 'Jimmy,' he repeated heavily. 'Jimmy.' He spat the name at her. 'I've named my son after your fancy man. The fellow you rolled in the hay with—or one of them, anyway. Did you give your bastard that name too? Did you?' He grabbed at the bodice of Amy's nightdress and shook her by it.

'No, no I didn't,' Amy gasped out between shakes.

'What's going on?' came a stern voice from the doorway. Charlie let go of her and they both turned to look at Mrs Coulson, who had appeared from nowhere.

'I… I don't feel very well,' Amy said. That was true enough; her stomach was churning with fear-induced nausea. 'I got a bit upset.'

'Mr Stewart,' Mrs Coulson said in a tight voice, 'I think you'd better leave now. Your wife's had enough visiting for today.' She met Charlie's grim stare with one far more hostile. He turned his face from hers and rose to leave.

'It's my job to look after your wife while she's with me,' Mrs Coulson went on coolly. 'If you're going to upset her when you visit, I'm afraid I'll have to ask you to stay away.'

Charlie narrowed his eyes as if he were about to argue the point, but all he said was, 'When's she coming home?'

'When she's fit to.'

'When?' he demanded.

'When the child's three weeks old. Not before.'

Charlie worked through the sum in his head. 'That'll be two weeks come Wednesday. I'll fetch her home then. And I'll visit when I please in the meantime.'

'Just as you wish, Mr Stewart. As long as you don't upset her while she's in *my* house.'

Just before Charlie reached the door he turned back and spoke to Amy, ignoring Mrs Coulson's presence. 'He'll be called David. I'll not change how I've registered him, or that clerk fellow will be thinking you told me to. But he'll be called David.'

Amy nodded, staring at her hands knotted in her lap rather than look at him.

'What was all that about?' Mrs Coulson asked when they were alone.

'Nothing,' Amy said, not raising her eyes from her lap.

'Nothing that's any of my business, anyway. I'm sorry, my dear. I won't pry any more. But I meant what I said,' she added sternly. 'I won't let him upset you while you're in my house.' She left the room, closing the door after her.

Still trembling, Amy laid her head on the pillow. *It's my fault. I thought it could all be forgotten. But it can't. He'll never forget what I did. Everything reminds him. And this poor little baby—now he'll remind Charlie too.* She reached out a hand to rock the cradle gently, careful not to disturb the sleeping child. 'David,' she whispered. 'He'll forgive you. It's not your fault. And you're his son—flesh of his flesh. He'll forget your name. But he'll never forget what I did, never.' She fought against the despair that threatened to overwhelm her. *It's no good being miserable. I have to make the best of it. I have to do my best to please him and to look after the children, and that's all I can do.*

She was still lying on her back with a look of grim determination on her face when Mrs Coulson came in with her lunch half an hour later, so obviously lost in her thoughts that the nurse put the tray down beside the bed and went out again without saying a word.

'I have to go home next week,' Amy said one afternoon a week and a half later. She and Mrs Coulson were sitting in the parlour, little David in his cradle beside Amy's chair. 'Charlie'll be glad to have Mal home, I don't think he likes Susannah having him very much. The time's gone so fast.' She smiled at the nurse. 'It's like a holiday, staying with you.'

Mrs Coulson snorted. 'A funny sort of holiday, having a baby. I'll miss you, dear—you and that pretty little boy.'

'I'll miss you, too.'

'You'll have to come and see me, and bring the children, too. I like to keep an eye on the babies I bring into the world. I've hardly seen you since young Malcolm was born.'

'I'd like to, but it's hard. I don't really get out of the house much, except church and sometimes Charlie brings me in to do the shopping with him. I don't even see Lizzie much, now she's got Maudie and it's not so easy for her to ride over. Charlie doesn't like me to…' She could not bring herself to say 'wander'. 'To go out by myself,' she finished awkwardly. 'I'm allowed to go to Pa's sometimes, but that's about all. I'll see if he'll drop me off with the children one shopping day.'

'That would be nice, dear,' Mrs Coulson said. 'I shouldn't think he'd mind that.'

'I expect I'll be back to stay with you before too long,' Amy said, trying to make her voice light. 'This is my life now—a baby every other year. I seem to get with child pretty easily. I wish I didn't get so worn out having them, though.' She frowned in thought. 'Mrs Coulson, how long do women keep on having babies for? When are they too old?'

'The change of life usually comes when you're not much over forty. Sometimes a bit later—I knew a woman once who had a baby when she was forty-six.'

'Forty-six,' Amy echoed. 'I'm eighteen now. I could keep on having babies for nearly thirty years. That's another fifteen babies—even more if I have them closer than two years. There's only twenty-one months between Mal and Davie. Fifteen babies!' The very thought was overwhelming. 'But women don't really have seventeen or eighteen children—well, not usually, anyway. Why don't they?'

Mrs Coulson was silent for some time, as if choosing her words carefully. 'There are ways of slowing the babies down a bit,' she said at last. 'A girl's mother usually tells her about it after she's been married a few years. Of course it works better for some women than others.'

'How? How do you slow them down? Please, Mrs Coulson, I don't want to have twenty children.'

'You'd never live to bear them,' Mrs Coulson said quietly. 'I'm sorry, dear, I shouldn't have said that. Take no notice of my ramblings.'

'Please tell me how to slow the babies down,' Amy begged.

She wondered why Mrs Coulson looked so sad. 'You really want to know?' the nurse asked. Amy nodded her head vigorously. Mrs Coulson sighed. 'Well, I'll tell you, for what it's worth. You see, my dear, women aren't fruitful all the time. Only around the middle of the time between each lot of bleeding, for a week or so—no one seems to know exactly how long. So if your husband leaves you alone for that week or two every month then you don't get with child, or at least you're less likely to.' She smiled ruefully at Amy. 'It doesn't seem so much to ask, does it, darling?'

'I see,' Amy said in a small voice. 'I thought maybe it was something a woman could do by herself. Thank you for explaining it to me.' *A baby every other year for the next thirty years. Except I won't live to bear them.* 'I think

I'll have a lie-down till dinner time. I feel like being by myself for a little while.'

'That's a good idea,' Mrs Coulson said. 'You have a nice rest. I'll keep an eye on the little fellow.' She watched Amy walking a little unsteadily out of the room, and knew it was because the girl's eyes were blinded with tears.

Why ever had they made that poor girl marry a man like Charlie Stewart? Mrs Coulson asked herself. That stepmother of hers must have taken a terrible dislike to the girl—though just how anyone could dislike that sweet little thing was beyond her—and had moved heaven and earth to get her out of the house. Jack Leith should have had more sense than to let himself be talked into such a dreadful mismatch, but perhaps he had been too besotted with his young wife to see what was going on.

But how on earth had they talked Amy into it? Mrs Coulson had counted on her fingers enough times to know that Malcolm had been born nine months after the wedding, so he certainly hadn't been the cause of it. And anyway, how would Charlie have got Amy to lie with him without putting a ring on her finger first, short of raping her?

All that talk about the terrible things the poor girl thought she had done, that must be the clue. Susannah Leith must have somehow convinced her that she had to marry Charlie, almost as some sort of punishment. Charlie would have been only too pleased to grasp the rich prize offered him. And yet, from what the girl said he was not at all grateful for his stroke of luck in getting such a wife.

Mrs Coulson shook her head. It was none of her business, and she had no right to be puzzling over Amy's private life. It was foolish of her, too, to get so attached to the girl. But she was such an affectionate little thing, so pathetically grateful for the tiniest kindness, that it was impossible not to love her. She was certainly not the first young mother Mrs Coulson had seen who had a bad-tempered husband, nor the first to show the marks of old blows. But Mrs Coulson had never seen a girl so frightened of her husband, a husband more than old enough to be her father. This was not some empty-headed girl going into marriage full of romantic notions that the cold reality of cooking, cleaning and child-bearing soon knocked out of her. The girl had obviously never had the least desire to marry that man, except to please other people. And now she was breaking her little heart trying to make him happy so that he might show her some sign of affection. That, Mrs Coulson thought grimly, assumed the man had a heart to feel affection with.

When Charlie left the bedroom after his visit the next day, Mrs Coulson intercepted him before he reached the front door.

'Mr Stewart, could I speak to you for a moment?' she asked, careful to sound very polite as she ushered him into her parlour. She sat him down in her best armchair and gathered her thoughts.

'I wanted to have a word with you about your wife. I'm a little worried about her.'

'What's wrong with her?'

Was that concern in his voice or just irritation? Mrs Coulson wondered. 'Having this baby has been hard on her. She had a difficult time of it with young Malcolm, too. I'm afraid I was rather remiss back then not to explain that to you. I want to be sure you understand it this time.'

'She looks all right,' Charlie said dubiously. 'Has she been playing up for you? I'll have a word with her.'

He made to rise, but Mrs Coulson put out a hand to stop him. 'There's no need for that. She certainly hasn't been "playing up". She's as good a patient as I could wish, and I'll miss her when she goes home. She's simply not very well, however she might look. Mr Stewart, your wife will be rather delicate for a few months.'

'Delicate? What the hell's that supposed to mean?'

'It means you'll have to be patient with her for a while. You might find she's inclined to get fits of weeping, that sort of thing. Childbearing takes some women like that.'

'I'll soon knock that nonsense out of her. I'll not put up with that sort of rubbish.'

'She won't be able to help herself, Mr Stewart,' Mrs Coulson said, wishing she could shake some sense into the stupid man. 'You won't help her by being harsh. You won't help yourself either,' she added, willing him to understand. But there was no hint of comprehension in his face.

'You're saying I should be soft on her. Let her get away with her nonsense, instead of correcting her when she plays up.'

'I'm saying the poor girl needs a rest. She needs to get her strength back before you expect too much of her. Mr Stewart, I'm a nurse, and you must excuse me if I say things that might offend you. She needs to get her strength back before she'll be ready to do her duty as a wife.'

Charlie's eyes narrowed, and she saw a red tinge mount in his face. 'She put you up to this, didn't she?' he said in a low growl.

Mrs Coulson struggled to maintain her composure. 'She did no such thing. The girl would be terribly upset if she knew I was speaking to you like this.'

Charlie went on as if she had not spoken. 'That little bitch with her airs and graces talked you into this. She'll not get away with trying to make a fool of me. I know my rights, and she'll do as I say. She can just try moaning to me—I'll show her what her duty is. I'll show her what happens if she tries to get out of it.'

Mrs Coulson felt her self-control slipping away as he spoke. 'Mr Stewart, you are the luckiest man alive to have a wife like that girl. If you were to show her just the smallest bit of kindness—just the tiniest bit of affection—she'd cling to you as if you were the most wonderful man in the world. Instead you make her shrink from you. You're so busy thinking about your rights that you're missing out on the best chance of happiness this world's ever going to show you.'

Charlie rose from his chair. 'You're a nurse. It's your job to get her well enough so she can come home and start doing her duty again. Beyond that, it's none of your affair. I'll thank you to keep your nose out of my business.' He walked towards the door.

'Mr Stewart,' Mrs Coulson called sharply. Charlie turned in the doorway. 'You're a fool, Mr Stewart. And one day you'll see it for yourself, if you live long enough to learn any sense. The trouble is, by the time you do it might be too late. Too late for you and for that poor girl.' The slamming of her front door was the only reply Charlie gave.

12

December 1887 – January 1888

Amy smiled back at the baby chortling on her lap.

'Not sleepy yet, Davie? Never mind, it's better if you're awake now, as long as you sleep well tonight.'

Not that that was usually a problem with David. At four months old he had already been sleeping through the night for weeks, much to Amy's relief. He seemed content to sleep most of the time. He woke when he was hungry, fed eagerly, then gurgled to himself until he dropped off to sleep again. Charlie could not complain about a baby who hardly ever seemed to cry.

'You're a good boy, aren't you, Davie.' David gave her a toothless grin. She hugged him, then put him down on the cradle mattress, which she had brought out to the kitchen. She raised the pillow a little so he could see her as she moved about the room.

'Mama.' She heard Malcolm call out in the high-pitched voice that managed to sound imperious for all its childish tones. 'Mama!'

Amy crossed the passage into Malcolm's bedroom, where she had tucked him in for his afternoon sleep only half an hour before. 'What do you want, Mal? You're meant to be asleep, you know.'

'Don't want to.'

'Aren't you sleepy?' Malcolm shook his head. Amy studied his face, the lower lip thrust well out as he gave his mother a sideways look. She sighed. 'I'll let you get up, then, but you have to be good. If you go getting grumpy you'll go straight back to bed. All right? Will you be good?'

'Yes!' Malcolm said.

He looked so little in a real bed, after being in a cradle for so long. When Amy had come home from Mrs Coulson's, Malcolm had been moved into the cottage's other bedroom, giving up his cradle to his baby brother. It had come as something of a relief to have Malcolm in his own room; it would not have been much longer before he was old enough to take far too much notice of what his parents were doing in the big bed.

Amy took off his napkin (Malcolm only needed them for sleeping now), praising him over its dryness, and dressed him, then took him out to the kitchen. A mug of milk and some biscuits kept him amused for a few minutes while she got on with her work, then she sat him in one corner with a pile of old newspapers that had been destined to do service as toilet paper, which he busily ripped to shreds.

When David whimpered, Amy stopped work and lifted him from the mattress to feed him. Malcolm left his newspaper ripping to stand close to them. She reached out and stroked down an unruly tuft of red hair.

'Do you want a cuddle, Mal?' She slipped her free arm around him. 'I can fit you on my lap, too.' Malcolm squirmed out of her embrace and took a step backwards. 'No? You're not much on cuddles, are you? You're like your Papa.'

Malcolm returned to his newspapers, but when he had finished making a mess with them he looked up at Amy. 'Play, Mama.'

'I can't, Mal. I'm feeding Davie, then I've got to finish cooking, then Papa will be here and it'll be time to have dinner. Wait a minute and I'll get you some more papers.'

'Don't want them. You play!'

'Malcolm, don't be naughty or you'll have to go back to bed.'

'He don't go to bed,' Malcolm said, glaring at David in Amy's arms.

'Davie's just a little baby, Mal. He sleeps lots and lots.'

'Stupid baby.'

'Don't say that,' Amy soothed. 'He's your brother. You'll be able to play with him when he gets bigger.'

'He too little,' Malcolm said.

'He'll grow up. You'll see, you'll like playing with him soon.' Malcolm gave her a dubious look. Amy laughed at his expression. 'I think you're a bit j-e-a-l-o-u-s. All right, then, I'll play with you for a bit when Davie's finished having a drink.'

When the baby stopped suckling she put him back on the mattress, then knelt on the floor with Malcolm. She lifted a sheet of paper that Malcolm had missed ripping, and thought back to games she and Lizzie had played as children.

'Wait a minute, Mal, I'll fetch my scissors.'

She picked a blunt pair out of her sewing box and sat down on the floor again. 'Look at this.' She carefully folded the sheet concertina-wise and cut a pattern into it. When she unfolded the paper a row of dolls holding hands was revealed.

Malcolm exclaimed with pleasure and made a grab at the dolls. 'Me!' he demanded.

'Yes, they're for you. Don't rip them too fast.'

Malcolm waved the row of dolls for a few minutes while Amy quickly finished mixing up a pudding and slipped it into the range. He dropped the paper, walked over to Amy and tugged at her apron. 'Horsies, Mama.'

'What about them? What do you want me to do?'

'Horsies!' Malcolm repeated, tugging harder at her apron and scowling at her lack of understanding. 'Make horsies.'

'Oh. I'm not sure if I can do horsies, Mal. I'll have a go.' She folded another sheet and looked at it, trying to visualize a horse-shaped outline, then cut out a form as horse-like as she could manage. 'How's that?' she asked doubtfully as she unfolded the result.

'Horsies!' Malcolm cried in delight. He dragged the trail of paper horses around the kitchen, making a clicking sound with his tongue as he did; imitating the noise his father made to gee-up the horses, Amy knew.

He was crawling under the table, still clutching his now bedraggled horses, when Charlie came into the house for dinner.

'Horsies, Papa,' Malcolm said, waving them at his father as he wrapped one arm around Charlie's leg.

'What's he on about?' Charlie asked. He freed himself from Malcolm's grasp and sat down at the table.

'Horses. I made him some paper horses to play with.'

Charlie peered doubtfully at Malcolm's toy. 'Are those horses?'

'Well, he thinks they are. They've kept him entertained while I was busy, anyway.'

'He hasn't been playing up, has he?'

'Oh, no,' Amy said hastily. 'He's been very good, really.' She had no intention of mentioning Malcolm's refusal to finish his afternoon sleep. 'He does get a bit bored, though, with just me to talk to. It'll be better in a year or two when Davie can play with him. Come on, Mal, sit up at the table now.' She lifted him bodily and placed him on the chair at her right hand before he could argue.

'He's growing up,' Charlie said, watching Malcolm as Amy served the meal. 'He's two now, isn't he?'

'Just over. He's big for his age, though.'

'Time you started teaching him a few things. I don't hold with bairns talking at the table.'

'What?' Amy looked up from encouraging Malcolm to hold his spoon properly. 'Why not?'

'It's not the right way to bring them up,' said Charlie. 'When they're wee babies it's different, but once they're old enough to know better they should keep silent at the table unless they're spoken to.'

'But Pa and Granny never—' Amy stopped herself. Charlie had made his opinion of her upbringing clear far too many times. 'I'll try to remember that. Until they're how old?'

'About twelve, I'd say,' Charlie said after some consideration.

'I think Mal's a little bit too young to understand that,' Amy said carefully. 'I mean, he's only been saying more than two words joined together for a couple of months. It might confuse him if we say he's not allowed to talk.' She glanced at Malcolm, who was turning his attention from one to the other as his parents spoke, hearing his name but probably understanding little else.

'Hmm. That's maybe right. Leave it a bit longer, then. A few more months shouldn't do any harm.'

Malcolm was so quiet during the meal that Amy wondered if he had understood more of Charlie's comments than she had thought. But it meant she did not have to worry about his saying anything Charlie might disapprove of.

When she had dished up the pudding she lifted David onto her lap so he could watch the others at the table. 'Davie's starting to sleep a bit less,' she told Charlie. 'He takes notice of everything, too. Look at Papa, Davie,' she prompted. David grinned and waved his arms at his father.

'Aye, they're fine boys, both of them,' Charlie said. 'I'll have some more pudding.'

Amy rose to take his plate and pile more custard pudding into it. When she took her seat again she noticed that Malcolm's bowl was still half full. 'Come on, Mal, eat up,' she encouraged.

'Don't want it,' Malcolm said, giving her a resentful look. Amy saw him rub his eyes and poke his lower lip out, and realised with a sinking heart that his lack of sleep had caught up with him.

'He's tired, Charlie,' she said. 'It's my fault—I should have made sure he had a good sleep this afternoon, but I got him up too soon. Don't be silly, Mal,' she said, trying to make her voice light. 'Of course you want your pudding. Eat up, then you'd better go straight to bed.'

'Won't! Won't go to bed! Don't want pudding!'

Charlie looked at his son in amazement, and Amy knew that this time it would be hard to shelter Malcolm. 'Hey, boy, you do as you're told,' he said. 'You eat what's put in front of you.'

'Won't!' Malcolm gave his bowl a shove away from him. It caught a roughness on the wooden table and tipped over, spilling custard on the table and onto Malcolm.

Amy spoke quickly, anxious to forestall Charlie's angry reaction. 'Malcolm! That was very naughty. You can go to bed right now—go on, off you go.'

'He don't go to bed!' Malcolm shouted, glaring at David. He flung his spoon in fury, and by sheer bad luck his aim was better than it had any right to be.

The spoon struck the baby a glancing blow on the cheek. For a moment there was a deathly silence in the room while Amy and Charlie were too shocked to speak, Malcolm absorbed the enormity of what he had done and David looked astonished. Then the baby opened his mouth wide and screamed his outrage.

Amy checked his face. 'Poor Davie,' she soothed, stroking the small red mark on his cheek, but a glance showed her that his screams were from shock rather than pain.

Charlie took an instant longer to recover his voice, but his expression told Amy it was too late to try and protect Malcolm. 'Come here, boy,' he roared above David's yells. He pulled Malcolm from the chair, at the same time undoing the heavy leather belt from around his waist.

Malcolm had never had more than the token slaps Amy occasionally gave him. He looked at the belt without any understanding, but the threat in his father's face was easily read. His face crumpled and he began to wail.

'He didn't really mean to hurt Davie,' Amy said. Charlie turned on her.

'Don't you go meddling, woman. I've been leaving it to you to bring the boy up till he was old enough to need a man's hand. Look what you're turning him into—a spoilt brat. I'll have to sort out your mischief before you ruin my son.' He yanked up Malcolm's little frock and swung the belt.

Amy turned away from the sight, holding David close to her to try and soothe him, as the repeated whack of leather against flesh and Malcolm's screams filled the room. The noise seemed to frighten David even more, so that he yelled louder than ever.

It took her a moment to realise that Charlie had stopped hitting Malcolm, as both children were still making as much noise as ever. 'You'll get that again if you play up—you remember that,' Charlie warned, his voice rising above the cacophony. 'Now you get to bed. You can stop that noise, too.'

Malcolm ran wailing from the room and into his bedroom, slamming the door behind him. His cries were muffled by the wall, and Amy managed to soothe David so that the room gradually became quiet once more.

'The little fellow's all right, is he?' Charlie asked, looking at David in Amy's arms.

'Yes, he's fine. He just got a fright.'

'Good.' Charlie frowned. 'I've been too soft on the boy. I should have been keeping a better eye on him—I can't expect you to have any sense.'

'He's not usually like that, Charlie. He really did get tired this afternoon, that's why he was grumpy.'

'You've been babying him. It's high time he learned to behave. All this climbing on my lap like a baby. It'll have to stop.'

'But… but you like him sitting on your lap,' Amy said in dismay.

'That was all very well when he was a baby. He's too old for that now.'

'Charlie, I don't understand. I know you want me to be firmer with Malcolm—you're right, I've been a bit soft with him—but what harm does it do for you to give him cuddles? All it does is tell him you love him.'

'I don't expect you to understand. You're stupid. But you can understand this all right—if the boy plays up, you tell me and I'll sort him out. My son's going to be brought up properly. You hear me?'

'Yes, I hear you,' Amy said, avoiding his gaze. 'Would you hold Davie for me while I get Malcolm undressed and put him to bed? Davie's still a baby—it won't do any harm if you cuddle him.' The bitter note that she could not quite keep out of her voice appeared lost on Charlie.

'All right. Just get him straight into bed, mind—no making a fuss of him.'

'I won't.' She placed David in Charlie's arms and went through to Malcolm's room.

Malcolm was lying face-down on his bed, his wails diminished to an occasional sob.

'Sit up, Mal, and I'll get your clothes off,' Amy said, determinedly matter-of-fact. 'Hurry up, it's high time you were in bed.'

'Don't want to.' Malcolm's voice came muffled through the pillow.

'That doesn't matter. You have to. Do you want Papa to come in here and see you being naughty?'

Malcolm sat up at once and looked apprehensively past Amy. She took off his clothes then made him lie down again while she put a napkin on him. As she pulled his nightshirt over his head she heard him mutter something that was lost in the folds of cloth.

'What did you say, Mal?' she asked when his head emerged.

'I hate Papa,' he said, glowering towards the door.

Amy took hold of his shoulders and gave him a little shake. 'Don't you dare say that. If I ever hear that from you again I'll smack you myself—I'll smack you really hard. You don't hate Papa at all. Papa only did that because you were naughty. Papa loves you. He just wants you to be good.'

She helped Malcolm under the covers and tucked him in snugly, for once not bothering to say prayers with him; persuading him to repeat 'God bless Papa' would be too difficult this evening. She planted a kiss on his forehead before he had time to twist away from her. 'Now, you go off to sleep and tomorrow you and Papa can be friends again.'

But she was sure that Charlie and Malcolm would never be quite the same again. Malcolm would soon get over his punishment; the three or four whacks with Charlie's wide belt had wounded his dignity more than anything else. But the next time he tried to climb on his father's lap he would be pushed away, and he would not understand why.

That's going to upset him. Poor little Mal, Amy fretted as she closed the door on him. *Granny used to give me lots of hidings when I was little. Much harder ones than Mal got, too. I probably got a hiding most weeks till I was old enough to know better.* She pictured her grandmother's face that had more often worn a broad smile than a look of reproof. *But I got cuddles every day. Every single day.*

It seemed that Harry and Jane did still have some energy left after getting their fill of fighting. A few weeks before Christmas Jane gave birth to a red-haired baby girl, who was at once the apple of her parents' eyes.

Early in the New Year the proud parents took little Doris Marion to church to be baptised. Amy was touched when Jane asked her to be a godparent, along with Bob and Marion Forster. After the service Marion invited anyone within range of her voice (which was most of the congregation) to an afternoon tea at the Forster's house.

Jane, with Doris on her lap, was given the place of honour in the centre of the Forster's verandah, on a comfortable chair from the parlour. Susannah had contrived to make a late entrance, befitting her self-appointed role of *grande dame*, but the attention she got as she swept up the verandah steps with the stiff silk of her skirts rustling, hauling by the wrists Thomas and George, squirming and self-conscious in blue satin suits, was short-lived. It was the new mother and baby everyone had come to admire.

Jane received with a serene smile the homage all the women present paid to the baby, secure in the knowledge that hers was the most perfect child the world had ever seen.

Pregnancy and motherhood had changed Jane, mellowing her fiery nature into one of calm happiness. Harry had gone around with a look of confusion for some months, wondering what had happened to his favourite sparring partner, but with the arrival of Doris the awesome responsibility of being a father had had its effects on him, too. Amy could see that her brother had grown up in a hurry over the last few weeks.

Amy chose a shady corner of the verandah to sit with David on her lap. She was glad of the outing, though she wished Lizzie could have been there with her; Lizzie's second pregnancy was now advanced enough to confine her to the house.

She cajoled Malcolm to stay close to her by feeding him bits of cake from her own plate. 'Papa's busy talking to the men, Mal,' she said when she saw him looking longingly at his father. 'We'll be going home soon, anyway.' She was quite sure that was true; Charlie had looked disgruntled at the modest amount of beer on offer, and Amy knew he would want to leave as soon as it was finished. 'You stay with me and Davie. Look, this is a yummy chocolate cake.'

'Well, that's everyone's plates loaded up, I'm going to take the weight off my feet,' Marion said, collapsing into a chair beside Amy with an exaggerated sigh. Her two-year-old daughter clambered onto her lap and smiled shyly at Amy. 'My other girl's staying with Bob's sister this week—I shouldn't have let her go! She's starting to be quite a help now. She'll be six in a couple of months. Your boys are growing, Amy,' Marion added, stroking David's mop of black hair admiringly.

'Mmm, they'll both be tall,' Amy said. 'Not like me.'

Marion's oldest, a boy of eight, emerged from the house having changed his Sunday best suit for a well-worn pair of dungarees. He reached out to take a large piece of sponge cake while his mother was talking to Amy, but Marion's eyes were too sharp for him.

'Leave that for the guests, Bobby,' she told him, slapping his hand away from the plate. 'You've had plenty already. Look at the state of you!' She turned Bobby's right hand palm upwards to reveal a liberal coating of icing, no doubt from pieces of cake filched earlier. 'You're not fit for polite company. Go and play somewhere—not too close, either.'

Bobby gave his mother a wounded look, but he skipped off cheerfully enough down the steps and towards a tree some distance away with a rope swing hanging from it.

'Boys!' Marion said, raising her eyebrows. 'You have to watch them all the time. He's got hollow legs, that one—it's all I can do to keep him fed. He eats nearly as much as his father! He attracts dirt like a magnet, too. How old are your two, Susannah?'

'Five and four. Far too close in age, I've never been the same since I went through all that.'

'Mmm,' Marion made a noise of sympathetic agreement. 'How do you get them looking so nice? Look at those beautiful suits—Bobby would have one of those ripped to bits in five minutes. That's if I could get him to wear it at all.'

Susannah smiled complacently. 'They are rather lovely, aren't they? My mother sent them from Auckland. You can't get anything like this in the country, of course.' She patted an imaginary wrinkle out of the white lace-edged collar of Thomas's suit. 'I'm afraid Thomas made a fuss about wearing this, but he just has to do as I say. George is still too young to worry about what he wears, thank goodness. Thomas is quite enough of a handful without having two naughty boys.'

'You look nice, Tommy,' Amy said, seeing the look of embarrassment on Thomas' face. 'I think they're a bit hot, though, Susannah. Can't they take their jackets off?' Perhaps the suits would look less excessively babyish without the jackets.

'Please, Mama?' Thomas asked, and George started to pull at his jacket.

'No, you can't,' Susannah said, giving George's hand a slap. 'I want you to look smart today.'

'You boys must be getting a bit bored, sitting with all us old women. Do you want to go and play with Bobby?' Marion asked.

'Yes, please,' Thomas and George chorused. Thomas turned to their mother. 'Please, Mama?'

'Go on, Susannah, let them have a run around,' Marion coaxed.

'Well, all right,' Susannah said. Both boys ran down the steps and towards Bobby without giving her time to change her mind. 'Don't you get dirty,' she called after them.

'Want to play,' Malcolm said, trying to pull away from Amy and follow the other boys.

'I don't know, Mal, they're a bit big for you,' Amy said doubtfully. 'Look, here comes Papa.' The men were indeed approaching the verandah, having exhausted the beer and being ready for tea and cakes. 'You run and see Papa.'

Malcolm toddled towards Charlie as fast as his plump little legs would take him, then walked back at his father's side, taking big steps to try and match Charlie's long stride. A few weeks before, Charlie would have picked him up and carried him, but now he would do no more than take Malcolm's hand rather self-consciously.

The first men to reach the verandah, including Charlie, took the few empty seats at the far end from where Amy was sitting, while the later arrivals made do with leaning against the railing. Amy noticed John standing in the far corner. She was about to beckon him over when Mrs Carr's strident voice rang out.

'Do come over here, John,' she called. 'There's room for one more on this bench—my girls don't take up much room.' That was not strictly true; while Martha was on the bony side of slim, Sophie in all charity could only be described as plump. 'Move over, Martha—you too, Sophie.' She yanked Martha towards her, making a gap between Martha and Sophie barely big enough for a man to sit.

Rather to Amy's surprise, her brother wandered over to Mrs Carr and took the offered place. 'Thanks,' he said, turning his smile on each of the three women in turn. Martha giggled and blushed, while Sophie smiled back with her usual somewhat vacant expression. Amy could not recall ever having heard Sophie string more than three words together at a time; though judging from her mother and sister there was no shortage of speech in the Carr house.

'Now isn't this nice?' Mrs Carr said brightly. 'You young people spending some time together. I'm afraid my girls get rather stale for company, John, with only their father and I around. And of course we hardly ever see Tilly, with her living way over in Katikati. Isn't it nice to have a handsome young man to talk to, girls?'

Martha giggled and turned what seemed meant to be a winning smile on John.

'I'll leave you young ones alone for a bit while I chat to a few more people,' Mrs Carr said, rising ponderously from the bench. 'Keep John entertained, girls.'

Freed from her mother's overwhelming presence, Martha took over the task of keeping John 'entertained'.

'It's a lovely day today. It's a really nice day to be outside in the fresh air. It's lovely here, isn't it?' she asked rather breathlessly.

'Mmm,' John agreed.

'Sophie and I were just saying what a nice time we were having. Weren't we, Sophie?' She leaned across John to nudge her sister with her elbow. Sophie looked mildly startled, smiled at John then returned to contemplating the middle distance. 'Doris is such a lovely baby, too. And you've got Amy's children living just next door. You must be awfully proud, being an uncle, John,' Martha said.

'Why? I didn't do anything,' John said, amusement in his eyes.

Martha seemed at a loss how to respond to this for a few moments. 'Well, no, but… well, you're an uncle,' she repeated, as if that explained all. 'Tilly's got two children now—did you know that? Sophie and I like being aunts, don't we, Sophie?' She nudged Sophie again.

'Yes,' Sophie agreed, not bothering to turn her broad, plain face towards her sister.

'It must be lovely to have children of your own, don't you think? You're so used to being an uncle, you must be looking forward to having your own.'

That, Amy thought, was going a little too fast; certainly no one could accuse Martha of being subtle. She studied John's face to see if he were showing any sign of wanting to escape, but he was still smiling.

'Dunno about that,' he said wryly. 'I'm in no rush to give up sleeping at night.'

Martha shrieked with laughter; John looked startled at the noise. 'What a funny thing to say! Babies don't wake up at night for long... do they?' she finished on a more uncertain note.

'Ask Harry,' John said, indicating his brother, who was standing behind Jane's chair. Harry did indeed have signs of weariness in his face, though they were overshadowed by his look of pride as he gazed at his wife and daughter.

A high-pitched voice dragged Amy's attention away from the little drama being acted out before her.

'I'm not! I'm not!' It was Thomas, fists clenched as he glared at Bobby Forster. The three boys were standing under a tree a few yards from the corner of the house.

'Yes, you are. You're a sissy. So's he,' Bobby added, casting a disdainful look at George. 'Look at those sissy clothes. You look like little girls.'

'Not a girl!' George protested.

'Why don't you want to climb the tree, then? Sissy,' Bobby taunted.

Marion stopped talking to Susannah in mid-sentence. 'Bobby, are you teasing those little boys?' she called, a warning note in her voice.

'No, Ma! I'm just trying to get them to climb the tree—I think they're too scared.'

'We're not scared of your stupid tree!' Thomas said, indignant at the slight. 'We've got much bigger trees at home, I can climb them all. But Mama said we mustn't get dirty.'

'Mama said,' Bobby repeated in a mincing voice. 'Mama said the little girls mustn't get dirty. Where's your hair ribbons, little girls?'

This was too much. With a cry of rage, Thomas threw himself at the older boy, the force of his unexpected assault knocking Bobby flat despite the difference in height and weight. He was on Bobby's chest and pummeling him with clumsy blows before Bobby recovered enough to roll Thomas over and push him hard against the ground, winding him and giving Bobby the chance to get back on his feet. George tried to grab Bobby round the knees, but a shove from Bobby knocked the four-year-old sprawling.

'You leave my brother alone!' Thomas screamed, scrambling to his feet and making an awkward attempt to swing a punch at Bobby, which the older boy easily warded off.

Susannah and Marion rushed from the verandah and dragged the combatants apart before they could engage again.

'You wicked boys!' Susannah slapped her sons across the side of the head, her cheeks crimson with rage. 'Rolling in the dirt like… like common little brats.' She slapped them again and shook them by their collars.

'Now, don't get upset, Susannah. It's Bobby's fault, he was teasing them,' Marion said, glaring at her son.

'I wasn't! I only said—'

'I heard what you said,' Marion interrupted. 'Teasing those little boys—they're visitors, too. Bob!' she called. 'Come here and sort your son out. Fighting like that—on a Sunday, too.'

'Two against one, though, Marion,' Bob pointed out, walking towards them without any apparent hurry.

'And he's twice their age, so that evens it up,' Marion retorted.

'That's true enough,' Bob said. 'Come on, Bobby, you and I are going to take a little walk.'

Bobby watched his father approaching and glanced around quickly as if weighing his options. He slipped from Marion's grasp and took to his heels, disappearing around the side of the house.

'The little brat!' Marion said, the amusement in her eyes matching Bob's. 'Never mind, his stomach will drive him back before long, you can sort him out then.'

'Yes, he'll keep,' Bob agreed.

'Don't take any notice of what my silly son told you,' Marion said to Thomas and George. They looked up at her, both whimpering quietly from their mother's slaps. 'He's just jealous because he hasn't got such nice clothes. Don't be too hard on them,' she said, turning to Susannah. You can't expect them to just take it when a bigger boy makes fun of them.'

'I *do* expect them to behave properly,' Susannah said, a spot of red still showing in each cheek. 'They should behave like young gentlemen— especially you, Thomas. You're old enough to be looking after your little brother, not teaching him to be rough and coarse. Look what you've done to your clothes!' Thomas's trousers had a large rent in the seat, and his left sleeve was flapping loosely where it had been ripped out of the armhole. George had managed to do no worse than get dust all over his own suit. 'Ruined! Just ruined, and Grandmama only sent them at Christmas. You're a horrible little monster. You know what Papa's going to do with you when we get home?'

She knelt down to spell out whatever the awesome punishment was to be in a voice too low for Amy to catch, but her words had the desired effect. Both boys began to howl.

'I can't stand the sight of you,' Susannah said, rising to her full height. 'Go and stand by the buggy till we're ready to leave. And stop that silly noise. Hurry up!' She gave them both a push towards the buggy. The boys ran off together, still sobbing.

'They're just being boys, Susannah,' Marion said, a look of concern on her kindly face.

'I think it was my boy who started it, really,' Bob added.

'I expect better of my sons,' Susannah said, making her stately way back to the verandah. 'They have to learn. I'm bringing them up to take a proper place in the world, not behave like animals.' She took her seat near Amy once again.

By this time Jack had wandered over to talk to Amy, and they had both witnessed the scene between Susannah and the little boys.

'Those children misbehaved terribly, Jack,' Susannah said. 'I'm very disappointed in them, showing me up in company like that. You'll have to punish them later.'

'You've already made a pretty good job of that,' Jack said ruefully, looking over at the little boys sitting in the shade of the buggy with an arm around each other's shoulders and tears running down their faces.

'Nonsense! I told them you'll give them a good thrashing as soon as we get home, then I'm going to put them straight to bed without any dinner.'

'A thrashing just for a bit of rough and tumble? They're boys, Susannah. You've got to expect them to get into scrapes.'

'They disgraced me, and I won't tolerate that. I told them you'd thrash them, Jack. They'll never learn to do as I say if you go against me—that would just teach them to play us off against each other. You do see that, don't you?'

Jack sighed. 'Yes, I see it. Well, we'd better get on home, then. No sense making the little fellows worry about it any longer than they have to.'

'We'll leave when I've finished my tea,' Susannah said, reaching for the cup she had abandoned to interrupt the fight.

'I'll have a bit of a walk, then. I need to stretch my legs,' Jack said, rising slowly. Amy was sure it was to escape from the sight of the unhappy little boys.

'Can I come with you, Pa?' she asked. 'Davie's getting a bit restless, a walk will settle him.' Jack smiled an invitation. Before she walked down the steps Amy took care to catch Charlie's eye so that he could see she was with her father.

'I've got soft, girl,' Jack said as soon as they were out of earshot. 'I've no appetite for beating children. Must be getting old, eh?'

'You're not old, Pa,' Amy protested. 'Anyway, I'm soft too, and I'm only nineteen. I hate it when Charlie hits Mal, even though I know he needs it.'

Jack smiled at her. 'You're like your ma. "Don't be hard on them, Jack, they're not really naughty," she used to say—even with Harry, and he could be a real little brute. Hard to believe he's the same boy,' he said, looking back at Harry hovering solicitously around Jane, adjusting a pillow behind his wife's shoulders.

'I don't think Granny ever got very soft. She gave me plenty of hidings. I always deserved it, though—I didn't always think so at the time, I suppose.'

Jack glanced towards the little boys just before he and Amy walked behind a shed, cutting them off from sight. 'I don't know, it's different with the little fellows than it ever was with the other two. Harry especially—he needed twice the hidings John did, and when he knew he was going to get one he'd say "I don't care," and try to stare me out. Then after I'd given him a couple of whacks he'd be bawling and saying he was sorry, he'd never do it again. You could feel you were doing the boy some good. George isn't too bad, nothing bothers him for long, but Tom... as soon as he knows he's in trouble he looks up at me with tears in those big eyes of his and says "I'm sorry, Papa, I didn't mean to be naughty." He means what he says, too, you can see it in his face. I feel like giving the poor little fellow a hug instead of a hiding—of course I can't do that. Susannah's right, it's no good her saying one thing and me saying another.'

'I know, Pa. I know just what you mean,' Amy said fervently.

'Well, she should have finished that tea of hers. Let's head back to the house.'

Jack and Susannah left soon afterwards, and Amy could see that Charlie would soon be ready to go. She would have liked the chance to spend a little time with John, but Martha Carr was still chattering away, so Amy made do with saying a brief goodbye to him in front of the Carr sisters.

'That's a pretty dress, Sophie,' Amy said, stroking the wide lace around Sophie's cuffs. The dark green of the dress minimised Sophie's overly buxom figure, and set off her pale skin nicely.

'Thanks,' Sophie said, smiling vaguely at Amy.

'I chose that material,' Martha put in. 'Sophie can never decide anything. I always have to help her choose things.'

Amy doubted that Sophie ever had the chance to decide for herself, but she made a noncommittal murmur as response. 'Bye bye, John, see you next Sunday.' She turned to hurry after Charlie, who was already making for the gig with Malcolm at his heels.

'I'd better be off, too. I'll walk you to the gate,' John said, rising from the bench.

'Are you going, John? Ma, John's going,' Martha said anxiously, but Mrs Carr had already moved to intercept him.

'It's been lovely seeing you today, John,' she gushed. 'You young ones getting on so nicely together. You know, we hardly ever see you to talk to—I know!' she said, as if the idea had only this moment struck her. 'Why don't you come for tea one night? You'd enjoy a good meal, wouldn't you?—oh, not that Susannah's not a good cook, I'm sure, but a change does no harm, does it? My girls are both fine cooks, though I say so myself. Martha does a wonderful roast dinner. These long summer evenings, you'd have plenty of time to get home before it was too dark.'

Amy wondered how John would manage to extricate himself from Mrs Carr's invitation without being rude. She caught his eye for a moment and almost thought she saw him wink, then he turned a wide smile on Mrs Carr.

'That'd be nice, thanks.'

Mrs Carr did not waste time pressing home her advantage. 'What about this Wednesday night?' she pounced.

'All right. I'll see you on Wednesday.'

'We'll all look forward to it. Won't we, girls?'

'Oh, yes,' Martha agreed. Sophie just smiled.

'What are you up to, John?' Amy asked when they were out of earshot. 'You know what Mrs Carr's after, don't you?'

'No. What?' John asked, feigning innocence. He grinned at her. 'I'd have to be pretty dopey not to catch on. I don't mind playing along with it, though—might get a decent meal out of it, anyway. I wonder if they make bread you don't have to break your teeth to get into?'

'I expect so. Do you... do you like Martha, John?'

'She's all right.' John gave her a wicked grin. 'Ask me again after I've tried her roast dinner!'

13

April – August 1888

Amy and Lizzie were so deep in conversation over their teacups when Frank opened the back door that they hardly looked up at his entrance.

'Well, he's never got much to say for himself, I suppose he thinks she could do the talking for him—she's pretty good at that,' Lizzie said. 'Not down there, Frank, put that baking powder on the top shelf.'

Amy waited until Frank went outside again before she replied. 'Like you and Frank, you mean? That's what everyone said about you two, you know. That'd be all very well if she talked sense. It's just chatter. You'd think it'd drive him mad.'

'Some men like not having to think for themselves—not that I'm saying Frank's like that. Just because he doesn't make a big song and dance about himself, people think he's a bit dim. Frank's not dim at all.'

'Neither is John. He just keeps his mind to himself. I don't think Martha would let him keep anything to himself, though.'

'Do you really think he might want to marry her?'

Amy frowned thoughtfully. 'I don't know. When I ask him why he keeps going there all the time he just grins and says it's the good food.'

'Hmm. John's so quiet, Martha might have to propose to him herself.'

'That's what people said—'

'I know,' Lizzie interrupted. 'And I'll have you know it's not true. Frank proposed all by himself, I hardly had to push him at all.'

'Mmm, I bet he even thought it was his own idea.'

'He still does.' Lizzie answered Amy's smile with a grin of her own.

'Who are you two old gossips pulling to bits?' Frank asked as he came back into the house and closed the door behind him.

'John. And we're not pulling him to bits, just discussing his future,' Lizzie said. 'Here, Maudie, go to Papa.' The little girl slid off what was left of Lizzie's lap and ran across the kitchen to Frank. He lifted her high in the air before sitting down with her on his knee.

'Him and Martha, eh? Mr Carr was saying the other day that his wife's had her eye on John for a while. It smells nice in here.'

'Amy's done a big lot of baking for me, she's filled up all the tins,' Lizzie said. 'It takes me all my time just to do the ordinary cooking now I'm such a lump.'

Amy slipped David from her lap and onto the floor. 'I'll get you a cup of tea, Frank.' She brought him the cup, along with some biscuits to sample, then sat and took up her own half-full cup again.

'Nice biscuits,' Frank said through a mouthful. 'I saw Charlie at the store with Mal, by the way, I don't think they'll be far behind me.'

Amy put her cup down at once, rattling it noisily against the saucer. 'I'd better go,' she said, taking off the apron she was wearing and hanging it behind the door. 'Come on, Davie, Papa will be here in a minute.'

'Stay and finish your tea,' Lizzie protested. 'He can wait for a bit. Oh, he can come inside and have a cup if he wants, if I stay this side of the table he won't be able to see much of me. We can all pretend not to notice I'm the size of a house.'

'No, it's all right, Lizzie, I don't want to keep him waiting or he won't let me come again. I was lucky he dropped me off today. Bye bye, Lizzie. Take care of her, Frank.' She kissed Lizzie and Maudie, scooped David up off the floor, and was half way to the door when they heard the rattle of gig wheels approaching. 'There he is,' Amy said, flustered by her hurry.

'Amy!' They heard Charlie's voice from outside.

'Coming, Charlie,' she called from the doorway as soon as she had it open. She was off down the steps at a run.

'Boy, she went like a scalded cat,' Frank said, looking after Amy in bemusement. 'She sure jumps when Charlie says to.'

'Ooh, that man,' Lizzie said, pursing her lips in irritation. 'He expects her to just drop everything when it suits him. Sometimes I'd just like to... oh, never mind him. Did you hear any news in town?'

'What sort of news?'

'Oh, you know—anyone having babies, or getting married or anything.'

Frank shrugged. 'I don't know, I didn't really talk to anyone, just picked up the stuff and came home.'

'Frank! Honestly, I never get to hear anything. Amy's not much use, *he* doesn't let her talk to anyone when they go to town. Here's Maudie and I stuck here getting sick of one another, and you don't even bother to fetch any interesting news for me.'

'I was in a rush to get home to you,' Frank said, letting Lizzie's reproaches wash over him. 'I was too busy thinking about my girls to bother listening to a lot of gossip. Anyway, I thought it looked a bit like rain, so I was trying to hurry.'

'Humph! Well, did you get all the stuff I told you to?'

'I think so.'

'What about those cloves?'

'Oh. Sorry, Lizzie, I forgot about them. I had to get some nails and stuff for the fence, and that drove those things out of my head, I suppose. I'll get them next week.'

'Frank Kelly, you're hopeless,' Lizzie scolded. 'I only asked you to get half a dozen things. Next time I'll write you a list and pin it to your shirt if you're not careful. How could you forget the cloves when I reminded you just as you were going out the door? I said—'

'Hey, what about a bit of respect for your old man?' Frank interrupted her tirade with a grin.

'What about my old man using the brains God gave him? It doesn't matter, I've still got a few cloves left. Your tea looks a bit stewed, shall I make a fresh pot? I wouldn't mind another cup.' Lizzie made to rise ponderously.

'I'll make it,' Frank said, getting up and putting Maudie on his chair. He brushed aside the thought of the fence repairs he had promised himself he would start on that morning; an extra few minutes sitting with Lizzie and Maudie was much more appealing. If he was lucky, that rain the sky had threatened as he rode home would start soon; then he would have to leave the fence for another day. 'I don't want you falling over, not the shape you are—if you once started rolling you'd be out the door and down the hill before I could stop you.'

'And whose fault is it I'm in this state?'

'Well, I'll admit to a share in it. Amy's right, I should look after you. Poor old lump,' he teased.

'Old lump,' Maudie echoed.

'Shh, Maudie! We'll have to start watching what we say in front of her, Frank, she's a real little parrot.'

'Mmm, I don't want her repeating some of the things you call me in front of your pa.' Frank carried the teapot over to the table and took a seat close to Lizzie. 'He'd give me a real talking to if he knew you don't treat me with proper respect.'

He leaned across Lizzie's bulge and planted a light kiss on her mouth, then glanced down to see Maudie trying to clamber onto his lap. He helped her up and gave her a squeeze. Was that respect, the way Amy acted around Charlie? he wondered. Running around like a frightened rabbit in case she annoyed him? If that was respect, Frank decided, then he'd just as soon do without it.

Joseph Arthur Kelly came into the world early in May, with no volcanic eruptions to mark his birth or terrify his parents. Frank had thought he could not possibly be any happier; with the birth of his son he found he had been wrong.

'He's amazing,' Frank said, watching Lizzie struggle to get a fresh napkin on the six-week-old Joseph. The baby was red-faced with anger as he flung his tiny limbs around, roaring in protest at the unwanted interference. 'Look at him kicking!'

'I've been *feeling* him kicking for months, don't tell me about how strong he is,' Lizzie retorted. 'He's strong-willed, anyway. I thought Maudie was bad for wanting her own way. Keep still, you little wretch—oh, don't say he's going to do *that* again when I've just got the last mucky nappy off him—ugh, he's peeing on my hand! Don't just stand there looking, help me! If I move my hand I'll get the lot in my face.'

Frank quickly soaked up the small fountain with a fold of napkin and wiped Lizzie's hand for her. 'He's a brat, all right,' he said proudly. 'Do you think he'll be tall?'

'I hope not—if he gets bigger than you, you'll never be able to make him do as he's told. He's a lot bigger than Maudie was at this age, though, so he'll probably be a fair size.' She gave an exaggerated sigh of relief when she had at last managed to get a clean napkin safely pinned and the baby warmly wrapped up. 'You men and your sons! You're all the same. Pa's made much more of a fuss about Joey than he ever did over Maudie—though goodness knows he spoils her rotten. What makes boys so special, for goodness sake?'

'Maudie's special,' Frank remonstrated. 'I mean, she was our first. I wasn't a father till you had Maudie. It was so neat when she was born—after I knew you were going to be all right, anyway—it was awful till then. I don't know, it's just… it's different having a son. It's like I've done something that'll carry on after I'm gone. No, that's not right, that just sounds dopey.'

'Yes, it does. And I don't see that *you* did so much, either.' But Lizzie's face softened as she looked down at Joseph, still red-faced but now quiet as he drifted towards sleep. 'He *is* pretty neat, isn't he? Come on, let's leave your precious son alone before he starts performing again.' She took Frank's hand and pulled him out of the bedroom.

'You're right, you know, Lizzie, men do make more of a fuss when you have a son. Even Charlie said something nice to me when Joey was born.'

'Did he? I hope he didn't do himself an injury—he's not even used to being polite, let alone pleasant.'

'Yes, he said congratulations, I must be pleased I'd finally managed to get a son after all this time.'

Lizzie rounded on him, her eyes flashing. 'You call that nice! That skitey old so-and-so. Just because he's got two boys—that's because Amy's so fruitful, there's nothing special about him. When I think how knocked out she gets when she has babies, and all he can do is skite about it! He should be telling everyone how lucky he is to have a wife like her, not how wonderful he is at fathering sons. Ooh!' She clenched her fists in anger.

'Hey, don't get in a state, Lizzie! Don't take any notice of Charlie, I sure don't.' He caught her around the waist and drew her close. 'I don't need anyone to tell me how lucky I am.'

Lizzie was so obviously in robust good health that neither she nor Frank thought anything of it when she started having occasional stomach pains. The cramps were never particularly strong, and Lizzie put them down to indigestion. Too much of her own good cooking, Frank teased; the waistline that refused to return to its pre-motherhood proportions seemed to support this.

Frank soon had something that seemed more serious on his mind. One day in the middle of July he was making his usual morning round of the in-calf cows when he realised three of them were missing. Puzzled, he counted them off again, but there was no mistake: where there should have been eighteen cows there were only fifteen.

Once he began walking the fence line of the paddock it did not take Frank long to discover how the cows had disappeared; indeed the small voice of conscience had suggested the reason as soon as he had double-checked the numbers. When he reached the section of fence Arthur had warned him about all those months ago he saw that one of the rotten posts had snapped off near the ground, probably when a cow had rubbed against it to relieve an itch. The rails slotted into it on either side had collapsed into an untidy heap.

Muttering under his breath in annoyance, Frank first moved the cows still in the paddock to another one before they could decide to follow their wayward sisters, then he fetched some rope from one of the sheds and set out to find the wanderers.

They had left a clear enough trail through the sodden ground, churning it into mud as they went. Once the trail entered the bush Frank followed the line of snapped twigs as much as the hoof prints. He saw clear signs that the cows had stopped by the creek and waded along its edge for a while, then had forded it and clambered up the opposite bank, bringing a load of earth into the creek in the process. His boots soon picked up a thick layer of mud, dragging heavily at him as he walked. How far had those stupid cows gone? he wondered. Knowing it was his own fault the cows had got out did not improve his mood.

He pushed his way through a patch of fern and felt something catch at his leg. Without thinking beyond the cows he was seeking he reached down to grasp at the obstruction then jerked his hand away, swearing as he pulled at the vicious thorns the cord of bush lawyer had hooked into his palm. He gingerly unhooked the weed from his trousers and pushed on.

A few minutes later he stopped for a moment when an odd sound reached his ear. It was certainly an animal, but he had never heard a cow make quite that noise before. Following the sound, he found himself in an area where the undergrowth was thinner. He looked around the small clearing and found what had been making the noise.

One of his cows lay on the ground, straining to get to her feet and moaning with the effort. Another was a few feet away, her unnaturally stiff limbs making it obvious she had been dead for some hours. Frank knew the cause even before he saw the scrubby plants around the edge of the clearing with their distinctive pattern of growth, each leaf directly opposite its pair on the long, thin branches instead of alternating up the stem: tutu, the bush farmer's scourge, and perversely attractive to livestock.

There was nothing to be done for poor old Brownie except bury her; Pudding might still be saved, though she was certain to abort the calf she was carrying. Frank hauled her to her feet and tied a length of rope around her neck, then led the stumbling creature well away from the lethal tutu bushes before tying her up and going in search of the remaining cow. Her track split off from the other two just outside the clearing; at least she hadn't been poisoned, Frank reassured himself.

Patches had not been poisoned, but that was cold comfort when Frank at last found her. She had made her way back to the creek, probably seeking her familiar paddock after her wanderings, but she had never made it. The creek bank was steep at the point where Patches had slithered down it; far too steep for the awkward, lumbering animal. She lay on the edge of the creek where she must have been all night, her head barely out of the water and one leg stretched away from her body at an unnatural angle that would have told Frank it was broken even if he had not been able to see white bone protruding from it.

The most horrifying thing was that Patches was still alive. Her breath gurgled horribly in her throat and there was blood trickling from her mouth, but it took more than a wintry night lying half in the creek with a broken leg to kill a tough Shorthorn.

The film over Patches' eyes cleared for a moment, and those big brown eyes looked at Frank with a flicker of recognition for the man who had handled her every day of her life. She roused herself to a last effort and shifted slightly where she lay, the exertion forcing a grunt of pain from her that would have been a bovine scream if she had not been too weak to make any real sound. Frank patted her shoulder and reached for the knife that hung in a sheath from his belt, then let his hand drop. Cutting the cow's throat would be a hellish task, especially if she found the strength to struggle, and Patches deserved a kinder death than that. He would keep the knife for skinning the dead cows.

Frank waded the creek, hardly noticing the chilly water that reached above his knees, then made his way back to the house at a run. He picked up the shotgun that was lying in the porch; Lizzie heard the noise and called out to him, but he ignored her, not trusting himself to speak. He made a short detour to one of the sheds and snatched up a spade for the graves he would have to dig, then retraced his steps to where Patches lay, too far gone now even to open her eyes as he walked up to her.

'Poor old girl,' Frank murmured as he pressed the muzzle of the gun against the cow's skull and pulled the trigger.

'What on earth have you been up to all this time?' Lizzie demanded when he at last got back to the house. 'I've had lunch waiting for ages, I've had to give Maudie hers, and...' She trailed off, taking in his ashen face and the state of his clothes, thickly caked with mud well above his knees. 'Frank, you stink! You smell like a dog that's been rolling in something dead. What's wrong? What's happened?'

Frank sat down heavily at the table. 'Three of the cows got out,' he said in a flat voice. 'Into the tutu, and Patches fell down a bank. Two of them dead, and Pudding only just alive—I think she'll pull through. I had to shoot Patches.'

Lizzie sat down beside him, too shocked to speak straight away. 'Two dead,' she breathed. 'That's awful.'

'Three calves lost, too. Pudding's sure to lose hers. Two cows and three calves, and all I've got to show for it's a couple of hides. A few shillings' worth if that.'

'It's such bad luck!'

'No, it's not,' Frank said bitterly. 'It's my fault. I was bloody lucky the whole lot of them didn't get out.'

'Don't say that,' Lizzie protested. 'How's it your fault?'

'Because I didn't mend that fence—I knew it was ready to fall down. Your pa gave me enough hurry ups about it. I was just too damned lazy.'

'Two cows and three calves,' Lizzie repeated anxiously. 'What are we going to do, Frank?'

Her obvious distress brought Frank to his senses abruptly. 'Hey, don't get upset, Lizzie. We'll be all right, it's just a bit of a blow. I've still got plenty of cows. I'm mainly wild with myself for being stupid.' He tried to laugh, but it came out as more of a snort. 'I don't know what your pa's going to say when he finds out.'

'Don't tell him,' Lizzie answered smartly. 'He'll only go on and on about it if you do, you know how bossy he is. It's none of his business, anyway.'

'I'd just as soon not tell him,' Frank admitted. He smiled at Lizzie, who had completely regained her usual assurance. 'I'm glad I've got you. Things never seem so bad with you around.'

'Things'll seem even better when you've got a decent lunch inside you.' Lizzie wrinkled her nose at him. 'You really do stink. Go and get changed, you're not going to sit at the table in that state. And don't you dare put those trousers in the wash basket to stink the room out,' she called after him as Frank headed towards the bedroom. 'You can throw them in the porch.'

Lizzie had been easily reassured, but there was a nagging uneasiness in Frank's mind over the next few days. When spring came, the milk yield would be even lower than the previous year's. Perhaps he should have kept a few of the calves last season. But there was no sense worrying about it now. They would still have plenty to live on, and Lizzie was a careful housekeeper, not given to waste.

By early August most of the cows had produced healthy calves, though Frank was disappointed at how few of them were heifers. But when he took his little family into town for shopping one Thursday, he was too busy feeling proud of them to think about much else. Lizzie recited her list of groceries, giving Mr Craig the storekeeper just enough time to fetch each item to the counter before she reeled off the next, while Frank watched her fondly. Joey lay in her arms, blissfully unworried by Lizzie's rapid movements as she strode back and forth in front of the counter keeping an eye on Mr Craig. The baby looked around the store, apparently taking a great interest in his surroundings when Lizzie kept still long enough for him to fix his attention on any one object.

'Papa?' Frank looked down to see Maudie tugging at his trouser leg. 'Lollies, Papa?'

She tilted her head to one side, showing off the tiny pink bow Lizzie had tied in her hair, and cast a fetching smile at her father. Frank bent to pick her up so she could see the row of sweet jars lining one end of the counter. 'You want some lollies, Maudie? What sort do you want?'

179

'She can have a halfpennyworth, that's all,' Lizzie said from the far end of the counter. 'See you wrap that baking powder properly, Mr Craig, I don't want it spilling. No sticky toffees, Frank, she'll make an awful mess. No big gob-stoppers, either, she might try and swallow them whole. A bag of sugar, and that's the lot, I think—no, not that one, the big size. Oh, I'll have some sultanas, too. She can have one lolly now, put the rest of the bag in your pocket, Frank.'

Frank sat Maudie in the buggy contentedly sucking on a sweet, and left Lizzie to finish off the shopping and supervise the loading of their supplies while he crossed the road to the bank. He wanted to get a little cash, and it was about time to settle his account at the store, too.

He wandered into the Bank of New Zealand, a vague smile on his face as he thought about Lizzie and the children, and he hardly noticed that the smile of welcome the bank manager gave him was rather strained.

'Frank, how are you?' Mr Callaghan greeted him. 'Haven't seen you for a while.' He went on without waiting for a reply. 'Ah, would you mind popping into my office for a minute?'

Frank followed Mr Callaghan, wondering what the manager could want. Mr Callaghan sat him down and closed the door before taking a seat behind his desk.

'How's the family?' Mr Callaghan inquired.

'They're great,' said Frank. 'Joey's really thriving, he's big for his age, Lizzie says. And that Maudie, she's a real hard case. Never stops talking, either. You know what she came out with the other day? Lizzie was—'

'That's good to hear, Frank,' Mr Callaghan interrupted. 'You're quite a family man now, eh? Is the farm going all right?'

'Pretty good,' Frank said, feeling a momentary rush of guilt about the cows that had died. 'Prices haven't been that good the last few years, but we get by. You know how it is.'

'Yes. I know how it is,' Mr Callaghan echoed. He sat and looked at Frank but said nothing for a few moments. 'Times are hard all over the country, Frank. They're hard for banks, too, even though everyone thinks the banks are rich.'

'I suppose that's right,' Frank agreed, wondering what on earth this had to do with him and how soon he would be able to get away. Lizzie had whispered to him not to be too long; Joey was getting restless and would be sure to want a feed soon.

'It's Head Office, you see. They're telling all the little branches like us to wake our ideas up. I've been letting things drift a bit, I must confess.'

Frank made what he hoped was a sympathetic noise and looked

blankly at Mr Callaghan.

'That loan of yours, Frank. The one Ben took out against the farm. You haven't paid anything off it for a while.'

'Oh. I suppose I haven't,' Frank admitted, struggling to recall just when he had last made a payment. Mr Callaghan had given him an occasional friendly reminder over the last few months, he remembered, but Frank had somehow not got around to doing anything about it.

'Not for over a year, actually. You've only ever paid ten pounds off it.'

'Have I?' Frank said guiltily. 'Well, you know, there always seems to be something that needs buying, what with the little ones. I sort of had to get a buggy now we've got the two of them, the cart wasn't too good. Maybe the milk price'll be better this season.'

'Maybe. I hope so, Frank.'

'Yes, it's sure to be. Well, I'd better be—'

Mr Callaghan raised his hand to wave Frank back into his seat. 'Wait a moment, I've something to give you.' He picked up a sheet of paper from his desk, holding it as though it burned his hand. 'I don't want to do this, Frank. I've got to. Head Office says I must with all the slow payers.'

Puzzled, Frank reached out to take the letter, which was addressed to him and written on the bank's letterhead. He began to read it, then looked up from the page and stared at Mr Callaghan in consternation. 'It says you're going to take my farm off me!'

'Believe me, that's the last thing the Bank wants to do. We don't know anything about running farms. The Bank wants you to get yourself straight, that's all.'

'But it says if I don't pay you'll take the farm off me. I can't pay! I haven't got two hundred pounds.' The bleak picture of being turned off his farm with a wife and two children to provide for made him feel physically ill.

'One hundred and ninety, plus interest,' Mr Callaghan corrected absently. 'Frank, you don't have to pay it all off at once. The letter says you have to satisfy the bank that you intend to make good your debt.'

Frank grasped at the straw of hope being held out to him. 'How do I do that?'

'Just make a good, solid payment by the end of September. That'll keep Head Office off my back.'

'That's less than two months. How much do I have to pay?'

'Seventy-five pounds would do it.'

Frank shook his head. 'I can't do that. I can't get seventy-five pounds.'

Mr Callaghan looked weary. 'Fifty, then. I think I could keep them quiet if you paid fifty pounds—it's a quarter of the loan. I'm sorry, Frank, that's the best I can do for you.'

'And if I don't pay that you'll take the farm away.'

'Let's hope it won't come to that.'

Frank shoved the letter into his jacket pocket and rose unsteadily. He walked out of the bank without speaking again, and made his way to where Lizzie and the children waited in the buggy.

14

Lizzie did not seem to notice Frank's quietness on the way home. She was busy soothing an increasingly fractious Joey until they reached a quiet spot out of town and she could put him to the breast, then she chattered away about the people she had spoken to in town. Frank let her voice wash over him, not taking anything in. Even when Maudie slipped her little arm through his and snuggled against him he hardly noticed.

He thought back to the time when the couple who had owned what was now Charlie's farm had lost it to the mortgage men. Frank had been only a child then, but he remembered hearing the adults talk about it in hushed voices. It had seemed the most dreadful thing possible. Was it going to happen to him?

He couldn't let it happen. Frank spent most of the afternoon walking around the farm, trying to work out how he could raise the money. It would mean selling all the new calves, of course. And maybe he could manage with one less horse, though it would mean working the remaining ones harder. He would have to ask the storekeeper if he could leave paying his bill for a while. On top of that, if he turned all the milk money over to the bank he might just be able to do it. But that would leave nothing to live on.

Well, they would just have to live frugally till the money was sorted out. Even then, he was not sure he would be able to scrape together fifty pounds in time. If worse came to worst, he would have to swallow his pride and ask Arthur for help, but things would have to be dire before he would admit to his father-in-law that he could not provide for Lizzie. In the meantime, there was no point worrying Lizzie about it.

His mind was so busy running the problem over and over that Frank had trouble doing justice to his dinner, especially the mountain of pudding that Lizzie put in front of him.

'Eat up, Frank,' she encouraged, looking up for a moment from spooning food into Maudie's open mouth. 'I made that sultana pudding specially for you, I know it's your favourite.'

'Yes, it's nice,' Frank said, toying idly with his spoon.

'You'd better eat it—I paid a fortune for those sultanas. Sevenpence a pound if you please! I gave that Mr Craig a piece of my mind, I don't mind telling you. I only bought enough for this pudding—six ounces, it takes, and I made him weigh them out just right. "I'm only buying these

183

because I promised my husband I'd make his favourite pudding tonight, Mr Craig," I told him, "so I've got to get enough for that. But you needn't think I'm buying any more while they're that price." That fixed him! Sevenpence a pound, indeed! He must think we're made of money.'

The food sat like lead in his stomach, though it was the turmoil of his thoughts and not Lizzie's light, fluffy pudding that made Frank feel ill. He pushed the bowl away. 'I don't want any more, Lizzie.'

'You'd better finish it. Honestly, if we're going to be ruined paying those prices for food you'd better enjoy it. Eat that up and don't be silly.' She pushed the bowl back towards him.

'I said I don't want it!' Frank shouted, shoving the bowl away roughly.

Lizzie dropped the spoon she was holding. She and Maudie both stared at Frank in astonishment. 'All right, I'm sorry I spoke. There's no need to bite my head off.' Frank turned away and looked at the far wall, but he was all too aware that Lizzie was studying him closely. 'What's wrong with you?' she asked. 'What's got you in such a sour mood?'

'Nothing.' He met her eyes and tried to sound unconcerned. 'I'm sorry, Lizzie, I didn't mean to yell at you. I've just got a few things on my mind, that's all. It's a really nice pudding, I'll have some more. Hey, don't be scared, Maudie, Papa's not wild really.' Maudie smiled, at once reassured, but Lizzie continued to look at him oddly. Frank knew he would have to be more careful if he wanted to keep his worries a secret.

Amy managed to snatch a brief visit two weeks later, hitching a ride on Charlie's spring cart when he took the milk to the factory. Lizzie greeted her warmly enough, but there was a tight look around her cousin's mouth that had troubled Amy the last few times she had seen Lizzie.

'I'll put the kettle on,' Lizzie said when they had settled the children in one corner. 'You don't mind not having any biscuits, do you? I haven't got all that many.'

'Want a bikkie, Mama,' Maudie piped up.

'No, Maudie. You can have one when Papa comes back,' Lizzie said. 'It's no good pulling faces, either. You can't have one now and that's that.' Maudie gave her a wounded look, which Lizzie took no notice of.

'I would have brought you some if I'd known you were running short, Lizzie. Did you run out of things for baking?'

'No, I'm just cutting down on things like that. As long as there're biscuits and things for Frank he won't notice. We're only having bottled fruit and cream for puddings all the time now, that doesn't cost anything. I've patched this petticoat till it's nearly falling to bits, too.' She turned up the hem of her dress to reveal a much-mended flannel petticoat. 'It should hang together till the end of winter, no sense wasting money on more material.'

'Why are you cutting down, Lizzie?'

Lizzie looked over her shoulder as if she half expected to see Frank in the doorway, then leaned a little closer to Amy. 'Frank's a bit worried about money. He thinks I don't know, and he doesn't want to tell me.'

'What's he worried about?' Amy asked, surprised. 'The farm's doing all right, isn't it?'

Lizzie pursed her lips. 'It *would* be if that Ben hadn't left a millstone around Frank's neck.'

'The money he borrowed, you mean? Why's that suddenly a worry?'

'I'll show you. Come up here a minute.' Lizzie rose from the table, then abruptly doubled over, clutching at her middle.

'What's wrong?' Amy rushed to put her arms around her, but Lizzie pushed her away.

'It's nothing. Just my stomach playing up again.'

'Are you still getting that?'

'Sometimes. Don't make a fuss.' Lizzie straightened up, but she was still in obvious discomfort.

'It's got worse, hasn't it, Lizzie?' Lizzie shook her head, but Amy persisted. 'Yes, it has. That's why you look so worn out lately—that and worrying about Frank. Have you told him you're crook?'

'I'm not crook. And I'm not going to tell him, not while he's worried about the money.'

'You should tell him. Maybe you should go to the doctor.'

'No! All I've got is the odd stomach ache, Frank doesn't have to pay good money for the doctor to tell me that. Anyway, I don't want the doctor poking around at me. I'll be better soon, shut up about it. Come on.'

Lizzie set off purposefully up the passage, and Amy followed in her wake. When they were in the front bedroom Lizzie closed the door behind them. She opened a drawer and lifted a crumpled sheet of paper from it. 'I found this in Frank's pocket when I was doing the washing. He doesn't know I've seen it, I put it in with his shirts afterwards and he must think he left it there himself. I can tell he's been reading it over and over from all the new creases in it.'

She passed the page to Amy, who read the bank's letter in growing shock. 'That's awful, Lizzie! Do you think Frank'll be able to get enough money?'

'Oh, he'll do it one way or another,' said Lizzie. 'Even if he has to borrow a bit off Pa—he won't want to do that, though. Pa would go on and on at him, he'd never hear the end of it. Frank must be really worried—he hasn't even been very interested in you-know-what lately. I wish he'd talk to me about it, that's all.' Her face set in firmer lines. 'I won't make him if he doesn't want to. If he wants to sort it out by himself, then he darned well can. I'm just making sure I don't ask for a penny more than I have to until this is all straightened out.'

'Yes, that's all you can do,' Amy agreed. 'But Lizzie, I do think you should tell him about those stomach aches being so bad. The doctor would—'

'No,' Lizzie interrupted. 'If I'm still getting them when we're straight again maybe I'll go to the doctor. Don't you dare breathe a word to Frank about it.'

It was no use arguing with Lizzie when her mind was made up, but Amy felt uneasy about her cousin when she left to go home.

She was so preoccupied with thoughts of Lizzie and Frank that she went through her tasks mechanically for the rest of the morning. As the afternoon wore on Malcolm became bored, wearying Amy with his constant demands to be entertained.

'I wish you were old enough to go out on the farm with your Papa, Malcolm,' she said when he tugged at her skirt yet again, whining for something to do. 'I can't play with you all the time. Oh, I suppose it's hard for you, stuck inside with me and Davie, but I can't do anything about it. You're too little to go wandering around all by yourself.'

'Want to go outside. Want to play with Papa.'

'Papa won't play, Mal. I don't think he knows how to. Anyway, he's busy doing fencing, you can't go way over the back of the farm looking for him.'

'Come out and play, Mama. Come and play with me.'

'Don't nag at me, Mal. I can't go out, I've got too much to do. I wish I *could* go out,' she said, looking out the window at the clear sky. 'It's a lovely day, and here's you and me stuck in the kitchen.' She looked at Malcolm's resentful expression and sighed. 'If I let you go outside by yourself, will you be a good boy?'

'Yes, Mama,' Malcolm said eagerly.

'Just play around the house. You can swing on that rope Papa tied to the tree for you. Promise you won't go far away?' Malcolm nodded. Amy took him out to the porch and put his shoes on. Malcolm ran towards the tree and was soon swinging back and forth.

The rest of the afternoon passed more quickly once she was left in peace. Amy soon had her cleaning finished so that she could start preparing the evening meal. When she took a break from cooking to feed David, she was surprised to see how late it was. *Mal's very quiet out there.* Suspiciously quiet, she decided. As soon as David finished feeding she put him back to bed and went outside to check on Malcolm, and was startled to find he was nowhere in sight. The rope he had been swinging on lay in a heap under the tree; when Amy examined it she saw that its hastily tied knot had come undone from being chafed against the branch. Her heart beating fast, she looked about her trying to decide which direction Malcolm might have wandered off in. *Not down to the creek*, she begged silently. *I shouldn't have let him go outside by himself, he's too little. Where's he gone?*

Since the creek was the most obvious danger, Amy was about to set off in that direction when Malcolm appeared around the corner of the cottage. Amy rushed to him and knelt down to throw her arms around him, at first too overcome with relief to notice his troubled expression or how muddy his clothes were.

'Where have you been, Mal? Mama's been worried about you! You told me you wouldn't go away from the house. That was naughty, wasn't it?'

'I'm sorry, Mama. I didn't mean to.' Malcolm looked up at her with tears in his eyes, much to Amy's surprise. The scolding died on her lips.

'Don't cry, love,' she soothed, holding him close. 'Mama got a fright, that's all. There's no need to cry.'

'Don't tell Papa,' Malcolm pleaded.

'All right, I won't tell him. But you mustn't go off by yourself again, Mal.'

'Rope falled down. I wanted a swing.'

'You should have come and told Mama. Mama could have fixed it for you.'

'I wanted a swing,' Malcolm repeated. 'I didn't mean to.'

'Didn't mean to what? What's wrong, Mal? Did something give you a fright? And how did you get so muddy?'

'I didn't mean to!' Malcolm began to cry in earnest.

'Shh, it's all right. You didn't mean to run off, did you? Come inside and we'll get some clean clothes on you.'

Malcolm slipped his grubby hand into hers and let her lead him into his room. 'I'm tired, Mama. I want to go to bed.'

'Do you? It's very early for you to go to bed, Mal. Do you feel sick?'

'Ye... es.'

Amy felt his forehead. 'You don't feel hot. I think maybe you just tired yourself out, running around this afternoon. I tell you what, you can have your dinner now then I'll pop you in bed. But you won't see Papa if you go to bed early, you know.' Malcolm looked solemnly back at her and said nothing.

Amy undressed him and put his nightshirt on, so that he would be ready for bed when he had eaten. He gulped down his dinner, looking up nervously from his plate at the slightest noise, then scurried off to bed as soon as he had finished. Amy tucked him in and looked down at him thoughtfully. Something had frightened him, she could see, but there seemed no point pressing him about it. By morning he would probably have forgotten whatever had upset him.

It was twilight before Charlie came in from milking. Amy had had the table set and his meal keeping warm for half an hour. Whatever had made him so late would not have put him in a good temper, she was sure. The ominous set of his face when he walked into the kitchen soon showed her forebodings had been correct.

'You've been a long time, Charlie. What happened? Is everything all right?'

'No, it's bloody well not all right. I've been chasing round the bush getting my cows back. The paddock gate was open and half a dozen of them wandered off.'

'Oh, no! Did you find them all?' It was no wonder he looked so grumpy. Especially since he must be furious with himself for having been careless enough to leave a gate open.

'Aye, I did. It took me half the afternoon, but I got the lot of them. I could have lost them, you know. They could have got clear away and gone wild, or maybe fallen in the creek where it's swift. I could have lost six cows.'

'It's lucky you didn't, isn't it? Your dinner's ready, I'll dish it up right now, shall I?'

'No,' he said grimly. 'Not yet. Where's the boy?'

'Mal's in bed. He said he was tired, so I didn't keep him up. He seemed a bit upset about something.'

'He would do.' Charlie turned to leave the kitchen.

'Where are you going, Charlie? You're not going to wake Mal up, are you?'

'I'm going to sort him out tonight.'

'Sort him out? What's he done?'

'What do you think?' Charlie stopped just before he reached Malcolm's bedroom door and turned to face her. 'Who do you think let the bloody cows out, you silly bitch? I didn't let them out myself, did I? Even you're not stupid enough to leave the gate open, and the little fellow's barely walking. Who does that leave? The boy.' He turned the door handle and went into the room. Amy followed him, knowing that what he said must be true. It certainly explained the state Malcolm had been in.

Malcolm was lying on his side with his eyes closed far too tightly for genuine sleep.

'Come on, boy, out of bed.' Charlie shook Malcolm by the shoulder. 'Hurry up about it.'

Malcolm opened his eyes and looked apprehensively at his father. 'Papa? I was asleep, Papa.'

'You're awake now.' Charlie pulled back the covers and hauled Malcolm into a sitting position. 'You let those cows out, didn't you?'

'No, Papa,' Malcolm said, all wide-eyed innocence. Amy could see at once that he was lying.

'Don't you lie to me, boy. You left the gate open, didn't you? Didn't you?' He gave Malcolm's shoulders a rough shake.

'I didn't mean to, Papa,' Malcolm said, abandoning all attempt at deception. 'I wanted a swing. I swinged on the gate. I opened it for a swing and the cows runned out and I couldn't make them come back. I chased them and chased them and they runned away and they wouldn't come back. I didn't mean to.' Tears ran down his face as he gasped out his confession.

'He didn't mean any harm, Charlie. Don't be hard on him,' Amy said.

Charlie turned on her. 'You keep out of this. If you'd been keeping a proper eye on the boy it wouldn't have happened. He's got to be taught a lesson. This place will be his one day, he's got to learn that you don't leave gates open for stock to wander.'

'He's too little to understand. He's had a fright, he won't do it again. Will you, Mal? Tell Papa you're sorry.'

'I'm sorry, Papa,' Malcolm said instantly.

'See? He really is sorry, Charlie. He didn't understand about the gate. You're right, I should have been watching him better. I won't let him go off by himself like that again.'

'I told you to keep out of this! Get out of here.' He swung his fist towards her, but the blow went wide of the mark. Amy moved closer to the door, but she could not bear to leave the room.

'Listen, boy, I'll tell you what's to happen. You and me are going over the back of the hill, and I'll cut a good, big stick. Then you're going to get a dozen whacks of it.' Malcolm stared as if hypnotized at his father towering over him.

'Charlie, you can't!' Amy said. 'Not twelve whacks, not with a stick!

He's not even three yet—you'll half kill him!' As if her voice had broken the spell, Malcolm began to wail.

'Shut up!' Charlie took a swift step towards her and gave her a slap on the side of the head that set her ears ringing. 'I'm going to bring my son up right. Don't you go interfering.' He left the room with Malcolm firmly grasped by one wrist, and Amy followed as soon as she had regained her balance. Charlie strode out of the house with Malcolm in tow, the little boy's legs pumping and his nightshirt flapping as he struggled to keep up with his father's stride without falling over.

Amy ran after them as quickly as she could, stumbling once or twice as she followed Charlie to where a stand of trees twined with supple-jack vines grew.

'Stay there—don't you move,' Charlie ordered Malcolm. The child appeared too terrified to disobey as he watched Charlie select a length of supple-jack and saw through the tough vine with his knife. When Charlie came towards him with the stick he howled louder than ever, as if he had only just realised what was going to happen to him. 'Stop that noise. Bend over and take your medicine like a man.'

'He's only a baby, Charlie! Please don't hit him with that,' Amy pleaded. 'Use your belt, that's hard enough for a little fellow like him.'

'Shut up!' Charlie turned on her and swung the stick, catching her just below the shoulder. Amy cried out in pain and shock, clutching at her arm, and Malcolm took advantage of Charlie's distraction to make a rush for her. He cowered behind his mother, trying to burrow under her skirts, but Charlie's long arms defeated him. He reached behind Amy and hauled Malcolm out, looking angrier than ever. 'I'll not have my son hiding behind a woman's skirts! Don't you try that again, boy.'

'He's only a baby, Charlie,' Amy sobbed helplessly. 'You'll half kill him. Please, Charlie, please.'

Charlie ignored her. He flicked Malcolm's nightshirt up and held the little boy by one arm while he swung the stick. Amy hid her face in her hands as Malcolm's screams pierced the air and she began to count the strokes.

When the whack of the stick against bare flesh stopped, she had only reached six. Charlie must have taken some notice of her pleadings after all. *Thank goodness. Poor little Mal, at least Charlie didn't give him twelve.*

'I'm taking this stick back with me. It'll be in the house from now on. You'll get more of the same if you ever do anything like that again. You remember that, boy,' Charlie said over Malcolm's yells. 'Get to bed.'

The moment he was released Malcolm ran wailing back towards the house. Amy made to follow him. 'Leave him be,' Charlie said sharply.

'He can find his own way back.'

'He didn't mean to do wrong, Charlie. He's just a baby.'

'He's *not* a baby, and I'll not have you treating him like one. He's got to learn. Spare the rod and spoil the child. And who's been spoiling him?'

'I have. I'm sorry, Charlie.'

'So you should be. Stop snivelling, woman.'

Amy walked slowly, hoping Charlie would get ahead of her and let her cry over Malcolm's punishment in peace, but he stopped and looked back, flicking the top off a thistle with his stick while he waited for her to catch up. She blinked away her tears and walked back to the house with him, wondering why there seemed such a brooding threat in his silence.

'Shall I dish your dinner up now?' she asked as she walked through the back door behind Charlie.

'Not yet. I've something to settle with you first. Get into the bedroom.'

A shiver went through Amy at his grim expression. Surely he didn't want to do *that* before he had even had his dinner? It wasn't even properly dark yet. But there was nothing to be done but obey him. She gave silent thanks that little David was such a sound sleeper; his father's grunts were unlikely to wake him. She trailed after Charlie into the bedroom. He closed the door behind her, still clutching the length of supple-jack in one hand, then turned to face her.

'You defied me, woman. You argued with me in front of the boy. I'll not put up with that from you.'

'I'm sorry, Charlie. I didn't mean to argue. I was just worried about Mal—he's so little to get the stick. I was wrong to contradict you, I know that. I won't do it again.'

'I'll see that you don't. Are you with child?'

The unexpected question startled her. 'Wh-what? No, I don't think so. Davie's so little, and I'm still...' She trailed off, anxious not to remind Charlie that she was still breastfeeding David even though he was now twelve months old, the age at which Malcolm had been declared too old for such babying. 'No, I'm sure I'm not.'

'That's as well.' He pointed to the chair that stood close to the bed. 'Bend down over that and lift your skirts.'

Amy stared at him blankly, then realisation dawned. 'You're not going to... please don't, Charlie. Please don't hit me with that thing. I'm sorry I argued, I won't do it again.'

He gave her a shove that sent her to her knees, and Amy grasped at the chair to steady herself. 'I have to teach you a lesson. You've got to learn how to behave. Hurry up, woman, or it'll be the worse for you.'

As if I was a child. As if I was a naughty little child. Amy leaned against the chair and fumbled at her skirts, bundling the layers of cloth up over her shoulders. The draught in the room felt chill on her legs and on her buttocks where her drawers gaped open.

'I said bend over,' Charlie growled.

'I don't bend in the middle very well,' Amy said through a muffling of cloth. 'It's my stays. This is as far as I can bend.' *I'm not a child. I'm a woman, and I wear women's clothes.*

'That'll have to do, then. Keep still.'

Amy looked at her hands lying on the seat of the chair and saw they were shaking. She knotted them tightly to try and steady them, closed her eyes and waited for the pain.

The stick bit into her flesh, and Amy barely stifled a scream. She was determined not to frighten David by making a noise, but the pain was hard to bear in silence. She stuffed a fold of cloth into her mouth to muffle the cries she could not hold back.

Each stroke left a burning sensation worse than the one before. Amy could count the stripes without needing to see them. *One. Two. Three.* The fourth missed its mark and fell on her thighs, hurting even more against the thinner flesh there. *Will I get more than Mal because I'm grown up? Or less because I'm a woman? Five. Ohh, it hurts. Six.* The seventh stroke gave her the answer. *More.*

Charlie had either lost count or decided that even a dozen strokes were not a severe enough punishment. When Amy realised after the thirteenth blow that he had stopped at last she spat out the gag she had made for herself, now soaked with saliva, and staggered on her knees over to the bed. She crawled onto it and sprawled face down, shuddering with the pain that racked her and heedless of the fact that her skirts were still high above her waist.

'I had to do that, you know. You've got to learn. Straighten yourself up and get out to the kitchen,' Charlie ordered. 'I'll have my dinner now.' Amy heard the door close.

It took several minutes before she was able to get up and put her clothes in order. Her flesh still burned when she walked into the kitchen and dished up Charlie's meal in silence.

'Where's yours?' he asked through a mouthful of stew.

'I'm not hungry.' The pain was too strong for hunger, and in any case she did not want to eat standing up and remind them both of her punishment.

'Don't you go sulking, woman. You deserved that.'

'I know I did. I'm not sulking, I'm just not hungry. Can I go and settle Mal, please? He's not used to putting himself to bed.'

'He'll be all right. He's not a baby.'

'No, he's not a baby,' Amy agreed wearily. 'But he's still a very little boy. Please, Charlie. I just want to see if he's tucked in properly—you know how cold it gets at night, and he's been getting a chesty cough lately. I won't baby him.'

'Be quick about it, then,' Charlie said. 'Just cover him up and get back out here.'

Amy slipped quietly into the half-darkness of Malcolm's room, where muffled sobbing from the bed told her he was still awake. She lit the lamp to see better. Malcolm cowered under the covers and peeped his tear-streaked face out, obviously expecting to see his father returning for fresh vengeance.

'It's only me, Mal, don't be scared,' Amy said, pulling back the covers. 'You've got between the top sheet and the blankets, silly. Hop out and let me get it tidied up.'

Malcolm twined his arms around her neck and let her lift him from the bed. He stood beside her, shivering in the chilly room while she smoothed out the sheets, then he climbed back onto the mattress and lay face-down.

'No!' he complained when Amy tried to lift his nightshirt. 'Don't, Mama.'

'Let Mama look,' Amy said gently. 'I won't touch, I promise I won't.' She drew in her breath at the lurid red marks on Malcolm's thin little buttocks, though she knew her own must look far worse. 'You're going to have some good bruises, Mal.'

'I didn't mean to let them out.'

'Of course you didn't. Shh, now, go to sleep. Papa won't be wild with you any more as long as you're good.' She patted the covers down over him and tucked them in, careful not to brush against Malcolm's tender flesh.

'It hurts, Mama.'

'I know it does. Try to keep still, then you'll go off to sleep faster. It won't be as sore in the morning. Don't, Mal,' she said, pushing him down flat when he tried to roll over. 'Lie on your tummy, it won't hurt as much like that.'

I wish I could, she thought as she kissed Malcolm and straightened her aching body. *I had to bend over and get beaten like a child, but I'll have to lie on my back like a woman tonight.* She shuddered at the thought, and pushed down the bitterness she felt rising. *I suppose I must deserve it.*

15

September – October 1888

Frank slapped the cheque down on the bank manager's desk, relief and resentment warring over which was his dominant emotion.

'That's my September milk cheque,' he announced. 'I talked the factory into giving it to me a couple of days early. And *that* makes fifty pounds I've paid you, and it's not the end of the month till the day after tomorrow.'

'Well done, Frank.' Mr Callaghan beamed at him. 'I knew you'd come through.'

'I wasn't so sure about it myself for a while there. It's not easy, you know, finding fifty pounds just like that. Not for someone like me, anyway.'

'I'd be a bit hard pressed to find fifty pounds myself. I know what you mean—especially with a wife, eh? Those women can spend money as if there's no tomorrow.'

'Not my Lizzie,' Frank said gruffly. 'She's as careful as anything. I don't know what she's been feeding us on this last couple of months, she's hardly run up any money at the store. I didn't let on to her about this,' he waved vaguely around the bank, 'but I've sort of wondered once or twice if she knew something was up. I've been a bit short with her a few times—with Maudie too, poor little mite.'

'Well, it's all sorted out now. But we don't want things getting in that state again, do we? We'd better make sure you make regular payments on that loan from now on, eh?'

'How much?' Frank asked anxiously.

'Say five pounds a quarter? Do you think you could manage that?'

'I suppose so. I managed to scrape up fifty pounds in the last couple of months—I wouldn't want to go through *that* again, though. Yes, five pounds a quarter should be all right.'

'Good lad.' Mr Callaghan examined the milk cheque then quickly jotted down some figures on a scrap of paper. 'Actually, this brings what you've paid up to fifty pounds, seven shillings and sixpence. Would you like the seven and sixpence in cash?'

'All right,' Frank said. Relief won out as he realised that the nightmare of the last two months really was over. He grinned at the bank manager. 'I might buy Lizzie a present, sort of make it up to her a bit for being such a rotten sod lately. Maybe something for Maudie, too.'

He left the bank feeling a great weight lifted from his shoulders. Now that the money was paid, everything was going to be all right. He would be able to tell Lizzie what had been going on, too; keeping it all secret from her had been one of the worst things about the whole wretched business.

A present for Maudie was easy enough: a bag of sweets would have her crowing with delight. Now he came to think of it, Lizzie hadn't let Maudie have any sweets for weeks and weeks. Well, she was going to have a whole twopence worth today. Some of those sticky toffees, too. She could make all the mess she wanted.

The sweets safely stowed in his pocket, he marched into Mrs Nichol's shop.

'I want a present for my wife,' he announced. 'Something pretty.'

Mrs Nichol beamed across the counter at him. 'I'm sure we can find something nice. What did you have in mind? A bonnet? Gloves? Perhaps a scarf?'

Frank looked around the unfamiliar items that filled the shop in growing bewilderment. 'I don't know—what do you think she'd like?'

'Hmm, let's see,' Mrs Nichol muttered, rummaging under the counter. 'I've got a nice lot of winter gloves in here somewhere.'

'Hey, this is pretty,' Frank said, fingering a fan that lay open on one end of the counter.

'Isn't it lovely?' said Mrs Nichol. 'I just got those last week, they're the latest thing from Auckland. I'll open up the others to show you.' She spread out five more fans. Frank glanced at them all, then returned to the one that had first caught his attention. 'You've got your eye on that one, haven't you, Mr Kelly? Dusky pink satin, that is, with ivory point lace. See the rose pattern on it? It's a beautiful fan, that.'

'It's not a very sensible thing, is it?'

'Well, I suppose not. It's very pretty, though. Just the thing for weddings and suchlike.'

'But it's not *sensible*.'

'No, it isn't,' Mrs Nichol agreed reluctantly. 'I can show you some good, warm scarves, they're sensible enough.'

'How much is this?' Frank asked, pointing to the fan.

'Three and sixpence.'

'I'll take it. Lizzie can have a rest from being sensible.'

Frank nudged Belle into a faster trot as he drew close to the house, eager to see Lizzie and tell her all about what had been happening. He could hardly wait to see how she would like the fan, carefully wrapped in tissue paper and stowed in his jacket pocket.

He had barely dismounted when he heard a high-pitched cry. He turned to see Maudie running towards him from the house as fast as her little legs would carry her, her face contorted with fright.

'Papa!' she screamed. 'Papa!'

Frank dropped the bridle, ran to Maudie and caught her up in his arms. 'What's wrong, Maudie?'

'Mama. Mama falled down,' Maudie wailed.

Frank ran for the house carrying Maudie, feeling sick with fear. He burst into the kitchen to find Lizzie lying on her side on the floor, clutching at her middle and groaning horribly, her face in a pool of vomit that was already matting her hair. Joey was howling from the bedroom, but Frank had attention for nothing but Lizzie.

He dropped to his knees beside her, let go of Maudie and took hold of Lizzie's hands. They felt hot and clammy to his touch. 'Lizzie! Lizzie, what's wrong with you?' he pleaded, trying to loosen her hands from their convulsive grip on each other. But it was obvious that Lizzie was beyond hearing him. She kept making inhuman groans as her body writhed.

'Mama's sick!' Maudie wailed from close to his ear, dragging Frank clear of the wave of panic that had threatened to overwhelm him. 'Papa, make Mama not sick!'

'That's right, Maudie. I've got to help Mama.' Frank forced himself to think clearly. He had to make Lizzie as comfortable as he could, then fetch the doctor.

He lifted Lizzie from the floor and carried her to the bedroom, hardly noticing the weight. He pulled back the covers and laid her down on the bed as gently as he could before wiping her face with his handkerchief. Lizzie seemed a little easier once she was lying on the soft bed; she still moaned and tossed her head from side to side, but her body's convulsive twitching subsided. Frank took off her shoes and undid the buttons of her bodice, but he was reluctant to risk giving her more pain by rolling her over so he could unlace her corset. He put the covers over her and knelt beside the bed for a moment, stroking her unresponsive face.

He stood up again and thought over what he should do next. Noticing Joey's distress properly for the first time, Frank picked him up from the cradle and paced around the room to try and settle the baby, Maudie trailing along clutching at his trouser leg. Joey's yells abated for a few moments, but he soon began roaring louder than ever when he realised there was no food to be had from that source. Frank felt the baby's napkin gingerly, and was dismayed to find it damp; changing napkins was a mystery he had always left in Lizzie's capable hands.

'You stink a bit, Joey, I think you've done more than just pee in that nappy. And you're hungry, aren't you? I can't do anything about that, boy. You'll just have to hang on for a bit.' He put the baby back in his cradle and tried to ignore Joey's indignant protests to concentrate on the real problem.

Lizzie desperately needed help, but the thought of leaving her alone tore him in two. 'Don't be frightened, Maudie,' he said to the little girl who still held fast, gazing up at him with tears pouring down her small, bewildered face. 'Mama's going to be all right, you'll see. Papa's got to go and get someone to look after her.'

'Papa!' Maudie wailed. 'Don't go away, Papa.'

'I've got to, Maudie.' He looked helplessly at her distraught face, and knew he could not leave her alone. But he could not possibly ride all the way into town at the speed the crisis demanded with Maudie perched in front of him. In any case, he could not bear to be away from Lizzie not knowing what was happening to her for as long as it would take him to fetch a doctor.

He made a sudden decision and swept Maudie up from the floor. 'Come on, Maudie, you and me are going for a ride.' He gave a last glance at Lizzie tossing about on the bed before he set off down the passage at a run, holding Maudie close while Joey continued to howl with frustrated hunger.

Belle had moved only a few steps from where Frank had left her. She looked up from cropping the grass in mild surprise as Frank ran towards her. He perched Maudie on the mare's neck before vaulting into the saddle.

He pulled Maudie close to him so that she was firmly held between his thighs. 'Hold on tight to her mane,' he told Maudie, coaxing her chubby little fists to take a handful of mane each. 'We're going to go really fast.'

Maudie was distracted from her fear for a few minutes by the excitement of galloping as Frank set off down the valley. The Aitkens were his closest neighbours as well as being nearer town and the doctor, so it was to their house that he rode. The sound of hooves thudding up the track brought Rachel Aitken to the door even before Frank had dismounted and lifted Maudie from the horse.

'Frank! Whatever's wrong?' Rachel asked.

'It's Lizzie. She's really sick. Can you help?'

'Of course,' said Rachel. 'What do you need me to do?'

Rachel's capable manner calmed Frank a little as she set to organising. Matt was despatched to fetch the doctor, and Maudie was delivered into twelve-year-old Bessie's care to be kissed and fussed over. The Aitkens' oldest son was to ride up and let Edie and Arthur know what was happening, and would drop Rachel off at Frank's on the way.

'You get back to Lizzie now,' Rachel said. 'You must be beside yourself worrying about her.' Frank was back in the saddle and urging Belle to a canter almost before she had finished speaking.

When a loud knocking made Amy hurry to open the back door she was surprised to see her aunt standing on the doorstep, puffing from her haste.

'Amy, I need you,' Edie said, cutting through Amy's questions. 'Can you come down to Lizzie's right now?'

'I'd have to ask Charlie—what's wrong, Aunt Edie?'

'The Aitken boy just came tearing up to our place. Lizzie's crook, I'm going down there to help Frank with her—she sounds pretty bad.' Edie looked over Amy's shoulder as Charlie walked across the kitchen to see what was going on. 'Charlie, I need to borrow your wife. Lizzie's crook, and I need Amy to help me look after Joey.'

'What do you want *her* for?' Charlie asked indignantly. 'You can look after a pair of bairns yourself, can't you?' Amy cringed at his rudeness.

'I can look after them, but I can't do Joey much good. He's still a little fellow, Charlie. He needs feeding, and Lizzie must be too ill for that. Amy's still nursing, I thought she might be able to give Joey a bit, too. There's only her and Jane with little ones, and to tell you the truth I never even thought about Jane until I was past their place.'

'Jane hasn't got much milk, anyway,' Amy put in. 'She's only just got enough for Doris. I've got plenty—please, Charlie, can I go and feed Joey?'

Charlie looked doubtful. 'You're sure you've got enough for young Dave as well as Kelly's boy?'

'Yes, I've got lots. Davie's not taking much now, anyway.'

'Well… all right, then,' said Charlie. 'I suppose there's no harm in it.'

'Thank you, Amy,' Edie said with evident relief. 'I won't wait for you to saddle up, I want to get down and find out what's happening to Lizzie.' She managed to smile, but strain was obvious in her face. 'You just ride down as soon as you can.'

'I will,' Amy said. *I'll have to walk, though.* 'I shouldn't be gone more than a couple of hours at the most, Charlie, I don't think Davie will wake up before I'm back.'

Amy was ready to leave within a few minutes of Edie's visit. She walked as briskly as she could to Frank's farm, her heart pounding more from the fear of what might be happening to Lizzie than from the exertion of the trek. *It's those stomach aches of hers, I'm sure it is. I knew she should have gone to the doctor. Poor Lizzie. Oh, I wish I could ride—it takes so long to walk.*

Rachel's son was sitting on the doorstep of Frank's house while his horse cropped grass just outside the garden fence. When Amy walked into the kitchen she found Rachel pacing the floor with Joey, whose cries were now more pathetic than outraged.

'Oh, thank goodness you're here, Amy,' Rachel said. 'Poor little Joey! I cleaned him up—he was in a terrible state—but I've no milk of my own to give him. I tried getting a bit of warm milk into him with a teaspoon, but he didn't know what to do with it, poor little mite. I was frightened he might choke.'

Amy had sat down and was already unbuttoning her bodice as Rachel spoke. She held out her arms for Joey. As soon as she guided a nipple into his open mouth, his lips closed on it and he began sucking greedily.

'Poor Joey,' she crooned. 'You're starving, aren't you?' Once she was sure Joey was feeding comfortably, she looked up at Rachel. 'What's happened to Lizzie?'

Rachel glanced anxiously at the open door that led into the passage. 'Doctor Wallace only got here a couple of minutes before you did, they haven't come out since. Amy, I should be getting home now, can you manage without me?'

'Of course,' Amy assured her. 'Thank you for helping us.'

Joey was on to Amy's other breast when the bedroom door flew open. 'Get that man out of here, for goodness sake!' Amy heard Doctor Wallace's irritated voice. 'I can't examine the woman properly with him hovering around.'

'I just want you to tell me what's wrong with Lizzie! Is she going to be all right?'

'Come on, Frank,' Amy heard Edie trying to soothe him. 'Let's leave the doctor to get on with his work. Please, Frank, come with me.' A few moments later she came into the kitchen leading Frank by the hand like a child. Amy twisted away to hide her exposed breasts, but it was obvious that Frank was in no state to take any notice.

'Why won't he tell me what's wrong with her?' Frank said, staring wild-eyed in the direction of the bedroom.

'He doesn't know,' Edie said, looking close to tears and keeping a tight hold on Frank's arm. 'He'll tell us what's wrong as soon as he can. Please, Frank, try and calm down. You don't want to disturb Lizzie, do you?'

Frank passed the back of his hand over his forehead and gave a shuddering sigh. 'Sorry, Ma. I just… it's driving me mad, not knowing what's going on. If anything happens to Lizzie, I don't know what—'

'Don't talk like that,' Edie cut in. 'We've just got to hope for the best.'

'Yes, I know we do. She'll be all right, eh?' Frank looked at Edie and Amy with a pleading expression, then a scream from the bedroom rent the air. 'Oh, my God, what's he doing to her?' Frank flung himself towards the passage door while Edie took hold of his arm and held on with all her might.

'Don't go up there, Frank,' Edie begged. 'The doctor knows what he's doing… oh, Lord, what's happening to my girl?' Edie broke into sobs. Her noisy loss of control distracted Frank. He put his arm around her and the two of them sank into adjacent chairs.

Amy disengaged an almost replete Joey from her breast, hastily closed her bodice and sat the baby on Frank's knee. She curled Frank's arm around his son and held it in place until he noticed the warm bundle on his lap.

'Joey,' he murmured. 'Poor little Joey.' He looked at Amy as if seeing her for the first time. 'You've settled him down. Thanks, Amy.'

'He was hungry. He's all right now.'

They sat in tense silence, Frank holding Joey close as the baby drifted towards sleep. There was no more sound from the bedroom until the door opened and Doctor Wallace walked down the passage to the kitchen, to three expectant pairs of eyes.

'She's very ill,' the doctor said sombrely. 'She has some sort of internal disorder. Perhaps a growth of some kind, or possibly an infection in one of her organs. She seemed very tender when I probed her.'

'But… but she's going to be all right, isn't she?' Frank implored.

'It's too early to tell,' Doctor Wallace said. 'All I can do for the moment is make her as comfortable as possible, and try to find out just what the trouble is. She has a high temperature, which suggests an infection, but I can't be sure. Now, she's going to need proper care.'

'What do we have to do, Doctor Wallace?' Amy asked.

'Keep her warm and comfortable, that's important. Whatever's wrong with her seems to be giving her a lot of pain. I've given her a strong dose of laudanum, that should keep her quiet for eight hours or so. If she seems at all restless, give her another dose. A spoonful or two should suffice. Is she normally a robust sort of woman?'

'She's hardly had a day's illness since she was a baby,' Edie said.

'That's something in her favour. Now, she'll need to be kept clean— her bodily functions will continue, you understand. One of you women should wash her at least once a day.'

'What about food?' Edie asked.

'You won't be able to get solids into her. I doubt if she'd keep down anything heavier than water today, see if you can coax her into taking some. Then from tomorrow make up a broth of some sort and give her a few spoonfuls. No warmer than lukewarm, you don't want to scald her. With the amount of laudanum she'll need to kill the pain she'll be no better than semi-conscious in the near future. Now, do you understand all that?' Doctor Wallace, observing the slender hold Frank had on his self-control, ignored him and addressed the two women. Amy and Edie both nodded solemnly.

'Good.' Doctor Wallace picked up his hat and coat from the chair where he had placed them. 'I'll be back tomorrow to see how she is.'

'Can't you do anything for her?' Frank begged. 'Can't you fix her up?'

Doctor Wallace stopped halfway to the door and turned a grim stare on Frank. 'Mr Kelly, if she has an infection then proper care and her own strength will give her a chance of pulling through. A chance, I said. Nothing's certain. If she has a growth... well, then there'll be nothing I can do for her except ease the pain. Good day to you.'

'That must be it,' Edie said when the doctor had gone, her voice a sad echo of its usual cheerfulness. 'She's got an infection. Lizzie's a strong girl, we'll get her fit again.'

'A growth,' Frank repeated, so quietly that Amy barely heard him. 'Nothing he can do. Just like with Ma.'

The entire Leith family was soon mobilised to do all they could to help Frank and Lizzie. Maudie was collected from the Aitkens and taken to stay with Arthur and Edie, while Amy took little Joey home with her, much to Charlie's astonishment.

'What have you brought him here for?' he asked when Amy carried Joey into the house.

'I have to feed him, Charlie. That means I've got to have him with me all the time. You said it would be all right for me to feed him.'

'I said you could go down today and suckle him—I didn't know you were going to bring the brat here!'

Amy sank into a chair, holding Joey tightly. 'Lizzie's very sick,' she said, struggling to hold back tears. 'She's got something wrong with her insides, but the doctor doesn't know what it is. She's not going to be well enough to feed Joey for a long time.' *Lizzie might die.* But she refused to say the words aloud, as if that would give power to the terrible thought.

'Well... can't they give him cows' milk or something? Why do you have to be a wet nurse?'

'Joey's so little—he's only four months old. If we tried to wean him all of a sudden like that he'd probably get really sick. He might even… he might even die, Charlie. Frank's beside himself with worry over Lizzie, how do you think he'd feel if Joey got sick too?'

Charlie looked thoughtful. 'It's that risky to wean him? Hmm, that'd be hard on Kelly to lose his son—it's taken him long enough to get one. I wouldn't want to take a man's son off him. You're sure you've got enough milk for the pair of them?'

'Quite sure.'

'All right, you can feed him for a bit. My son gets fed first, mind—I'll not have you starving him for Kelly's boy. He's such a scrap of a bairn, he can't need much milk anyway.'

'Thank you, Charlie,' Amy said with heartfelt gratitude.

'Where's he going to sleep, then?'

'I'll put him in with Davie for now, there's plenty of room to top and tail them in the cradle. Aunt Edie said she'll get Uncle Arthur to bring Joey's cradle down tomorrow. It was too heavy for me to carry.'

'Two of them in the bedroom,' Charlie said grimly, as if already regretting his magnanimous gesture. 'I hope he doesn't bawl at night.'

So do I, Amy agreed silently.

With two nursing babies it was difficult for Amy to leave the house, so she was not able to help care for Lizzie as much as she wanted to. In any case, Edie would have insisted on taking the lion's share of the nursing herself. But the rest of the family did what they could, with a constant flow of cooked meals being sent down the valley to Frank's house and his washing done in turns by Amy, Jane and Susannah, while Jack and Arthur sent whichever of their sons they could spare to help Frank with the farm work. Early in the crisis Jack pointed out to Susannah that she was the only one of the three younger women without a baby to look after, and suggested she should go next door and do Edie's cleaning while Edie was busy caring for Lizzie; when Susannah seemed reluctant he made one of his rare assertions of authority and insisted she do it.

After a grinding nightmare of a week Doctor Wallace announced that Lizzie's illness was definitely an infection rather than the dreaded growth, and Frank's barely-controlled terror subsided into a dull misery. The doctor was quick to stress that he still had no idea whether or not Lizzie would recover, but there was no invisible monster slowly devouring her from the inside as Frank remembered so clearly from his mother's long wasting illness.

Day after day Lizzie remained unchanged, tossing about on the bed flushed and moaning, or when she had been dosed with laudanum lying so motionless that her stillness made Frank think of death rather than healing sleep. He could hardly bear to watch her, but even less could he bear to be away from her for any length of time, imagining that she might suddenly take a turn for the worse.

One afternoon two weeks after Lizzie's collapse, Amy was cleaning the kitchen when she heard the noise of hooves approaching the house.

'That's Papa!' Malcolm said, rushing to the kitchen door.

'I don't think it is, Mal,' Amy said as she followed him. 'He only went out half an hour ago, he said he'd be gone all afternoon.'

She opened the door to see her aunt standing in the porch. Edie smiled at her, but lines of strain were worn deep in her face and she swayed as she stood.

'Aunt Edie! Is everything all right? How's Lizzie?' Amy asked.

'She's the same as ever. No better, no worse. Hello, Mal.' Edie managed a smile for the little boy staring up at her. 'You looking after Mama, are you?'

'I thought you were Papa,' Malcolm said accusingly.

'Charlie's gone out by himself,' Amy explained. 'Mal's having a bit of a sulk because he couldn't go too. I've told you, Mal, sometimes Papa likes to go out by himself. I expect he'll take you with him when you're old enough. Come inside, Aunt Edie, you look worn out. I'll put the kettle on.'

Edie shook her head. 'No, I'd better not sit down or I'll fall asleep on you. Amy, I wondered if you could do me a good turn?'

'Of course. What can I do?'

'I've been down at Lizzie's from morning till night every day, but I've just got to go home for a spell this afternoon. Maudie's fretting for her Mama—your uncle's trying to look after her, but she needs a woman. Susannah's over there most mornings, but she's not much on cuddles and things. And Ernie's got a bad cough, he keeps going out without his jacket on, and your uncle never thinks to make him wear it. I'd like to give the place a decent clean up, too—not that I'm not grateful for Susannah coming over to help, but she's not too keen on getting down on her knees and scrubbing.'

'You look as though you need a good sleep, Aunt Edie.'

Edie smiled ruefully at her. 'Well, maybe I'll even manage a nap if I get everything sorted out quickly enough. You're right, that's what I feel like more than anything—taking little Maudie to bed with me and having a doze. But Amy, dear, someone needs to look after Lizzie this afternoon. She needs a wash, and I only got a couple of spoonfuls of soup into her this morning. Do you think you could go down there? I know you're busy with the little ones, but I'd take it kindly if you could spell me.'

'Oh, Aunt Edie, I wish I could,' Amy said in distress. 'But Charlie's out.'

'Yes, so you said, dear. Does that matter?'

'I can't ask him if it's all right, you see. Oh, I wish I could go. I really want to help.'

'But you'd just be popping down the road to Lizzie's,' Edie said, looking puzzled. 'He wouldn't mind that, would he?'

'I'm not allowed... I'm meant to ask...' It sounded ridiculous, Amy knew. She could see that Edie had no idea what she was talking about, and no wonder. After all, other women were allowed to leave the house without having to beg permission. *Other women aren't as bad as me, I suppose. But Lizzie needs me! And Aunt Edie's just about dead on her feet. Oh, what can I do?* She saw the puzzlement in her aunt's face turn to disappointment.

'That's all right, dear,' Edie said. 'I shouldn't have asked you, you've got enough on your plate just now. I'll go back to Lizzie's, I don't really need to go home at all. You just forget I troubled you.' She turned to leave.

Charlie will be really wild with me if I go down there without asking him. He'll give me an awful beating. She saw Edie stumble a little with weariness as she negotiated the porch steps. 'Wait a minute, Aunt Edie,' Amy said, making up her mind abruptly. 'Of course I can go down there this afternoon. I was just being silly, saying I couldn't.' *So I'll get a beating. I've had beatings before, I know what to expect. It won't kill me.*

'You're sure?' Edie asked.

'Yes,' said Amy. 'I want to go, and it's time I helped a bit more. You go home and have a rest. Let's see,' she said, thinking aloud. 'I'll have to take the little fellows with me, they'll both need feeding. Mal, we're going down to Aunt Lizzie's.'

'Don't want to,' Malcolm said.

Amy studied him anxiously. She could try insisting he do as he was told, but dragging an unwilling Malcolm down the road would not be easy. The only thing he seemed to take any notice of was a belt or a stick, and they both knew she would not use either on him. 'Aunt Edie, would you take Mal for me and drop him off at Susannah's?' she asked.

'Of course, dear—I'll take him home with me, if you like.'

'No, don't do that. He's in a mood, you've got enough to do without putting up with his sulks. Susannah will just send him off with Pa and the boys, he'll like that. Mal, I want you to go with Aunt Edie.'

'No,' said Malcolm.

Persuasion seemed more likely to succeed than coercion. 'Aunt Edie will give you a ride on her horse. You'd like that, wouldn't you? He's mad on horses,' she explained to Edie.

Malcolm weighed up the offer. 'Can we go fast?'

Edie laughed. 'We'll have a go, Mal. I've ridden more in the last couple of weeks than I have in years—it just about killed me the first day or so. Oh, Amy, see if you can get a bit of food into Frank while you're there, too. I made him some lunch, but I bet he's left it. You'll have to stand over him like you would a child to make him eat it. Poor boy, he's beside himself over Lizzie.'

Amy hoisted Malcolm in front of Edie and waved them off, then went inside to get ready. She wanted to leave quickly; because she knew she was needed, but also so as not to give her courage time to fail.

She took a scrap of brown paper that had been wrapped around a tin of baking powder and flattened out the creases, then wrote a quick note on it:

'Charlie,' (*Dear* would have been too blatant a lie) 'I have gone to Lizzie's for the afternoon to help look after her. Mal is at Pa's and I have the babies with me. I'll be back in time to make dinner.' She hesitated for a moment, then added, 'I'm sorry,' before signing the note with a simple 'Amy'.

'I'll be a lot sorrier when your Papa's finished with me,' she told an oblivious David, who chortled away as she put a warm coat on over his gown. 'Well, it can't be helped. I've got to go.' David crawled around by her feet while she wrapped Joey warmly for the journey and thought over just how she was going to carry the two children down the valley.

Amy improvised a carrying sling for Joey from a length of old sheet that had been consigned to her rag bag. She hoisted David onto one hip and set off down the road.

The mile or so to Frank's house had never seemed so long. Amy's arms were aching well before she got there. She sighed with relief when she walked into the kitchen and let David slide to the floor. There was no sign of Frank, though she saw the pan of chops Edie had left for him lying untouched on one side of the range close to a pot of soup. Amy decided he must be out working somewhere on the farm.

'You can walk for yourself now we're inside, Davie,' Amy said. 'I've carried you far enough. You're such a heavy boy!' She kept hold of his hand and steadied his tottering steps as they slowly went up the passage to the bedroom.

Amy walked through the open bedroom door and stopped in her tracks. Frank was sitting on a chair beside the bed, close to where Lizzie lay pale and still, the slight rise and fall of the blankets over her chest the only sign of life. He held her limp hand in both of his while tears flowed unchecked down his face.

She hesitated in the doorway, unsure whether to speak or to slip away quietly, till David broke the silence with a burst of childish babble. Frank turned an unseeing face to them, then rubbed his sleeve over his eyes to clear them of the tears blinding him.

'Amy?' he said, sounding confused. 'I didn't know you were coming.'

'Aunt Edie asked me to, Frank.'

'Did she? Maybe she told me, I don't remember. Hey, you've brought Joey with you,' he said, a tiny look of animation softening the naked grief that twisted his face. 'Look, Lizzie, Joey's here.' He turned back to Lizzie and stroked her unresponsive cheek.

Amy walked closer to the bed. 'She can't hear you,' she said gently.

'I know. I just sort of hope she can, you know? I don't want to treat her like she's... like she's...' He trailed off, unwilling to voice the thought.

He loves her so much that he can't bear the thought of losing her. Amy stood in silence for a few moments before she could bring herself to speak. 'I need to do a few things for her, Frank,' she said at last. 'She'll need washing and things.'

Frank let go of Lizzie's hand and stood up. 'I know, you want me to get out. Edie always shoos me out of the way when she's looking after Lizzie.'

'It's not that you're in the way. It's just that... well, I'll need to...'

'You have to take her clothes off, and you don't want me around. Don't hurt her, eh, Amy?'

'I don't think she can feel anything. Have you given her any laudanum this afternoon?'

Frank shook his head. 'Edie gave her a dose before she left, that's why she's lying so still now. I can't bear to give it to her. I want her to have it so nothing hurts her, but I hate the way it makes her look as though she's... as though she's *dead.*'

'Frank, you mustn't think that! She's asleep, that's all.'

'No,' Frank said wistfully. 'Lizzie's not like that when she's asleep. She wriggles and makes little snuffly noises, and she pushes against you till she's lying in the middle of the bed.'

'I know,' Amy said. 'She used to push me right out of bed sometimes when we were little.'

'Did she?' For the first time the ghost of a smile passed over Frank's face. 'She hasn't done that to me yet. It's a good thing I'm a bit bigger than her, eh?' The ravaged look came over his face once more as he stared at Lizzie. 'I wish she'd get better,' he murmured. 'She looks so awful. See how thin she's got? And Edie cut her hair off. All that pretty yellow hair. She said it would drain Lizzie's strength if she didn't cut it off.'

Amy stood beside him and looked down at Lizzie's pale face. Its usual soft covering of flesh had been honed away so that Lizzie's cheekbones, which had always been invisible, were now prominent. 'She'll put on some weight when she's well again,' she said, trying to sound far more confident than she felt. 'It's because it's so hard to get any food into her. I'll try and give her some soup when I've finished washing her. Where can I put Joey while I'm looking after Lizzie? He's sound asleep, the good little chap.'

Frank dragged his attention back to her. 'The cradle's just... where's it gone?'

'I've got it at home, Frank. Joey's staying with me, remember?'

'Oh, yes, I forgot for a minute. It's been really quiet without him and Maudie around the place. I'll put him on my bed. I'm back in my old room now. It's like before I had Lizzie.' He reached out for Joey, and Amy laid the sleeping child in his arms.

As soon as Frank had gone out, she closed the door behind him and got on with the task of washing Lizzie. David, unaware of the tribulation around him, crawled about on the floor of the unfamiliar room. Edie had wrapped lengths of cloth around Lizzie's middle like a loose napkin. Amy undid them, washed the soiled flesh underneath, then replaced the cloths with clean ones. She sponged Lizzie all over and dried her carefully with a towel, and smoothed the short hair that framed her face. Through it all Lizzie lay limp and unknowing, her shallow breathing only slightly disturbed by Amy's interference with her body.

When she had finished, Amy gathered David up from the floor and went out to the kitchen. Frank was sitting at the table with his gaze turned inwards. He did not look up at Amy's approach.

'I'll dish you up some of this lunch, shall I?' Amy said, lifting the lid off a pot of boiled potatoes.

'What? Oh, no thanks. I've had lunch.'

'No, you haven't, Frank,' Amy said gently. 'I can see you haven't eaten any of this.' She loaded a plate with chops and vegetables and put it in front of him. 'Come on, now, eat up.'

'You sound like Lizzie,' Frank said, taking up his knife and fork.

'You need to keep your strength up, you know. Lizzie wouldn't want you missing your meals.' Amy put a little soup into a bowl and took it to the bedroom, where she managed to slip a few spoonfuls into Lizzie. It took her some time, pausing between each mouthful to make sure Lizzie did not choke, but when she went back out to the kitchen, leaving the bowl of soup by the bed, Frank's plate was still almost full.

'Frank, you've hardly touched that food.'

'I've had a bit.'

Amy sighed and sat down beside him. 'I'm going to sit and watch you till you've eaten that,' she said, remembering her aunt's words. Under her watchful gaze Frank began eating more diligently, and it did not take him long to finish the meal.

'That's better, isn't it? I'll wash these few dishes, then I'll give the floor a wash.'

'I'll go out and do some work in a minute,' Frank said, but he made no move to rise. 'I can't understand how she got sick so fast,' he said, his brow furrowed. 'The doctor said she would have been having pains before she got really crook, but she can't have. She got those little cramps for a bit, but she stopped saying anything about it, so they must have come right. How did it happen so fast? Doctor Wallace was so sure it must have been hurting her for ages. Maybe he's wrong about what she's got. Maybe she's got something worse.' He looked dangerously close to tears again.

'No, Frank, I'm sure that's not it,' Amy said. 'The doctor's right, she's got something infected inside her.'

'Then why didn't it hurt her before that day?'

Amy thought for a moment before speaking. Lizzie had said she wasn't to tell Frank about those stomach aches, but Lizzie's illness was no secret now. Frank was so worried, it seemed the kindest thing to tell him the whole truth.

'Lizzie knew she was sick weeks and weeks ago. She didn't know how bad it was, though. She kept getting awful stomach aches, but she thought it'd get better by itself.'

Frank turned to her in shock. 'She knew?' he echoed. 'But... but why didn't she tell me? Why did she keep quiet about it? I would have taken her to the doctor.'

'She didn't want to upset you. She knew you were worried about... about things.' She had said too much, she realised when Frank gave a start.

'What do you mean, worried about "things"?' he demanded. 'What things?'

'I…' It was no use pretending, and against Amy's nature to try. 'Lizzie knew about the money. She found the letter from the bank. She didn't want to ask for any money while you were so worried, so she just kept quiet about those stomach aches and hoped they'd go away.'

Frank was staring at her, open-mouthed with shock. 'You mean she was in pain for ages, but she kept quiet because of me? Because I'm such a useless bastard that I can't even provide for my wife? Lizzie!' he cried. He slammed his fists onto the table so hard that his plate fell to the floor, breaking in two where it landed.

'Frank, stop it,' Amy said in alarm. 'I'm sorry, I shouldn't have told you.'

'When I asked for her Arthur wanted to know if I could provide for her,' Frank railed against himself. 'Oh, yes, I was so sure I could! Provide for her? I bet she's been half starving herself to save money. I didn't even have the brains to see she was sick. Arthur never should have let me have her. He should have kept her at home where she was safe. Now she's going to die, and it's my fault! It's all because I've been such a lazy, good-for-nothing bastard!'

'She's not! You mustn't say such things. Lizzie's going to get better, you'll see. Frank, you mustn't blame yourself like that. You've made Lizzie so happy. She's wanted to marry you since she was fourteen, it's all she's ever really wanted. She's not going to die, Frank!' Amy took hold of his hands in hers and held them tightly. 'We won't let her. We're going to look after her, and she's going to get better.' She held Frank's hands until she felt him relax a little.

'Let's start now,' she said. 'I hardly got any soup into her before, she might take it better from you. Come on.' She led Frank by the hand up to the bedroom and sat him beside the bed. Frank propped Lizzie's pillow a little higher, and Amy showed him how to spoon the soup carefully into Lizzie's mouth. 'There, you see?' she said triumphantly. 'She *is* taking it better from you. You can tell Aunt Edie you want to feed her from now on.'

'Yes, I will,' Frank said quietly. He stroked Lizzie's face. 'I'm going to look after her. I'm going to look after Lizzie properly from now on.'

She left him in the bedroom and finished doing the cleaning, then gathered up a still-sleeping Joey and slipped him back into the sling, picked up David, and left the house without disturbing Frank to say goodbye.

Frank loves Lizzie so much, she thought as she began the long, weary trudge. *She mustn't die! It would be such a waste. It would just about kill Frank if he lost her. I never knew anyone could love another person as much as he does.* Amy could not help but wonder how Charlie would react if it was her lying ill instead of Lizzie. He would be worried about how he would manage the house and the children, and about his loss of home comforts, but she could not imagine he would feel any grief. The tears that began to trickle down her face were only partly for Lizzie and Frank.

David grew sleepy, and both babies dragged more heavily against her arms as she walked. Amy grew clumsy with tiredness, her feet stumbling against rocks on the road. Her right foot twisted on a large stone, almost making her lose her balance. She forced herself to pick out her way with more care. The day was bright although cold, and the glare soon made her head ache. Joey began to squirm, making her more uncomfortable than ever. She saw his mouth working, and knew he would soon demand to be fed.

Amy was too absorbed in the necessity of putting one foot in front of the other even to think about what might be in store for her until she turned off the main valley road and up the track towards Charlie's house. Then the memory of what she had done rushed in on her: she had left the property without permission. He had told her within two days of their marriage that she was never to do such a thing, and now she had broken the rule.

For a few moments she let herself hope that perhaps Charlie might not yet be home; sometimes his visits to town lasted till late in the day. But that idea was dashed when she came near the horse paddock and saw Smokey grazing. So Charlie was home. Home and aware of her absence.

He was standing in the doorway as Amy walked up to the porch. She stood at the foot of the steps and waited for him to speak.

'So, you're back,' he said grimly. 'You went out by yourself. You went out without asking me.'

Weariness dragged at Amy. 'Yes, I did. Can I come inside and settle the babies, please?'

Charlie took a step back from the door to let her pass, then followed her through the kitchen and into their bedroom. His stick rested against one wall; Amy shuddered as she saw it. Joey was now whimpering with hunger; Amy was about to feed him when she remembered the rule about feeding David first. There was no sense getting in even more trouble, even though she could see that David was not at all hungry.

She untied the sling and laid Joey on the bed, then undid her bodice and tried to coax David to take a nipple into his mouth. 'I had to go,' she said, too weary to feel more than a vague fear of what was to come. 'Someone had to look after Lizzie, and Aunt Edie was just about ready to drop. I couldn't ask you because you weren't here.' David took a few desultory sucks, then let the nipple fall out of his mouth as his eyelids drooped.

'I had to, you see,' Amy went on. If she didn't look at him she would not become too frightened to speak. She undressed David and put him in his cradle, careful to lay him on his side facing away from them so that he would not see her punishment if he woke too soon, then she took up an increasingly irate Joey and put him to the breast. 'Lizzie needed me. We're family, and we have to help one another. Lizzie would do the same for me if I was sick. So would Aunt Edie, and Jane. Even Susannah—Pa might have to make her, but she'd help me. That's what being a family means. It's so that—'

'All right, that's enough,' Charlie interrupted. 'Don't you lecture me, woman. You disobeyed me—you wilfully defied me. You know what that means, don't you? You know what's going to happen?'

'Yes, I know. But I can't help it. I had to do it.' Amy sat in silence while Joey suckled, shifting him to her other breast after a few minutes. 'I'm sorry it meant disobeying you. I'm very sorry.' She raised her eyes to his for a moment, then dropped them as she disengaged Joey from her breast and fastened her bodice. Her eyes flicked to the stick then away before she put a clean napkin on Joey and tucked him into his cradle.

Amy stood up from the cradle and looked straight at Charlie. *Better get it over with.* She dropped to her knees in front of the chair, lifted her skirts to her shoulders, and waited for the first blow to fall.

She waited and waited, wondering why Charlie did not move. At last she twisted around to look at him, and saw his hand reach out towards the stick then drop to his side again. His brow was furrowed in thought.

'There's something in that,' he said at last. 'I suppose you thought you were doing the right thing, going down there. You can't have got up to much mischief with two bairns to lug about, either. We'll say no more about it this time.'

Amy raised herself slowly upright and sank onto the bed, shaking in reaction to the unexpected relief.

'That doesn't mean you can wander off by yourself whenever the fancy takes you, mind. I'll let you off today, but you're to ask if you want to go again. Understand?'

'Yes, I understand. Thank you, Charlie.'

Frank sat at Lizzie's bedside holding her hand, but there were no tears on his face now. He looked grim and determined as he stroked her cheek.

'I've let you down,' he whispered. 'But I'm going to make it up to you. I'm never going to let anything hurt you again. When you're well again you're going to have whatever you want. I'm going to make things right for you.' He raised her hand to his mouth and kissed it. 'I love you, Lizzie.'

16

October 1888 – August 1889

On a mild spring day late in October, Lizzie opened her eyes and looked at Frank with recognition as he sat by her bedside.

When his rush of elation had settled into a calmer happiness, Frank spent the afternoon mending the stretch of fence whose collapse had, in his eyes, marked the beginning of their troubles, and to which he had done no more than rig a temporary repair up till now. There would be no more falling down fences on his farm, he pledged to himself.

It took many weeks for Lizzie to recover her full strength. All through her long convalescence, Frank hovered solicitously over her whenever he was not busy on the farm. As she became stronger Frank spent more and more time working, amazed at all the things he had left undone or done half-heartedly over the years. Even the weeds scattered through his paddocks, which he had always accepted as the natural state of the pasture, now seemed an inarguable sign of his neglect, and he set to work destroying them.

Seeing how much Lizzie was fretting for the children, within a few days of her return to consciousness Frank insisted that Edie let Maudie come home, and he gladly took on the task of looking after her until Lizzie was well enough to get up. He soon gained new skills in feeding, washing and dressing little girls, but he reluctantly admitted that caring for a baby was beyond him. Amy gradually weaned Joey over the next few weeks, and by the time Lizzie was well enough to care for him Joey was ready for solid food.

By autumn Lizzie was so well that it was hard to believe she had ever been ill. But the illness had left its marks. Her hair would take years to regain its former length, and it was months before she could easily pin it up under a bonnet. The weight she had lost was more readily replaced; Frank soon found he had a warm armful to cuddle again.

The changes in Frank were not so visible, but they were deeper and more long-lasting. Never again would he take happiness for granted. It was something to be worked for, and to give thanks for every day. No longer did he surprise Lizzie by coming back to the house an hour or two before she expected; now she had to get used to keeping meals warm in the evening while she waited for Frank to finish some vital piece of work that simply would not wait until the next day. Whenever he had to go out he spent most of the time away from the farm thinking about what he should do when he got back.

'Frank, you've gone mad,' Lizzie complained one evening when Frank finally came in for his dinner half an hour after sunset. 'I was beginning to think I'd have to come looking for you with a lantern.'

'I've got a lot of wasted time to make up,' said Frank. 'I'm going to make this farm pay.'

'That doesn't mean you have to work all hours of the day and night! You'll knock yourself out.'

'No, I won't. I'm just working hard for a change.' He stepped up behind Lizzie as she stood at the range dishing up his meal, and slipped his arms round her waist. 'I nearly lost you,' he murmured in her ear. 'I nearly lost my Lizzie. I'm never going to risk that again.'

There was one resolution he found more difficult to keep. The first night he once again joined Lizzie in their bed, he told her very solemnly that it would be for the best if she did not have any more babies for some time; at least until she was back to her full strength. Lizzie agreed with equal solemnity, and explained that since she had had to stop breastfeeding Joey so early she would be likely to get with child almost at once if they did not take care. But they soon found that good intentions were no match for natural impulses. In March Lizzie told Frank there would be another child in November, when Joey would be barely eighteen months old.

When he had got over the guilty awareness of his lack of self-control, Frank could not help but be pleased, especially as Lizzie was so delighted. He watched her anxiously for any sign of illness as her pregnancy advanced, but Lizzie bloomed as she swelled.

Late in the month John Leith startled his family with the announcement that he was going to get married. Not the news of the marriage itself; most of the population of Ruatane had been expecting to hear that was imminent for many months, ever since John had first started his frequent visits to the Carrs'. What caused such surprise was his choice of wife. No one was more astonished than Martha Carr when John went to see her father, not to ask for her hand but for her younger sister Sophie's.

'It's not fair!' Martha wailed to her mother. 'He was meant to ask me! What's he want her for, anyway? She's *fat*.' She was doomed to an unsympathetic hearing; after she got over the surprise, Mrs Carr was philosophical about having disposed of one daughter when all her efforts had been devoted to placing the other.

Martha soon decided to make the best of it, especially once her mother had comforted her with assurances that it would be her turn before too long. Mrs Carr insisted Martha have a bridesmaid's dress at least as elaborate as Sophie's wedding gown for the April wedding; after all, as she told her husband, Sophie had already got herself a man. Making the most of Martha's attractions was much more sensible.

By the time of the wedding Amy was almost four months gone with a new pregnancy, and she fretted over whether or not she should attend. Desire to go to her brother's wedding outweighed the worry that her condition might be visible; she comforted herself with the memory that at the same stage of her three earlier pregnancies she had barely shown. For a while it had seemed that nausea, far more violent and dragging on for longer than she was used to, might deny her the outing, but at last it subsided into mere morning sickness instead of attacking her all through the day.

Lizzie's baby was due two months later than Amy's, so she had no such worries about appearing at the wedding. In fact, Frank would have found it difficult to keep her away from her first important social occasion since her illness.

'Now, you're sure you feel up to it?' he asked as they drove to the Carrs' house after the wedding service. 'You just tell me if you get a bit tired, we can go home whenever you like.'

'Frank, for goodness sake,' Lizzie said. 'Stop treating me like I was still sick. Honestly, I hardly even get the chance to talk to anyone when we go to town, you're always in such a tearing hurry to get back to work. You needn't think you're going to do me out of a bit of fun today.'

'I just don't want you getting worn out. I'll make sure there's a proper armchair for you.'

'Oh, no, you won't! You can leave the armchairs for the old women, thank you very much.'

Lizzie gathered up her two children and made straight for the corner of the parlour where most of the other women had congregated. She and Amy took full advantage of their chance to chat.

'What I can't understand,' Lizzie said, 'is just how he ever got around to asking her. I mean, look at them now—have you even seen them speak to one another?'

'No,' Amy agreed, studying John and Sophie where they stood in the centre of the room, close by a table which Mrs Carr and Martha, helped by the Carrs' oldest daughter Tilly, were busily loading more and more food on. 'But I've seen them smile at each other a few times.'

'Smiling's all very well, but it's a bit hard to propose like that. Now, if it had been Martha I could understand it. She would have asked him herself—either that or he would have asked her just to shut her up.'

'Shh, Lizzie! Martha will hear you.'

'No, she won't. She's not taking any notice of us, she's too busy eyeing up all the men to see who she can chase after next.' Martha was indeed showing no sign of feeling rejected; she was clearly making her best effort to be charming to any unattached young man whose attention she managed to catch.

'Well, that's another of those girls married off,' Mr Carr remarked to any of the men standing close to him who cared to listen. 'It's an expensive business, getting rid of daughters. You'll have that one day, Frank.'

'Hey, hang on! Maudie's not even three yet,' Frank protested with a laugh.

'The time goes fast enough. Sophie'll make John not a bad wife— she's the best of the lot of them, really. She's the only one who didn't inherit her ma's tongue, anyway. Can I pour you a beer, Charlie—oh, you've already helped yourself.' He poured himself a mug instead, and topped up Frank's glass.

'Yes, she's not a bad girl, is Sophie,' he went on. 'John won't have got anything out of her, either, she'll have kept herself decent. Her and Martha both, they'd never dare open their legs till they had a ring on their finger. Not after that trouble we had with Tilly.' He glanced over his shoulder towards Tilly's husband, a sullen-faced young man with an expression that said he wished he were elsewhere.

'He's a no-hoper, that one,' Mr Carr muttered to his listeners. 'Good at making babies, but not too keen on any other sort of work. He's had jobs on half the farms around Katikati, he gets sick of it after a couple of months and tries another place. I'll probably have to have the two of them here in the end. Well, if he plays his cards right he'll get this farm when I'm gone. He reckoned it wasn't his brat, but Tilly swore it was, and her ma believed her. She's no soft touch, my old woman—if she believed Tilly, then it was the truth. She gave that girl a hell of a hiding when she found out there was a child on the way.'

'Wasn't it a bit late for that?' Frank asked.

'Too late for Tilly, right enough. But she made the other two stand and watch while she did it. I don't know which girl was yelling the loudest by the time she'd finished. No, John'll get his first go at Sophie tonight. I don't know if he's tried it on before, but she'll have given him short shrift if he has.' He looked across the room at Martha, who was taking animatedly to an amused-looking Bill. 'Course, the trouble with Martha is, I don't know if she's got much chance of getting a husband

217

bar using the same way Tilly did. She hasn't got much going for her. She's got her ma's looks and her ma's tongue, but she didn't get her ma's cunning.'

Charlie downed the last mouthful from his mug and refilled it. 'You wed the woman,' he said, voicing the thought that Frank had kept to himself.

'Well, we all do stupid things when we're young. Don't you go being so bloody smug, Charlie Stewart, not when you're drinking my beer. Just because you scored that tasty little piece.' He looked across the room at Amy. Frank saw Amy turn and stare back, then quickly look away, as if she had sensed she was being observed. Now that his eyes had drifted in that direction, Frank studied Lizzie, taking pleasure in the sight of her blooming health. She did not catch his eye, but she waved her new fan in a rather ostentatious way, making Frank smile even more broadly. 'I don't know how you did it, Charlie,' Mr Carr said, openly envious. 'The best looking bit of skirt in this town, and barely ripe when you got her.'

'I'll thank you to keep your eyes to yourself,' Charlie said, fixing Mr Carr with a grim expression.

'All right, all right, I'm just looking. I'll leave the baby snatching to you. When you've got a looker like that, Charlie, you've got to expect to have her stared at. I notice you've got her with child again.'

'That's right,' Charlie said with evident self-satisfaction.

'You don't muck about, do you? Making up for lost time, eh? What are you grinning about, Frank?'

'What?' Frank dragged his eyes back to his companions. 'Oh, I was just thinking about Lizzie. She looks good, eh?'

Mr Carr laughed. 'Now, that's the sign of a man who hasn't been married long—a room full of women, and he's only got eyes for his wife. She's got over that bad patch all right?'

'Yes, she seems really well now. I still keep an eye on her, try and stop her from overdoing things.'

'My wife fed his son while his wife was poorly,' Charlie put in. 'My son was still on the breast then. But she had plenty of milk for two bairns, so I let her feed both.'

'Ah, yes, Charlie, I think you might have mentioned that once or twice,' Mr Carr said, rolling his eyes at Frank. 'Maybe a few more times than that.'

Susannah glided towards Amy in her gown of bronze silk with brocade bodice, choosing a moment when Lizzie had gone to refill her plate. It was the dress she had worn on her first Sunday in Ruatane, but even now almost eight years later it still outshone any other outfit in the room.

'You shouldn't be here, Amy,' Susannah said in a low voice. 'You're *showing*.'

All Amy's pleasure in her outing evaporated in a moment. She looked down at the blue silk gown that had to do service as her only good dress. It was true that its close fitting style meant the dress was already uncomfortably snug. 'I'm only just showing. I don't think anyone will see. No one's taking any notice of me today, anyway.'

'I'm afraid you're wrong about that. Your condition's quite obvious.'

Amy looked around the room, imagining all eyes on her in disapproval. She knew it would be no use asking Charlie if they could go home, not when there was so much free beer still to be drunk. 'I can't help it,' she said bitterly. 'I'd never get out of the house if I had to wait for a time when I wasn't with child or nursing a new baby. I'm always in this state.' She turned her back on Susannah and walked away to what she hoped was an inconspicuous corner.

'Hey, I don't think I've had a wedding kiss from you yet,' she heard a voice behind her. Amy turned and saw John advancing on her while Sophie circulated among some of the guests.

'Haven't you?' Amy put her arms around his neck and kissed him. 'Congratulations, John. I hope you and Sophie will be really happy.'

'We'll be all right,' John said. He glanced over to where Sophie was showing off her new wedding ring to an admiring audience, and Amy saw a complacent smile play around his mouth. 'Sophie's good. I tell you what, she's looking forward to getting out of here. Martha's been giving her a real hard time since she found out we were getting married.'

'Poor Sophie,' Amy said, at the same time wondering how John had managed to get so much information out of Sophie when Amy had rarely heard her say more than two words together. 'But John, Martha might have been hurt, you know. I mean, she thought you were interested in her. I hope you haven't been leading her on.'

'I never touched her, if that's what you're getting at. I never said anything to her, either, bar "pass the salt" or that sort of thing. I can't help it if her and her ma made things up.'

'No, you can't,' Amy agreed. 'It's just that everyone thought it was Martha you were after.'

'Yes, that's what Sophie said at first. She said Martha would make a heck of a fuss about it—that's why it took me so long to talk Sophie round.'

'John, Sophie seems to say an awful lot more to you than she does to anyone else.'

'That's because I shut up and let her talk. Do you think her ma and sisters ever gave her much chance to get a word in edgewise? Sophie mightn't be the brightest, but she's not as dim as people think.'

'You're not so slow yourself, John. Oh, I've got to ask, tell me to shut up if I'm being too nosy. What made you notice Sophie when you must have had Martha hanging round you all the time whenever you came out here?'

'That's easy,' John said, the twinkle in his eye making it hard to judge how serious he was. 'It was the first day I realised it was Sophie who was doing all the cooking!'

This pregnancy seemed more uncomfortable than any of her previous ones. After the nausea at last disappeared, Amy seemed to swell so rapidly that at times she wondered if her skin could stretch fast enough to hold her body in. She knew she was bigger than she had been when carrying the two boys; perhaps this would be an even larger baby.

Maybe it'll be too big for me. Maybe this will be the one that kills me. She thrust the brooding thought aside whenever it slipped into her mind. Self-pity was a luxury she could not afford.

But pregnancy had its advantages. Although it made every day an ordeal for Amy as she dragged her growing burden around, the way Charlie softened in his manner made up for much of the discomfort. Sometimes Amy could almost delude herself that he might be about to say something kind to her, or even show her some token of affection, though in her more sensible moments she knew that was too much to expect. But he tolerated her increasing clumsiness with only mild complaints, carefully refrained from hitting her when she was slow in serving his meals, and only rarely called her 'bitch'.

One evening in early July, when Amy was a little over six months pregnant, the two of them sat in the parlour in a silence that was almost companionable, the fire crackling cheerfully on the hearth. Charlie scanned the *Weekly News* idly while Amy sewed at an old pair of his trousers that was beyond mending and which she was cutting down for Malcolm. She glanced up and caught him looking at her with an expression so self-satisfied that it came dangerously close to being a smile.

Charlie looked away and buried his nose in the newspaper before speaking. 'Felt the bairn move much?'

'Quite a bit. Not as much as Mal did, but about the same as Davie.'

'Mmm. Another big, strong boy, eh? I might have to think about putting another room on in a couple of years.'

When I have another baby. Won't he ever let me stop? A faint cough, muffled by the intervening wall, dragged her thoughts from their fruitless course. 'Mal's nearly over that bad cough now. He's much better since he's been in his new bedroom.' Distressed at the signs of illness in Malcolm, Charlie had readily taken up Amy's hesitant suggestion that he make a new room by walling in half of the cottage's verandah. Malcolm now slept there instead of in the chilly back bedroom that saw no sunlight all day. 'The weather'll be getting warm again when the new baby comes, so Davie should be all right in the back room till next year. He's a bit too young to share with Mal yet, I think. We shouldn't need another room for a while.' Charlie grunted something that might have been agreement.

'Charlie,' Amy said carefully, gambling on his mellow mood. 'It might… it might be a girl this time.'

Charlie dropped the paper on his lap and looked at her in astonishment. 'A girl? What do I want with a girl child? What use would that be on the farm?'

'No use at all, I suppose. But it might be one anyway. I've had two boys now, it can't keep on being boys forever.'

'I never thought of it being a girl child. Do you think you're carrying a girl?'

'I don't know. I don't think you can tell. I just wanted to sort of… well, warn you. I hope it'll be another boy, really I do.' And it was true. A girl would try to take the place in her heart that would always be Ann's, and Amy feared she would resent the child instead of giving her the love she deserved. It had been hard enough learning to love Malcolm; if she had a daughter she could not be sure of winning the struggle.

'A girl,' Charlie repeated. His look of amazement slowly faded as the notion settled into his mind. 'Well, I suppose there's no harm if this one's a girl,' he said at last. 'There's plenty of time for more boys. If it's a girl you can name it,' he added as he took up his newspaper again.

'Thank you,' Amy said in surprise. It was a gift; the only one he had ever given her, and Amy at once felt she wanted to give him something in return. She thought for a moment, then asked, 'What was your mother's name, Charlie?'

'Eh?' He looked up from the paper, and a faraway expression spread over his face. 'Her name was… Margaret. Yes, that was it, Margaret. Maggie, they used to call her. I remember her standing in the doorway and calling out to me to come in for supper, holding a wee bairn in her arms. She was tall and straight, and she had blue eyes. And they killed her,' he ended bitterly.

221

Amy gave a start. 'Wh-what? Who killed her, Charlie?'

'The bloody English,' Charlie spat. 'Called themselves Scots—called themselves clan chiefs—they never came near the Highlands till they decided to play farmer. There was only one sort of clansman they wanted, and that was the four-footed clansman.'

'What's a four-footed clansman?'

'Sheep. Bloody Cheviot sheep. That was the way to make easy money—run thousands of sheep on the hills. Only trouble was, there were people on that land. Good, honest clansmen—my father's family had worked that land time out of mind— and loyal to the chief—my mother and father both had grandfathers out in the '45.' That meant the Jacobite rebellion of 1745, Amy knew; though she suspected Charlie would not allow it to be called a rebellion. 'That lot weren't going to let that stop them. "Pack your belongings and get out," the steward said. Then him and his men set fire to the cottages so there'd be no going back—never even gave us time to get our things out before they threw in the torches. There was one old woman still in hers when they burned it, I remember my father saying. Our land. It was ours, and they took it away from us,' Charlie said in a voice raw with outraged loss. 'My father had no bit of paper to say it was his—the lairds had the paper. They kicked us off our land as if we were animals—no, they treated animals better. They treated the sheep better! Every time I cut a ewe's throat I tell myself it's the Countess of Sutherland.'

Amy shivered at the force of his hatred as he spoke about things she had scarcely even heard of, despite her own Scottish blood. History at school had meant English history, and had rarely strayed north of the border; certainly it had never discussed anything critical of the country most of Amy's classmates were taught by their parents to call 'Home'. Part of her wanted to stop him before he got himself in too much of a state, but the story held a horrible fascination. 'What did your family do? Where did you go?'

'We walked. We carried what we could—what we'd pulled out of the cottage before they torched it. My mother carried the little girl, and my father and me what our backs would bear. We walked and walked. I don't know how far, or how long it took. I only remember the walking, sleeping in the fields at night, my father putting his coat over Ma and the girl when it rained. She was far gone with child, bigger than you are now.' He frowned in thought. 'She seemed old. She was grey and worn-looking, and bowed down instead of erect like she used to be. She can't have been as old as all that, though, not to be still bearing.

'We got to some port. I don't know where it was, my father never spoke of it after. We got to within sight of it, then her pains came on. Too early, she said it was, but the walking was too much for her. She lay down in the dirt of the road and cried out with the pain. There were other women, they helped her. Someone took me off, but I could still hear her. For a while, anyway.' He fell silent.

'The poor, poor woman,' Amy murmured, hardly noticing the tears streaming down her face. 'You must have been very young.'

Charlie shrugged. 'I don't know. Five or six, maybe. They said some dirt got in her, she got some childbed ailment with a fancy name.' He gave a bitter snort. 'Not that she had a bed to give birth in, nor one to die in. She died in a field by the road. Some woman took the baby, but it only lived a day.'

'So you and your father—and your little sister—left Scotland?'

'Aye. There was nothing for us there any more. We went to Canada, the whole village on the one boat. The girl died on the way. She wasn't strong enough for that boat.' He shuddered at memories he chose not to speak of. 'There was work in Canada, and the chance of land. Cutting forests, that was good work for a strong man. Till one day the blade slipped in the sawmill. Took off my father's arm, and he bled to death while we watched.'

'Oh, Charlie! Who looked after you? Who took care of you?'

'Care?' he repeated, looking puzzled. 'I didn't need anyone to take care of me. I must have been ten or eleven by then. Old enough to do a man's job—for a boy's wage.'

Still a child, Amy thought, tears coursing down her face. *With no one to cuddle him when he got scared at night, no one to talk to about the things that upset him. Oh, Charlie, no wonder you don't know how to play with the children. No wonder you don't know how to be gentle.* 'It's a long way from Canada to Ruatane,' she said softly.

'A hell of a long way. Took me twenty-five years to do it. Twenty-five years of living rough, wherever there was work to be had and a chance of putting a bit of money aside. Across Canada, down through California, then worked my passage to Dunedin. Cutting stone blocks for building—that's work for a strong back. Fencing, digging the roads, whatever paid the best. Hauling loads to the gold-fields, there was money in that. I made my way north bit by bit—I heard there was land to be had in these parts, good land for a man not scared of hard work to break it in. Took me another five years working in the sawmills and the mines before I had enough money. No time to think about getting a wife, and no women in most of those places—not the sort you marry, anyway. Then it seemed to be too late,' he said, looking pensive. 'But I

223

got my land,' he went on, fire in his eyes again. 'This farm is mine, and I've the bit of paper to say so. No one's ever taking it off me or my sons. I've got sons now,' he said triumphantly. 'This land is ours forever.'

His eyes focussed on Amy instead of into some unseen distance, and he appeared to become fully aware of her presence for the first time since his diatribe began. 'You were just a wee mite when I got this place. A plaguey brat you were for a bit, you and that cousin of yours running wild on my land. But you blossomed,' he mused, his eyes on her in a way that made Amy grateful for the bulkiness exempting her from his demands. 'You blossomed, all right.'

Amy sat in silence as she tried to absorb the magnitude of all he had said. 'I'm glad you told me all that, Charlie,' she said at last. 'I wish you'd told me years ago.'

'Why? What's it got to do with you?'

Amy looked away to hide the hurt. *I'm your wife, aren't I?* 'You should tell the children about it when they're old enough to understand. It was their grandparents, after all.' She felt the hard bulge of her belly under her hands and thought about the woman who had been Charlie's mother; the woman made old and grey before her time. 'And if this baby's a girl,' she said quietly, 'I'd like to call her Margaret.'

The weight dragged at Amy more and more as the weeks passed and she grew bigger. The simplest task became a trial, and the heavier work such as washing became almost too much to bear. But it had to be done, so she struggled on.

On a Monday early in August, with six weeks still to go before the nine months would be up, Amy was taking the dry clothes off the line while David toddled about near her feet. Every time she reached up for a piece of washing a sharp pain stabbed under her ribs, and she had wait for it to subside before she could carry on.

David tugged at her skirt. 'Mama,' he said excitedly. 'Tommy coming!'

Amy looked in the direction he was pointing and saw that her little half-brother was indeed making his way up the track towards them. 'Hello, Tommy! What are you doing here?' She held out her arms, and he let himself be embraced. He tried to put his own arms around her, but when Amy let him go he stepped back and gave her a puzzled look.

'You're fat, Amy. You're much fatter than Sophie.'

'Yes, I'm really fat,' Amy agreed. 'Don't worry, I won't be for long. You'll see, by Christmas I'll be as skinny as ever. Tommy, it's lovely to see you! I haven't seen you for months. But why did you come today? And where's Georgie?'

'He's got a cough. He had to stay home today. I just wanted to see you.' Thomas looked up at her and his lower lip trembled. 'That's all right, isn't it?'

'Of course it is. I've been missing you. Does Mama know you're here? Oh, you say "Ma" now, don't you? Now you're a big boy going to school. And you'll be seven soon, won't you?'

Thomas looked troubled. 'I'm meant to say "Mother". That's what she tells me I'm to say. But I forget sometimes. And kids at school laugh when I say "Mother". They reckon I should say "Ma". That's what they all say.'

Trust Susannah to make it hard. 'Well, maybe you should say "Ma" at school and "Mother" at home.'

'I do try and say that. It's hard to remember, though.' He looked far more worried than this problem seemed to justify. Amy was sure there must be something else on his mind that he would tell her in his own time.

'Yes, it must be hard, Tommy. I think you'll get used to it, though. Does Ma… Mother know you're here?'

'No. She won't care. She'll think I'm still at school.'

'Well, I suppose it's all right as long as you go home before it gets late. Hold on, I'll just get these last few things off the line then you can help me carry it all back to the house.'

Thomas took one handle of the tin bath that Amy used as a clothes basket, and they made their slow way back to the house while David danced happily around them.

'Thank you, Tommy, that was a big help, you carrying one side. We'll just leave it on the floor for now,' she said as they entered the kitchen. 'I'll get you some milk and biscuits, shall I? I bet you're hungry, boys are always hungry.'

She piled biscuits onto a plate and poured mugs of milk for the three of them, sitting David on the floor to drink his while she took a seat close to Thomas.

'Now, you must tell me all about school. I bet you're learning lots of things. Is Miss Radford a nice teacher?'

'Ye-es,' Thomas said. 'She's quite nice. But she gives you the strap when you do things wrong.'

'That's so you won't do them wrong again, Tommy. That's why teachers strap you. You're a clever boy, you don't get things wrong much, do you?'

'Not much. I did my spelling wrong last week. Miss Radford only growled me and said I should try harder, then she helped me with the hard words. She's quite nice. But…'

'What?' Amy probed, seeing his face grow troubled.

'I told M-Mother about it, and she was really wild. She said I'll disgrace her if I'm dumb at school. What does "disgrace" mean, Amy?'

'That's a hard word to explain. It means… well, it means when someone does bad things and then everyone thinks they're awful. Don't worry, Tommy, you'll never disgrace anyone. Mother only said it because she was annoyed.'

'She said I wasn't going to be a stupid farm boy. She said if I carry on being stupid it'll have to be b-beaten out of me.' He looked plaintively at Amy. 'I didn't mean to do it wrong.'

'Of course you didn't. Mama… Ma… oh, you've got me doing it now, *Mother* didn't mean it. She was just angry.'

'She *did* mean it, she did! She'll make Pa give me a hiding. M-Mother hates me,' he finished in a wail.

'Tommy, no! You mustn't say that. Mother doesn't hate you.'

'She does! She hates me. She said I was a hateful little devil—she said it just yesterday. She said she wished I'd never been born. Mama hates me,' he sobbed.

Amy reached out and tugged him gently from his chair towards her. 'Come on, cuddle up. Climb on my lap, never mind my fat tummy.' She put her arms around him and he laid his head on her breast as his sobs slowly eased. 'There, that's better, isn't it? Tommy, sometimes when grown-ups are tired or annoyed they say things they don't mean. I know it's hard, but you have to learn not to take any notice when they say silly things.'

'Mother and Pa have awful fights sometimes. I hear them through the wall.'

Amy remembered hearing muffled shouts through that same wall. 'Put your head under the pillow when they start. You won't hear them if you do that.'

'They had one last night. Mother said she hated living on the farm. She said Pa shouldn't have made her come. She said she wished she'd never met him. Pa said he wished she never had either.'

The wall wasn't *that* thin. 'Tommy, have you been listening at the wall?' Amy asked.

Thomas's guilty expression was answer enough. 'She said George and me would drive her to distraction if Pa didn't sort us out. She said we were turning into horrible little brutes. She'll make him give me a hiding,' he wailed.

'Shh, Tommy, shh. Pa doesn't really give you many hidings, does he?'

'No,' Thomas admitted. 'But Mother said he will if I get in trouble at school. She said he'll give me a really awful hiding. And... and I got two sums wrong at school today, and Miss Radford hit me with the ruler. See?' He held out his palm and Amy studied it, but there was no sign of any red mark; the strokes must have been very soft. It was not Miss Radford's mild chastisement that had got Thomas in such a state. 'Papa will hate me too!' He lapsed into sobbing once again. Amy held him tightly and kissed the tears as they welled out of his eyes.

'Tommy, Pa will never, ever hate you. And you're not hateful, you mustn't believe that. You're my little brother, and I love you. Pa does too. So does Mother, she's just not so good at showing it.' She brushed a lock of black hair away from his face. 'Do you remember how I used to look after you when you were little?'

'Yes,' Thomas said, his voice muffled against her bodice. 'I remember. But you went away. You came to live here at Uncle Charlie's instead. Why did you do that, Amy?'

How could she begin to explain to a six-year-old? 'I... I just had to.'

'Why did you go away, Amy?' Fresh tears welled up as he gazed at her. 'Was it because I was naughty?'

'Oh, no, Tommy.' She pressed him against her so that he would not see her face. 'It's because *I* was,' she said softly.

Thomas looked at her without understanding. 'I remember once we all went on the big boat up to Auckland. You and me and Mother and George. We went to visit Grandmama and Grandpapa. I didn't like it there. Their house was full of things you weren't allowed to touch. But you weren't there, Amy.'

'No. I had to stay with another lady. I didn't know you remembered all that.'

'I do. We came home and you still weren't there.' He looked confused. 'But then you were there again.'

'That's right. Pa came up to Auckland to fetch me.'

'I don't remember that bit. You were there, then you went away. Can't you come back again, Amy?'

Amy forced herself to smile so that the tears she could feel pricking at her eyes would not upset him. 'No, Tommy. I can't come back. I have to look after Uncle Charlie, you see, and Mal and Davie. Who'd look after them all if I went home?'

'I see.' Thomas looked disappointed. 'Could I come and live here with you?'

'Wouldn't you miss Pa? And what about Georgie?'

'Maybe they could come and live here, too.'

Amy laughed. 'This is only a little house, Tommy. There's no room for a big boy like you, let alone all those others. And anyway, Pa has to look after the farm.'

'But I could sleep in your bed.'

'No you couldn't, Tommy. I have to sleep in Uncle Charlie's bed.' She made herself smile again as she looked at his serious face. 'It's not very easy being little, is it? You know something, darling? Sometimes it's not that easy being a grown-up, either.' She glanced at the clock; it was high time she got the washing folded and dinner underway.

'Tommy, I'm glad you came to see me, and you can come and visit me another day. But you'd better go home now.'

He clung to her. 'I don't want to.'

'Why? Because you're scared Pa will give you a hiding?' Thomas nodded solemnly.

Amy studied him. If she forced him to go off by himself, he might well decide to run off into the bush rather than face the wrath he feared. But what could she do to calm him? Only one thing, she decided.

'I tell you what, Tommy. What say I take you home, and we go and see Pa first. I'll have a talk with Pa, and I promise he won't give you a hiding. Do you trust me?'

'Ye-es,' Thomas said doubtfully, then he gave her a watery smile. 'Yes.'

'Good boy. We'd better take Davie—oh, Davie, what a worried face!' She laughed at the sight of David staring wide-eyed at them. 'Here's us two being all serious, we've got Davie doing it too.' David grinned back when he saw her smile.

After a detour to the milking shed, where Charlie was getting the cows into the yard while Malcolm trailed at his heels, to ask permission for the outing, Amy set off holding a small hand in each of hers.

She made straight for the cow shed, where she knew she would find her father and older brothers.

'Amy! I didn't expect to see you here,' Jack greeted her, standing up from a milking stool and enfolding her in a careful hug. 'You're puffing like a steam engine, girl!' he said in concern as her chest heaved against him.

'It's the walk,' Amy said. 'Everything's a bit of a struggle just now. I'll be all right when I catch my breath.' She paused for a few moments to let her breathing slow. 'Tommy came to see me, Pa. He's worried about something. Tell Pa, Tommy,' she coaxed, holding his hand tightly.

'I got two sums wrong, Pa. Miss Radford hit me with the ruler. I'm sorry.' He looked up at his father with a pleading expression.

'Only two?' Jack laughed. 'That means you must have got a lot of them right, boy. I'm not much good at sums, your sister used to help me with mine. Hey, it's nothing to cry about, Tom.' He patted his little son on the shoulder. As she watched the two of them together, Amy was struck by how much Thomas looked like their father. It occurred to her to wonder whether that was one of the reasons he seemed to attract so large a share of his mother's resentment.

Amy chose her words with care. 'Pa, Tommy thinks Mother will be annoyed with him. He thinks she'll want you to give him a hiding. I told him you wouldn't—I *promised* him you wouldn't. Please tell Tommy that's right.'

Jack gave a heavy sigh. 'It doesn't take much to make her wild with him. Don't worry, Tom, I won't give you a hiding for getting two sums wrong. She can go crook at me instead.'

'Thank you, Pa,' Thomas said, his face breaking into a smile.

Amy left them in each other's company and took David's hand to make her way home. She wished there were not quite so many fences to climb, each of them making her uncomfortable burden stab at her ribs.

'Carry me, Mama,' David begged when they were barely halfway back.

'Oh, Davie, can't you walk? You're very heavy for me, and Mama's tired.'

'Please, Mama.' He held out his arms; Amy sighed and gathered him up. She had to lift him over each fence before clambering over it herself.

Weariness made her clumsier than ever. As she crossed the last fence, she lost her balance and went sprawling on the ground. She tried to stand, then crouched on her hands and knees until the wave of nausea her fall had brought on passed. She clambered to her feet, picked up David and forced herself to walk on.

Black spots began to interfere with her vision as she stumbled up the last hill before the house. She almost tripped on the doorstep, catching herself on the jamb at the last moment. She staggered into the kitchen and let David slip to the floor. 'Time to start making dinner. Ohh, I feel awful, Davie. I wish I could lie down. Mustn't be lazy, though. Mustn't keep Papa waiting.' Amy took a step, and the room tilted alarmingly. She reached out for the nearest chair, but it jumped away from her grasp. She groped wildly for it; there was a crash as the chair tumbled to the floor. Amy fell across it, her belly landing heavily on the edge of the seat. She screamed with pain as she rolled off the chair and onto her back.

Red shafts of agony stabbed at the backs of her eyes. She clutched at her belly, trying to lift herself upright. *It's the baby. The baby's coming. It's too early! I'm going to die.*

229

17

There was a high-pitched wailing echoing around the room. *Stop it*, Amy wanted to cry out, but she had no voice for any sound but inhuman groans. It was David, she knew, howling at the sight of his mother writhing in agony on the floor.

The noise faded away. Amy tried to raise herself to see what David was doing, but the attempt made blackness come more thickly over her vision. She lay back and let the convulsions rack her body as they wished.

There was no sense of time. She did not know how much later it was when a face loomed over her.

'What's going on? It's the child, isn't it? It's started early.' It was Charlie's voice, grating painfully in her head.

Amy nodded, the movement making black dots swim across her eyes.

'I'd better get you into town, then.' He made to lift her. Amy screamed with the pain of being moved.

'No, Charlie,' she forced rasping words out of her tight throat. 'You can't. I'd never bear the trip.'

'Well, what am I supposed to do?' he demanded.

Amy could hear the fear in his voice. *Scared he'll lose his new son.* 'Bring the nurse out here. Bring me Mrs Coulson.'

'I said you weren't going to that woman again. I don't care for her, she's no idea how to speak decently.'

'Please, Charlie, please!' Amy begged, her voice cracking with the effort. 'She'll look after me. She'll make it stop hurting. I'm going to die. I don't want it to hurt when I die.'

'Hush! There's no need to speak like that.' He was silent for a moment. 'All right, you can have the woman. She knows her work, even if she's an interfering bitch. But you can't lie on the floor.' He put one arm under her head and the other under her knees and lifted her easily. After one loud scream, Amy fell into a half-swoon till he had laid her on the bed.

She was aware of Charlie standing over her, but it hurt too much to open her eyes. 'You'll be all right while I'm gone?' he asked. 'The child won't come till the nurse is here?'

'I don't know. I don't think it'll take long. There's blood coming out now, I can feel it. Please hurry, Charlie. But… but where are the boys?'

'Outside. Dave came running down to the cow shed yelling his head off—I couldn't understand a word of it. Mal said he was telling me you were ill. I told them to stay put down there. Shall I take them to your pa's?'

Amy forced herself to think, though thinking made her head hurt. 'Yes, take them over there. Take them now. Bring Mrs Coulson. Bring her soon. Hurry!'

'I'll go like the devil was after me,' he said grimly. A door closed, and Amy knew she was alone again.

Waves of agony came at random, convulsing her body in a way unlike any birth pangs Amy could remember. At times she seemed to be floating above the pain as if it hardly belonged to her; at other times it seemed larger than her body could hold. *You're going to kill me, baby. You and me are going to die together.* Her thoughts travelled their own jumbled route to the other baby she had thought would kill her in the bearing. It hadn't killed her. But she had been in a nursing home then, with a woman who knew what she was doing even if she took pleasure in the cruelty of it. *I wish I could have seen you again before I die, Ann. I wish I could know if you're happy.*

In a kind of calm that settled over her during an interval between bouts of pain, Amy heard the door opening and a woman's light tread coming through the house. *Mrs Coulson? No, it's too soon. Who?*

'Amy?' A voice made thin with apprehension. 'Where are you?'

Susannah. Why her? Amy lay quiet and let Susannah find her own way to the bedroom.

'Oh, here you are.'

The time spent lying very still on the bed had given Amy strength enough to speak. 'What are you doing here, Susannah?'

'I've come to look after you, of course. Your father said to—I wanted to, anyway. You need a woman with you.'

'Where are my boys? Have you brought them with you?'

'You don't want them to see you while you're in this state, do you? You look dreadful.'

'Where are my boys, Susannah?'

'Why?'

'Because I'm going to scream with the pain in a minute, and I don't want to frighten them. Where are they?'

'They're with your father. He said—' Amy's scream interrupted her. When it died away, Susannah was quiet for some time. 'What do you want me to do for you, Amy?' she asked at last, her voice quavering.

'Nothing. Go away.'

'Don't be silly. I can't leave you in this state. Shall I... shall I have a look at you?' She pulled back the covers Charlie had placed over Amy, and gave a little scream. 'There's blood everywhere!'

'I know. Leave me alone. I don't want you touching me.'

'I should undress you or something, but I... I don't want to hurt you.' Susannah covered Amy's limbs again. 'I'll just sit with you, shall I? I'll keep you company till the nurse comes.' She reached for Amy's hand and patted it, but Amy pulled it away.

'I don't want you here, Susannah. I don't want you to watch me dying. I'd sooner be by myself.'

'Now, you mustn't talk like that! There's no need to say such dreadful things. You're not dying—you're a strong, young girl having a baby. You'll be right as rain in no time.'

'What do you know about it?' Amy spat out the words.

'Don't be ridiculous. I've had two children myself, and I think I suffered as much as any woman. That's why I've come to look after you. I'm older than you, I know more about such things.'

'Do you? Have you felt the pain like it was going to split you in half? I've felt that once. It's starting again now.' She tilted her head back to scream the louder, but screaming brought no relief beyond not having to listen to Susannah. The pain died away, but not the memories it dragged up. 'It hurts you till you think you're going to die. Then there's a little baby, and you love her all the more for the pain she cost you. Then they take the baby away. That's what happens. It's no good loving her. They take her away. It's better if you die.'

'Stop that, Amy. Don't say such things. You feel terrible, I know, but it'll pass. You'll feel well again soon.'

'Will I? This is the third baby I've given Charlie. I'm still doing my duty, Susannah. I can't decide I'll stop doing it. I can't tell him two sons is duty enough. Why was it enough for you?'

'It's none of your business. That's between your father and I.'

'Why, Susannah? Why?' Amy persisted.

'Because... because I'm a decent woman,' Susannah snapped. 'I've had my share of that horrible business with men. I didn't choose to do it like you did. I only did it when I had to.'

'I thought I was decent, too. I thought that was part of the bargain. If I married Charlie I'd be decent instead of what you called me. Now he calls me that instead. And I have to go on having babies till I die.'

'Stop talking about dying! Women have babies every day, you're no different. And anyway, you'll be too old to have them one day. You'll only be fruitful till you're forty or so.'

'Till I die,' Amy repeated. 'I'm not good at having babies, for all I get with child so easily. But I've got to keep on having them till I die.'

'Oh, I can't bear to listen to you going on like that! I will leave you alone if that's what you want!' Susannah stormed out of the room, slamming the door after her.

A few screams later she crept back and sat beside Amy again. 'Is it getting worse, Amy?'

'Yes. And it'll get worse than this.' *You're fighting me, baby. Because I fell over and hurt you. You're trying to tear your way out of me instead of giving me time to push properly.*

'I've got to do something! Shall I... I don't know, wash you, maybe?' Her face was twisted with disgust; Amy could see how much the offer had cost her.

'No. You'll hurt me more if you touch me down there. I... I think I'd like a drink of water,' she said, as much to shut Susannah up as from a desire to moisten her cracked lips.

Susannah hurried over to the chest of drawers and filled a glass from the tin of water. Amy lifted her head to sip at it, then fell back against the pillows. She let Susannah take hold of her hand as she waited for the next wave of pain.

At last there came the noise of hooves approaching. 'That must be the nurse!' Susannah said, jumping up from her chair and peering out the window. 'Thank Heavens!'

A moment later Mrs Coulson rushed into the room and put her arms around Amy. 'Poor darling,' she soothed. 'Don't be frightened, sweetheart. I'll have you comfortable in no time. I'll just have a quick look at you, then you can have a nice dose of chloroform.'

She pulled back the covers and raised Amy's dress. 'Mrs Leith, give me a hand to get her undressed, will you?' she asked without turning towards Susannah. 'I'd like you to—' She glanced over her shoulder, and abruptly stopped speaking when she saw Susannah's white face. 'Whatever's wrong with you, woman?' Mrs Coulson asked. 'Haven't you ever seen a child born?'

'No,' Susannah admitted in a faint voice.

'For goodness sake! Who sent you here?'

'My husband... I wanted to come. I came to look after Amy.'

'Oh, yes, I can see that. You'll have been a great help to the girl. Get out, please. If you can't be any use, you can at least keep out from under my feet.'

'But I'm meant to be helping! It's just... it's all so revolting,' Susannah said weakly, looking away from Amy's exposed loins.

'Well, you're not helping. Go and make a cup of tea or something. I'm

233

sure Mr Stewart's feeling the need of one.' Susannah went out, closing the door after her.

'That woman's worse than useless,' Mrs Coulson muttered. 'Never mind, that's her out of the way.' She sat down on the chair beside Amy and lifted the bag she had brought. 'I'd better put you out before I try undressing you. I'll hurt you too much doing it by myself.' She lifted out the chloroform bottle and a pad of cloth.

'Am I going to die, Mrs Coulson?'

'Shh, darling. Of course you're not,' Mrs Coulson said, with a cheerfulness that Amy knew was forced.

'Please tell me the truth. I want to know.'

Mrs Coulson stroked Amy's face. 'It isn't given to us to know the hour of our deaths. But I'll do my best to see that your hour doesn't come for a long time yet.'

Her kindness made Amy let go of her fear. 'What about my baby? It's too early. My baby's going to die, isn't it?'

'You shouldn't talk...' Mrs Coulson began, then she sighed. 'How early? Your husband said about a month.'

'Six weeks.'

'As much as that?' She hesitated before speaking again. 'Well, my dear, anything can happen. But... six weeks early? I'm sorry, darling.' She held the pad over Amy's face.

When Amy was lying still and quiet, Mrs Coulson undressed her. The nurse gave a sharp intake of breath when she untied Amy's drawers and saw the livid bruises across her abdomen. The marks of a heavy boot? The bruises didn't seem quite the right shape for that, but she could not imagine what else might have caused them. So that was what had brought on this untimely labour. Mrs Coulson knew it was going to be difficult for her to speak civilly to Charlie, for all she had promised herself she would.

She fought with the baby till both of them were near exhaustion, but the child was its own enemy far more than it was the nurse's. It seemed to want to fight its way out of Amy's womb, but at the same time tried to cling to its safe home. The nurse's probing soon told her the baby was in the breech position, and as fast as she could tease a little leg free of the tangle of limbs it twisted away from her fingers. But the convulsions of the uterus at last proved stronger than the child within, and it expelled its struggling tenant buttocks first.

The tiny boy weighed barely four pounds, the nurse was sure. He waved his little fists and howled, making no more noise than a kitten.

Mrs Coulson shook her head over him, wrapped him in a blanket and laid him on the bed beside the unconscious Amy after pulling a sheet over Amy's lower body. She did no more than wash the blood off the baby's face. There was no sense disturbing the doomed little creature any more than she had to.

Charlie and Susannah were sitting at the table, Charlie with a half-eaten plate of something Susannah had managed to throw together for him. They both looked up as Mrs Coulson came into the room, each with their own different face of fear.

Susannah gave a small scream. 'Look at your hands!' she gasped. 'They're covered in blood!'

Mrs Coulson looked down. Her hands were indeed thickly coated with dark blood, now drying; she had hardly noticed it till now. 'She always bleeds a lot when she bears. That's one reason it takes her so long to get over it. This time's worse than usual.' She pursed her lips at Susannah. 'Mrs Leith, if you're going to be sick I'll thank you to do it outside. I've no intention of cleaning up after you, and I doubt if Mr Stewart has either.' Susannah looked away shamefacedly.

'Well?' Charlie asked. 'What's happening?'

'If you want to see your new son while he's still living you'd better hurry up about it. He won't be with us for long.'

She turned and made her way back to the bedroom, with Charlie following. Somewhat to Mrs Coulson's surprise, Susannah came along a few moments later. Mrs Coulson eyed her warily, but she seemed in control of herself.

'Here he is,' Mrs Coulson said, turning the blanket down a fraction. 'A beautiful boy. Nothing wrong with him except he's on the wrong side of the womb. Poor, innocent creature,' she murmured, but her eyes shifted to Amy as she spoke.

'There's no hope for him?' Charlie asked.

Mrs Coulson shook her head. 'No. There's nothing I can do for a baby that small except keep him warm and comfortable.'

Charlie stared at Amy lying small and still on the bed. 'How is it with her?'

'I don't know. We'll hope for the best, but I won't be sure till morning. If the bleeding gets worse things won't be good. If she does pull through, the poor child's going to be very weak for a while.'

'What brought it on? Why did she have the boy ahead of time?'

Mrs Coulson stared hard at him. 'I thought you might be able to tell me that, Mr Stewart.'

He looked blankly at her. 'What are you talking about?'

'Her belly's covered in bruises. That's what knocked the baby about so that he decided to come out too early. I'd like to know how she got them.'

She heard Susannah give a sharp intake of breath, but Charlie looked puzzled. 'Bruises?' he repeated. 'How would she have got bruises?' He frowned in thought. 'When I found her she was on the kitchen floor,' he said slowly. 'There was a chair tipped over beside her. She maybe fell on that.'

Well, for all the harshness she was sure he inflicted on the girl, Mrs Coulson could see he was not guilty of that atrocity. The news of Amy's bruises had clearly come as a surprise to him. 'I see,' Mrs Coulson said. 'Yes, that must have been it. Poor child.'

Charlie looked at her through narrowed eyes as he belatedly took in her meaning. 'Did you think I'd done it to her? Kicked my own child out of her?'

Mrs Coulson stared back at him. 'You'd be surprised what some men do to their wives, Mr Stewart. At least I hope you would.' She could see Susannah looking at Charlie with horror in her eyes. And it would do Susannah Leith no harm, Mrs Coulson thought, to consider just what this man she had forced onto her stepdaughter might be capable of doing to the girl.

'You'll want him baptised?' Mrs Coulson asked.

'Aye. I'd best go and fetch the minister.'

'Yes, you'd better. We might need him for your wife as well. But the child mightn't live that long, Mr Stewart,' she said matter-of-factly. 'If I think he's slipping away too fast I'll say the words over him myself. The Lord will listen to me as much as He would to the minister. What do you want him called?'

Charlie stood over his tiny son and reached out to touch him, pulling his big, clumsy hand away when it was still inches from the baby's face. 'Alexander.' He must have had the name picked already, Mrs Coulson knew. 'And John—that's for her pa. Alexander John.' He turned and left the room.

'I should go home,' Susannah said. 'I like to keep an eye on Sophie when she's getting dinner on. I'll stay if you need me, though.'

'I think I can manage without you, thank you,' Mrs Coulson answered shortly.

Susannah took a few steps towards the door, then turned back to Mrs Coulson.

'Do you really think he kicked her?' she asked.

Mrs Coulson grimaced. 'As it happens, I don't. It was my first thought, but I don't think he would have been able to lie that well. Anyway, the man's besotted with the idea of having sons—he wouldn't have risked damaging one of them. He thumps her freely enough the rest of the time, I'm quite sure. You do know that, I suppose.'

'I... I saw a bruise on her face once. She must have annoyed him. I warned her—I told her when she married him she'd have to try hard to please him.'

'Oh, she does that all right,' Mrs Coulson said grimly. 'She breaks her little heart trying to please him. And he's breaking her body to give him sons.'

Susannah moved close to the bed to look at the baby. 'So tiny,' she murmured. 'Such a pretty baby. Poor little thing.' She seemed reluctant to look at the unconscious Amy, but her gaze was drawn to the pale face that had scarcely more colour than the white nightdress below it, her cloud of dark hair spread out on the pillow around her. 'Amy's not going to die, is she?'

'I don't know.' Mrs Coulson stroked the pale face, then studied Susannah's troubled expression. 'I don't think she will,' she said. 'Not this time, anyway. There's still enough strength left in her to bear this. She must have been a healthy girl before she married him. No, this time I think she'll pull through. Maybe the next time, too, and maybe even the time after that. But one of these years it'll be too much for her. One day the bleeding will be too bad, and I'll have no way of stopping it when it is. I'll watch her die in front of me, her lifeblood soaking into a heap of rags. That little body of hers can't put up with too many more of that man's babies ripping it apart.'

'It's men,' Susannah said, her voice shaking. 'They're just... they're like animals. It's all they think about. And women have to suffer.'

Mrs Coulson stared coldly at her. 'Do they?' Who was Susannah Leith to go setting herself up as an expert on suffering? That frame of hers was big-boned enough, for all she carried so little flesh on it, and her husband was little more than average in build. She showed no sign of having been damaged by the mere two children she had borne. 'Some women certainly do.' She tried to will herself to keep silent, but her hurt and indignation were stronger than her self-control. 'Mrs Leith, if you couldn't stand seeing that pretty little face looking back at you across the table every day, couldn't you have found a better husband to bully her into taking?'

Susannah's expression tightened into anger. 'No, I couldn't,' she snapped. 'He was the best I could do for her. She brought it on herself.'

'Did she? She must have committed some dreadful sins to deserve this.' She turned her back on Susannah, lifted the sheet and began mopping up the fresh blood pooling between Amy's thighs. The noise of the door closing told her she was alone with Amy, and with the baby whose cries were already dying away.

It was late the following afternoon before Amy struggled up through the darkness into consciousness.

'How do you feel, darling?' Mrs Coulson asked.

'My head's all thick.'

'Wake up slowly, dear. I've kept you under for a long time, I kept spooning laudanum into you as soon as you stirred. There was no sense letting you wake up straight away.'

I'm alive. Pain hovered at the edge of Amy's awareness, not touching her for the moment but ready to bite when the numbness faded. 'My baby's dead, isn't she?'

'He, darling. Another boy. I'm sorry, sweetheart, we lost him.'

'A boy?' Amy frowned in confusion. 'I thought it was a girl. They took her away.'

'He's with the angels. The poor little fellow struggled hard, but he's where there's no pain now.'

'Dead. My baby's dead.' The words fell flat and heavy in the air between the two women.

Mrs Coulson sat down on the bed and slipped her arm around Amy. 'Come on, darling, have a good cry.'

'I'm not allowed to make a fuss about it. My baby's gone.'

'Who says you can't make a fuss? Don't try and be brave, dear. There'll be time for that when you've got the tears out of the way.'

Amy shook her head. 'I knew I couldn't keep my baby. They told me I'd have to give her away. What's the use making a fuss? It doesn't matter how much I love her. They've taken her away. I'm not allowed to keep her. It's better if you don't love them.'

'You're a bit muddled in the head, aren't you? I think I'd better leave you by yourself for a bit.' She patted Amy on the arm and stood up. 'I won't tell your husband you're awake yet. There'll be no one to see whether you're being brave or not.'

But when she heard the door close, Amy lay dry-eyed and stared at the ceiling. There was a small gap between two of the boards that she could not remember having seen before. It held her eyes as her thoughts wore a groove in her awareness.

My baby's dead. There's no use crying over it. I knew I couldn't keep her. I knew he'd die.

When Frank told Lizzie about Amy's premature labour and the loss of her baby, Lizzie's immediate response was distressed helplessness at being confined to the house by her own pregnancy. That reaction lasted less than a minute; Lizzie did not take easily to feeling helpless.

'I've got to go and see her,' she announced, the determined set of her jaw giving Frank a sinking feeling. They were about to have an argument, and he was probably doomed to lose it.

'But Lizzie, you can't go up there. You don't want to see people now you're big.'

'It's not "people", it's Amy. I've got to go and see her.'

'I don't think you should. You might do yourself harm if you go rushing around like that. And you might get upset if you see her.'

'Don't talk rubbish—how would it do me any harm going for a little ride in the buggy? Anyway, I'll get a lot more upset if I'm stuck here thinking about Amy instead of being able to help her.'

'I don't know, I don't want you wearing yourself out. Amy's got plenty of people looking out for her, she doesn't need you.'

'She *hasn't*, Frank. How would you like to be stuck in a house with Charlie if you were feeling miserable? Aunt Susannah will be hanging around, too, and she'll make Amy feel even worse. I'm going up there myself.'

'No, I don't think I should let you.'

Lizzie gave him an obstinate look. 'How are you going to stop me?'

'Lizzie, don't go making it hard. I don't want to row over this. I'm not taking you and that's that.' He put all the authority he could muster into his voice, but Lizzie did not appear in the least cowed.

'If you won't take me, I'll walk.'

'You can't walk way up there in your state!'

'Drive me, then. That's your choice, Frank.'

'Lizzie!' But Frank was sensible enough to know when he was beaten. He went outside and harnessed the horses to the buggy while Lizzie got the children ready for their unexpected outing.

They pulled up in front of Charlie's cottage after a trip punctuated by resentful looks from Frank and an occasional toss of the head from Lizzie. 'You'd better wait outside,' Lizzie said. 'No, Maudie, stay with Papa. You'll have to keep hold of Joey, Frank, or he'll try and get away.' She plumped Joey on Frank's lap and climbed down from the buggy before Frank had time to help her.

*

239

'Mrs Kelly,' Mrs Coulson said, looking up in surprise from a small pot of milk she was warming on the range. 'I didn't think you were still out and about.'

'I'm not meant to be. I wanted to come and see Amy.'

Mrs Coulson frowned in concern. 'It might upset her, you know. Seeing you swelling and healthy when she's just lost her own little one.'

'Oh.' Lizzie looked crestfallen. 'I didn't think of that. Maybe I shouldn't have come, then.'

'Well, I don't know.' Mrs Coulson thought for a few moments. 'I think perhaps it'll do her more good than harm. She's very fond of you, she's always talking about you and your husband. You might get her to let go a bit, she won't do it for me.'

'Let go? How do you mean?'

Mrs Coulson sighed. 'She's determined to be brave. She keeps going on about how she mustn't make a fuss. Do you know, it's nearly a whole day since I let her wake up and the poor girl still hasn't shed one tear over the baby.'

'Really? Poor Amy. Right, I will go and see her,' Lizzie said resolutely. 'Is that milk for her? I'll take it.' Mrs Coulson poured the warm milk into a mug, and Lizzie carried it off with her.

Amy looked up at Lizzie's approach and felt something close to a smile flit across her face.

'Hello, Lizzie. However did you talk Frank into letting you come out?'

'I've got my ways. How are you?'

Amy looked down at her hands and toyed with the edge of the blanket. 'I'm all right. There's no need for people to fuss over me.'

'We fuss over you because we love you. I do, anyway, and I think that nurse does too.' Lizzie put the mug down on the chair within Amy's reach and sat on the bed. She leaned forward and kissed Amy's cheek. 'I'm sorry,' she said softly.

'Don't be. I'm all right. I'm not making a fuss, am I? I'm not talking about him. That's what everyone wanted me to do last time, just pretend it never happened.'

'There's nothing wrong with mourning your own baby, Amy.'

'What's the point? It won't bring them back. I've had four children and I've lost two of them. I've still got the other two, haven't I? So why should I go bawling over the lost ones? Talk about something else, Lizzie.'

Lizzie kept up the losing battle for a quarter of an hour, but Amy's determination was stronger than hers. At last she rose a little ponderously. 'I'd better go. Joey's probably peed in his nappy by now, and Frank's going to go on enough at me about coming up here without Joey bawling for him.'

Amy nodded. For a moment she was tempted to ask Lizzie to bring Joey in to see her; she had grown very fond of the little boy while tending him during Lizzie's illness. But some instinct warned her it would be hard to cling to her stubborn composure if Joey started winding his chubby little arms around her neck and giving her his soft baby kisses. She turned her face away from Lizzie and stared at the blank wall.

'Did you do any good?' Mrs Coulson asked when Lizzie came back out to the kitchen.

'No,' Lizzie said, pursing her lips in frustration. 'She won't let herself go. I don't know what to do for her.'

'Hmm. I don't think she's going to come right in herself till she grieves properly. He could do it easily enough.' Mrs Coulson made a vague gesture to indicate the absent Charlie. 'If he'd show her a bit of affection she'd melt, I'm sure of it.'

'Might as well try and get blood out of a stone.'

'Exactly. And I'm going home tomorrow. I hate leaving the girl in this state, but her husband's not that pleased to have me here. Young Mrs Leith, the red-headed one, was over today, she said she and the other young Mrs will bring over meals and do the cleaning till our girl's well again. They seem capable enough, so she'll be all right there. I just wish I could get her out of this state she's in.' Mrs Coulson frowned in thought. 'It's very odd, the way she's taking this. She hasn't lost any children, has she? I haven't seen her since little Davie was born. Did she miscarry a baby before this one?'

'No. Amy hasn't miscarried any babies.' The slight emphasis she placed on 'miscarried' struck Mrs Coulson as curious.

'She's been saying some strange things about this baby. Something about not being allowed to keep him. She keeps saying she's not allowed to make a fuss, but I'm sure no one's said that to her. I haven't let her husband in to see her except when I'm there, and no one else would tell her that—I don't know that even he would, come to that. Sometimes she seems to think the baby was a girl, too, even now she's not muddled in her head. What do you think's making her talk like that?'

'I wouldn't know, Mrs Coulson,' Lizzie said, answering rather too quickly. 'I'd better be going now.' Something in her manner made Mrs Coulson look at her sharply. Oh, yes she did. Lizzie Kelly knew something, all right.

Lizzie left the room, and Mrs Coulson stared after her thoughtfully. Was there more to Amy's semi-conscious ramblings than she had assumed? Whatever the guilty secret Jack Leith's family was hiding, Amy's cousin knew as much about it as anyone.

'None of your business,' Mrs Coulson muttered to herself. 'Don't poke your nose into other people's affairs.' But her eyes kept drifting towards the door that led to where Amy lay, while her mind turned over half-formed conjectures.

Frank was walking around Amy's little garden, steadying Joey with one hand and matching his pace to the little boy's uncertain steps while Maudie clung to Frank's free hand.

'Hurry up, Frank, I want to go now,' Lizzie called as she clambered into the buggy.

'So you've had enough outings for today?' Frank said when he had unhitched the horses and started down the track. 'I thought you might want me to take you into town while you're about it, so you could run up and down the street for a bit.'

'Don't be so silly.' Lizzie frowned in thought and did not speak again for some time. Frank shot her a look that was meant to be stern and was met with a glare in return.

Maudie sat between her parents and looked wide-eyed from one to the other. At last she could contain herself no longer. She tugged on Frank's sleeve until he looked down at her. She beckoned to him to lower his head before she spoke in a hoarse whisper.

'Have you been naughty, Papa?' she asked, glancing apprehensively at her mother.

'No, Maudie,' Frank replied in an equally audible whisper. 'Mama's been naughty.' Lizzie looked straight ahead, pretending not to hear either of them, but Frank saw her eyes flick in their direction.

'Oh!' Maudie tried to take in the magnitude of this idea. 'Are you going to give her a smack?'

'I don't know, love,' Frank said solemnly. 'It depends if she keeps on being naughty or not.' A toss of her head was the only response Lizzie made.

Lizzie gathered up the children as soon as they had reached home and Frank had lifted the three of them to the ground. She was about to take them into the house when Frank reached out for her arm.

'Go inside, Maudie,' he told the little girl. 'Go on, don't be nosy,' he added, giving her a small push when she showed more inclination to stay where she was.

'Lizzie,' he said when their only audience was the oblivious Joey, 'don't do that again. I mean it.'

'Don't do what?' Lizzie said indignantly.

'You know what I mean. Don't force me to let you do something I don't want to. I only took you to Amy's because you threatened to go rushing up there by yourself.'

'Don't be so bossy! Anyway, I'm not sick like you keep making out. I'm only having a baby, for goodness sake!'

'Yes, well, you shouldn't really be having this baby, you know. It's only because I couldn't keep my hands off you.' Frank abandoned sternness and slipped an arm around Lizzie's shoulders. 'I worry about you, Lizzie.'

Lizzie relaxed against his arm. 'I didn't exactly try and fight you off, did I? Don't worry about me. There's no need, honestly there's not.'

'Well, will you behave yourself? Take things a bit easy, no more going visiting till the baby's come?'

Lizzie sighed. 'I didn't do her any good going to see her, anyway. I can't give her back her baby, and that's the only thing that would really help. She needs something to love. I might as well have stayed home.'

Frank took this as acquiescence, and was satisfied Lizzie had seen sense. So he was all the more astonished two days later when she announced that she wanted to visit Amy once again.

'Lizzie, I thought we agreed,' Frank said helplessly. 'You said you'd take things easy.'

'No, I didn't. *You* said I would. Shut up a minute and listen. I know I shouldn't be going out, but this is important. I promise if you take me up there once more—just this once—I'll stay home and not complain until the baby's born. Cross my heart I will. Please, Frank,' she begged, taking hold of his hands and looking at him with a pleading expression Frank had no weapon against, especially when he saw tears forming in her eyes.

He sighed. 'If I don't say yes I suppose you'll only threaten to go by yourself again. You'd better mean it, though, Lizzie. No more tricks like this.'

'Of course not. I've promised, haven't I?'

'Yes. And I'll keep you to it.'

When he helped Lizzie into the buggy, Frank was startled to see that she held a small ginger kitten in one hand. 'That's one of Tab's latest litter, isn't it? What are you doing with it?'

'He's a present. Hurry up, I want to be back in time to get lunch on.'

Charlie was filling a jug of water from the rain barrel when they pulled up. 'I'm just going to pop in and see Amy for a minute, Charlie,' Lizzie said. 'We won't stay for a cup of tea, thanks—I see you're just getting water for one,' she added impertinently.

'Those women from next door don't seem to bother fetching the water,' Charlie grumbled. 'What have you got there?' he asked, eyeing the kitten suspiciously.

'This? It's a kitten,' Lizzie said, all wide-eyed innocence. 'I meant to get Frank to tell you—when I was up the other day I saw a couple of mice hanging around your safe.' It was the first Frank had heard of it; and, he suspected, the first the mice had heard of it. 'You want to watch that, Charlie, mice can gnaw right through a safe quick as look at it.'

'Mice?' Charlie echoed in alarm. 'I hadn't noticed any.'

'Oh, you would have noticed them soon enough. So I thought I'd better bring you a cat. We've got plenty. Don't let me keep you talking, I'm sure you're busy,' she said, sweeping past Charlie and into the house.

There were dark rings under Amy's eyes that betrayed sleepless nights, and she looked at Lizzie with a strange, faraway expression. Recognition took several seconds to reach her eyes.

'I didn't expect to see you again so soon, Lizzie,' she said wearily. 'I hope you're not going to try and talk about my babies again. I don't talk about them. I don't make a fuss.'

'I'm not going to talk about anything,' Lizzie said briskly. 'I'm not even staying.' She walked to the bed and kissed Amy's cheek. 'Our Tab's had seven kittens, she can't feed them all properly. You'll be doing me a favour if you take one, it'll save Frank drowning it. Here you are.' She placed the kitten on the blanket over Amy's chest. 'I'll be off, then.' With that, Lizzie was gone as suddenly as she had arrived.

Amy looked down at the tiny kitten. It mewed feebly, with a sound that Amy fought against recognising. It was far too much like the cry of a tiny baby. She reached out to push the kitten away from her, but her fingers brushed against fur as soft as baby's hair.

Almost against her will, her hand stroked the kitten. Its mewing stopped, and the kitten made its laborious way up the blanket towards Amy's face, hooking its claws into the cloth to steady itself as it went. It reached its goal and pressed its nose against Amy's cheek, giving a questioning little miaow. Amy stroked it again and again, feeling the vibration of the purr that was too soft for her ears to catch. A tiny pink tongue reached out and tickled her face as the kitten licked at the salt tears that had begun to trickle down Amy's cheeks.

18

Before she returned home, Mrs Coulson impressed on Amy that she should stay in bed for at least two weeks. But it was less than a week after Alexander's birth and death when Amy announced to Charlie that she was well enough to get up.

'So you'll be able to bring the boys home, Charlie. Could you fetch them today, please?' she asked, ignoring the grinding discomfort she still felt when she moved about. 'I don't want Susannah looking after them. She doesn't like children.'

Charlie took her assertion of good health at face value, and did not need persuading to want his sons back. He collected the boys that same morning. Amy studied them anxiously, but neither child seemed much the worse for their time away from home. David spent the first few days not wanting to let Amy out of his sight, and he climbed onto her lap whenever she sat down for long enough to give him the chance; but he was soon reassured that his mother was not going to become ill again suddenly, nor was he to be sent away next door for some mysterious reason.

David was enraptured at the sight of Amy's kitten sitting on her lap when Charlie brought the boys home.

'Pussy cat!' he said in delight. 'My pussy cat?'

'No, Davie,' Amy said with a smile, ruffling David's curls as she held a possessive hand over the tiny kitten. 'He's my pussy cat. But I'll share him with you. His name's Ginger. Look, I'll show you how to stroke him—you have to be very gentle, because he's so little.' She took hold of David's hand and guided it down Ginger's back, but David did not need to be taught. He touched the kitten with a gentleness that seemed instinctive, and Ginger learned to purr at the sight of David as quickly as he learned to hide under Amy's skirts and out of the reach of anyone's boot if he happened to be in the kitchen when Charlie's heavy tread sounded on the doorstep or Malcolm bounded into the room.

Frank kept an anxious watch over Lizzie as her pregnancy advanced, alternating between looking forward to the new baby's arrival and feeling guilty that there was to another child so soon. Lizzie seemed healthy enough, but it distressed him to see her working as hard as ever while she got bigger and more awkward.

'Do you have to do that, Lizzie?' he asked when he found her scrubbing the kitchen floor one day in her seventh month.

'Yes, I do,' Lizzie said firmly. 'I won't be able to do it at all when I get a bit bigger, but I'm going to make sure it's clean as long as I can manage. I'm not having dirty floors in my house, thank you.'

'Well, maybe I could—'

'No, you couldn't,' Lizzie interrupted. 'You've never scrubbed a floor in your life, there's no need for you to start learning now. Anyway, it's my job. I don't go out ploughing paddocks, do I?'

'No, but I'm not having a baby, am I?'

'Anyone would think you were, you're making such a fuss about this one. It's my third baby, Frank, I should know what I'm doing by now.'

'You know what you're doing, all right. I just wish... oh, I don't know. I wish I could make things easier for you, that's all.'

'I'm not complaining, am I? Stop talking rubbish, Frank. And don't you dare walk on the wet part,' she warned as she returned to her scrubbing with renewed vigour.

Frank did not stop worrying over Lizzie's health until November came at last and with it the arrival of their second daughter. The birth was as uneventful as either of the baby girl's parents could have wished, and for the first time in months Frank could forget his feeling of guilt and indulge in the delight of being a father once again.

'What are you going to call her?' Amy asked when she had admired the tiny girl with her fuzz of brown hair.

'Oh, I've had a lot of trouble with Frank over that,' Lizzie said, smiling fondly at her new daughter. 'We thought... well, I know this sounds a bit soft, but I wasn't really meant to have another baby just yet, so she's sort of a special present for us. So we want her to have both our names.'

'Where's the trouble, then?' Amy said. 'You knew what to call her straight away.'

'Well, yes, but I wanted Frances Elizabeth, and Frank wanted Elizabeth Frances.'

'I see.' Amy smiled knowingly at her cousin. 'She must be Frances Elizabeth, then, if that's what you want.'

She was surprised when Lizzie hesitated in answering. 'Oh, Frank can be silly about things like that. He gets really soft sometimes. So I thought if it means that much to him, and it doesn't really matter... well, she's Elizabeth Frances.'

Amy laughed aloud. 'You mean you let Frank win? That must have given him a shock. And two Lizzies in the one house? Two in the one valley will be a bit much!'

'She won't be Lizzie, that's too confusing. She'll be Beth. And less of your cheek, Mrs Stewart. Anyway, I think Beth's going to be more like Frank. She looks like him, don't you think? Her mouth's just the same as Frank's.'

Amy had never considered Frank's mouth to be at all like the sweet little cupid's bow Beth had, but she humoured Lizzie. 'Yes, she'll probably be just like Frank. I don't think she'll have much hope of bossing anyone around, not with you and Maudie in the house. Maudie even starts telling Davie what to do as soon as she sees him.'

'He lets her get away with it. Joey doesn't take the least bit of notice, so that's good for her.'

'Mmm, it'll teach her to be clever about it, like you are.'

Lizzie pulled a face at Amy but did not bother arguing. 'What have you done with your boys?'

'Frank took Davie as soon as he saw us coming up the road. He's got the three of them out in the paddock with him—Maudie, Davie and Joey all on the one horse! I don't think the horse has really noticed, he's still pulling away at the plough as if there was no one on his back. Davie's smiling all over his face at having a ride on the big horse. Frank's wonderful with children, isn't he?'

'Mmm. That's because he's just a big kid himself. But you're right, he is good with them. I suppose Charlie's got Mal.'

'Yes, he said he'd take him into town today.' Amy sighed. 'Mal always gets excited when Charlie says he can come. He gets in a real grump if he has to stay home with Davie and me—oh, he can be a menace sometimes. Last week Charlie wouldn't take any of us in with him, it was one of those days when he wants to go out by himself. Mal really played up for me. He kicked over the bucket of dirty water when I'd just finished scrubbing, and he knocked a whole tray of biscuits onto the floor because I told him he'd have to wait until Charlie came home before he could have any. Then when I gave him a smack he bit my hand—hard, too.'

'He's a real little brat,' Lizzie said, looking shocked.

'No, he can't help it. It's boring for him when he's stuck with me, and he just loves being with Charlie.'

'Well, he's out of your hair this morning, anyway. You don't look that pleased about it,' Lizzie commented, seeing Amy's worried frown.

'Oh, I'm pleased Charlie's taken him. But sometimes Mal plays up when they go out... well, he usually does, really. He behaves better for

Charlie than for me, but Charlie wants him to be perfect. He forgets Mal's only a little boy still. You can't expect a four-year-old to sit quietly and wait while Charlie's busy at the store or down at the factory. Mal starts running around and knocks things over, or touches things he's not meant to. Half the time he gets a hiding when they come home. He still wants to go out with Charlie the next time, though—it's better to have a hiding than to be left with his boring old mother, I suppose. Charlie's very hard on Mal.'

'Sounds like he needs it,' Lizzie said. 'I bet Charlie gave him a good hiding for biting you.'

'Well, no, he didn't. I didn't tell Charlie,' Amy admitted. 'Mal gets plenty of hidings without me telling on him.' She did not divulge the fear she never quite voiced even to herself: that Malcolm would hate her if she did not do her best to keep him happy. The duty she owed Malcolm seemed much heavier than anything David claimed; loving David had been easy from the day he had been born.

'You've got to be firm with children sometimes,' Lizzie pronounced. 'That's the only trouble with Frank, he's a bit soft. I bet he's letting Maudie get away with murder while I'm stuck in bed. Mind you, Mrs Parsons doesn't stand for any nonsense from Maudie and Joey, so she's keeping them in line. Of course she's a bit bossy, really. I had to tell her off for ordering Frank around, she's been better since then. But she's good with the children.'

'I know it doesn't do to be too soft. I wish Charlie didn't expect so much of Mal, though. Mal can't be perfect, any more than I can.'

'Who says you're not?' Lizzie said indignantly. 'Charlie's got no reason to complain.'

Amy shook her head. 'I don't think Charlie would agree with you, Lizzie. Never mind about me, let's have another look at this pretty little girl. Can I have a hold of her?'

When she visited Lizzie and the newborn Beth, Amy did not know that she herself was already carrying another child. She had barely begun to wonder when her normal bleeding would return when the reason for its over-long absence became obvious; not from any of the signs of a normal pregnancy, but from the painful spasms and heavy, clotted bleeding of a miscarriage.

She told no one of the miscarriage except Charlie; it was his child, and in Amy's eyes he had the right to know of its brief existence and death. It was difficult for her to gauge Charlie's response. She knew he must be disappointed at losing another child, but he showed no more sign of wanting to talk to her about it than he had after Alexander's death. The only comment Charlie made was 'There'll be other bairns'; and once the bleeding from the miscarriage had ceased he set about seeing that there would indeed be others as soon as possible.

Amy did not want to cloud Lizzie's happiness with her own loss, and there was no one else to share her feelings with, her occasional hesitant requests to be allowed to visit the 'interfering' Mrs Coulson being curtly refused. Her ginger kitten seemed to sense her grief, and he was more than usually affectionate while she was mourning the loss of a child she had not even known she was bearing. Ginger's endearing habit of licking away the tears Amy only let herself shed when she was alone made them flow all the more freely.

Frank was unsure whether to be relieved or concerned when Mrs Parsons finished her two weeks of looking after the household and went home. It was a relief to have the house to themselves again; he found Mrs Parsons rather daunting, even after Lizzie had somewhat cowed the nurse by laying down the law to her. But it troubled him to have Lizzie back in her round of cooking and cleaning, with three small children to look after now, especially when he saw how tired she was at the end of each day. She brushed aside Frank's concern, but it did not stop him wishing he could make her life easier.

Lizzie stayed at home with Joey and the month-old Beth while Frank took Maudie into town with him one day for the weekly shopping expedition. Maudie was delighted at having her father to herself, and Frank was glad of his daughter's company as she sat on his lap and prattled away. The trip into town went almost as quickly as when Lizzie was with him.

When he had made his purchases, including the sweets that Maudie cajoled him into buying her, Frank loaded the supplies into the buggy then took Maudie by the hand and headed for the Post and Telegraph Station. They were just about to cross the road when Frank's eye was caught by the tiny display window of Ruatane's watchmaker and jeweller, old Mr Hatfield.

It was some years since Frank had set foot in the shop; his last visit to the jeweller's had been to buy Lizzie's wedding ring more than five years previously. Today his attention was caught by a shaft of sunlight glinting on the contents of the window. In one small corner was a tray of rings, and close beside the rings lay a box with a lining of black velvet that set off to advantage the string of pearls it held. They glowed warmly in the sunlight. Their creamy colour made Frank think of Lizzie's thick mane of hair that was slowly recovering its former length.

'Papa?' Maudie tugged at his arm. 'Can I see, Papa?'

Frank hoisted her up so she could press her nose to the window. 'See the nice necklace, Maudie?'

'Oh, it's *pretty*,' Maudie said, her breath misting the window as she gazed at the pearls. 'Is that for Mama?'

'Do you think Mama would like it?' Frank asked. Maudie nodded vigorously, still staring wide-eyed at the window. 'Yes, I bet she would. It's probably too dear for me.' He turned away from the window, still holding Maudie, but the pearls drew him back. He could almost see himself fastening them around Lizzie's neck. 'Let's have a better look at them. It doesn't cost anything to look, eh?' Frank pushed open the door of Mr Hatfield's shop, setting a bell jangling as he did and making the silver-haired proprietor look up from his high stool behind the counter.

Mr Hatfield was something of an anomaly in Ruatane. His precise mode of speech, and manners that would not have been out of place in any drawing room, set him apart from almost all the other inhabitants, and he chose to keep to himself, not taking any part in the social life of the town. Frank could remember hearing adults speaking over his head when he was a small boy referring to Mr Hatfield as a 'remittance man'. It had been many years before his mother explained the term to Frank, so he could understand that Mr Hatfield had been encouraged to leave England by a family who had sent him a modest allowance ever since to ensure that he would not come back. His mother had hinted there was some sort of scandal behind Mr Hatfield's family's earnest desire that he leave the country, but she had never elaborated, and Frank had slowly come to realise that none of the people who speculated on Mr Hatfield's background had any real idea what his past might have held. The allowance was sufficient for a man to live comfortably on if his needs were simple, and at the same was small enough to make it unlikely he would ever be able to save the fare home.

Some time in the years since he had left England, the remittance man had acquired skills as a watchmaker. Ruatane was too small for much money to be made from such a business, and it was well known in the town that Mr Hatfield used his little shop as much to indulge his hobbies as to supplement his allowance. On entering the shop Frank remembered the few times his father had brought him into it. It had seemed a magician's cave to him then, the shelves lined with arcane instruments and obscure artifacts. Today he could give a name to more of the objects. One of Mr Hatfield's cameras had wandered into the main part of the shop from the small room he called a studio out the back, along with a pile of photographs. Frank recognised a telescope on one shelf, and assumed that some of the lenses stacked around it made up part of the telescope's equipment. There were lumps of various minerals, some polished and some in their natural state. Frank saw chunks of kauri gum among the minerals, some with insects trapped within the clear resin. Other insects, notably a large collection of dragonflies, were arranged in shallow boxes, each insect with a neatly written label below it.

'How do you do, Mr Kelly?' Mr Hatfield said, lowering his jeweller's eyepiece to the workbench before he stood up to shake Frank's hand. 'And this charming young lady must be your daughter? Delighted to meet you, Miss Kelly.'

Maudie, never usually at a loss for words, was nonplussed at being referred to in such terms, as well as being rather overwhelmed by the unfamiliar surroundings. She clung to Frank and pressed her face against his chest.

'Come on, Maudie, don't be shy. This is Mr Hatfield—he took that nice big photo of me and Mama when we got married. Say hello to the man,' Frank coaxed. He persuaded her first to peer at the watchmaker then to smile at him. She held out her little hand and Mr Hatfield shook it very solemnly.

'This is a funny shop,' she told him.

'Thank you, Miss Kelly,' Mr Hatfield answered as if she had paid him a compliment. 'Is there something I can assist you with, Mr Kelly?'

'We want that necklace for Mama,' Maudie put in before Frank had a chance to answer.

'Necklace? Are you interested in the pearls?' There was the hint of a smile in the look he gave Frank, and Frank knew without being told that Mr Hatfield was sure the necklace was too expensive for him.

'Well, I wouldn't mind having a look at them,' Frank said, trying to sound nonchalant as he let Maudie slide to the floor.

Mr Hatfield reached into the window and carefully lifted out the box containing the pearls. 'Yes, rather lovely, aren't they? It's a foolish fancy of mine—I think a jeweller should have some real jewellery in his shop apart from the odd wedding ring. I bought these on a trip to Auckland. I suppose they'll sit in the window forever now, but I do get the pleasure of having something worth displaying. Here, touch it,' he encouraged, holding the necklace out to Frank. 'Run your fingers over the pearls, feel how silky they are. Like a woman's skin,' he said dreamily. Frank looked at him in surprise. As far as he knew Mr Hatfield had never been married, but from the faraway look in his eyes it seemed the pearls conjured up an old memory.

Frank stroked the pearls softly. 'They feel nice. Have a look, Maudie—don't touch, though,' he added hastily, seeing her sticky little fingers reaching out to grab at them. 'How much?' he asked, dragging himself back to reality. Now that he had seen the necklace up close, he was more sure than ever that it must be beyond his means.

'Fifty pounds,' Mr Hatfield said, and Frank suppressed a gasp with difficulty. 'Yes, I know, it's a terrible price. It's what I paid for them, foolish though it was.' He replaced the pearls in their box and put it back in the window.

'I'm sorry,' Frank said. 'That's a bit much for me.'

'But they're for Mama,' Maudie protested.

'No, I can't afford them, Maudie. I'll get something else for Mama. There're lots of nice things in here, there's sure to be something Mama would like.' Frank looked along the counter, wishing a gift would make itself obvious.

'What sum of money did you have in mind to spend, Mr Kelly?' Mr Hatfield asked.

'I didn't have anything in mind,' Frank admitted. 'I just saw that necklace and thought it'd be nice for Lizzie. I want to get her something, though. Let's see.' He struggled to decide how much he could afford to spend, and came to the conclusion that he had no idea. He knew there was enough money coming in to supply the family's needs, including the five pounds a quarter for the bank, but jewellery for Lizzie did not form part of his usual shopping. 'Something small,' he said reluctantly.

'These bangles are quite popular with the young men,' Mr Hatfield suggested, pulling a box of slim silver bangles towards him. 'I believe a good number of the girls in Ruatane are sporting them. They're one and sixpence each.'

Frank picked up a bangle. 'It's quite pretty,' he said, turning the bangle around so that its patterned surface caught the light. 'I think Lizzie would like it. What do you think, Maudie? Would Mama like this?'

Maudie gave the matter serious consideration. 'The beads are nicer. But that's nice, too.'

'All right, I'll take it,' Frank said, trying not to sound disappointed. Lizzie would like the silver bangle, he was sure, and he would enjoy giving it to her. But it was frustrating to be unable to buy her something really beautiful, something that would make her gasp with delight. He gave a last glance towards the window where the pearls lay. Lizzie would gasp if he came home with something like that, all right; but it would be with horror, not pleasure. She would scold him soundly and send him straight back to return it, knowing as well as he did that he could not afford such an extravagant gift. In fact, he realised, even one and sixpence might be more than was sensible.

He reached in his pocket and was dismayed to find he had barely a shilling on him. 'Um, I don't think I can pay for that just now,' he said awkwardly. 'Is it all right if—'

'No trouble at all,' Mr Hatfield assured him. 'I'll send an account at the end of the month.'

'Papa?' Maudie looked wistfully up at Frank and pressed his hand. 'Can I have one too?'

'Aw, heck, Maudie, I don't think I can afford to buy two bangles. And it's a bit much for a little girl like you, I don't know what Mama would say. Do you really want one?'

'Yes,' Maudie said, winding her arms around his leg and squeezing. She gave her father a look that reminded him of Lizzie, and he could almost hear her mind ticking over. 'Or a hair ribbon.'

'A ribbon.' Frank seized on the chance, sure that a length of ribbon would cost no more than a few pence. 'I'll buy you a nice new hair ribbon. We'll go over to Mrs Nichol's as soon as we've finished here.'

'There you are,' Mr Hatfield said, handing Frank a neatly wrapped parcel. 'And a little something for Miss Kelly.' He placed a small piece of polished kauri gum on the surprised Maudie's palm.

'Say thank you,' Frank prompted.

'Thank you,' Maudie said, turning her most winning smile on Mr Hatfield. 'Would you like a kiss?'

Somewhat to Frank's surprise, the elderly jeweller bent down to Maudie's level and offered his cheek for a wet, rather sticky kiss. 'What a delightful little girl,' he said to Frank when he had straightened up again.

'Yes, she's hard to say no to, eh?' Frank agreed. 'She's just like her ma.'

Maudie insisted that no colour but red would do for her ribbon, although the effort Mrs Nichol put in to trying to persuade the three-year-old into a soft pink or blue made Frank wonder if Lizzie would quite approve of scarlet. But letting Maudie choose the wrong coloured ribbon was not going to worry Lizzie overmuch, he was sure.

It was not Maudie's new ribbon that occupied Frank's thoughts as they walked to the Post and Telegraph then headed for home. It was the frustrating awareness that he could not give Lizzie all that he wanted to. He was not sure just what he did want to give her, but it was something more than her daily grind of hard work looking after him and the children. He could feed and clothe her, and keep a roof over her head, but there should be more to life than that. His Lizzie deserved more, whatever the 'more' might be.

But how could he make life better for her? There never seemed to be much money left over after the bills had been paid. He struggled to make the musings that trod the same aimless circuit over and over come to some useful conclusion. Maybe the problem was that he never had more than the vaguest of ideas just how much money he was likely to make in a season, nor how much he would need to spend.

He grasped hold of the thought. Perhaps if he kept a careful note of everything he earned and spent, it would be easier to plan for extra outgoings. The diary he bought every year was scarcely used, with only such momentous events as the births of his children being recorded. Frank resolved that he would start writing every transaction in his diary, down to the threepence he had just spent on Maudie's ribbon. Then he would be able to work out the totals and know how much he would have left over, though he shuddered at the thought of the sums he would have to struggle with. Perhaps if he did that he would be able to buy some nicer things for Lizzie. What would she like? he wondered. Apart from food, the only thing she ever seemed to ask for was the plainest of material to make dresses, and even that not very often. He would have to try and wheedle out of her what things she secretly craved.

He pulled his thoughts up sharply as he realised what a fruitless path he was wandering down. It was all very well deciding to keep a record of what money came in and out; it was a good idea, and he would go ahead with it. But he knew without doing any sums that he did not earn enough to buy Lizzie the things she deserved. Milking twenty cows and selling a potato crop once a year was not going to make him a rich man. But it was all he knew, and all he had to offer. Perhaps he could get more cows? He rejected the idea as soon as it was formed. Twenty were as many as he could milk by himself. It would be different when Joey was older, he thought, brightening for a moment. Once he had a son big enough to help, he would be able to increase the herd.

Of course by that time there would be more children to feed; plenty more, judging by the rate he and Lizzie were producing them. And he did not want to wait until a child not yet two years old was big enough to help before he started making life better for Lizzie.

Maudie, worn out by the excitement of her outing, laid her head in his lap and went to sleep. Frank stroked her fair hair softly and smiled at his daughter, quiet at last. He was lucky. He had Lizzie and he had the children. Lizzie was happy, he knew that. But there must be something more he could do for her. Some way to give her the life she should have. But what? And how?

19

May 1890

The day after Amy had her second miscarriage, barely five months after the first one, Charlie made one of his solitary visits to town.

'You're sure you don't want to take Mal?' Amy asked, not with any great hope of success.

'Not today,' Charlie answered curtly. 'It doesn't suit.'

'I see.' It was no use even to think of arguing.

Amy dreaded the thought of putting up with one of Malcolm's tantrums, especially today when she was still suffering the after-effects of her contractions. The butter-making she had done that morning had made the discomfort even worse. She had to find some way of keeping Malcolm entertained while his father was away; perhaps an outing would at least tire him out.

She hurried outside to catch Charlie before he left, and found him patting Smokey, murmuring into the horse's ear as he adjusted the bridle. Amy was struck by Charlie's almost tender manner; she had certainly never seen anything so close to affection on his face when he looked at her.

He cares a lot more about that horse than he does me. I suppose that's fair, she thought wearily. *The horse does his job—he even likes doing it.*

'Please may I go over to Pa's?' she asked. 'I'd like to take the boys for a visit. I haven't been there for a couple of months.'

'All right,' Charlie said as he mounted. 'Go straight there and back, mind. And be sure you're back in time to get dinner on.'

I've never, ever been back late from anywhere. 'I will.'

'Are you going to tell any of them?' he asked, jerking his head towards Jack's farm. 'About losing another bairn, I mean.'

'No. It's our business, no one else's.'

Charlie nodded his agreement. 'The women are all breeding over there, aren't they?'

'Well, not Susannah. But Sophie and Jane both are, yes.'

'Mmm. Your brothers look pleased about it all.' His mouth worked oddly as he looked at her. Amy was unsure whether he was irritated with her or upset by their loss. Perhaps he was not sure himself.

'Charlie, I… I'm sorry about the baby,' Amy said.

'All right, there's no need to go on with a lot of nonsense,' Charlie said brusquely. 'Don't you go weeping and wailing. There'll be another before long.' He dug in his heels and set off down the road at a trot.

I know there will. That doesn't make it any easier to lose this one. She waved as he rode away, but Charlie did not turn to look back at her.

Amy wrapped some biscuits in a cloth and set off with the two boys. Malcolm ran ahead, darting around as things caught his attention, and Amy was pleased to see him tiring himself out.

'Hurry up, Mama,' he called from a few yards ahead, giving up on the hare he had been chasing.

'No, Mal, you'll just have to wait for me. Mama doesn't feel like hurrying.' If she plodded along at her own pace, the walk was not too uncomfortable. 'Go on, Davie, see if you can catch up with Mal,' she encouraged. David toddled off towards his brother, and Amy noticed how much he had grown in the last few months. David was going to be tall, she could see; perhaps even taller than Malcolm.

Jane greeted her with pleasure, and Dolly (as Doris was universally known) climbed onto Amy's lap and gave her a wet kiss before Jane coaxed all three children into one corner of the kitchen with biscuits to share.

'It's nice to see a different face,' Jane said as she poured tea for them both. 'I can't really get up to the big house now, not that it's very exciting up there. I don't see much of *her.*' A toss of her head and a disapproving scowl indicated the invisible Susannah. Amy hid a smile at how much Jane looked and sounded like Harry as she spoke. 'Your pa's sweet, though, he's always been nice to me.'

'Yes, Pa's lovely,' Amy agreed.

'I'll be glad when this is over,' Jane said, pointing to her swollen belly. 'Nearly two months to go.' She pulled a face. 'I bet Sophie's a size now, she's a couple of weeks ahead of me. I don't think we'll need to send the nurse home between babies. Harry says we should ask for a sale price.' She giggled at the thought, and Amy laughed with her.

'You're having a bit of a rest from having babies?' Jane asked.

'I seem to be,' Amy said, careful to sound nonchalant.

'That's good. I know things are a bit hard for you at home. Harry's often said... well, never mind. Harry talks too much. He's very fond of you, though—so am I.' Jane rose impulsively and kissed Amy on the cheek, then took her chair once more and fussed over pouring a second cup of tea.

Amy squeezed her hand. 'I'm fond of you too, Jane. It's nice to see how happy you and Harry are.'

'Oh, he drives me up the wall half the time!' Jane raised her eyes heavenwards, but her smile belied her words. 'I suppose he'll be just as silly over this baby as he was with Dolly—honestly, you'd think no man had ever fathered a child before. I remember seeing John grinning at him behind his back—I bet John's just as bad now.'

'Probably,' Amy agreed.

Malcolm became fidgety once all the biscuits were eaten, and Amy knew it was time to leave.

'I'd better pop up and see Sophie,' she said. 'She must be getting a bit bored now she's stuck at home.'

'I'm not sure Sophie gets bored.'

'No, I suppose you're right.' Amy sighed. 'Sophie's nice, and she seems to make John happy. But she's a bit... well, she's hard work talking to.'

'Oh, I know,' Jane agreed fervently. 'She smiles and nods, but you can tell she's not taking in a word you say. Still, she must be easy to get on with. I bet they never have any fights.'

'She wouldn't suit Harry,' Amy said daringly.

'Cheeky!' Jane pulled a face at her. 'You're right, my grumpy old husband wouldn't like her at all. Poor old Sophie, though, she has to put up with Madam breathing down her neck all day long. Sophie never seems to mind. If it was me it'd be a different story. Honestly, that Susannah! She used to go on about Harry when I first came to live here—you know, making nasty little remarks the way she does. She called my Harry bad tempered,' Jane said indignantly. 'What a cheek! I gave her a piece of my mind, she never tried that again. Ooh, Harry hates her.'

'That's my fault, I'm afraid.'

'Rubbish! She's just a... well, she's what Harry calls her.'

Malcolm was already standing by the door waiting impatiently. 'Hurry up, Mama. I'm sick of this,' he complained.

'Shh, Mal! Say thank you to Aunt Jane for having you.'

'No.' Malcolm yanked at the door and hauled it open with difficulty, then disappeared through it.

'The door sticks,' Jane grimaced. 'Harry's had dozens of goes at fixing it—he doesn't really know what he's doing, but he won't ask anyone else. At least the roof doesn't leak any more, it used to, did you know?'

'I think I remember hearing that,' Amy said, smiling at the memory.

'Yes, I finally managed to get Harry to fix it when we found it dripping water on Dolly's cradle.'

'I'm sorry Mal was rude, Jane. He always plays up for me.'

Jane dismissed Amy's apologies with a wave of her hand. 'Don't worry. Boys are more trouble than girls, just look at Harry! Oh, don't those two look sweet,' she exclaimed. Amy looked past Jane to see Dolly and David taking turns rocking a miniature cradle that Harry had made for his daughter's doll. 'Why don't you leave Davie here while you go up to the house? It's nice for Dolly to have someone to play with. Oh, you can leave Mal too if you want,' she added without any great show of enthusiasm.

'No, I won't saddle you with him, he'd wear you out. Thanks, Jane, I shouldn't be long with Sophie.'

She hurried off to catch up with Malcolm, who was swinging on Harry's gate. 'Come on, Mal, we're going to see Aunt Sophie now.'

'I want to see Tommy and Georgie.'

'They mightn't be home from school yet. You can see Grandpa, though. And I bet Aunt Sophie's got some yummy cakes to eat, she makes nice things.'

'Don't want to see Aunt Sophie. Where's Grandpa?'

'I don't know, Mal, I suppose he's working somewhere. We'll find him after I've had a little talk with Aunt Sophie. Look, there's Uncle John,' she said, glad of the distraction.

John waved when he saw them, and waited for them to catch him up. He greeted Amy with a kiss and grasped Malcolm around the middle, turned him upside-down and held him wrong way up until the four-year-old squealed in delight. 'I was just popping up to see how Sophie is,' he said. 'She was looking a bit down at lunch-time. She'll be pleased to see you, it'll take her mind off things.'

'She must be getting worn out,' Amy said as she walked beside John, Malcolm scampering around them.

'Well, she doesn't say much, but she's puffing and blowing a lot. Do you think I should tell her to have a lie-down or something?'

'That's a good idea,' said Amy. 'It's not so easy to do that once you've got little ones to look after, but she should try and get the weight off her feet when she can. Have her legs been aching, or anything like that?'

John had just begun to reply as he held the door open for Amy and walked into the kitchen close at her heels, but the words died on his lips. Sophie was on her hands and knees, scrubbing the floor as vigorously as her massive bulk would allow, her face red with exertion.

'What are you doing, Sophie?' John asked.

Sophie looked at him in mild surprise. 'Scrubbing,' she answered simply.

It took John only a moment to recover from his shock. 'Not any more, you're not. Come on, Soph, up you get.' He prised the scrubbing brush from her grip and dropped it into the bucket, then helped Sophie upright and eased her onto a chair. He sat down next to her and took one of Sophie's hands in both of his. 'You shouldn't be doing that stuff,' he told her, concern in his face.

'But it's Thursday. I always scrub on a Thursday,' Sophie said, glancing guiltily at her bucket.

'Amy, tell her she shouldn't,' John appealed.

'John's right, Sophie,' Amy said, taking a seat on the other side. 'It's not good to do heavy things like that. You've got enough to do just moving yourself around.' If Sophie had been plump before she got with child, she was huge now. It was hard to believe she could expand much more in the six weeks she still had to wait till full term. Her chest was heaving as she sat and struggled for breath, and Amy wondered if she would have been able to get up off the floor without John's help.

'You don't want anything to—' Amy began, then remembered Malcolm's presence. 'Why don't you go outside for a bit, Mal? Tommy and Georgie have got a lovely big swing out the back, much better than yours at home. You go and play on that.' Malcolm weighed up the idea for a moment, till the attractions of a swing won against the dubious amusement of listening to adults talk over his head. 'You don't want anything to go wrong with the baby,' Amy went on when Malcolm had gone. 'It's no good wearing yourself out.'

'The floor's dirty,' Sophie said uneasily.

'Let it stay dirty, then. You can always give it a sweep, you don't have to bend for that.'

John watched Sophie anxiously until her breathing steadied. 'I didn't know you were doing this stuff, Sophie. From now on you just leave it all. I don't want you hurting yourself.'

'But…' Sophie's brow furrowed in thought. 'There's the water,' she announced. 'We've got to have water.'

'Sophie!' said Amy. 'Have you been carrying water up from the well?'

'It hasn't rained for a bit, there's none in the barrel,' Sophie said apologetically. 'I've got to get it from the well. I make lots of trips, 'cause I can only carry two buckets at a time.'

Amy turned to her brother. 'John, that's really heavy, hauling buckets of water all that way. You mustn't let her do that.'

She saw John's concern turn into something sterner. 'Where's Susannah?' he asked. 'What's she doing, letting you do this stuff by yourself?'

'Having a lie-down,' Sophie answered, nothing more than acceptance of the fact in her voice.

'A lie-down!' John echoed.

'Yes. She likes a lie-down in the afternoon. She loosens her stays.'

'I'd like to throttle her with her bloody stays,' John said, his eyes smouldering though he did not raise his voice.

'She asked if I'd mind cleaning up while she had a rest. I don't mind scrubbing and doing that other stuff,' Sophie said, staring at John's angry face in confusion. 'I always scrub on a Thursday.'

'Shh, Sophie, it's all right,' John soothed. 'You leave it to me, I'll get things sorted out.' He disentangled his hands from Sophie's, stood and made his way towards the passage door.

Amy got up and followed him halfway up the passage, leaving Sophie at the table. 'John, don't do anything silly.'

'I'm not going to do murder, Amy, don't worry.'

John hammered on the bedroom door, waited a moment, and when there was no response hammered even louder.

'Who's that?' Amy could hear a slight nervousness in Susannah's response, despite the muffling of the door. 'What do you want?'

'I want a word with you, Susannah.' John rattled the door handle, but made no attempt to turn it.

'You can't come in,' Susannah called. 'Wait a minute, I'm not dressed.'

There was the sound of rapid movement within the room, then Susannah opened the door a fraction and peered around it, clutching her dressing-gown closed with her free hand. 'Well?' she said, managing to maintain a certain haughtiness despite the indignity of the situation. 'What are you making such a fuss about?'

'What the hell do you mean making Sophie do all the work while she's in this state?' John demanded. 'There's the poor girl hardly able to drag herself around, and you've got her on her hands and knees scrubbing the floor!'

'I didn't tell her to do it! I just told her to tidy things up a bit. How was I to know she'd start scrubbing? I don't see that I can be blamed if the girl's silly enough to do that sort of thing.'

'She's good-natured and willing, and you've ordered her about ever since I brought her home,' John shot back. 'Who did you think was fetching the water? Did you think it came up from the well by itself?'

'Why should I have to do everything? It won't do her any harm to fetch a bit of water. She's carrying far too much weight, that's why she gets tired. It'll do her good to get a bit of exercise.'

'Exercise!' John spat the word. 'My poor Sophie making herself ill, and you're sitting on your backside doing nothing.'

'Don't use such language to me! It's none of your business how I spend my time. Go away.' Susannah made to close the door, but John interposed his body in the doorway, pushed the door open and went into the room. Amy crept further down the passage so that she could see into the bedroom.

'It's my bloody business all right when I see my wife working like a servant for you, you lazy bitch!'

'How dare you speak to me like that! Get out of my bedroom. Go on, get out of here.' Susannah made a little movement of her hands as if she were about to push John away, then appeared to think better of it and instead took a step backwards. 'Get out,' she repeated, but Amy heard a tightness in her voice that revealed fear. 'Where's your father? I want to speak to him.'

'Never mind about Pa. This is between you and me. I won't put up with it, Susannah. I won't let you treat Sophie like that. You've been a bitch to my sister, you're not going to be a bitch to my wife. You're going to do your share.' He took a step towards Susannah. 'You're going to—'

He was interrupted by a shrill scream from Susannah. 'Don't touch me! Get away from me!' She scurried across the room so that the bed was between them, letting her dressing-gown gape open as she ran, revealing the top of her camisole with the corset pressing against it. 'Go away!' she cried.

Amy rushed into the room and made a grab at John's arm. 'John, you mustn't. Leave Susannah alone. Come out of here.'

'What's going on?' Amy heard a voice from the passage, and turned to see Jack standing in the doorway. 'I could hear you lot shouting from halfway up the hill, and Sophie's in the kitchen saying you're all killing one another.'

'Jack, tell him to leave me alone,' Susannah said, still wild-eyed but no longer terrified now that her husband had appeared. 'He burst in here and started abusing me—he used the most awful language—he's gone quite mad.'

'What are you doing, boy?' Jack asked. 'Susannah, you're not even dressed properly.' Susannah looked down at her gaping dressing-gown and snatched it closed, tying it hastily. 'You've no business in here,' Jack told his son.

'That bitch should—'

'There, you see?' Susannah demanded. 'He's doing it again—in front of you, too. Make him stop. Make him go away.'

'That's enough of that talk, boy,' Jack said. 'Will one of you tell me what the hell is going on?'

John took a deep breath and spoke more calmly. 'I came up to the house to see how Sophie was—I thought she looked a bit weary this morning. I got here and found her on her hands and knees scrubbing the floor because *she*,' he shot a venomous look at Susannah, and she glared back, 'told her she should clean the place up. I got Sophie talking, and I found out she's been doing all the work—'

'She has not!' Susannah interrupted, but John went on as if she had not spoken.

'While Susannah's done nothing. Sophie's been hauling the water every day! The state she's in, Pa, and she's been doing that. And then I find out this b… this woman's having a lie-down, if you please!'

'Is this true, Susannah?' Jack asked.

'Why shouldn't I have a lie-down? I've the most awful headache. And I'm *not* going to haul water like a servant! If he doesn't want Sophie to do it he can fetch the water himself. I don't see why Sophie can't help me with the work, no one ever gave me much help when I was in her condition.' Tears started from her eyes. 'You dragged me to this awful place. You expect me to work like a slave—you want me to be like some rough farm girl. Now you won't even stand up for me against them all. Everyone's against me. You all hate me!'

'No one hates you, Susannah,' Jack said wearily.

'I do,' John put in. 'She's caused nothing but trouble since the day—'

'No one asked for your opinion,' Jack interrupted. 'And you can treat my wife with a bit of respect. There's no need to come bursting into my bedroom when she's barely decent.'

'No,' John said. 'She doesn't deserve respect.'

'I'm your father, boy. I expect you to do what I say. Get out of here.'

'I'm going.' John made to leave, then turned back to his father. 'Maybe I shouldn't have come in here after her, I'll grant you that. But I'm not going to put up with how she's been treating Sophie. If you won't make her do her share I'll… well, it just won't get done. And that's that.'

'Right, you've said your piece. Out you get.'

'Come on, John,' Amy encouraged. She pulled at his arm. 'Are you coming, Pa?'

Jack turned to look at Susannah, who had sunk into a chair, weak with relief. 'Not just yet.'

'Leave me alone, Jack,' said Susannah. 'My nerves are in a dreadful state. I'll have to close the curtains and lie down in the dark until my head stops throbbing.'

'That'll have to wait,' Jack said. 'We need to have a talk first, Susannah.'

Susannah shot him a resentful look. 'I thought at least you might take my part—though goodness knows you never have before. I suppose you're going to abuse me now, like your brute of a son.'

'No, I'm not going to abuse you. Out you get, you two,' he said over his shoulder to John and Amy, who were looking at him from the doorway. 'This is private.' He closed the door firmly on his audience.

That was a funny sort of visit, Amy mused as she made her way home with her sons. *I'm sure we never used to fight all the time before Susannah came. I don't think I've ever seen John in such a state.*

Charlie was late home from town, as he often was after his solitary outings. Amy gave the children most of their dinner before he came home. He was so late that she had time to get the bread dough mixed and kneaded for the morning baking after getting Malcolm and David ready for bed. By the time Charlie finally arrived, she had the boys sitting at the table in their nightshirts, hair brushed and faces washed as they waited for their father's arrival and the chance to eat their pudding.

'Did you have a nice time in town?' Amy asked as she dished up the food.

'Passable,' he answered. 'These two behave themselves?' he asked, glancing at his sons. The boys, to Amy's relief, had been tired out enough by their outing to sit quietly at the table, according to Charlie's rules for the behaviour of children.

'Yes, they were both good boys,' said Amy.

She studied Charlie as he ate, trying to gauge whether or not he was drunk. He smelt of beer and more than a whiff of gin, but she soon decided he was sober, much to her relief. He went through to the parlour when he had finished eating. Amy stacked the dishes on the bench while the boys finished off the last of the pudding.

'Time for bed, you two,' she said. 'Come and say good night to Papa.' She picked up David and carried him into the parlour, while Malcolm went in ahead of her.

'Good night, Papa,' Malcolm said. Amy smiled to see him thrust out his hand to have it shaken. Malcolm was always so eager to seem grown up.

''Night, boy,' Charlie said, shaking the outstretched hand. He watched Malcolm go off to his bedroom with a look of satisfaction, and Amy did not distract him for a few moments.

'Kiss Papa good night,' she said, carrying David over to his father's chair. She leaned across Charlie to bring David within kissing distance, trying not to wrinkle her nose at the unpleasant smell thus brought so close to her. It was the smell he usually carried home from town, and

Amy had never quite managed to make it out. There was the beer and gin she had already noted, along with an acrid smell of sweat that surprised her when she considered it. He seemed to have worked up as much of a sweat on his outing as he did when working on the farm, and although Amy had never spent an afternoon drinking in a hotel she did not think it would be a place of great exertion.

But there was another element in the blend, one she could not identify; no, two of them. Both seemed familiar, and one made her shudder a little, at an unpleasant association that she could not grasp hold of. What was that smell?

David pressed his lips to a part of his father's cheek not covered with beard, but he screwed up his little face as he did so. 'Pooh! You smell funny, Papa.' He closed his eyes tightly for a moment, then opened them wide and smiled at having solved the riddle. 'You smell like a lady!'

'Stop talking rubbish,' Charlie growled. 'And that's enough of all this kissing me like you were a baby.'

He made to push David from him, but Amy had already snatched the child away. She turned from Charlie, knowing that her face would betray what she had just realized.

'Out of the mouths of babes and sucklings.' That had been one of her grandmother's sayings, usually uttered when Amy came out with something unexpected. The missing elements of that smell were now so obvious that she wondered at her stupidity in not recognising them before. Beer and gin, that was easy. And sweat; he had been working hard, all right, though not at any honest labour. But now she knew what made up the whole: cheap perfume that accentuated rather than hid the smell that had made her shudder. It was the smell of their bed after Charlie had mounted her.

A woman! He's been with another woman! 'Lady,' David had said, but that was not quite the right word. It would not have been a 'lady' that Charlie had found to drink gin with and roll among dirty sheets. He had been with a whore.

She schooled her face into a bland expression, and turned back to Charlie. He was staring at her; she returned his look as if nothing out of the ordinary had happened.

'What a silly thing to say, Davie! Come on, I'll put you to bed so you won't annoy Papa with your nonsense.' She even managed a small laugh.

When she had seen both boys settled in their bedrooms, she walked briskly through the parlour. 'I'm going to bed now, Charlie,' she said, still careful to sound untroubled. 'I'm a bit tired, I don't think I'll do any sewing tonight.'

'Please yourself,' he grunted in reply.

Once safely out of sight of Charlie and the boys, Amy dropped her rigid self-control. She caught sight of herself in the mirror, white-lipped and eyes wide. *Whore. Whore. Whore.* The name Susannah and Charlie had both flung at her echoed in her mind.

Amy moved mechanically, and was vaguely surprised to find herself in her nightdress and lying in bed. She stared up at the ceiling, clenching and unclenching her fists until she realised what she was doing and forced herself to relax her aching hands.

Anger was not something Amy had allowed herself to feel for many years, and the strength of her emotion frightened her. She wanted to smash something; preferably something Charlie valued. She wanted to shout at him; to hurl back some of the abuse he had heaped on her over the miserable years she had spent with him, trying so desperately to please him, trying vainly to earn his respect since affection was not to be hoped for. She thought back over those mysterious outings he had made over the years, and remembered with startling clarity the first of them: it had been the morning after Malcolm turned six weeks old, when she had had to do her duty and had been unable to hide the agony it gave her. 'Useless bitch.' She heard the words again, felt once more the hurt of them. And he had left her alone with Malcolm, the places where she had been torn still throbbing from his thrusts, while he diverted himself with a whore.

But she could not afford to feel anger. She gradually became calmer as the reality of the situation pressed in on her. He was free to do what he wanted. He had been free to do as he wished with her since the day she had married him, and his betrayal did not change that. He called her a whore for her sin with Jimmy, but now that she had discovered his faithlessness the only thing she could do was pretend to be as ignorant as ever. If she confronted him with what she knew he would beat her, perhaps using the stick that leaned against one wall of their bedroom, and then order her not to speak of it again. She could at least save herself the beating if she kept silent.

She heard him moving about in the parlour, and knew he would soon come to bed. Another flash of anger shook her, followed by a stab of fear. He was going to come into the room and climb into bed with her. What if he chose that night to mount her? *I can't. I can't pretend not to know. Not when he still smells of another woman.* Disgust was a bitter taste in her mouth at the idea of having him thrust that thing inside her when it had so recently been in a whore.

It suddenly struck her that it was not going to happen. Charlie could only manage to take out his lust on her once or twice a week, and even then he sometimes had to admit defeat and roll off her exhausted but unsatisfied. He had spent the afternoon with a whore; that was a guarantee of an undisturbed night for his wife.

Amy closed her eyes and pretended to be asleep when Charlie came to bed, while her mind turned the puzzle over and over. But when she at last dropped off into genuine, if uneasy, slumber she had still not decided what emotion she felt most strongly at the idea of Charlie with a whore. Was it anger? Or hurt? Or (a small voice whispered in her head) relief?

20

July – November 1890

The Leith family gained two new members that July. Early in the month Sophie gave birth to a sturdy boy for whom no name but John, after his father and grandfather, was considered. To avoid the confusion of three generations in the house with the same name, the youngest John was from the beginning referred to as 'Baby' by the rest of the family.

The nurse did not have to wait two weeks for her next patient to need her; Jane's baby decided to come a week early, so that there was a mere nine days between the two cousins. If Harry was disappointed at having a second daughter he showed no sign of it to those around him, declaring staunchly, 'There's nothing wrong with girls, there're plenty of boys around here, anyway.'

There should have been three new grandchildren for Jack that year, but it was not to be. Amy had her third miscarriage late in July, and in September she had several days of bleeding that seemed too heavy for a normal monthly flow, accompanied by painful cramps. She was not sure if it should be counted as yet another miscarriage, but whether or not it meant another dead baby the loss of blood left her weary and dejected.

Every miscarriage left Amy a little weaker, and getting through her daily tasks was becoming more of a struggle. Often she would have to stop for a few seconds and gather strength to go on with heavy tasks. Sometimes she lost awareness of what was going on around her for a moment or two, and the resulting lack of concentration earned her many slaps when she did not respond quickly enough to Charlie's biddings.

She hated telling him about the miscarriages, but she felt it was his right to know. Each time he looked grimmer and more irritable, though he said little.

After the ordeal of telling Charlie, she wanted to hide from the sorrow of another lost baby, not talk to anyone else about it. Lizzie noticed Amy's increasingly wan appearance, but her attempts at probing for the reason were met with assurances that nothing was wrong, that Amy was just 'tired'.

On a mild day in early November, Frank was driving the family home from their weekly trip to the store, having with difficulty curtailed a long discussion between Lizzie and the storekeeper's wife, when Lizzie tapped his arm as they passed the Royal Hotel.

'Look at that,' she said. 'There's Charlie going into the hotel. In the middle of the day! Isn't that disgraceful?'

Frank followed Lizzie's disapproving stare. Charlie had tied his horse to a hitching rail outside the hotel and was making his way up an alley. The path led to stairs at the rear of the hotel, giving access to the upper floor. With a start, Frank realised just where Charlie was heading.

'Well, I do think that's shocking,' Lizzie declared. 'He should be home working—he could give Amy a hand with a few things, too, instead of wandering off by himself. Do you know, she has to chop her own kindling half the time? She says he doesn't think of it and she doesn't like to bother him. And Mal wears her out with his nonsense, too, it wouldn't hurt Charlie to cart him into town even if he won't take Amy. Fancy him going out drinking! He should be ashamed of himself.'

'Shh, Lizzie,' Frank said, looking around to see if anyone was within hearing distance.

'I don't see why you're shushing me,' Lizzie said, making no attempt to keep her voice down. 'It's not me parading about drinking in broad daylight. And Amy's not even very well. All he thinks about is his own comfort. You'd think he could make do with a bit of beer at home.'

'It's not beer,' Frank said quietly.

'Well, gin or whisky or whatever it is.'

'No, it's not drink at all—well, maybe he drinks a bit up there, I don't know.' Frank glanced at Maudie and Joey on the rear seat of the buggy, but they were too busy sharing out their haul of sweets to take any notice of the adult conversation. 'Men don't go round the back and upstairs at the Royal for a drink.'

'What do they go there for, then?'

'It's... well, there are women there,' Frank said half under his breath.

Lizzie frowned at him in puzzlement, then her eyes grew wide. 'Women?' she echoed. 'You mean *whores?*' She mouthed the word silently.

Frank nodded. 'That's right.'

Lizzie opened and closed her mouth several times without saying anything. It was so unusual to see Lizzie lost for words that Frank could not quite hide a smile. They were out of town and rattling along the beach before Lizzie had regained her composure.

'Well,' she said at last. 'Well, I never. Women like that, right there in the main street. I never would have thought—' She broke off in mid sentence and stared at Frank through narrowed eyes. 'You seem to know an awful lot about it all.'

'Me?' Frank laughed aloud as he caught her meaning. 'Hey, don't go looking at me like that, Lizzie. I've never been up there.' He shifted the

269

reins into one hand so that he could slip one arm around Lizzie as she balanced Beth on her lap, letting the horses slow to a walk as he did so. 'I thought that was pretty obvious when we got married,' he murmured in her ear, thinking back to the fears that had so racked him before his wedding with the detached amusement years of happy marriage gave.

'You sounded quite an expert on those women,' Lizzie said, but there was no real suspicion in her tone. Frank was sure she was remembering his first clumsy attempts on her virginity.

'Well, men talk among themselves. You can't help picking up things like that in the hay paddock or whatever.' He gave her a squeeze. 'Lizzie,' he whispered, 'there's never been anyone else, you should know that. Why would I ever have bothered with other women when I had you to look forward to?'

'Oh, I don't know. Never mind about that, I was being silly.' Lizzie looked back over her shoulder in the direction of Ruatane. 'Why on earth would Charlie want to go to a place like that?'

Frank loosed his hold on Lizzie to urge the horses into a trot as he considered her question. Amy wasn't his Lizzie, but she was pretty and sweet-natured. And it was obvious she put everything she had into trying to please Charlie; he must be hard to please if that wasn't enough for him.

He glanced around at his family with a warm feeling of satisfaction. There was no one else like his Lizzie, but Charlie surely had nothing to complain about with his own wife and sons. 'I don't know, Lizzie,' Frank said. 'I can't imagine why.'

'These buttonholes are a beggar,' Lizzie complained as she knotted a fresh length of white cotton. 'That last one came out a bit funny. Never mind, it won't show under your jacket.' She stabbed the needle into the cuff of the new shirt she was making for Frank. 'Amy's always been so fussy about things like that, if she did a buttonhole that didn't look right she'd unpick it and start again, even if it was just for Charlie—as if he'd even notice. He wouldn't be a bit grateful, anyway. Ooh, I had a hard time being polite to him yesterday, after what we saw him up to in town the other day.' She pulled a face.

'I know. The filthy look you gave him after church—you weren't exactly polite, Lizzie.'

'Well, I didn't say anything, did I? When I think of him going to that place—whorehouse, did you say it's called?'

'So I've heard,' Frank said. 'I wouldn't know, really.' He turned his attention back to the magazine he was reading as he and Lizzie sat close together on the sofa, sharing the lamplight and each other's warmth.

'I had to be careful not to let on to Amy what I was so annoyed with Charlie about, too. Not that I had much chance to talk to her, that grumpy old so-and-so always makes her rush away.'

'You don't think she knows about him going there?' Frank asked idly, not lifting his eyes from the page.'

'Of course not! She wouldn't put up with that.'

'What could she do about it?'

'She could tell him off, for a start. Tell him he wasn't to go back there.'

Lizzie's indignation had run away with her usual good sense. 'Could she really, Lizzie? I don't think Amy does much telling in that house.'

Lizzie looked deflated. 'No, you're right—she's too scared of him for that. Well, I wouldn't put up with it.'

'You won't have to.' Frank gave her arm a quick squeeze before trying to find his lost place on the magazine page.

'Amy's very pale lately, don't you think?' Lizzie asked. She had been musing off and on over Amy's pallor and air of distraction since seeing her the previous morning.

'Mmm?' Frank looked up from the magazine, abandoning his attempt to concentrate on it. He thought back to how Amy had appeared at church, but Lizzie was right: Charlie had dragged her away too quickly for Frank to take much notice of her. Amy certainly did not have Lizzie's air of robust good health. 'I suppose she does a bit. Do you think she's sick or something? Maybe she's got a baby on the way.'

Lizzie shook her head. 'No. She would have told me if she was—I thought she would've been with child again by now, but I'm glad she's having a rest from it. I don't know, she just doesn't look right. I suppose she might be pining over the baby that died.'

'She needs to have another one, eh? Take her mind off the one she lost.'

'That's what people always say,' Lizzie said pensively. 'If a woman has another baby she forgets all about losing one. I don't think it's that simple, you know. Not for someone like Amy, anyway—she feels things harder than other people. Poor old Amy.'

Frank looked at Lizzie in surprise, wondering what had suddenly made her sound so sad. 'Are you really worried about Amy? What do you think's wrong with her?'

'Oh, nothing,' Lizzie said, briskly matter-of-fact again. 'Amy's got a lot to put up with, that's all. Sometimes I get upset about it because it's not fair. What are you reading, anyway? You've had your nose stuck in that magazine for ages.'

For a moment Frank almost felt that Lizzie was trying to distract him by changing the subject, but he was willing enough to be distracted. 'Your pa's been giving me these magazines when he's finished with them for years, but I've only started reading them properly the last few months. This one's really interesting. It's about these cows—Jerseys, they're called—do you want to have a look?' He held his open magazine out towards Lizzie.

'Cows?' Lizzie said in amazement. 'Don't you have enough to do with cows every day without reading about them?'

'Not cows like this. Have a look at them.' He placed the magazine on her lap. Lizzie gave an exaggerated sigh, pushed her sewing to one side and studied the picture.

'Oh, they're pretty!' she exclaimed. 'Not like ordinary cows at all. They're a bit thin, though. Are they healthy?'

'They must be. I was reading this bit down here,' Frank traced his finger down the page until he found what he was looking for. 'Here it is—look at how much milk they produce. About four gallons a day each—that's about the same as the Shorthorns. But it's got more cream in it than any other sort of cow gives—see, it says that over here. You can get over five parts in a hundred butterfat.'

'Is that a lot?'

'Well, it's more than our old Shorthorns give. They reckon here that Shorthorns give about four parts in a hundred, but that's for the best Shorthorns, not my old mongrels. Shall I have a go at working out how much more it'd be?'

'No, don't worry about it. Take your magazine back, Frank, I want to get these buttonholes finished, then you'll be able to wear this shirt tomorrow.'

The germ of an idea was starting to form in Frank's mind. If these fancy cows produced milk so much richer than he got from his Shorthorns, a herd of Jerseys the same size as Frank's would deliver far more butterfat, and thus more money. And it would not be too many cows for one man to milk. 'I think I will work it out, Lizzie.'

He fetched his diary from the bedroom, careful not to wake Beth who was sleeping peacefully in her cradle. 'Have you seen my pencil?' he asked when he was back in the parlour.

'I tidied it away somewhere. Look in the drawer under the window.'

'I looked there. That's where I left it.'

'No, you didn't. You left it lying on the dressing table, that's why I tidied it away.'

'Where did you put it, then?'

'Oh, I don't know, Frank. I'll find it tomorrow, I'm busy now with this sewing.'

'Don't worry, I'll find it.' Frank crossed the passage to the bedroom again and rummaged around in several drawers until he seized on the missing pencil and carried it back to the parlour. 'Found it!' he announced.

'Where?'

'In the drawer you said,' Frank admitted. Lizzie glared at him, but without any real wrath, and returned to her sewing while Frank began writing figures on a blank page in his diary.

In the few minutes that followed, the silence was broken only by occasional sighs from Frank that gradually grew deeper and deeper. He glanced at Lizzie from time to time, but she stitched away determinedly, not meeting his eyes, till at last Frank had to admit defeat.

'Could you give me a hand with this, Lizzie?' he asked.

'No, I couldn't,' Lizzie said sharply. 'I told you, I'm busy. Stop going on about those cows, for goodness sake!'

'Aw, go on.' Frank slipped his arm around her and gave her a squeeze.

Lizzie held herself stiff for a moment, then gave a sigh and relaxed into his hold. 'All right, I haven't a hope of concentrating on this with you going on. What do you want?'

'I'm trying to work out how much money I'd get from all the cream a herd of these Jerseys would give, but it's all full of so many pence a pound and all that. I can't do it by myself.'

Lizzie gave him an apprehensive look. 'I don't think I'll be much help. I was never much good at sums.'

'Neither was I. That's why I need you to help.'

'No, honestly, Frank, I'm hopeless at them. Adding up and things, that's easy enough, but I hate those really hard sums with lots of things to multiply and stuff. I think Miss Evans must have worn a whole strap out on me, trying to get me to do them properly.'

'She must have worn out two on me, then. She used to be nice about it, you know. Sometimes she'd keep me behind after school and have a little talk about sums and things. I remember her saying, "Frank, I'm sure you could do this work if you'd only try and concentrate. You'd have no trouble at all if you stopped dreaming and took more notice of your lessons."' He pulled a rueful face at the memory. 'Then she'd pull out the strap and get stuck into me.'

'Humph! She never used to bother saying all that to me. She'd just get straight into giving me the strap. Just for getting a few stupid sums wrong! And for talking, too, she was always going on about talking. "Lizzie Leith, I've told you before about talking in class. Come out to the front." As if there's any harm in talking! I think she enjoyed it.'

'She must have got sick of strapping you for talking, she would've had to do it every day,' Frank said. 'I don't think she enjoyed it really, though. She used to look quite sad sometimes when she did it to me.' He grimaced. 'And sometimes Pa would find out I'd got in trouble at school, then he'd give me a real hiding.'

'Why'd he do that?' Lizzie asked.

Frank slid away from her gaze as he recalled the unpleasant memory. 'He used to say no son of his was going to be an idiot. He reckoned I'd remember my sums better if he beat a bit of sense into me.'

'That's not fair! Giving you a hiding when you'd already got the strap! Honestly, people can be so mean.'

Frank laughed at the sight of Lizzie with her eyes flashing. 'Well, you can't do anything about it now. Pa's too far away for you to give him a piece of your mind. Let's have a go at these sums, eh? With the two of us on the job we should be able to muddle through it, even if neither of us are much good.'

Lizzie still looked reluctant. 'It's Amy you should be getting to help you, really. She was always good at sums. Maybe you should wait until she comes around some time.'

'I don't *want* Amy to help me. I want *you* to. I want us to do this together, Lizzie. It's important.'

'All right, don't get in a state about it,' Lizzie said in surprise. 'I'll have a go.' She gave him a sly grin. 'Shall I go and get one of your belts? You might be better at doing the sums if I stand over you and threaten you with it.'

Frank grinned back at her. 'You could try. Of course I might just take it off you and teach you how to be a good, meek little wife.'

'You'd only try it the once,' said Lizzie. 'Forget about the belt, then, I'll just have to trust you to behave. Here, pass that diary over so I can have a go.'

Accompanied by much head-scratching and pencil-chewing, they had soon covered several pages of the diary with sums, most of them crossed out. 'I think that's the answer,' Lizzie said at last. 'Five hundred pounds of fat a year—that's the hard part, eh? I hate those long division things.'

'Mmm, do you think we divided the right bits into each other?'

'Well, we worked it out all the different ways and that was the only one that ended up with a sensible answer.'

'And then we had to times it by the sevenpence a pound the factory pays and change it from pence into pounds and shillings—that was awful. I wonder who decided to make it so hard, you know, with twelve pence in a shilling and twenty shillings in a pound.'

Lizzie looked blank. 'How else could it be?'

'Oh, I don't know, just so's it worked out easier. Don't worry about it, no one's going to change the way money works just to make it easier for us.' He studied their hard-won answers with interest. 'So that's about six shillings a week, and fifteen pounds in a year from one cow. Three hundred pounds for twenty cows. That's a lot! It's just about twice what I get now. I bet those cows cost a lot to buy.'

'Mmm, the people who have that sort of cow must be well-off.' Lizzie closed the diary and put it on the floor, then snuggled into the crook of Frank's arm. 'Never mind, Frank, we've got enough money. Don't go thinking about things you can't have.'

'I wonder if they advertise cows like that in the paper,' Frank said thoughtfully. 'It'd be interesting to know how much they cost. Then I could work out if it was worth—'

'Not more sums!' Lizzie interrupted, rolling her eyes at the idea. 'Not tonight, anyway, I couldn't bear it.' She covered her mouth as a yawn escaped from her.

'Tired?' Frank asked.

'Mmm. I'm always worn out on a Monday night, washing's hard work. I remember hearing Ma talking to Mrs Carr once, the two of them were saying Monday should be the wife's night off. I didn't know what they were talking about then, but Ma was giggling like an idiot.' She yawned again. 'I can hardly keep my eyes open. Do you want to come to bed?'

'Yes, figuring all that stuff out's hard work too, eh?'

It took Lizzie much longer to extricate herself from her layers of clothing than it did for Frank to undress, and he was already in his nightshirt by the time she was ready for him to help her out of her stays. She gave a sigh of relief when he had unlaced her.

'Ahh, that feels better. That dress is getting tighter and tighter,' she complained as she stepped out of the stays.

'I wonder why,' Frank teased. He slipped his arms around her and squeezed, enjoying the soft feel of her body through her chemise.

'Having all your babies, that's why. Let go, Frank, it's too cold to stand around in my underwear.'

Frank released her. He climbed into bed and watched as she shed the rest of her clothes and pulled on her nightdress, then bent over Beth's cradle.

'She's sound asleep, the good little thing,' Lizzie said, a fond smile playing around her mouth. 'She's the best sleeper of the three of them, and we've been lucky with them all, really.' Lizzie tucked the little girl in snugly before climbing into bed beside Frank.

'Frank?' she whispered as Frank leaned over to the bedside table to put out the lamp. She sounded half-asleep already.

'Mmm?' he answered as quietly, both of them careful not to wake Beth.

'You know how you said you used to get in trouble for dreaming at school?'

'I sure did. Miss Evans was always telling me off for staring out the window instead of doing my work.'

'Well, what were you thinking about all the time?'

Frank pulled her towards him in the darkness. They snuggled close against the night chill. 'I don't know. All sorts of things, I suppose. Like... well, how the valley must have looked when it was all trees. And how the different sorts of trees grow—you know, some are tall and pointy, and some are bushy. Why tuis have got those white feathers on their chests. Why sometimes there's smoke coming from White Island.'

'No wonder Miss Evans got annoyed with you. You must have hardly got any work done, looking out the window all the time.'

'There was Ma, too.' Frank lay quietly for a few moments, holding Lizzie a little tighter as the feeling of loss washed over him. 'I used to wonder why she had to be so sick. She never moaned or anything, but her face was all sort of pinched from it. Some days she was better, then I'd think she was going to get well again. Then she'd get worse.' And she had slowly faded away, till one day she had died in this very bed, but Frank could not bring himself to finish the story aloud. 'She was nice, Lizzie.'

'I know,' Lizzie whispered, pressing against him. 'Ma liked her a lot. I wish I remembered her.'

'I didn't go to school all that much, anyway,' Frank went on more lightly. 'Sometimes Pa needed me to help him and Ben. I got up to Standard Three, then I just stopped going. Miss Evans was probably pleased to see the back of me.'

'Probably,' Lizzie agreed in a sleepy voice. She rolled away from him a little, and Frank lay waiting for a drowsiness that refused to come.

Instead his mind turned half-formed ideas over and over. If he could get some of those better-producing cows. If he could make more money. He could get nice things for Lizzie. She had looked so tired that evening, after spending most of the day scrubbing at dirty clothes. Maybe he could even pay someone to help her with the washing, outlandish though the idea seemed.

From her breathing he thought Lizzie was deeply enough asleep not to be easily wakened. He reached out towards her. Lizzie's nightdress had ridden up around her hips, and Frank stroked her thigh with a light touch, savouring the satin feel of her skin. He wished her hands might have the chance to be as soft as the rest of her body, instead of chapped and reddened from all the rough work she had to do.

'Don't go getting any ideas,' Lizzie said drowsily. 'I'm too tired. It's Monday, remember? The wife's night off.'

'Sorry, I didn't mean to wake you up.'

'Go to sleep,' she mumbled.

Frank rolled onto his back and tried to sleep, but his mind refused to rest. He listened to Lizzie's breathing and decided that she was also awake, though only just.

'Lizzie?'

'What?' came a muffled response.

'If you could have anything you wanted, what would you have?'

'A good night's sleep. Shut up, Frank.'

At least that much was in his power to give her. Frank rolled away, and was careful not to disturb Lizzie again. He at last dropped off into a sleep that seemed full of dreams of Lizzie wearing pretty dresses and displaying rings on smooth, unblemished hands.

The house was full of the noise of three lively children all day long, so it was the following evening before Frank had the chance to raise the subject that had been filling his head for much of the day. With the children all tucked up and asleep, Frank broke the companionable silence as they sat in the parlour, Lizzie stitching away as usual.

'Lizzie?'

'Mmm?'

'Remember what I asked you last night? About what you'd have if you could have anything you wanted?'

'Did you? I must have been asleep. Oh, that's right, you kept talking when I was trying to get to sleep. I didn't take any notice.'

'Well, what would you have?'

'I don't know what you mean, Frank. I've got everything I need.'

'But what do you *wish* you had?' Frank persisted. 'There must be things you dream about.'

'Of course not,' Lizzie said, looking at him with an utter lack of comprehension. 'What would I want to do that for? I've got healthy children, a nice house, and you're all right when you're not going on with a lot of nonsense.' She pressed against him for a moment to take any sting out of her remark. 'We've got plenty to eat, and we've no worries now we're over that bit of bother with the bank.'

'I know, Lizzie, but what about other things? I mean, there's more than just what you need.'

'Like what?'

'Like…' Frank tried hard to think of something to illustrate the point he had trouble seeing clearly even for himself. A fancy of his mother's slipped into his head, taking him by surprise. 'Well, what about music?'

'Music? What about it?'

'You don't *need* music, do you? But people like having it. It's sort of something extra, just to make you happy. I remember Ma used to say she went to a concert once, some man playing the piano. She said it was like hearing the angels sing. Sometimes I used to hear her humming away to herself, and she'd have a special little smile. I think she was remembering the music. You see what I mean?'

'Not really. You'll be telling me we should get a piano next.'

'That'd be good. Maybe we will one day.'

'Frank, we can't *play* the piano. You're getting silly.'

'But just because this is how things are now, it doesn't mean they've always got to be like this. Can't we think about how things might be different? I want special things, Lizzie, things for you.'

Lizzie put down her sewing and stared at him with a troubled expression. 'You sound like Amy. Going on about things you can't have, dreaming about things till you talk yourself into believing they'll come true. It's no good thinking like that, Frank. It's… well, only bad can come of it. Look what happened to Amy.'

'Did she used to dream about things?' Frank asked, surprised. As little notice as he took of her, he could see that Amy's life did not leave room for such luxuries as dreams. Lizzie's remark raised a curiosity in him. 'Why did she marry Charlie, anyway? They're a strange match.'

'They *made* her,' Lizzie flashed, her eyes burning with indignation. She opened her mouth to speak again, then snapped it shut abruptly. 'That's none of our business, Frank. Don't ask me about it.'

'All right,' Frank said, his momentary interest easily diverted. 'What about you, Lizzie? Didn't you ever have dreams?'

'I wanted a place of my own, and lots of children, and a nice husband. I've got all that. I'm lucky, aren't I?' She turned a glowing smile on him, and Frank gave her a hug.

'Not as lucky as me. But you must have dreamed about some things— things that weren't sensible, I mean.'

Lizzie gave him a sidelong glance, then spoke almost shyly. 'Maybe,' she allowed. 'When me and Amy were little we used to read stories. You know, things about castles and princesses and stuff. We used to make up our own stories sometimes and act them out, up in the bush where no one could see us and laugh. I used to think about those stories sometimes—only when I was little, I mean. It was all a load of nonsense.'

'What did you used to think?' Frank probed.

'Oh, just how it'd be nice if some of that stuff was true. You know, if I could live in a castle and wear pretty dresses and jewels and things. And if...' she turned her face aside slightly. 'Well, sometimes I wished I could be beautiful, and have some handsome prince ride up and carry me away with him. Silly, eh?'

'Hmm,' Frank said thoughtfully. 'Well, I can't do much about the castle. A farm might have to do. And if any princes come sniffing around here after you I'll see them off the place with a shotgun, never mind how good-looking they are. I want to get you the pretty dresses and things, though. I'm going to do it, too, Lizzie, you wait and see. I'm going to get better cows, and I'm really going to make a go of this place. And Lizzie,' he slipped his hand under her chin and gently pulled it around to face him, 'you're already beautiful,' he whispered as he leaned over to plant a kiss on her open mouth.

21

November 1890

Amy wondered why washing day seemed even harder than usual as she lifted the heavy sheets, dripping their burden of scalding hot water, out of the copper and into the first rinsing tub. After the recent hot weather the rain barrel did not contain nearly enough water for the tubs, so she had had to carry load after load from the well. A dull ache had started low in her abdomen during one of those wearying treks up the hill, and it grew worse and worse as the morning wore on.

Even when she had finished hanging out the last load of washing, the cramping pains did not ease. Late that afternoon, after she had carried the dry washing inside, the pains became severe enough to make Amy double over and clutch at herself. She thrust some cakes at the boys to keep them amused and shut herself away in the bedroom to expel what would have been a baby had it been able to remain in her womb for seven more months.

She could not allow herself to lie down and rest. She had the boys to watch, the clothes to fold away ready for next day's ironing, and it would soon be time to start making dinner. And before any of that, she had the miserable job of cleaning herself up. There was a harder task later. That evening she had to tell Charlie she had lost yet another baby.

The tiny hope she still held that Charlie might show her some sympathy, might open his heart over the loss they shared, was soon dashed. When Amy tried to say something of her own sadness he silenced her at once, burying his nose in the newspaper though she could tell he was not actually reading it.

There was nothing to be done but try to go on as if nothing had happened, although the latest miscarriage seemed worse than the ones that had gone before. Her body complained as she dragged herself around the house, trying her best to do her work properly. She got up every morning already tired, and by the end of the day she was often dizzy with weariness and with the dragging pain that refused to leave her entirely. She was barely twenty-two, but she felt like an old woman.

Amy had no one to share her sadness with, and there was no one to tell her that she should rest for a few days to recover her strength. It did not occur to her, much less to Charlie, that she might be due any special care. For all the pain of the miscarriages there was no baby to show for them, and thus no right to the two or three weeks of rest giving birth would have entitled her to.

'I'm taking the boy milking with me this afternoon,' Charlie announced a few days later over his afternoon tea. 'It's time he got used to being around the cows. He'll maybe be ready to start helping next year, the rate he's growing.'

Malcolm was delighted at the idea of being treated in such a grown up way. 'I'm going to milk the cows,' he said proudly as he sat on the back doorstep and Amy tied his boot laces for him.

'Now, you must do what Papa tells you,' she cautioned him. 'Stand just where he tells you, and don't get in Papa's way.' She could not help but be relieved at the thought of having a rest from Malcolm for an hour or two, but when she saw how excited he was at the thought of 'helping' his father she had misgivings. An over-excited child a few days past his fifth birthday was not likely to stay calm and quiet, especially a child as lively and self-willed as Malcolm.

'I know what to do,' Malcolm said indignantly. 'You don't know.'

'I know more about it than you do, Mal, and don't be cheeky,' Amy said, looking over her shoulder to see if Charlie was within hearing. But he had disappeared around the corner of the house after finishing his second cup of tea, and she had time to finish tying Malcolm's laces before he reappeared.

'Can I come too?' David asked plaintively as Charlie walked up to them.

'No,' said Charlie. 'You're too small.'

David's lip trembled. Amy slipped an arm around his shoulders as they stood and watched Charlie and Malcolm out of sight, Malcolm scampering excitedly around his father as they walked.

'Mama, when will I be as big as Mal?' David asked.

Amy twisted one of his long, dark locks around her finger. 'Mal's got a head start on you, Davie, you mightn't ever be as big as him. But you'll be big enough to go out with Papa one day, don't worry. Next spring maybe you'll be able to help Papa feed the calves. Would you like that?'

'Yes,' David said, brightening.

'Anyway, I've got to have someone to keep me company. Come inside and help Mama make some cakes.'

She gave David scraps of pastry from the tarts she was making, and he shaped them with his chubby little fingers ready for her to drop spoonfuls of jam into the centre of each lump.

'Those are beautiful tarts, Davie,' she praised him. 'Now we'll have to wait for them to cook.' She carefully placed David's tarts on one corner of the baking tray, slid it into the range and closed the door, then started mixing up a batch of biscuits.

David wandered out of the kitchen, but Amy did no more than listen to make sure he did not open the front door. David was not likely to get up to mischief pottering around in the house. He was not a boisterous child, and even if he had been there was nothing to break.

She wondered vaguely where the day had gone as she tried to rush through her baking. Normally she would have had most of her cake tins filled by lunch-time, but everything seemed to be taking so much longer lately. She was tired all the time, and pain was something that never quite left her, merely varied from nagging aches to sharper thrusts. The bleeding from the miscarriage had subsided into a flow no heavier than a normal monthly blood loss (though it was longer than she could remember since her cycle of bleeding had been anything like normal), but it still seemed to be draining away what was left of her health.

When she closed the oven door on the last batch of biscuits, she decided she had better check just what David was up to. She had barely taken a step towards the door when a cry of pain made her run into the parlour and thence into the bedroom she shared with Charlie.

'What's wrong, Davie?' she asked, but the sight that met her explained it all. She would have laughed if David's sad little face had not made comforting him her first thought. Ginger was trying to scramble out of the cradle that stood against one wall of the room, hampered in his escape attempt by the baby's dress through the neck of which his head and one front paw had made their way. He had a look of panic on his face, and as soon as Amy had seen that David's cry had been from nothing more serious than a small scratch she caught Ginger and disentangled him from the dress.

'Poor Ginger,' she soothed, stroking the cat until she managed to coax a purr from him. 'I'll give you a nice dish of milk in a minute.'

She put the little dress back in the drawer that David had left open, then sat down on the bed and drew him into her arms, kissing his scratched finger and wiping away his tears with a clean corner of her apron. 'Shh, Davie, it's all right. Ginger didn't mean to scratch you, he just got a fright. What were you trying to do with him?'

'I wanted to rock him,' David sniffed. 'Like Dolly does.'

'Oh, you mean like when you and Dolly rocked the doll in the little cradle?'

David nodded. 'Ginger doesn't like me any more,' he said plaintively.

'Of course he does, Davie. Ginger loves you.' As if to illustrate his agreement, Ginger rubbed against David's legs as the little boy sat on Amy's lap. 'But you can't play with him like that, darling, he doesn't like being rocked. It's like when you tried to cuddle that chook the other day—she scratched you too, remember? Just stroke Ginger. I'll tie a bit of paper on some string for you later, then you can play a game with him.'

'Why don't we got a baby, Mama?'

His innocent question sent a jolt through Amy. 'Why do you ask that, Davie?'

'Dolly's got a baby. Aunt Sophie's got a baby. Why don't we got one?'

Amy did not want David to see her crying, but it was difficult to hold back the tears. 'I don't know, Davie. Maybe we'll have one soon.'

'Don't Papa want a baby?'

'Oh yes, Davie. Papa wants lots of babies.' Amy hugged him tightly. 'It's too hard for Mama to explain, sweetheart. You'll have to be my baby for a bit longer.'

'I'm not a baby!'

'No, that's right, of course you're not a baby. But you're my little boy, aren't you? You love Mama, don't you?'

'Yes, Mama.' David wound his arms around her neck and planted a wet kiss on her mouth. His big blue eyes studied her solemnly from under his long, dark lashes, and Amy stroked his hair, twining her fingers in the thick mass that fell in natural ringlets. Edie had always said David was too pretty to be a boy, and in his little dress with his hair falling to his collar he looked far more like a girl.

Sometimes the force of her love for him almost frightened Amy. David's sunny temper and affectionate nature made him easy to love, but she was never quite sure whether she loved him more for himself or for the likeness she knew he must bear to her daughter. If she loved him too much she would lose him, just as she had lost Ann. In her sensible moments she knew that was nonsense, but it was hard to be sensible when she was so tired, and when everything hurt so much. 'You won't go away and leave Mama, will you, Davie?' she murmured.

'No, Mama,' David said, confusion in his face.

'Of course you won't, Mama's being silly. Come on, let's go and try out some of these cakes I've been making.' She stood up with David in her arms, ignoring the pain his weight gave her.

'And play a game with Ginger!'

'That's right, Davie, I'll make a paper and string toy. Just as soon as we've given poor old Ginger some milk.'

After Ginger had been compensated for his indignities with a saucer of milk, David skipped around the kitchen dragging the makeshift toy, Ginger scampering after him, until the two of them curled up on the floor together, tired out by their game.

Amy put away the last of her baking and glanced at the clock. 'Look at the time! I'll have to hurry and get dinner on or it'll be late.'

But try as she might to rush, the hands of the clock raced on cruelly. The pot of potatoes had barely begun to boil and she was still mixing up a pudding when Ginger disentangled himself from David's arms and jumped over the windowsill. 'That must mean Papa's coming,' Amy said, glancing anxiously through the window. 'I hope Mal was a good boy.'

Charlie did not come in as quickly as she expected, and a loud wail a few moments later told her why. He must have taken Malcolm behind the shed to use a stick on him. Malcolm burst through the room a short time later, howling as he ran towards his room, and Charlie soon entered in his wake, grim-faced as he sat down heavily at the table.

'What happened?' Amy asked, glancing over her shoulder as she replaced the lid on a pot of beans, willing the vegetables to boil faster.

'Had to give the boy a hiding.' Charlie banged his fist on the table. 'He won't do as I tell him. Racing around like a fool, scaring the cows. That white-faced brute kicked me before I could get the leg rope tied because the boy rushed up behind her and yelled out some nonsense.' He rolled up one trouser leg and revealed a red blotch already darkening into a livid bruise.

'He's lively, Charlie. I'm sure he didn't mean to be naughty, he just gets excited and forgets what you tell him.'

'He's got to learn. He's got to do as he's told.' Charlie repeated it like a litany. Amy glanced down at David, who was standing close to her, wisely avoiding his father for the moment. It had troubled her earlier to see David upset at not being allowed to go out with his father and brother; now she was glad he was still considered too young.

Charlie looked at the table as if noticing for the first time that there was no food laid before him. 'Where's my dinner?' he demanded.

'It'll be a couple of minutes yet,' Amy said. 'I'm a bit slow today, I'm sorry.'

'What have you been doing all day? Can't you even get a bit of food on the table? God knows you're no use for anything else.' He shoved himself upright and crossed the kitchen to tower over Amy as she stood by the range. 'You lazy, good-for-nothing bitch!' He slapped her across the side of her head, making her eyes water.

'Mama!' David cried out. 'Don't hit Mama!'

Amy pushed him behind her and held him there, out of Charlie's sight. 'I'm sorry. I just... I feel a bit sick today. I'm going as fast as I can.' She had both hands busy holding David, so she could not wipe away the tears she felt brimming over.

'Don't whine at me, woman, for God's sake. Hurry up.' Charlie took his seat once again and watched Amy, a scowl on his face, until the food was at last dished up and placed in front of him.

'Is Mal allowed any dinner?'

'All right,' Charlie said after a moment's thought. 'If he behaves himself.'

There were few words spoken during the meal. Charlie kept a stern eye on Malcolm, who sniffed from time to time as he sat perched on the pillow Amy had placed under him to protect his tender buttocks. 'No snivelling, boy,' Charlie warned. Amy's head ached from the slap he had given her. She fought against dizziness as she rushed back and forth between the table and the range.

Charlie scowled at her tear-streaked face as she placed a bowl of jam pudding in front of him. He cast a glance around the table, taking in Malcolm's red eyes and David's trembling lower lip. 'Look at you all. Three babies at my table. You drive a man to distraction.' He fetched a bottle of beer from a shelf and poured himself a mug full.

Amy put the boys to bed as soon as they had finished eating; neither of them showed any reluctance to get out of their father's brooding presence. She did the dishes and mixed up the next morning's bread dough under his watchful gaze, wishing he would go into the parlour, but instead Charlie finished his bottle then switched to a large glass of whisky.

'What the hell's wrong with you, woman?' he said in a growl.

Amy kneaded at the bread dough, each punch sending a jolt of pain through her head. 'I'm tired, that's all. It makes me slow. I'm sorry dinner was late, Charlie. I'll try and do better.'

'Why can't you hold a child any more?' So that was the real cause of his anger.

'I don't know. Maybe next time it'll be all right.'

'You must be doing something wrong. It's not natural, dropping your bairns early all the time.' He took a gulp of whisky. 'Why aren't you carrying my children properly?'

'I don't know, Charlie. I don't know.'

'Kelly's wife's got three bairns now,' he said, emptying his glass and pouring another, his hand shaking slightly. 'She's a good breeder. What's wrong with you?'

'I don't know.'

'You didn't get rid of the other fellow's bairn, did you? You held on to that one all right. You could carry a bastard.'

Amy caught her breath in shock, but there was no reply she could give that would not anger him. She carried on kneading the dough as if she had not heard him.

'Well? What's going on with you? Answer me, woman!' His voice rose, and he slapped down his glass, spilling a little whisky.

Amy weighed up whether ignoring him or telling the truth would anger him more, and chose frankness. 'I think maybe I'm having them a bit too fast. Maybe if I could… if I could have a rest from bearing for a few months, I might come right…' She stopped, frightened at what she saw in his face.

'Bitch!' he roared, lashing out with one of his long arms to slap her across the cheek. 'Who put that in your head? Was it that interfering shrew of a nurse? You'll not get away with it, woman. You're not sneaking out of my bed.'

'I'm sorry, Charlie. I didn't mean to annoy you. But you asked me and that's what I think—no one told me to say it. I won't say it again. I'm sorry.' She wanted to cry, but that would only make him angrier.

He glowered at her as he took another swig from his glass. 'Stupid bitch,' he muttered. 'Useless, good-for-nothing bitch.'

Amy finished kneading the dough at last, and placed it in front of the range, relieved at having finished the heavy work of the day. 'I'll just check on the boys,' she said. Charlie did not answer.

David touched the red mark of Charlie's latest slap as she leaned over to give him a goodnight kiss, his face crumpling with threatened tears. 'Why Papa hit you, Mama?'

'Because I was silly, and I annoyed him. We all have to try and do what Papa says and not annoy him. Papa works hard and he gets tired. Shh, Davie, Mama's all right. Go to sleep now.' She tucked him in and closed his door.

Malcolm's room was silent. Amy thought he was asleep until she heard a muffled sob as she tucked him. 'Are you all right, Mal?' she asked softly.

'It's not fair,' Malcolm mumbled into his pillow. 'I didn't do nothing wrong.'

'You annoyed Papa, Mal. I know you didn't mean to, but you must do what he tells you. Never mind, maybe Papa will take you milking again tomorrow and you can show him what a good boy you are really. Good night.' She tried to sneak a kiss, but Malcolm thrust his head under the pillow to avoid it.

The lamp had still not been lit when Amy went back into the parlour. She saw that the door of the main bedroom was open; perhaps Charlie had left his newspaper in there. She bent down to the lamp, but Charlie's voice stopped her before she had taken hold of it.

'Get in here,' he called from the bedroom. She straightened and hurried through, seeing to her surprise that Charlie was already in his nightshirt. 'Come to bed,' he said, his voice slurring a little.

'Now?' Amy said stupidly. 'It's very early.'

'Are you arguing with me, woman?'

'No. I was just... surprised.' She turned her back on him and began taking off her clothes, her heart pounding. *Should I tell him he can't do that thing? He'll get annoyed. I've got to tell him.* She felt his eyes on her as she took off her chemise and pulled her nightdress over her head, leaving her drawers on underneath. 'Charlie, I'm... I'm still—'

'What are you mumbling about?'

She turned to face him. 'I'm still bleeding from the baby.'

'A bit of blood won't kill you,' he said, his voice harsh.

Amy closed her eyes for a moment against a wave of fear and disgust. She untied her drawers and rolled them up around the blood-soaked rag they had held between her thighs all day, pushing the wadded mass under the bed before climbing between the sheets.

He was groping at her nightdress before she had had the chance to lie down properly. Amy heard the ripping noise of a seam giving way as he snatched at the fabric. She kept her eyes tightly closed, hoping that he might at least be quick about it.

It was much like being beaten. There was the same sense of a rhythmic series of blows to her body; the same blend of pain and degradation. And, like a beating, she never knew how long it was going to last.

Tonight the alcohol seemed to be hindering his efforts, but he was determined. When he at last rolled away from her, Amy choked back the bitter-tasting vomit that was trying to make its way out of her throat; she felt too weak to trust herself to get up and scrabble under the bed for the chamber pot.

There was blood trickling between her thighs, mingled with what he had left there. In the morning she would have to face stained sheets and a torn and bloodied nightdress. Charlie would find her blood on himself when he got out of bed.

Why did he have to do that to me while I'm bleeding? Why couldn't he have gone to one of his whores? She knew part of the answer before the thought was fully-formed: he wanted her with child again. But there was more to it than that. There were things he wanted from her that Amy was only dimly aware of, but aware enough to know that she could not give them. Try as she might to be obedient, she could not make herself feel what he

287

wanted her to feel.

She shifted a fraction, trying to find a more comfortable position for legs that had been constricted by Charlie's weight. But even the slight movement made her body rub against his in the narrow bed. She would sooner lie still in the awkward pose he had forced her into than touch him again.

There was a bone-aching weariness all over her body. She felt her blood drying stickily between her thighs while fresh blood seeped out from what felt like an open wound. She did not move. If she moved she would vomit; if she stood up she would faint.

I don't know if I can put up with much more of this. The bleak thought edged into her awareness, and made her angry at her own stupidity. *I have to put up with it. He can do whatever he likes with me. I can't stop him. I can't do anything.*

22

November 1890 – January 1891

If Lizzie had thought Frank would soon forget the idea of improving his herd, she was in for a surprise. He read and re-read his farming magazines, and pored over all the newspaper advertisements for stock, until he had decided how many cows he would need to buy and from whom he should buy them.

'There's a bloke south of Auckland who's advertising cows,' he told her one evening while Lizzie washed the dishes. 'They talked about him in the *Farmer*, his herd's meant to be really good. I think he'd be the one to buy them off.'

'Mmm,' Lizzie said, scrubbing at a plate. Frank could tell that she was only giving him a small part of her attention.

'I think I'd better write to him,' he said.

Lizzie put the plate down with a thump. 'What did you say?'

'This bloke with the cows—I'm going to write to him, see if I can order some. What's wrong?' he asked, seeing Lizzie's mouth hanging open.

'You really mean it, don't you?' she said, shaking her head in disbelief. 'You're really going to buy those cows.'

'Lizzie, I've been talking about it for weeks. Didn't you believe me?'

'I thought it was just something to talk about. I didn't know you really meant it. If you're going to write a *letter* you must be serious. You never write to anyone.'

'I've never had to before. You'll have to help me with the letter, see I do it right.'

'How would I know? I've never written to anyone either.'

'That doesn't matter, all we have to do is tell him we want to buy some cows. Three cows and a bull, that's what I want. That should be enough to set up a bit of a herd—I'd buy a dozen cows if I could, but I wouldn't have a show of affording that many.'

Lizzie dried her hands on her apron and sat down beside him, a worried look on her face. 'Frank, those cows cost a lot, you told me that. Where on earth are you going to get all the money?'

Frank slipped his hand over hers. 'That's the hard part. You'll have to help me with that, too.'

'Me? I don't know anything about money.'

He gave her a rueful grin. 'More sums, Lizzie. Even harder ones this time.'

Mr Callaghan looked mildly surprised when Frank marched purposefully into the bank and asked for a private word in his office, but when he heard what Frank had come about he was openly astonished.

'Am I understanding you properly, Frank?' he said when he had recovered something of his composure. 'You want to borrow money to buy some cows?'

'That's right,' Frank said, hoping he appeared more confident than he felt.

'A hundred and fifty pounds—for four cows?' Mr Callaghan's voice cracked for a moment. 'It seems an awful lot. And... well, we both know you got in a bit of strife with that loan you already have. I wouldn't like to see that happen again.'

'Neither would I,' Frank said fervently. 'This is different.'

'Is it?' The bank manager looked dubious. 'You'd better explain it all to me slowly. What's given you the idea of buying cows?'

Frank launched into his explanation with enthusiasm. 'They're special cows, these ones are. I've read everything I can find about them. They produce more cream, you see—the richest milk of any cow there is, Jerseys give.'

'That's interesting, but is it important?'

'Yes, it is. The factory doesn't pay by how much milk we produce, not since they started making butter instead of cheese. They pay us for the cream. The *cream*,' Frank repeated. 'The more cream I produce, the more money I make.'

'I begin to see what you're getting at,' Mr Callaghan said, a glimmer of interest in his face. 'But these cows are rather expensive—very expensive, judging by the amount you want to borrow.'

'The really good ones are,' said Frank. 'I don't want to get just any old Jerseys, I want these real pedigree ones. I need a bull as well as some cows, then I'll be sure to get decent calves out of the cows I've already got.'

'A hundred and fifty pounds, Frank. It's a good deal of money.'

'I know. But I can pay it back, I'm sure I can. Take a look at this.' Frank reached into his jacket and brought out two carefully rolled sheets of paper covered with Lizzie's neatest writing. He spread them out on the bank manager's desk, handling the pages almost reverently as he recalled the labour that had gone into producing them. Mr Callaghan was not to know how many rough copies, full of crossings-out and sums that refused to add up, had gone before this impressive-looking document.

'We worked it all out. Look, here's the money for the cows up the top. And here's what I'll get for the extra cream the first year—it's not much, because I'll only have the three Jerseys producing. The second year's the same—I wouldn't be able to pay anything back the first two years.' He glanced at Mr Callaghan, then went on speaking quickly so as not to give the older man time to remonstrate.

'But the year after that the calves from the first three Jerseys—they'll be in calf when I get them, and I'm sure to get at least one heifer—will be producing, so that's a little bit more money, see?' He pointed a few lines down the page. 'I'll be able to start paying back a bit on the loan then. And I'll put the bull in with my cows next year, so I'll have a bunch of half Jersey calves the second year. That means in four years when that lot are producing milk I'll be earning a lot more... let's see, that starts on this other page. And after that it'll just get better and better as there's more and more Jersey blood in the herd.'

Explaining the figures to Mr Callaghan had given Frank a clear picture of Lizzie sitting at the kitchen table painstakingly drawing up the good copy by lamplight, the tip of her tongue poking out between her lips as she concentrated on the task. He smiled at the memory as he sat back in his chair and looked expectantly at Mr Callaghan. 'What do you think?' he asked.

Mr Callaghan's eyebrows had risen in surprise as Frank had begun his explanation; now he studied Frank's figures carefully, not speaking for some time. At last he looked up from his desk.

'Did you work all this out by yourself?'

'Lizzie helped me with the sums. And she wrote it out nice and neat, she's got much tidier writing than me. But us two did it by ourselves,' Frank said proudly.

'I'm impressed. Very impressed indeed. You've obviously thought this all through most carefully. I'm not used to seeing this amount of preparation when someone asks for a loan.' Mr Callaghan bent his head to scrutinise the figures once again. 'Hmm, no repayments for three years... it's a long time, but...' He looked across the desk at Frank. 'How old are you, Frank?'

The unexpectedness of the question took Frank aback. 'What? I'm... um, I'm twenty-eight. Why?'

'Twenty-eight,' Mr Callaghan mused. 'Your whole life before you, eh?'

'I've had quite a bit of it already,' Frank said, not sure just what the bank manager meant but unwilling to have marriage and the fathering of three children ignored.

'I think perhaps the best is yet to come,' Mr Callaghan said with a smile. 'Frank Kelly, if this country is ever going to drag itself out of the slump we've been in for so long, it's going to be young men with a bit of gumption like you who'll do it.'

'Does that mean…' Frank said, hardly allowing himself to believe it.

'Yes, Frank. The money's yours.'

'I don't know whether to be pleased or annoyed,' Lizzie said when Frank told her the news. 'I sort of hoped Mr Callaghan would say no—but I wanted him to say yes, too.'

'Be pleased,' Frank urged her. 'This is really going to work out for us.'

'But all that money, Frank. Aren't you worried about it?'

'It scares the pants off me,' Frank admitted. 'But it's worth doing, I'm sure it is. I mean, Mr Callaghan wouldn't lend me the money if he didn't think it was a good idea.'

'He doesn't know anything about cows, though. What say… oh, I don't know, what say the cows don't thrive or something? It'd be awful to see all that money down the drain.'

'Don't even think about it,' Frank said with a shudder. 'I thought I might have a word with your pa before I arrange ordering these cows, sort of run the idea past him and see what he has to say.'

'Hmm. I don't think Pa will think much of it. You know what he's like, always so sure he's right about everything. He'll go on at you about it.'

'I know, but if I didn't tell him he'd make a heck of a fuss when he found out, eh? It's better to let him know now. Anyway, he might have some good advice.'

'What'll you do if he says you shouldn't buy them?'

Frank paused to consider. Arguing with his father-in-law was not a prospect he relished, but his ideas for improving the farm were more important than the risk of offending Arthur. 'If he's got really good reasons why I shouldn't buy the cows, maybe I won't buy them. Otherwise… well, I'll listen to him, then I'll go ahead and do what I want.'

'You're going to do *what?*' Arthur exploded. 'Pay a fortune for a few funny-looking cows? Frank, I've stuck up for you over the years when people have said you're a bit dopey, but right now I'm wondering. Have you lost your senses, boy?'

Well, they had not got off to much of a start, Frank thought. He and Arthur had been having a pleasant enough stroll around Frank's paddocks with Maudie and Joey trotting at their heels, Arthur proffering

292

advice on improving the pasture as they walked, until Frank had plucked up courage to raise the subject. 'I don't think so. I just want—'

'Now, I don't mind telling you that you weren't much of a farmer till a couple of years ago, but you've got a lot better. This place of yours isn't too bad at all since you woke your ideas up. As a matter of fact you've gone a bit silly about it sometimes, out working after dark and all that, but I've said nothing—I'm not one to interfere, you know that. But this nonsense you're on about now... Do you need more cows? Is that the trouble? Frank, I'll *give* you some cows if you need them, you've only got to ask. You don't want to go buying scrawny cows from someone you've never met. They probably wouldn't last the season, anyway.'

'Thanks a lot, Pa, but I don't want more cows—I've got as many as I can milk, anyway. I want better ones.'

'What's wrong with my cows? I offer you some of my cows and you tell me they're not good enough for you!'

'I'm really grateful, honestly I am, and your cows are good, much better than mine. But Jerseys are better. They give more cream.'

'They'd have to give a hell of a lot more cream to pay for themselves.'

'Ooh, Grandpa,' Maudie said, looking wide-eyed at Arthur. 'You said a bad word. You said *hell*,' she said with relish.

'Shh, Maudie, don't give cheek,' Frank admonished, but Arthur patted his little granddaughter on the head.

'She's all right. She's got more sense than some people around here,' he said, giving Frank a stern look.

'They *do* give a lot more cream. Me and Lizzie worked it out, and after a few years I'll be getting—'

'Lizzie?' Arthur looked suspicious. 'Is this Lizzie's idea?'

'No, it's mine—Lizzie thinks it's a bit mad,' Frank admitted. 'But it's Lizzie I really want to do it for, Pa. It's her I want the money for.'

'She's not sick again, is she?' Arthur asked. 'If it's money you need, Frank, don't be scared to ask. If you and Lizzie are in trouble I expect you to come to me for help, not go borrowing money for some hare-brained scheme.'

'No, Lizzie's not sick. But she looks so tired sometimes. She works so hard all the time, I'd like to make things easier for her. I want to get her nice things, too.' Frank had hoped Arthur might understand, but he saw only a growing exasperation in his father-in-law's face.

'She's been trying it on, has she?' Arthur shook his head. 'Frank, I thought you knew how to handle Lizzie. You've made a pretty good job of keeping her in line, I'll give you that. I didn't think you were up to it at first, but you sorted her out before she got out of hand.'

'Lizzie's all right—no, she's great. I don't know what I ever did without her.'

'Oh, she's a good wife, I won't dispute that. Her ma brought her up properly, she knows how to do her work. But remember what I told you, Frank—she likes her own way. You settled her down back when you first got married, but it sounds to me like it's time you did it again if she's trying to plague you into buying her a lot of fancy nonsense. A belt across the backside would do that girl no harm at all.' Maudie gave a squeal of alarm, but the men took no notice. 'You mustn't put up with nagging. You can't let your wife tell you what to do.'

'She doesn't really... not about the cows, anyway. It's my idea. Lizzie never asks for nice things. She deserves them, though.'

'You're talking a load of rubbish, Frank. I'm thinking of my daughter, you know. She's the one who'll suffer when the mortgage men turn the lot of you off the place. Of course I'd take you all in, but we none of us want that. See a bit of sense, boy. Forget about those fancy cows, and next spring I'll give you a few decent calves if you still think you want more cows. All right? That's the end of it, then.'

Frank was silent for a few moments, choosing his words with care. 'Thanks a lot for the advice, Pa. I really appreciate it. I'll have a think about it.'

'There's nothing to think about, I've done the thinking for you. I'm telling you, boy, forget about it.' Arthur's eyes narrowed. 'Are you listening to me?'

'I think... I think buying those cows is the right thing to do,' Frank said. 'I've thought about it a lot, and it seems right to me.'

'What the hell did you ask my advice for, then? Wasting my time getting me to come around here, then you tell me you've already made up your mind?'

'I didn't—' Frank began.

'Why don't you just call me an old fool to my face?'

'I don't—'

'Right, I know when I'm not wanted. I'll get out of your way now.' Arthur turned on his heel and made for the horse paddock, where he had left his horse grazing.

'Pa, don't go off in a huff,' Frank called after him. 'I only meant—'

Arthur turned to face him. 'You mark my words, Frank, you'll regret it if you go getting into debt over this stupid idea of yours. And you'll have no one to blame but yourself.' He strode away at a brisk pace.

'He didn't kiss me bye-bye,' Maudie said. 'Grandpa's in a bad mood, Papa.'

'He sure is, Maudie. Don't worry, he's not in a bad mood with you.'

Maudie was unusually silent when Frank led the two children into the kitchen where Lizzie was busy peeling potatoes. Her gaze flicked from one parent to the other as Frank and Lizzie spoke.

'How did he take it?' Lizzie asked.

'Not too well. He thinks I'm being stupid.'

'No wonder—I think you're pretty stupid about those cows myself, half the time.'

'Don't be cheeky, Mama,' Maudie piped up.

'Cheeky yourself!' Lizzie said indignantly. 'Don't you go butting in, Miss.'

Maudie looked up at Frank with a serious expression. 'Are you going to give Mama a belt, Papa?'

'No, Maudie. Keep quiet, love.'

'What did you say, Maudie?' Lizzie looked incredulous.

'Grandpa said Papa should give you a belt on the backside,' Maudie recited self-righteously.

'Did he, Frank?'

'He only said it because he was fed up with me. Stop looking so keen, Maudie, I'm not going to.'

'Oh.' Maudie looked disappointed.

'But I'll give *you* one if you don't behave yourself.' Lizzie inspected Maudie more closely. 'How did you get your face so mucky—Joey, yours is even worse.'

'Grandpa gave us lollies,' Maudie said, beaming at the memory.

'Trust him! Go and wash your face—take Joey, you can wash his, too. Go on,' she said, giving Maudie a push when the little girl showed no sign of moving.

'What were you and Pa doing, talking about me like that?' Lizzie said. 'In front of the little ones, too! That Maudie picks up everything you say.'

'It's just how your pa talks, take no notice. He's got ideas about how wives should be… well, kept in line.'

'Humph! Don't *you* go taking any notice of him either.'

'No,' Frank agreed absently. 'He said people say I'm stupid. I suppose they're all laughing at me.'

'Well, they've no business saying it. It's not true, anyway. If anyone ever says it to me I give them a piece of my mind.'

Frank sat down at the table beside her. 'Do you really think I'm stupid, Lizzie?'

'Of course not! Don't be stup—I mean, don't talk rot.'

'You said you did a couple of minutes ago. I don't know, maybe I shouldn't buy those cows after all. I'd only make a mess of it, get us in trouble.'

Lizzie put down a half-peeled potato and looked seriously at him. 'You should listen properly, Frank. Like I said, half the time I do think it's mad. Then—' her head swivelled to the passage door, and barely skipping a beat she spoke in a louder voice. 'That's not clean! Wash your face properly, and Joey's too.'

'But Mama, I want to—' Maudie said from the doorway.

Lizzie lifted a finger in warning. 'You heard me, Edith Maud.' Maudie disappeared as quickly as she had come. 'Then I listen to you talking,' Lizzie said, turning back to Frank, 'and I believe it all—I think it's the best idea anyone's ever thought of.' She wiped a damp hand on her apron and placed it over Frank's. 'Do what you think's right, Frank. Whatever you decide, I'll be behind you.'

'Lizzie,' Frank said, clutching her hand, 'you make me feel like I could do anything in the world.'

The day Frank's cows arrived, half the male population of the town seemed to find some excuse to be hanging around near Ruatane wharf when the *Douglas* came in. Frank was pacing up and down the wharf a full hour before the little boat appeared, rounding the bend in the coast just before it crossed the bar into the river mouth. Frank let out his breath in a sigh of relief as he saw the boat gain the safety of the calmer water.

'Not long to wait now, eh?' The voice at his shoulder startled Frank. He turned to see Bill standing close behind him.

'I'll be glad when I've got them safe at home,' Frank said, glancing back at the approaching boat.

'I'll bet. Me and Alf have come to give you a hand driving them.'

'Hey, thanks, Bill,' Frank said. 'I was a bit worried about doing it by myself. Won't your pa go crook, though? He's been funny with me ever since I said I was buying them.'

'It was Pa's idea,' Bill said with a grin. 'He said if you were going to ruin your family buying fancy cows we'd better at least see that you didn't lose them on the way home—he reckoned the Feenans might pinch them off you when you went past their place! Anyway, Pa won't let on, but he wants to know all about these cows—he'll be pumping us for all the news later.'

The boat was still several yards from the wharf when they heard a loud bellowing, and as soon as it was tied up the noise was almost drowned out by a human voice.

'Where's Frank Kelly?' the captain roared. 'Come and get this mad bull of yours off my boat before I chuck him over the side.'

Frank was on the boat before the captain had finished speaking. He rushed anxiously to the open area near the stern where the animals had been tethered. The three cows stood quietly, and raised their heads to gaze at Frank with what looked like pleading in their soft brown eyes. But the bull was tossing his head and bellowing furiously, tugging at the rope that tethered him as he tried to hurl himself towards the dry land now so tantalisingly close.

Frank studied the animals, pride swelling in his chest. They were beautiful. The cows had soft coats of a rich, warm brown, and their eyes were huge dark pools in sweet faces. They were smaller than his Shorthorns, and finer-boned, but their proportions were perfect, though Frank would have preferred to see more flesh on them. And in Frank's eyes the bull was magnificent. Like the cows, he was smaller than a Shorthorn, but he looked sturdy and heavily-muscled, and his coat was thick and healthy.

'How are we going to get him off?' Alf asked, eyeing the angry animal nervously.

'He'll be all right,' Frank said. He walked up to the bull and patted him on the head, and the bull quietened a little. 'Come on, boy,' Frank said in a soothing voice as he tied a length of rope through the animal's nose ring.

'He knows you,' the captain said. 'Crazy animal. Jerseys, eh? Remind me never to carry Jerseys again.'

The three of them walked beside their horses, leading the cattle on ropes, till they were safely through town. All along the main street, Frank saw women peering through lace curtains and men staring more openly over fences or standing outside the hotels.

'These your fancy cows, eh?' someone called out. 'Pretty skinny, aren't they?' Frank ignored him.

'Pa says they won't last six months,' said Alf.

'Shut up, Alf,' Bill admonished.

'He did!' Alf insisted.

'He only said it because he was in a bad mood. Here, that cow's going to wrap her rope around a pole—keep an eye on her.' Thus distracted, Alf said no more on the subject.

Once they had reached the beach, they mounted and drove the cattle along the sand at a quiet pace. The animals seemed too relieved at being back on dry land to show any inclination to stray.

It was a long journey, since they were restricted to the slow pace of the cattle, but at last they turned off the beach, went the mile or so up the main track, then drove the cattle on to Frank's farm. Lizzie saw them from a distance and came rushing out to meet them with Beth in her arms, Maudie and Joey running ahead of her.

'Aren't they beautiful!' Lizzie exclaimed. 'So thin, though.'

'A few weeks of good feed, they'll soon have plenty of flesh on them,' Frank assured her. 'It's a good job I sorted out all those thistles, eh? Can't put fancy cows like these on scruffy pasture.'

When the cattle had been put into paddocks, the bull in solitary splendour with one to himself, Bill and Alf went straight home, refusing Lizzie's offer of afternoon tea. 'It's nearly milking time,' Bill said. 'Anyway, Pa will be standing on one leg waiting to find out all about this lot, we'd better put him out of his misery.'

Frank checked the animals over carefully, assuring himself that the long walk after their voyage had done them no harm, but the vigour with which they were cropping grass showed they were settling in happily. Satisfied, he went up to the garden gate, where Lizzie was standing with the three children.

'Well, we've done it, Lizzie.'

Lizzie's smile had a hint of anxiousness. 'You're still sure it's a good idea?'

'Surer than ever.' He held out his arm for Lizzie to slip her own through. 'Let's take another look at this fellow.'

They stood by the fence and stared at the bull, who was ripping up great mouthfuls of grass. 'He's a beauty, eh?' Frank said. 'I've never had a bull before. No more borrowing your pa's bull for my girls.'

'What do you want a bull for, Papa?' Maudie asked.

'Don't ask so many questions,' Lizzie said briskly. 'Take the little ones up to the house, Maudie, and give them a bikkie—you can have two if you like.'

Maudie stood there for a moment, apparently considering pressing the point. The alternative won, and she led Joey and Beth away.

'He looks healthy,' Lizzie said, studying the bull. 'He's not very big, though, is he? He's smaller than Pa's bull. Do you think he'll be... well, up to the job?'

Frank slipped an arm around her waist and gave her a squeeze. 'I'm not very tall, either. You've never complained,' he said with a grin.

'*You* haven't got twenty-odd wives,' Lizzie retorted.

Frank patted her bottom. 'A good thing, too. One's enough. Don't you worry, he'll be up to it.' He gazed proudly at the bull. 'This herd is going to be really good, Lizzie. This is just the beginning.'

23

February 1891

The last week of haymaking was spent on Frank's farm, and all the men involved took full advantage of the opportunity to study 'Frank Kelly's funny-looking cows', as they were generally called. Frank put up with the jokes and comments cheerfully enough; he was quietly proud of his Jerseys with their rich, creamy milk.

The fine weather held throughout the week, and the work went smoothly in spite of the time lost discussing the Jerseys. Charlie took Malcolm out to the haymaking most days. Malcolm usually so tired himself out running around with the other boys and swimming in the creek that he had no energy left to be troublesome when he did come home.

On the last day of the season, Lizzie invited everyone in the valley to her house for a supper to celebrate the end of the annual task. Charlie returned home to do his afternoon milking, and when he had finished the four of them walked down to Frank's farm in the golden light of late afternoon. While the men built the last of the haystacks, Amy helped Lizzie and the other women carry mountains of food out to the verandah.

To David's delight, Charlie had for once decided his younger son could join him and Malcolm with the men. From the verandah Amy saw Malcolm and David running about with the other children, carrying armfuls of hay missed by the workers over to the stacks, then climbing all over the haystacks chasing one another until one of the men would see them and yell threats.

The men worked harder than ever, seeing the end in sight, and well before dusk the last stack was finished and everyone had gathered on the shady verandah to attack the food. There was a huge ham surrounded by mounds of sandwiches, pies, and savouries of all kinds, followed by several of Lizzie's most magnificent sponge cakes as well as cakes brought by the other women; lemonade for the women and children, and generous amounts of beer for the men. The evening had a holiday feel about it. Even though most of the men would have to get up at first light to milk, the hay was safely in for another year and the winter feed was assured.

Charlie made the most of the free beer. He installed himself in a corner near the barrel and drank glass after glass, showing no inclination to join in any of the chatting groups. Amy was aware of the occasional glances he cast at her, but as long as she kept within sight he seemed willing to let her move about freely.

People plumped down in seats as they found them, but with the wariness she had learned over the years Amy was careful where she sat. Since Rachel Aitken was confined to the house by her latest pregnancy there was an empty place beside Matt, but Amy avoided taking it, knowing how Charlie would react to the sight of her sitting close to Matt Aitken.

She looked around the verandah for somewhere safe, and saw her cousin Bill waving her over. Amy smiled at him and picked her way through the press of people to his side.

It was delightful to chat away about old times with Bill, bringing to life again years in which, looking back, it seemed to Amy that she had never known what unhappiness was.

'Remember how I used to talk you into giving me half your lunch when you'd just started at school?' Bill said. 'I kept telling you I'd forgotten mine, and you believed me.'

'I think I gave you the whole lot once or twice,' Amy said, smiling. 'I must have felt sorry for you.'

'I liked those little cakes your granny used to put in with your sandwiches. I had to be careful Lizzie wasn't around when I was getting them off you, though.'

'Lizzie figured it out before long, of course,' said Amy.

'Yes, and she said she'd tell Miss Evans if I didn't cut it out—heck, I think she might even have said she'd tell Pa.' He grinned at Amy. 'You kept giving me the odd cake, though.'

'I got Granny to put in extra so I'd have some for you.'

'You always were a soft-hearted little thing,' Bill said. 'And Lizzie was always good at making everyone do what she thought they should. You've neither of you changed much, have you?'

Amy glanced over at Charlie, and saw him looking at her with a face like thunder. *What have I done wrong now?*

She looked away. Even if there was to be a reckoning later for whatever transgression she had committed, right now she was enjoying herself. It was a joy to relive those long-ago days when they had all been playmates together. For a few hours she could forget what she had made of her life, forget what she had to go home to, and pretend to be a little girl laughing with her cousin, not a care in the world.

'Lizzie's been a mother hen to us all since she was little,' Amy said. 'What would we do if she changed? No one to boss us around and tell us when we're wrong. Do you remember the school picnic when we all went down the coast on that old wagonette, and a wheel fell off when we were just leaving to come back?'

Bill snorted. 'That's right. Lizzie had us all organised in no time—the biggest boys to lift up the wagonette, other fellows to have a go at putting the wheel back on, then when that didn't work she sent out the two fastest runners to bring someone back with tools.'

'And the older girls had to look after the little ones, and see they didn't wander off. She had it all worked out. Miss Evans just laughed and said she might as well have stayed home, Lizzie had everything in hand. No wonder she's so good at running a house.'

'She's got a good man,' said Bill. Amy saw him glance at Charlie. There was a moment's awkward silence before Bill went on.

'Remember that time Lizzie talked us into coming down here so she could give Frank those pies?'

'Oh, that was so *funny*,' Amy said. 'Frank standing in the back doorway looking like he wished the ground would open up and swallow him. Then you and me sitting in that dusty parlour trying not to laugh out loud while Lizzie got a cup of tea organised and Frank trailed around after her like an orphan calf.'

'Frank never had a chance, eh?' Bill looked over at Frank, who was sitting on the far side of the verandah with a drowsy Maudie sprawled on his lap. 'I don't think he regrets it. Hey, do you remember those New Year picnics we used to have when we were little? There was so much food! And it always seemed to be hot and sunny. I wonder why the summers seemed longer then.'

'Because we hadn't lived so long,' said Amy. 'Remember how the food tasted better, too?' And so they continued their agreeable series of 'do you remembers'.

It was the pleasantest evening Amy had spent in a long while, and she was quite sorry when the time came to go home. The evening had drawn in, more food had been brought out and eaten, and the beer had all been drunk. Charlie had had more than his share of it.

Amy retrieved her boys from a pile of children asleep in a corner, and the four of them set off in the soft darkness. A huge yellow moon hung low in the sky, shedding ample light to see their steps by.

Malcolm was buoyed by the novelty of being up at such an hour, and he chattered away as they walked, but within a few minutes David was stumbling with drowsiness. Amy picked him up to carry the rest of the way. He nestled against her side, winding his arms around her and burying his head with its thick, dark curls into the curve of her neck. She could soon tell from his breathing that he was fast asleep.

She became aware that Charlie's silence was from something more than just tiredness and having drunk too much. She remembered the black looks he had been casting at her, and wondered what trouble was brewing. Perhaps if she could get him home and into bed quickly enough, he would forget whatever had upset him. She noticed his steps were a little unsteady, and hoped he wasn't too drunk to make it back to the house; tempting though it might be to leave him in a ditch, the consequences did not bear thinking about.

They got home without incident, and Charlie sat at the kitchen table while she put the boys to bed. Malcolm was still full of the excitement of the day and insisted he wasn't sleepy, but a warning growl from Charlie, who heard his protests from the kitchen, settled him. Amy could see that he would be asleep within minutes.

David did not stir as she carried him to his own bedroom, tucked him in and kissed him softly on the cheek. Malcolm had been refusing kisses from her since he was younger than David was now, and she dreaded the day when David would announce that he was too grown-up for kisses and cuddles.

Amy returned to the kitchen to get things ready for morning. She would be up late making bread for the next day; that would be the price of her pleasant evening, but well worth paying.

Charlie had brought out some beer for himself and was downing it by the mugful. He would have trouble getting up in the morning, Amy thought, but she was not foolish enough to tell him so. At least all that beer on top of a hard day's work in the hay paddocks made it unlikely he would disturb her rest when she at last had the chance to go to bed.

He finished a bottle and sat, still silent, staring at her as she kneaded the bread.

'Don't wait for me, Charlie,' Amy said, working away at the dough. 'I'll be a while yet. You go to bed if you like.' Silence. She looked at him, then looked away from his black stare. He stumbled over to the dresser, got something from inside it, and sat down again.

'Would you like me to get you a cup of tea?' Amy offered. When she turned to face him, she saw that he had brought some whisky from the dresser and was taking swigs of it straight from the bottle. Her heart sank; whisky always put Charlie into the foulest of moods. He was concentrating on his bottle for now, so she turned back to her kneading and hoped he would ignore her.

Amy caught his movement out of the corner of her eye and assumed he was walking back to the dresser. When she felt his hands on her shoulders she gave a small cry.

'Charlie, you frightened me.' She tried to still the trembling of her hands by gripping her apron, twisting the cloth between her fingers. He turned her round to face him, still with his hands on her shoulders, lowered his head and crushed his mouth against hers, grinding her lips against her teeth. His breath stank of beer and whisky, and his beard rasped at her. She tried without success to suppress a shudder. He drew back. Still he said nothing, and still he stared at her with the same black intensity.

'Please, Charlie,' Amy said, struggling to make her voice calm, 'it's very late, and I've got to finish this. Please, couldn't it wait? You go to bed, and I'll come along as soon as I can. Please?'

He made a sound in his throat like a growl, and gripped her shoulders more tightly. Again Amy shuddered.

'Why do you shrink from my touch?' he snarled. 'Any man but your lawful husband, is that it?'

'I'm sorry, Charlie, I didn't mean to annoy you. I'm tired, and I said the wrong thing. I'll come to bed now if that's what you want.'

'And what do *you* want, you dirty little bitch? To crawl into bed with any other man who'll have you?' He shoved her away from him; she staggered, but kept her feet.

'I don't know what you mean—of course I don't want anyone else. Please don't call me those names.'

'Slut!' He gave her a slap that made her ears ring. 'I'll call you whatever I like. You think you can make a fool of me right under my nose with other men and then come over all dainty and coy when I touch you. Tired! Who's tired you out? I'm not blind—I can see what you're up to.'

'*Please* tell me what I've done wrong,' Amy begged. 'I don't know what I've done.'

He lashed out again, this time with his fist closed, and caught her a blow on the cheek. The crack of his fist against her cheekbone was like a gun going off beside her head. She fell to the floor, catching herself with one hand. He grabbed her by the arm and hauled her to her feet, then pulled her higher so that her face was close to his, forcing her to stand on tiptoe. Her head ached and her heart was pounding. She had never seen him so angry before.

'I saw you playing up to the men tonight, flashing your eyes and smirking and giggling. You were just about sitting on that Bill's lap. You wanted to get into his trousers, didn't you?' He shook her. 'Didn't you?' He hit her across the mouth with the back of his hand. 'Or have you already been there?'

He let go of Amy suddenly, and she fell back a few steps. She felt the wall against her back, hard and cold. *I will not cry out.*

'He's my *cousin*,' she pleaded. 'He's like my brother.'

'That wouldn't stop you, would it? If it wears trousers you're after it. I saw you hanging around your fancy man from the city that summer— right here on my farm you were throwing yourself at him when he was meant to be making hay. You opened your legs quick enough for him. Until he got sick of you and left you with a swollen belly.' Amy put her hands over her ears to shut out the dreadful words and turned away, but he stepped forward and caught hold of her hands, pushing them back down against her sides, then took a handful of her hair and jerked her head back, forcing her to look up at him.

'You liked it with him, didn't you?' he hissed. 'You enjoyed tumbling in the hay with him. Didn't he believe it was his brat you were carrying? How many men were there?' He tugged at her hair.

'Just one,' she whispered. He pulled her head back further and spat in her face. Amy forced down a rush of nausea. Still tightly gripping her hair so that she couldn't move, he hit her again across the lips. She tasted salt from the blood filling her mouth.

'You hung around him like a bitch in heat.' A slap across the cheek. 'You yelled and panted for him.' A blow to the side of her head. 'But you shrink away from *me*.' His voice rose in a howl of rage and anguish as he lashed out again, and at last Amy understood what enraged him. She had hurt his pride, and he was making her pay.

Now she could no longer distinguish words through the roaring in her ears, but she could hear his voice as though it were coming from a great distance. She prayed that he would not wake the children; with each blow she willed herself to think of her boys. She would not cry out; she would not disturb them and have them come in to the room and see this. She would bear it in silence until he tired of his sport. If she screamed it would only inflame him more. Surely he would stop soon. His hands must be hurting by now.

He swung out again. Her head reeled with dizziness and nausea. Perhaps he would stop if she fainted. But she could not will herself to faint.

His fist slammed against the side of her head, catching the edge of her eye with the knuckles, but she sensed that his left arm was tiring. Its grip on her hair loosened, and at the same time the force of his forearm lashing across her face knocked her to the floor and sent her skidding into a leg of the table. Through the roaring she heard a rattling noise above her head, and felt something wet on her shoulder. It was whisky from Charlie's bottle. He snatched at the bottle before it tipped completely over, and held it high in front of him.

She could only see out of one eye now. She watched him with his bottle, and for a moment she thought he was going to smash it over her head. But instead he cradled it to his chest like a baby. He gave her a savage kick in the stomach, thudding her spine against the table leg, then turned and lurched out of the room. She heard the thump of his steps go erratically out of the room, then for a time the world went dark.

Amy felt the floor's cool solidity. The roaring in her ears had faded, and she lay motionless, empty of everything except the relief of being alone and in total silence. At last her mind began working again, forming fragments of emotion into coherent thoughts. He despised her for what she had done before she married him. Because she had given herself to another man, and borne that man a child. A sob convulsed Amy as she thought of her little girl. She thrust the memory aside; she did not have the strength for it tonight.

But it was more than her shame, as she had been taught to call it, that had enraged him. It was because he knew his very touch repelled her, and she barely endured his demands, while he knew, too, that she had gone willingly to another man.

She had been soiled, but Charlie had taken her. That was the bargain: he had got a young wife from a good family; a wife who was obedient, would work for him uncomplainingly, and would bear his children. In return she had gone to a husband who was meant to give her a home, protect her, and give her back her respectability. She had kept her side of the bargain faithfully; only now had it been borne in on her that she, too, might have some rights.

From the first night she had come to his house, whenever he had touched her it had been a punishment, whether it was a blow when she had annoyed him or just the rough way he used her for his lust. She had come to him eager to please and desperate for approval, and he had hurt her and reviled her. And now he had beaten her savagely for shrinking from him.

Awareness of her body crept back, and Amy slowly absorbed the details of her pain. She felt on fire all over. It was a long time before she attempted to move, and when she did try she thought she would faint.

She lay still until her head stopped spinning quite so violently, then dragged herself to her hands and knees, took hold of a chair, and pulled on it until she was squatting.

A new spasm racked her. She clutched at her belly until the

306

convulsions eased a little, then stared at the pool of blood on the floor between her thighs, slow to comprehend what it meant. So there had been another child growing within her; another child lost. A child killed by its father.

When the pain no longer threatened to make her faint, Amy slowly pulled herself to her feet, using the edge of the table for support. She felt something hard in her mouth, and spat a mouthful of blood into one hand. In the middle of the pool were two teeth. She closed her hand on them and squeezed until she felt them cut into her palm, then slipped them into her apron pocket.

The habit of guilt was strong in her. She deserved everything bad that had happened to her from the time she had lain with Jimmy; she had been told so over and over. She had accepted it as her due. But had she really deserved this from her husband? Hadn't she been punished enough now?

She wiped up the blood as well as her trembling hands would allow, lit a candle and put out the lamp, then walked quietly through the parlour and up to the bedroom door.

Charlie was sprawled half on the bed with his legs dangling over the edge, clutching his empty bottle in one outflung arm. She paused in the doorway, watching and listening. His snoring told her that he was sound asleep, and unlikely to be easily disturbed. Amy felt that the very last thing in the world she wanted to do was touch him, but she forced herself to go over to the bed. In the early hours of the morning it could be cold even at this time of year. He should not lie there all night with no covers over him.

She prised his fingers from the bottle, a shudder running through her at the touch. There was something wound around his hand: long strands of her hair, ripped out by him. The pain in her scalp was a small part of the whole, and she had scarcely noticed it till now. A treacherous memory from her last day with Jimmy crept into her awareness; so Charlie wanted a lock of her hair, too.

She put the bottle on the floor near the wall where he would be unlikely to trip over it. She managed to get his boots off, but when she tried to lift his legs onto the bed the weight sent stabs of pain through her, forcing her to abandon the attempt. Instead, she took a blanket from the wardrobe and draped it over him. She took her nightdress from a drawer and walked out of the bedroom, closing the door quietly behind her.

The photograph on the mantelpiece caught Amy's attention as she came into the parlour; she paused to study it. Something had put the idea of a family portrait into Charlie's head two years before, and he had summoned Mr Hatfield out to the farm to make a visible record of Charlie and his heirs.

It showed Charlie standing before the fence in front of the house, holding Smokey by the reins. Malcolm was perched in the saddle, beaming with pride at being allowed to sit on the horse. Amy had not ventured further than the gateway in the fence. She looked at the image of herself with David in her arms, clutching the child to her as much to hide the signs of pregnancy as for the pleasure of holding him.

Charlie's kingdom. His farm, his sons and his wife. She had thought she belonged to him then; belonged as much as his farm and his animals did, and had as little right to complain.

Amy heard the soft sounds of David's breathing as she slipped into his room. She put out her candle and undressed in the dark so as not to wake him; unwilling, too, to face her injuries before she had to. She slid into bed alongside him, trying to find the position that would cause least pain, and snuggled up to his warm little body. He stirred, and pressed against her. It hurt, but she clung to him. In the morning she would have to move David's things out to the verandah room; he was old enough to sleep out there with his brother, and she needed this room now. Because she was never going to share Charlie's bed again.

24

February 1891

Amy woke much later than usual the next morning, with the sun already bright in the sky. For a few moments she looked around the walls and wondered where she was. Memories of the previous evening came flooding back and she was suddenly wide awake.

She realised what had woken her: it was the bellowing of the cows. They were hours late in being milked, and were making their disquiet obvious. Charlie must have been even drunker than she had thought to sleep through this.

David had rolled away from her in the night. He was still asleep, with his head on the other edge of the pillow and one arm flung out over the covers. He had the thumb of his other hand in his mouth; she pulled it out gently. He stirred a little without waking.

Amy slipped out of bed, and groaned as her body complained at the movement. Steeling herself, she walked over to the wall mirror. The face that looked back at her was almost unrecognisable. Her cheeks were a swollen mass of bruises, she could only just see out of a half-closed black eye, and one lip was split by an angry-looking cut. Her hair was tangled, giving her an even wilder appearance.

She turned from the apparition and crept out of the room, then through the parlour till she stood outside Charlie's door, every step running shafts of pain through her. She listened for any sound of movement, but heard nothing. Summoning her courage, she opened the door and went in. Charlie lay just as she had left him, still sound asleep and breathing noisily; he looked as though he might sleep the day away, and she was in no hurry to confront him.

But the cows needed milking. Amy remembered the pain in her breasts when they were full of milk after Ann had been taken from her; she felt them aching in sympathy for the poor beasts with their swollen udders. Charlie was obviously in no state to milk them, so she would just have to do it herself.

She gathered up her hairbrush from the chest of drawers, closed the door on Charlie and went back to David's room. He stirred as she came in, turning a sleepy face to her. His eyes widened, and he opened his mouth to cry out. Amy went to his side, crouched on the floor by the bed and put her arms around him, hiding her face until he had got over the fright.

'It's all right, Davie, it's Mama,' she soothed. When she released him he stared at her wide-eyed, then reached out and touched her cheek very lightly.

'Your face is funny, Mama.'

'I fell on the floor and I got hurt.' It wasn't a lie, it just wasn't all of the truth; but enough of it for a three-year-old.

She couldn't leave the boys here while she went down to the cow shed; they would be sure to wake Charlie, and he would be like a bear with a sore head this morning. He was hard enough on them even when he didn't have a hangover.

'Davie,' she said, 'would you like to help Mama today? Papa's not very well, and he has to stay in bed. We have to whisper so we won't wake him up. I need you and Mal to help me milk the cows. Will you do that?'

David nodded, his eyes alight as he climbed out of bed. It was all a game to him. She helped him get dressed, putting a finger to his lips when he got too excited.

'Now, you must creep *very* quietly out to the verandah and wake Mal up and tell him our secret. When he's dressed you can both come back here—see which one can be the quietest.'

She lifted her nightdress over her head when David had gone, and saw the injuries on her body for the first time. Charlie's vicious kick had been effective in more than bringing on a miscarriage. Her back and her rib cage both had livid bruises discolouring them. She tried to check her ribs for any damage, but found that even a light exploratory pressure was unbearable; one or more must be cracked. Angry red lines had etched into her skin around the site of his kick; they puzzled her until she realised they had been made by the bones of her corset when his foot and the table leg had ground them into her.

It was obvious she would not be able to lace herself in while she was in this state. She shoved the corset into the wardrobe and closed the door on it. *That's one good thing, anyway. An excuse not to wear that for a while.*

Dressing was awkward enough without it. Twisting her body around to fasten bodices and petticoats rubbed her tender skin and set all her bruises throbbing. But she managed to get her clothes on before David came back with Malcolm. The five-year-old looked at her in awe.

'I'm all right, Mal, there's no need to stare at me like that,' she said, trying to reassure him. But he was not frightened, merely impressed.

'That's a *huge* black eye,' he said. 'How did you get one like that?' He sounded as though he wished he could have one, too. *It's not that hard, Mal. Just make your father angry enough and he'll give you one.* No, that wasn't quite fair; Charlie might be harsh, but he didn't hate his sons as it seemed he hated his wife. In his own way he loved them; especially his precious first-born.

'I fell on the floor,' she repeated. 'You two sit on the bed and wait while I do my hair.'

They sat obediently enough and swung their legs for a few minutes. Amy tugged at the knots, trying to tease out the worst of them with her fingers. Her scalp was tender on the back of her head where Charlie had grabbed at it. When she probed gingerly with her fingertips she could feel that a small patch of hair was missing; a little dried blood came off on her fingers.

The boys, growing bored, started kicking one another's legs, and scuffling in an idle way. 'Stop that!' Amy said. 'You'll wake your father.' That quietened them briefly, then Malcolm tickled David, who gave a high-pitched squeal of indignation. It was unfair to expect them to sit still.

'How about you go down to the cow shed and wait for me there,' Amy said. 'See if you can let the cows into the yard,' she added, not with any great hope they would manage it.

The boys erupted from the room and raced out the back door. Amy stood very still for a moment to listen for any signal that Charlie might have been disturbed, but the house was silent.

The raw patch on the back of her head meant she couldn't pin her hair up or put on a bonnet, so she left it falling around her shoulders and down her back. It felt strange to wear it loose; she hadn't left the house with her hair down since she had been declared a woman at sixteen.

On her way out of the house, she paused in the kitchen to get something for the boys to eat. Her dough of last night was still lying on the table, cold and hard now. She found some of yesterday's bread, not too dried out yet, and cut thick slices from the loaf. That and two apples from the box by the back door would have to keep them going till she could get them breakfast.

To her agreeable surprise, the boys had all the cows in the yard with the gate closed behind them. The two of them looked very pleased with themselves.

'What clever boys!' Amy said. 'You got them in all by yourselves— that'll save us a *lot* of time.' She knew that all they had had to do was open the gate, hold it open until the cows, eager for relief, had all filed in, then close it after them; but they could easily have upset the animals by rushing around or shouting, making the job of getting them into the yard a good deal harder.

'I know how to do it,' Malcolm said proudly. 'I help Papa sometimes.' And he often enough earned a beating for upsetting the cows. Today

Malcolm seemed to be taking the responsibility seriously enough to overcome his usual boisterousness.

Amy led two cows into bails and showed Malcolm how to tether their heads and tie a leg rope to one hind leg. He tied the second one while she milked the first. Crouching on the hard little stool was painful, but there was something soothing about pressing her face against the cow's warm, soft flank as she squeezed its teats and heard the satisfying swish of milk going into the bucket.

She and the boys got into a pattern of work together: Malcolm leading the cows in and tethering them, and letting them out into the paddock when they were done; Amy milking; then the two boys carefully carrying each bucket between them over to the row of milk cans and pouring the milk in. They spilled a little each time, but they were trying so hard that Amy could not possibly scold them. The spilt milk puddled into the cow dung on the earth floor of the milking shed; even at such close quarters the pungent smell was too familiar for Amy to do more than twitch her nose at it.

Amy found herself becoming sleepy as the morning wore on. Her hands got into a rhythm that took little concentration; the shed was warmed by the sun as it rose higher, and by the body heat of the cows. Each cow seemed to have a look of trust and even gratitude in its liquid brown eyes as it was led in. It was only pain that stopped her from dozing off where she sat.

It took them more than three hours to finish, and Amy was exhausted by the time they let the last cow back into the paddock. She had no idea where Charlie would have moved them after milking; they would have to stay where they were until he finally appeared. She and Malcolm carried a can of milk between them as they walked up to the house. She hoped Charlie would wake up before it was time for the afternoon milking; she had no desire to see him before she had to, but she did not think she would be able to cope with a second session that day. All she really wanted to do was lie down and sleep; though that was out of the question. She was already behind with her work for the day.

When they got near the house she saw a small plume of smoke rising from the chimney. So he was up, and had lit the range. At the thought of facing him, her grip on the handle of the milk can slackened. 'Watch out, Mama, you're spilling it,' Malcolm said, bringing her attention back to their burden. She took hold of David's hand as they went into the house, and held it tightly.

Charlie was in the kitchen, sitting at the table with a mug of tea cupped in his hands. She saw that he had hacked the remains of the previous day's loaf into rough slices. The spoiled bread dough lay in front of him, cold and pale like a dead thing. He looked up as they walked in. When he saw the state of Amy's face he winced and turned away.

The boys rushed over to him, full of their own importance, while Amy carefully lifted the heavy can onto the bench.

'Papa! We milked the cows!' David squealed.

'Mama milked them, you mean,' Malcolm corrected him. 'But we got them in the yard, and I tied them up, and we carried the milk. Didn't we, Mama?'

'Of course you did, and I couldn't have managed without you.' Amy ruffled his hair, and gave David a squeeze. She was avoiding Charlie's eyes as much as he was avoiding hers.

'Are you sick, Papa?' David asked.

Charlie flinched at the boys' high-pitched voices. 'No, I'm not.'

'Mama said you were,' Malcolm chimed in. 'She said you had to stay in bed because you were sick. That's why *we* had to milk the cows—us and Mama.'

'Stop your blethering,' Charlie grumbled. 'Keep quiet or leave the room.'

'But we haven't had any breakfast!' Malcolm said. 'I want breakfast.'

'I'll make you something,' Amy said. 'You two sit down and wait nicely.' They sat and looked at her expectantly, but she suddenly felt overcome with weariness and sank into a chair herself. 'I'll do it in a minute. I just want to have a little rest first.'

'But I'm *hungry*,' Malcolm wailed.

'So am I,' David added, not to be left out.

'*Don't speak at the table*,' Charlie thundered. He lashed out with his fist. Malcolm was unlucky enough to be near him, and he caught the blow on the side of his head. Amy rose, scooped both boys off their chairs and put an arm around each of them. She stroked Malcolm's hair as he buried his face in her apron and forgot to be grown-up.

She led the boys over to the door. 'Go outside and play for a while— it'll be lunch-time quite soon, anyway. Wait a minute.' She went to one of her cake tins to fetch them a handful of biscuits each. 'There, that'll keep the worms quiet.' She was rewarded with smiles from both boys, though Malcolm's was rather watery. Cakes for breakfast were an unexpected treat. 'Take an apple each, too,' she called out the door after them.

She turned back to Charlie, unable to put off talking to him any longer. 'They're just tired,' she said. 'They were up late last night, and

313

they've worked very hard helping me with the cows. They're not really being naughty.' She sat down again, not wanting to stay in the room with him but too weary to leave. Her head was throbbing, and she ached all over. On the floor close to her feet, she saw the marks of the blood that she had only managed to clean up in a cursory fashion the night before. *My blood. My baby's blood.*

'They've got to learn to do as they're told. I'll not have them prattling at the table. You shouldn't have done it,' Charlie said, still not looking at her.

'Shouldn't have done what?'

'Milked the cows. You should have woken me up.'

Amy stared at him in blank amazement. 'Woken you up?' she echoed. She gathered her thoughts and answered carefully. 'I didn't wake you up because I thought you wouldn't be very pleased to be disturbed. I didn't want to… annoy you.'

'It's *my* job to milk them,' Charlie said, sounding more distressed. '*I* should have done it. You had no business doing it. You'll have upset my cows with your flapping skirts, too.'

'Does it really matter, Charlie? It needed doing, and I did it. I'm sorry if I've annoyed you, and no doubt I didn't do it very well, but the cows were bellowing and I was too scared to wake you up.' She had not meant to admit her fear, but the words slipped out before she could call them back.

'You'd have no reason to be scared if you behaved yourself,' he grumbled. 'You push a man too far with your nonsense.' She said nothing; she was not going to apologise for having been beaten. 'I don't know why I didn't wake up,' he fretted.

Because you were blind drunk, of course. 'I expect you were tired.' *Beating me like that must have taken a lot of energy.*

'I didn't hear you get up.'

Now it starts. 'No. I wasn't there.'

He looked at her, shocked. 'You didn't… stay out here?'

'No, I didn't lie on the floor all night,' she said bluntly. 'I slept in David's room.' *Did you really think I'd crawl into bed with you after that?* She shifted on her chair, trying to find a position that did not hurt so much.

'Sit still, woman! Stop squirming like that.'

'I'm sorry.' She apologised out of habit, and was at once vexed with herself. She rose to leave the room.

'Where are you going? I've made some tea. Drink it,' he ordered.

Amy sat down obediently, and poured herself a cup without thinking. But when she put the hot china to her cut lip, she gasped and lowered it, slopping a little tea in the saucer.

'I can't drink this,' she said.

'Why not?'

'My lip's too sore. I'll have some when it's cooled down.'

'Eat something, then,' he said, pushing the plate of bread towards her. Amy shook her head. 'Why not? You're a bag of bones now—you've got to eat, woman.'

'I can't eat that. It's too hard.'

'You don't need to use your lip to eat bread! Shove it in your mouth.'

'I can't.' She put her hands on her lap, and found again the small lump in her apron pocket.

'Why not?'

'Because of *this*,' Amy flared, taking the teeth in her hand and thrusting them in front of his face.

There was a moment's shocked silence. 'Did I...' Charlie said uncertainly.

'Yes, you did.' She put the teeth back in her pocket.

He rose unsteadily and walked to the door. When he reached it he turned and looked at her. 'You behave yourself and it maybe won't happen again.'

No, it won't happen again.

All Amy's work took twice as long because of her injuries. She knew she would only be able to do the essentials for many days. The floors would have to stay unscrubbed, the rugs unbeaten, and there would not be as many cakes as usual; butter making, too, would have to be abandoned for the moment. She could only bear to carry half-full buckets of water, so fetching it took twice the normal number of trips. There would be no chance at all of weeding her vegetable garden; she would just have to hope that the plants were well-grown enough to survive the neglect. Doing the work that could not be avoided was going to be hard enough when lifting anything heavy meant agony, and twisting her body to reach shelves or lift pots from the range sent shafts of pain through her bruised flesh.

Charlie came back from the afternoon milking to find her moving David's things out to the verandah room, David imagining that he was helping her as he trailed along getting underfoot.

'What are you doing?' Charlie asked.

'Davie's old enough to sleep out here now.' Forcing her voice to sound casual, Amy added, 'I'm going to sleep in his room.'

Charlie nodded. 'That's for the best, until you're well again. You'll be yourself in a few days.'

It's not just for a few days. But she said nothing, postponing the confrontation while she could. She wanted to build up as much strength as possible before the battle began.

'I took the boy milking with me,' Charlie said. 'He behaved all right. He's old enough to make himself useful around the place.'

'Yes,' said Amy. 'Mal's growing up. He was a big help to me yesterday—you were, too, Davie,' she added, seeing his hurt expression. 'You're a bit too little to go milking every day, though.'

'He'll grow up fast enough,' Charlie said. Amy had to resist the urge to remonstrate. She did not want to lose her baby boy before she had to; especially now she knew there would be no more babies.

Malcolm came in swaggering with self-importance.

'I've been helping with milking,' he said. 'You were slow this morning, Mama—it's much faster when Papa does it. Milking's man's work,' he added, standing close to his father as he parroted him. Amy turned away from the sight. Today Malcolm's startling likeness to his father was hard to bear.

Malcolm was still boasting about milking and doing 'man's work' when Amy put the boys to bed that evening. 'Papa won't take you, you're just a baby,' he said to David.

'I'm not a baby!'

'Why won't Papa take you, then?' Malcolm countered.

David could not come up with any argument against this, and his lower lip trembled. Amy gave him a hug.

'Never mind, Davie, you can help me, can't you? Shall we go and look for blackberries tomorrow, if Mama feels a bit better?' His face lit up at this. The walk would be uncomfortable, and she could not really spare the time to go blackberrying this early in the season, but Amy couldn't bear to see the little boy looking unhappy.

Despite her aches, Amy slept better that night than she had in years. To sleep without fear of being roughly awakened seemed a great luxury; she felt almost guilty for enjoying it so much. But she needed her sleep. She needed to get strong.

Amy's bruises deepened in colour over the next few days. Her swollen eye subsided a little, but her face still looked appalling three days later when Sunday arrived. It was clear to both her and Charlie that she would not be able to appear at church that morning.

'Now, you be a good boy for Papa,' she told Malcolm as she watched Charlie hoist the boy up to sit in front of him on the horse. She waved them off, hoping Charlie would not be too impatient with Malcolm, and relieved that he had been so easily persuaded to leave David at home with her. Her little David had never yet felt his father's wrath at its most frightening; she would hate him to get his first beating while she was still too frail to comfort him properly.

But Charlie looked no more sour than usual when he and Malcolm returned, and Malcolm had clearly enjoyed the adventure of riding with his father. Amy sent the boys outside to get rid of Malcolm's pent-up energy while she worked on the midday meal. Charlie stood in the kitchen doorway and watched her going to and from the range for some time before he spoke.

'People asked after you,' he said, an uneasy note in his voice. 'I had to say you were poorly.'

'That was true enough, Charlie. I'm not exactly feeling well.'

'They thought I meant you were with child. I could see them thinking it.'

'Let them think what they like. It doesn't matter.'

'Your pa...' The uneasy note was stronger. 'Your pa said he might call in and see you before lunch.'

Amy dropped a pot lid heavily. 'Oh, I hope he doesn't. You should have told him not to.'

'What could I have said? And don't you go ordering me around, woman—telling me what I should and shouldn't say. He maybe won't come, anyway.'

But Jack did come, striding across the paddocks and up to the back door of Charlie's house, beaming in the anticipation of seeing his daughter happy, healthy and swelling with new life.

'Where are you, girl?' he called from the doorstep. He came into the kitchen, full of the familiar smell of roast mutton, without waiting for a reply. 'I thought I'd just pop over and see how—' He stopped abruptly when he saw Amy standing at the far end of the table. 'No,' he said in a voice scarcely above a whisper. 'What's happened to you?'

Amy put down the plates she was holding and rushed to him. 'Shh, Pa, it's all right,' she soothed, as if she were talking to a child. 'Don't get upset. Here, sit down.'

She led him to a chair. He sat at her urging, staring at her face in dumb horror. Amy took a seat close to him. 'I know I look awful, but you mustn't get upset. It looks much worse than it is—you know how faces are for swelling up if they get a bit of a knock.'

'No, I don't,' Jack said, finding his voice again at last. 'I don't know how women's faces are when they've had a man's fists slamming into them. It's not a sight I've seen before.' He reached out to brush his fingers over her swollen eye and bruised cheeks. Amy could not help flinching at his gentle touch. 'Where is he?' Jack asked heavily.

'Over the back somewhere. Keeping out of your way, I expect.' She took his hand in both of hers. 'I'm all right, Pa, really I am. I wish you hadn't seen me like this, but you mustn't worry about me.'

'Worry? That bastard I gave you to does this to you, and you tell me not to worry! How long's this been going on?'

'This was the first time—the first time like this, anyway. And Pa,' she said, clutching at his hand, 'it's the last time, too. Nothing like this is ever going to happen again.'

'Damned right it's not! You're coming home with me right now. I never should have let you go in the first place.' He stood and held out his hand to help her rise. 'Come on, girl.'

Amy closed her eyes for a moment, gathering strength. How easy it would be to take the offered hand, how easy to run away. But the battle had to be fought, and it was her battle with Charlie, no one else's. Only if she lost would she flee.

'No, Pa. I'm staying here. He's still my husband, and he's the father of my sons.'

'I can't leave you here with him!' Jack protested.

'Yes, you can. I'll be all right.' She stood up slowly so as not to jar her cracked ribs. 'Pa, it's not going to happen again. I promise you that.'

'You can't know that. You can't know what he'll do.'

'I do know.' Her voice rang with certainty. 'I wouldn't say it if I wasn't sure it was true. Have I ever lied to you?'

'Never,' he admitted. 'But, girl—'

'Grandpa!' David cried out in delight as he burst through the doorway and flung himself at his grandfather. 'I seed you coming! I runned real fast—faster than Mal. Mal and Papa are coming. Mama looks funny, eh? Mama fell down on her face. Are you having lunch with us, Grandpa?'

'No, Davie,' Amy said. 'Grandpa's going home now. Aunt Susannah and Aunt Sophie have cooked lunch for Grandpa.'

Jack looked helplessly at her. 'I can't do it, girl. I can't leave you here.'

'You have to,' Amy insisted. 'I'll be all right. I promise.'

'What's wrong, Grandpa?' David asked, looking in confusion at Jack's stricken face. 'Are you crying?'

'Shh, Davie, Grandpa's all right. Don't upset the little fellow, Pa,' she urged quietly. Jack opened his mouth to argue, then shut it again.

Amy took his hand and led him to the door. 'Go home, Pa, and try not to worry about me. It's like Davie said—I fell on the floor and got hurt. That's nothing to get upset about, is it? I'll come and see you when

318

I don't look so awful.' She offered the less bruised of her cheeks for a kiss; her split lip was still too tender for caresses.

Jack went obediently through the back door, just as Charlie appeared around the corner of the house with Malcolm. Amy stood in the doorway, holding her breath as the two men stared at each other.

It was Jack who broke the silence. 'My girl tells me she fell down and got hurt,' he said coldly. 'An accident, I suppose you'd call it? I don't want my daughter having any more accidents like that. If she did I'd have to do something about it. Do you understand me?'

Charlie looked away before he answered. 'I can't help accidents. She'll be more careful now, I've no doubt. There'll maybe be no more accidents after this.'

'There'd better not be,' Jack said. He cast a last helpless glance at Amy before turning his face toward home.

Charlie watched Jack's retreating back, then turned to Amy. 'You didn't tell him.' He sounded confused.

Amy leaned against the door frame for support, aware of the weakness of her body now that the immediate need for strength had passed. *That was hard. Poor Pa, I wish he hadn't seen me like this.* 'I didn't need to. He knows. Lunch is nearly ready,' she went on in a determinedly light tone for the benefit of the children. 'You might as well come to the table.'

'There's a buggy coming up the road,' Charlie said, shading his eyes as he peered in the direction of the rattling noise that Amy now noticed for the first time. 'It's Kelly and his brood.'

'Is the whole valley going to come and see me today?' Amy said wearily. 'Charlie, can you make sure Frank and the children don't come inside? You won't be able to keep Lizzie out.'

She retreated to the relative privacy of the kitchen, and had time to sit down facing away from the door before Lizzie came up to the house.

'It's only me,' Lizzie called from the doorstep. 'We're on our way to Ma's for lunch, I just dropped in to see how you are. Charlie said you were a bit crook this morning, I wondered—'

'Lizzie,' Amy interrupted, still facing away from her cousin. 'I don't want you to make a fuss. It's not as bad as it looks.' She twisted around in her chair, wincing at the pain of the movement, and saw Lizzie's puzzled expression turn to shock.

'Amy, what's he done to you?'

'I know I look awful. You should have seen me the morning after he did it.' She managed a small laugh. 'It'll get better.'

'Why, Amy? You look as though he tried to kill you or something.'

319

'No, he didn't want me dead. He just wanted… well, never mind what he wanted. That's all over now.'

Lizzie knelt in front of Amy's chair and put her arms around her. 'I didn't know he treated you like this. I knew he hit you sometimes, I've seen the bruises. But like this! Oh, Amy, what can I do? How can I help you?'

Tears had begun to tumble down Lizzie's face. She clung to Amy as if she wanted to comfort her, but it was Amy who stroked Lizzie's hair and whispered soothingly in her ear. 'There's no need. It's over, Lizzie. I'm not going to let him hurt me again.'

'How can you stop him?'

'Don't worry about that. That's between me and him.' Amy took Lizzie's face in her hands, enjoying the feel of soft flesh that had never known a cruel touch. 'Now, Lizzie, I want you to forget all about how awful I look. In a few weeks I'll look the same as I ever did, so there's no need to make a fuss. I do want you to do something to help me, after all.'

'What?' Lizzie asked. 'What can I do?'

'I want you to go up to Aunt Edie's and act like nothing's wrong. Don't let anyone see you're upset—I don't want the whole valley talking about what's happened. I want you to go now, Lizzie. You've got Frank and the children waiting out there, they'll be wondering what you're up to. Help me up, I'm a bit clumsy just now.'

Lizzie helped her to her feet, and let Amy lead her to the back door. 'Off you go now, Lizzie. I won't come out the door or Frank will see me.'

Lizzie hovered uncertainly in the doorway. 'You're sure you'll be all right by yourself?'

'Quite sure. Hurry up, Lizzie.' Amy submitted to a kiss, painful though it was. 'Now, you go off and have a nice lunch.'

'I'll come and see you next week.'

'Only if you promise not to get upset.'

Frank turned with relief from his awkward attempts at making conversation with Charlie when Lizzie appeared through the doorway.

'You right, Lizzie?' he said as she climbed into the buggy and took Beth onto her lap. 'We'll be off, then, Charlie. See you tomorrow at the factory.'

'Don't talk to him,' Lizzie hissed under her breath.

Frank glanced at her in surprise. 'What's wrong? Hey, have you been crying?'

'No,' Lizzie muttered. 'I'm not crying now, anyway. Drive faster—I want to get away from here.'

Frank urged the horses to a gentle trot. 'What happened? Is Amy really sick?'

'She looks *awful*,' Lizzie wailed.

'Is Aunt Amy sick?' Maudie asked from the rear seat, sounding frightened. Joey babbled away in the private language no one but his mother and big sister could understand, but it was clear enough that he was about to start crying at the thought of his much-loved aunt's being ill, and little Beth picked up enough of her mother's distress to let out a whimper of her own.

'Settle down, you lot,' Lizzie said. 'Aunt Amy's not sick. She hurt her face, and she looks a bit funny. Mama got a fright, that's all.'

The children were easily reassured, but Frank looked at Lizzie in concern. 'What's wrong?' he asked under his breath.

'I'll tell you later,' she murmured. 'There're too many ears flapping here.' She gestured towards Maudie.

Lizzie's façade slipped from time to time over lunch, and Frank saw her brush an occasional tear away when she thought no one was watching. He kept an eye on the clock, anxious to get home and find out what had so upset her as soon as they could politely leave.

'You look a bit down in the mouth today, Lizzie,' Arthur remarked. 'What's the matter, cat got your tongue?'

'Nothing's wrong with me,' Lizzie snapped. 'Mind your own business.'

'Here, you keep a civil tongue in your head, my girl,' said Arthur. 'Frank, why don't you keep your wife in line?' he added, forgetting to keep up the haughty manner he was still trying to use with Frank.

'Lizzie, don't talk to your pa like that,' Frank said. Lizzie cast an anguished look at him, rushed from the table and went out the back door. She was back a few minutes later, only her swollen eyes betraying her lapse.

Arthur glanced from Frank to Lizzie, frowning, but he said nothing until he and Frank were sitting on the verandah after lunch while Lizzie helped her mother with the dishes. 'You boys go and see to Frank's horses,' he told Bill and Alf.

'Don't worry about that, there's no need,' Frank said.

'Yes, there is—that bay of yours hasn't got much condition on her. Spending all your time looking after your fancy cows, are you? Give them a nosebag each, Bill. Ernie, you go too.'

Arthur waited till his sons were out of earshot before turning back to Frank. 'Now, Frank, you'll say it's none of my business, but Lizzie's my daughter and I'm making it my business. There's such a thing as being too hard on a wife, you know.'

'Eh?' Frank said in blank astonishment.

'It's not natural to see Lizzie in such a misery. You want the girl to have a bit of spirit. Respect, that's one thing, but having her scared half out of her wits… well, that's not right.'

'But Pa, I haven't—'

'All right, Frank, that's enough,' Arthur interrupted. 'I've said my piece, I'll say no more. I think you know what I mean.'

'I suppose so,' Frank said dubiously. Whatever had upset Lizzie, he was quite sure he was not responsible.

At last it was time to go home, and he trotted the horses all the way. He unharnessed them while Lizzie got the children out of their good clothes, put Beth down for her afternoon sleep and sent the two older children outside to play. By the time he got back to the house, she was alone in the kitchen.

'What's wrong?' he asked.

Lizzie collapsed into his open arms, dissolving into sobs. 'Oh, Frank, if you'd only seen her.'

Frank patted her back. 'Seen what? What's wrong with Amy?'

'He's beaten her. Poor little Amy. And I can't do anything about it!'

Frank held her in silence for a few moments, wondering what he could say to soothe her. 'It's none of our business, Lizzie,' he said carefully. 'I know you think he shouldn't have done it, but… well, some men do give their wives a slap sometimes, love. It's nothing for you to upset yourself over.'

Lizzie pulled away and glared at him. 'Do you think I don't know that? I'm not talking about a slap or two—Lord knows he's given her plenty of those over the years. She's usually got a bruise somewhere, though she never says anything about it. Never like this, though. Her face is all cut and bruised—she's bruised all over, I think. You can see it hurts her just to move. He's had a real go at her with those horrible great fists of his—fought her as though she was a man instead of little Amy who never hurts anyone. Her face, Frank—you can hardly recognise her, it's so black and swollen.'

'What the heck's he done that for?' Frank said in astonishment.

'How should I know?' Lizzie shot back. 'How am I meant to know what a man like that thinks?' Her face crumpled, and she let Frank enfold her in his arms again.

'Poor old Amy, eh?' Frank tried without success to fathom why any man, let alone one with a sweet-tempered wife like Amy, would want to beat her as savagely as Lizzie had described. 'She's such a little thing, too. She's not very strong.'

Lizzie's voice came muffled from where she had laid her head on his shoulder. 'You wouldn't say that if you'd seen her today. I was the one crying like a baby, she just sat there all calm and quiet. It was like she was looking after me, not the other way around. Amy's strong, all right. She's stronger than any of us.'

25

March 1891

Amy's injuries slowly healed as the weeks passed. Her bruises faded from livid purple to a dirty yellow; the swelling of her black eye subsided until the injured eye no longer looked half the size of its mate; and her split lip closed up, leaving a red scar that would fade in time to be barely noticeable. Her ribs seemed as painful as ever, but that injury was not visible.

The healing of her wounds was accompanied by a return to strength not confined to her body. The weariness of spirit that had grown in Amy as a response to years of rough usage, broken nights, and nothing to look forward to but more of the same, more pain and more dead babies, began to lift, and to be replaced by a tiny thread of conviction that things might be otherwise.

To sleep properly at night, a deep sleep not disturbed by a hand snatching at her nightdress or a heavy body heaving itself onto hers, was blissful, and she wallowed in the luxury of it. After years of having to spend every night lying flat on her back for Charlie's convenience, even when he had beaten her buttocks raw, she indulged herself trying out different positions to sleep. On her front, on either side, her head on two pillows or on none, changing position a dozen times if she wanted instead of lying very still so as not wake Charlie; Amy tried them all, until at last she decided the way she liked best was to lie on her side right in the middle of the bed and curl her knees close to her chest so that her body made a half circle. It was the way she had slept as a girl, she remembered now, in the days before she had known anything of men.

By the end of March, though her face was far from back to normal she no longer looked horrifying. Indeed, there was a new calmness about her that a more perceptive man than Charlie might have wondered at. She had been aware for days that his scrutiny of her face must be telling him the worst of her injuries had healed, so it was no real surprise when the crisis came.

It was a cool evening at the end of a bright day. The boys had been in bed for hours. Amy sat at her sewing and Charlie read his newspaper, casting occasional glances at her.

He folded his paper noisily and put it down on the floor by his chair, then stood up and lit a candle from the lamp. 'I'm going to bed,' he said, extinguishing the lamp as he spoke.

Amy stopped in mid-stitch when the lamplight disappeared. She slipped her needle into the cuff of the shirt she was mending and bundled the shirt into her sewing bag. 'Good night,' she said as she struck a match to light her own candle. She gathered up their tea cups from beside the chairs and carried them through to the kitchen, expecting Charlie to go straight into the bedroom.

Instead she heard his heavy tread following her into the kitchen. *So it's to be tonight.* She put the candle and the cups down on the table and shut her eyes for a moment, gripping the rough wood of the table as if to gather its strength into herself, then turned and looked straight at Charlie.

'I thought you were going to bed.'

'Aye, so I am. And so are you. There's nothing wrong with you now.'

'Nothing that shows, no.'

'So there's no need for you to go off to the other room any more. You can come back where you belong.' He had half turned to go, too sure of being obeyed to bother waiting, when Amy answered.

'No.'

The word dropped heavily into the silence of the dim room, like a stone flung in a pool. Charlie turned back and stared at her, his face grim in the flickering light of the candle.

'What did you say?'

'I said no.' Her voice rose on the last word. 'I'm not coming to bed with you.'

'I'm telling you you're coming—you're coming right now.' Amy knew the irritation in his voice would soon turn into something stronger.

'And I'm telling you I'm not.'

'Are you defying me, woman?' Still he seemed to doubt that he was hearing her properly.

'Call it that if you want. I'm not coming back to your bed. That's all over between us.'

'I'll not have you talking to me like that—I'll show you what happens when you don't do as you're told.' He took a step towards her; Amy held her ground and stared back defiantly. 'You're going to feel that stick on your backside—I'll teach you not to disobey me.'

'No, you're not going to do that, Charlie.'

The calmness of her voice brought him up short, and almost despite himself he asked, 'Why not?'

He towered over her; Amy had to crane her neck to look him in the eye. She spoke slowly, enunciating each word clearly. 'Because if you ever lay a hand on me again, I'll walk out that door and I won't come back.'

'You can't! You've no business talking of leaving—you belong here. You belong to *me.*'

'I'm not going to put up with what you did to me. I won't let you touch me again.'

'I'll do what I like with you,' he said, his face a fierce red. 'You're mine, woman, and I'll show you what that means.'

'What are you going to do, knock some more of my teeth out?' It was dangerous to taunt him, she knew; but she was beyond fear. He had done his worst to her and she had survived it; he had no weapons except the strength of his body, and she was not going to let him use it against her any more. 'You could only force me once. If you do I'll walk out. I mean it, Charlie.'

'Do you think I'd let you go?'

'You can't stop me. You're not always here to watch me. It's not far to Pa's, I could be over there before you'd noticed I was gone.'

'I'd fetch you back—I'd not have you making a fool of me, running home to your pa.' He still thought he was winning, Amy could tell, but her new-found self-assurance was confusing him.

'Would you? You'd have to deal with Pa and the boys first. Pa wanted to bring me home with him when he saw what you'd done to me—he'd never let you take me back if I asked him to look after me.'

'You've no right—the law would be on my side, you know. I'd get the sergeant out here to fetch you back.'

'I thought you didn't want to be made a fool of. What do you think the town would say when they heard you'd had to get the policeman to drag your wife home for you? And then I'd run away again, and you'd have to get Sergeant Riley out again. How long would you keep it up? How long do you think Sergeant Riley would keep coming out before he told you to stop bothering him?'

'You... you couldn't.' Now he was struggling to hold on to his certainty. 'What kind of a woman abandons her children? Eh? What sort of evil bitch runs off and leaves her bairns?'

'Leave them? I wouldn't leave my boys with you. I'd take them with me.'

'No!' He howled the word, fear and fury mingled. 'You're not taking my sons away from me—not my sons! I'll not let you take them.'

'If you force me to run away, then they'll come too. You can't stop me doing that, either. You can't have them with you all the time, not every minute of the day. They love going to see Pa, I'd have no trouble getting them to come with me. And Pa wouldn't give his grandsons back to you any more than he'd give me.'

'You want to take my sons away from me!' he raged.

'No, I don't, Charlie,' Amy said, her voice calm although she had to raise it to make him hear her. 'I don't want to take the boys off you—they need their father, and I know you love them, whatever you feel about me. I'll only take them away if you make me leave.'

'I won't let you,' he repeated.

'Otherwise, things can carry on just the same as before. I'll keep house for you, I'll do the same cooking and cleaning I've always done. I'll do everything I've always done. All except that one thing. Just that one thing.'

'You've no business saying what you will and won't do—it's your duty to do as I say—damn it, you're my wife! What about my rights?' He shouted the question at her.

'What about mine?' Amy shouted back, allowing herself to feel anger at last.

He stared at her blankly. 'What are you talking about?' Amy could see that he truly had no idea what she meant. 'For years I've fed and clothed you—kept a roof over your head—what do you mean, going on about rights?'

'I think you've had your money's worth out of me.'

But that was too subtle a concept for Charlie. 'The rights of the marriage bed—it's your duty to share my bed,' he floundered.

'I don't think it is. Not any more. You've made it very clear to me over the years that I don't... please you in... in that way.' Amy fought down the embarrassment she felt in speaking of such things. 'And it seems there are women who do.' She saw him give a start. 'I think we'd both be a lot happier if you stopped trying to force the rights of the marriage bed and just carried on taking your pleasure where you've been taking it for years—in the whorehouse.'

'Who told you that?' Charlie demanded. 'Who's been running to you with tales?' Amy could tell from his voice that he was struggling to keep up his belligerence in the face of the jolt she had just given him.

'You told me yourself. I smelt the whores on you.'

'And why shouldn't I go to the whores? What pleasure do you think it is mounting you, the nonsense you carry on with? All that trembling and bawling, and making out you're too much the fine lady for me?'

'Stop doing it, then. Stick to your whores.'

'What makes you think you're so much better than them? Eh? You bore a bastard to the first man who offered to tumble you—what does that make you, then?'

'I've never been a whore, Charlie. I didn't even know what the word meant till I married you, but you flung it at me often enough that I took notice of what people say until I'd figured it out for myself.'

'So you're trying to make out that you were a decent woman when I wed you? That you came to me in the state a wife should?'

'Of course I'm not.' For a moment the vision of her tiny daughter lying in her arms flashed before Amy, but she shut it out at once. She had to be strong, not dissolve into tears. 'Yes, I sinned. I did wrong. But that was before you had any claim over me. I've never wronged you, Charlie. I've never sinned against you.' Despite her best efforts, she could not keep a catch out of her voice. 'I've done my best. I've tried so hard to please you.'

'Well, you haven't.'

'No, I know that. So there's no use trying any more, is there? I'll go on doing the things I do seem to be capable of—you've never complained about the way I keep house—and you use the women who suit you.'

She could see in his face that he knew he was losing the fight, and that the frustration of knowing it was making him angrier. 'It's not your place to tell me what to do—there's more than pleasure in it. I've the right to get sons on my wife—it's your duty to give me sons.'

'I've given you two strong sons. This isn't a big farm, you know—it'll be hard enough to make it support two families when the boys are grown.'

'So you despise my farm, do you? Not good enough for the fine lady? Not good enough for Jack Leith's daughter?'

'I didn't say that. All I said was it's not big enough for a tribe of sons—don't do that, Charlie,' she warned as he balled his fist.

'I'll decide how many sons I can support, not you. I'll decide when I've enough sons to help me work the place. Don't you go telling me you'll give me no more, bitch. You'll give me sons, all right.'

She stared dispassionately at his fist. 'You shouldn't have got rid of the last child, then.'

His face clouded with confusion. 'What are you talking about?'

'The one I was carrying the night you knocked my teeth out. The one you kicked out of me when I was lying on the floor.'

He paled visibly at her words. 'No,' he whispered. 'Why didn't you tell me you were with child?'

'It's hard to think clearly when you're being beaten like that. Anyway, I didn't know it myself. I've been with child so much this last year, I can't tell the signs any more. I think I'd carried that one a bit longer than some of the others, though. Maybe I wouldn't have lost it this time. Maybe you would have had another son.' She stabbed the knife in further. 'But you'll never know. Because you killed it. Why should I carry more babies for you to kill?'

'Y-you're lying,' he stammered, but they both knew he did not believe his own words.

'I dragged myself up off the floor and held on to that chair. That's when I felt the child coming. There was a lot of blood. There's a bloodstain where you're standing. It's not as dark as it was, but you can see it if you look properly. I haven't been able to give the floor a good scrub since, not with the state you left me in. Some of it's my blood, but most of it's from the baby.'

'It wouldn't have happened if you hadn't driven me to it, you and your nonsense—you brought it on yourself.'

'Did I? Did I ask you to leave me all bloodied and bruised? Did I ask you to kill our child?'

Charlie gave a roar of rage and frustration. He raised his fist, and Amy resisted the almost overpowering urge to cringe away as he swung it.

There was a resounding crack as his fist hammered into the wall behind her. He stormed from the room, slamming first the door into the parlour and then the bedroom door. Amy found herself alone in the kitchen.

Her legs gave way under her, and she sank heavily into a chair. She realised that she was shaking, but not with fear. It was exhilaration; the exhilaration of having faced Charlie and won. He was never going to hurt her again.

When her heart stopped pounding so fiercely she stood up, leaning on the edge of the table for support. She was aware of a deep weariness creeping over her now that the immediate need for strength had passed. She examined with dispassionate interest the dent Charlie's fist had left in the wall. *That could have been my face. A few weeks ago it was.*

She walked slowly into the tiny bedroom that was now hers, closing the door behind her. When she had undressed she slipped between the sheets, the touch of the smooth linen like a caress. She extinguished her candle and felt the darkness of the room enfolding her in a safe embrace before she fell into a deep, dreamless sleep.

Charlie sat in silence while Amy dished up his breakfast the next morning. She was about to go and fetch the boys from their bedroom when he spoke.

'I think you're maybe not over that bit of trouble yet.'

Amy stopped in her tracks, wondering what was coming next.

'It might be for the best if you keep to the back room for a wee bit longer,' he went on. 'We'll speak no more of what was said last night when you were feeling poorly.'

Pretending I'm sick won't change things, Charlie. And I'm never coming back to your bed. But Amy said nothing aloud. If he wanted to try and save face with himself by believing lies about what had gone on between them, let him believe them. The truth would force itself upon him soon enough.

Later that morning, when Amy had finished making Charlie's bed and tidying his clothes away, she opened his wardrobe and saw her silk dress hanging there beside his suit. It was time she did something about that, as well as the three drawers that held the rest of her belongings. There was no need to leave her things in his room any longer, not now that she had told him how matters were going to be.

She hung the silk dress in the tiny wardrobe that stood in a corner of the second bedroom, with her work dresses beside it and her precious hat on a shelf above them. She had already filled with her underwear two drawers of the little chest Charlie had made for what had been the children's room, when she came to empty the lowest drawer of Charlie's chest. It surprised Amy with its weight as she tugged at it. She opened the drawer to discover the books that she had carried from her father's house in her heavy bundle on the night of her marriage six years before.

Amy had always vaguely remembered that the books were there, but just getting through each day had taken all her endurance through the intervening years, leaving no room for such indulgences as reading. She sat down on the floor and began to lift the books from the drawer.

She gave little cries of delight as she pulled out each one. There were books of poems, one or two volumes of plays, and several novels. Amy remembered clearly when she had received each one of them; and she had loved them all. They had been her window on a world beyond the valley; a world she had dreamed of living in. The dreams were gone now, or at least were too deeply buried to have any conscious sense of yearning attached to them; but now that she had changed her reality to make it bearable, if no less narrow, she could once again take pleasure from the dream-windows. Now that she had her own room, her books would not be hidden away as if they were something shameful.

When the books had all been taken out and lined up against one wall of her little bedroom, Amy found tucked away in a corner of the drawer, safely wrapped in lacy doilies, the silver-framed photograph of her family. *I'm not going to hide you away, either, Mama,* she told the image. The photograph given pride of place on her chest of drawers, Amy sat down on her bed and gazed with pleasure at the look of love on her mother's face.

I don't know what you'd think of what I've done about Charlie, Mama. I bet you never would have done anything like that to Pa. She smiled at the picture of her father as a young man. *Pa never hurt you, did he? He loved you. He still does.*

So now she had all her worldly goods in her own bedroom; all except one thing. She went back to Charlie's room and stood in the doorway, studying the bed and its covering.

It was her bedspread, made by her own hands and her grandmother's. But she had brought it to Charlie, and it had covered both of them for six years. She had promised him she would still be an obedient wife in every way except sharing his bed; would taking the bedspread be a breach of that? Charlie might think so. As far as he was concerned, the few things she had brought to their marriage had become his property, just as she had. It was the way she had thought about herself for years: his property, for him to do with as he wished.

But not any longer. Her body didn't belong to him any more, and neither did her bedspread. She gathered it up quickly, so as not to give herself time to change her mind, and carried it through to spread over her own little bed. She allowed herself to survey the room with satisfaction before she hurried off about her work. Her own small domain, with her precious things around her.

That evening, Amy took a candle through to her bedroom and heard Charlie go outside; to relieve himself, she assumed. The sound muffled by the wall, she heard him come back through the kitchen and parlour, then into his bedroom. The footsteps stopped abruptly. It struck her that he must have seen the bedspread had gone, and with it his 'wee bit longer' pretence.

There was a banging and thumping; it took Amy a few moments to realise Charlie had opened the wardrobe and was now pulling out all the drawers to see if she had taken all her clothes. *Yes, I have, Charlie. Every single thing I own.*

The footsteps started again, and she heard Charlie's heavy tread making its way towards his bedroom door. *He's annoyed now. He's going to come in here and... what? Drag me back in there? Rip my clothes off and force me right here?* She held the candle in front of her and stared into its light until her eyes hurt. *Don't do it, Charlie. Don't make me take the boys away from you.*

Amy sat unmoving, listening to the progress of Charlie's steps. She heard his door handle turn and the door squeak as it opened, but then the steps stopped. There was a long silence; Amy knew that Charlie's slow brain was weighing up the consequences of what he was about to do.

The door closed and his steps began again. But they went back to his own bed, not towards her. Through the thin wall she heard him muttering as he undressed and climbed into bed; curses against her, she had no doubt.

Amy let her breath out on a sigh, and realised she had been holding it for some time. She put the candle on the chest by her bed and got undressed, then took a book from the neat row and held it close to her as she slipped between the sheets. She propped the pillow behind her and snuggled down to indulge in the almost forgotten luxury of reading in bed.

Dark glares and a stony silence from Charlie were her reward at breakfast the next morning. Amy looked back calmly when she had to look at him at all, smothering an occasional yawn. She had indulged herself a little too long with reading, but to be weary from self-indulgence was almost a pleasure in itself.

The sky threatened rain; not strongly enough to keep Charlie from his work, much to Amy's relief, but enough for her to keep David inside with her all morning. She was grateful for the placid nature that made David content to potter about the house after her while she worked. He played with Ginger, dragging a piece of paper on a string behind him to entice the cat, while Amy made the beds and tidied the bedrooms, scrubbed the kitchen floor and dusted all the rooms. When Ginger grew tired and curled up in a sunny corner of the now-dry kitchen floor to sleep David curled up with him, stroking the cat's soft fur.

Amy left the potatoes she was peeling and sat down for a moment to watch them, smiling at the sight. She was lucky to have a child like David; he was as delightful as Malcolm was difficult.

'Ginger's asleep, Mama,' David said, looking up at her.

'That's right, Davie. Pussy cats need a lot of sleep.' She held out her arms. 'Come and have a cuddle with Mama, just for a bit. I've got to start making pudding in a minute.'

David readily clambered onto her lap, put his arms around her neck and planted a wet kiss on her lips. 'You're pretty, Mama. Your face not funny now.'

'Thank you, Davie.' She squeezed him tightly. 'Ooh, you're good at cuddles, sweetie. Mama loves cuddling her Davie.' She wound one of his dark ringlets around her finger and smoothed his curls down over his collar. *My pretty little baby. Too pretty to be a boy.*

'When can I go to school, Mama?'

'Like Mal? Not till you're five. That's a year and a bit away. So soon,' she mused. 'You're growing up so fast.' *Ann's six now. I bet she looks just like Davie, except even prettier.* If anyone could be prettier than David.

'I going to be big like Mal.'

'Of course you will, Davie. Big and strong, so you can help Papa. Hop down now, darling, Mama's got to finish making lunch.'

Charlie came in for the meal looking as sour as he had at breakfast; Amy was glad that Malcolm was safely away at school and unable to make his father any grumpier. Charlie did not usually take much notice of David, even had the younger boy been inclined to naughtiness. There was an element in Charlie's expression that made her a little uneasy: a touch of malice along with the surliness. It made her wonder if he had spent the morning plotting some way of getting even with her. But frustrated annoyance was much plainer than the malice; if he had indeed been trying to plot retaliation it seemed to have been in vain.

Amy lifted David onto his chair and tucked a napkin into his collar before she dished up for the three of them. When Charlie had said a rapid grace and begun eating his own food she started to cut up David's chop into manageable pieces for the little boy.

'What are you doing?' Charlie asked.

'Cutting Davie's meat up for him,' Amy answered simply, wondering why he should suddenly take an interest in something she did every day.

'He's big enough to feed himself. Leave him alone.'

'He can't manage the chop, Charlie. His hands are still a bit little to handle a knife and fork with meat.'

Charlie fixed her with a grim stare. 'I said leave him alone. You're babying that boy.'

It was not worth making a fuss about. He would see soon enough that David was not capable of cutting his meat. She took up her own knife and fork and began eating in silence.

David looked from Amy to Charlie and back again, a puzzled expression on his face as he tried to fathom what was going on over his head. Amy motioned towards his plate. David picked up his fork and stabbed at the meat.

The chop was too heavy for his little hand. It fell off the fork and landed on his helping of carrots. David stabbed at it again, knocking a few slices of carrot onto the table. He looked guiltily at his father, picked up the carrot slices and stuffed them in his mouth, then picked the chop up in both hands.

'Here!' Charlie said sternly. 'You eat that properly—don't go eating with your fingers like a savage.'

'I can't, Papa—'

Charlie pointed a warning finger at him. 'Don't speak at the table, boy. You know the rule.'

David cast a pleading look at Amy, but she could only look back helplessly. He dropped the chop back onto his plate and tried stabbing it again, more energetically this time.

The chop skidded across his plate and slid into the boiled potato opposite it. Meat and potato flew off the plate and onto the table. David reached out to grab at them, and in his haste he flipped the whole plate over, scattering what was left of his meal over the table and the floor.

David stared at the mess he had made, and turned to his father with tears filling his eyes. 'I'm sorry, Papa. I didn't mean to.'

Charlie reached out and gave David a clout over the ear. 'I told you to keep quiet! Look at the mess you've made, you young fool.'

David let out a wail of pain and fright. He clambered down from his chair to bury his face in Amy's lap. She put her arms around him and held him close, stroking his hair. 'It's all right, Davie,' she soothed. 'You couldn't help it.'

'Why can't that boy eat properly?' Charlie demanded. 'It's high time he learned. You still feeding him like a baby, at his age.' He glared at David sobbing in Amy's lap. 'How old is he?'

'Only three, Charlie. Just a little fellow.'

'Old enough to behave himself. When does he turn four?'

'In August,' Amy admitted.

'He's nearer four than three, then. What are you doing, keeping him in dresses at that age? Eh? Time he was in trousers.' He looked at Amy's hand stroking David's long curls, and Amy could almost hear his mind ticking over.

'Time that boy had a haircut,' Charlie said suddenly.

'No!' The cry of protest was out before Amy could call it back. 'Don't cut his hair, Charlie, not his pretty curls. He's too little.'

'Aye, it's time he had a haircut,' Charlie repeated, grim satisfaction on his face as he saw how much the idea upset Amy. 'He's nearly four. I gave his brother his first haircut at three years.'

But Malcolm had not had beautiful black ringlets tumbling down to his collar, framing a face with huge blue eyes and a rosebud mouth. Malcolm had not been a walking image of a lost daughter. Amy clutched at David, and her distress communicated itself to him, making him sob more than ever.

Charlie went off to his bedroom, returning with a pair of scissors. He took hold of David's arm and yanked him from Amy's grasp.

'Right, get on this chair, boy. And stop that bawling.' He gave David a slap across the head which, if it was intended to still the child's sobs, failed miserably. Amy felt tears running down her own cheeks, but she bit back the words of protest that rose to her lips, knowing she would only make things harder for David by arguing.

When Charlie had dumped him unceremoniously on the chair, the sight of the large scissors waving around close to his face made David wail even louder. He tried to squirm away from the terrifying blades, but Charlie took a tight grip on his arm and lowered his face till it was close to his little son's.

'Now, you behave yourself, boy. Keep still and don't make a sound, or I'll teach you a lesson. Understand?' He shook David's arm. 'Understand?'

David gulped back a sob and gave a little nod. 'Yes, Papa,' he said in a voice that was more of a squeak. He held himself rigid, following the movement of the scissors with nervous flicks of his eyes.

The blades sliced off long coils of black hair at every cut. Amy watched helplessly as the pile of shorn curls around the chair grew thicker.

Charlie had nearly finished when the scissors brushed against David's ear for a moment. The child gave a yelp of fright and a small start, then screamed as the blades nicked his ear.

'You cut my ear off!' he wailed.

'Stop that,' Charlie roared, emphasising his words with another slap. 'Stop crying like a baby. It's your own fault—I'd not have cut you if you'd kept still.'

But David only howled the louder, patting at the ear that now had a small spot of blood on it.

'I warned you, boy. I told you to behave yourself.' Charlie snatched a handful of hair at the top of David's head, where it was still long enough to grab at, and held it tightly so that the child could not move. He snipped the last few curls off close to David's scalp, then dropped the scissors on the table.

Charlie let go his grip, and the little boy began to scramble off the chair towards his mother. 'No, you don't,' Charlie said, taking hold of his arm. 'You played up for me, boy. I'm going to teach you a lesson.'

David looked at him with fear but no understanding, but Amy understood only too well.

'Charlie, no,' she begged.

'He's got to learn.' But the look of triumph on Charlie's face said clearly that it was her he sought to punish, not the trembling child held firmly in his grasp. 'I'll teach you to do as you're told, boy. I'm going to give you a good hiding.'

David had never had anything close a beating, but he had seen his older brother sobbing from the effects of one often enough. He howled his terror and tried to pull out of Charlie's grip. 'Mama,' he wailed. 'Mama!'

'Don't go crying for your Mama like a baby, or you'll get a worse hiding.' Charlie tried to drag David from the room, but the child struggled so hard that instead his father picked him up and carried him outside tucked under one arm.

'Don't hit him, Charlie, please don't,' Amy pleaded, hurrying after them. 'He didn't mean to annoy you. He's just a little boy, don't hurt him.'

Charlie said nothing until the three of them were behind the shed where he kept a length of supple-jack handy for chastising Malcolm. He turned to Amy and gave her a scornful look.

'What are you going to do about it? Run to your pa and tell him I gave my son a bit of correcting? It's your fault, in any event—you've been babying the boy. It's time I took him in hand.'

Amy stood silent and helpless. Charlie was right; she could not take the boys off him just because he punished them when he considered they deserved it. He did nothing to the children that she had not seen her own father do to his sons, and if he did it more harshly and at a younger age he was still within his rights.

She turned her face away so as not to see the blows falling, but she could not shut out David's screams.

There were six strokes. David's wails hardly abated when the blows stopped. Amy reached out her arms for him, but Charlie kept him firmly in his grip. He put David under his arm once again and carried him to the verandah bedroom, where he shoved him through the doorway.

'You can stay there till you stop that noise. You don't leave this room till I say you can.' He shut the door on the sobbing child. 'Keep away from him,' he warned Amy, and though she looked with longing at the closed door she followed him obediently back to the kitchen.

'Food's cold,' Charlie muttered as he finished his chops and vegetables. Amy had no stomach for her own meal. She served up Charlie's pudding, willing him to get on and leave the house so that she could comfort her miserable little David.

He stood up at last, but before he reached the door he turned back and stared at Amy. 'Leave that boy alone. You keep away from him until I say you can go in there.'

'I just want to see if he's all right, Charlie. Please let me—'

'No,' he interrupted.

Amy glared at him. 'You can't keep me away from my little boy. I won't let you.'

He gave her the same look of triumph she had seen earlier. 'You go near that boy without my say-so and I'll give him another dose of the same. Understand?'

So that was how he wanted to fight the next round: using David as a weapon. Amy turned away from him and nodded.

When Charlie had gone, she selected one of the longest locks from the mournful pile of shorn curls, tied it with a piece of ribbon, and placed it on her chest of drawers beside the photograph of her mother.

It was a wretched afternoon. Amy was torn between an almost overpowering desire to rush to David and comfort him, and the knowledge that she would be responsible for getting him beaten again if she did.

When Malcolm arrived home from school, she was almost grateful for the distraction he provided as she gave him some milk and biscuits.

'Where's Dave?' he asked, looking around the room for his brother.

'In the bedroom. He got in trouble with your father, and he's not allowed out of the room.'

'Did Pa give him a hiding?'

'Yes, he did. Leave Davie alone, Mal. Malcolm!' she called as Malcolm, ignoring her, made for the door into the parlour.

'Where are you going, boy?' Charlie said from the door, coming in for his afternoon tea.

'I want to see Dave.'

'You can't. He'll stay in that room by himself till he stops his bawling. Come here and sit down.'

Malcolm did as he was told, but he cast almost as many glances at the intervening wall as Amy did.

Charlie took Malcolm off to help him with the milking, leaving Amy once again alone in the house with the weeping David. From time to time she heard the little boy crying out to her.

When he came back for dinner, Charlie went out to the verandah while Amy stood and listened in the doorway between the kitchen and parlour.

'Are you going to stop that bawling?' The sound of weeping came to her through the open doorways between them. 'Then you'll stay there till you do. There'll be no dinner for you tonight.'

'Mama,' David sobbed as the door closed on him once more.

'He's very little to go without his dinner, Charlie,' Amy said when Charlie had come back to the kitchen and sat down at the table. 'He hardly had any lunch, either.'

'It'll teach him a lesson. It's time he grew up a bit,' Charlie said.

Malcolm was visibly subdued during the meal. When he had finished eating he looked expectantly at his father for permission to go to his room.

'I need to put the boys to bed now, Charlie,' Amy said, trying hard to keep her feelings out of her voice. 'I have to help them get undressed and tuck them in.'

Charlie stared narrowly at her. 'All right,' he said after a pause. 'Put them straight to bed, mind. None of your babying nonsense.'

Malcolm pushed ahead of her, eager to get into the bedroom. 'Did you get a hiding, Dave?' he asked breathlessly the moment he was in the room.

David was curled up against the wall on the side of the bed furthest from the house. He turned towards them at the sound of Malcolm's voice, and his wretched, bewildered face sent a pang through Amy. His eyes looked bigger than ever now that his hair had been shorn; they were full of fear like a captive creature's.

'Mama,' he whimpered, holding out his arms to her. 'Cuddle me, Mama.'

'I can't, Davie. I'm not allowed.' Amy blinked away tears as well as she could manage at the sight of her poor, shorn little boy. 'Come on, Mama will help you get your clothes off.'

She unbuttoned his frock and lifted it over his head, careful not to touch his bruised buttocks. 'My bottom hurts, Mama,' he said, his voice trembling.

'I know, Davie. Lie on your tummy tonight, it won't be as sore in the morning.' Her arms ached to hold him close, but she half expected Charlie to burst in on them at any moment.

Malcolm started pulling off his own clothes when Amy had helped him with the buttons. 'Hey, your hair looks good, Dave,' he said. 'You look like a boy now.'

'Do I?' A tiny spark of animation came into David's tear-streaked face.

'Yes, not like a stupid girl.'

When Amy had buttoned his nightshirt David reached up to where his curls had been, fingering the cropped hair with new interest. 'Papa cut my ear off,' he said when his hand brushed against the tender spot, a small note of pride in his voice.

'No, he didn't, Davie,' Amy corrected gently. 'He just nicked it a tiny bit.' She pulled back the covers and watched David scramble into bed, making sure that he lay face down. 'Don't be rough with Davie tonight,

Mal,' she said. 'He's got a sore bottom.'

'I know that,' Malcolm said scornfully. 'I know all about getting hidings. Let's see your ear, Dave.' He checked the ear and whistled his appreciation. 'He nearly cut my ear off too, once. You've got to sit real still when he cuts your hair, and it takes *hours*. What did you get a hiding for?'

'I don't know,' David said, bewildered again. 'I must have been naughty.'

'Nah, Pa just gets wild sometimes,' said Malcolm. 'He gives me hidings just for nothing. The other day he—'

'Good night, you two,' Amy interrupted. She did not dare give David a kiss in case she were caught in the act. 'Don't talk loud or Papa will hear you.'

'I'm hungry, Mama,' David said plaintively.

'I'm sorry, darling, I can't give you anything to eat. Try to go to sleep, then breakfast time will come around faster.'

She put out the candle and closed the door on them as Malcolm went on whispering his own experiences of his father's rough justice. It was not a topic she would have chosen for David on such an evening, but it was a small comfort to her to see Malcolm treating his brother as an equal instead of with the indifference he usually showed the younger boy.

Charlie was sitting in the parlour with his newspaper. He looked up at her entrance.

'Behaving himself now, is he?' he asked.

Amy sank into her own chair and cast a bitter look at him. 'He's miserable, and he's very hungry, and he doesn't understand why you hit him. Is that what you wanted?'

'I want him to behave. What do you mean, he doesn't understand? I told him what he was getting it for.'

'He's only a baby. He didn't know what you meant.'

'He's not a baby, for all you've been treating him like one,' Charlie said. 'Keeping his hair like that and him in dresses all this time. Making a fool of the boy.'

'Better than making him miserable, isn't it?'

'Making him grow up, you mean. He's not your baby, woman. You've got no baby.' He looked at her through narrowed eyes. 'If you want a new bairn to fuss over, you know how to get one.'

'And you know how to get rid of one,' Amy thrust back. She rose to go to the kitchen. In the doorway she turned and looked back. 'Charlie, don't make your son hate you just to try and upset me.'

339

'Don't talk crap,' Charlie said from behind his newspaper. 'I gave him a lesson, that's all.'

Amy shut the door on the sight of him and began on her breadmaking. *I suppose it was silly to think Charlie would just give in. He's no right to use Davie like that! Poor little Davie.*

When the mindless work of kneading dough had given her time to mull everything over, she felt calmer. Charlie might think he had found a way to force her back to his bed by being cruel to David, but it would not work. His sense of justice was different from hers, but he had one nevertheless, and it would not allow him to go on punishing David without cause. He loved his sons in his own impenetrable way.

The battle with Charlie would not be over quite so quickly as she had hoped. Fighting it might take the rest of her life. She accepted the knowledge without dread. *If that's the way you want it, Charlie.*

26

Frank knew there was a good deal of scoffing going on around Ruatane about his 'funny looking cows', and not all the scoffers bothered to hide their derision. He took the sly grins and occasional rude remarks in good humour, confident that he was doing the right thing. And when the results of the butterfat tests Frank had the factory run on the Jerseys' milk became noised abroad the jibes began to fade away. There were a few die-hards who insisted the Jerseys were too thin and frail to last a winter, but the richness of their milk gave the lie to any insinuations of ill-health.

His mind was so busy with self-satisfied musings on the quality of his Jerseys and speculations on how many heifer calves he might get out of them in spring that he almost forgot to tell Lizzie about the small good turn he had done on his way to the factory one morning. But he remembered the incident in time to mention it idly to her over lunch, and in the process changed the course of at least two lives, though he did not know it.

'I ran into the teacher this morning,' he remarked as he buttered a thick slice of Lizzie's fresh bread. 'Poor thing was in a bit of a state. You know she's got a horse and gig she hires so she can get out here? One of the buckles on the reins had snapped where it joins on to the bit, and she was standing beside the gig looking as though she couldn't decide whether to bawl or swear.'

'Miss Radford wouldn't swear, Frank,' Lizzie said. 'She's a teacher. Joey, hurry up and eat those carrots instead of pushing them round your plate.'

'Don't want them,' Joey muttered.

'Do you want a belt on the bottom instead?' Joey shook his head vigorously and began shovelling carrots into his mouth, and Lizzie turned her attention back to Frank. 'What did you do?'

'I looped a bit of string around the rein and tied it on to the bridle, but it won't hold for more than a couple of days and she won't be able to trot the horse with it like that. I told her she'd better get a new buckle fitted as soon as she can.'

'She was lucky you came by. That was early for her to be on her way to school, wasn't it?'

'She said she has to get there early to write the work up on the board. She has quite a day of it, I think. She's got to catch that horse, then harness it, then get all the way out to the school in time to get all the stuff written up.'

'I never thought about that. When you're at school you never wonder how the teacher gets there or anything. I hope that old Mrs Lawler she boards with makes her a decent breakfast.'

'Then when she gets back to town at night she's got to see to the horse before she can have her dinner. And she was telling me she's got to mark the kids' work and write up the lessons and stuff after tea. It's a long day, eh? She said she won't have a show of getting to the blacksmith's to see about that buckle before Saturday. I hope the rein holds for her till then. It's going to take her even longer to get to and fro, too, with only being able to walk the horse.'

'The poor thing. I don't suppose you could mend it for her?'

'Yes, I could do it quite easily. I've got plenty of buckles, too. It's a matter of getting her gig here, though—she hasn't got time to stand around waiting for me to do it after school, she's got to get home.'

'I know!' Lizzie said with a burst of inspiration. 'Why don't we have her to stay the night? Then you'll be able to fix the reins for her and she'll have a rest from doing that long drive. You can pop down to the school this afternoon and tell her to come and stay tomorrow.'

Thus decreed by Lizzie it could not fail to happen. A grateful Miss Radford arrived the next evening to find herself bustled inside by Lizzie while Frank took charge of her horse and gig.

Lily Radford was a tall, slender woman in her late twenties. She had a not unattractive, though very pale, face under her severely scraped back light brown hair, but the fine lines that years of poring over exercise books by candle light had etched prematurely around her eyes gave an impression of weariness and disappointment. But when she smiled, as she did at Lizzie and the three staring children, a kind nature and a wry sense of humour showed through.

'It's very good of you to have me, Mrs Kelly, and very kind of your husband to repair the harness for me.'

'No trouble at all,' Lizzie assured her. 'There's five of us, one more makes no difference. You don't mind sleeping with Maudie, do you? I can put her in with Joey if you'd rather have the bed to yourself.'

Maudie had no intention of missing out on her full share of the novelty of having a stranger in the house. 'I want to sleep with Miss Radford,' she said. She hung onto the teacher's arm and looked up at her with her most winning expression. 'I can, can't I?'

'It's your bed, dear, I wouldn't dream of putting you out of it.'

'See?' Maudie said triumphantly to her mother.

'Don't you go wetting the bed, then. She probably won't,' Lizzie added to Lily, seeing her expression. 'She hasn't done that for months.'

'Oh, good,' Lily said.

She begged Lizzie to let her help prepare the meal, despite Lizzie's protests that Lily must have work to do for the next school day.

'But I wouldn't normally get back to Mrs Lawler's for another hour, and I don't have to see to the horse tonight, either. Anyway, I haven't done any cooking for... oh, I don't know how long. It'd be a nice change—if I won't be in your way?'

By the time Frank came in for dinner the two women were on first name terms and were chatting away merrily. He smiled at the sight of Lizzie enjoying herself with someone new to organise.

After he had finished his meat and vegetables, Lizzie placed a lemon pudding before him. 'Hey, this is nice,' Frank said.

'Lily made it,' Maudie piped up.

'Miss Radford to you,' Lizzie said, waving her serving spoon in Maudie's direction. 'Lily made this lovely pudding, Frank. You're a good cook, Lily.'

'Not really,' Lily said with a smile. 'I'm terribly out of practice. Mother was a wonderful cook, though she had to learn rather late in life, and she taught me. I never get near a kitchen now.'

When the dishes were done Lily cuddled little Beth until it was time for the children to go to bed, but she refused Lizzie's invitation to join her and Frank in the parlour, instead fetching the exercise books she had to work on and setting them out on the kitchen table.

'I'll make sure Maudie goes on the pot before she goes to sleep, you shouldn't have any trouble with her in the night. Don't stay up too late, you'll wear your eyes out doing all that,' Lizzie said.

'I'm all right, this is a lovely bright lamp you have here,' Lily assured her.

Maudie did not disgrace herself, and Lizzie had enjoyed Lily's company so much that it was not long before she invited the teacher to stay a whole weekend on the farm.

'She's nice,' Lizzie whispered when she and Frank were alone in bed. 'I thought she'd be a sour old biddy. It doesn't seem right, her being an old maid. She's twenty-eight, poor thing, not much chance of getting a husband now.'

'Found out how old she is, eh? Trust you. I suppose you know all her business.'

'I found out a few things, just from being friendly. Let's see, she was born in England, her parents came out here when she was a little thing, her father died when she was... three, I think she said. She's got no brothers or sisters, and her ma died nine years ago. She started teaching when... are you listening, Frank?'

'Eh? Sort of. I think I nodded off for a minute. Hey, I was worried about Orange Blossom this morning, she looked a bit lame.'

'You and your precious cows! What's wrong with her, anyway?'

'Nothing, I think she was just a bit stiff. She was right as rain this afternoon.' He smiled into the darkness at the thought of his beautiful Jerseys. 'Good old Orange Blossom.'

'Such fancy names they've got, eh? Orange Blossom and Countess and Golden Dawn.'

'Don't forget Duke William. I bet he's looking forward to getting to work come summer.'

'We'll have to think of some more names when the calves arrive. It'll be harder than finding names for babies.'

'Yes, fancy names for the Herd Book. None of your old "Patches" or "Brownie" for those calves.'

'I hope that bull of yours is up to the job.'

'He's up to it,' Frank said confidently.

'I don't know, he's not very big—hey, what are you up to?'

'What do you think?' he murmured in her ear as he slid her nightdress higher.

'I don't know why I feel sorry for Lily, having no husband,' Lizzie complained unconvincingly. 'At least she doesn't have to put up with—' Frank's mouth on hers silenced her. The way she slipped her arms around him gave the lie to her pretended irritation.

Lily's weekend visits became more frequent. She and Lizzie had little in common, but a genuine friendship was growing between them, and Frank was happy to see it. He knew that Lizzie still fretted at times over what she saw as her failure to settle Amy's life properly, and if she enjoyed feeling she was doing Lily some good then he would cheerfully encourage her.

When Lizzie invited Amy for afternoon tea one Saturday while Lily was visiting, Amy was in two minds whether or not to accept. It would be a pleasant change to see a face other than Charlie's across the table, but spending time with a woman who had managed to do what Amy had dreamed of might be a little hard to bear. Just as she had determined to go after all, Charlie decided to be difficult over whether or not he would let her. By the time he finally said she could, it was so late that she had to walk at a near-trot all the way to Frank's farm, with David scurrying beside her as fast as his little legs would carry him.

344

'Now, you and Lily will get on well,' Lizzie said when Amy arrived. 'You're interested in some of the same things. Amy used to be a teacher, too.'

'Were you, Mrs Stewart?' Lily said. 'I didn't know that.'

'No, I wasn't.' Amy sat down and gathered David onto her lap. 'I was going to, but... well, it didn't work out. I just helped Miss Evans for a while, that's all.'

'You're lucky,' Lily said. Amy looked at her in astonishment.

'Don't you like being a teacher?' she asked.

Lily pulled a face. 'No, I'm afraid I don't particularly enjoy trying to beat knowledge into children who'd rather be just about anywhere than sitting in school. Forcing grammar down their throats isn't going to help them milk cows or rear babies, and that's all most of them are ever going to do—oh, I'm sorry, Mrs Stewart, that sounds terribly snooty. It's not how I mean it. There's more value to the world in milking cows and bringing up children.'

'Is there? I suppose you're right, but... I don't know, sometimes it doesn't seem much to do with your life. Not that I don't love my boys.' She squeezed David. He nestled against her, tired out by his brisk walk and content to be held in her arms. 'I don't know what I'd do without my Davie.'

'So this is Malcolm's brother.' Lily did not quite manage to hide a grimace. 'He doesn't look much like him.'

'They're as different as chalk and cheese,' said Lizzie. 'Davie's a lovely child, and Mal's just like his pa—a right little—'

'Lizzie! Don't talk about Mal like that,' Amy remonstrated.

'Suit yourself,' Lizzie said. 'I'm going to change Beth's nappy, that'll give you two a chance to talk about schools and things for a minute.'

'Mal's not really a bad boy,' Amy said, wishing there was more conviction in her voice. 'He's very lively, and he likes his own way.'

'He certainly does,' Lily said. 'I've never known a five-year-old as... determined... as your son. I'm afraid I'm not managing to teach him much. Actually I'm not teaching him anything at all, except how to put up with being smacked on the hand with a ruler.'

'He wouldn't take any notice of that,' Amy said ruefully. 'Not with what he gets from his father. He's always been better behaved for men, anyway.'

'I'm afraid I can't do anything about not being a man,' Lily said. 'I don't like using a strap on the little ones, but I must say Malcolm tempts me. When will this boy start school?'

'Next August my Davie'll turn five.' Amy stroked David's cropped hair, silently grieving for the lost curls. 'I'll miss having him around all day.' She smiled at Lily's dubious expression. 'Don't worry, Miss Radford, Davie really is very different from Mal. He's a lot more like my little brothers.'

'Tom and George? Now they *are* nice children. Poor little Tom, though, I hate having to hit him when he gets things wrong. You can see he feels dreadful about it, but... well, it's just the way it's done. I can't let Thomas get away with making mistakes just because I like him more than I do most of the others.' She snorted. 'As if it matters whether he knows how to parse a sentence properly. It's what they pay me for, though.'

'Miss Radford, why...' It was hard to find a way to ask the question that did not sound rude. Amy trailed off awkwardly.

'Why am I a teacher?' Lily prompted. 'Certainly not from any sense of vocation. Sheer necessity, Mrs Stewart. There aren't many jobs a poor woman with pretensions to gentility can take. Father didn't leave anything to us beyond what Mother called "good breeding", and that doesn't pay the rent. Mother had an annuity that used to be sent out from Home, but it was only during her lifetime, and I always knew I'd have to provide for myself one day. I have a sort of uncle—he's a cousin of Mother's, I think, but not a very close one—he paid for me to go to secondary school. A proper school, too, not some trumped-up dancing class teaching young women deportment and a word or two of French. He paid for my piano lessons, too. I had two years at the school, that was enough to get me a pupil teacher's job. By the time Mother passed away I already had my teaching certificate, so she knew I'd be able to support myself in some sort of decency. She didn't know how much I hated it.'

'I'm sorry,' Amy said, wishing it didn't sound so inadequate.

'I suppose you're wondering why I didn't get married,' said Lily.

'No, not really. It's... well, it's not exactly the easy way out either, Miss Radford.' Amy had not meant to be so blunt, but Lily's frankness made her lower her own guard.

'I suppose not. I think perhaps it depends on the husband.'

'You're right,' said Amy.

'Mother had rather grand ideas, you see. She always thought I'd marry a professional man. She conveniently didn't notice that I never went anywhere I was likely to meet such men.' Lily sighed. 'Poor Mother, she was always saying we were sure to get invited to a ball at Government House one day and I'd meet what she called a "suitable" man there. Of course we never did. And if I ever did get an invitation, say if one of the other pupil teachers' mothers asked me to dinner, Mother would never let me go. "I'm sure they're worthy people, Lily, but they're not quite our type, dear." I heard that so many times I just stopped asking her, and of course people stopped inviting me. The classroom, the house and the shops, that's where I spent my days. And I'm afraid I've never had the sort of face that turns men's heads.' She smiled wryly. 'Well, that's all past now, anyway. I'm much too set in my ways to put up with a husband, and I'm sure I'd make a dreadful wife.'

Lizzie came back into the room. 'You two talking about husbands? I thought you'd be on about books and all that nonsense. Here you go,' she said, plumping Beth on Lily's lap. 'She smells a bit sweeter now.'

Beth laid her head on Lily's chest and smiled up at her. Lily planted a soft kiss on the little girl's forehead. 'She's a dear child. Marriage does have its compensations, doesn't it, Mrs Stewart? Little ones like these two?'

'Oh, yes,' Amy agreed. 'Do you read much, Miss Radford?' she asked, hardly daring to hope that she might at last have found someone she could talk about her beloved books with.

'You must call me Lily, or you'll make me feel terribly old—though I am years older than you, aren't I?'

'I'd like to do that—and you should call me Amy.'

'Thank you, I will. I don't think I've read a book from beginning to end in years, Amy. Just exercise books till I want to throw them on the fire.'

'You're very good with children, Lily,' Lizzie put in. 'Beth just loves you.'

'It's easy to be good with them one at a time,' Lily said, stroking Beth's soft baby hair. 'It's when you've fifteen or twenty of them to try and keep under your thumb. Oh, Lizzie, I didn't tell you—I had a letter from the inspector this week, he said they're going to do something about that Irish family who never send any of their children to school. They're going to make them—that'll be another five or so children next term.' She rolled her eyes at the thought.

'Feenans? Those bog Irish?' Lizzie said in disgust. 'Waste of time making them come to school, half of them'll end up in jail anyway. They'll drive you mad, Lily.'

'As bad as that?' Lily asked Amy and Lizzie both nodded. 'Ah, woe is me,' she said, putting on a tragic face. 'I sometimes wish I was a washerwoman married to a street sweeper.' She laughed at her own attempt at melodrama. The other two women laughed with her, and the children joined in with giggles despite having no idea what the women were talking about.

'It's such a shame about Lily,' Lizzie said more and more often to Frank over the next few weeks. 'She's so nice, it's not right that she's an old maid. She's very lonely, too. And she's so good with the children, I bet she'd love to have some of her own. I blame her mother, not making sure Lily was properly settled.'

Frank made noncommittal noises of sympathy when Lizzie ran on in this vein. He could not raise much interest in Lily's prospects, and thought it was none of their business in any case, but it was in Lizzie's nature to try and organise the lives of those around her, and when she was in full flight it was as much use trying to curb her as to dam the creek when it flooded.

But Lizzie gradually stopped railing against what she saw as Lily's cruel fate of spinsterhood. Frank thought she had resigned herself to her own inability to do anything about it. As he later reflected, that just showed that even after knowing her for so many years he could still be very wrong about Lizzie.

He thought little of it when Lizzie remarked one evening after supper, 'I bet Bill would love to have a look at the Jerseys.'

'Do you think so?' The thought of showing off his precious Jerseys to an interested audience held great appeal.

'Mmm. Well, it stands to reason, doesn't it? He helped you get them out here the day they arrived, he'd like to see how they're getting on. Just because Pa makes smart remarks about the Jerseys doesn't mean Bill agrees with him. I think you should ask Bill to come around some time.'

'Maybe I will.'

'Yes, that's a good idea, Frank. You'll probably see him at the factory tomorrow, tell him to come for lunch on Saturday.'

'It doesn't have to be Saturday, does it? Friday would do.'

'No, it's *got* to be Saturday,' Lizzie insisted. 'Saturday will suit just right. Tell him to get here a good bit before lunch, so we won't be in a rush. And you'll have time to show him the cows, too.'

'That's what he's coming for, isn't it?'

'Mostly,' Lizzie said, a rather smug smile playing about her mouth.

Frank studied her in amusement. 'You're plotting something, aren't you? You've got that look on your face. What are you up to?'

'You'll see,' was all Lizzie would say. 'You just tell Bill to come on Saturday, that's all I need you to do.'

Frank invited Bill for the following Saturday as he had been instructed. It was only when Lily arrived on Friday night straight from school to spend the weekend with the Kellys, as she so often did now, that realisation of just what Lizzie was up to dawned on him. 'Does Bill know Lily'll be here?' he asked Lizzie in the privacy of their bedroom.

'Not if you didn't tell him,' Lizzie said. She gave a small giggle. 'It'll be a nice surprise for him.'

As Frank lingered over his morning tea the next day, he thought Lizzie seemed oddly restless. She kept finding reasons to go over to one of the kitchen windows and peer out down the track. After one of these darting visits to the window she turned to Lily.

'I've just had a thought,' Lizzie said, somewhat breathlessly. 'I need some figs. Do you mind picking me some?'

Before Lily had a chance to say whether she minded or not, Lizzie had thrust a basket into her hands and practically pushed her out the back door.

'Now, mind you pick plenty,' Lizzie said. 'Take your time, there's no need to rush back. You might have to climb a little way up the tree, just in the low branches. It's easy enough to climb. No, Maudie, you can't go and help Aunt Lily,' she said, restraining the eager child by one hand. 'I want you to help me in here for a bit.'

She closed the door on Lily and smiled at Frank, her eyes dancing. 'Bill's coming up the road.'

'Is he? I'll go down and meet him. We might as well go out and take a look at the cows right now.'

'No, you won't,' Lizzie said. 'You can bring him straight up here. There'll be plenty of time for looking at cows later.'

Lizzie insisted that Bill sit down and have a cup of tea as soon as Frank ushered him into the kitchen, but just as she seemed about to pour it she remarked in a tone of studied casualness, 'Bill, how about you just pop out and help Lily with those figs? She's probably got a basketful now, and it'll be a bit heavy.'

'Who's Lily?' Bill asked.

'You know—Miss Radford, the teacher. Didn't Frank tell you she's staying the weekend with us? Hurry up, you can have your tea when you and Lily get back.'

Bill went outside, and Lizzie scurried over to the kitchen window opposite the one that had held such fascination for her earlier.

'What are you up to with all this fuss about the figs, Lizzie?' Frank asked, wandering idly over to stand beside her.

Lizzie craned her neck to see the tree that stood some distance from the house. 'Lily will have climbed a little way up it—yes, she's a couple of branches up.' She gave a small giggle. 'She's going to get a shock when she looks down and sees Bill.'

Frank followed Lizzie's gaze and saw Lily a few feet up the tree, standing on a broad branch. She had hitched her dress up halfway to her knees to make climbing easier, unaware that she had an audience.

'Hey, Lily's showing a bit of leg, eh?' he remarked with a grin.

'Maybe you'd better not look—make sure you don't look at her legs, anyway,' Lizzie said, not turning away from the window.

'I'll do my best,' said Frank.

They watched as Bill approached the fig tree. When he got close enough to see Lily clearly he hesitated, then stepped forward and looked up into the tree for a few moments before speaking. Although they could not hear what was said, they saw Lily give a start and almost let go of the basket. Bill reached up and took it from her, then helped her clamber down.

'That's just right,' said Lizzie.

'That was a bit mean on Lily, wasn't it? She'll be embarrassed now.'

'It doesn't matter. She'll forget about being embarrassed soon enough.'

'Why did you want Bill to catch her like that?'

'Lily needs a bit of help, that's all. She's not all that pretty, but I noticed the other day when she was showing me some new stockings she had on that she's got a nice pair of legs. I'm just helping her show her best features off.'

Frank laughed. 'You're a wanton little hussy, Lizzie.'

They watched as Bill and Lily began to walk back to the house. 'Oh, good, I thought she might be a bit taller than Bill, but she's about the same height,' Lizzie said. 'She's two years older than him, but you'd hardly know. Don't you go telling Bill Lily's twenty-eight, not till things have got on a bit further. She looks quite pretty just now, don't you think?'

Lily certainly looked flustered, but the pinkness of her cheeks was more becoming than her usual paleness. She seemed to be covering her confusion by talking in an animated way, moving her hands about as she spoke. Bill was listening in silence, smiling as he watched her. Frank saw his brother-in-law's gaze drift down towards Lily's now discreetly covered ankles once or twice, and he was not surprised at Bill's wandering eyes. 'No one else looks pretty to me when you're around,' he said, giving Lizzie a squeeze. 'But you're right, she's got nice legs.'

'You rogue, Frank Kelly! I told you not to look at her legs.' She patted his hand absently where it rested on her shoulder and continued her scrutiny through the window.

When the strolling couple neared the house, Lizzie pulled Frank away.

'I don't want them to know we were watching,' she said, making a great show of fussing about with the teacups.

Frank noted the lively pleasure on her face. 'You must think a lot of Lily.'

She stopped her activity for a moment and gave him a serious look. 'Bill could do an awful lot worse for himself, Frank. So could Lily.'

When they had had a hurried cup of tea, Lizzie let Frank take Bill out to look at the cows that were the ostensible reason for his visit, while she and Lily got on with the lunch preparations. Bill did not mention his dramatic encounter with Lily, and Frank had no desire to raise the subject; matchmaking was something he was happy to leave to Lizzie.

Bill seemed genuinely interested in Frank's plans to improve his breeding stock, but Frank suspected that part of his attention was directed towards the other visitor to the Kelly household. He seemed eager to get back to the house when they heard Lizzie calling them for lunch.

'I think we'll have our cup of tea in the parlour,' Lizzie announced as she and Lily cleared the pudding plates away, with Maudie self-importantly helping. 'Lily, put the tea things on that tray and take Bill through, we'll be along shortly.'

'I know the way, Lizzie,' Bill said, the corners of his eyes crinkling in amusement.

'Yes, I know you do,' said Lizzie. 'You can keep Lily company in there for a minute, Frank and I just want to have a talk about something. Go on, off you go.'

Bill and Lily went obediently off to the parlour, leaving a smug-looking Lizzie and a grinning Frank.

'Have you known my sister long, Miss Radford?' Bill asked as he stood back to let Lily through the parlour door ahead of him.

Lily was about to give an innocuous response, when something in Bill's impudent grin touched a spark of humour in her. 'Long enough,' she answered with a matching smile as she placed the tray on a small table. 'Shall we wait for them before I pour?'

'What do you think?' Bill asked, grinning more broadly.

'I think that if we do, this tea will get very cold indeed.' She poured two cups, and handed one to Bill before sitting down on the couch.

Bill glanced at the armchair opposite, then indicated the empty place next to Lily on the couch. 'May I, Miss Radford?'

'Please do, Mr Leith.'

Frank felt Lizzie press against him and give a little wriggle as they lay huddled together in the island of warmth their bed made in the chilly darkness.

'Pleased with yourself?' he whispered.

'It's a start,' Lizzie answered quietly. 'We've a fair way to go yet, but we're off to a good start.'

'"We"?' Frank teased. 'Are you and Lily plotting this together?'

'Don't say "plotting", Frank, it sounds awful. I'm just giving Bill and Lily a helping hand. They're just right for each other, wouldn't it be a shame if they never got around to getting to know each other properly? It's time Bill found himself a wife, anyway, and he hasn't been doing much about it, has he?'

'What say Bill and Lily don't think they're as suited as you do?'

'Don't talk rubbish—of course they'll think it when they get to know each other a bit better. They're not silly.'

'That's true,' Frank said. 'And anyone who knows you knows it's pretty silly to try arguing once you've made up your mind.'

'Only when I know I'm right.'

'But you always *do*, Lizzie.'

May – December 1891

It was not a whirlwind courtship; neither Bill nor Lily was prone to being swept along on a tide of passion. But what began as shared amusement at Lizzie's blatant attempts to manipulate them soon turned into a hard-headed appraisal of each other that led them both to the conclusion Lizzie had already come to on their behalf: they could each do a lot worse for themselves.

From there it was only a small step, given the many opportunities of spending time with each other that Lizzie made sure of putting in their way, to a mutual respect that seemed likely to turn into something warmer in time. The only thing that bothered Lizzie was that neither of them seemed in any rush to move matters beyond friendship and into romance.

'I wish Bill would hurry up and ask Lily,' she fretted to Frank. 'Lily'll be twenty-nine next year, they should get on with it. She's only got so many child-bearing years, she's already wasted half of them. It might be harder for her to get with child, too, not being very young.'

'She's not an old woman, Lizzie,' Frank protested in amusement. 'Heck, she's a year younger than me!'

'Of course she's not old, but she's not getting any younger, either. You should have a word with Bill about that when you see him at the factory some time, tell him to get on with it.'

'Now, don't you try that on me. I'm not about to tell Bill in front of half the men in Ruatane that he needs to get Lily between the sheets before she's too old for it.'

'Well, you wouldn't need to say it like that,' Lizzie said, pursing her lips. 'I wish Lily would give him a bit more encouragement, though. She told me he's only kissed her three times, once when they were—'

'Hey, never mind telling me all that, Lizzie,' Frank interrupted. 'I don't want to know their business. I hope you don't go telling Lily things about me and you—I'll never be able to look her in the eye again.'

'Of course I don't! That wouldn't be decent, not with her being an unmarried woman.' She sighed deeply. 'I don't know what I'm going to do about those two. I'll have to give them a hurry-up somehow.'

But it was not Lizzie who precipitated Bill into action. The two groups of people responsible never realised what an effect they had had, and in the case of one pair would have been furious had they been told.

It was Mrs Carr and her daughter Martha who gave Bill the first push.

After leaving him in relative peace over the winter, Mrs Carr began badgering him with invitations to dine at their house that became more and more difficult to refuse politely. On each of these occasions, usually outside church but sometimes at the store, Martha would be standing nearby fixing Bill with what she seemed to imagine was a winning smile and giggling foolishly. She would then launch into a long, prattling tale about someone's wedding or new baby, before pressing her mother's invitation on him.

With such a contrast before him, Bill could not help but appreciate Lily's quiet voice and the way she clearly thought far more often than she spoke; the soft laugh he could sometimes coax from her made him want to laugh with her, while Martha's high-pitched whinnies made him cringe. The more foolish Martha let herself appear, the more sensible Bill realised Lily was.

The other group who intervened on Lily's behalf would not have been particularly interested had anyone ever bothered to tell them the effect they had had. When the last term of the year began, Lily gained the new pupils she had so dreaded: a cohort of Feenan children, impelled by the threat of the law into reluctant school attendance.

'They're as bad as you said, Lizzie,' Lily lamented when she half-staggered through Lizzie's kitchen door at the end of the first week of the new term. 'They start fights every lunch-time, they throw things in the class room, and they don't take any notice of me except when I drag one of them off his bench and get stuck into him with the strap. That's the only good thing about them—at least they're all small enough for me to manhandle—so far, anyway. The biggest one will be beyond me by next year, I'm sure.'

'Honestly, I don't know what they think they're doing, making those horrible brats come to school,' Lizzie said as she helped Lily off with her cloak. 'They should just let them stay ignorant if they can't behave like civilised folk.'

'I won't stay civilised myself for much longer with that lot to cope with. You know what they did today? When we'd finished school and I sent all the children home, those Feenans opened the paddock and let my horse out.'

'The little brats!' Lizzie exclaimed.

'They made sure they frightened him, too, yelling at him and slapping him with a stick. It took me ages to catch him, that's why I'm so late. I'd probably still be chasing him if your little brother Ernie hadn't helped me—Thomas and George did, too.'

'Well, I'm glad Ernie was some use.'

'Mmm. Ernie's not a bit interested in learning anything, I'll never get him past Standard Three, but he doesn't give me much trouble. Thank goodness I'm staying here this weekend, I couldn't have faced that long drive tonight. Ohh, I'm exhausted,' she sighed as she sank into a chair. 'And it's *months* till the holidays.'

Things did not improve at the school under the Feenans' reign of terror. Lily grew paler than ever in the ensuing weeks. Dark circles appeared under her eyes, and her cheekbones became more prominent as worry spoiled her appetite. She tried to keep up a brave face, but Lizzie could see that Lily was becoming despondent. Lily hid her feelings successfully enough that Bill had no idea how much of a struggle her work had become, and it was sheer accident when he did find out.

It was on a Thursday afternoon, and Lily was to stay the night. Bill had dropped in on his way home from town, hoping he might find Lily already there. Having found that she had not yet arrived, he was standing by the door about to leave when the door burst open and she rushed in.

One glance at her showed how distraught she was. Her hair had come loose from its pins, and wisps were falling around her face; her eyes brimmed with tears; and down the front of her beige skirt was a large blotch of black ink.

'Lily, what the heck happened?' Bill asked.

'I can't bear it any more, I can't,' Lily sobbed. 'Not those horrible children. They're monsters!' Tears streamed down her face. She staggered a little as she took a half step forward. Bill reached out and Lily flung herself against him, letting his arms close around her. 'Th-that Des Feenan. I w-was just t-trying to get him to—' the next word was lost in a sob. 'And then h-he threw the ink—and the other one s-said—'

'Shh, Lily, shh,' Bill soothed. 'One of those brats did this?'

Lily nodded and gulped back a sob. 'They're getting worse and worse—they don't take any notice of me—I can't—'

'Right, that's settled,' Bill announced. 'You're not going back to that school, not for those kids to drive you up the wall.'

'I've got to, Bill—it's my job—I've got to.'

'No, you don't. Or... well, I suppose you'll have to for a couple more weeks, you'll have to give notice or something.'

'I can't stop working. I've got no money.'

'That doesn't matter. I'll be providing for you soon enough, once we're married.'

'Hallelujah,' Lizzie remarked to the room at large before she shepherded three fascinated children out of the room without disturbing the pair who had eyes and ears only for each other.

And so it was decided, just like that. Lily was not foolish enough even to consider saying no, though she did insist that she would not give up her teaching till the end of the year.

'I'm meant to give a term's notice, Bill,' she said. 'It wouldn't be right for me just to walk out. Anyway, I'll be able to put up with the worst those Feenans can do to me, now I know it'll only be for a few more months.'

Bill reluctantly gave in, but he had no intention of seeing Lily again tried as sorely as she had been. The morning after he had made the proposal that had taken him by surprise more than it had anyone else, he paid an unannounced visit to the school, made a startled Lily point out the perpetrator of the ink incident, and administered summary justice on the villain with his riding crop, afterwards giving dire warnings to his wide-eyed audience of what might be in store for anyone else foolish enough to give Miss Radford any trouble.

Thus cowed, most of the class behaved in an exemplary fashion for many weeks, while the Feenan children's attendance became more and more haphazard until, a week after Bill's visit, they stopped coming altogether.

'The education people will catch up with them next year and make them send their children again,' Lily told Frank and Lizzie. 'But I won't be there then!' She gave a laugh of pure happiness.

While he was pleased for Bill and Lily, Frank followed the progress of their romance with no more than vague interest. He had other things to think about in the last months of the year. Calving time was like no calving he had ever overseen before; this year he had his three Jersey cows to fuss over.

The three calves arrived over four days in early August, interspersed among the almost-unnoticed Shorthorns. After the first Frank was delighted, after the second triumphant, and when the third shiny golden creature slid wetly into the world Frank could hardly contain his jubilation.

'Another heifer,' he shouted to Lizzie as he burst into the house, and for once Lizzie did not scold him for wearing his boots inside. 'Three heifers! Twice as many Jerseys to milk!' He flung his arms around Lizzie and lifted her off the floor, twirling her around despite her laughing protests.

'It's like a sign,' he said when he had calmed down a little. 'A sign I'm doing the right thing.'

'Well, you already knew *that*,' Lizzie said with the assurance that he loved so much in her. He hugged her again until she protested that she could not breathe.

The new calves thrived, fussed over by Frank and by his older two children, who vied with each other for the honour of feeding the Jerseys when the calves had been taken away from their mothers. Maudie insisted it was only right that she should have two of the calves to feed, as she was the oldest; Joey tried to argue the point, but Maudie's skill in disputation was too much for him.

When November arrived, the event came that Frank had been awaiting almost as eagerly as the birth of the calves: it was time to put his bull in with the cows. It did not take long to see that, Lizzie's doubtful comments notwithstanding, Duke William was approaching his job with energy and enthusiasm.

'I hope he doesn't wear himself out,' Lizzie remarked as she and Frank leaned over the fence and watched Duke William at work one day.

'Him? He's only getting started,' said Frank. 'There's plenty of go in that fellow. Hey, Maudie was asking me the other day what Duke was doing with the cows, climbing on them like that.'

'Trust her not to miss a trick. What'd you tell her?'

'I just said he was playing games with them. I suppose she'll work it out for herself one day.' He thought for a moment. 'I don't think anyone ever told me what the bull's really up to—I can't remember when I figured it out.'

'I think it was the night we got married,' Lizzie said, ducking nimbly out of his reach before Frank could give her the playful slap on the bottom she was asking for.

Frank tried to tell himself that he needed to keep an eye on the bull while he was in with his harem, making sure Duke William did not overtire himself. He went around sporting a foolish grin all during Duke William's weeks of pleasure, but he did not realise just how obvious his empathy with the bull had become until Lizzie pointed it out to him one night.

The moment he had put out the lamp, he reached for the soft body lying close to him and began lifting her nightdress. He had only got it up to her thighs when Lizzie murmured, 'You've been watching that bull again, haven't you?'

'A bit,' Frank admitted.

'I thought as much. Honestly, Frank, you're as bad as when we were first married, now you've got a bull.'

'Stop complaining,' Frank whispered. He heard a smothered giggle, and enjoyed the pleasant reflection that there was one room in the house where Lizzie was happy to let him boss her.

By December, Frank was confident that all the cows were in calf except the two who would be their house cows over the coming winter. It was also December when Lizzie told him she thought there would be another baby the following August.

'And that's the fault of your bull, too,' she added, though 'fault' was hardly the right word for news that made them both so happy.

'No, I'll take the full blame for that piece of work myself,' said Frank.

Lily moved in with Lizzie and Frank soon after her engagement was announced, abandoning her weary treks to and from town with relief.

'It's more convenient for Bill to come and see you, too,' Lizzie had said when pressing her hospitality.

'Bill will see all he wants of me soon enough,' Lily said wryly. 'Perhaps I shouldn't give him the opportunity to think better of it while he's still got the chance.'

'Lily, you say some silly things at times!' Lizzie scolded. 'Of course he's not going to change his mind. Bill's not stupid. Anyway, he'd never dare let you down, he'd never hear the end of it.'

'Thank you, Lizzie, that's very encouraging,' Lily replied, laughing. 'We were going to leave the wedding until February—do you think we should have it as soon as possible, before Bill gets tempted to run away from home?'

'You should have it in December, as soon as school's finished,' Lizzie pronounced. 'No sense keeping everyone waiting—you two have been slow enough already.'

When Lizzie became aware of her pregnancy, she was more pleased than ever that she had urged Lily into an early wedding. 'I might be too big by February, I could have missed out on going to it,' she said to Frank, indignant at the very thought.

'That'd be a bit rough, eh?' Frank agreed. 'Specially when it was all your idea.'

Lily insisted on a small wedding, her own determination not to make a show of herself strengthened by the discovery that Bill was putting up with a good deal of half-serious complaints from his father over the fact that it was Arthur who would have to pay for the occasion.

'Your father's always charming to me, but he's said some dreadful things to Bill,' Lily said to Lizzie. 'He told him no wonder Bill was marrying an orphan, he'd never get any girl's father to let him have her.'

'I've never heard anyone call Pa charming,' Lizzie sniffed. 'He thinks a lot of you, Ma told me. Right after that first time you went around there for lunch, he said you've got plenty of sense.' Lizzie did not bother to quote her father's comment in full: that Lily was not very young, but she seemed to have a good head on her shoulders.

'Did he? That was nice of him. Bill said your father told Alf and Ernie they'd better make sure they didn't marry orphans or he'd be bankrupt. Bill says he's joking, but I don't want to cause any trouble, not when I'll be living with them soon enough. Just your family and your Uncle Jack's, that's all we'll have at the wedding.'

'Pity that means you've got to have Charlie as well. Haven't you got anyone of your own to invite?'

'I don't really have any relations. I'd better send an invitation to Uncle Fred and Aunt Helen—he's the one who paid for me to go to school. I'm sure they won't come, though, I haven't seen them in four years, and even then it was only for afternoon tea the day before I left Auckland for good.'

'Yes, make sure you invite them,' Lizzie agreed. 'They'll probably send a present.'

Sure enough, a few weeks before the wedding a parcel arrived at the Post and Telegraph Station for Miss Lily Radford, care of Mr F. Kelly.

'It's from Uncle Fred,' Lily said when Frank placed the parcel before her. She ripped open the outer layer of brown paper, revealing a large envelope and a well-wrapped package. 'Well?' she asked Frank and Lizzie, her eyes sparkling with amusement at Lizzie's eager expression. 'What shall I open first, the letter or the present?'

'The present,' Lizzie said. 'Letters can wait, I want to see what your rich uncle's sent.'

'It won't be anything much, Lizzie, he's not really an uncle, remember.' But Lily duly unwrapped the layers of paper until she had uncovered a neat enamelled box and a small silver dish. She studied the gifts with her brow furrowed, opened the box and drew out one of the small pieces of cardboard it held.

Lily looked at the card in disbelief, smiled, then laughed aloud. 'Oh, Aunt Helen,' she gasped out through her mirth. 'Whatever possessed her?'

'What are they?' Lizzie asked. She picked up one of the cards and peered at it. ' "Mrs William Leith",' she read aloud. 'That's nice, that'll be your married name.' She passed the card to Frank, who looked at it equally blankly. 'But why would you want a lot of cards with your name on?'

It took some time for Lily's merriment to subside enough for her to explain. 'They're visiting cards, Lizzie. They're for women who've nothing better to do than parade around town paying calls on other idle women.'

'Why do you need bits of card to do that?'

'Well, this isn't going to make much sense because it's really just a lot of nonsense, but I'll do my best. The idea is that you call on someone when you know she'll be out—probably paying calls on someone else, in fact. Then you leave one of these cards to let her know you've called.'

'But why do you call when she's out? And couldn't you just tell whoever comes to the door?'

'You do tell whoever answers—probably the parlour maid if it's someone rich like Aunt Helen. But you leave a card anyway, that's the whole point of calling. It's all to do with exchanging these cards, that's why you call when the other lady will be out. You write on the card to let her know what day you'll be "at home".'

'Eh? You mean those women are out so much that they have to write people notes to let them know when they'll be at home? When do they get their work done? Their houses must be a disgrace.'

'That's what they have all those servants for. Not just at home, Lizzie, at home to visitors. They might decide they'll receive callers one afternoon, and they'll leave these cards telling all their acquaintances what day they can call. If anyone called any other day, they'd just have the maid tell the caller that Madam wasn't home. Oh, and this little tray is to display all the cards other women have left for you. I believe the idea is that you only put the most impressive ones on show.'

'What a load of rubbish,' said Lizzie.

'Yes, it is,' Lily agreed. 'Aunt Helen's obviously never been anywhere like Ruatane. Ah well, I shall have to write and thank her profusely for her lovely gift. And I'd better see what she says in the letter.'

There was a smaller envelope inside the large one, as well as a sheet of writing paper. Lily scanned the letter quickly.

'They won't be coming to the wedding, of course, but Aunt Helen thanks me very politely for thinking of them. The rest is all news of her family. Their little girl must be growing up now, Aunt Helen says she's going to school. Such a dear little thing, Sarah was.' She put the letter to one side. 'Now, what's in here?'

She opened the smaller envelope and pulled out a folded piece of heavy paper. 'What's this?' Lily asked aloud, then gasped as she unfolded it. 'Now *this* is from Uncle Fred,' she said brightly. 'Look at this—it's a banker's order.' She held the paper up to show them.

'Ten pounds,' Frank said, impressed at the sight. 'What are you going to do with it, Lily?'

'Well...' Lily thought for no more than a few seconds. 'I'm going to buy a wedding dress,' she announced. 'I wasn't going to get a new dress, not when it'd mean Bill's father having to pay for it, but now I've some money of my own I'll be silly and have a dress made.'

'That's not silly,' Lizzie protested. 'It's just sense—you only have a wedding once, you want to make the most of it.'

'And I've waited long enough for it, haven't I? Now, don't look so eager, Lizzie, I'm not going to go mad. Just a nice, sensible dress that I can wear for years and years.'

'You should get a good one for ten pounds,' Frank remarked idly, thinking of how far that amount would go towards the improvements he was contemplating for his cow shed.

'Goodness me, Frank, I'm not going to spend ten pounds on it! No, I suppose I'd better give the rest to Bill.'

'You'll do no such thing!' Lizzie said. 'You're going to spend all that money on yourself.'

'I don't think I should, Lizzie. I mean, don't you think I should ask Bill what he wants me to do with it? I'm afraid I'll have to get used to asking him things like that—it'll be quite strange, I've only had my own opinion to consult for so many years. I'd better get into the habit now, it'll save trouble later.'

'There's no need to rush, you're not married yet. Now, Lily, you're being a bit silly over this. You know perfectly well you need all sorts of... well, not things you'd ask Bill about, not yet anyway... oh, you know,' she ended feebly. She grimaced at Frank; he knew it was a signal that she wanted him to leave them alone. Perhaps she wanted to talk about Lily's underclothes. He grinned as he remembered the first time he had seen Lizzie's lace-edged drawers, after having wondered for so long what she kept under her skirts; it had been a delightful revelation.

'What do you think, Frank?' Lily asked. Frank glanced guiltily at her, wondering if she had read his thoughts.

'About what?' he asked.

'What should I do about the money? I thought perhaps Bill could use it towards our wedding, so his father won't have to pay for it all. You're a man, tell me what you think Bill would want.'

It was a heavy responsibility, and Frank considered the question carefully. 'Well, I can't say for sure what Bill would think. But if Lizzie got a bit of money of her own, I know what I'd want.'

'More fancy cows,' Lizzie put in, raising her eyes heavenwards. Frank ignored her pert remark.

'I'd want her to spend the lot on things for herself, the sillier the better. Heck, Lily, Bill doesn't want money from you—he'd probably be a bit put out if you offered it to him. So would Arthur, come to that. I think you should buy yourself a whole lot of pretty things. Bill will enjoy seeing them,' he added daringly before leaving the two women to plan Lily's trousseau in fine detail.

December brought the end of the school year, and two weeks later came the day of the wedding.

The warm, golden light of the late afternoon sun gave a richness to the green of the valley as Frank drove the family up to Arthur's house, Lily on the front seat beside him in her dove grey silk dress while Lizzie and the children squashed themselves into the back seat for the short drive. The small group of guests was waiting on the lawn when the Kellys arrived. Frank saw Bill smiling at them from the verandah, Alf looking uncomfortable in his good suit at Bill's side. Lily's cheeks were pink and her eyes shining as Frank helped her down from the buggy. She took Maudie by the hand, and slipped her other arm through Frank's.

Lizzie gave Lily a kiss, issued a stern warning to Maudie, who was the bridesmaid, to walk like a little lady, then shepherded the other two children over to the knot of guests.

'Ready?' Frank asked. Lily nodded, fixing him with a brilliant smile, and for the first time Frank decided that perhaps she was just a little bit pretty. 'I didn't think I'd be giving any girls away for a few years yet, you know,' he told her with a grin. The three of them began their stately procession across the garden and up to the verandah where Bill waited.

After the service, the Leith family began the celebrations welcoming their newest member. Despite his grumbling, with such a small wedding Arthur had found little enough to spend money on. The bulk of the food had been produced on the farm, and killing one more sheep than usual was no hardship; nor was serving up one of the large hams from the larder. Edie had used a vast amount of dried fruit for the wedding cake, but that was the only thing she had had to buy specially from the store.

Determined to show that he welcomed Lily's arrival, Arthur had been careful to provide a generous amount of beer; far more than the eight grown men at the wedding could reasonably be expected to consume. It was not his fault that one of the men had no intention of being reasonable.

Amy had been pleased at the chance of an outing with her family, but

362

she almost wished she had not come when she saw how heavily Charlie was drinking. She turned her back on him, determined not to let him spoil the day for her.

Not that it was ever possible to ignore his brooding presence completely. She could not show any but the coolest of interest in her male cousins, and had to duck her head away when Bill attempted to kiss her, instead taking his hand and shaking it. She had laid down one new rule of her own for her marriage, but she would still do her best to obey all the rest of Charlie's orders, however unreasonable they were. To flout any of his rules would be to risk goading him into breaking hers.

She found plenty to talk about with the other women; getting permission from Charlie to leave the house was always haphazard, and over the previous three weeks he had decided to be more difficult than usual, refusing even to let her visit her father's house. Lizzie had been too busy organising Lily to have had time to come and see Amy, so she had had no congenial adult company for some time.

Amy thought she detected a slight bulge in Jane's front, so it was no great surprise when Jane whispered to her that she would be having her third baby the following June.

'Madam's got wind of it,' Jane said, indicating Susannah with a toss of her head. Susannah glanced over at them from where she sat with Edie, and Amy saw her purse her lips in disapproval. 'She said to me the other day what a shame it was that I wouldn't be able to come to this—she looked down her nose well and truly when I told her I was coming all right, but I just gave her a look like *this*.' Amy laughed at Jane's fierce grimace. 'I'm not showing yet—well, not so that men would notice, they're half blind about that sort of thing. I told Harry that Madam didn't think I should come—you should have heard what he said about her. I had to tell him off, using language like that in front of the girls. It's a good thing he doesn't speak to Susannah, or she'd learn some new words.'

'I don't know, Jane, I think he used them all to her face before he stopped speaking to her. I bet he's pleased about the new baby.'

'Oh, yes, men always seem to act as though they've done it all by themselves.' Jane looked over at Harry, who was explaining in fine detail to Frank his plans for extending his house. 'I hope it's a boy this time,' she confided. 'Harry loves the girls, and he never let on he was a bit disappointed when Esther came along, but I know he'd love to have a son. Well, it stands to reason, doesn't it? Men always want sons.'

'Charlie did,' Amy agreed. 'He wasn't interested in having daughters.' She realised she had put Charlie's days of fathering children into the past tense, but if Jane had noticed her slip she gave no sign of it.

Lizzie soon joined them, and shared the news of her own new pregnancy. Amy saw the other two women study her flat belly then glance at David, now nearly four and a half. She knew her family all wondered why she had had no more babies since Alexander; she had no intention of satisfying their curiosity and thereby exposing Charlie to ridicule. Let them think she had become barren; she might as well be, since she would never bear another child.

She looked over at the group of children running about in the garden, ranging in age from Jane and Harry's seventeen-month-old Esther up to nine-year-old Thomas. It would be hard to watch the other women with their new babies; especially if either of them had a pretty little dark-haired girl. Now that David was so visibly a little boy, she felt as though she had lost her window on what Ann must look like. It had been a little like losing her all over again.

'Amy? Are you all right?' Lizzie's voice interrupted her reverie.

'What? Oh, yes, I'm fine.'

'Are you sure?' Lizzie pressed. 'You haven't been having any… any trouble at home, have you?'

'No, Lizzie, I haven't. I'm perfectly all right.'

'You just looked a bit down in the mouth. You look well, though. You know, I think you've grown a bit taller the last few months.'

'Lizzie, what a silly thing to say! I'm much too old to be growing. Anyway, I was just thinking about something.'

'Something sad?' Jane asked. 'You looked a bit upset.'

'Did I? Well, I shouldn't have,' Amy said. 'Today's a really happy day, Bill and Lily don't want long faces at their wedding.' She looked at the newly-weds sitting side by side on the verandah, and it was easy to smile at the sight. 'They look so happy, don't they?'

'Mmm,' said Lizzie. 'They're a good match, all right. It was silly, Lily struggling on looking after other people's children when what she really needs is to get on and have some of her own.'

David ran over to Amy and began to clamber onto her lap. 'Can I have another cake, Mama?' he asked, looking up at her with the wide-eyed smile of anticipation that she could never resist.

'Don't climb up on me, Davie, you know Papa says you mustn't do that any more. Of course you can have one, there's plenty. You go inside and ask Aunt Edie—she's in the parlour. Come out and eat it on the grass, though, you mustn't drop crumbs on Aunt Edie's rugs.' She glanced over swiftly to check that Charlie was not watching, then gave David a quick squeeze and a kiss before he ran up the steps and into the house in search of his aunt.

There was no risk of Charlie's noticing her forbidden 'babying' of David; he was far too engrossed in his beer. While the other men filled their mugs from time to time at the barrel that stood under a shady karaka tree, Charlie had not moved more than a few feet from it ever since the service had ended.

The day cooled pleasantly as the sun dipped towards the hills. The noise of the children's voices faded gradually as, one by one, they found spots well out of the way of large, careless feet and lay down, tired out with playing.

Amy saw Jack and Arthur wander over towards the beer, deep in conversation as they walked. Arthur filled both mugs, and the men stood under the tree and chatted for a few minutes longer. But when Charlie forced himself on their attention by pouring himself yet another drink Jack gave him a look of disgust and walked away.

He dragged a chair close to Amy and sat down beside her. 'How's my girl?' he asked, resting his arm across her shoulders. 'Haven't seen you in weeks, except at church.'

Amy leaned her head against his chest. 'I know, it's been hard for me to get out just lately. You should come over and see me sometimes, maybe bring Tom and George now school's finished.'

'I might just do that. I worry about you when I don't see you, girl.'

'You shouldn't, Pa, there's no need. Everything's fine, really it is. You come over tomorrow—I'll make some of those ginger biscuits you used to like if you promise to come.'

'I haven't had those in years,' Jack said. 'I don't think I've had them since you went away.'

'Maybe I'll give the recipe to Sophie—no, I won't,' Amy amended. 'That way I can talk you into coming and visiting me a bit more often.'

Arthur was still leaning against the tree trunk, sipping his beer. Amy saw her uncle cast an occasional irritated glance in Charlie's direction. He took a step or two closer and made a comment on the weather, which Charlie did not answer. After a short silence, Arthur spoke again.

'Go a bit easy on the drink, eh, Charlie,' he said with a joviality that was clearly forced. 'Leave some for the rest of us.'

Charlie muttered something that Amy did not catch. He drained his mug, but made no move to fill it again.

'That's right, let one lot hit bottom before you send the next one down to join it,' Arthur said. He topped up his own mug and leaned against the tree trunk again. 'If you kept downing it at that rate you might find your wife having to carry you home.'

Charlie looked grimly at Arthur, then shot a black look in Amy's direction. She turned her head away, but not before she had seen him shape the word 'bitch' at her.

'Hey, hey, there's no need for that sort of talk,' Arthur remonstrated. 'I think you've had enough for one night.' His eyes flicked to Amy just long enough for her to see the sympathy in them, then he scowled at Charlie, his face full of disgust. Amy realised with a jolt that her father must have told Arthur about the beating.

'She's a *bitch*,' Charlie said, his voice easily reaching Amy and her three companions. 'Sour-faced little tart. She's—'

'That's enough, Charlie,' Jack said. 'Speak to my daughter with a bit of respect or keep your mouth shut. I'll shut it for you if you don't.'

Amy reached out and put her hand over his. 'It's all right,' she said quietly. 'Don't take any notice.'

'I'm not going to listen to him talking to you like that, girl.'

'It doesn't matter, Pa,' Amy said. She squeezed her father's hand. 'It's only talk, nothing else. Nothing else,' she repeated. 'Words don't hurt, not really.' She looked over her father's shoulder to see Charlie muttering to himself, but his eyes shied away from Jack's and he said nothing audible.

'I think perhaps we'd better go home now,' Amy said. She turned to Lizzie and Jane to see them both looking a little shaken as well as, in Lizzie's case, furious. 'I'm sorry,' she told them; but it was not an apology, merely an expression of regret that the other women had had to witness the unpleasant scene. 'Now, where are those boys of mine?'

'I don't want to see you going off by yourself with him,' Jack fretted.

Amy slid out from under his arm and took both his hands in hers. 'Pa, you mustn't worry about me,' she said, looking up into his troubled eyes. 'It's all right, I promise it is. He won't do anything but talk, and he won't even do that for much longer tonight. He'll go to sleep as soon as I get him home, then in the morning he'll wake up with a sore head feeling sorry for himself.'

She planted a kiss on her father's cheek and stood up. 'Come and see me tomorrow, I'll be expecting you. Bye bye, Jane, and you too, Lizzie— don't look so fierce, Lizzie!' She kissed them both and went searching for her children, whom she found sleeping in a corner of the verandah.

Leading a drowsy child with each hand, she walked up to Charlie. 'Do you want to go home now?' she asked.

Charlie glanced from Arthur to Jack, who were both glowering darkly at him, and it was obvious even to him that if he did not take the opportunity Amy held out of leaving with some dignity the two men would take great pleasure in evicting him, and quite possibly keeping his wife and sons behind.

'Aye, we'll go now,' he said. 'Hurry up.'

'We're ready now.' She turned to wave to her father, then walked off beside Charlie.

For once it was not hard for her to match his pace. The beer was taking its toll; he had to put much of his attention into treading at all steadily. They walked in silence, and Amy concentrated on guiding the sleepy little boys' steps, carrying David for the last stretch up the track to Charlie's cottage.

She led the boys through to their bedroom and undressed them. Both children were half asleep by the time she had tucked them in; she even managed to steal a kiss from Malcolm. While she got the children into bed she listened for the sound of Charlie making his own way through the house, but she did not hear him come any closer than the kitchen. So he was going to be silly; it was no more than she had expected from the way he had behaved at her uncle's.

She closed the boys' door softly, then went through the parlour and into the kitchen. Sure enough, Charlie was sitting at the table. He had lit a candle and stuck it roughly into a candlestick; Amy corrected its precarious angle before speaking.

'Pa's coming over tomorrow,' she said, as if it were of only slight interest. 'Do you want something, Charlie?' She spoke in the same calm voice she had used to him earlier. 'I'll make you a cup of tea if you like.'

'Bitch,' he muttered. 'Miserable little bitch.'

'I mixed the bread this afternoon before we went out, so I've no need to sit up now. But I'll make you some tea if you want. And would you like a biscuit? Or maybe a sandwich? What would you like?'

'I want my rights, that's what.'

'Charlie, I've said all I'm going to about rights. There's no sense going on and on about it. Now, if you don't want me to get you any supper I'm going to bed.' She took a candle from a shelf and lit it from the one on the table. 'Do you want any supper or not?'

'Dirty little whore. You're a useless, good-for-nothing trollop.'

'I'm not listening, Charlie.' She walked across the room, shielding her candle from the draught with one hand.

'Stupid bitch of a woman. Sour, tight little bitch.'

Amy went through her bedroom door and looked back at him. 'Good night.' She shut the door on the sight of his scowling face.

28

December 1891

The hangover he woke with the morning after Bill and Lily's wedding left Charlie rather subdued all that day, but he had fully recovered from his overindulgence by the following Sunday, when Bill and Lily made their first appearance at church as a married couple. As she watched the newly-weds talking to well-wishers after the service Amy noticed the way their fingers sought excuses to brush against each other's hands and arms, and she smiled to herself. Bill and Lily were happy, and they did not mind the world's knowing it.

Amy saw Charlie cast a scowl over his shoulder at Bill and Lily as he started the gig homewards. *He's jealous. He's thinking about Bill and Lily, and what they've been doing at night. I hope he's not going to carry on silly again.*

'She's nothing to look at,' Charlie muttered.

'Lily's very nice,' said Amy.

Charlie directed his scowl at her instead of at Bill and Lily, over the heads of the two boys squeezed between them. 'Aye, maybe she is. Not a sour little tart like some.'

'What's a tart, Mama?' David asked, looking up at her expectantly.

'It's something nice to eat, Davie,' Amy said. 'It's like a pie with no top. I might make an apple tart for pudding tomorrow—I'll put lots of sugar in, then it won't be sour.' Charlie scowled more fiercely than ever, but said nothing more about tarts, sour or otherwise.

Amy was up at five o'clock the next morning to start the weekly washing. She paused from hauling piles of steaming hot clothes between the tubs to get morning tea ready, calling Malcolm and David down from the tree they were playing in as she walked back to the cottage.

Charlie was already sitting at the table when she went into the kitchen with the boys. She expected him to complain at having been kept waiting a few minutes, but he seemed too busy rummaging in his pockets to take much notice of their arrival. She put the kettle on to boil and got the tea things ready.

Charlie brought his hands out of his pockets and formed a small heap of coins on the table in front of him. He muttered his calculations aloud as he laboriously counted the coins, then counted them again, clearly dissatisfied with the first answer.

'I thought I had more than that,' he grumbled to himself. 'I'll have to go to the bloody bank, try and talk that miserable beggar of a manager into letting me have a bit until the cream cheque comes.' He began to count the coins a third time.

Amy poured the tea, and put his cup beside the small pile. She took her own seat at the other end of the table. As she let one hand drop into her lap she felt a small lump in the pocket of her apron.

'These were in your trousers,' she said, pulling out the two coins she had found when checking Charlie's pockets before hurling his trousers into the copper. She placed the coins before him. 'A sixpence and a threepenny bit.'

Charlie snatched at the coins and added them to his little hoard. 'That should do it,' he said, studying the pile with some complacency.

'What do you want money for?' Amy asked, taking a sip of her tea. It was rarely that she saw cash; the provisions of the household were always bought on credit at the store.

'Mind your own business, nosy bitch,' was all the reply he gave her, but remembering his mood of the day before it was no great surprise to Amy when Charlie, having finished his tea, pushed back his chair and announced that he was going into town.

'I see,' Amy said, clearing away the cups without looking at him. The boys hovered around her as she stepped over to the bench, eager to beg another biscuit each. *So whores have to be paid in cash, do they?* 'I suppose you'll have lunch there?'

'I might.'

'Can I come, Pa?' Malcolm asked.

'No, you can't,' said Charlie.

'But I want to. I want to go with you. Why do I have to stay with her?'

'Don't you whine at me, boy,' Charlie growled. Malcolm had the sense to take a step backwards out of his father's range. He did not dare complain again in Charlie's hearing, but his face wore a black scowl.

'I wanted to go with Pa,' he muttered when Charlie had gone outside to catch his horse.

'Well, you can't,' said Amy. 'Don't pull such awful faces, Mal, the wind might change and you'll be stuck like that. Now, don't get under my feet, I've got to get the washing finished.'

She went outside, the two boys trailing after her. Charlie had saddled up his bay gelding and was mounting. As she watched he rode away without looking back at them.

'I wonder why he's not riding Smokey,' Amy remarked. The grey was always Charlie's preferred mount.

'Smokey's a bit stiff, so Pa doesn't want to ride him far today. Pa told me that when we were milking yesterday afternoon,' Malcolm said, full of self-importance. 'You don't know anything about horses.'

'Don't talk to me like that, Mal. I used to ride every day when I was little, I know more about horses than you do.'

'No, you don't,' Malcolm said. 'You're just a silly bitch.'

Amy turned on her heel, took hold of Malcolm by the sleeve and gave him a slap on the bottom. 'Don't you dare say that to me,' she told the startled child. 'I don't ever want to hear language like that from you again.'

Malcolm stared at her, astonished. 'Pa calls you that,' he said indignantly. 'He says it all the time.'

'Your father can do—' she stopped to correct herself, 'can *say* whatever he likes to me. He's a grown man, and this is his house. But you can just behave yourself.'

It did not take Malcolm long to regain his composure. 'Anyway, that didn't even hurt. You can't even do hidings. Silly bitch.' His expression told Amy he was daring her to hit him again.

She gazed back at him and sighed, resigning herself to defeat. He looked so startlingly like his father when he scowled at her like that, but Malcolm was not Charlie, and she had no right to treat him as though he was.

It was one thing to assert her rights with Charlie; he had chosen to marry her, he was a grown man, and he had to bear the consequences of having gone too far in his treatment of her. She would give him what duty she still owed him, and give it ungrudgingly.

But she owed Malcolm more than mere duty; he was her son as well as Charlie's, born out of her body, and she owed him love. Always at the back of her mind when she thought of Malcolm was a vague feeling of guilt that she did not love him as much as she should. It was not his fault that his parents had married with no trace of affection between them, and it was not his fault that he bore his father's face. However much he might hurt her, she could not bear to hurt Malcolm in return.

'Please yourself, then, Mal,' she said. 'Just don't let your father hear you talking like that—even if he does say it himself, that doesn't mean he'll let you.'

She walked the rest of the way to her copper and tubs, the boys ambling along in her wake. 'Why don't you two go and climb trees again?' she asked.

'Don't want to,' Malcolm said, more because she had suggested it than from any real disinclination, Amy suspected.

'You're in a real mood, aren't you? All right, then, don't. Stand around here and watch me do the washing if that's more fun.'

'I want to climb trees, Mal,' David protested.

'Oh, all right,' Malcolm said. He went off readily enough with David, leaving Amy free to finish off the last load of washing in peace.

Now that the day had reached its full heat the sun beat fiercely on her despite her wide-brimmed straw hat, plastering her hair down with perspiration and making her head ache. She had often wished Charlie would build a roof over the copper and tubs wide enough to shelter her from the sun, but she knew it would be no use asking him.

She hung the last of the clothes out to dry and stood for a moment enjoying the shade of the tree that one end of her clothesline was attached to. Close to the tree trunk Ginger was sprawled luxuriously, almost invisible against the dry ground there. Amy paused to stroke his warm fur, feeling the rumbling purr deep within him, then headed back to the house. She glanced over at the small stand of trees where the children had been playing earlier, but there was no sign of the boys. Weary from her morning's labour, at first she did no more than wonder idly where else they might have gone. As she remembered Malcolm's defiant mood a vague foreboding crept over her. Just what was that boy up to?

'Mal?' she called. 'Where are you? Davie? Mal?' There was no answer, and with an inward groan she set off in search of them.

The snort of a horse caught her attention as she passed the house and started down the track. She stopped for a moment and listened, then walked quickly in the direction of the sound.

The boys had climbed onto the fence of the horse paddock, and Malcolm had attracted Smokey over with a few small carrots filched from Amy's garden. The horse snatched at the carrots, coming right up to the fence to get at them. Giving Charlie's horse a treat was a harmless enough activity, but something about Malcolm's stance made Amy stand and watch the boys instead of turning away and leaving them to it.

Dangling one of the carrots just out of Smokey's reach, Malcolm clambered onto a fence post, waving his arms until he had his balance and could stand upright. He let Smokey take the carrot, then as Amy watched Malcolm darted out and caught hold of Smokey's mane with both hands and flung himself onto the horse's back.

For a few moments Amy was too startled to move, then she gathered up her skirts and ran the rest of the way to the horse paddock. 'Malcolm!' she called. 'What on earth do you think you're doing? Get off there!'

'Mal's riding Papa's horse!' David squealed.

'Mal's a naughty boy,' Amy said, unsure whether to feel angry or anxious. 'He's no business getting on Papa's horse by himself when he doesn't even know how to ride. Malcolm!'

But Malcolm was too busy keeping his precarious seat to take any notice of her. He clutched a fistful of mane in each hand and gripped tightly with his knees, kicking the horse with all his might. Smokey had looked aggrieved when he had been unexpectedly mounted; as Malcolm dug in his ankles the horse's ears went back and he broke into an awkward trot. Malcolm bounced up and down on the bony back, but his hands kept their hold on Smokey's mane and he clung limpet-like with his knees.

'Gee up,' he urged the horse. 'Go faster! I want to gallop!'

Malcolm's eyes were flashing with excitement. It was no use calling out to him; he was beyond hearing her, even if he had been likely to take any notice. So Amy stood close to the excited David, keeping a tight hold of the little boy's hand in case he decided to dart into the paddock after his brother, and waited to see how Malcolm's wild ride would end.

He did not manage to persuade Smokey into a gallop, or even a canter. Instead Smokey's trot became faster and more jolting, his ears flat to his head, until the horse decided he had had enough of this unpleasant little burden who kept kicking at his sides so uncomfortably.

It took Amy a moment to realise what was happening when she saw Smokey lower his head, then she shouted a warning.

'He's going to buck, Mal! Let go his mane and jump. Go on, jump off now!'

Instead Malcolm clung on tighter, but he had no chance of keeping his seat when Smokey lashed out with his hind legs. It only took a few good bucks till Malcolm went flying over the top of the horse's head to land in a heap on the grass.

Amy was over the fence and at Malcolm's side before she knew she had moved. She dropped to her knees beside him and reached out to touch his face, her heart pounding at the sight of his still form.

'Mal?' she said, her voice shaking with fear. 'Talk to me, Mal!'

Malcolm's mouth hung open, his face dazed. He took a great gulp of air and his eyes lit up. 'Did you see me riding him? That was *neat*.' He made to sit up, but his mouth twisted into a grimace.

'You're dizzy, aren't you?' said Amy. 'Lie still for a minute.' She laid his head in her lap and stroked his cheek. 'You're going to have an awful headache later. Serves you right, too,' she added, annoyance finding its way to the surface as her fear faded. 'All right, you can sit up now if you want. Let's have a look at you. I don't think you've done yourself much damage, though it's not for want of trying.'

She checked Malcolm over, feeling her way gently along his body. He had taken most of his weight on one hip; he winced a little as she touched it, but it was clearly nothing serious. The most painful-looking souvenir of his escapade was a long scratch along the back of one hand and halfway up to his elbow where his arm had scraped over a piece of wood lying in the paddock, leaving a bleeding graze that had stained his shirt sleeve.

'You've made a good job of that,' Amy said. 'You've ripped your sleeve, too, and this is the only shirt that still fits you properly.' She dabbed at the blood with her handkerchief. 'I'll give this scratch a wash when we go inside, it'll be sore for a bit. You're going to get a huge bruise on that leg, too. That'll go with the ones your pa's going to put on your bottom. He's going to be very angry with you, Mal.'

'Are you going to tell on me?' Malcolm asked, giving her a resentful look.

Amy studied his face. Malcolm was trying hard to look defiant, as though he did not care what his father might do to him, but she could see fear in his eyes. They both knew only too well what Charlie's anger meant.

After a year of going to school, the only thing Malcolm seemed to have learned was how to defy another woman besides his mother. At least school meant the hours Malcolm and Charlie spent together, and therefore their opportunities for falling out with each other, were limited.

But now that the long summer holiday had begun, that small relief had disappeared. Again Malcolm was spending most of the day with Charlie, and again there was trouble most days. Malcolm did not cry as much as he once had when his father punished him; perhaps Charlie saw that as a sign his son was growing up, but Amy suspected it only meant Malcolm was getting better at hiding what he felt.

She sighed. 'No, I won't tell him, Mal. But he might figure it out for himself—look what you've done to poor Smokey.' The horse was grazing on the far side of the paddock, keeping his distance from them, and he was walking with a distinct limp. 'He needed a rest, that's why your pa didn't take him out today—you told me that yourself, you silly boy.'

'I didn't ride him far. I just wanted a little go at it. I wanted Pa to take me out on the horse with him,' he finished, his lower lip quivering. The shock of his fall, coupled with the fear of retribution that Amy had put into his head, made him look dangerously close to tears.

'Well, maybe your pa won't notice. He probably won't even look at Smokey when he comes home, he'll be thinking about other things.'

Except that he would have to turn his bay out into the horse paddock with Smokey; Malcolm would need to be very lucky for his father to miss seeing Smokey's lameness. But there was no sense frightening the child, and perhaps he would indeed be lucky. 'Let's go back to the house and I'll clean you up.'

By the time she had washed Malcolm's grazed arm and helped him into a clean shirt, the morning had almost gone. It was high time she started making lunch. Amy glanced at the kitchen clock and thought for a moment. Despite his refusal to commit himself, she knew Charlie would not be home until well into the afternoon; it would have been close to eleven o'clock by the time he got to town, and he always stayed several hours when he treated himself to such outings.

'How do you feel now, Mal?' she asked, smoothing down his tousled hair and carefully picking a dead leaf out of it.

'I'm all right. This shirt's too hot,' he complained.

'I can't help that, it's the only clean one you've got left until the washing's dry. But you're right, it's really hot today, much too hot for a proper cooked lunch like your pa always wants. How would you boys like a picnic instead? We could take it down to the creek and sit under the trees. You two could have a swim if you like.'

'Yes!' both boys chorused.

'That's what we'll do, then. A swim might help your sore head, too, Mal. Come and help me pack a basket.'

She made a pile of sandwiches, using some of the cold meat from the previous day's roast dinner, and put them into a basket along with a few scones left over from morning tea, some cakes and several peaches, with a bottle of her home-made lemonade to wash it all down.

'Have a swim first, that'll make sure you're good and hungry,' she told the boys when they reached the bank of the creek. She helped David with his buttons while Malcolm undressed himself. The naked boys jumped into the waist-deep water with whoops of delight.

Amy smiled as she watched them, happy at the sight of her sons enjoying themselves. She took off her boots, and turned her back to the boys while she undid her garters and pulled off her stockings, then she sat on a rock that jutted into the creek to dangle her feet in the water, gasping at the delicious coolness. 'Don't you dare splash me,' she said, seeing the mischievous look on David's face. She squealed with laughter as the two boys flung handfuls of water at her. It was far too hot to worry about a few splashes.

'Come and have a swim, Mama,' said David.

'No, I'll just dip my feet in. That's enough for me.' She was already exposing more of her flesh to daylight than she had in years, with her skirts pulled up to her knees.

Malcolm threw himself under the water and came up snorting. 'Can you swim, Ma?' he asked.

'I used to be able to. I suppose I still can.' She thought back to other warm days when she and Lizzie had slipped away to a sheltered part of the creek where they could strip off and splash about to their hearts' content, as carefree as these two children. Lizzie had always taken the precaution of threatening Bill and Alf with dire retribution from their father if the boys disturbed them while they were swimming, so the girls could cavort without fear of being observed. It seemed so long ago, those days when she had not worn ankle-length dresses, nor been laced into corsets that barely allowed her to bend in the middle, let alone run about climbing trees and leaping over fallen logs the way she and Lizzie had done. And yet, when she came to work it out, the memories were little more than ten years old.

'Come here a minute, Davie, and hold on to my hands, then you can practise kicking,' Amy said. 'That's right. Kick a bit slower, though, you don't want to splash all the water out of the creek.'

Malcolm watched with interest, then let Amy persuade him into taking his own turn at holding her hands and kicking vigorously. 'You've got strong legs, Mal, you're kicking really well. I can't teach you properly, though, not when I can't get in the water with you. It's about time you two learned to swim, I don't want you drowning yourselves.'

'Will Pa show us how?' Malcolm asked.

'I don't know, your pa's always busy working or he's tired. I'm not even sure if he can swim himself, anyway. Maybe I'll see if he'll let me take you over to Grandpa's a bit more over the summer, then we might try and talk Uncle John or Uncle Harry into teaching you. Uncle Harry hasn't got any boys of his own, he might like borrowing you two for a bit.'

After their lesson in kicking, the boys leapt about in the creek until they began to shiver from the cold water. They scrambled over the rocks to the creek bank and collapsed onto the grass, panting from their exertion.

'The sun's so hot it'll dry you quite fast, then you can get your clothes on and we'll have some lunch,' Amy said. She lifted her wet legs out of the creek and went over to lie on her side between the boys, watching the sunlight glistening on the little rivulets of water that ran down their bodies.

The two boys looked so different that she sometimes found it hard to believe they had both come out of her, but the pair of them had inherited Charlie's long legs and strong build. 'You two are growing so fast,' Amy said. 'You'll be taller than me in a few years. Maybe you'll even be taller than your father one day.'

She kept a close eye on the boys as the sun dried them, anxious that Malcolm's fair skin should not burn. As soon as they were no longer visibly wet, she coaxed them into rolling onto their fronts so that their backs would dry.

'This grass is prickly,' Malcolm complained when he was lying face down.

'I know, but you won't be there for long, just till you're dry.'

The fine, downy hair on Malcolm's arms looked almost blond in the sunlight as she checked his graze. 'That swim's given your arm a good rinse, it looks quite clean now.' She brushed the dried grass and small sticks off Malcolm's back, stroking the smooth skin down his spine.

'That tickles, Ma,' Malcolm said, wriggling away from her touch.

'It's fun tickling you.' She took advantage of his face-down position to plant a kiss on his damp hair while he could not see what she was doing, then she turned to brush David's back clean.

His hair had dried enough to form tiny curls where it lay against his neck. A small pool of water had formed at the tip of the longest lock. Amy kissed it away. David must be due for another haircut if his hair was long enough for visible curls. That meant seeing her little boy looking like a frightened rabbit as his father waved the big scissors around his head, with David doing his best to hold back the tears that he would be punished for if they were seen. To Malcolm haircuts meant boredom and having to sit unnaturally still; for David they had taken on nightmare proportions since his first experience of his father's wrath. She did her best to promise him treats to follow each haircut, but it was hard for the four-year-old to cling to the hope of something nice to eat as he perched terrified on a chair watching the scissors and knowing that a stick was close at hand if he misbehaved.

David slithered across the grass to nestle close. He laid his head on Amy's chest and pressed his warm little body against hers. 'I like it when Papa's not here,' he said, smiling up at her.

'You shouldn't say that, Davie,' Amy admonished. 'We wouldn't have anything to eat if Papa didn't work hard on the farm growing things and milking the cows.'

But she could not put any real rebuke into her voice; not when it was such pleasure to lie in the sun with her boys, Charlie's sobering presence too remote to cast any shadow on them. Malcolm had dropped his usual belligerence towards her, too warm and languid to feel the need to be defiant. For a moment she considered trying to draw him close for a cuddle so that she would have a child in each arm, but when she ran her fingers across Malcolm's shoulders she felt him stiffen. She contented herself with patting his arm.

'My two boys,' Amy murmured. 'I'm lucky to have you, aren't I? It's nice being together, just the three of us.'

'I wanted to go with Pa,' Malcolm said quietly.

'I know, Mal. Don't get upset about it, lovey, you can go with Pa another time.'

'I wanted to go with him,' Malcolm persisted. 'He wouldn't take me. He left me behind like I'm a baby.'

'He just likes to go off by himself sometimes. He'll take you when you're old enough.' Only when the words were out did she realise their full import: when her son was old enough, his father would take him whoring. She fought back a rush of anger at the thought.

'You always say that. When will I be old enough?'

'You won't be old enough to go to the hotel for years and years, Mal, and a good thing, too. But your pa takes you out other places with him—he often takes you to the factory.'

'Yes,' Malcolm allowed. 'But then we just go on the cart. It's not like riding a horse. Pa took me into town on the horse once, we went real fast on the beach. He doesn't take me any more.'

'He never takes me,' David put in.

'You're too little,' Malcolm said, proud of his two years' superiority.

'Would you like to go with Papa, Davie?' Amy asked.

David thought for barely a second. 'No. I like it with you best, Mama.'

'It's good going with Pa, even just to the factory,' Malcolm argued. 'You get to see lots of horses, and Pa talks to the men and things. It's all men down there. Pa says women talk a lot of rubbish.'

It's all women where your father's gone. I don't suppose he bothers talking to them, though.

'But Papa gets grumpy. Then he hits us,' David countered.

'Yes.' Malcolm lapsed into silence as he pondered the problem.

'He doesn't hit you all the time, Mal, and he hardly ever hits you, Davie,' Amy said, anxious that the boys should not paint their father in a worse light than he deserved. 'Only when you're naughty. Or sometimes just because he's really grumpy,' she added in deference to the truth.

'Why does he get grumpy, Mama?' David asked.

'Papa works hard, Davie. When people get tired they get grumpy.' *Going to whores tires him out, too.* 'You just have to try not to annoy him when he's tired.'

She disentangled herself from David and sat up, stretching her arms. 'We'd better see about eating this lunch. You boys have had enough sun for one day, you're going a little bit pink, Mal.' Malcolm would have trouble enough if his father found out about his riding escapade without painful sunburn.

It was well into the afternoon by the time they had finished lunch and then sat in the shade digesting it.

'It's nice here, but I'd better get back and see if any of that washing's dry,' Amy said. 'I need to butter some scones for afternoon tea, too—your father will be home any time now, he wouldn't be very pleased to see me lazing around here instead of working.'

From a slight rise on their way back to the house Amy saw a horse and rider coming up the valley in the distance.

'That's probably your pa. You'd better try and stay out of his way this afternoon, Mal, in case he goes looking at Smokey—oh, you'll have to help him with milking later, won't you? Well, stay away from the house till then, anyway. I'll come and call you when it's time. Don't say anything about your sore arm and maybe he won't notice.'

Malcolm did not need any persuasion to make himself scarce. He and David were well out of sight before Charlie was much closer.

Amy hurried down to the horse paddock to meet Charlie as he rode up a few minutes later. He dismounted, and glanced at her approach in surprise.

'What are you after?' he asked.

'Nothing. I just came to say hello.'

Charlie grunted in response. He led the horse into the paddock and took off the saddle and bridle, leaving the bay free to crop the grass. Charlie looked across the paddock to where Smokey stood near the opposite fence, but before he could take a closer look at the horse Amy spoke.

'I've got scones buttered, and the kettle's on. You must be ready for a snack.'

'Aye, I've a fair appetite,' said Charlie. Thus distracted, he walked up to the house, stopping only to put the tack away in one of the sheds.

'Where's the boy?' Charlie asked when he had joined Amy in the kitchen.

'They're both playing over the back.' It vexed Amy that Charlie tended to forget he had a second son, but she knew it worked to David's advantage to be largely ignored by his father. 'I'll call them when you've had your afternoon tea.'

Two cups of tea and a plate of scones later, Charlie looked pleased with himself. Amy studied his face, wondering if she could succeed in shielding Malcolm. She had not realised how avidly she was watching until Charlie narrowed his eyes at her and said, 'What are you staring at?'

Amy lowered her eyes. 'I'm sorry, I didn't mean to stare.' Now instead of his face she could see Charlie's boots, a layer of dried mud thick around the edge of the soles. It was hard to remember what Charlie's feet looked like without boots, now that she no longer shared his bed. That seemed to be the only place he never wore them. *I wonder if he takes them off at the whorehouse. I suppose he must before he gets into bed there. He's got that whorehouse smell again.* 'Do you want another cup of tea?'

'No, I can't sit around here all day. It'll be time to get those cows in shortly.' He pushed his chair back, but remained sitting. 'The boy can help me with that.'

'I'll call him, then.'

The boys appeared soon afterwards, both of them standing in the kitchen doorway and eyeing their father nervously. Charlie stood up and went outside, Amy and the children following. As Charlie turned in the direction of the cow shed, Malcolm a few steps behind him, Amy relaxed a little. She was sure that once Charlie started the long job of bringing in the cows and milking them he would forget all about Smokey, and by the morning the horse would probably have got over the worst of his lameness.

Charlie stopped abruptly. 'I'd better have a look at Smokey first, see if he's over that bit of stiffness. You wait there, boy, don't go wandering off.'

'I'm sure Smokey's all right, Charlie,' Amy said, a little too quickly. 'He can wait till tomorrow, you don't want to waste time now rushing around after him.'

Charlie ignored her and headed for the horse paddock. Amy's mind raced as she tried to think of ways to distract him. But he would either disregard her or get angry if she obstructed him, and neither of those would do Malcolm any good.

Malcolm's eyes ranged around with a hunted expression, but he did not stir from the spot where his father had told him to stay. Amy moved to stand close beside him. She let her arm rest on his shoulders in a helpless attempt at comfort, but he did not seem to notice.

They were not left waiting for long. Charlie strode back up to them, his face livid.

'He's lame! My horse has gone lame! What the hell's happened to him?'

None of them made any answer, and Charlie ranted on.

'Something's frightened him—he shied away from me, he never does that. Something's made him bolt, and he's strained himself in that stiff leg. He'll be no use for days.'

He slowly became aware of the unnatural silence of his audience, and looked at the three of them with dawning suspicion.

'Do you know anything about this?' he asked Amy.

'He... he must have got a fright, like you said,' Amy hedged.

'What frightened him, then? Eh? What's been going on behind my back?'

While Amy struggled to think of an answer that might satisfy him, Charlie's attention turned to Malcolm.

'What have you been up to, boy? Have you been plaguing my horse?'

'I... I didn't...' Malcolm began. But the threat in his father's face pushed him over the edge into panic, and he made an ill-conceived attempt to run for it.

Charlie's thought processes might have been slow, but his reflexes were fast enough to react at once to a calf trying to dodge away from him. He snaked out his long arms and caught Malcolm before the boy had gone two strides, twisting Malcolm around to face him and holding him firmly by both shoulders.

'I didn't mean to lame him, Pa,' Malcolm gasped out.

'Don't be hard on him, Charlie, he didn't mean any harm,' Amy said. Charlie ignored her.

'Haven't I told you not to interfere with the horses?' he demanded. 'Haven't I said you're to keep away from them when I'm not here?' He shook Malcolm roughly.

'I-I didn't mean to—I just wanted—' Malcolm took a gulp of air and spoke in a rush. 'I wanted to ride him—I just went for a little ride—I wanted to ride him like you do—I wanted to go to town with you but you wouldn't take me—you never take me—you think I'm too little—I wanted to ride him but he kicked me off—'

'You've lamed that horse, you little bugger,' Charlie said, angrier than ever. 'I told you to keep away from them. That bloody horse could have killed you,' he finished in a roar, but Malcolm was far too frightened to understand that his father's anger was all the worse because of his fear for Malcolm's safety. 'Right, I'm going to teach you a lesson,' Charlie said, half dragging Malcolm out of sight behind the shed where he kept a stick handy.

Amy sank onto the back step holding a fearful David close to her, weeping quietly at the familiar sound of Malcolm's yells. 'Davie, you must try and be a good boy,' she said through her tears. 'You must always do what Papa says so he won't get angry with you. Promise me you'll try.'

'Yes, Mama,' David said.

When Charlie reappeared, trailed by a sobbing Malcolm, David stared at his father and clung harder to Amy.

'You get down to that cow shed and you wait for me there. Understand?' Charlie said.

He watched Malcolm run off, then turned to David and gave him a hard look. 'Now, what about you? Did you try riding my horse?'

David pressed his face against Amy's chest, his voice a muffled squeak. 'David!' Amy said sharply, pushing him away from her and gripping his shoulders to steady him. Charlie in his current mood was quite capable of giving the child a beating merely for being babyish. 'Stand up straight and answer Papa properly.' She gave his arm an encouraging squeeze.

'No, Papa,' David said in a voice that, although high-pitched with fright, was clear. 'I didn't ride the horse. I just looked.'

'Good. See that you don't.' Charlie gave Amy a look that told her she would have been liable for a beating herself for letting Malcolm commit his offense if she had not put a stop to such treatment, then turned on his heel and made off towards the cow shed.

That evening Amy watched Malcolm during the dismal silence of the family's dinner time. His tears had disappeared, but in their place was the sullen expression he so often wore. The sullenness had been replaced by the merry, open face of a happy little boy during the pleasant few hours she had spent alone with the children, but now it was back with a vengeance. She could do nothing to comfort him; instead she had to watch him eat in silence, then put both boys to bed while Charlie stood in the doorway to see that there was no forbidden babying.

She would have liked to have gone straight to bed rather than sit in the parlour with Charlie, but there was the never-ending pile of sewing to be tackled and no light brighter than a candle in her room. The candle was enough to read by if she stood it close to her bed, but it was too hard on her eyes to do tiny hand stitches by its light. She tried to ignore Charlie's presence as she stitched away at a new chemise for herself, until he demanded her attention by speaking.

'Did you see the boy riding Smokey?'

'Yes, I did,' she said, wondering if he was going to make more of a fuss. 'I got down to the horse paddock just as he was jumping on.'

'You didn't stop him.'

'I called out to him, but I don't know if he even heard me, he was so excited about it all.' She dropped her sewing into her lap and looked across the lamp at him. 'Charlie, I don't think Mal did anything so awful today. He's mad on horses, and he wanted to have a go at riding. It's a shame he lamed Smokey, but Smokey'll come right soon enough.'

'I've told him before not to go near the horses when I'm not here. He's got to learn to do as he's told.'

You would have been here if you hadn't been out whoring. It wouldn't have happened then. 'He forgot. Children forget what they've been told when they get excited. It doesn't mean Mal's wicked. It means he's just a little boy.'

'It's time he grew up, then.'

Charlie lapsed into silence, and Amy took up her sewing, then he spoke again.

'What sort of a job did he make of it?'

'What? Oh, riding, you mean?' She stopped and thought. 'He was quite good, actually. Especially for the first time he'd ever been on a horse by himself. He's got good balance, I think. He hung on tight, and he's got strong legs for kicking. That was the trouble, Smokey's not used to being belted like that.'

'Was he scared?'

'Mal? Not a bit. Mal's not frightened of anything.' *Except you when you're wild with him.* 'Even when Smokey bucked him off, he was too excited to notice the knocks he got.'

'Hmm. He's no coward, that boy.'

'No, he's very brave.' *Charlie's proud of Mal for doing that. He gave poor Mal an awful hiding, and now he's calmed down he's thinking what a brave boy he is. I bet he won't tell Mal that, though. He only ever tells him he's done wrong.*

Charlie turned the page of his newspaper noisily. 'I might buy the boy a pony.'

'A pony?' Amy echoed. 'That'll cost a lot of money, won't it?'

'That's none of your concern. You keep your nose out of my affairs and get on with your work. Aye, I'll ask old man Carr if he's any ponies he's not wanting.'

'Mal will love that. He'll be beside himself,' Amy said. *He'd be even happier if you told him you're proud of him. But you won't.*

29

Malcolm took to riding more naturally than he had to walking. It was barely a matter of weeks before he was trotting his little pony confidently around the paddock. Charlie's idea of teaching consisted of giving the boy a leg-up onto the pony's bare back then slapping the animal on the rump until he broke into a trot, and Malcolm took many tumbles before he mastered the art of keeping his seat. He never so much as whimpered, no matter how painful the fall; he was too busy enjoying himself. It was not long before he was managing to coax the pony, a steady little bay called Brownie, into an occasional canter, and even attempting to jump over logs, though this led to more falls than successes.

By the time school started again there was no question but that Malcolm would be riding there and back each day, even though by the time he caught the pony before and after school it would have been almost as fast for him to walk. Charlie insisted he care for the pony himself, but there was no difficulty in making Malcolm do all Brownie's grooming and feeding. He adored his pony.

Amy was glad to see his new-found happiness, but she wished it did not have to be at David's expense. Malcolm was too busy now with his precious pony to have any time for his little brother, and Amy could see that David missed his company. He was still her affectionate little boy, eager for cuddles and kisses when his father was not around to see, but Amy could not provide the rough-and-tumble play David was used to from Malcolm.

For all his harshness, Charlie was a better father than some Amy knew of. She remembered from her own school-days a few children falling asleep over their desks, having been dragged out of bed to help their fathers with the morning milking then sent off to ride to school with no time for a proper breakfast. Charlie was not so demanding of his sons while they were very young. Malcolm had to help him with the afternoon milking, but he was left to sleep until Amy got the boys up for their breakfast, and David was considered too young to help at all.

Even so, it was a long day for Malcolm. After breakfast he had to catch his pony, put on the bridle and throw a blanket across Brownie's back (Charlie had no intention of paying for an extra saddle, and Malcolm would have been the only child in the school with such a luxury if he had), then ride down the track to school. In the afternoon he groomed the pony and put him out to graze, and after some milk and biscuits it would be time for him to help his father round up the cows for milking.

Amy's own days were so full that it was some time before she began to suspect that Malcolm did not always come straight home from school. Sometimes he seemed more out of breath than the short ride warranted, and when her suspicions grew strong enough for her to begin taking note of the time on the kitchen clock she soon realised that on the days Malcolm rushed into the kitchen flushed and panting he was at least a quarter of an hour later home than he should have been.

'Where have you been?' she asked him one day when the fifteen minutes had stretched to twenty-five and Malcolm had had no time to groom the pony before racing up to the house for his afternoon tea.

'At school,' he said, giving her a look that dared her to deny it.

'You haven't come straight home, though, have you?' said Amy. 'It only takes a few minutes for you to get home, especially the pace you bring Brownie up the road. Come on, Mal, tell me. Where have you been?'

'Nowhere,' Malcolm said, his face set. 'Just riding around a bit.'

'I thought as much. You should come straight home from school, you know. Your father thinks you do.'

'I didn't do nothing wrong,' said Malcolm. 'Just went down the road a bit and over a couple of ditches. It's boring just riding to school and back. Don't you tell on me.'

'I won't tell on you, but... oh, if you must go off riding by yourself, at least try and get home a bit sooner than this. Your pa will notice if you keep getting back this late, you know. He expects you here well in time for milking.'

'I'm sick of milking,' Malcolm muttered.

Amy gave a little laugh of surprise. 'Sick of milking? It's no use being sick of it, Mal, it's got to be done. I might as well say I'm sick of cooking dinner every night.'

'But I'm sick of it,' Malcolm persisted. 'I want to do more riding and things.'

'You can do riding when there's no school. You've got to help your pa, he needs you. It's going to get harder for him to manage when he gets older, too. Anyway, you used to love going out and working with him.'

'That was *years* ago,' Malcolm said, overstating matters. 'That was before I had Brownie. I hardly ever get to go for a good ride.'

'Yes, you do, you go for a ride every Saturday. Stop moaning and eat your biscuits, your pa will be up in a minute.' It was hard, she knew, for a six-year-old to accept the inevitable. 'We all have to do things we don't want to, Mal. You're always so keen to be grown-up—well, that's what being grown-up means. Come on, now, be a good boy and get rid of that grumpy face. It'll be winter soon enough and only the house cows to milk.'

Malcolm grumbled most afternoons about having to milk and help with other farm work, though he had the sense not to do so in front of his father. Amy would still sometimes catch a hurt look on Malcolm's face when Charlie went into town without him, as he generally did once a fortnight or so, but Malcolm did not look aggrieved for long. Instead he would spend the few hours of his father's absence practising more and more ambitious jumps over logs and stumps, dragging brushwood into heaps to make a more challenging course. Ditches were soon no problem, and before autumn had begun to turn into winter Malcolm was able to coax Brownie into leaping obstacles that Amy would have thought quite beyond the pony's capability. There was no role for David beyond that of admiring audience in any of these riding exploits, and it wrung Amy's heart to see the little boy feeling left out.

One afternoon as she was walking back from the vegetable garden with a load of carrots to go in that evening's soup, Amy stopped to watch the two boys. Malcolm had just managed to take Brownie over a slim tree trunk he had set up between two stumps. He leapt from the pony's back, grinning.

'Did you see that?'

'That was neat,' said David. He took a few steps towards Malcolm and the pony. 'Can I pat your horse, Mal?'

'All right,' Malcolm said magnanimously.

David stood on tiptoe to pat the pony's neck. 'He's nice. I wish I had a horse.'

'Pa might get you one when you're six,' Malcolm said, but this was too far into the unimaginably distant future to give much comfort to the four-year-old.

The memory of David's wistful little face would not leave Amy. With no money of her own and no influence over Charlie she could not do anything about getting David his own pony, but she wanted to cheer him up somehow.

The best she could do for the moment, she decided, was to give him a little outing. A few mornings later she got permission from Charlie to visit Lizzie, and set off down the road with David at her side.

It had seemed a fine idea to give herself and David a change of company, and they were both disappointed at the end of their walk to find Frank's house deserted, a note from Lizzie on the kitchen table to tell anyone who popped in that the Kellys had all gone to town for the morning.

'I wanted to play with Joey, Mama,' David said as they walked back down Frank's track after their fruitless attempt at visiting.

'I know, darling, I'm sorry. We'll try and come down another day.'

David was silent for some time, then he said, 'Maudie's got a horse, too.'

'Not her own horse, Davie. It's just one of Uncle Frank's horses she uses to get to school.'

'But she's allowed to ride it. She can ride good now.'

'You'll learn soon. You'll be able to ride on Brownie with Mal when you start school.'

'I wish I had a horse.'

'I know, Davie. I know.'

They walked on in silence to the end of the track and then turned on to the road up the valley.

A cart was coming down the road towards them, a man waving at them from the driver's seat. When the cart got closer, Amy recognised Matt Aitken.

Matt drew the cart to a halt, and Amy went over to exchange polite greetings with him, annoyed with herself at being so nervous speaking to a man not within her immediate family. It took an effort of will before she could meet Matt's eyes and speak sensibly to him.

'I've just been up to see to a couple of your uncle's horses,' Matt said. Amy knew that he occasionally did some farrier work in the district. 'I'm on my way home now—would you like to come with me and see Rachel? She doesn't get a lot of visitors, and her and Bessie get a bit fed up with each other's company all day. I could give you a ride home afterwards.'

'I should be getting home, really,' Amy said. Charlie had given permission for a visit to Lizzie, not to Rachel Aitken. And he would be furious at the thought of her riding about unsupervised with Matt Aitken.

'Maybe another day, then,' Matt said. 'Hey, I bet this boy would like to see Peg's pups, wouldn't you, Dave?'

'Pups?' David echoed, his eyes lighting up.

'That's right. She's got eight of the little beggars. I'm bringing a few of them with me when I go out, trying to talk people into taking them off my hands! Come on, up you come.'

He leaned down and hoisted David into the back of the cart, where Amy now noticed a wooden crate lined with sacking. She looked in and saw four puppies snuggled together in a tangled mass.

David dropped to the floor of the cart beside the crate and stared at the puppies.

'Aren't they *pretty*,' he breathed in wonder.

Matt laughed. 'I thought they were pretty ugly, myself. You're more than welcome to one of them, Amy, I don't know how I'm going to get rid of them all.'

As Amy watched, one puppy separated itself from its fellows and clambered over to stand with its paws pressed against the side of the crate. It nosed against David's hand and whined in its little voice. David stroked it, and the whines grew more excited. He lifted the puppy carefully into his lap, laughing in delight as the pup's long tongue snaked out to lick his face.

'He likes me, Mama,' David said, so excited that his voice came out as a squeak.

'Yes, he does,' Amy agreed, her heart sinking. She knew what must come next.

'Can I have him? Please, Mama? Can I take him home?'

'I'm sorry, Davie, I don't think Papa would be very pleased. He thinks he's got enough mouths to feed without a puppy around the place.'

'Please, Mama. I'll look after him. Papa might like him.'

'I don't think so, darling. I'm sorry, I think you'll have to leave the puppy here.'

'A dog around the house isn't a bad idea, Amy,' Matt put in. 'I got Peg after Te Kooti's lot came through a while back. The soldiers sent them packing before they caused any trouble that time, but you never know when something like that might happen again. I can't always be home with Rachel, I like the idea of a dog barking its head off if anyone came poking around who had no business to.'

'Charlie was a bit worried about Te Kooti,' Amy mused. She remembered the time well. Te Kooti had arrived in the town with a band of followers a little over two years before, causing consternation among the settlers. He had left the area peacefully after talking to the troops that had been hastily despatched from Gisborne, but the incident had been a talking point around Ruatane for months afterwards. 'I wonder...' She looked at David, who was still stroking the puppy. He raised his gaze to her, the barest hint of tears making his eyes even brighter.

'Please, Mama? He could play with me. Please?'

It was too hard to resist. 'I tell you what, Davie, I'll see what Papa thinks about us getting a dog.' She had to extricate herself from David's rapturous embrace, complete with puppy tucked into the crook of one arm, before she could speak again. 'Now, don't get too excited, he might say no, but I'll ask him.'

'It costs nothing to feed them,' Matt said. 'Just chuck them the bits of offal you don't want.'

'I'll see what Charlie says,' was all Amy would commit herself to.

She rummaged in her drawstring bag until she found a leftover skein of wool she had meant to give Lizzie. She snapped off a short length and tied it around the pup's neck.

'Just so you can tell him apart from the others if you need to,' she said to Matt. 'But if Charlie does say he'd like a dog, there's no need to tell him I put that wool on.'

'Trying to pull the wool over his eyes, eh?' Matt said, and she laughed with him. 'When do I send the pup over, then?' he teased. 'He's ready to leave Peg now.'

'We'll have to see,' Amy said, careful not to promise anything to David. But she was becoming more and more determined that he would get his pet.

'Now, Davie, don't say anything about the puppy, not even to Mal,' she warned as they drew near home. 'If Papa says we can have one it'll be our secret that you've already picked him.'

David agreed to secrecy readily enough, but she could see that he could hardly contain his excitement. She was relieved that Charlie paid as little attention as usual to David that day.

Amy waited until the children were safely in bed and Charlie was settled in the parlour before she remarked in a carefully casual tone, 'I heard some people are getting dogs in case there's Maori trouble again.'

'Trouble?' Charlie said, taking more notice of her remark than he usually did. 'What sort of trouble?'

'You know, like when Te Kooti came through. Some men are a bit worried about leaving their farms when they have to go out, in case someone interferes with their stock. Men who only have women and children around. They think a dog barking might scare the Maoris off.'

'Hmm.' Charlie pondered the problem. 'There might be sense in that.' He frowned. 'A dog might worry stock.'

'You'd want the sort of dog that was used to animals,' Amy suggested. 'One born on a farm would be best.'

'It'd need feeding,' Charlie said, and Amy knew she was almost there. 'There's already enough mouths around here.'

'I've heard they don't take much feeding,' she said as if it were of only slight interest to her. 'They just eat the rubbishy bits of meat that you don't like anyway. All those bits you have to bury when you kill a sheep.'

Charlie creased his brow in thought. 'I might ask around about a dog.'

'I think Aitkens might have some they don't want,' Amy said. 'Someone said their bitch had a litter, and they were trying to give the pups away.'

'Give?' Charlie echoed. 'They're not wanting anything for them?'

'I don't think so. They've got more pups than they know what to do with.'

'Hmm.' He went back to reading his newspaper, but before he rose to put out the lamp that evening he said, 'I might pop over to Aitkens tomorrow, see about a dog.'

'That's a good idea,' Amy said, hiding her elation.

In the privacy of her own room she hugged herself in anticipation of the joy she would see on David's face when Charlie came home with the puppy. She lay in bed and savoured the knowledge that for the first time she had managed to manipulate Charlie into doing what she wanted while thinking it was his own idea. It was a pleasant reflection.

The beginning of a bumper crop of babies for the Leith families that year was marked by the arrival of Jane's in June. Yet another baby in the valley appeared a small enough event to those outside it, but to Harry Leith the birth of his son seemed the most momentous event of his life.

'You know what Robert did the other day?' Harry asked Frank one Sunday after church when the baby was a little over a week old. 'He looked at me! Looked me right in the face. You could see he knew who I was.'

'Boy, that's pretty good, Harry,' Frank said obligingly. He saw John grinning at him over Harry's shoulder.

'He's bright, that son of mine,' Harry went on. 'You know, I just about expected him to open his mouth and say something, he was looking at me that knowing.'

'I bet he wishes he could talk, Harry,' John put in. 'He'll probably start talking pretty young.'

'Sure to,' Harry agreed.

'Yep, one day he'll look you right in the eye and say, "Shut up, Pa." Then the rest of us will know he's bright, all right.'

Frank tried to smother a chuckle and failed badly. Harry glared at them both, then joined in the laughter even though it was at his own expense.

Frank was pleased for Harry, but he had other things on his mind.

Calving would start in a month or so, and right in the middle of it Lizzie was due to have the new baby. She assured him it got easier with each birth, and this one being her fourth would be no trouble at all, but he knew that when the time came he would worry as he always did. Lizzie was too precious ever to be taken for granted.

When June turned into July and the heavy rain started, at first the farmers were relieved that the run of dry years that had made raising crops difficult in recent times was over. But as July wore on and the rains grew heavier, it became obvious that this was far more than normal winter weather.

For years afterwards they would talk about the Bay of Plenty floods of 1892, but in those middle weeks of July everyone was too busy coping with the deluge to give any thought to their historical significance. It was much later that the people of Ruatane had time to exclaim over the almost forty inches of rain had fallen in twelve days. As the flood waters rose, the farmers in the Waituhi Valley moved their stock to higher ground and prayed that the creek would stop rising before it reached their houses.

Frank shrugged off his coat and hung it in the porch, water streaming from it onto the wooden floor and down the back steps. A yell from Lizzie met him as he opened the door, but it was not directed at him; the load of mud his boots carried after trudging around the sodden paddocks was far too heavy for him to forget to pull them off as soon as he reached the shelter of the porch.

'You go out that door and I'll give you a good hiding, Joey,' she warned. 'Then your pa'll give you a better one.'

'I want to go outside,' Joey protested, torn between the desire for freedom and the sure knowledge that his mother's threat should be heeded.

'No, you don't, Joe,' Frank told him. 'I wouldn't be going out myself if I didn't have to. Now, you be a good chap and don't give your ma a hard time. She's looking a bit weary on it.' He sat down at the table and poured himself a cup of tea from the pot Lizzie had ready, two-year-old Beth clambering onto him as soon as he had made a lap. 'You all right?' he asked Lizzie.

'I would be if that son of yours wasn't driving me up the wall wanting to go outside all the time,' Lizzie grumbled. She shifted in her chair, trying to find a more comfortable position for her bulky body. 'No, I'm all right. I'm as sick of being stuck inside as the kids are, and I think I've forgotten what the sun looks like, but there's nothing wrong with me.'

'I've been helping Ma,' Maudie said self-importantly. 'I made some biscuits.' She basked in the glow of her father's approving smile.

'So you did, love,' said Lizzie. 'I'm glad of the help, too, it's a good thing she can't get to school just now.' Frank could see that Lizzie was trying to appear her usual unflappable self, but there was a tightness about her mouth that reflected the strain they were both feeling. 'How are the animals, Frank?'

'Looking miserable, but they're right enough. They should be all right in those top paddocks—the water will never get that high.'

'It must stop raining soon, mustn't it?'

'It'd better,' he said. Seeing the fear in Lizzie's eyes he added in a lighter tone, 'It's sure to. Probably another day or so, that's all. I've put the Jerseys in the cart shed.'

'Spoiled things!' Lizzie exclaimed. 'What about the poor old Shorthorns?'

'They're all tough as old boots, and I didn't get a mortgage on the place to buy them. Anyway, I might put a few of them in there, too, if they start calving before the rain stops. I sledged a fair bit of hay over to the shed, that'll keep them going.' He did not remind her that all the hay stacks in the creek paddocks had been lost; nor did he tell her of the cow he had seen floating down the swollen creek that day. His own stock were all safe and sound, and that was all he could spare concern for at the moment. Except, of course, for the concern that was in his thoughts day and night: the heavily-pregnant Lizzie.

'That shed's going to get pretty full if you've got to keep all the calves in there.'

'No, it won't. The flood's sure to die down before calving gets going.'

She only half believed him, he could tell, though they were both careful to sound confident in front of the children. Later that evening, when Frank had helped an awkward Lizzie into her nightdress, he looked up from buttoning the bodice and saw in her face the strain she had been hiding all day. The thought of the baby loomed between them, as impossible to ignore as the bulge it made in Lizzie's nightdress.

'I let Maudie use just about the last of the sugar in those biscuits today,' said Lizzie. 'It'll be all bottled fruit for pudding from now on until you can get to town again.'

'That doesn't matter,' Frank said, trying to sound reassuring. 'I like your fruit. Anyway, the flood will be over before we run out properly.'

'Will it?' She turned from him and clambered into bed. Frank put out the lamp and climbed in beside her, angling his body to fit snugly around the curve her back made. He felt her tenseness as he pressed against her.

'Don't worry, Lizzie,' he murmured. 'It'll be all right.'

'Will it?' she repeated.

Frank held her in silence for some time, wishing that Lizzie did not have to be so very pregnant just when they were completely cut off from their neighbours, let alone the town and its nurses.

'I'm sorry, Lizzie,' he whispered.

'What for? You didn't make it flood.'

'No, but I got you in this state, didn't I?' Lizzie did not answer; nor did she respond when he stroked her arm.

'I shouldn't have watched that bull so much last summer, eh?' he said, more to himself than to her. He felt Lizzie give a start at his words, then begin making little jerking movements. He closed his arms around her, trying to soothe her sobs, then realised with a jolt that they were not sobs at all. 'What are you laughing about?' he asked, somewhat indignant at her response to his attempts at comforting.

'You, of course, you great fool! What a dopey thing to say.' He felt Lizzie relax against him. 'Honestly, Frank, you can be a real idiot sometimes. Anyone would think you'd planned it so I'd be the size of a house right in the middle of all this.' He laughed with her, content to know that Lizzie had for the moment forgotten to be afraid.

Lizzie wriggled herself closer. 'I don't know why I have to have babies at such ridiculous times. Maudie comes right in the middle of a mountain blowing up, and now this one's going to arrive when we're stuck in a flood.'

'It's not going to come that quickly, is it?'

He felt Lizzie shake her head, her hair tickling his face in the darkness. 'It shouldn't be for a few weeks. Maudie was early, though.'

'We'll be right, then. It'll all be over by the time the baby starts.' His hand crept down to caress the warm bulge of her belly. 'And even if it isn't, I'll look after you. We know more about the whole business now.'

'Oh, no you won't,' Lizzie said. 'I'm not one of your precious cows, Frank Kelly. You needn't think you're sticking those great hands of yours up inside me.'

'We'll see,' he murmured, chuckling at the fierceness of her tone. 'You might be glad of a bit of help.'

'Not from you, thanks very much. I've no intention of having this baby until the flood's over and you can fetch a nurse out, or at least another woman.' She said it with utter certainty, and Frank felt himself sharing her confidence. When Lizzie was like this it was impossible to imagine even the forces of nature daring to disobey her.

'You're right, Lizzie,' he said with mock solemnity. 'The baby won't be born till you're good and ready.'

Which turned out to be quite true. Late in July the torrential rain began to subside into weather that was merely stormy and unpleasant, and the creeks and rivers slowly returned to their usual confines. The people of the valley emerged from their isolation to compare notes with one another on their losses, and to begin the task of rebuilding fences washed away by the flood.

They had been luckier than many, they discovered when they were no longer cut off from the rest of the world. Sheep were being found washed up all along the coast, but losses within the valley had been slight. Jack had lost one cow, and Arthur and Jack had both lost a few of the sheep that served no other purpose than to provide meat for the family table. Much to the delight of all the older children, water had gone through the school, and cleaning it up so that lessons could resume was well down on the list of priorities.

The only dwelling to be flooded was Harry's, built well above the level of the usual winter floods but no match for this freakish deluge. Harry, Jane and the three children moved into the homestead until their house had been thoroughly cleaned and the timbers damaged by the flood replaced, and that the Leiths survived the ensuing weeks of strife was a source of wonder to the rest of the family for long afterwards. The apparent miracle was put down to the fact that Jane had not yet recovered her full strength after Robert's birth, so was unable to put much energy into fighting with Susannah.

Life had almost resumed its usual patterns when Michael Kelly made his way into the world, with nurse and grandmother duly in attendance. Relieved of his burden of worry over Lizzie, Frank could give more attention to tending his cows and acting as midwife to whichever of them needed his help. The new Jersey calves spread their arrivals around the baby's, one heifer and a bull calf a few days before, and a second heifer a week after Michael's birth.

With a total lack of justice, Lizzie told anyone who would listen that Frank had worried more about the Jerseys than he had about her, but now that they had weathered the latest storm Frank was too contented to rise to her teasing. Two more heifers to add to his growing tally of pedigree Jerseys; a dozen half-breeds to replace the older Shorthorns and thus improve the cream content of the milk he sold to the factory; another son who in a few years would help him on the farm; and best of all: Lizzie hale and strong as ever, Lizzie supporting whatever he did, Lizzie giving him a reason to do it at all.

30

December 1892 – March 1893

That December Sophie produced her second son, a little dark-haired child they named Andrew, in the way she did most things: placidly and uncomplaining. The family took Andrew's arrival in much the same way as Sophie did; a second son and fifth grandson was an occasion for no more than mild celebration, and the most obvious effect was that the youngest John graduated from being known as 'Baby' to the more appropriate 'Boy' now that there was a real baby.

Later in the month, two days after Bill and Lily's first anniversary, came a birth that caused far more excitement. In fact, Arthur's reaction to the birth of Lily's son came dangerously close to straining Lizzie's friendship with Lily beyond mending.

'Come and see my grandson,' Arthur greeted Frank and Lizzie when they arrived the day after the birth to pay their first visit to the baby. 'No, don't worry about the horses—Ernie, see to Frank's horses.' He drew the Kelly family towards the house in his wake. Mickey stirred for a moment in Lizzie's arms, then settled again as she walked.

'Edie?' Arthur called as they trooped in the back door. 'They're here to see him.'

Edie emerged from Bill's bedroom. 'For goodness sake, Arthur, don't make so much noise,' she scolded. To Frank's amazement, Arthur looked abashed.

'Sorry,' he mumbled. 'I didn't wake the little fellow, did I?'

'He's already awake,' Edie said, smiling. 'He's just had a feed and he's all sleepy and nice. Now,' she said, taking charge of the situation and clearly in her element with a baby in the house for her to fuss over, 'you children can just have a peep at him, then go outside and keep out of the way. The rest of you try not to make too much row. Lily's worn out, poor love.' She hurried up to Lizzie and said in a whisper loud enough for Frank to catch, 'In labour for two days and two nights, the poor dear. Bill's been beside himself.'

Lizzie clicked her tongue sympathetically as they walked into the room, which had not been designed to hold six adults and five children. Edie led the three older children over to inspect the baby, then firmly escorted them to the door and sent them down the passage, leaving the adults free to move around more comfortably.

Lily lay against a pile of pillows, the linen pillow cases looking scarcely paler than her face, but a faint smile played on her lips as she gazed at the child in her arms. Bill sat beside the bed staring at the baby with a look of bemused delight, one hand resting proprietorially on Lily's shoulder. He glanced for a moment at Frank and Lizzie, then his eyes returned to the baby. Frank watched the three of them and recalled the way he had felt when he had first seen Maudie, a tiny bundle snuggled up against Lizzie. He smiled as much at the remembered joy as at the sight before him.

'Did you ever see a better looking baby?' Arthur demanded. 'He's a fine boy, my grandson. How are you feeling now, my dear?' he asked Lily.

'Tired,' Lily said in a weak voice. 'But better than I was this morning, thank you… Father.' She added the last word hesitantly, but his beaming smile said clearly that Arthur had forgotten he had ever wondered whether Lily might not be a little too old, a little too well-educated, and a little too finely bred to become the bride of a farmer's son. The way Lily had thrown herself wholeheartedly into helping Edie run the house had overcome most of his doubts; now that she had produced this wondrous child, her place in his heart was sealed.

Lily moved a little in the bed as if to ease some discomfort, and her face contorted. She shot a helpless look at Edie, who clearly understood the signal at once.

'Out of here, you men,' Edie said briskly. She had to give Bill's shoulder a shake before he took any notice of her. 'Go on, Bill, you can come back later. You too, Arthur. Give the poor girl a rest for a bit.' She bustled the three of them out and shut the door in their faces.

'A fine boy, that grandson of mine,' said Arthur. 'Time we had a drink to celebrate.'

Frank soon found himself sitting in the parlour with Arthur and Bill, each of them holding a generously filled glass of whisky.

'To my grandson,' Arthur intoned.

'To my son,' Bill added, looking at the wall in the direction of his bedroom.

'To… hey, what's his name?' Frank asked.

Arthur's smile grew even wider. 'Didn't I tell you?' he said smugly.

Two walls away Edie replaced the covers over Lily and patted them down gently. 'Nothing wrong that a good rest won't fix,' she said. 'It'll be sore down there for a bit, but you'll forget it all soon enough now you've the little fellow to think about.'

Lizzie had taken the seat vacated by Bill. She opened her bodice to offer a nipple to a now-wakeful Mickey. 'What are you going to call him,

Lily?' she asked.

Lily smiled at the baby, now dozing in his cradle. 'Well, I'd decided he was going to be William, and Bill had no objection to that,' she said, a touch of wry humour showing through her weariness. 'But then when it was all over and I'd woken up properly, and Bill had come in and seen us, your father came in—'

'I'd had a beggar of a job keeping him out till then,' Edie put in. 'I said you and Bill were to have a bit of time just the two of you and the little fellow, once you'd woken up. He only gave you five minutes.'

'Was it that long?' Lily said musingly. 'Well, he came in and looked at the baby as though he'd never seen one before. He gave me a kiss as if I was really his daughter, and...' Her smile took on a touch of sadness. 'I don't remember my father very well.' She gave her head a little shake and went on. 'Then after he'd asked how I was, he asked what we were going to call the baby. I opened my mouth to say "William", and found myself saying, "We'd like to call him Arthur, if you don't mind." ' She laughed, but the movement made her wince. 'He doesn't mind,' she said softly, her eyes drooping as she spoke. As soon as Mickey had finished feeding, Lizzie and Edie rose and quietly left the room to join the men in the parlour.

Lizzie was not normally given to fits of jealousy, but when she felt her husband or one of her children was being slighted she could be fierce in their defence. When she had heard her father refer to 'My grandson' one time too many, she tartly reminded him that he already had four other grandchildren.

'That's all very well, but they're Kellys,' Arthur responded. 'This boy's a Leith.'

'What a load of old rubbish,' Lizzie said. 'Babies are babies—what on earth does it matter what their name is?' But Arthur laughed at her, and only Frank saw that Lizzie was hiding hurt under her show of pique.

'Take no notice,' he urged when they were on their way home, with Arthur safely out of earshot. 'He's just being silly, just because it's a novelty for him to have a Leith grandson. Not to mention one named after him. He'll get over it soon enough and be moaning that the little fellow keeps him awake at night.'

'Serves Pa right if he does,' Lizzie muttered. 'I hope he bawls all night.'

But Lizzie's sense of fairness would not allow her to feel any resentment towards Lily for the place the young Arthur was clearly going to hold in his grandfather's heart. Her father might be being ridiculous, but Lily was her friend, and Lily was sore and weary from travail that no man could really understand. Lizzie teetered on the edge of blaming Lily for the way Arthur was ignoring his other grandchildren, then abruptly swung the other way.

'Pa fussing over that baby's probably getting on Lily's nerves,' she said. 'Poor Lily's worn out, too. Ma said she had an awful time of it.'

'Mmm. Bill said the same to me. It doesn't come natural to her like it does to you, eh?'

The appeal to Lizzie's pride in her own womanly gifts coaxed a smile from her. 'No,' she said. 'I'm lucky. Still, the first time's the worst, especially with Lily not being so young. It'll be easier next time.'

'Bill said something about not wanting her to have another one for a good long time, after this one being so hard on her.' Frank shifted the reins into one hand so that he could slip his free arm around Lizzie. 'Hope he's better at keeping to it than I was when you'd been ill, eh?' he murmured close to her ear.

'He couldn't be any worse,' Lizzie said. They shared pleasant memories in silence for a few moments.

'I don't remember you looking as bad as she does, Lizzie. You always look as pretty as ever, even when it's only just over.'

'Flatterer,' Lizzie scoffed, but she smiled as she said it. 'She does look awful, doesn't she? Ma told me she'll be fine, and Ma knows all there is to know about it, so there's no need to worry, but I bet she'll be a while getting over it. She looks nearly as bad as Amy did.'

'Worse,' Frank said idly.

'Oh, no,' Lizzie insisted. 'Amy looked shocking that first time. You wouldn't know, you didn't see her.'

'Yes I did,' Frank said. 'I took you in to see her after she had Mal.'

He felt Lizzie stiffen against him. 'So you did,' she said in an odd voice. 'I'd forgotten about that. Sorry.'

An apology from Lizzie was startling. 'What's up, Lizzie?'

'Nothing. Nothing at all. I might make a sultana pudding tonight.' She faced his scrutiny with a disarmingly open expression.

The idea of Lizzie's hiding something from him was too ridiculous for Frank to waste any time on. Her strange behaviour, he decided, should be put down to lingering jealousy over the new baby. He patted her arm, then returned his full attention to the track in front of him.

Ruatane had held its first ever Agricultural and Pastoral Show the previous year, though the name seemed too grandiose for the small gathering that had taken place. But when it was announced that a second one would be held that March, the show took on the status of an institution. There were few enough opportunities for the farmers of the area and their families to waste most of a day on fun and call it work, and nearly all of those close enough to town managed to attend.

The competitions were for the most part light-hearted; the farmers who had bothered to bring some of their animals along paraded them around in a roped-off area of the paddock in front of other farmers, while their wives compared baking and gardening skills under a hastily-erected marquee. Children darted about from one part of the paddock to another, admiring cows and horses then trying to beg biscuits from their mothers. But the organisers had made a fair attempt at setting up ordered judging, with animals divided into various categories according to age and breed.

Most of the animal entries were from farmers who lived within a mile or two of the town, but Frank was keen to show off his best despite the inconvenience of getting the chosen animals to the show. It meant spending a fair part of the morning driving Duke William and Orange Blossom into town, leaving Lizzie to come in later managing the buggy and the children on her own, but when he had groomed and fussed over the animals in their small pens until their coats were glowing in the sunlight Frank knew it was worth it. He stepped back and studied the two creatures with satisfaction; he was sure they were the best in the show, even if the rest of the town might be too foolish to see it.

As he hung over Duke William's pen, waiting for the judging to begin, Frank became aware that he was being scrutinised. He turned to see a man whom he did not recognise, which was something of a novelty in so small a town.

'That's a fine animal you have there,' the stranger remarked.

'Yes, he is,' Frank agreed readily. The man was obviously someone of discernment, to have seen Duke William's superiority. 'That's one of my cows over there, too.'

The man admired Orange Blossom to Frank's satisfaction, then introduced himself as Ted Jackson, a farmer from near Thames (though he mentioned in passing that he also owned two farms at Tauranga) who treated himself to attendance at some of the more distant A and P shows from time to time.

As they chatted, it soon became clear to Frank that although he and this Ted Jackson both called themselves farmers they meant something rather different by the term. The quality of Mr Jackson's clothes, made of the sort of cloth reserved for Frank's best suit, gave him the first clue. After Mr Jackson had talked casually of managers and staff, and the pressures of overseeing several farms, Frank guessed that this was a man who had staff quarters more elaborate than Frank's own house. He nodded and smiled at much of what the older man said, contributing little to the conversation.

But on the subject of his Jerseys he waxed eloquent. He could quote the pedigrees of the four he had purchased back for several generations.

'Good lines you've got there,' Mr Jackson said. 'You must be getting good stud fees.'

Frank mumbled a noncommittal reply, unwilling to admit that no other farmer in the area had as yet shown any interest in hiring his bull.

'Do you sell many of your calves?' Mr Jackson asked.

'Um, not... many,' Frank said, narrowly avoiding an outright lie. 'I'm still building up the herd.'

'Fair enough.' Mr Jackson fished around in his jacket pocket and produced a card with his name and address. 'I'm a bit fed up with the prices some of these fancy breeders try to screw out of me for pedigree cows. If you decide you can spare one or two this spring, drop me a line.'

Frank glanced at the card and stowed it in his pocket. 'I might just do that.' He shook hands with Mr Jackson before the latter moved off to admire some heavy horses. Then Frank heard the call for bulls to be led out and promptly forgot the stranger.

There was some good-natured grumbling over Frank's cheek when he was awarded a ribbon for the best Jersey bull in the show; as the only Jersey bull, Duke William had not had to face competition to win his prize. But after Orange Blossom had been awarded her own ribbon as the best Jersey cow of any age in the show, again having been paraded around the ring in solitary splendour as the sole example of her breed, she was involved in a more genuine contest.

A small group of cows were arranged in a ring, with their owners crouched beside them on stools to milk them. When the buckets were full they were passed over to the panel of men who had been appointed judges: the manager of the butter factory, an elderly farmer from the other side of Ruatane whom Frank barely knew, and a Dairy Advisor who had conveniently been visiting Tauranga and had had his return fare to Ruatane paid so that he could give the show a little extra status.

In terms of quantity there was not much in it. Orange Blossom was much smaller than any of the Shorthorns, and by rights a good Shorthorn should have had the edge over her in sheer volume produced. But when the contents of the buckets were carefully measured, Orange

Blossom's production was found to be second only to one huge Shorthorn.

That would have been enough to make Frank prouder than ever of the dainty Jersey, but there was better to come. With elaborate care, milk from each cow had been poured into graduated glass cylinders and left to stand in the shade of the judges' tent while other competitions went on in the ring. When the milk had stood long enough for a clearly discernible layer of cream to have formed, the percentage of cream was measured and the winner announced.

Frank knew well enough that his Jerseys produced creamier milk than any other cows in the area; the payments he was getting from the factory showed that more tangibly than any afternoon competition could do. But to have it loudly announced in front of everyone he knew made his chest swell with pride. He owned the cow that produced the best quality milk in the whole district.

Lizzie squeezed his hand so tightly at the announcement that he knew she was almost as excited as he was himself. She gave him a little push to start him on his way over to the tent to collect his prize: a small silver cup and five shillings.

'Congratulations, Mr Kelly,' the Dairy Advisor said, fixing Frank with a friendly smile. 'Even for a Jersey that cow of yours is producing impressive milk. You must have a fine herd.'

'They're not bad,' Frank said, then he plucked up the courage to express his true thoughts. 'I haven't got many Jerseys yet, but the ones I've got are really good. I'm going to have a really special herd.'

'I'm sure you are,' the advisor said. 'Perhaps I should pay you a visit while I'm in the area, have a look at these fine cows of yours and talk over your plans?'

'That'd be good,' said Frank. 'Come out for lunch one day, my wife's a great cook.'

The advisor laughed. 'You're obviously a very fortunate man, Mr Kelly.' And Frank silently but wholeheartedly agreed.

Frank was not used to attention. Elation had carried him over to the tent, but when he stepped back clutching his prizes and looked around at what seemed a sea of faces all staring at him, his courage nearly failed. It was only when he picked Lizzie's face out of the anonymous mass that he found the strength to make his way back past his applauding audience, fixing his eyes on Lizzie like a beacon to safe harbour. He hugged each of the children in turn, then gave Lizzie the biggest hug of all despite the baby in her arms, heedless of the amused looks turned on them.

Amy clapped with the rest, though Charlie did not bother. 'Load of rubbish,' she heard him mutter. 'Making all that fuss over a funny-looking cow.' He had said nothing when she showed him the ribbons she had won for her baking and preserves, but she had not expected him to. She glanced down at her handful of ribbons and reflected on how little it took please her; being told that her strawberry jam was better than anyone else's would not have excited her in the days when she had dreamed of going to live in Auckland, of discovering what wonders the world outside her little valley held.

She shoved those thoughts back into the recesses of her mind where they belonged. Dreams were for people who had some hope of making them come true.

The cattle judging over, she held David by the hand to stop him racing ahead as they walked beside Charlie. An event was about to begin; an event the thought of which had filled Malcolm's waking hours for weeks.

Malcolm was already there, holding Brownie by the reins and looking eager for action. As soon as all those interested had found places to stand, the riders were told to mount and bring their horses up to the rope lying across the ground that marked the start and finish line.

The race was meant to be for boys aged twelve and under, but Amy was sure that one or two of the dozen or so who lined up were thirteen or even fourteen. It was ridiculous for a boy of seven to be riding against them, and Amy had been worrying about Malcolm ever since Charlie had said he could compete. But it would have been no use her speaking out against it; even if Charlie were to take any notice of her, which would be a near miracle, Malcolm would hate her for it. That would be harder to bear than watching any tumble he might take.

A pole had been stuck in the ground a few paces in front of the start line, and a hundred yards or so in front of that a second pole marked the other end of the course. The riders would have to gallop up to the far pole, turn around it, race back to the near pole, then repeat the performance twice more before sprinting for the finish line. It occurred to Amy to wonder whether Malcolm, with his total disdain for school and all it had to offer, would be able to manage the necessary counting, but as he listened to the man who was explaining the rules she saw him repeating them under his breath and glancing back and forth at the poles, picturing what he would have to do. He would manage, she decided. The race meant enough to him to make him try, something he never did at school.

A lowered handkerchief signalled the start. The riders dug in their heels and the horses broke into a run. Malcolm's pony was soon left several strides behind some of the longer-legged mounts, and Amy hoped he would not be too disappointed if he ended up trailing the field.

But there was more to this race than speed. Malcolm was the fifth rider around the far pole, but Amy could see that he made by far the tightest turn. By the time they approached the near pole he was barely behind the leading bunch of four, and again he made a turn so tight that the pony seemed to fold back upon himself. Amy began to cheer for her son, though she knew he was too occupied to hear her, and David joined in with his higher-pitched voice.

'Come on, Mal,' they shouted. 'Go, Mal!'

As the leading group, with Malcolm now firmly part of it, rounded the far pole one of the bigger boys swayed for a moment, clutched at his reins, then slid almost gracefully to the ground. He scrambled up to get his horse and himself out of the way of the other riders, and made his way off the track kicking disgruntledly at the dirt.

His example made the remaining riders more cautious, and they took the next two bends making a wider berth around the poles. All except Malcolm. He sat his little pony as if they were two parts of the same creature, sliding his legs instinctively so as to urge Brownie into the tightest of turns while giving the pony's spine all the freedom it needed to bend.

With the end in sight, the other boys kicked their mounts into faster gallops, then leaned into the turns so recklessly that two more fell off on the last pass of the far pole. Malcolm did not appear to lean at all, but Brownie passed the pole so closely that he all but brushed it, and when he had rounded it he and Malcolm were in the lead.

'Go, Mal! Go, Mal!'

Amy and David were not the only ones shouting now. She could hear voices all around her taking up the cry, including Charlie's deep one. Brownie would have been no match for the fastest of the horses in a long gallop, but the flashiest two were riderless after that last turn, and although the remaining riders tried desperately to swallow up Malcolm's lead he crossed the finishing line a full stride ahead, to a roar of admiration from everyone watching.

Malcolm sprang from Brownie's back and rushed to them, eyes shining. Amy flung her arms around him and gave him a hug, but Malcolm hardly seemed to notice. All his attention was on his father. 'I won, Pa!' he cried. 'Me and Brownie won! Didn't I do good? Didn't I?'

Amy followed Malcolm's gaze. *Tell him, Charlie. Tell him you're proud of him.*

Charlie looked away, and began fiddling with his pipe. 'Not bad. You took that second-to-last turn like a fool, you were bloody lucky not to come off.' He glanced at Malcolm, to see the boy's face crumple. 'Don't stand there gawking like an idiot, boy, go and see to that pony. Leaving the beast standing there in a sweat! I'll take him off you if you won't look after him properly.'

Malcolm stared at him a moment longer, all the happiness that had been in his face souring into the bitterest of disappointment. He shook Amy's arms off and ran back to his pony, ignoring the cries of congratulation that were shouted out to him as he passed. Amy saw him press his head against Brownie's sweaty flanks, but she knew it was not the pony's sweat that left damp trails on Malcolm's cheeks when he lifted his head to look back at his father. He turned away, and led the pony off to the privacy of a shady willow near the river bank.

Amy managed to force a smile for the people around her who commented on Malcolm's skill. When she trusted herself to look at Charlie again, she saw pride on his face as he agreed that his son was a remarkable rider, and began to enlarge on just how gifted Malcolm was with a verbosity that was unusual for Charlie and soon drove even the most sincere admirers away.

She sent David off to join a group of boys around his own age who were being organised into teams for a tug-of-war, then walked away to pretend fascination over a prizewinning Shorthorn cow as an excuse not to have to stand close to Charlie. For a moment she considered joining Malcolm, but she knew she could offer nothing to comfort him. Only his father could do that. She glanced at Malcolm hugging his pony's neck, then back at Charlie, his face full of the pride he would show to everyone except the one it mattered to.

You don't even know what you've done. You don't know you've hurt Mal. She did not realise how viciously she had kicked the ground in front of her until the cow gave a snort of surprise and backed away from the unpredictable woman standing so worryingly close.

Amy went into the boys' bedroom that evening to tuck them in, opening the door just in time to hear the whack of a body landing on the floor. A pair of soulful brown eyes stared up at her and a tail thumped in greeting.

'Davie, you're not meant to let Biff on the bed with you,' she said. 'He'll drop fleas.'

'Biff doesn't have fleas,' David assured her, with more sincerity than accuracy. Biff, named by David for the sound of his bark, thumped his tail even louder at the sound of his name. He was not the most beautiful of dogs, though he had a nature of irreproachable sweetness towards the children, and tonight he looked more ridiculous than usual, with the ribbon Amy had won for her bottled peaches tied around his neck. Despite his supposed status as Charlie's guard dog, Biff had swiftly become 'Dave's dog' to everyone in the family. Even Charlie occasionally referred to 'That bloody dog of Dave's' when they drove up to the house to be greeted by wild barking.

Malcolm lay silent, facing away from her. Amy found the trophy he had won flung into a corner of the bedroom. She picked it up and placed it on the boys' chest of drawers, then leaned across David to squeeze the older boy's arm.

'I was so proud of you today, Mal.' But it was not her he wanted to hear the words from. He pulled his arm away.

'Your pa was, too,' she tried. 'He told everyone how well you'd done.' A stony silence greeted her.

One last attempt. 'They'll all be too scared to ride against you next year, you were so good today.'

Malcolm rolled onto his back and stared at the ceiling. 'I'm not going in that stupid race again,' he said with more bitterness than any seven-year-old should have been capable of. 'I'm not ever going in any races again.'

Amy knew better than to argue. 'No one's going to make you, Mal. Good night.' She patted him on the arm, and kissed David. The little boy was looking at his older brother with a puzzled expression, but his eyes were already drooping.

Charlie looked up as she came into the parlour and took up her sewing. 'Asleep?' he asked.

'Davie nearly is. Mal's wide awake. He's still wound up from today.'

He grunted and pretended to be engrossed in his newspaper. 'He's a bloody good rider, that boy,' he remarked to the room at large.

'Why don't you tell him?' She had not meant to voice her thoughts aloud, but the words came out of their own accord.

'Don't want him getting above himself. It'd only fill his head with a lot of nonsense.'

Amy stabbed the needle into the thick moleskin of the trousers she was mending and pictured Malcolm as she had last seen him, staring fixedly at the ceiling and trying to look as though he did not care what anyone thought of him. *Better than what it's full of now. Better than that poor child lying awake wondering why nothing he does ever seems to please his father. He's going to stop trying one day, Charlie. He might have stopped trying already.*

31

With his two-year-old heifers now calving for the first time, that spring Frank had six new Jerseys to add to his herd. The four heifers were a welcome addition to his tally of future milking cows, but the two bull calves made Frank consider more closely just what he should do with the one-year-old bull he had kept from the previous year.

Frank's normal practice with the Shorthorn bull calves, as well as any unwanted Shorthorn heifers, was to keep them for a year then sell them as fat cattle, and he had vaguely assumed he would do the same with the yearling Jersey bull. But a few days before he was due to ship out these unwanted calves, he remembered his conversation with Ted Jackson at the A and P Show.

Had the older man really meant he might be interested in buying some of Frank's cows? Perhaps he had only said it to be polite. Mr Jackson would probably give him a brush-off if Frank tried contacting him. He had almost decided not to bother when he casually mentioned the idea to Lizzie.

That settled the matter. Lizzie was as doubtful as he was that Mr Jackson would genuinely be interested, but, as she pointed out, the worst the man could do was say no. Accordingly, Frank sent off a wire to Mr Jackson and decided to delay shipping the calves for a short time while he waited for a reply.

The reply came within days, but not in the form Frank had expected. When the *Waiotahi* made its next trip to Ruatane it carried a passenger: Mr Jackson in person. He arrived at Frank's farm on a hired horse later that same day, apologising for having invited himself but keen to look at the herd.

Frank was only too pleased to show off his precious Jerseys to someone who appreciated their qualities. He explained something of the background and nature of every single one, right down to the new calves, and he noticed Mr Jackson nodding approvingly as he studied the good condition all the animals were in.

'Well, that's a fine lot of animals you've got there,' Mr Jackson said when he had finished his tour, ending up by the fence where Frank had tethered the yearling bull for his closer inspection. 'Have you ever thought of taking a couple up to the Auckland Show?'

'Eh? I couldn't do that,' Frank said, startled at the outrageous idea.

'Why not? They're as good as any I've seen up there most years.'

'Auckland's, well... it's so *far*. I'd have to leave the farm and everything.'

'I'm sure that wife of yours could run the farm by herself perfectly well for a few days, as long as you could get someone to help with the milking,' Mr Jackson said. 'Mrs Kelly strikes me as a very capable woman. You should consider it—you'd find a readier market when you came to sell stock if you could boast of a prize from Auckland.' He glanced around the paddock at the cows grazing contentedly between the remaining stumps. 'Funny, they look almost out of place here, royalty like them with that old cow shed of yours in the background.'

'I'm thinking of doing up the cow shed, when I get a bit of money to spare,' Frank said, trying not to sound too defensive.

'Eh? Oh, yes, I'm sure you are.' Mr Jackson flashed him an apologetic grin. 'Sorry, I suppose that sounded rather rude. I just meant it's a bit surprising to find such fine animals on a bush farm like this. You've obviously got... well, *vision*, if that's not too grand a word.'

'Vision,' Frank repeated thoughtfully. 'Like I imagine things then make them happen? That sounds good—I'll have to tell Lizzie that one.'

'Mmm, I'd be interested in hearing Mrs Kelly's reaction to that,' Mr Jackson said, smiling. 'Now, about these animals you want to sell—'

'Um, it's just the one I want to sell,' Frank interrupted. 'I did say that in the wire, didn't I?'

'Yes, you did, but I was hoping I could talk you into more—especially now I've seen them all. One or two heifers would fit into my herds nicely.'

Frank shook his head. 'No. I'm sorry, I know you've come a long way and all that, but I can't sell you any heifers. I've only got six milking Jerseys, then the two yearlings and now these four heifer calves, I need the lot of them if I'm going to build up the herd as quick as I need to.'

Mr Jackson nodded. 'You're quite right, of course. It was worth a try.'

'You can have the bull calves as well as the yearling if you like,' Frank offered, without any particular hope of being taken up on it.

'No, there's only room for so many new bulls, and calves are too risky. I can see that yearling of yours is already well-grown and healthy-looking. He's not a proven stud, of course, so he's a bit of a gamble. He's got good blood lines, though, so I'm prepared to take the risk.'

'There's no risk,' Frank said stoutly. 'He's raring to go, that fellow. Come spring, you won't be able to keep him away from your girls.'

Mr Jackson smiled. 'I hope you're right. Well, let's get down to a price, then. What sort of amount were you thinking of?'

This presented Frank with something of a problem. Sold as part of a mob of fat cattle, the yearling would have been worth no more than a pound or so, but sold as a pedigree Jersey he must be worth a good deal more. But how much? 'Ah… what do you think's a fair price?' he asked, knowing this was not the best way to set about bargaining but unsure what else to try.

'Well, he's only a yearling.'

'A good, healthy one,' said Frank.

'That's true, but he's not a proven stud,' Mr Jackson reminded him.

Ten pounds, Frank decided. It seemed an outrageous price to suggest for a calf he had bred himself, but it would do no harm to ask. Maybe Mr Jackson would offer five.

Mr Jackson walked around the bull, studying him from all angles. 'He's filling out nicely. Going to take after his father, eh?'

'Sure to,' Frank said.

'Hard to tell at that age, of course.' Mr Jackson leaned on the fence and took a pipe out of his pocket, then spent an inordinate amount of time filling and lighting it. At last a puff of smoke emerged. Mr Jackson pulled the pipe from his mouth and pointed it at the bull.

'Twenty pounds.'

'What?' Frank tried to bite back the stunned outburst, but it was too late. He realised his mouth was hanging open, and snapped it shut before going on. 'You're offering me twenty pounds for that bull?'

'All right, twenty-five,' Mr Jackson said. 'Now, I know it doesn't sound much for a pedigree Jersey, but he's only a yearling, and I'd pay all the shipping costs, too. I'll take him back with me when the *Waiotahi* leaves if we can come to an agreement.'

Twenty-five pounds? Frank tried to appear calm as his mind raced. Take the money, part of him screamed, but a small core thought rapidly. Just because he had bred this bull himself didn't mean there was anything inferior about it. He had paid seventy pounds for Duke William. Duke William had, of course, been a lusty three-year-old and a proven stud, but this bull was William's son and might well be just as good. Yes, Mr Jackson was taking a gamble on the yearling, but not a foolish one. If he had offered such a staggering amount so quickly, perhaps he could be persuaded…

'He's got really good blood lines, that bull,' Frank said, forcing a note of reluctance into his voice. 'On both sides, too. He's Orange Blossom's calf, and she—'

'All right, all right,' Mr Jackson cut in. 'Thirty pounds. And that's my final offer.' Frank could see in his face that he meant it. Mr Jackson offered his hand. 'Shake on it?'

Frank grabbed the hand and shook it heartily, beaming all over his face. Wait till Lizzie heard about this!

Mr Jackson accepted Lizzie's invitation to stay for dinner, but turned down her offer of a bed for the night, explaining that he had a room reserved at the Masonic Hotel. Lizzie declared that the two men could not possibly discuss business with four lively children around, so she put the little ones to bed early. Left in peace, Frank and Mr Jackson made their final arrangements for the bull to be brought into town the next day, when Mr Jackson would pay over the money for it. They shook hands again when Frank saw the older man to his horse.

'You know, you should think seriously about taking some of those animals of yours up to Auckland,' Mr Jackson said just before he left. 'It's not going to be all that long before you start having heifers to sell, you want to make a name for yourself before then. You think about it.' Frank assured him that he would think about it, then promptly put the idea out of his head.

Lizzie was waiting to hear all the details when Frank went back to the house. 'So you sold that bull, then?' she said, looking up from the basin where she was washing the dishes. 'What did you get for him?'

'Oh, not a bad price,' Frank said nonchalantly. 'A bit more than I expected.'

'That's good. How much? More than you would have got selling him for meat?'

'Mmm.' Frank looked at her very seriously. 'You know when we did all those sums about borrowing money to buy the Jerseys?'

Lizzie groaned. 'I'll never forget! I thought my head would never stop spinning from that lot. Why? Oh, Frank, you don't want to do any more, do you?'

'No, not just now. I just thought I'd better tell you that we did them all wrong.'

'What?' Lizzie said in dismay. 'We can't have!'

'Yes we did, we left something out. We never put in anything to do with selling bulls. It doesn't matter, don't worry about it. That was a nice pudding you made tonight.'

Lizzie studied him narrowly. 'Are you teasing me?'

'Maybe,' Frank confessed. He laughed aloud, crossed to Lizzie in two strides, and put his arms around her waist to pick her up and swing her around, making Lizzie shriek. 'Thirty pounds, Lizzie! Thirty pounds he's paying me for that bull!'

'Put me down!' Lizzie squealed, waving her soapy hands ineffectually. 'You'll do yourself a mischief, Frank!'

'Not carrying a little thing like you, I won't,' Frank teased. He swung Lizzie around a few more times, then let her gently down to the floor.

She clung to him for support against her dizziness, and Frank took advantage of her helplessness to kiss her soundly. 'Thirty pounds,' she breathed when her mouth was free. 'What are you going to do with all that money? Buy more cows?'

Frank shook his head. He sat down at the table and drew Lizzie to the chair beside him. She wiped her wet hands on her apron and looked expectantly at him. 'For a minute I thought I might,' he said. 'But then I thought about it a bit more, and I've decided it's better for me to breed my own from now on. I've got really good cows, why should I pay a fortune to buy someone else's?' Lizzie nodded her agreement.

'It'll be no problem making the payment to the bank this year, that's one thing,' he said. 'But I was already pretty happy about that, the milk cheques have been good this last year.

'No, I think I'll put most of it into doing the place up a bit. That cow shed of mine's not fit for the Jerseys, it's time I built one with a decent concrete floor like that dairy advisor fellow told me about.'

'Do you know how to do concrete?'

Frank shrugged. Right now he felt as though he could do anything. 'I'll figure it out. I'll ask a few people, there must be someone around here who's done concrete.'

'Pa'll say you're mad. He'll say there's nothing wrong with a dirt floor in a cow shed.'

'Your pa said I was mad to buy the Jerseys.'

'I know. Pa's a real know-all, I'm glad you don't take any notice of him.'

Frank savoured the thought of telling Arthur what the bull had sold for. 'You know, I'd only ever thought about how much money I'd get from milking the Jerseys. I'd never really thought about being able to sell them. Maybe in a year or so when I've built the herd up a bit I'll be able to sell the odd heifer. Not for anything like thirty pounds, of course, but those girls'll be worth a bit. Especially if... no, that's a mad idea.'

'What?' Lizzie prompted.

'Oh, that Jackson fellow said I should take a couple of the Jerseys up to Auckland. They have a really big show up there, he says, much bigger than the Ruatane one. He said my cows are as good as any of the ones they show up there.'

'Of course they are,' Lizzie agreed at once.

'He reckons if they won a prize up there I'd be able to sell them easy as anything. I won't do it, of course.'

'Why not?' Lizzie asked. 'Why shouldn't you?'

'I couldn't do that! Heck, I've never even been to Tauranga! Go all that way without you—we couldn't take the kids, and Mickey's too young to leave.'

'Oh, I wouldn't go. Who'd look after this place while you're away?'

'Lizzie, you couldn't!' Frank protested. 'Not run the farm as well as look after the house and all the little ones.'

'I wouldn't try doing the farm work. What's the point of having all those brothers if they're never any use to me? Pa's got more sons than he knows what to do with, he can lend us one for a few days. No, two,' she corrected herself. 'One to do the work here, with me keeping an eye on him to see he does it properly. And another one to see you behave yourself in Auckland.'

'Your pa would never lend me your brothers. He'd think it was a mad idea, racing off to Auckland,' Frank said, forgetting that he had thought it a mad idea himself a few minutes before.

'Not when you tell him how much money you've got for that bull,' Lizzie answered smartly. 'That'll knock him back a bit.'

'Maybe,' Frank allowed. 'I don't know, I don't think I want to go, really. Anyway, it's not for months yet, forget about it for now. Hey, doing up the cow shed isn't going to take anything like thirty pounds. I thought I might slap a new coat of paint on the house, too, smarten it up a bit. I might even fix the verandah roof where it's saggy. Would you like that?'

'As long as I can keep those kids out of the paint. Yes, it'd be good, the place does look a bit scruffy on the outside.'

'Mmm. Hey, when did you last have a new dress?'

'I made this one just last month.'

'No, not a plain dress for every day like that, a really fancy one.'

'What do I want fancy dresses for? I've got one dress that's good enough for church, that's all I need. For anything special I've got my wedding dress. Frank, you're not getting silly ideas, are you?'

'I don't think it's a silly idea for you to have nice things. I haven't seen you in a really nice dress since... I don't know when.'

'So you think I'm like the house, eh? A bit scruffy on the outside?'

'Well... the outside doesn't match up to the inside, anyway. I think you need a new dress, Lizzie.'

'Rubbish. I told you, I've got my wedding dress for when I need anything flash.'

Frank digested this for a moment, then frowned. 'I haven't seen your wedding dress for a while. You don't seem to be wearing it.'

'I haven't been anywhere flash.'

'What about little Arfie's christening? You just wore the same dress you wear every Sunday.'

'Oh, stop going on about it,' Lizzie said. She seemed to be avoiding his eyes. 'If you want to spend some money, Maudie could do with a new pair of boots.'

'She can have some, then. But you're going to have a new dress, Lizzie Kelly.'

'No, I'm—'

'Yes, you *are*,' Frank interrupted. 'I've decided you are. I know why you're not wearing your wedding dress these days, too.' Lizzie shot him a look that spelled danger, but he ploughed on regardless. 'It doesn't fit any more, does it?'

Lizzie scowled at him. 'I can't help it, it's all these babies. Every time I have one I seem to slip on a bit more weight. I don't need you throwing off at me about it.'

'Hey, I don't mind.' Frank took hold of her hand and persuaded her on to his lap, then slipped his arms around her and squeezed. 'There, you see? I can still get my arms around you no trouble. I don't want you any skinnier than that—I like plenty to cuddle.'

'I can't fit my dress any more,' Lizzie muttered. 'Amy still fits her wedding dress.'

'Amy's too skinny. Anyway, she's got to fit it—her miserable old so-and-so of a husband probably wouldn't buy her a new one. *Your* husband says you're to have a new dress.'

'It's just a waste of money. Oh, I suppose I could make a new one—I saw some cheap cotton the other day in town, it looked quite nice.'

'No,' said Frank. 'Nothing cheap. A really flash dress, like your wedding dress.'

'Silk, you mean?'

'Is that flash? All right then, silk.'

Lizzie shook her head. 'No, I'm not wasting money on a silk dress. Cotton's good enough. I'll—'

'How about doing what you promised for a change, Lizzie?' Frank interrupted, speaking as sternly as he was capable of.

'What are you talking about?'

'I remember hearing you promise to... what was it? "To love, cherish, and to obey"? How about doing some obeying?'

Lizzie opened her mouth to argue, then snapped it shut. 'All right,' she said, though Frank found her sudden docility less than convincing. 'What colour, then?'

'I don't know, what colour do you want?'

'No, you have to say. I don't want a new dress at all, remember?'

'Well…' He looked at her eyes staring boldly back at him and admired their colour. 'Blue,' he announced.

'Right. What sort of material?'

'Silk. I already said that.'

'But what kind of silk?'

'Are there different kinds?' Frank asked with a slight sinking feeling.

'Oh, yes, lots of them. Silk satin, silk crepe, silk—'

'Heck, I don't know about that stuff. You pick a nice kind.'

'Frank, if you're going to get all bossy on me,' Lizzie said in a voice of irreproachable sweetness, 'you've got to do it properly. You'll have to tell me exactly what sort of material, and then what style you want. *I* don't trust myself to choose, I might do it wrong.'

Frank let his arms drop to his sides, leaving Lizzie perched awkwardly on his lap. 'You know, sometimes I wish I'd taken your pa's advice about teaching you how to behave. Here you go pretending to do as you're told, and you're just getting your own way as usual. How the heck am I meant to know what sort of material? All right then, forget about the dress and suit yourself. You always do.' For a moment he considered pushing her off his lap, but he could not quite bring himself to. Instead he pretended to ignore her; this took some doing, with her very tangible presence making itself felt on his knees.

Lizzie looked at him in apparent astonishment, while Frank kept up what he hoped was a dignified silence. The corners of her mouth turned up in a smile, and she nestled against him.

'Taffeta,' she announced.

'Eh? What are you on about now?'

'Silk taffeta. That's what I want. A blue silk taffeta dress, all stiff and nice. That'll hide the cuddly bits.'

Frank gave in and put his arms around her again. 'Lizzie, you're an annoying old chook sometimes, you know that? You've got to have your own way, don't you?'

'Well, now I've had a chance to think about it, maybe it's not such a waste as all that, not when you've got that money you didn't expect to. I didn't like you getting all bossy on me, that's all.'

'Silly of me to try, really. You're so good at it, there's no need for two bosses in the one family.'

'I am not,' said Lizzie. 'One of us has got to be sensible, I don't see how that makes me bossy.' She let herself be cuddled for a few minutes, then extricated herself from Frank's embrace and went to finish washing the dishes. 'Make sure you save a bit of money after you've done all this stuff with cow sheds and silk dresses,' she remarked over her shoulder. 'You'll need it.'

'What for?'

'For that trip to Auckland, of course!'

All that year, Amy followed with interest the increasingly intense discussions in the newspapers over the question of whether women should be allowed to vote. Her reading was of necessity often several days out of date, as she had to wait until Charlie had discarded his newspaper before she got a chance for more than a glance at it, but if a particular issue discussed the suffrage question she usually had advance warning in the disgusted mutterings she would hear as Charlie worked his way slowly through the paper.

'Those interfering bitches, trying to poke their noses in to stop a man having a drink when he pleases,' indicated that there was some news about the temperance movement.

'There's some useless men out there, don't know how to keep their wives in line.' That was equally likely to mean more temperance news or an item on women's suffrage.

'Those politician fellows are all half mad. They surely can't be that stupid.' That was a sure-fire clue to news about the voting question; and as the year wore on, though the exact phrasing varied, it was an opinion Charlie expressed more and more often.

It was early in September when Charlie looked at his newspaper and flung it down in disgust. 'Mad buggers in Wellington! They've bloody well done it!' Amy knew better than to make any comment, but after that introduction it was no surprise when she gathered up the discarded paper and found that the Legislative Council had at last passed a Bill for women's suffrage.

She studied the details, lost in admiration of the women who had worked so hard, and the men who had had the sense to support them, then tidied the paper away and got on with her work. But while her hands were busy all the rest of that afternoon, she set her mind to work on a more subtle task: how she would persuade Charlie to let her vote in the November election.

Even if he had not been so vocally opposed to the very idea of women's franchise, Charlie seemed to think she was little better than a simpleton, and therefore not worth wasting the privilege of a vote on. It would be of no use merely to ask him; she would have to make him want to let her vote. Amy bided her time as the election drew nearer, observing Charlie's mood carefully, and in the meantime she read everything she could get her hands on about the candidates for the Bay of Plenty electorate. She fully intended to cast her vote intelligently.

A few days before the deadline for voter enrolment, Charlie still seemed to be grumbling as much as ever.

'They'll be giving votes to the cows and horses next,' he complained one day. 'Might as well do, for all the use votes are to a pack of meddling women.' That was not a good opening, and Amy let it rest.

On his return from the factory next day, Charlie came into the kitchen and sat down at the table muttering under his breath. 'They're mad, the lot of them,' he announced.

'Who is, Charlie?' Amy asked as she poured his tea.

'Those men. The lot of them.' He took a gulp of tea, then put the cup down heavily. 'They're letting their women vote!'

He obviously expected her to look surprised, and Amy did her best. 'Are they really? What, all the other men?'

'Aye, pretty much the lot of them. That uncle of yours—you know what he came out with? "Edie's got more sense than some men I could name." ' Amy could imagine her uncle saying it, and the look he would have cast at Charlie as he made the remark; Arthur's sentiment had clearly been lost on Charlie.

He made a noise of disgust. 'Henpecked lot of fools. They'll regret it,' he said sententiously. 'Women should learn to keep their place. Give them an inch—no good will come of it.'

'Have another biscuit,' Amy said, pushing the plate towards him. He took two biscuits, then studied her narrowly.

'You needn't think you're voting.'

'Oh, no, I can tell you don't think it's right for women,' Amy said, careful to sound unconcerned. 'It's a shame, though. It's not fair on you, really.'

'Eh? What are you blethering about?'

'Well, it's not fair when you think about it. I mean, here you are sticking up for what you think's right, and you're worse off than all the others.'

'What's this crap? Talk sense, woman.'

'Those other men. They'll tell their wives who to vote for—Lizzie was saying just the other day she'd asked Frank how she should vote—so it's like the husbands will all get two votes.' She raised her eyes to look straight into his. 'But you'll only get one.'

Charlie leaned back in his chair and slowly digested this idea. 'Two votes each,' he muttered. 'The cunning buggers.'

Amy kept silence, careful not to interrupt the process of his thoughts. He was still muttering under his breath when he left the kitchen, but she smiled to herself when she was safely alone. He had taken the bait.

She had to wait until the eve of the enrolment deadline to be certain. Charlie rose to put out the lamp, making Amy hastily bundle up her sewing for the night, then remarked as he bent over it, 'I'm taking you into town tomorrow to sign up for the voting. I'll not be missing out on my rights—there'll be two votes from this farm.'

'Just as you say, Charlie,' Amy said, turning her head aside to hide her smile.

On election day Ruatane had a festive air when Charlie drew the gig to a halt and tied the horse to a hitching rail a block from the court house. It was no use trying to find a closer hitching place; the main street was full of people milling about, coming in and out of the court house or standing around talking to friends and neighbours.

At first glance Amy thought women far outnumbered men, but as they worked their way through the crowd she realised that the numbers were roughly equal. It was simply that the men, universally dressed in black or grey, were overshadowed by their womenfolk parading in dresses of every shade, their clothes in many cases decorated with ribbons in the suffragist colours of purple, gold and white.

And what an array of dresses there were! Amy had never seen so many women in the one place all obviously wearing their best clothes. She did not feel at all out of place in her wedding dress complete with her special hat.

'Now, do you think you can remember what I told you?' Charlie asked her yet again. 'You're to vote for Burton. Can you remember that?'

'Yes, I think I can manage,' Amy said, trying not to allow her irritation to show. He had catechised her on the subject all the way into town, making her repeat the name of his chosen candidate every few minutes.

'They'll give you a bit of paper, and you're to mark the one you want...' Charlie looked around disapprovingly at the women laughing and joking near him. 'You'll maybe get in a muddle, trying to find your way around the bit of paper.'

'I can read, Charlie,' Amy said in a tightly controlled voice. 'Perhaps they've made it easier this time, anyway, with all the women voting.'

Sarcasm was always lost on Charlie. 'Aye, they maybe have.'

'There's Frank and Lizzie! Oh, and Harry and Jane are over there.'

Lizzie spotted Amy at the same time, and ploughed through the crowd towards them, her new taffeta dress swishing as she walked. 'This is fun, eh?' Lizzie said, eyes sparkling. 'All these people! I've cast my vote,' she said, full of self-importance. 'You know, just like Mr Seddon said.' She looked around at the sea of faces. 'Nearly everyone's here. Jane said Aunt Susannah didn't want to come, she says it's not ladylike to vote, so Jane and Sophie left all the kids with her! I bet that put her nose out of joint. Lily's here somewhere, come and see—'

'You didn't come here to gossip, you came for the voting,' Charlie interrupted. 'Come on, woman, we've not got the whole day to waste.' He pushed ahead of Amy, clearing a path, and she followed in his wake with the children close at her heels.

Charlie waited for her at the top of the courthouse steps. 'That wife of Kelly's will have put the name out of your head with her prattling. They'll all have voted for William Kelly, I'll be bound.'

'Lizzie says she thinks he might be a cousin of Frank's father,' Amy said.

'Aye, I've heard that rubbish. He's a Liberal, I know that. I'm not voting for a Liberal—that's Seddon's lot.'

A few steps more and they were inside the courthouse, where a man stood ready to issue them with papers and direct them to booths. 'Now, you're to vote for Burton. Can you remember that?'

'Yes, Charlie. Mr Burton.'

Charlie reached into a pocket of his jacket. 'I maybe should write it down on a bit of paper for you.'

'There's no need for that. Mr Burton, Mr Burton, Mr Burton. That's right, isn't it?'

He rummaged around in the pocket without success. 'No, I'll have to come into the booth with you, see you don't get in a muddle.'

'No!' She could not keep the indignation out of her voice, but could see no way of stopping him.

'Come along, Mr Stewart, don't block the door, please,' said the clerk. 'Mrs Stewart, will you come this way?'

Amy made to follow him, with Charlie a step behind, when the clerk stopped abruptly. 'No, you wait here, please,' he told an astonished Charlie. 'Your wife must go into the booth by herself, then you can go in and cast your own vote.'

'I'm going to see she doesn't get in a muddle,' Charlie said indignantly.

'No, you're not, Mr Stewart,' the clerk said. 'You're not the first man to make a fuss about it today, either.' He went on before Charlie had a chance to interrupt. 'No, I'm sorry, it's the law. Either Mrs Stewart goes in that booth by herself or she doesn't vote.' He stood with arms folded and one foot tapping the floor lightly while he waited for Charlie to make his decision.

'All right, she can go in by herself,' Charlie allowed. He turned to Amy. 'Now, have you got the name sorted out?'

'Mr Burton,' Amy said one last time. She smiled at the clerk as she took the paper he held out, then strode into the booth, leaving Charlie with the two boys.

What had Mr Seddon said? She closed her eyes for a moment to recall the Prime Minister's words that she had read in one of Charlie's newspapers.

'A great power has been given to women with the granting of the vote. Let she who has a husband, whom she loves and respects, be guided by that husband.'

Loves and respects. But I don't. So that means I can please myself.

With a bold stroke she marked her choice: William Kelly.

32

November – December 1893

From soon after the time Malcolm started school, Amy had had to accept that he was not going to be much of a scholar. To Malcolm school was something that got in the way of what he wanted to do, and occasionally he decided it was worth arguing over whether or not he had to go at all. He generally had the sense to keep these arguments between himself and Amy; on the few occasions he was foolish enough to ask his father why he had to waste time going to school, he usually received a clip over the ear and was sent packing. Charlie kept the boys home from school whenever he decided he needed them on the farm, but teachers at country schools were used to such absences.

With Malcolm's attitude to women already set in a mould of disdain, Amy had hoped that the teacher who replaced Lily might be a man. But when term had started the previous year, yet another woman had been appointed.

The new teacher, Miss Metcalf, was well over forty, grim-faced, and built on sturdy lines. As soon as they heard that another woman teacher had arrived, Frank had teased Lizzie that she would have the Education Board on her back if she married off another of their teachers, forcing them to find a replacement again, but one look at Miss Metcalf convinced them both of the folly of such an idea.

'You'd never talk Alf into taking her,' Frank remarked.

'The very idea! She must be nearly as old as Ma.'

'And with a face that would sour milk.'

'Mmm. No wonder she's never found a husband. Honestly, some women have no idea.'

With Lizzie's help withheld, it seemed that Miss Metcalf was doomed to spinsterhood, and that the pupils of the Waituhi School were doomed to having her as their teacher. She was as stern as her appearance suggested, and her pupils learned belatedly how lucky they had been in Lily. Miss Metcalf had a strong right arm, and she exercised it several times a day wielding a strap on any children who stepped out of line.

With such a daunting personage, David's first day at school had been far more alarming than Malcolm's. Amy had taken him down that morning while Malcolm rode on ahead; parting with her little boy for the day had given her a pang. David arrived home that afternoon, clinging around Malcolm's waist on Brownie. Dried tears made two trails down his grubby face, and his right hand bore a red welt.

'Davie! What happened, darling? Did you get in trouble?' Amy had asked.

Malcolm had volunteered the explanation. 'He bawled, and that grumpy old Miss Metcalf gave him the strap. She was wild!'

'I wanted to stay with you, Mama,' David had said, his eyes wide with the memory of his frightening day. 'The teacher growled me. Everyone was singing a song, but I didn't know how to sing it, and I wanted to see you, and I cried. She said I was being a baby, and she hit me with the strap. She's horrible.'

'School's stupid,' Malcolm had chimed in.

'But lunch-time was good,' David had said, brightening visibly. 'I went and played in the bush with all the other boys. It was fun.' It was also, Amy was sure, how he had got his face and clothes so dirty. 'Then I wanted to come home, and I cried again. The teacher hit me again. See my hand?'

Amy had kissed the grubby little paw and comforted David with milk and biscuits, and had tried to explain to him that school had more to offer than day-long torture sessions interrupted by running around in the bush for an hour.

But David was by nature eager to please. He had now been at school a little over a year, and lunch-times were still the high point of his day, but he generally got the strap only when Miss Metcalf decided to punish the entire classroom of children for some unruliness. As far as schoolwork went, David seemed to be keeping up with the other children of around his age.

It was Malcolm who worried her. Whenever Amy tried to quiz him on how he was getting on at school he brushed her aside. But she could see no sign that he was making any progress at all, and from the occasional muttered complaint he let slip she knew he was regularly being punished for getting his work wrong.

Malcolm never referred to any lessons at school. The only things he spoke of were the lunch-time escapades in the bush and, just occasionally, some mischief that the bigger boys had got up to. The older boys figured frequently in his after-school conversation, with the name of Des Feenan, the main actor of the ink-throwing incident, often coming up, always in tones of admiration.

As far as Amy was concerned, Feenans meant trouble. She could never hear the name without remembering the fight at the hay dance and what had happened after it. Her whole life had been shaped into its present mould by that night.

But she knew that forbidding Malcolm to spend time with Des at school would only give the older boy more glamour in his eyes. Malcolm did not usually take any notice of her forbiddings, other than as something to rebel against.

Charlie seemed never to have wondered what progress Malcolm might be making at school; he apparently took for granted that his son was learning whatever he needed to. The reality had to be forced upon him.

The day of reckoning came at the end of the school year, when the district inspector had made his annual visit to examine children for entry to the next Standard. Now that Malcolm was in Standard One, for the first time he had to face an examination by the inspector, and all Amy's fears on his behalf proved to be justified.

Charlie was thunderstruck when he received a note saying that Malcolm would not be advancing to Standard Two in 1894 because he had failed the examination.

'There's been a mistake,' was his first response. 'That teacher's got the boy muddled with some other lad.'

But there had been no mistake, and a visit from Miss Metcalf confirmed it. When she arrived at Charlie's house she resisted Amy's attempts to draw her into conversation, insisting that she wished to speak to Malcolm's father.

Amy ushered the teacher into the parlour, put the kettle on for tea, then sought out Charlie. Malcolm and David did not need her whispered warning to make themselves scarce once they heard who the visitor was.

Charlie walked into the parlour just after Amy had carried through tea and biscuits on a tray. He sat down opposite Miss Metcalf and gave her a stony-faced stare.

'You say there's something wrong with my boy,' was how he introduced the subject. 'You're trying to make out he's simple.'

'I've said nothing of the sort, Mr Stewart,' Miss Metcalf answered.

'Why isn't he to move up a class, then? Why are you holding him back?'

Miss Metcalf matched his stare with one just as grim. 'Because he failed his examination. He failed it very badly indeed.'

'What's in this fancy examination, then? Some load of foolishness, I'll be bound.'

'Charlie, please—' Amy began, but Charlie cut in on her.

'You can keep your mouth shut or get out of here. I'm talking to this woman, trying to find out what nonsense she's holding the boy back over.' Amy cringed at his rudeness, but Miss Metcalf looked no more sour than before.

'I'll tell you what's in it, Mr Stewart, then you can judge for yourself how foolish the examination is. The child was asked to read a few words of one syllable—words like "house", "fence", "stream", and so on. Then he had to write down on his slate the small letters of the alphabet, and then he was given some numbers to add together. Call those things nonsense if you will, but that's what's required to pass Standard One, and Malcolm made a very poor showing.'

Charlie was speechless for a few moments. 'That's just reading and writing,' he said at last. 'The boy's been at school three years and he's not reading and writing?'

'That's correct. He's barely able to read, and his writing is even worse. I didn't put him forward for the examination last year because it was so obvious he wasn't up to it, but I'm obliged to present any child of eight or older for the examination or make excuses to the inspector. Malcolm is the only child his age who still can't pass Standard One. Maud Kelly, for instance, is almost a year younger than him, and she passed the examination with no trouble, though I'd hardly call her a brilliant scholar.'

'He's behind the rest?' That, Amy could see, was in Charlie's eyes worse than Malcolm's inability to read and write. 'Well, why is he, then? It's your job to teach him. You said yourself he's not simple—why can't you do your job?'

'I'm doing my best, Mr Stewart,' Miss Metcalf answered. 'I don't think there's anything much wrong with your son's mind. If the boy would only apply himself he'd get on well enough, even if he's not particularly gifted.'

'Apply himself? What's that supposed to mean?'

'Malcolm is a most troublesome child,' Miss Metcalf announced. Amy's heart sank. It was obvious what was in store for Malcolm. 'He talks in class, his work is messy when he does it at all, when he goes off into the bush at midday he sometimes chooses not to come back at the proper time, and he generally ignores what I tell him even though I punish him whenever he's disobedient. I'm constantly having to give him the strap for getting his answers wrong, but it seems to be doing no good. There's only so much I can do with a child like that. Your son is wilful.'

'Wilful, is he? We'll see about that,' said Charlie.

Miss Metcalf demolished a biscuit in two large bites, took a last gulp of her tea, and rose to leave. 'Well, I don't think there's any more to be said on the subject. I'll be on my way.' She turned as Amy led her to the front door and remarked, 'The younger boy's not too bad. David behaves reasonably well.' But Charlie hardly seemed to notice what she said. Muted praise of David was no compensation.

'Where's the boy?' he asked as soon as Amy had closed the door on Miss Metcalf.

'I don't know,' Amy answered truthfully. 'He went off somewhere with Dave.'

'I'll have to find him, then.'

'Leave it for now, Charlie, can't you?' Amy said. 'You'll have to go trudging around after him, he could be anywhere. If you wait for lunchtime he'll turn up of his own accord.' And with a little luck, she hoped, Charlie's anger would have cooled from its current pitch.

'This won't wait,' he said grimly.

It took Charlie some time to find Malcolm, and the effort of searching for the boy did nothing to improve his temper. Malcolm had learned to take punishments with increasing stoicism, but his yells told Amy this was a worse thrashing than usual. In between the sounds of the stick falling on flesh and Malcolm's cries of pain she heard Charlie's voice in snatches:

'Shamed me before the whole valley—Wilful, she says—Disgrace to your name—Even Kelly's girl did better than you—I'll knock some sense into you, boy.'

The only reference Amy made to the examination that day was to whisper to Malcolm that evening as she tucked the boys in, 'You're not a disgrace, Mal. You haven't shamed anyone. Your father didn't mean that.' No child of hers was going to believe itself a disgrace while she had breath in her body to tell it otherwise. But tonight was not the right moment to tackle Malcolm about his school work; that could wait.

She bided her time for a day or so, then chose a Saturday morning when she had the boys to herself while Charlie took the milk to the factory. When both boys were sitting at the table with milk and biscuits, Amy fetched a small bundle from her room and sat down beside Malcolm.

'Mal, I want to talk to you about that exam.'

'Leave me alone,' Malcolm said, clearly unwilling to be reminded of the unhappy subject.

'No, I won't leave you alone. I don't like seeing you get hidings any more than you like getting them. Miss Metcalf says you haven't learned anything this year, and if you go on like that you'll fail again next year. You know what that'll mean, don't you?'

Malcolm glared at her, but his defiant expression could not hide the fear behind it. 'I can't help it.' He shifted uncomfortably on his chair; his new crop of bruises must be troubling him. Amy remembered the pain of such bruises all too well.

'I think you can, Mal. You're not silly, you've just wasted a lot of time at school and now it's hard for you to catch up. You don't like Miss Metcalf much, do you?'

'She's crabby,' David volunteered, but Amy shushed him. Malcolm was her concern for the moment.

'The trouble is, it's not Miss Metcalf who gets the hidings if you keep failing. It's you.'

Malcolm shot her a hostile look. 'It's stupid, all that stuff at school. Dumb stories about old kings and stuff, and stupid poetry things about flowers.'

'Yes, I suppose that stuff can be boring. But if you never learn to read, you won't be able to find out all sorts of interesting things from books.'

'Books are stupid.'

'Not all of them. Some things are pretty good. I was reading this the other day.'

Amy pulled a page ripped out of the *Weekly News* from the bundle of papers on her lap. 'It's about some horses they were selling at a special sale up in Auckland. They sound like good horses, really fast ones. Shall I read it out to you?'

Malcolm looked at her suspiciously. 'It's not about horses. It's about old kings or something.'

'Not everything that's written down is boring, Mal. Listen to this.' She read a few lines aloud from the newspaper item describing the horses offered for sale. Out of the corner of her eye she saw Malcolm following her words with keen interest.

Amy stopped in mid-sentence and put the paper down. 'That's enough of that, I think.'

'Read the rest!' Malcolm protested. 'You were just up to a good bit.'

'If you got better at reading you could read those things for yourself, couldn't you?'

'I can't,' Malcolm muttered. 'It's too hard.'

'No, it's not, Mal. If you just try a bit you'll be able to read properly in no time.' She pulled her chair over so that Malcolm's shoulder brushed against her arm. 'Look at this. It's what I was reading just before. Do you know any of these words?'

Malcolm looked where she was pointing and shook his head. 'Not when the writing's all small like that.'

'No, it's hard with newspaper writing. Do you know your letters?'

'Some of them.'

'I know mine,' David put in. 'A, B, C—'

'I know them like that,' Malcolm said scornfully. 'Just saying them one after the other. That's not what Ma means.'

'That's right, Mal, I mean looking at the letters all muddled up and knowing which is which. Here, I've written them out, let's have a go at making the sounds.'

'That's boring,' Malcolm complained. 'That's what old Miss Metcalf tries to make me do all the time. "Ba-Ba-Ba" and all that. Anyway, then if you look at words and try and say the sounds it doesn't work properly.'

'Yes, it does!' David protested. 'C-A-T, that's cat.' He beamed at Amy.

'Well, it works for easy words like that, but not for real words.'

'That's true, it doesn't always work, but it gives you a clue. You sound it out, then you can usually figure out the word. And once you can read properly you just look at the word and you know what it is without sounding it.'

'But it's boring!' Malcolm insisted. 'Just making stupid noises from the letters.'

'All right, then, let's see if we can make it not so boring. I'll write a few words out big from the paper. Look at this.' Amy carefully copied out words that might appeal to Malcolm onto a scrap of blank paper ripped from the edge of the newspaper. She pointed to the first one. 'Sound this out for me.'

Malcolm turned his face away. 'I can't.'

'Try, Mal. Just try a bit.'

'It's stupid!'

'Do you want your pa to give you another hiding like that?' She hardened her heart against the frightened look her words elicited. 'Do you want one every week? Your pa's going to start taking a lot more notice of how you're getting on at school. Come on, be a good boy and look at this. See, it starts with H. What does H sound like? Ha-Ha-Ha. Then there's an O. Ho-Ho-Ho. Then R. Hor-Hor—'

'Horse?' Malcolm said hesitantly.

'That's right! Good boy. See, you're clever really, I knew you were. Now, Mal, I'll tell you a secret. Yesterday I made some of that special fudge you like—you know, the sort with nuts in it—and I've hidden the tin, so it's no use you looking around the kitchen. If you can get all three of these words right for me I'll give you three pieces—yes, you can have some too, Davie, don't look so worried.' Counting out the pieces of fudge would serve as the day's arithmetic lesson, she decided; it would be almost too trivial, but would guarantee success for Malcolm.

Thus motivated, Malcolm let himself be coached through reading 'mount' and 'saddle', and Amy praised him profusely for having managed the two-syllable word. Next she made up a quiz by listing all the colours of horse she could think of, and turned helping Malcolm guess the right answers into a game, with David trying to guess them first. It was already obvious that David was reading at least as well as Malcolm, and Amy was grateful that Malcolm knew so much more about horses than his younger brother did. It was important that Malcolm won such games.

As soon as she saw Malcolm's enthusiasm begin to flag, Amy folded up the pieces of paper and made the boys close their eyes while she fetched the tin of promised fudge from beneath her bed. 'How about you and me do some reading and things again soon, Mal? Not every day, just sometimes.'

'Will you make more fudge?' Malcolm asked.

Amy laughed. 'I might. You'll have to see.' She put her arm around him and hugged him before he had time to pull away. 'Now, you boys go outside out of my way, I've got to make some scones for your pa's morning tea.'

David rushed out the back door, eager to let Biff off the chain and take his dog for a run, but Malcolm stopped just inside the door. 'That wasn't as boring as it is at school, Ma,' he said. 'It sort of makes more sense when it's real things like horses.'

Amy smiled at him. 'That's good, Mal. I'll have to make sure it keeps on making sense.'

She breathed a sigh of relief, and realised how much she had been enjoying herself. She could not hope to do more than help Malcolm scramble through the first few Standards; he had missed too much work to have any chance of reaching one of the senior Standards before it was time for him to leave school. But at least she could save him a few beatings.

It was fear of his father's stick that had moved the boy to take notice of her, Amy knew, not any desire for learning, and that fear tended to fade along with the bruises. But rewarding him with treats when he did his work properly would help.

Rewards for work well done, and lessons that were made interesting for Malcolm; that was how she would go on. *How on earth am I going to bring horses into it when he gets into Standard Two or Three and he has to start learning history and geography?* she wondered briefly, then smiled to herself. *I'll manage.*

*

There were few enough incidents out of the ordinary in an area like Ruatane, and when something as dramatic as Frank Kelly's selling a yearling bull for thirty pounds occurred the population made the most of it. Within days of the sale it seemed that everyone within ten miles of the town knew about it, and with the news coming on top of Orange Blossom's success in the show earlier that year Frank found to his astonishment that he had become something of a celebrity.

He could not appear in public without several men asking how his cows were doing. After Frank had learned to overcome his initial response, which was to shuffle his feet, mumble a reply and wish he were elsewhere, he began to find the interest rather gratifying. There were no jokes about 'Frank Kelly's funny-looking cows' now.

The new status that Frank had gained in the community had an effect more concrete than improving his confidence when speaking to people beyond his immediate family. When the time came to put Duke William in with the cows for the bull's annual recreation, Frank found that there were a few farmers whose interest in the qualities of his Jerseys went beyond mere admiration: they wanted to hire Duke William to service their cows. Although the money exchanged was only a matter of a few shillings for each hiring, Frank swelled with pride.

'They all know Duke William's the best bull in Ruatane,' he told Lizzie one night as they lay in the darkness, Mickey's breathing a gentle soughing from his cradle under the window.

'He won't wear himself out, will he?' Lizzie asked. 'Doing all those other cows as well as yours?'

'Not that fellow,' Frank said stoutly. 'He could do twice that number and not notice the strain.'

'You and your bull! Anyone would think it was you they wanted to hire.'

'No thanks, you're trouble enough.' Frank patted Lizzie's belly, searching for the as yet imperceptible bulge. 'Well, you can't blame William for the state you're in this time. I started this one well before he got on the job.'

'Mmm. I'm not going to be able to wear my new dress much longer, eh? Never mind, it's got good, deep seams, I'll be able to wear it after the new baby comes even if I do put on a bit of weight.'

'All the more to cuddle.' Frank rolled onto his back and drew Lizzie towards him until she laid her head on his shoulder. 'It'll be just about time to start building that new cow shed when the baby arrives.'

'Well! It's easy to tell what matters most to you, isn't it? That's a fine way to talk about your child.'

'Don't go getting huffy, you know what's most important to me.' He planted a kiss on her nose. 'You are, you old chook. But I've got to think about the cow shed and all that, or I'll never get things how I want them for you. They won't just happen by themselves.'

'You think about things too much,' Lizzie said, the beginnings of drowsiness in her voice. 'We're all right.'

'I know we are, but "all right" isn't good enough for you.' He shifted slightly, finding a more comfortable position. 'You know, I reckon it'd be better for us if we had one of those co-operatives.'

'What on earth is that?'

'I've told you about them—the dairy advisor mentioned it when he came out that time, and I've been reading about them in the *Farmer*. You know, butter factories the farmers own themselves instead of just a few businessmen making all the money.'

'That's right, you did go on about it for a while. It's hard to remember that stuff when I'm half asleep.' She was quiet for a few moments, then spoke again as if interested despite herself. 'But if the farmers own the factory themselves, doesn't it take a lot of money to buy it in the first place?'

'A heck of a lot.'

'So where does the money come from?'

'The banks loan it, then every month a bit of money from the butter goes to the bank to pay it back.'

'Well, that's no use, then. You must have borrowed about all the money Mr Callaghan had in the bank.'

Frank chuckled. 'I expect he's still got a few pounds to lend. The dairy fellow said it costs about two thousand pounds to set up a factory.'

He felt Lizzie jolt into wakefulness. 'What?' she said in a voice that was nearly a shriek.

'Shh!' They both lay in frozen silence, listening for any sign that Lizzie's exclamation had woken Mickey, but the little boy merely snorted in his sleep and sank back into peaceful breathing.

'You could fire a gun beside that child and he wouldn't wake up,' Lizzie said. 'Frank, you're not going to try and borrow two thousand pounds, are you?'

'Of course not! Mr Callaghan would laugh me out of the bank if I even suggested it. No, the idea is you get twenty or so farmers into it, then you each only have to borrow about a hundred pounds.'

'Oh, that doesn't sound nearly as bad. I thought you'd gone silly for a minute. So, when are you going to start up this factory?'

The magnitude of the task loomed before Frank. Unlike buying the

Jerseys, this was not something he could do alone, with only the bank manager to convince. 'I don't know, Lizzie, probably never. No one else around here is interested in that sort of thing.'

'Then you'll have to talk them into it,' Lizzie said, as though describing the simplest of tasks.

'How would I do that?'

'Tell them why it's a good idea, just like you've been telling me. It sounds like sense to me.'

'But you take notice of me, Lizzie—when it suits you, anyway. No one else does.'

'*Make* them. You must know more about that sort of thing than anyone else around here, with all that stuff you keep reading. The other farmers are mad if they don't listen to you.'

Frank's mouth found its way to Lizzie's lips and pressed against them. 'You make me feel ten feet tall—when you're not making me feel like I'm two years old and I've been a brat, anyway.'

'I don't do that!'

'Well, not very often. Maybe I will try talking to some of the other men about a co-operative, see what they think. The worst they can do is laugh.' Being laughed at, though still something he disliked, no longer held the terrors it once had for Frank.

'They won't laugh! Look at all those men who want to hire Duke William.'

'Three of them so far, Lizzie. That's not exactly the whole town. And there's a big difference between giving me a few shillings to hire my bull and letting me talk them into borrowing a hundred pounds. I wonder if...'

'What?' Lizzie prompted.

'Oh, just getting mad ideas again.'

'What mad ideas? Tell me.'

'I was sort of thinking... maybe if I did take a couple of the cows up to Auckland—you know, to that show I was talking about—and if they did all right there—'

'Then they'd take notice of you!' Lizzie finished for him. 'That's just what'll happen.'

'Maybe. If I go—I still haven't made up my mind, you know.'

'Oh, yes you have,' said Lizzie. 'You're going to that show. It's decided.' Having made her announcement, she rolled onto her side and promptly fell into the deep sleep of the utterly self-assured.

33

January – March 1894

Frank was not one to struggle against the inevitable, especially when it was something he wanted to do. Once Lizzie had stated so categorically that he was to go to Auckland for the show, the idea took on the status of a settled thing, and Frank began working towards making it happen.

There were letters to be written, entering his animals for the show and booking a room in a boarding house for himself. Then he had to book passage on the *Waiotahi* to Tauranga, and from there to Auckland on the *Wellington*; he could not leave it to chance that the boats would have room for one bull and three cows on the days when he would need to travel, especially on the slightly smaller *Waiotahi*. The cost of his adventure mounted steadily, but as the time drew nearer Frank grew more and more certain that it was the right thing to do.

The arrangements for the trip were not difficult. They were simply a matter of dealing with people who were ready and willing to provide what he needed in return for his money. Such people did not need to be convinced that the trip was a sensible idea.

Getting what he wanted from Arthur would be another matter altogether. He could not possibly leave the farm without someone trustworthy installed to do the heavy work while he was away. Using one of Lizzie's brothers was the obvious solution. And while he did not concede Lizzie's teasing claim that he needed someone to see that he behaved himself while he was away, he would welcome some help with the animals on the trip, as well as the company of someone familiar when among so many strangers. That meant getting Arthur's acquiescence, even if his enthusiasm was too much to hope for.

The memory of how terrified he had been when asking for Lizzie's hand made Frank smile. Arthur had given him the most precious thing he had had to offer; it was a small enough favour by comparison that Frank wanted now.

Early in February Frank's letter-writing tasks were complete, and he was ready to tackle Arthur. His opportunity came soon enough, when he took Lizzie and the children up to his father-in-law's for Sunday lunch, on what would be one of Lizzie's last outings before pregnancy confined her to home.

After the usual huge family meal, the women shooed the older children outside to play and began carrying the dishes to the bench. Ernie made himself scarce before anyone could suggest he should play with the children, and the men went into the parlour to digest their meal in comfort.

As Frank discovered when he questioned Lizzie later, she had not quite trusted him to raise the subject, and had taken her own precautions. When she had seen her mother a few days earlier, Lizzie had let slip the news of Frank's proposed journey, knowing that Edie would report it to Arthur, albeit in a garbled state.

Sure enough, Frank had barely settled comfortably into an armchair before Arthur assailed him.

'What's this I hear about you going to Auckland?'

'Well, I was sort of thinking of going,' Frank admitted, taken aback.

'Edie says you're taking all those Jerseys of yours up there to show someone.'

'Not all of them!' Frank said, trying to hide a smile.

'Yes, well, Edie gets a bit muddled sometimes. I didn't think you'd be that stupid. What mad idea's got into your head now, Frank?'

Frank saw Bill and Alf exchange an amused glance, and Bill rolled his eyes at Frank in sympathy. This was not quite the way he had planned to launch into the subject, but it was too late to worry about that now.

'There's a big show on in Auckland next month. I want to take Duke William and three of the cows up to it.'

Arthur sighed, and shook his head. 'Frank, you don't want to do that,' he said, speaking slowly as if to a very young child. 'You've no idea what you'd be letting yourself in for. You'd have to take them up on the steamer, then organise grazing for them—in the city, mind you—as well as find a place to stay yourself. You'd never get all that sorted out, certainly not by next month.'

'Oh, I've done all that,' said Frank.

'What?' Arthur erupted. 'You haven't!'

'Yes, I thought I'd get that settled before I mentioned it to you—I didn't want to worry you about that stuff. I've booked all the passages, I've got a place for myself, and the animals will stay at the place where the show's going to be. It's all set.' He studied Arthur, and was gratified to see how disconcerted his father-in-law looked.

'You're a bit of a dark horse, aren't you?' said Arthur. 'How much is this jaunt going to cost you?'

'A fair amount,' Frank admitted. 'That's all right, though, I'm using a little bit of what I sold the bull for.' Arthur winced at this reference, and Frank pressed the point home. 'Thirty pounds I got for him.'

'Yes, I know that, Frank. You'd steal the crutches from a cripple, you would—taking thirty pounds for that bull! The man must have been a simpleton.' Frank hid a grin, aware of the reluctant admiration behind Arthur's invective. 'Never mind all that, it's still a mad notion.'

'I don't think it is,' said Frank.

'I know you don't, that's why I'm explaining it to you. This isn't like driving a couple of cows into the Ruatane show.'

'I know. That's why I need to go there.' Frank hurried on before Arthur had time to interrupt. 'No one's going to hear about my cows if I never go out of Ruatane. There'll be hundreds of farmers at that show, and they'll all get a look at my Jerseys. Next thing you know, I'll have a few more people wanting to buy the odd animal. Thirty pounds for that bull, Pa,' he reminded Arthur.

'Don't you go getting big-headed, Frank. The world isn't full of fools lining up to get fleeced by you.'

Frank laughed. 'It doesn't have to be! I don't need to sell many at that price, do I?' He saw that Arthur was on the verge of irritation, and assumed a more serious expression. Now came the hard part. 'I want to ask you a favour, Pa. Quite a big one.'

'Oh, you do, do you?' said Arthur.

'Mmm. I need someone to stay at my place and look after the farm while I'm away. Just to do the milking and see to the horses. Everything else can wait, I'll only be gone a week.'

'You've got a cheek, Frank! You march up here and tell me what you will and won't do, then you want me to let you have one of my sons so you can go off on this jaunt.'

'That's right,' said Frank. 'I'd like it to be someone I could trust to do a good job. Of course, if it doesn't suit you to do without them I thought I might ask Matt Aitken if he could lend me one of his boys.' He held his breath to see if this bluff would come off; he had no intention of asking such a favour of the Aitkens.

'You'll do no such thing!' Arthur said indignantly. 'Getting strangers to look after your animals when you've family here!'

'I'd much rather one of you helped me out. I just thought if it didn't suit—'

'Never mind whether it suits or not, that's what's going to happen. One of the boys can go down there.' Arthur glanced across the room at his older two sons. Before he had the chance to make any announcement on which one was to be chosen, Alf spoke up.

'I'm not going. I don't want Lizzie bossing me around—it was bad enough when she lived here.'

'You'll go if I tell you to, boy,' Arthur said, sounding affronted, but Bill cut in before an argument could develop.

'Send Ernie down, Pa,' he suggested. 'You were saying just the other day he's been getting a bit unruly lately, Lizzie'll sort him out for you.'

'Yes, she might just do that,' Arthur said thoughtfully. 'Especially with Frank not there to keep her in line.' He smiled at the notion. 'That'd teach him to know when he's well off. Right, Frank, you can have Ernie.'

'Thanks, Pa,' Frank said. 'That'll be a real weight off my mind.'

That was the essential task achieved; he might as well see if he could manage the other one. 'It's going to be a bit of a beggar taking those cows up to Auckland by myself.'

'Oh, not so sure of yourself after all, eh?' said Arthur.

'Well, I think I can manage. It's just not going to be all that easy.'

'At least you've got the sense to know that.' Arthur stroked his beard as he studied Frank. 'I don't like the idea of you going up there by yourself,' he said, looking troubled. 'Auckland's a big place. I don't want you getting in strife.' He mused for a few moments, then appeared to come to a decision.

'Maybe I should go up there with you,' he said.

'No!' Frank said in alarm. Fond though he was of Arthur, his father-in-law was not the companion he would have chosen for such a journey. Uncomfortable visions sprang into his mind: Arthur ordering him about on every stage of the trip, Arthur exhorting the judges on how they should select the winning animals, Arthur bailing up any hapless person who showed interest in Frank's cows and expounding on the virtues of Shorthorns as opposed to Jerseys.

'I couldn't put you out like that,' he said, forcing his voice back under control. Panic fed inspiration. 'And anyway, who'd look after the farms? Yours as well as mine. I mean, it's really good of you to lend me Ernie, but I was hoping you'd sort of keep an eye on things for me, see that nothing goes wrong. I wouldn't really be able to leave the farm if you weren't around.'

'Well, that's sensible enough,' said Arthur. Frank sank back into his chair in relief. 'It's no good thinking these boys could manage by themselves. Still, I don't want you going up there on your own, not with all those animals to cope with.' He gave an exaggerated sigh. 'I suppose I'll have to spare you one of the other boys as well as Ernie.'

'I'll go,' said Alf. 'I wouldn't mind seeing Auckland.'

'You!' Arthur scoffed. 'Frank'd be spending more time keeping an eye on you than he would on the cows. No, you'd better go, Bill. You've got more sense. There's nothing like a wife and child for steadying a man.'

'That'd be great, Bill, if you want to come,' said Frank.

'All right,' Bill said. 'I wouldn't mind seeing it, either.' He gave a sidelong grin at the scowling Alf.

'As long as Lily doesn't mind,' Frank added. 'It's a bit mean taking you off her, especially while Arfie's just a little fellow.'

'Bill doesn't have to ask leave of his wife,' said Arthur. 'I've said he's to go, that's all you lads need to worry about. Anyway, she's a sensible woman, is Lily. She's not one for making a fuss about nothing.'

'No, Lily won't mind,' said Bill. 'It's only for a few days.'

'I don't see why Bill gets to go and I've got to stay home,' Alf muttered.

'You could always stay with Lizzie if you're that set on a change,' Bill suggested, and was rewarded with a deeper scowl from Alf. 'Not so keen on that? Never mind, you'll be so busy doing mine and Ernie's share of the work, the time'll be gone before you know it.'

'That's not fair!' Alf protested. 'You get a holiday and I've got to do your work for you.'

'You doing someone else's work as well as your own?' Arthur said. 'I'll believe that when I see it. Well, I'll just have to manage with what's left me.' He looked at Frank through narrowed eyes. 'You've just talked me into letting you have two of my sons so you can go off on this mad fool trip of yours.'

'That's right,' Frank said. 'I really appreciate it.'

'I should hope you do! You're not as silly as you used to be, are you, Frank?'

'I suppose I'm not,' said Frank.

'I can't get over how well they did,' Frank said. 'Especially Spring Blossom—did I tell you she got best two-year-old, Amy? She's one of the first ones I bred, too, she's out of Orange Blossom, and—'

'Frank, Amy doesn't want to hear all about your cows,' Lizzie interrupted. 'And anyway, you told her about Spring Blossom half an hour ago.'

'Oh. Did I? Sorry, Amy.' Frank grinned sheepishly at her. 'I'm going on a bit, aren't I?'

'Yes, you are,' Lizzie agreed.

'No, I'm interested really,' said Amy. 'You must be so proud, Frank—I know Lizzie's proud of you, too.'

'Don't encourage him, you'll make him worse,' Lizzie said. But Amy saw her rest a hand on Frank's for a moment and give it a squeeze.

Frank had hardly been home a day, and was still full of his trip to Auckland. Lizzie maintained that he had kept her awake half the night talking about the show, but despite her claim of broken sleep she looked happier than Amy had seen her since the day Frank had sailed out of Ruatane. It was well worth the walk down to Frank's house for afternoon tea to see the two of them together; the sight of Lizzie without Frank had seemed almost unnatural.

'I got a third prize for Countess, and Duke William got fourth in his class,' Frank reminisced happily.

'Frank!' Lizzie scolded. 'That's enough about your cows, for goodness sake. Drink your tea before it gets cold.'

'How about hopping off my lap for a bit, love?' Frank told Beth, who had her head pressed against his chest as she hung on her father's every word. 'Go on, there's a good girl.' He unwound Beth's arms from around his neck. 'You can come back when I've had my tea.'

'Come and sit with me, Beth,' Amy invited. 'See what Maudie and I are doing.'

Beth trotted over to the couch and snuggled up to Amy, peering closely as Amy helped Maudie do fine hemming stitches around a handkerchief.

'You know, that was one of the funniest things about being away,' said Frank. 'I'd sit down and no one rushed to sit on my lap. There's always a couple of them ready to climb on here. It felt sort of funny, having no weight on me.'

'Beth fretted over Frank more than the others did, and the whole lot were pretty bad,' Lizzie remarked. 'I had to have all four of them in bed with me the first night, they were all in such a state with their Papa gone.'

'You cried too, Ma,' said Maudie.

'Oh, did you just?' Frank looked pleased at the idea. 'You didn't tell me about that.'

'No one asked you, Miss,' said Lizzie. 'I told you I'd only let you stay home from school to see your pa today if you promised to behave, not go butting in with your opinions when they're not wanted. You watch your step, or I'll tell your pa about a certain girl who had a hiding the other day for giving me cheek.'

Maudie tossed her head in a manner so like Lizzie's that Amy and Frank both had to hide smiles.

'Anyway,' Lizzie said, 'who could help having a bit of a weep with four kids bawling? We all settled down after a couple of days.'

'Ernie looked a bit down in the mouth when he met us at the wharf,' Frank remarked. 'He reckoned he thought you were going to belt him once or twice.'

'The little wretch! What did you say to that?'

'I told him off—said he'd better not have been giving you a hard time. He said it was you who'd been giving him the hard time.'

'Just because I made him work properly! He thought he could get away with sleeping in.'

'Ma poured a jug of water over him to make him wake up,' Maudie said, eyes sparkling.

'He didn't sleep in again. Then he tried being a bit slack about some of the work. I gave him a piece of my mind about that, don't you worry. I made sure he had plenty to do, that kept him out of mischief. He's cleaned all your tack, Frank, and polished your boots, too. And those horses have never looked so shiny—I made him groom them all every day.'

Frank laughed. 'No wonder he looked sorry for himself! Bill told him that's why Alf wouldn't come down here. Ernie was just a little fellow when we got married, he's forgotten how good you are at getting your own way.'

'I just wouldn't stand for his nonsense, that's all. I had enough to put up with, what with Pa coming round all the time poking into everything, looking in the sheds and nosing around the animals.'

'Gee, it's a big place, that Auckland,' Frank mused. 'When the boat was coming up to the wharf there, Bill and I sort of looked at one another, and I knew he was thinking the same as me—we'd just as soon have stayed on the boat and come home again. All those people! And they're all rushing around, no one taking any notice of anyone else. I never thought there could be so many buggies on the road, either—it's a wonder they don't bang into one another all the time.'

'It's not healthy, all those people living jammed up against each other,' Lizzie said. 'It doesn't seem right to me.'

'There's a lot to see there, though. There were some really fancy machines at the show, too—even machines for milking cows, if you please! We had a bit of a look in that Queen Street place, too. After me and Bill got the animals settled in we went for a ride on one of those tram things.'

'What's a tram, Pa?' Maudie asked, abandoning her sewing to Amy for the moment.

'Sort of a great big buggy, love, with dozens and dozens of people riding on it. Hey, Amy, did I tell you the boarding house we stayed in had that Edison electric light?'

'Did it?' Amy said, with a more genuine interest than she had managed to rouse for Frank's cows. 'I'd love to see that.'

'I can't imagine what that looks like,' Lizzie said, frowning. 'Frank's told me and told me about it, but I just can't. I'm not sure it's safe, either. It's not natural, that electric business.'

'I bet you'd like it,' said Amy. 'No more filling lamps, and having to clean them out and keep them trimmed all the time.'

'You'd like the running water, too, Lizzie,' Frank put in.

'Yes, I wouldn't mind that,' Lizzie said. 'Still, that's only sense, getting water an easy way. It's still water, that's natural enough. What's so funny?' she asked, noticing that Frank and Amy were both laughing at her.

'You are,' Frank said.

'You always know exactly what you think about everything,' Amy said. She bent more closely over the handkerchief with Maudie.

'Hey, I forgot to tell you, Lizzie!' Frank said suddenly. 'You'll be interested in this, Amy.'

Amy looked up from her stitching, needle poised in the air as she waited for Frank to tell her something else about his cows.

'It was when Bill and I had that trip into Queen Street. We went in a tearoom, and afterwards Bill ducked out the back and I walked down the street a bit while I was waiting for him. I was wandering along—half the people in creation there, mind you, the last thing I expected was to see a face I knew. And there he was—I just about walked into him—it was that Jimmy fellow, you know, Susannah's brother.'

Amy's body gave a jolt as if a shock wave had passed through it. Every muscle seemed to have gone rigid. She could no longer feel the warmth of the two little girls pressed against her. It was a moment before she could make out Frank's voice again through the roaring that filled her ears.

'Hey, watch out, Lizzie, that's my foot you're kicking. It took me a minute to recognise him, it's years since he was here—ten years, we worked out. He gave me a funny look at first, as if he—ow! Stop it, Lizzie.' His chair scraped as he moved it out of Lizzie's reach. 'As if he didn't want to talk to me. He was friendly enough once he got over that. Boy, you should have seen his wife. Talk about a fancy outfit—sleeves you could stick a leg of beef in, and the whole dress all covered with fancy stitching and lace and stuff. Jimmy said she's from—'

'Never mind all that, Frank, Amy doesn't want to hear,' Lizzie cut in.

'Of course she does!' Frank protested. 'Jimmy's sort of her family. He met his wife—Charlotte, her name is—in Australia, he said. Seems he was living there for a bit.'

'Frank, I want—'

'In a minute, Lizzie, just let me finish the news or I'll forget what I was going to say. Then his pa started ailing, so he came back to Auckland. Boy, that Charlotte! You could see just by looking at her she's always had money. I was talking with Jimmy about that hay dance—you know, when he knocked down Mike Feenan—and she was really looking down her nose. I saw her checking her glove after she shook hands with me, like she thought I might have got it dirty. Then she looked at me as though I hadn't had a wash for a few weeks, and she said,' he made an attempt at a mincing voice, ' "Oh, from a farm, are you? How very interesting." Then Jimmy—'

'Aunt Amy, look what you've done!' Maudie wailed. 'Ma, look what Aunt Amy's done! Let go!' Amy was vaguely aware of Maudie tugging at her arm, and in obedience to the pleading in the little girl's voice she looked down at her hands. The sight of the needle buried deep in her finger confused her; however had it got there?

Lizzie hurried over to the couch, took hold of Amy's right hand and tugged at it. 'Poor love,' she murmured.

Amy stared down at her hands and saw a drop of blood welling up on her finger. It was deep crimson, darker than she had known blood from a finger could be, and it grew in size as she watched.

She gave a great shudder, and realised that she had not breathed for some time. With the movement came feeling. Amy let out a strangled sound that might have been a shriek if it had had any real volume. But the cry was not from the pain in her hand; she had many times felt far worse pain than that and kept silent.

Her loss of control lasted only moments. By the time Lizzie had finished dabbing the blood away and tying a strip of cloth around the finger, Amy had assumed something close to her usual calm appearance.

'I'm sorry I gave you all a fright,' she said, trying unsuccessfully to smile. 'I felt a bit faint, that must be why my hand slipped.'

'It's the heat,' Lizzie said. 'It's bad in here this afternoon. Would you like to lie down for a bit? Frank, help her into our bedroom.'

Frank was standing over Amy, looking concerned. He bent to slip an arm behind her back. 'Shall I carry you?'

'No, Frank. Please don't worry about me, I'm all right now.' She accepted Frank's support to stand up. 'I'd better go home now.'

'Have a lie-down first,' Lizzie urged. 'You're white as a sheet.'

'No, I've got to go, or there'll be a fuss. It'll be time to get Charlie's afternoon tea ready, it was good of you to have yours early so I could come. He doesn't like being kept waiting, and I don't want trouble today—I do feel a bit odd.'

'You can't walk home in that state,' Lizzie said. 'Frank, you'd better take her home. You can pop her behind you on the horse, she hardly weighs more than a feather.'

'No,' said Amy. 'I'll walk.'

'Are you sure, Amy?' Frank said. 'I don't mind taking you, and you look pretty pale.'

'Thank you, Frank, but I can't. I'd never hear the end of it from Charlie if I went off by myself with you.'

'Ooh, that man,' Lizzie muttered. 'All right, then, Maudie can take you. Maudie, go and catch one of the horses, then you can double Aunt Amy home.'

'There's no need—' Amy began.

'Yes, there is. Don't argue, Amy.'

Amy submitted to Lizzie's orders, relieved that she did not have to attempt the walk home while her head was still spinning. She let herself be lifted onto the horse behind Maudie, and clung on to Maudie's waist when the little girl told her to.

The slow ride, with Maudie scrupulously keeping the horse to a walk, offered few distractions. Maudie prattled away, but she did not seem concerned whether or not Amy answered her, and Amy took the opportunity to put her jangled thoughts in order.

I haven't even thought of him in years. If her thoughts had turned even vaguely to Jimmy, she had imagined him in Australia, as remote as if he were dead. And now it seemed he was no further away than Auckland. *Auckland. Where Ann was born. Does he ever wonder what happened to his child? Does he ever wonder about me?* The memory of loss was a raw, open wound. Not the loss of Jimmy himself, but the things he had taken from her: innocence; the right to stay in her father's house and not feel herself a shameful burden; the possibility of a life that did not include marrying Charlie. And Ann. *My daughter. He gave me Ann, but I couldn't keep her because he ran away. He never wanted me. Not as a wife, anyway. I suppose he's got what he wants now—a fancy wife, the sort he can show to his elegant friends. Not a rough farm girl without proper manners. I was only good enough to make a baby with.*

Amy thrust aside the picture of the baby in her arms. The place for weeping was in the privacy of her own room, not on a bright afternoon out on the road where anyone might see her.

Maudie turned the horse off the road and on to the farm track. Charlie looked up from the paddock where he was digging potatoes, and shaded his eyes to see who was coming. When he saw that Amy's companion was only a child he turned back to his digging, no longer interested.

'Let me off here, Maudie, I'll walk the rest of the way.'

'No, Ma said I'm to take you right to the house,' Maudie said self-righteously, and Amy let her have her way.

When they got to the fence in front of the cottage, Maudie brought the horse to a halt for Amy to dismount. 'Shall I help you down, Aunt Amy?'

'No, thank you, I can manage.' Amy tightened her arms around Maudie's waist and leaned over her shoulder to plant a kiss on her smooth cheek. 'You're a good girl, Maudie. Your ma's very lucky to have a daughter like you.' She slid from the horse's back and waved to Maudie as she rode off.

Amy stood on the porch steps for a few moments, watching Maudie shrink into the distance. Charlie would come up for his afternoon tea now he had seen her returning; she had better make a batch of scones for him. And the boys would be home from school before long, wanting something to eat. She would have to try and give Malcolm a reading lesson; it had been several days since his last one. Perhaps she could slip a lesson in before it was time to start preparing dinner. The rain barrel was almost empty; there would not be enough in it for the vegetables and to wash the dishes afterwards, so that would mean a trip to the well to fill a pair of kerosene tins. The kitchen floor was due for cleaning, too; she would have to remember to save the soapy water for scrubbing it in the morning.

Work doesn't get done by standing around thinking about it. That's what Granny used to say. She turned from the sight of Maudie trotting briskly away and went into the kitchen, the heat of the sunny room washing over her like a wave. *I don't suppose women who wear dresses all covered in lace and embroidery ever do scrub floors.*

'What's wrong with Amy?' Frank asked as soon as Maudie had ridden away with Amy clinging on behind her.

Lizzie glanced at Beth watching them with interest. 'I'll tell you later,' she said, and Frank left it at that.

Maudie persuaded her mother to let her stay up later than usual that evening so that she could sit on her father's lap, and Frank knew better than to ask again about Amy with such an attentive audience. Lizzie finally sent Maudie to bed, and suggested an early night to Frank.

Lizzie undressed and put on her nightgown, then sat in front of the mirror brushing her hair. Frank watched her from the edge of the bed, wondering at her pensiveness. Perhaps she was anxious about Amy.

'Is Amy poorly?' he asked. 'She's not expecting, is she?'

'No, she's not,' Lizzie said, not turning away from the mirror, though the brush paused in its movement through her hair. 'I asked her about that again the other day, she just laughs me off and says I'm having enough babies for the whole valley.'

'So why did she take that funny turn? Has that old so-and-so been knocking her around again?'

'I don't think so. I don't know if she'd tell me if he did, mind you. But whenever I ask her if she's having any trouble like that she says he never hits her any more. I suppose I've got to believe her.'

'Good. That great lump of a man thumping a little scrap like her. I'll never forget how she was when you were sick.' He stood and walked the few steps to Lizzie, and rubbed her shoulders. 'I think she's almost as fond of you as I am.'

Lizzie took one of his hands in hers for a moment, then began brushing her hair more rapidly, pulling at it almost roughly. After a few strokes she slapped the brush down on the dressing table and turned to face him.

'Frank, I'm going to tell you a secret,' she said, so solemn that Frank had to laugh.

'Secret? I didn't think you had any secrets from me.' He let his hands slide down her arms towards her waist. 'I don't know where you keep them hidden.'

Lizzie twisted out of his grasp. 'No, listen properly, or I won't tell you. I haven't got any secrets—not from you, anyway. This one isn't mine to tell. It's Amy's.'

'Then you'd better not tell me,' Frank said, suddenly serious.

Lizzie sighed. 'I think I had better. I've been thinking about it all evening. I don't want you upsetting Amy like you did today. She's got enough to put up with.'

'Me?' Frank said, startled. 'I didn't mean to upset her. What did I do?'

'It wasn't your fault, you didn't know any better. That's why I'm going to tell you—so you'll know not to do it again.'

Frank waited for Lizzie to speak, but having announced her intention, she seemed reluctant.

'Put out the lamp and hop in bed,' she said at last. 'I don't want to talk loud.'

Frank did as she said, and Lizzie pressed close to him so that her mouth was beside his ear.

'You remember that summer Jimmy was here,' she began in a whisper.

'I should do,' Frank said, smiling into the darkness. 'That was the summer we started courting properly.'

'Yes, we did. That was half the trouble—I was so busy thinking about you that I didn't take as much notice as I should have of Amy.'

Lizzie fell silent again. 'Well, Jimmy was doing his own sort of courting,' she went on after a long pause. 'You must remember the way him and Amy were hanging around each other all summer.'

'I was too busy watching you,' Frank murmured in her ear. He cast his mind back ten years, remembering the tall young man with the infectious laugh, and the way Amy had been like his shadow while they were bringing in the hay on the Leith farms. 'I suppose they were. And at that dance—he thumped Mike Feenan because Mike was giving Amy trouble.'

'That's right.'

'But hang on, Lizzie—you're not saying Amy got upset just because they had a bit of a romance ten years ago and I reminded her of it? Heck, she's been married for years and she's got two kids—she's surely not still pining for Jimmy!'

'I hope not,' Lizzie said. 'He's not worth it.'

'So why did she get upset today?'

Lizzie sighed. 'It was more than a bit of a romance—as far as Amy was concerned, anyway. Amy... well, she sort of feels things stronger than other people. When she loves someone she puts her whole soul into it. She loved him, Frank. He didn't deserve it, but she loved him. And then he asked her to marry him.'

'Did he? I never knew that! Did she turn him down?'

'Of course she didn't! She was absolutely besotted with him—she would have crawled a mile on her hands and knees if he'd asked her to. She said yes, all right. She believed him.'

'So why didn't they get married? Did her pa break it up?'

'He never knew about it. Not till it was too late, anyway. Jimmy told Amy it'd have to be a secret engagement for a while, and she went along with it. She was so young, Frank! She believed everything he said. And then he ran off and left her.'

'Just ran off with no warning?'

'Yes.'

'That was pretty mean! Even if he'd changed his mind about marrying her, he could have let her down gently.'

'That man didn't care about anyone but himself. That's why he deserted her instead of facing up to his duty. He took what he wanted, and then...' Lizzie trailed off, and when she started speaking again her voice was so quiet that Frank could hardly hear her. 'Then he ran away. Because she told him she was going to have a baby.'

442

A jolt ran through Frank. 'What?'

'Don't you dare think badly of her,' Lizzie said fiercely. 'It wasn't her fault—it wasn't!'

'I shook his hand the other day,' Frank said, his voice unsteady. 'I shook the bastard's hand. I should have knocked him down into the gutter. To leave her like that, and her carrying his child!'

'He might have knocked you down first. He was a lot bigger than you.'

'Huh!' Frank said in disgust. 'He was all right when he was down here, but I don't think he's done a day's real work since. His hand was just about as soft as his wife's when I shook it. Hey, it's no wonder he looked worried when he spotted me—he must have thought I knew what he'd done.'

'Probably. We've managed to keep it pretty secret.'

'But... hang on,' Frank said, struggling to rearrange the assumptions he had made about Amy over the years into some sort of sense after Lizzie's revelations. 'You're not saying Mal's Jimmy's son, are you?'

'Of course not. Don't be stupid, Frank, you can count on your fingers as well as I can. Mal was born nine months after Amy married Charlie, and he's the image of his father, anyway.'

'What happened to the baby, then? Did she lose it?'

'Yes, she did. But not the way you mean it.' Lizzie's voice trembled a little. 'That was before I'd had babies myself, I didn't understand it properly then. I thought it was a good idea about her baby. I thought it was for the best.'

'Hey, don't get upset, Lizzie,' Frank soothed, stroking her arm.

'You remember how I kept telling you she was sick for months? That's when she was with child. And then they sent her up to Auckland, to get her out of sight. She had the baby, and they made her give it away. Give *her* away—it was a little girl.' Frank heard Lizzie gulp back a sob.

'That must have been hard on her, giving away her baby.'

'I think it just about broke her heart. She had no fight left in her after that—she hadn't had much even before the baby was born, not after Aunt Susannah had had a good go at her. Aunt Susannah arranged it all. She made Amy do it. She made her marry Charlie.'

'Why did she want her to do that?'

'To get her out of sight. Aunt Susannah told Amy she was so dirty and ruined that no one would ever want her—no one but Charlie, anyway. She got it into Amy's head that it'd make Uncle Jack happy if she married Charlie. So she did. And she's been paying for it ever since.'

They lay together in silence while Frank absorbed the enormity of what Lizzie had told him. Amy was always gentle and kind. And she loved Lizzie almost as much as Frank did himself; that in itself would be reason enough for him to be as fond of her as if she were a sister. 'And I made her think about all that again today,' Frank said. 'I wish I could say sorry. That'd only make it worse, though, wouldn't it?'

'Yes, it would. Pretend you still don't know, Frank.'

'I don't know how she's borne it, all these years. That ratbag deserting her like that. And having her baby taken off her—that must be hard on a woman. And she didn't even want to marry Charlie, then he goes knocking her around. She must be tougher than she looks.'

'She is. She's the strongest person I know.'

34

April – December 1894

With a combination of bribery and reminders of the wrath he would face from his father if he failed his Standard One examination again, Amy managed to cajole Malcolm into letting her give him occasional lessons all through that year. Though she racked her brain to make the lessons interesting, she could not raise any spark in him of her own love of books for the sake of the window they opened on the wider world. It did not surprise her; she had never been able to discern anything of herself in Malcolm.

But Amy could see that the sporadic lessons were doing some good. By hunting through her books and Charlie's newspapers for any references to horses, she had managed to teach Malcolm to recognise an increasing range of words. She taught him writing by having him copy out the names of all the farm horses on sheets of paper she saved from the wrappings of their weekly supplies. When he had written them out neatly enough she helped him nail the decorated sheets onto the boys' bedroom wall. And the simple arithmetic that was all he would need to pass his examination she taught by writing out several different prices of horses from newspaper advertisements and showing him how to compare the amounts.

It was the best she could hope to achieve with Malcolm, and Amy tried to be satisfied with it. David could not be left out of these lessons; in fact he entered into them with enthusiasm, and it was soon obvious that he would have no trouble at all passing his Standard One test that year. He had caught up with his brother despite the two years between them, and there was a strong chance that he would eventually pass Malcolm at school.

Not that Malcolm would mind if his younger brother did pass him; except that his father would make him mind, Amy reflected. Malcolm hated school; she almost had to push him out the door on school mornings, and he would usually come home scowling and full of complaints about whatever Miss Metcalf had tried to make him do.

Which made it all the more suspicious the day Malcolm came home half an hour after David and grinning smugly. When quizzed by Amy, David had said that he did not know where Malcolm was, but he would be home soon; pressed further, David had begun to look distressed, and Amy had left him in peace, guessing that he had been sworn to secrecy.

'Where on earth have you been all this time, Mal?' Amy demanded when Malcolm finally swaggered through the back door.

'At school,' he said, eyeing her boldly.

'You haven't been at school till after half-past-three, have you? Dave's been home for ages.'

'I didn't tell on you, Mal,' David said.

'Shut up,' Malcolm said, directing a scowl at his younger brother. 'Anyway, you can't stop me doing what I want,' he told Amy.

'It's not me you have to worry about. Mal, you mustn't go wandering off by yourself. You know how wild your pa would be if he found out—you're just lucky he hasn't come up for his afternoon tea yet. I know you like to go off riding—well, you just can't on school days. Come on, hurry up and put your working clothes on before your pa gets here.'

She took his arm to hurry him through the house, but Malcolm shook her hand off.

'I can get changed by myself,' he said. 'I don't need you hanging around me.'

'I want to see that you don't muck about. Hurry, Mal.' She gave him a push to send him on his way, and followed closely on his heels as he went through the kitchen and parlour, then out the front door to his bedroom, David trailing along in their wake. 'There's a funny smell on your clothes, too. You'll have to wear a clean shirt tomorrow, and you haven't got many left till wash day.'

Ignoring Malcolm's protests that he would rather do it by himself, Amy unbuttoned his shirt while he undid his trousers. She sniffed at the shirt and frowned. The smell was familiar, but not one she associated with Malcolm.

Realisation came abruptly. Amy grabbed at his arm and pulled him towards her. He was too taken aback to pull away before she had got a good whiff of his breath.

'Mal!' she said in horror, 'you smell of beer! You've been drinking, haven't you?'

'You leave me alone,' Malcolm said. He took a step away and glared at her.

Amy took hold of his shoulders and gripped them hard as he tried to wrench himself free. She had to resist the urge to slap him. 'Listen to me, Malcolm. You might think it's grown up and clever to drink beer, but it's not. Drink is a terrible, terrible thing. Men go... well, sort of mad when they drink a lot. They don't know what they're doing, and they do things they didn't mean to. And it's too late afterwards to wish they hadn't.'

'Pa drinks,' Malcolm said.

'Yes, and look how grumpy he gets when he has a lot to drink.'

'He's always grumpy.'

'He's a lot worse when he's drunk,' said Amy. 'I don't want you to be like that.'

'Des says that's the only time his Grandpa isn't grumpy, when he gets drunk. His Grandpa never belts them when he's got some whisky, and he sings songs about Ireland.'

'What about his pa, Mal?' David asked. 'Does he get grumpy like our pa?'

'Des hasn't got a pa.'

David looked confused. 'Why not? Everyone's got a pa.'

Malcolm shrugged. 'I don't know. Des says he never had one.'

'So you've been out with that Des Feenan, have you?' Amy pursed her lips. 'Did you sneak off from school with him?'

'Huh! I never went to school today. I just left Dave there and went off and met Des and his brother. They pinched some beer off Des's Uncle Mike and they let me have a bit of it. It was nice.'

'Mal wouldn't take me,' David said plaintively. 'He said I was too little.'

'At least you had that much sense, Mal. Don't you dare take Dave off with that boy. And you shouldn't be going yourself, either. For goodness sake, don't you want to get out of Standard One this year?'

'You said you could teach me enough so I'd pass.'

'I can't do miracles. You've got to do a bit of work yourself. You haven't let me help you for a couple of weeks, and if you won't even go to school you'll never pass.'

'I'll go sometimes,' Malcolm muttered. He looked away from her and said grudgingly, 'We can do some reading tomorrow if you want.'

'We'd better, if I'm ever going to get you through that exam. Mal, I wish you wouldn't hang around with those Feenans. And drinking beer with them! I didn't think you'd be so stupid.'

'They're fun. And I don't have to do what you say. You're just a silly—'

Amy put a hand over his mouth. 'Don't call me names, or I just might tell your pa what you've been up to. Just because he drinks doesn't mean he wants you to when you're not even nine yet. And I'm not that bad word, either. I'm your mother, and you shouldn't talk to me like that.' *At least I know who fathered my children, not like those Feenan girls.*

There was little time to waste on trying to convince Malcolm of the folly of what he had done. She put a clean shirt on him and began buttoning it up while Malcolm pulled on his old trousers.

447

'You must have spilt half that beer down your front, from the smell of you. Better than drinking it, I suppose, but the smell lasts longer. It's quite strong,' she fretted. 'Your pa might notice it.' She stopped her buttoning abruptly. 'I'll have to see he doesn't.'

She hurried from the room, and returned moments later with a small bottle of lavender water that Lizzie had given her for her birthday the previous year. She had the stopper out and had sprinkled the perfume liberally over Malcolm before he had time to take a step backwards.

'Pooh, that stinks!' he complained.

'So do you. I'm covering up one stink with a nicer one.' She flung some of the perfume over her bodice and put her arms around Malcolm, resisting his attempts to pull away. 'Hold still a minute and let me give you a cuddle.'

'Ugh,' Malcolm said, trying to twist out of her grip. 'I don't want to.'

'I don't care. I'll do my best to keep you out of trouble, Mal, but I'm not going to tell lies for you.'

Amy barely had the boys dressed in their work clothes and in the kitchen ready for their father when Charlie came through the back door.

'Stinks in here,' he said, sniffing the air with a look of distaste.

'It's my scent,' Amy explained airily, pouring his tea.

Charlie screwed up his face. 'You've no need to choke everyone else with that crap.' He sniffed again. 'Come here, boy,' he said, taking hold of Malcolm's arm and pulling him closer. 'You smell of it too!'

'That's my fault,' Amy said. 'I was giving Mal a cuddle before—I know I'm not really meant to cuddle him, but it was only a little one—and I got my scent all over him. It's a bit strong, isn't it?'

'You've no call to go making a fool of the boy like that,' Charlie grumbled. 'He'll likely be frightening the cows away with that stink.'

'I hope not,' Amy said, trying to sound properly concerned. 'Never mind, it'll wear off.'

She stood on the back doorstep and waved them off, relieved that Malcolm had the sense to be walking on the far side of David from his father. It was worth using half her bottle of perfume if it could protect Malcolm from his father's wrath, but she wished he would not keep straining her inventiveness. The thought of Malcolm's sampling beer at his age left her feeling nauseated; how many of his father's other habits was he going to inherit?

Maybe Mal will grow out of all this silliness, she tried to convince herself. But Amy had no skill at lying, least of all to herself.

Jack Leith's sixtieth birthday provided an excuse for the entire Leith family to gather together that December, for the first time since Bill and Lily's wedding three years before. The clan had expanded substantially in those three years. Arthur's namesake grandson was now two years old, just a few months younger than Harry and Jane's Robert and Frank and Lizzie's Mickey, and four weeks the junior of John and Sophie's Andrew. Robbie had a little brother now, though it would be some time before eight-month-old Donald was much of a playmate for him.

The prestige that went with having the newest baby of all belonged to Lizzie, with little Daniel barely six months old. The baby gurgled cheerfully as he was passed around the verandah from lap to lap, showing the placid temperament all Lizzie's children seemed to be blessed with, at least during babyhood.

Amy felt herself the odd one out as she watched the other women with their babies. She was the youngest of them all, but David was over seven years old and had long ago left babyhood behind. *He doesn't even call me Mama any more*, she thought wistfully.

Her thoughts were shaken out of their fruitless course when Lizzie plumped Danny onto her lap. Amy took full advantage of the opportunity to feel a warm, plump little body pressed against hers, and to smell the sweet, milky odour of the baby as she kissed him and stroked his hair.

When they had all talked long enough to catch up on any newsworthy events that had happened in the few days since most of them had last seen one another, Amy helped Susannah and the other women carry dish after dish of food outside. The men spread rugs under a small group of trees near the house, while the children raced about excitedly at the sight of their delayed lunch.

A picnic lunch was the most sensible way to cope with a family group that numbered sixteen adults plus their assorted children, but the informality of the occasion seemed to be troubling Susannah. Something was annoying her, anyway, Amy could see. Susannah's lips were pressed together in an even thinner line than their usual one, and she glared at anyone who spoke to her. Even the normally imperturbable Sophie looked somewhat cowed, as though she had received a tongue lashing from Susannah that morning.

'My goodness, you look down in the mouth today, Susannah,' Edie remarked. Amy tried to make herself inconspicuous as she squeezed past her aunt, who was taking up a good deal of the free space in the passage. 'Whatever's wrong with you? And on a happy day like this, too,' Edie chided mildly.

'Happy, is it?' Susannah said, a wounded note in her voice. Amy decided to lurk in the safety of the kitchen, where she could peek at the two women through the door jamb, until Susannah finished talking to Edie. It was better to be accused of listening at keyholes than to give her stepmother a fresh target for her complaints. 'Perhaps you wouldn't think it was quite so wonderful if you'd been up since daybreak making food for that horde out there. And after the night I've had. I hardly had a wink of sleep. Not that I expect anyone to be very concerned about me, of course. No one ever is.'

Edie put the platter of meat she was carrying down onto a small table and slipped her arm through Susannah's. 'Now, we've all done our best to help you out today,' she said, her kindly tone softening the rebuke. 'We've all brought things, and quite right, too. There's far too many of us for you to have to feed on your own. I can see you look worn out, though. So does Jack, come to that—I don't suppose he had much sleep either if you had a bad night. Now what's wrong, dear? You mustn't say no one takes any interest in whether you're upset. I'm asking you now, aren't I?'

'You wouldn't understand,' Susannah said distantly.

'Try me.'

'It would be a waste of time. You'd say I'm being stupid, just like Jack did. None of you care what I want.' She sounded close to tears, but it was difficult for Amy to judge how genuine her distress was.

'Are we really all so horrible to you, Susannah?' Edie asked gently.

'Yes,' Susannah snapped, followed almost immediately by a reluctant, 'No.' She sighed. 'You've always been kind to me, Edie. You're the only one who has.'

'Don't talk like that. You couldn't ask for a kinder husband than Jack, could you? Now, don't pull such faces, my girl. Tell me what the trouble is. Are you feeling a bit left out?' Edie probed. 'All these babies around and you with only those big boys of yours? But Jack thinks he's past putting up with babies, is that it? Are you thinking you'd like another little one?'

'Certainly not! Edie, you helped me through that frightful business of having the children, you know what a dreadful time I had of it. I don't think it's anything to laugh about,' she said haughtily.

'You're a funny girl,' Edie said through a chuckle. 'I've never known a woman have an easier time of it than you, and you go on as if—now, don't get so huffy, dear, I didn't mean to offend you. You know, it'd take your mind off things if you did have another baby, and you're young enough. You could talk Jack round if you put your mind to it.'

'I do not want another child! I've quite enough to worry about as it is, trying to bring up the two I have properly so that they won't turn out to be brutes like—' Susannah broke off, biting back the words that would have given even the easy-going Edie offence. 'Like they will if I'm not careful. Jack certainly doesn't seem to care what becomes of them. Leave me alone, please, Edie. You wouldn't understand. None of you would.' She pushed past Edie with her head held high. Amy slipped out the back door to take the long way around the house rather than face Susannah in her role of tragedy queen.

'I'm afraid it's all very informal,' Susannah said when she brought the last platter out from the house. 'You can all sit wherever you want. I do hope there's enough for everyone—children are inclined to help themselves to the best bits.'

She cast a disapproving look at Lizzie, who was herding her family towards the picnic area. 'You do seem to have a *lot* of children, Lizzie.'

Frank half expected Lizzie to snap at Susannah, but she said, 'Only five,' calmly enough, apparently more inclined to take the remark as a compliment than otherwise.

'Really? It seems like more when they run about all the time. It must be difficult to teach them proper table manners when there're so many of them.'

'Not difficult at all,' Lizzie said, bridling.

'Oh? You do surprise me.' Susannah glided off to take her own place at what would have been the foot of the table, had there been a table, ignoring the glare Lizzie sent after her.

'Now listen, you lot,' Lizzie told the four children old enough to take any notice when she had sat them down. 'You're to behave yourselves, right? If I see any of you taking something then putting it back, or any of those things you're not allowed to do at home, there'll be *trouble*. She turned to Frank. 'Isn't that right, Papa?'

'Yes, bad trouble,' Frank said, trying to look solemn. 'Mama will leave you here with Aunt Susannah, and she'll—' At the sight of Beth, who was more sensitive than her siblings, and Mickey, who was too young to know any better, both looking dangerously close to howling, he broke off. 'No, Mama won't do that—she'll only give you a hiding. I wouldn't look as pleased as all that about it, though, Mama can be pretty bad when she gets wild.'

'And if you're *very* naughty, Papa might get angry with you,' Lizzie said, bringing out her ultimate threat. As an angry Papa was something none of the children had ever seen, the notion held all the menace of the unknown, while a Mama bent on justice was only too familiar. 'So just watch yourselves.'

Jack sat at the opposite end of the rugs from Susannah. 'Come and sit beside me,' he invited Amy. She took a place at his side, but made no attempt to beckon Charlie over from the solitary spot he had found for himself under a tree a short distance from everyone else; he would happier by himself, and more easily ignored by her family. It would be no use trying to persuade Malcolm to sit with her, not when there were older boys for him to hover around, but David sat beside her and looked longingly at the food spread out before him.

'And I'll have the little fellows over here,' Jack added, patting the ground at his left hand and beckoning Thomas and George.

'No, they can sit down here with me,' Susannah said. 'Come along, boys.'

'But Pa said—' George began to argue.

'Your father has forgotten what a trial you two have been to me lately,' Susannah interrupted. 'I want you here where I can keep an eye on you and see that you behave decently.' Her voice sounded cool and composed, but her eyes glittered warningly.

'Let them sit where they want, Susannah,' said Jack.

'Oh, yes, and watch them disgrace me in front of everyone.' Susannah's voice rose in pitch as she spoke. 'Is it asking too much to be allowed to bring my own sons up to have proper manners?'

'Stop making a fuss over nothing,' Jack said, clearly only too aware of his large and interested audience.

'Of course, I know you don't think that sort of thing matters. That's why you won't let me see that they grow up like young gentlemen.' Susannah had abandoned her attempt to sound coolly aloof, and her voice was growing dangerously close to a wail. 'You think it's a waste of time, I know. It doesn't seem to matter what I think. You begrudge them the chance—'

'For God's sake, Susannah, don't bring all that up again,' Jack said wearily. 'All right, they can sit by you if it means that much to you. Just let me have my lunch in peace, will you?'

The two boys sat down on either side of their mother, George looking as though he would like to be rebellious while Thomas had an expression of stoical misery. There was an awkward silence for a few moments, then Jack said with forced heartiness, 'Right, I'll say grace before the flies carry the whole pile off. Then you can all get stuck in to this lot or we'll be eating leftovers for a month. Cheer up, you fellows, this is a birthday, not a funeral.'

When he had intoned a short prayer, Amy squeezed his hand in silent support. Jack smiled and drew her close in the circle of his arm, forgetting for the moment his own injunction to start eating. He glanced down to where Susannah was lecturing the two boys, though inaudibly from this distance, and his smile faded.

'I didn't think she'd perform today,' he said. 'She hasn't been so bad lately, I thought she'd got over all that nonsense she used to go on with. Now she's got this new idea in her head. She doesn't mind making me look a fool.'

Careful not to make her father dwell on an unpleasant subject, Amy refrained from asking what Susannah's new idea might be. 'Don't worry, Pa, no one takes much notice of Susannah. Even Tom doesn't get as upset as he used to.' She followed her father's gaze. 'At least she doesn't dress the boys like little dolls any more.'

'No, I put my foot down about that. No need for her to make fools of the little fellows too.'

'Shh, Pa, no one thinks you're a fool. You mustn't say such things. Now, how about you start eating some of your birthday lunch?' She slid out of his grasp and began picking out the choicest bits from the platters within reach to load onto her father's plate. 'I brought over some of my ham—you know, cured that special way with honey the way you always liked it. Do you want some?'

'As much as I can get,' Jack told her with a smile. 'No one else does ham like yours.'

Demolishing the generous lunch took everyone's attention for most of the next hour, though there was enough left over to guarantee that Jack's family would indeed be eating the remains for several days. The trees provided shelter from the worst of the heat, but the warmth of the day relaxed those who were capable of it, and the company, congenial for the most part, made for amicable conversation.

'Hey, Frank,' Harry called across the rug, 'I hear you're getting rid of all your fancy cows.'

'Not flaming likely!' Frank protested with a laugh, sure he was being teased. 'Someone's been having you on, Harry. You shouldn't believe everything you hear, you know.'

'No? I heard you'd been selling Jersey cows in calf.'

'That's right.' Frank smiled at the chance to share his latest success without being accused of boasting. 'Just the one, mind you. I sold a one-year-old in calf, sent her up to the Waikato.'

'I thought you'd be dead keen on building up your breeders, Frank,' John remarked. 'What are you up to, selling them?'

'Just one,' Frank reminded them. 'It was because I went up to that show in Auckland. Lots of people got to see my cows, and they thought they weren't too bad. Well, come spring I had a few men asking if I had any for sale.'

'A few?' Lizzie said. 'Frank had dozens of people asking! No wonder, too, with all the ribbons and things he won in Auckland. I've never heard of anyone getting as many letters as Frank's had this year.'

'Well, there were quite a few, all right,' Frank said. 'Anyway, I was a bit troubled about that. I mean, if I'd sold cows to everyone who wanted to buy them, I'd have had no Jerseys left. But if I just told them I didn't want to sell any heifers, they'd all decide I was a dead loss as a breeder— and in a few years when I've got the herd better set up I want to be able to sell the extras, eh?'

His smile grew broader. 'Then I got this idea. I wrote back to the ones who sounded keenest, and I sort of hummed and ha'd about whether I'd have enough cows to sell, and I got them to say what price they'd go up to. Then I sold a heifer to the one who offered the most money, and I wrote to all the others to say sorry, I'd sold all the heifers I could spare this season, and maybe I'd be able to supply them next year or the year after. I've already had a few wanting to put their names down for next season,' he added, trying not to sound too smug.

'That was pretty cunning,' Harry said.

'Thanks,' said Frank. Out of the corner of his eye he saw Arthur looking uncertain whether to boast about Frank's success or scoff at it, and Frank decided to tip the balance. 'Of course Pa helped me think of it. I talked it all over with him and he helped me decide what to do.'

That was stretching the truth to the limit; after carefully deliberating, Frank had told Arthur what he intended to do, and Arthur had not actually said it was a stupid idea. But his remark had the desired effect: Arthur glowed with pride and said, 'Frank's got the sense to take good advice, I've always said that. Even if he did go off half-cocked over buying those cows,' he added, careful not to encourage a swollen head in his son-in-law.

Frank sprawled on the grass with his plate balanced on the uneven ground. Lizzie sat beside him with Danny on her lap, the plump baby crushing the taffeta of her blue dress paid for with a little of the money from Frank's bull, while the other four children clustered around giving full attention to their pudding. A family for a man to be proud of, and proud he was. Five healthy children, and a wife like Lizzie. As if that wasn't enough to be thankful for, the farm was doing better than ever and the Jerseys were thriving. He knew the heifer he had sold would be the first of many. Lizzie was never going to wear patched petticoats again.

Mr Hatfield, the watchmaker-cum-photographer, arrived as most of the family were polishing off their second helpings of dessert. He looked mildly bewildered as he found himself being sat down on a cushion and plied with cakes and puddings, despite his protestations that he had already eaten. He had politely refused to intrude upon the family occasion when Jack had told him to come out in time for the meal, but he was no match for a group of women all firmly convinced this must be the first decent food the elderly Englishman had had in years.

He was not allowed to set up his camera on its stand until he had eaten three plates of pudding and downed two glasses of beer, after which he disappeared behind his camera with the expression of a man seeking safe harbour. There ensued an orgy of photograph taking, Mr Hatfield standing as aloof as possible from the complex operation of deciding who was to stand where for each photograph, and where any missing children could possibly have got to in the few seconds since their mothers had last seen them.

Fitting the entire gathering into one frame was a challenge only accomplished after a great deal of muttering and lip-chewing on Mr Hatfield's part, and he relaxed visibly when Arthur's branch of the clan moved aside. Having stared grimly at the camera for the group photograph, Charlie took up his station by the beer barrel and ignored all the activity around him.

Photographing Jack and Susannah with Jack's five children was the next task. 'I want my girl on this side,' Jack instructed, patting the right arm of the chair Thomas had carried out from the parlour for him. Amy sat down, took her father's hand in hers and squeezed it. Jack seemed to have put whatever it was that he and Susannah had been arguing about out of his mind. It was good to see her father happy, though Amy could not help but notice how deeply the lines on his forehead and around his eyes seemed to have been etched in the last few years. The knowledge that her father was growing old sent a pang through her, but she thrust it down. Today was a day for celebrating, not for thinking mournful thoughts.

'John, you stand here,' said Jack. 'You're the oldest. Harry, you stand beside Amy, and the little fellows can sit on the grass in front of me.' Susannah stood behind the chair, resting her hand lightly on Jack's shoulder, and Mr Hatfield took several shots so as to be sure of success.

'What about one with the kids?' Harry said, beckoning Jane over.

Jack agreed, declaring that he wanted a picture of himself with all his descendants. Sophie and Jane retrieved those of their children old enough to walk and lined up for the photograph, and David ran over to stand beside Amy when he saw his cousins lining up.

'Do you want him in it?' Jack asked Amy, flicking his hand in Charlie's direction. Charlie settled the issue by refusing to participate, and no one seemed disappointed at his absence.

Malcolm eyed the group dubiously and looked reluctant to join in. 'You ask him, Pa,' Amy said when her attempts at cajoling met with a defiant look. 'He doesn't take any notice of me.' She tried to ignore the disapproving sniff from Susannah.

'Come on, Mal,' said Jack. 'We can't have a photo without you. You're the most important fellow here.'

'Am I?' Malcolm asked, drifting a little closer. 'Why?'

'Come and sit by me and I'll tell you,' Jack encouraged. 'I might even have a toffee in here somewhere.' He patted his jacket pockets.

'Pa!' Amy protested. 'Mal doesn't need lollies, not after the feed he's just had.' She could not help laughing at the sight of Malcolm letting himself be tempted by the mention of sweets.

Malcolm came over to sit by Jack's feet, close to Thomas and George. 'That's the boy,' Jack said. 'Now, you know why I've got to have you in my birthday picture?' Malcolm shook his head. 'Because you're my oldest grandchild, that's why!'

Jack slipped the promised toffee into Malcolm's hand, too engrossed to see that all trace of laughter had been wiped from Amy's face. *He's not. He's not your oldest grandchild. Ann is. My little girl—my little Ann. Everyone pretends you never happened.*

It took Amy some time to get her feelings sufficiently under control to manage a shaky smile for the camera. As soon as the photographs were finished she walked away from the rest of the group to get what privacy she could. She wanted to run away into the bush, to hide from everyone and fling herself down beside the Waimarama to weep in solitude. But Charlie would follow her, intent on retribution; she was not allowed to 'wander'. Instead she pretended to study with interest the climbing rose that trailed up one side of the house, reaching out a hand to stroke the small pink blooms that she could see only through a blur of tears.

'They're pretty, aren't they?' Frank's voice close behind her made Amy jump. 'We've got some like that at our place.'

Amy blinked rapidly to clear the tears, and wiped the back of her hand across her eyes before turning to face Frank. He was leading Mickey by one hand, steadying the two-year-old's attempts to run.

'I had to take Mickey around the back,' Frank said. 'All that lemonade he's been drinking.'

Amy nodded, swallowed to clear the lump in her throat, and knelt to straighten Mickey's clothes, which Frank had left twisted at the front after pulling the little boy's drawers closed. 'That's better, isn't it, Mickey.' She gave him a kiss before standing up.

'Thanks, Amy, I didn't notice that,' said Frank.

'Lizzie's left you in charge of him, has she?'

'Mmm, just for a bit. She's gone inside to give Danny a feed. Boy, can that kid drink! He wants feeding all the time. Lizzie says he's slowing down now, though. It's a good thing, too—I reckon Lizzie was a bit more tired with him than she's been with the others. She's all right now, but it took her a while to come right. She had that trouble with sore legs, too, before Danny arrived. Of course, he was a big baby,' Frank added proudly. 'The biggest of them all.'

'Yes, he was,' Amy agreed. 'More like one of my babies. He's growing well, too.'

'He sure is. He's taken it out of Lizzie, though. I think she should have a bit of a rest before the next one.'

Amy was more touched that Frank trusted her enough to share such a personal thought than embarrassed that he should do so. She was about to rest her hand on his arm and say something reassuring when she saw Charlie look up from his seat near the beer barrel and stare at her through narrowed eyes.

She was too weary to think of some polite excuse; the truth would have to do. 'I'm sorry, Frank, I can't talk to you by myself—I'll get in trouble if I do.' She walked away before he had the chance to reply.

Amy almost collided with Thomas and George as they ran from the house wearing their everyday dungarees.

'Watch out, you two.' She lifted her arms as if to fend off an attack. 'Now, how did you talk Mother into letting you put your old clothes on?'

'We didn't,' George said. 'Tom asked Pa, and he said we could.'

'But he said to keep out of Mother's way, so we're going down to the creek,' Thomas added. 'You want to come?'

Amy glanced over at Charlie, who seemed to have once more lost interest in her now that she was only talking to children. It was tempting to let the boys' enthusiasm drive out her dark mood. 'I wouldn't mind a paddle. I'd better not, though. Uncle Charlie's starting to look a bit tired, we might have to go home soon.'

'Come and see our tree house first, Amy,' said Thomas. Amy let herself be tugged over to a large puriri that had been left standing for the sake of the small amount of shade it gave the lower part of the garden.

She admired the rough platform the boys had made in the tree, but refused all attempts to persuade her to climb up for a better look at it.

'Ladies don't climb trees,' she told them. 'Not in their good clothes, anyway,' she added, remembering her first clumsy attempts at rigging a clothesline.

The boys slithered down the trunk and dropped to the ground beside her. 'I'm going to have to stop calling you my little brothers soon,' Amy said, noticing how much they had grown in the last few months. 'You're taller than me now—even you, George. Sit down with me a minute before you go rushing off to the creek—you won't make me feel so little if we're sitting down.'

'Where's Ma?' Thomas asked, looking anxiously over at the guests.

'She's talking to Lily, see? Don't worry, she won't think of looking for you for a bit. And don't forget you're meant to say "Mother".'

'Only when she can hear,' George said with a scowl in his mother's direction.

The three of them sat down with their backs against the broad trunk. 'Have you two had a falling out with Mother?' Amy asked.

'Sort of,' said Thomas.

'Her and Pa had a big row last night,' George volunteered. 'It was about us.'

'Mother wants to get rid of us, and Pa doesn't.'

'Of course she doesn't!' Amy protested. 'You mustn't say such things!'

'She does,' said George. 'She wants to send us away.'

'Pa won't let her, though,' Thomas said. 'He says he wants us here with him.'

'You two have been listening at the bedroom wall again, haven't you?' said Amy. Both boys refused to meet her eyes. 'That's how you've got such a silly idea in your heads. Now, why would Mother want to send you away?'

'To school,' Thomas said. 'She wants us to go to Auckland, to a special school.'

'A grandma school,' George put in.

'It's not a grandma school,' said Thomas. 'It's a word like that, but it's not grandma.'

'It is,' George insisted. 'Mother says we could live with Grandma and Grandpa and go to a grandma school.'

'A grammar school, I think she must have said,' Amy suggested. 'The Church of England Grammar School. That's in Auckland.'

'Yes, that's it!' said Thomas.

'Mother said that'd cure us of being rough farm boys,' said George. 'She said a grammar school would teach us to be young gentlemen.' He pulled a face at the prospect.

Thomas looked puzzled. 'Pa got really wild then. He said, "Did your brother go there?" That's Uncle Jimmy,' he explained to Amy, not noticing her sudden change of expression. 'He came to stay with us once when I was real little—I sort of remember him, but George doesn't. I think Mother said yes, but I couldn't hear her properly. Pa said he didn't care for what they taught boys at that school. He said he didn't mind if people called his sons rough, but they weren't going to call us...' he trailed off and looked at Amy rather shamefacedly. 'He said some bad words.'

'I'm sure he did. He didn't know your big ears were flapping away, listening to their private talk. That's what comes of listening at the wall, Tom. You hear things you've no business to.'

The boys were not used to having Amy speak sharply to them, and Thomas's bewildered expression sent a pang of guilt through her. 'Oh, don't look at me like that, Tommy,' she said, giving the boy a quick squeeze. 'I'm not really grumpy. Not with you, anyway. But you shouldn't listen to other people's business, you know.'

'Isn't it our business too?' Thomas asked. 'I mean, they're talking about what they're going to do with us.'

'And then you go hearing things you don't understand and getting all muddled about them. You'd be better off waiting till Pa tells you the whole story.'

'They talked about you, too,' George put in.

'I'm sure they did.' It would be difficult for Jimmy to be dragged into the argument without her own name coming up. 'No, I *don't* want to hear what they said about me,' Amy said, forestalling George's attempts to enlighten her. 'I'm quite sure you didn't understand it, anyway. And don't you go listening to gossip about me, either, or I really will get grumpy with you.'

'Well, anyway, we're not going to some stupid school,' George said.

'No,' Thomas agreed. 'Anyone would think we're little kids. I'm going to finish school next year, then I'll work with Pa all the time,' he said proudly.

'Is that what you want, Tom?' Amy asked.

'Of course,' said Thomas.

'You wouldn't like to go to a High School and learn lots of interesting things?'

'Pa knows all sorts of stuff about the farm and all that. That's what I want to learn.'

'Me too,' George put in. 'Only I have to wait two years,' he added, screwing up his face. 'She won't be able to tell us what to do once we're working.'

'Yes, that's right,' said Thomas.

Amy studied their avid expressions. 'That's what you really want, is it? To help Pa on the farm?' They both nodded vigorously. She gave them each a hug. 'That's good, then. It's good when people get to do what they want.'

Frank was freed from his baby-sitting task when Lizzie returned from the house, a contented Danny in her arms. He left Mickey with her and went to get himself a mug of beer.

He paused on the way to chat with Mr Hatfield, interrupting the photographer's attempts to pack his equipment away.

'Have you still got those pearls in your shop?' Frank asked, keeping his voice low so that no one else would hear.

'Oh, yes,' Mr Hatfield said. 'I'm not likely to get rid of those. Sometimes I take them home with me of an evening and keep them there for a change. If you don't see them in the window, that's why.'

'Well, don't go selling them to anyone else,' said Frank. 'I'm going to buy those off you one day, you just wait. Lizzie's going to have those pearls.'

Mr Hatfield gave him an indulgent smile. 'Yes, I think I could bear to part with them to you. You'd give them a good home.'

Despite his kind words, Frank knew that Mr Hatfield thought there was little chance Frank would take him up on the offer. It would be a long time, he admitted to himself, before he would be able to afford fifty pounds for such a luxury, but he was prepared to be patient.

Going to the beer barrel meant standing closer to Charlie than he would have chosen, but the warmth of the day and the several mugs he had downed earlier had left Frank feeling too mellow to be particularly concerned. In fact he felt ever so slightly dizzy, but the drowsiness the beer had given him was more pleasant than otherwise. When he had filled his mug it seemed too much of an effort to walk straight back to Lizzie; instead he leaned against a tree trunk, from where he had a good view of her with their two youngest children.

It was a pleasant sight. Danny lay on a rug close to Lizzie, waving his plump little arms and legs around and chortling to himself, while Mickey rested his head in Lizzie's lap with his eyes half closed. Lizzie stroked Mickey's hair, her eyes darting around keeping watch on the other three children. A lock had escaped from beneath her bonnet to lie across her neck; it glinted golden in the dappled sunlight. She looked very young and, in Frank's eyes at least, very beautiful.

'So those funny-looking cows of yours are doing all right, are they?' The voice made Frank start. He gave the merest nod of acknowledgement to Charlie. 'Feeling pretty pleased with yourself, eh, Kelly?'

He *was* feeling pleased with himself; there was no denying it. Too pleased to let Charlie Stewart annoy him.

'Yes, things are going all right,' Frank said. 'I'm getting more cream than ever from the Jerseys. A fair few of the rest are half-breeds now, so they're giving richer milk than the old Shorthorns. You don't want to put your name down for one of my heifers, do you?' he said cheekily.

Charlie spat on the ground. 'I've better things to spend my money on than dopey-looking cows.'

'Please yourself,' said Frank. 'There's plenty of people that do want them.' He gave a laugh. 'It's a good thing I can get a bit of cash out of selling the odd animal, too! The way the family's growing, I'm going to have to think about building on to the house in a couple of years.'

Charlie gave a grunt that Frank took as encouragement. He went on, warming to his subject. 'There's things to do with the farm, too—there's always something that needs planning. Now I've got the cow shed decent, I thought I might get a bit more of the bush broken in this winter. I'm trying to build up the Jersey herd as quick as I can, so I'll need the extra pasture in a few years. I mean, I've got three sons now. I've got to think about providing for them, eh?'

'You think you're bloody clever, don't you?' Charlie growled.

'I don't know about that,' Frank said, taken aback by the ungracious response. 'I've sort of tried to figure out how to do things, then just done my best, that's all. Things are working out pretty well, anyway.' He glanced around the garden and saw Maudie re-tying Beth's hair ribbons, which had worked loose as the younger girl ran around with the other children. Such pretty daughters he had, Frank reflected proudly. Especially Maudie, who was the image of her mother at the same age.

That thought led Frank's attention naturally back to Lizzie. A warm feeling flowed through him as he watched her. 'I couldn't do it without Lizzie,' he said, more to himself than to Charlie. 'It wouldn't be worth it.'

461

'You must need the money, all right,' Charlie said sourly. 'That woman of yours looks as though she eats plenty.'

The smile disappeared from Frank's face. 'You can keep your opinions on my wife to yourself, thank you.'

But his show of irritation seemed to encourage Charlie. 'You make sure she's with child all the time, eh? Going on to me about how many sons you've got! You don't get much pleasure out of her when she's got a swollen belly, do you?'

'You shut your mouth,' Frank said, speaking rather louder than he had intended. He was aware of Lizzie's attention suddenly on him as the unfamiliar sound of Frank's voice raised in anger reached her. Amy, too, looked up from where she sat with Harry when she heard the angry voices; no doubt she had learned to be alert to such danger signs.

'Don't think I didn't see you talking to my wife before, either. I'm warning you, Kelly, you keep your hands off her or I'll kill you. She's still my woman, I'll not let any other man have her.'

'I don't want her! Don't be such a bloody idiot, thinking every man who talks to your wife wants to take her off you!'

'You wouldn't have the gumption, would you? You didn't have the guts to get a woman of your own—you had to wait until that one started chasing after you.'

'Who asked your opinion?' Frank demanded, genuinely angry now.

'No wonder you want to keep her with child all the time. She doesn't order you about so much when she's got a big belly, eh?' Charlie spoke in rapid bursts, pausing only to take gulps of air. 'You watch out, Kelly—you think you've got her where you want her right now—it won't last, you smug bastard. She'll turn on you, you mark my words. They're all bitches, these Leith women.'

All other conversation had died, but Frank hardly noticed. 'You say one more word like that about Lizzie and I'll knock your teeth down your throat,' he growled.

'You?' Charlie spat in disgust. 'A little runt like you? I'd break your arm before you knew what had hit you.'

Charlie was a head taller than Frank, but twenty years older. Frank was not sure what the outcome of a fight might be, but he felt willing to give it a try. He smelt the sour odour of the older man's sweat, and saw his massive fists. Frank caught a glimpse of Amy's worried face out of the corner of his eye, and remembered Lizzie's description of that little face bruised and bloodied by those same huge fists.

'Well, at least I don't go knocking around women half my size,' he flung at Charlie.

462

The silence around them grew more tense, and Charlie's face turned grimmer than ever. 'What business is that of yours?' he snarled. 'Keep your nose out of my affairs or I'll teach you to—'

'That's enough, you fellows,' Arthur said, striding up and interposing his body between the antagonists. 'This is a birthday party, not a bar for you to brawl in.' He met Charlie's black stare with one far sterner, holding his gaze until Charlie turned away and affected indifference. 'You're only here because of Amy,' he told Charlie. 'If you don't want to behave, you can take yourself home. No one'll miss you.'

He turned his back on Charlie. 'Frank, you can behave yourself, too. Carrying on like an idiot! Go and sit down,' he said, giving Frank a cuff on the shoulder to emphasise his words. 'And you can apologise to your Uncle Jack—giving him all this bother on his birthday,' he called after him as Frank made his way back to the rest of the family.

'Sorry,' Frank mumbled in Jack's direction, but Jack waved his apology aside. Frank saw Susannah staring at him with a disdainful expression, and her mouth shaped a word that might have been 'animals'. She then made a show of looking in the other direction, thin-lipped with disapproval.

Already regretting his outburst, Frank dropped to the ground beside Lizzie. When he met her eyes he regretted it far more. Lizzie glared at him, barely able to speak for the anger that was making her eyes flash. She would not make a fuss in front of everyone, but there was going to be trouble later, Frank realised with a sinking feeling.

'What on earth do you think you're doing, rowing with Charlie like that?' she hissed under her breath.

'I couldn't help it,' said Frank. 'He was saying things about you, and I got wild. I was just trying to shut him up.'

'Yes, and making more trouble for Amy. That's just what she needs, isn't it? You putting the old so-and-so in a worse temper than usual.'

'I didn't mean to—he shouldn't have gone on like he did.' Frank caught Amy's eye to send a silent apology, and was relieved to see that she appeared surprisingly calm. She even managed to direct a small, rueful smile in his direction. 'She looks all right, anyway.'

'No thanks to you,' Lizzie shot back.

Amy watched Charlie settle himself against a tree trunk beside the beer, then turned her attention back to Harry. 'Funny how we can't have a family get-together without a row,' she said, smiling to make a joke of it. 'Never mind, I think some of you think the fights are the best part. No wonder Susannah looks so disgusted with us all.'

'What'd he mean?' Harry demanded. 'What'd Frank mean about knocking around women?'

'Don't go making a fuss, there's no need. You'll upset Pa if you go on about it.'

Harry was not to be put off. 'What'd he mean? Has that old bugger been thumping you?'

'Leave it, Harry,' Amy said. 'It's all right.'

'If he's laid a finger on you—'

'Harry,' Amy interrupted, 'I want you to leave it. Please?'

She let her hand rest on his arm, gripping it more tightly to be sure of his full attention. Harry's eyes darted from her to Charlie and back again, and she felt the muscles of his arm tense as he clenched his fist.

But Harry was no longer the fiery twenty-year-old with no one but himself to think about that he had been ten years before. The responsibilities of a wife and four children had had a steadying effect on him, and he had learned a degree of self-control that his family would hardly have believed possible once.

'All right,' he said. 'I won't do anything about him just now. Not in front of everyone.' He sent a baleful glare in Charlie's direction. 'I'll leave it till a better time.'

He raised his voice to be sure Charlie would hear. 'Maybe I'll come over and see you some time soon, Amy. John'll come with me, I expect. If there's anything troubling you, we should be able to sort it out. We might come tomorrow.'

'There's nothing troubling me,' said Amy. 'But you and John are welcome to come over any time you want.' Impulsively, she flung her arms around his neck and kissed him soundly. 'You're a dear—even if you do like to make a fuss about nothing.'

Amy released Harry and smiled. It was good to know that if the power of her threat to leave Charlie ever wavered, the thought of the vengeance her father and brothers would exact would not be far from his mind.

She looked over at Charlie, and could not help feeling a little sorry for him in his so obvious isolation. But feeling sorry for him was vastly preferable to being frightened of him.

I haven't got anything to be frightened of now. After so many years of wariness and fear, it was difficult to comprehend their absence.

35

December 1894 – May 1895

After the fracas at their father's birthday party, Amy saw more of her older brothers than she had since her marriage. Their first visit to Charlie's house took place the morning after the party. Harry was determined to elicit the details of what Charlie had done to deserve Frank's invective, and Amy was equally determined to avoid trouble. She eventually admitted that Charlie had, indeed, hit her in the past; at the same time assuring them that that had been long ago, and there was no risk of any more such violence.

Charlie had wisely made himself scarce as soon as he caught sight of Amy's brothers approaching. John and Harry looked grim at her revelation; Harry scolded her, and said she should have told them when Charlie had first hit her. He insisted that she do so if anything of the sort ever happened again.

'Maybe we should sort him out anyway, just to let him know what he'll get if he tries anything like that again,' Harry said, and John looked ready to go along with the idea. But they allowed themselves to be persuaded by Amy to let well enough alone.

That visit was the first of many. Harry and John took to popping over together or, more often, alone, for unannounced visits. Since Jack also now made a habit of dropping in on Amy, hardly a week went by without her enjoying the company of one or other of her family.

She had worried that after his skirmish with Frank Charlie might forbid her to have anything to do with Lizzie, but that fear was soon laid to rest. Charlie, it seemed, saw the incident as a humiliating defeat, and chose to pretend it had never happened.

To her huge relief, Malcolm managed to pass his Standard One examination, as did David, so Malcolm was safe from that particular focus of his father's wrath for at least another year. Charlie had not yet become aware of Malcolm's occasional truancy; Amy resigned herself to the knowledge that it could only be a matter of time before he did discover it. But there was no sense worrying about that before she had to.

Her life had assumed a sort of tranquillity that Amy could not in strict honesty call happiness, but was content to make do with. There was no more fear, and no more vain yearning for what might have been; or at least if there was still yearning, she had buried it too deeply for it to give pain. The moments of affection she managed to snatch with David, already few and far between, were becoming even rarer as the boy grew up and spent more of his time with his father and brother, but she accepted that as inevitable. She knew David loved her as much as he ever had, even if he was learning not to show it so openly.

Contentment was not the stuff of dreams, but it was sufficient; it had to be. It was in May that Amy discovered just how fragile her tranquillity was.

Charlie had gone into town by himself that morning to get the supplies; the briefness of his absence told Amy that he had not paid a visit to the hotel. After lunch he lingered for a short time over the newspaper he had brought home, then dropped it on the floor as he rose to leave.

Left alone, Amy picked up the crumpled newspaper. A minute or two scanning the main stories; that was all she intended to allow herself. But it took only seconds before her eyes were caught by a story that made her give a sharp intake of breath, then stop breathing altogether until her body forced her to expel the stale air and take a great gulp to replace it.

'No,' she whispered, her eyes wide with horror. 'What have I done? What have I done to my baby?'

Frank had collected a copy of the same newspaper when he and Lizzie had done their shopping that morning, and over lunch he glanced at it. The pages of farming items were what he usually found most interesting, but he let his eyes run over the news stories first, and stopped at the most dramatic one.

'Hey, listen to this, Lizzie.' He spread the newspaper flat on the table and began reading snatches aloud.

' "Shocking case... woman charged with murder... two bodies in garden—" '

'Frank, don't ramble on. Tell me the story so it makes sense, not just bits and pieces like that.'

'All right.' Frank read ahead, then looked up from the paper to check that Lizzie was still listening. 'It's about this woman down south somewhere—Winton, the place's called, I've never heard of it.'

'Neither have I,' said Lizzie. 'It can't be much of a place.'

'No. Anyway, she had all these babies at her place—not her own, other people's babies. She was meant to be looking after them, but apparently she was doing them in and burying them in the garden.'

'She didn't! Does it really say that, Frank?'

'It sure does. They're going to hang her, it says. Well, they'll have a trial first, but it sounds like she's guilty, all right. That'll be the first time they've ever hanged a woman in New Zealand.'

'She must be mad or something. What were people doing, leaving their babies with a madwoman?'

Frank shrugged. 'I suppose they didn't know she was crazy. It says in the paper there's a lot of women doing what she did—not killing the babies, just looking after them for money. Baby farming, they call it.'

'Looking after them for money?' Lizzie frowned. 'Why would anyone pay that woman to look after babies?'

Frank glanced down at the paper again. 'Well, it says the mothers were mostly girls with no husbands. This Minnie Dean woman would find people to adopt the babies, and the mothers would give her money to look after their babies until someone adopted them. Maybe she got sick of looking after them all. They think there's a lot of these baby farmers around—they say the government's going to do something about it. It's awful, eh?'

He raised his eyes from the newspaper, and was startled to see that Lizzie had gone pale.

'Hey, don't get upset,' he said, reaching across the table to take hold of her unresponsive hand. 'I didn't mean to worry you, reading that stuff out. It's probably a load of rubbish, anyway—you know what the papers are like.'

Lizzie's first words when she recovered her voice startled Frank. 'Saddle up one of the horses for me.'

'Eh? What do you want me to do that for? You haven't even finished your pudding yet.'

'Now, Danny shouldn't wake up for half an hour or so as long as you don't go making too much noise. You can put Mickey down as soon as he finishes his pudding—hurry up, Mickey, don't play with your food,' she exhorted the three-year-old. She took hold of his bowl and began spooning food into his mouth, talking to Frank as she did so. 'Give Danny some bread and milk when he wakes up, that should keep him quiet till I get home. I might be a while, but you'll just have to wait till Maudie's back from school to look after the little ones before you can go out on the farm.' She looked over her shoulder and frowned. 'Don't just sit there, Frank! Hurry up and get that horse ready for me.'

'Where are you going?' Frank asked.

'Use your head! How do you think Amy's going to feel about all this?'

'All what? You mean that story in the paper? What's it got to do with Amy?'

'Don't be so stupid! Of course it—' Lizzie stopped abruptly, and pulled a face. 'No, I'm the one who's being stupid, not you. I never did tell you the ins and outs. You know that trouble of Amy's before she got married? Well, she tried a few times to talk to me about it when she first came home from Auckland. I used to just shut her up. I thought she was upsetting herself more, thinking about it all the time.'

'That's probably right,' said Frank.

'Maybe. I'm not so sure now. Anyway, she told me that when she was in the nursing home some woman came to see her. Aunt Susannah had arranged it, apparently. The woman came and talked to Amy, then later she came back and took the little one away. She told Amy she took little ones like that—you know, with no fathers—and found people to adopt them. Uncle Jack gave her money to do it for Amy's.' She looked seriously at Frank. 'Now do you see why I've got to go up and see her?'

'You think the woman was like the one in the paper?' Frank asked, shaken.

'I don't know. But I know what Amy'll be thinking.'

Amy felt hands gripping her arms, shaking her. Her eyes gradually focussed on the figure leaning over her. *Lizzie? What's Lizzie doing here?*

'Poor love.' The distress in Lizzie's voice drew Amy into full awareness of her surroundings. She found that she had slid from her chair on to the floor and was slumped against one leg of the table, the newspaper still clutched in one hand. 'Come on, get up,' said Lizzie. 'I'll help you.'

Amy's body seemed to have gone limp, but Lizzie managed to lift her onto the chair. 'There, that's better, isn't it?' Lizzie said.

'She's dead,' Amy said bleakly. 'They've killed her. They've cut her throat and buried her in the ground. I gave her away, and now she's dead.' She collapsed against Lizzie's encircling arms, her body racked with sobs.

Lizzie held her close and made crooning noises. When the flood of tears began to subside, she eased her grip.

'You don't know that, Amy. You've no reason to think anything awful happened to her. Just because there was one mad woman down south, it doesn't mean they're all like that.'

'No, I don't know,' Amy said. 'I don't know if she's dead or alive, or if she's being looked after, or anything. I gave her away. That tiny little thing, all soft and trusting, and I gave her away to a woman I'd never seen before.'

'It was because you wanted the best for her—that's why you did it. You wanted her to have a good home.'

The kind rationality in Lizzie's voice stabbed like cruelty. 'The best for her? To be murdered and thrown in someone's garden like a bit of old meat?' Amy fought for a moment against Lizzie's embrace, then went limp, too weak to struggle.

'I could bear it, you see,' she said, her voice muffled against Lizzie's shoulder. 'I could bear not being allowed to keep Ann as long as I could think about her, and imagine them making a fuss of her. How she'd be dressed in pretty clothes and have fancy dolls and things, and how they'd love her. I thought they'd love her nearly as much as I did. I do love her,' she whispered. 'And now I don't know if she's dead or alive. I don't know if I can bear it.'

'Amy, don't. You'll make yourself ill or something.'

'I can't help it. I keep seeing her lying on my lap looking up at me, then lying all still like she's dead.' Amy gave a violent shudder, and made an effort to calm her voice. 'I'll come right in a bit, Lizzie—I'll have to, won't I? I can't sit about feeling sorry for myself all day. You go off home now, I'll be all right.'

'No, I'm going to take you home with me for a bit,' Lizzie said, suddenly decisive. 'Just so you can have some peace and quiet.'

'I can't,' Amy said, shaking her head.

'Yes, you can.'

'Lizzie, I can't just wander off with you like that—it's lovely of you to worry about me, and I'm sorry I haven't been very grateful, but I've got to stay here. I've baking to do, and I'll have to start getting dinner on in an hour or so. The boys'll be home in a while, too, and they'll be after something to eat. And Charlie'll want his afternoon tea, I've got to make something for that.'

'Too bad,' Lizzie decreed. 'They can look after themselves for once. Now, don't you start arguing with me.'

She stood up and began bustling around the kitchen, gathering biscuits from several tins and piling them onto a plate. 'See, there's plenty of biscuits left. And Charlie must know how to make a pot of tea, for goodness sake! You'll have time to get dinner on after you've had a little rest at my place.'

The thought of escaping briefly from Charlie's house, with its constant reminders of his brooding presence, was cruelly tempting. 'I can't, Lizzie.'

'Why not? What excuses are you going to drag out now?'

'How can I go and ask Charlie when I'm in this state?' Amy said. 'He'll want to know what's wrong with me, and I couldn't bear talking to him about it.' Belatedly she recalled the promise he had extracted from her on their wedding night. *And I'm not allowed to talk about Ann, anyway. He'd hit me if I told him.*

'Don't tell him, then. You won't be gone for long—just leave him a note or something.'

Amy shook her head. 'I can't do that. I'm not allowed to leave the farm without asking.'

'That nonsense of his! Why on earth does he make you do that all the time?'

'Because I'm a bad woman, Lizzie,' Amy said, her slender self-control threatening to slip away as she spoke. 'I'm bad and I can't be trusted. I'm the sort of woman who'd give away her baby to someone she'd never seen before.'

'Stop that,' Lizzie said sharply. 'I won't listen to that sort of talk. Now, don't you worry about him—I'll ask him myself.'

'You'd better not—you'll get him in an awful mood if you're rude to him. Charlie's not like Frank, you know.'

'I'm never rude to Frank! No, I'll sort it out with His Lordship—don't worry, I'll be as meek and mild as anything.'

'You?' Amy said dubiously.

'Yes,' said Lizzie. 'I saw him from the road as I came up, he's not far away. You get your cloak and boots on, and by the time you're ready I'll be back.' She hurried from the house, leaving a dazed Amy to obey her.

Though Lizzie was capable of playing a wide variety of roles when the need arose, meekness was one she was rather rusty on. But she did her best.

'Charlie, is it all right if I take Amy down to my place for a little while?' she asked. 'She's taken a bit poorly, I want to get her sorted out.'

'What's wrong with her?' Charlie asked, his eyes narrowing.

'Oh, just a woman's problem.'

Charlie looked blankly at her. 'What does that mean?'

His ignorance took Lizzie aback. 'It's... well, you know... things women get wrong with them. Things to do with their insides and all that.'

Charlie grunted. 'Some nonsense of hers.' But Lizzie was pleased to see that he looked discomforted by the reference to women's 'insides'.

'So you won't mind if I take her home for a bit?' she pressed. 'Just an hour or so.'

Charlie considered for a few moments, then said, 'All right. See you get her back in time to get the meal on,' he called after Lizzie's retreating form.

'You're sure he said I was allowed?' Amy asked as she accepted Lizzie's leg-up onto the horse.

'He said you can stay as long as you like.'

The outrageous suggestion shocked Amy into disbelief. 'He did not say that, Lizzie!'

'Well, he should have,' Lizzie said briskly. 'He said you could come with me, that's all you need to worry about.' She clambered onto the saddle and they set off at a lively walk.

Amy leaned against Lizzie's back, content to do as she was told. But when they passed the school a fresh wave of guilt assailed her.

'I shouldn't be wandering off like this,' she fretted. 'I should be there to get the boys their milk and cakes.'

'Rubbish,' said Lizzie. 'They're not babies, they're capable of finding the milk jug. Why do you have to be there to wait on them?'

'I want to look after them. I gave my baby away to a stranger—at least I can try and be a good mother to the boys.' She loosened her hold on Lizzie's waist, ready to slide from the horse. 'Let me down, I'm going back.'

'No, you're not,' said Lizzie. 'Hold on tight.' She gave the horse a sharp flick with her riding crop, along with a hard kick, and the startled beast broke into a canter. Amy gave a yelp of alarm, flung her arms around Lizzie and held on desperately as she was shaken and bounced on the horse's bare rump all the way to Frank's farm.

She slid to the ground and leaned against the horse's heaving flanks, rubbing her own tender rump. 'That was a mean trick, Lizzie—cantering with me stuck behind you.'

'I had to do it, you were being silly. Anyway, you're here now. Let's get you inside, then you can have a lie-down.'

Amy pushed an unruly lock of hair away from her face, aware of how much had escaped from its pins. Her fingers touched the stickiness of dried tears, and she knew how red and swollen her face must be. 'I must look a fright—what'll Frank think when he sees me in this state?'

'I'll tell him you're not well. Don't worry about him, men never take notice of that sort of thing.' Lizzie took hold of Amy's arm and led her into the house.

Frank was sitting at the table, attempting to add up a column of figures while he balanced Danny on one knee. Mickey sat opposite them, his face wreathed in smiles as he crammed jam tarts into his mouth.

'What are you doing out of bed, Michael Kelly?' Lizzie demanded.

The little boy's grin disappeared when he saw his mother's expression.

He turned to his father for support. 'Papa said I could.'

'He said he wasn't sleepy,' Frank said, looking guilty. 'I put him in bed and told him he had to stay there, but he started bawling, and that woke Danny up, then they were both bawling. So I thought I'd better get them up. He's been pretty good—aw, heck, Mickey, look at that stuff all over your face! Sorry, Lizzie, the cakes were keeping him quiet and I sort of forgot to watch him. Nice to see you, Amy,' he added as an afterthought. Amy could see that he was avoiding looking closely at her tear-streaked face.

'Right,' Lizzie said. 'I'm going to get that belt. If anyone who's meant to be in bed is still in this kitchen by the time I get back...' She let the statement hang in the air as she led Amy up the passage and into the front bedroom.

'Let your hair down and loosen your stays,' Lizzie instructed, closing the heavy drapes so that the room grew dim. 'I'll make sure the children don't make any noise and disturb you. You just try and forget about everything except having a nice lie-down. See if you can go to sleep.'

'I can't stay long, Lizzie.'

'You'll stay as long as I tell you. Don't worry, I'll get you home in time to make His Lordship's dinner.' She gave Amy a peck on the cheek and left the room, carrying one of Frank's belts.

Mickey was nowhere to be seen when Lizzie came back into the kitchen.

'I've never seen that kid move so fast,' said Frank. 'He wouldn't do it for me, that's for sure. Put that belt down, eh Lizzie, you'll make me nervous waving it around like that. I tried giving Danny some bread and milk like you said, but he wouldn't eat it.'

Lizzie laid the belt across the back of a chair and sat down. 'Give him here.' She held out her arms, and Frank passed Danny over. 'Did you warm the milk?'

'Oh. Was I meant to?'

'Honestly, Frank! You can't expect a little fellow like him to drink cold milk.' She unbuttoned her bodice and guided Danny's mouth on to one of her nipples. 'Never mind, mine comes out warm.'

'How's Amy?' Frank asked. 'She looked like she'd been pretty upset.'

'She was in an awful state, poor thing. She's quieter now, she might drop off to sleep with a bit of luck. I wish I could do something for her, though.'

'You're doing your best.'

'Oh, I can give her a bit of a rest, and I'll send her home with pudding and some vegetables so she'll only have to do the meat for their dinner—remind me to give her some of my baking, too, she didn't get her own done today. That's all very well, but I don't know how she's ever going to be easy in her mind again with this worry about what happened to her baby.'

'No, it's pretty hard, all right,' Frank said. 'I don't suppose… oh, I don't know.'

'What?' Lizzie prompted.

'Well, do you think you could find out what happened to it—her, I should say, it was a girl, wasn't it? I mean, couldn't she write to the woman or something?'

'She doesn't know anything about her. She keeps saying she gave her baby to a woman she didn't know a thing about, and now she thinks this woman's done away with the baby. I've got to do something, Frank— Amy's going to hate herself if I don't. What can I do?'

The sight of Lizzie in distress always roused Frank to his greatest efforts. 'I reckon we could do it, Lizzie. We could figure out who this woman was and write to her.'

'How?'

'Well, Amy must know something about her, at least her name and where she came from. You try and get as much as you can out of her, then we'll see what we can sort out. We'll think of something.'

Lizzie's sudden smile was reward enough. 'You really think we'll be able to find out what happened to the baby?'

'We'll have a darned good try, anyway.' Frank hated to cloud Lizzie's relief, but he had to prepare her for the worst. 'You know, we might find out Amy's right. Maybe the little girl died. What'll you do if that happens?'

It took Lizzie no more than a moment to consider. 'I'll lie to her,' she said simply. 'I'll tell her I couldn't find out anything about the woman. Bad enough that she should *think* she gave her baby away to a murderer—if she *knew* it I think it'd kill her.'

24415484R00277

Printed in Great Britain
by Amazon